CONTENTS

PREFACE — i

ACKNOWLEDGEMENTS — viii

COLLECTED PUBLISHED WORKS
Under The Nom De Plume "Craig Ellaichie"

Background — 1

SHORT STORIES

The Lengthsmen's Camp (1893) — 2

Twice Missed — 12

POEMS

Football — 18

Poetry and Trifles — 12

The Two Ships — 21

The Valley of the Children — 23

Ballade of Convict Days — 25

Ballade of Regret — 26

Omar's Wish — 27

Loss of "The Victoria" — 29

The Colonist's Return — 31

Gladstone — 33

Under The Nom De Plume "MacDonald Grant"

Background — 35

SHORT STORY

An Amateur Providence (1903) — 38

COLLECTED PUBLISHED WORKS
Under Isabel Grant 47
Poems
The Two Tides 48

Miss Grant's Poem 50

The Empire's Greeting (1902) 52

Short Stories
A Stolen Game (1904) 55

The Making of Men 69

Paddy's Love Story 81

The Prospector's Christmas Dinner.(1910) 105

A Tale of a Turkey (1910) 124

Pharaoh's Daughter (1912) 135

Saint George and the Dragon (1922) 146

The Point of View (1922) 156

A White Carnation (1923) 165

At the Sign of the Thermometer (1923) 192

Article
The Bronte Family (1908) 203

A Novel
The Furnace for Gold (1905) 220

PREFACE

The work of Isabel Grant is representative of popular writing in Australia at the close of the Victorian years. Her writing included fiction and poetry for newspapers and magazines. Professionally she presented papers before her peers in the Teachers Association and submitted articles for the state Queensland School Paper, which was established in 1905 to provide additional reading and wider information to school children. She also wrote stage and radio plays which it has been impossible to trace to their end use.

The original purpose of this book was to preserve Isabel's writings for the family in a semi permanent form. These came to light during a family history research project. From a beginning of one poem and one short story the volume found of her work increased until it became evident that she was one of the pool of Australian writers who kept newspapers and magazines supplied with short stories, serials and poems. She was principally an educator and writing was a sideline, as indeed it had to be for all Australian writers of the time where it was not possible to make a living by the pen.

As the collection grew in volume it grew in value as a useful tool for future researches. Her collected work gives another look at history through literature. It gives a view of the language and expressions used at the turn of the twentieth century and the style the public demanded for their popular fiction. Her work opened vistas both for the family's history and for the history of country town Australia particularly of Central Queensland where she lived and worked most of her life.

Her literary output spanned a dynamic time in the development of Australian writing.

On the world stage, Australia, which began as a colony for the transportation of convicts by Britain in 1788, cannot be said to have produced any literary classics in its first hundred years. There was an abundance of useful books for the prospective emigrant, and travelogues which were thinly disguised as a story. Other so-called Australia novels used the colony only as an exotic setting for a formula story for the readers in England. Such writing was significant historically but not of great literary merit.

By the 1880s Australia had long since ceased to receive convicts and with an overwhelming freeborn society Australia was developing a distinct, more confident, character. People at last began to identify themselves as Australian and were inspired and energized by the ideals of nationalism, unionism and socialism. The love hate relationship with Britain was losing intensity, although the cultural cringe had not. Altogether Australia showed a more distinct, settled and confident mien to the world.

Such was the environment that Isabel and her family returned to from Scotland early in 1882.

The first Australian books that could be considered significant were Marcus Clarke's "For the Term of his Natural Life," (1874) and Rolf Bolderwood's "Robbery Under Arms." (1882). Both were serialized before they were published in book form. Serialization was the accepted form of publication in Victorian times and with such a small population base this became a safe way in Australia as well to test for success and popularity. "Robbery Under Arms," written in colloquial language was extremely popular in Australia and read world wide when it was published. It would have influenced the young Isabel as did the Victorian authors whose books the Grants read - Sir Walter Scott, Dickens, Thackeray, James Fenimore Cooper, Bulwer-Lytton, Charles Lever and Mark Twain. Another influence on her writing would have been the Bulletin Magazine, first published in 1880, which either created the environment or tapped into the growing predilection for a good Australian yarn.

Authors Henry Lawson and "Banjo" Patterson, who have become icons in their field, were published in the Bulletin. They and other writers were instrumental in expressing the spirit of the Australian male as a bush dweller, tough, sentimental, laconic, a man of action, capable and independent.

Isabel's writing owes something to this ideal although her characters are all set in her own milieu, professionals in small country-town Australia. Isabel resisted the popular genre for tales to make the readers flesh creep. She also resisted the tragic or the siteing of her characters in crushing isolation in the bush. She uses plots with a twist and her setting is Australia.

Her style was very popular at the time. The fact that in her writing she uses far too many adjectives and adverbs, is frankly sentimental and is tempted by the melodramatic is a present day criticism. Her serialized novel was said in its day to be "a capital story, full of human interest, capitally told" and that "our author does not give way to sentiment."

While her sentimental element has not worn well her humour has. It is the humour of misadventure and typically Australian, a broad but sympathetic style in which everyone can participate including the victim. The humourous situations she uses are as funny today as they were when written. It is a pity that so few of these were found.

Like most Scots, particularly Highlanders coming, as she says from a "toilsome life," she made an excellent settler and her writing shows she identifies herself with the consciousness and traditions of Australia. She shows none of the torment of fellow Australian Ethel Lindesay who wrote acknowledged classics such as "The Getting of Wisdom." Ethel, better know under her pen-name of Henry Handel Richardson was born within a day of Isabel. Richardson, as often with the really gifted, shows a compulsion to show up the inequalities of life. She writes with a simplicity so unlike the popular and rather ponderous prose of her era. Isabel, on the other hand, shows no torment with the lot of women. There is no hint of dissatisfaction with Australian culture, sophistication or life, and her prose while not ponderous could be crisper.

The Victorian and Edwardian society demand that women assume a restrained demeanor suited Isabel. She *was* gentle and self-effacing but this overlaid a strong will. She admired restrained capable professional women who also remained deferential to their men folk. A niece of her daughter's age who visited regularly found her overbearingly prim and proper. Youth in the 1920s, to Isabel's consternation, had left Victorian ideals behind. While the niece did not warm to her Aunty Belle she did admire her capabilities. She particularly remembers an excellent teaset Isabel made at pottery classes.

Isabel's literary career was precipitated in 1892 when the editor of Rockhampton's *The Capricornian* Newspaper, Mr. W. McIlwraith, instigated a competition "with a view to encouraging native talent and enhancing the attractions of" his Christmas Supplement. Her entry under the nom de plume Craig Ellachie did not fit the formula to win a prize but was used in the next year's supplement. Mr. McIlwraith was looking for stories for "the enjoyment and <u>instruction</u>" of his readers. The winning entries were therefore very similar; strongly moralistic and sentimental love stories. Isabel's story which appears on page 3 is a charming little tale but without the necessary 'young man goes bad but finds salvation in God and the love of a pure woman" element to be chosen in the top three.

Her background shapes her writing. Isabella Grant was born in Milton, Glen Urquhart, Scotland on the second day of the year 1870. During her life she was called Belle or Isabel. Her father, William Grant, had at that stage taken up farming on a large tract of land called locally Tychet.

His history is worth recording as her later material bears witness to his adventures on the gold fields of Australia and to the easy Australian egalitarianism he developed there. After finishing his indentures as a tailor he emigrated on an assisted passage in 1851 as a young 19 year old. He arrived in Melbourne at the time when ships were being abandoned by their crews in harbour – the great gold rush had just begun! It would seem that he joined the mad rush with a group of friends.

He did well at the diggings and sailed home to wed a hometown girl, Jessie McDonald. William returned a second time to Australia shortly after the wedding in 1858 with his new bride. He and Jessie farmed in a fertile area outside Melbourne which again seems to have brought him wealth as he was able to return to Glen Urquhart after eight years with their four surviving children to buy a home and a farm, which would certainly been beyond his means had he not emigrated. Five more children were born in The Glen, of whom Isabel was the second.

William's Australian friends were writing to tell of new finds of gold, this time in Queensland, so after 14 years William left for the third time for Australia, this time their destination was Brisbane. His enthusiasm and Jessie's strong sense of family caused the whole family to emigrate together. Isabel was 11 and a scholar. From Brisbane they moved to Rockhampton, the port city for the fabulously rich gold town of Mt. Morgan.

1884 was a tragic year for the family with her sister Mary dying at 16 of typhus and her father a few months later of pneumonia.

Jessie, with the aid of her two working sons, managed to keep all four younger children at school.

Isabel did six months of domestic duties at home after reaching her fourteenth year but quickly returned to the academic life. She sat for and passed her Teacher's examination and took up her pupilage in July 1885 which she completed in 1889.

Comments from inspectors reports over 15 years range from –"very intelligent, bright and kind." "The most cultured member of the staff;" "remarkably intelligent;" "is studious and well read." "The most intellectual and cultured member of the staff." "Her method of teaching formerly somewhat erratic has grown to be steadier and more impressive." Her only problem in the beginning seems to stem from being "not as vigorous and assertive in discipline as is necessary."

Her career in teaching spanned twenty four years, the last five as Head Mistress of the Central Girls' Schools first in Maryborough and then finally back to Rockhampton.

She retired in 1909 to marry Jack Murray from Maryborough, having lived until her late thirties at home with two brothers, two sisters and her Mother.

After her marriage she wrote the Kiddies Corner for the Maryborough newspaper. That work is not within the scope of this collection.

Isabel's male siblings influenced her writing strongly. Her eldest brother John, a carpenter and later Mayor of Mount Morgan, gave her access to the experience of living in the environment of a mining town where she was able to see the behind the scenes of the lives of mine managers, city fathers and the working men. She used that to good effect in her novel "A Furnace for Gold."

All three brothers played rugby and continued a strong involvement on committee work long after their playing days were over. She wrote one poem on "Football" and a short story based around the time of convalescence from injuries of a teenage football player.

Her brothers Kenneth and Hugh both studied the classics. Their books and influence were therefore at hand for Isabel to absorb. Hugh became a solicitor, and legal understanding is pivotal in two of Isabel's short stories.

At the turn of the century both brothers were inspired by the nationalism, unionism and socialism movement sweeping Australia.

Kenneth was elected to State Parliament and eventually became Minister for Mines and later Minister for Education. Isabel was living in the family home with them during this active time but she made little use of what must have been passionate political debates. Neither did the suffragette movement capture Isabel's interest. This can be attributed to her luck in the goals she wanted to achieve and in her brothers' liberal attitude to women's rights.

She enjoyed freedom to expand and achieve within her chosen pursuits. She wrote and was published, she succeeded and was recognised in her profession and she married for love and with motherhood she achieved another desired goal. That she was able to continue earning an income with her writing after marriage was a luxury.

Only once is the plight of the working man alluded to and she shows that her brothers' ambitions for the working man has not awakened any crusading zeal in her. In her novel, written during these years, she has a character suggest that "those fellows in there ought to get a fair share of the gold they work for." The mine owner replies "Poor wretches; indeed they do not get it. I should not care at this day to earn my bread under their conditions ... however as we are on our way to a ball, we needn't stop now to discuss the labour problem in the mine need we?" This sums up her attitude of acceptance of conditions and a disinterest to challenge the status quo.

She valued hard work and long term commitment and saw them as the way to succeed. She was a committed Christian without being hypercritical or narrow minded which is unfortunately sometimes the case. She was a kind person with a sense of humour as well as a touch of easy melancholy, characteristics inherited from her father. Her profession of teaching encouraged a desire to manage people which she thought of as "gently guiding." A robustly confident husband and daughter did not let this trait become too evident but she did suffer from the clashes.

The big sea voyage by sailing ship from Scotland to Australia lasting three months impressed the young Isabel and in later years the sea was her chosen method of travel to visit Sydney and other coastal cities. Two of her poems deal with voyages by sailing ship and I consider one of them, "The Two Ships" to be one of her more powerful poems. Her birth and childhood in Scotland show in occasional phrases and quotations in her writings which also have a preponderance of trim, blue eyed male characters.

Her teaching background shows in her skilful handling of children's language and actions and in the interaction with adults. Her child characters are treated with more matter-of-factness than her adults, who often suffer from the cloying sentimentality of the era. The works have been presented as close to their original layouts as possible showcasing popular writing at the turn of the century which also happens to give a history of Australia, the people and the times.

Gail Grant is the wife of Hugh Grant, Isabel's great nephew. They are one of five families still living in the Central Queensland area who are descended from Isabel's parents, the first Grant immigrants to settle here.

Acknowledgements

I would like to thank Margaret Berry for allowing me the free use of Isabel's work. Margaret is Isabel's grand-daughter and the custodian of nearly half of this collection.

I would like to acknowledge my debt to Jennifer Lentell for her major effort in all aspects of research into Isabel Grant's life. With her guidance at the State Archives in Brisbane we found the records of Isabel as a pupil and later as a teacher. This initial research gave a rich and vibrant background to Isabel's life and was one the deciding factors in pursuing her literary work for this collection.

Jennifer is a member of the Central Queensland Family History Society and deserves her reputation of being one of the most prolific and knowledgeable researchers in Queensland. She also unearthed many references to Isabel from the local newspapers all of which have added to the understanding of Isabel's early life with her family in Rockhampton.

Thanks also to John Rowland for sharing extra finds of Isabel's life and literary progress which he came across in local newspapers while pursuing his own research.

My thanks to Michael Roser, then editor of *The Gympie Times* for generously supplying information on the history of that paper and to the staff at the Gympie Library for finding a second story Isabel wrote for *The Gympie Times*. That story, A Tale of a Turkey, was published in 1910 and appears on page 124.

Thanks to my many friends for helpful advice and particularly to Pat Handley for many hours of practical help with the computer as well as support and interest. To Renee Millar for her great help in typing out most of the novel for me. Also to my son Duncan, husband Hugh and sister in law Barbara for their interest and help.

THE COLLECTED PUBLISHED WORKS OF ISABEL GRANT

Craig Ellachie

BACKGROUND TO THIS WORK

Isabel Grant used the *nom de plume* Craig Ellachie. This name derives from a mountain in the highlands of Scotland called Craigellachie. In the turbulent past the mountain was used during times of trouble to rally Grant clansmen by lighting bonfires on its sides to signal a call to arms. From this comes the Grant crest: a flaming mountain, and war cry: "Stand fast Craigellachie."

It was common in the late nineteenth century for women to use a male name in the hope of wider acceptance by editors and readers. For example Ethel Florence Lindesay, born in the same year as Isabel and one of Australia's first internationally acclaimed writers used the pen-name Henry Handel Richardson.

Isabel put cuttings of the work published under this name in a leather bound book. Her hand written title page is used above. Unfortunately the book has suffered the fate of age and the surviving work is predominately poems. None of the cuttings from this scrapbook retain the date or identity of the publication. However one story published under this *nom de plume* was found in The Capricornian newspaper in the Christmas edition 1893. Because this is the earliest published work to be traced I have elected to start the collection with the stories and poems written as Craig Ellachie.

CRAIG ELLACHIE

THE LENGTHSMEN'S CAMP

BACKGROUND TO THE PUBLICATION

A hint of the existence of this story came in 1905 from a speech by Mr. W. McIlwraith, co-owner and editor of Rockhampton's daily *Morning Bulletin* and weekly *Capricornian*, when he farewelled Isabel on her transfer from the Central Girls' School. He speaks of her "literary development, of which he was a keen observer" and mentions that she had submitted a story for a competition he was running "in connection with *The Capricornian*."

After some research the competition was found in 1892. The winning entries were all chosen with exactly the same format of a love story with the moral – Australia gives to those who practice habits of thrift, sobriety and persistence.

Isabel's story did not fit into this mould but was published in the next Christmas supplement in 1893. Her story is a lot less sentimental. It gives a snapshot of domestic life in her time and perfectly captures the rub of irritation between her two contrasting female characters and the distance both husbands keep from the emotional turmoil. She has used a mundane situation with skill to create an interesting and pleasant story.

With a verve typical of the pioneering spirit of the times Rockhampton's first paper was brought out in 1861 shortly after settlement and with a population of just 689. By 1870 Charles Buzacott, who had taken over ownership from his brother decided to follow a venture proving successful with the southern newspaper and launched a synopsis of his daily paper in a weekly version to be sent to the outback with the mails. Named *The Capricornian,* it proved a great success with both country and city readers. It contained a mixture of news, local events, agricultural and pastoral information and included a significant portion devoted to fiction. William McIlwraith was a successful and influential editor and public figure guiding both his papers from 1880 -1911 into a dominant position.

TALES FOR CHRISTMASTIDE.

THE LENGTHSMEN'S CAMP

By CRAIG ELLACHIE

"Well, I hope Darrawell is settled now, and I shall have no more trouble." The superintendent spoke in a tone that did not seen to indicate much hope, as he turned to his dinner with a vexed air.

"How is it that you have so much trouble with these lengthsmen's camps?" his wife asked curiously.

"There's always a woman in it, my dear, women I ought to say, for we have none of this bother with a bachelors' camp. But let there be two or three women together with little to do, and they raise a shindy to pass the time. Half of my time I'm settling quarrels, separating those who can't get on together. But I hope there will be none of this at Darrawell."

After a few minutes' silence he broke out again. "Do you remember Biddy Finucane?" His wife nodded. "Well, I've sent her and Pat up there. She is the best old soul in the world, and the only other woman is that pretty, quiet young wife of Sandy Gordon. These two women are sure to get on, and I can be quite easy about Darrawell for three months at least."

The lengthsmen's camp at Darrawell was a very rough affair. Two little two-roomed houses for the married couples, and six or seven tents for the single men. By the first Saturday in December they had all reached their new homes. Biddy might be seen bustling in and out of her little house, preparing breakfast. Little personal beauty had been granted to Biddy, except her sparkling Irish eyes that shone out of her brown, wrinkled skin with a merry, kindly look. The withered skin clung to the bones as tightly as in a mummy.

Boots were articles of fine attire to Biddy; in the house they were always laid aside, and the large knobby feet moved as easily over the stony ground as though her soles had been changed to leather. Pat, a picture of lazy contentment, leant up against the side of the door, smoking a short, black pipe, and giving now and then a word of encouragement to his busy wife.

Some ten yards away, in the other little house, the reverse of the picture might be seen. Just inside the room, and out of the rays of the morning sun, sat Rose Gordon with a beautiful baby boy in her arms, directing her husband as he set about preparing the breakfast for both. So fair a picture they made that Sandy stopped now and again with the fryingpan in his hand to admire. The tall, powerful figure of the Scotsman moving about the little room with the little frying-pan in his large hands looked both comical and pathetic. But this seemed to strike neither the husband, who was bending all his energies to his task, nor the young wife sitting so comfortably on the large trunk. When breakfast was over Sandy began to prepare a substantial lunch in a way that showed it was no unaccustomed task, and then to gather his tools for the day's work. At last he turned to go, but paused at the door, "You won't feel lonely will you, Rose? This is different from our last place."

The wife looked up with unmistakable love in her beautiful eyes, and said softly, "Why, Alick, how could I, when I have baby: Besides that, Mrs. Finucane seemed real nice when we came up in the train yesterday." It was characteristic of Sandy's English wife that she would on no account call her husband "Sandy." Alexander, Alick, and even Lex she had attempted, to her husband's amusement, but nothing so common as "Sandy." For the same reason she had insisted on her little son receiving the overpowering name of Charles Albert Edward.

Biddy had had a busy time of it until the men were gone to work, for she had volunteered in her hearty way as they came up in the train to cook and wash for the single men as well as Pat. In this way Biddy turned many an honest penny. Biddy was proud of her cooking abilities, and if the food was not served in too particular a manner, few lengthsmen were fastidious. After breakfast was over and the little houses set in order, the women were free for the rest of the day.

Biddy soon got through her work; so feeling inclined for a gossip she put on a battered old hat of Pat's and ran up to her new neighbour. Rose had taken her work in a more leisurely manner, and had hardly finished dressing the baby when a shadow fell on the doorway, and Biddy stepped in. Rose looked up with her usual placid smile, though truth to tell she felt rather vexed that her new neighbour should find her work behind-hand on her first visit.

Biddy came forward with such real kindliness that the slight vexation vanished.

"You see," Rose explained in the proudly apologetic tone of a young mother, "Baby kept me." "Let me hold the purty little lad while you fix things;" cried Biddy, then added in a tone unlike her ordinary one, "Ah, I buried five children, nivir a one left of them all, five boys, and the last one had the same eyes as your baby. My little Michael he would have been twenty-one come Christmas if he had lived."

Rose laid her boy in Biddy's arms, with a pitiful look in her eyes for the woman who had lost her children.

Before the men came home the violent and often fleeting surface friendships that women conceive for each other had begun between the two. This friendship is apt to pass away in indifference or actual dislike, unless something awakes the deeper feelings, when it becomes firm, faithful, and lifelong.

When Sandy came home he was delighted at the state of affairs. While Rose got the supper ready she talked incessantly of Biddy, how kindhearted she was. "Fancy, Alick, the poor thing told me she buried five children, you should have seen the look she gave to Charlie when she said it."

Sandy was busy scrubbing his big head in the little tin basin at the door and could not reply, but Rose needed none, and chattered happily until her husband was ready to sit down. Sandy was a man of few words, and though he was really delighted that the only woman neighbour should prove so friendly, he only said, " She is a real good woman, I'm glad you have got such a sensible one near you."

Curiously enough Sandy's praise of Biddy seemed hardly to please Rose, and she changed the subject.

Sandy was quite at ease now about his wife. Somehow to this big-hearted Scotsman, Rose had made a very poor match in marrying such a rough fellow as himself; and as far as it lay in him he tried to make her life smooth for her. Rose little knew what a noble fellow was the man on whom she fancied she had almost thrown herself away. Rose prided herself on her correct English, and Sandy's slips in moments of excitement into his mother tongue—the tongue of Burns, were matters of real mortification to his wife. What would she have done with a fellow like Pat?

For a week the friendship was at fever beat. If Rose was not down, Biddy was up. Then it began, naturally, to cool. Biddy's cooking was a matter of pride to the whole camp, and really, considering the materials, Biddy worked wonders. Then, perhaps, Biddy was inclined to be boastful, and Rose resented the implied superiority. Sometimes Sandy, though rarely, would complain of his own badly-prepared meals, and contrast them with what Biddy supplied with the same materials.

No woman cares to hear another praised at her expense, and Rose began almost unconsciously to herself, to strive to outdo Biddy in the superior comfort and cleanliness of her little house. Then began a tacit, though openly friendly rivalry. However slatternly Biddy was in dress, her house was as neat as a pin, and Biddy would not let her neighbour out-shine her. When Pat's house was resplendent in white curtains Rose had bought curtains and matting too. Not to be outdone Biddy sent down the line for a rocking chair (an ordinary one); Rose immediately retorted by buying a sofa. Perhaps it was a petty thing, but the rivalry was very real to the two women, who had little else to occupy their time.

The state of immaculate cleanliness in which both houses were kept was something to admire. Pat complained there was no rest for the soles of his feet, Biddy made him take off his boots at the back before he came in. Sandy bore it all with invincible good humour, but even he began to feel slightly irritated as day by day Rose grew more fastidious. Biddy was very open in her ways, and often talked to the young fellows about the latest thing Rose had bought; and what she intended to get; and the young men out of sheer, thoughtless fun would work up Biddy and even Pat to a passing anger. A sore feeling had arisen on both sides.

Sandy alone scorned to notice the petty rivalry, even when hot-tempered Pat would become almost aggressive. "Leave the women alone, Pat," he would say, "it will come right in time."

Events came to a crisis one day in the middle of December. Biddy had been washing hard all day. In the first week of friendship she had proposed to Sandy that Rose should help and share the profits. But Sandy, said sharply, "As long as I live my wife will never need to do such a thing, and if I die, my life's insured and she won't want; my bonnie little lass."

Biddy thought with some bitterness of easy-going Pat, who was quite content to let his wife slave on, as long as he had money for his periodic drinking bouts.

Rose had finished her own little washing in the early morning, and now at sunset in her pretty pink print, had gone out to meet her husband. Sandy hurried home before the others, and when he met her, took little Charlie from her. Rose carried his billy and sauntered slowly homewards. They made a pretty picture, and so thought Biddy, as she was out emptying her last tub. Poor Biddy, the contrast was bitter, and evident even to herself, as she stood there, barefooted, disheveled, and worn out. Rose looked up, and in her careless happiness, glanced with ill concealed pride, from her own trim attire to poor Biddy. Sandy had at this moment made some comical remark, and Rose laughed a sudden, shrill, sweet laugh. Biddy saw the glance and heard the laugh, and her whole fiery Irish nature was roused. It seemed to her a deliberate insult. At this moment the rest came into sight, and Biddy caught up her tub and hurried to her own door.

Sandy and Rose lingered for a moment to speak to Pat. Pat eyed with approving eyes the pretty little woman so neat and fresh. As be passed on and entered his own door, he found Biddy bending over the fire. Pat glanced with disapproval at the untidy figure, and said in an injured tone, "Why don't you try and look a little more like Sandy Gordon's wife, Biddy. She looks so clean and neat."

Biddy turned round with blazing eyes, though a tear was slowly coursing down her withered cheek. "Why don't I look like her? Why don't you work like him, Pat Finucane? I slave from morning till night, and the first chance you get you drink all my money in one big booze. Thirty years since I married you, Pat Finucane, and nivir was I insulted like this day." For a moment Biddy faltered, but soon burst out again. "Yes, she's young and pretty, and has a happy life. I'd like to see her in my place. "Biddy's voice rose higher and higher. Pat was cowed by the storm he had so unwittingly raised, and bent all his energies on soothing his wife.

Rose had no idea of the storm brewing, and was surprised after breakfast to see Biddy coming up dressed in her finest, with a look on her face that caused Rose some wonder. Biddy knocked—another wonder; and came in at Rose's invitation. Her eyes looked even brighter than usual, but their light was no longer friendly. In some ten minutes Biddy had relieved her mind, and Rose began to understand her visitor. Biddy had a vigorous Irish tongue, and once fairly started, her own vehemence carried her away. Rose felt herself innocent of intentional insult, and tried to say so; but Biddy stormed on unheeding. Biddy shouted and gesticulated, and Rose listened in angry silence. At last there was a lull, and Rose went to the door. "Leave my house, and don't darken my door again," Rose spoke in the quiet tone of intense passion, her nature was that slow one that once angered finds it almost impossible to forgive.

"Oh! Indeed," said Biddy, with a toss of her old head, "tisn't me ever stays where I'm not wanted." The assumed dignity was intensely comic, but neither woman noticed it. The loud talking had wakened little Charlie, who now broke into a loud wail. The mother turned with an utter change of manner, and caught up her boy. Biddy's face softened, and unconsciously she took a step forward. Rose saw the movement, and clasped her baby closely to her, crying "Don't come near him, you wild Irish thing, you might do him harm."

Biddy turned away with a pitiful, chidden air, and went slowly homewards. When she reached her own room, Biddy sat down on the bed and looked drearily round. Her anger had left her, and only sadness remained. The poor old face quivered now and then, but no tears came.

Once her lips moved, "So like my Michael!" But that was all. She remained in this position for some time, then glancing at the clock, she rose slowly and painfully and began to damp some white garments from yesterday's wash.

Sandy found a very different wife to the one he had left in the morning. Rose for some time held her peace, but soon broke into an indignant account of Biddy's visit. It did not strike Sandy as of much importance. "Bear in mind, Rose, her hard life, and don't you be too hard, lassie, on the words an old woman says in haste."

"In haste," cried Rose, with bitter emphasis. "Why she had all the night to get over it, and one thing is certain, I'll never speak to her again, and there's only one thing you can do, that is, get shifted to another camp."

Sandy reasoned, explained that instead of a removal he might get a dismissal, but Rose was firm. At last Sandy lost his temper, and gave Rose the first real scolding since their marriage. Rose burst into tears; but with all the quiet obstinacy of her nature would not yield. A very unhappy night passed in both houses. Next day whenever Rose met Biddy, she stared in an unseeing way before her, and the half-hearted attempts of Biddy to heal the quarrel, shrank away before the frozen air of Rose

Life at Darrawell became a very dreary affair, even easy-going Pat felt the unhappy atmosphere. At last Sandy determined to end this uncomfortable state of affairs, and wrote to the Superintendent respectfully asking for a transfer to another camp. When the letter arrived the Superintendent tossed it aside, with the remark. "Thought as much; even two women can't get on together, for I'll bet anything it's his wife who wants the transfer. And such a quiet looking woman, too."

Sandy received a letter saying that a week would be given to reconsider the matter, as the Superintendent expected to be at Darrawell the day after Boxing Day, and would see to it personally. The letter ended with the hint that times were hard, and many would be glad of the billet.

Sandy showed the letter to his wife, but she was firm, and four days of the allotted week passed in the usual uncomfortable manner. The last four days had been intensely hot, and though Rose prepared everything, it did not seem to her that next day could be Christmas.

A thunderstorm had threatened each day, but did not break, and so at sunset, though the sky was dark, the air was so close and hot that Rose dressed little Charlie in a light muslin frock, and went to meet Sandy.

Before she had gone far the storm broke, and the rain fell in torrents. Rose turned and ran home, but before she had reached the door they were both drenched, and Charlie's little body was blue with cold, for as usual in a thunderstorm, the atmosphere had lowered rapidly several degrees.

Rose had literally no experience of nursing. Charlie had been a remarkably healthy child, but even she could see the boy was distressed. She undressed him quickly, and covered him up; then she went to remove her own wet clothing. She came again and again to feel his hands. He seemed feverish, she thought, and waited with a heavy heart for Sandy.

When Sandy came in the sight of his wife's troubled face startled him. But he took the matter more easily than Rose. "Charlie is a strong boy, a ducking won't hurt him," he said hopefully.

Rose was relieved, and went to prepare supper with a lightened heart, and Christmas Eve passed happily enough at the little house at Darrawell. Towards midnight Rose woke up with the sound of a cough in her ears. She struck a match and came to Charlie's crib. The baby stirred in his sleep, then came the hollow cough again. Rose lit the lamp, and turned to the crib again, when Charlie threw up his little hands and began to fight for his breath. The little face was purple, the limbs rigid. Rose flew to Sandy, crying, "Wake up, wake up, Charlie is dying. In an instant Sandy was on his feet, he glanced to the bed.

"Oh what shall we do?" moaned Rose. 'Look, he is choking." Sandy was as helpless as Rose, and could only look on in speechless agony. Suddenly Rose sprang to her feet, "Run Sandy, run and get Biddy, she can help us, and she's too kind not to come."

Sandy lost no time in obeying, and Biddy was wakened by a loud rapping at the door. "Quick!" Sandy was shouting. "Come up, Charlie is choking."

In no time Biddy was at the door, ready for anything. "What's up," she cried. "Don't wait," cried Sandy, in agonized tones. "I tell you the baby's choking."

"Croup," said Biddy promptly. "Here, take this tub; what a blessing I left the kettle on, the water must be near boiling." As Biddy was speaking, she seized the tub, handed it to Sandy, took up the kettle, and felt in her little safe for a bottle of brandy.

They found Charlie still struggling for breath, while Rose hung helplessly over him, her tears falling on the baby's distorted face.

Without a word Biddy took the tub from Sandy, poured the hot water into it, found it too hot and poured in some cold water that, fortunately, was in the billy on the table. Then with tender, loving hands she got Charlie ready, and popped him into the hot bath. In a few minutes the breathing became easier, and as Biddy rubbed the little hands and chest with brandy, the blue, rigid look passed away. Biddy then lifted him out of the bath, and when she had dried him a natural perspiration broke out.

"He'll do now, bless his little heart. Cover him up warm, and let him sleep."

Rose broke into the tears of relief, and seizing Biddy's hard, toilworn hand, she raised it to her lips and kissed it passionately.

"You gave me back my baby. Oh! May Heaven bless you and forgive me." Rose could say no more, and sank on her knees beside Charlie's little crib, and pressed her lead against her recovered treasure The old woman laid her hard, brown hand softly on the bowed golden head and said with a tenderness that was infinite.

"Oh, my dear! My dear! Don't thank me, thank the Lord that he has spared your boy, though he took mine from me; I am a poor, proud old woman, and should think shame of what I said in this very room. But wasn't it this day, the book says, that brought peace and goodwill to the earth, for," said Biddy, with a quick change of humour, as she glanced to the little clock on the shelf, "Tis the Christmas morn, and a Merry Christmas I wish you both." And in the wish for Christmas time the petty strife between the two women passed away. When the Superintendent arrived on the twenty-seventh, he was agreeably surprised to find Gordon had changed his mind, and no vexatious transfer would be necessary, though, after all, if he had only known, there was "a woman in it," in fact two.

THE COLLECTED PUBLISHED WORKS OF ISABEL GRANT

THE FOLLOWING ITEM WAS REPORTED IN *THE CAPRICORNIAN* ON THE 31ST. OF October **1891** AND PROVIDES AN UNDERSTANDING OF THE JOB OF A LENGTHSMAN.

Mr. Archer, the member for Rockhampton. remarks the *Brisbane Courier* of Wednesday, yesterday presented a petition to the Legislative Assembly from a number of lengthsmen on the Central Railway line, stating that they are now charged ground rent for the land upon which their "humpies" are erected at the rate of 2s. per month, and also freight on their rations. These new impositions, coming on top of the reduction made in their wages some months ago, affect them very severely, and indeed they say it cuts down their poor earnings by from fifteen to twenty-five per cent. The petition asked relief from these disabilities, and pointed out that although it might be considered desirable to place all the employees on the same footing, it should not be forgotten that the circumstances of the Central Railway are different from those of the Southern lines, as it runs through unoccupied country, whilst the latter pass through flourishing agricultural districts, whence supplies may be obtained at a low rate. The petition was received.

CRAIG ELLACHIE

The following story was found in the scrapbook containing some of the work Isobel submitted under the *nom de plume* Craig Ellachie. It is not dated and the identity of the newspaper has not been established.

TWICE MISSED
(By Craig Ellachie)

(Written for the News.)

The other day I came across an announcement in an English paper of the marriage of the Earl of Cardorn, with Muriel, second daughter of the Duke of Sillford. A full description of the dresses, presents, &c followed in the usual style but I paid little attention to anything except the bare names; for, strange as it might seem, I was at one time the chosen friend of the man whose marriage the paper was announcing with such pomp. To me, I might say he owed the greatest benefit one man may bestow on another. It was no very difficult thing in those days to make his acquaintance; probably I am not the only one who says, as he sees this notice, "Oh! I knew him very well when he was George Carew;" for, at the time I mentioned, he was book-keeper in the employ of Jacobs and Anderson, at Waruinga.

The firm presented the awful combination of a Jew and a Scotchman, and it was a particularly smart man who got the better of either in any transaction. They had a practical monopoly of all the trade in the little bush town, which consisted of some fifty houses, a bank, and a combined post and telegraph office. Jacobs and Anderson owned the general store which sold all the necessaries and most of the luxuries of bush life. At the same time the only good hotel in the place belonged to them. Their employees, by a sort of tacit understanding were expected to board there. The board was high, the wages received at the store not great, so that, as a matter of fact, Jacobs and Anderson did little more than board their employees in return for more labor than any other firm would have managed to get for twice the money.

I had charge of the drapery establishment, and as Carew and I, of course, boarded at the same place, we were thrown a good deal together. Carew was a big, fair fellow, with a face that had already begun to show the signs of steady drinking. He was weak, yet with most people a kind of hearty bluffness carried this off, while his ready tongue gave him the reputation among the rest of being a bit of an orator. He was certainly the quickest impromptu speaker I have ever met. His scholarship alone should have given him a good position (for he had received an university education) if he were not evidently destroying all his chances and going to the dogs. Yet he was the most generous, kind-hearted fellow to be found—one who would sell his coat for a needy mate; the black sheep of a family; one of the many who seek a new country, in the vain hope of leaving behind the vices that have cursed their career in the old.

The barmaid at the hotel was reckoned a very pretty girl. I didn't think much of her beauty myself, but all the men raved about it. Perhaps it was "sour grapes," for she never once looked my way after a remark I made the first day I came. Nelly was a bit of a cockney, but such a quick, clever girl that she knew her own shortcomings, and was trying hard to remedy them. She was particularly sensitive about this failing, but of course I did not know this, and when the girl said, "It's dreadfully 'ot; I'll go out and get some fresh 'air," I couldn't resist the rather mean remark—"I'm sure, Miss Wilson, you have no need; your beautiful hair is all your own."

I'll never forget the look the girl gave me as she turned from the open door on the way to the verandah. One or two of the fellows laughed, and the girl never forgave me or took any more notice of me than she was obliged to. Not that I cared—she was not my style, and I could watch quite calmly the struggles of the rest. The two favorites seemed to be Grahame, the bank manager who boarded here too, and Carew. Grahame was a wide-awake Scotchman, and could take good care of him; and Carew was the sort of fellow who falls in love with some girl or other periodically and recovers easily. Nelly was not the sort of girl to do a foolish thing, and would think twice before she threw herself away on Carew, though she might keep him dangling round.

The great excitement of the third week after I had come was the "Melbourne Cup". Nearly every man in the town had a ticket. This was the year when "Zelinda" was running, Zelinda, who had won last year's cup, and was all but certain to win this year's too. The list was expected to be out on Thursday. The first prize in the consultation was £30000.

On Thursday evening as I was coming up the street I met Carew, who was in a very excited state. I stopped him and asked what was the matter, though I expected to find him partly drunk. He was quite sober, however, and told me he had drawn Zelinda, and that Jacobs had offered him £5,000 for his chance. He had refused; he meant to stick to it, for his luck had turned at last, and it was about time. I advised him to take the £5,000, but he would not listen, but went on talking in his mad way. "It was a sure thing, he would be fool to let it go; Jacobs was not the kind of man to risk his money unless he were morally certain of a return." I turned and walked back with him to the hotel. I saw a girl's figure on the verandah, and knew it was Nelly's. Carew recognised it too, for he suddenly stopped, caught me by the arm, and broke out, "By Jove, I'll propose to Nell; she'll not refuse me; my luck's on to-night; I'll win everything."

I tried to say something about the foolishness of it all—how the girl would be a fool to have him; he would be a worse to have her; that if she did accept him it would be for the sake of the money, and she'd lead him a life with it; that, after all, Zelinda was a shaky chance, and a lot more, for I really liked the fellow. But he only laughed good-naturedly and sprang up the steps. I passed on to my own room.

Next morning at breakfast I guessed by Grahame's glum face, and the excellent look on Carew's, that he had been successful after all. I thought Nelly was hardly the shrewd girl I expected when she would take Carew—careless, unsteady Carew on the mere chance of the £30,000. I had expected her to hold him off until it was certain. At the store all day Carew was overflowing with fun, and quite sober. I saw Nellie and him walking together in the evening. On Friday the races would come off, so we would know the result next day.

On Saturday morning, about eleven. I had to go over to the post office, and I saw a bit of a crowd gathered; the result of the race had come. Zelinda was nowhere, and I had to go back and tumble down poor Carew's castle in the air. He burst into a perfect yell of laughter when I told him, though his eyes had a dazed look in them, and his face quickly settled into a hard, melancholy expression.

He sprang from the desk where he was sitting, with an oath, and came up beside me, his big form towering over me, dilating with sudden passion, "Nelly is a brick, this won't make any difference to her; it's not the money she cares for, and I'll break every bone in your body if you say a word against her;" he finished with another oath. But in spite of all his bluster there was a look of furtive anxiety in his eyes, and I felt that Nelly was not the sort of girl to sacrifice herself for love. I was agreeably surprised again when, that evening, he told me Nelly held to her engagement. Money, she said, made no difference to her, and she thanked me, he said, for my opinion of her; for, of course, like a lover, he had told her everything. How that girl hated me!

For a week or two affairs went on smoothly enough; then, I fancy, Nelly had begun to repent of her bargain, and began flirting with Grahame. George spoke to her about it; they quarrelled, made it up again, but Carew began once more to take to the drink, which he had given up for the girl's sake. Nelly threw him over at once; it seemed to me she was only waiting for an opportunity to do it decently, but perhaps I was too hard on her. Carew had been hard hit this time, for he collapsed utterly. He remained away from the store next day, drinking heavily. He came on the day following, and Jacobs promptly sacked him. For three days he hung about the hotel, drinking the remains of his month's salary. On the fourth day I had gone over to the post office, and the postmaster asked me to give a letter to Carew if I saw him; it had been there two days. I took the letter—a big blue one—and promised to deliver it. I saw no sign of Carew all day, but after tea I had gone for a solitary walk in the moonlight by the Yarriwell, the little creek on which Waruinga stands. I saw a tall figure lounging some distance ahead that looked familiar. It was Carew, I saw at once, but his attitude was a strange one, and one glance at what he carried in his raised hand sent me running towards him. It was a pistol, and the wild, haggard look on the man's face in the clear moonlight told me his purpose. He did not hear my approach over the grass; to snatch the pistol from him and fling it into the creek was the work of an instant.

He turned savagely upon me, but as he saw who it was his expression changed and it was with the pitiful look of the boy in pain which he does not understand that he said, "Oh! Jack, Jack why didn't you let me do it and get out of my misery?"

In the moonlight the dissipated look seemed to have left the man's face and a great pity for the wrecked life before me swept over me.

"Oh! It's not only the girl; it's everything. I've made a mull of my life from first to last, and it's not worth finishing," he said wearily and his great arms hung loosely by his side.

I turned without a word, and he came quietly with me. Together we entered my room, where I remembered the letter. He sat down and opened it. As he read, a change passed over him; every feature became tense, the listlessness gone. The letter was a bulky one and contained several documents. He read them slowly without a word, still with that look of strange intensity. When he had finished he handed them to me in silence.

What was my surprise to find that the letters were from a large firm of solicitors in London, informing him that, owing to the death of his uncle and his only son, he had succeeded to the title and estates of Cardorn. They enclosed a draft of money sufficient to pay any expenses connected with his return to England. Talk of luck! I knew he was of a pretty good family, and he was quite free; Nelly had given him up.

"Well," he said as I looked up, "what do you think of that turn of fortune's wheel? If you had been five minutes later Cardorn would have another master, and there would be another weak fool less in the world."

"Not many men get a chance like you; take my advice, go straight off in to-morrow's coach, you have nothing in the world to keep you."

"And Nelly?" He said in my own words some time ago. "What sort of a countess do you think she would make?"

"Thank your stars she has set you free."

He gave me a queer look, and asked, "Would she take the position if I offered it?"

I knew the weakness of the man- a generous weakness—and I determined to save him. If Nelly knew his rank, and had fire minutes with him, she could twist him round her finger. For some time he held to the opinion that he ought to tell her and let her decide. At last he agreed to ask the girl to renew the engagement, giving her a solemn promise to reform—that would be giving her a "fair show," as he expressed it.

"Come with me," he said with an embarassed laugh. "I'm such a fool; the girl will have it all out of me."

I hardly cared for the position, yet did not like to refuse, and we left the room together. We found Nelly on the verandah steps, the moonlight streaming down on her bright hair.

I felt awkward, out of place, as the first greetings over, which on Nelly's part were cold enough, and Carew plunged at once into his request to be forgiven. She looked to where I stood leaning against the verandah post, as if asking what my unwelcome presence meant. Carew saw the look, and said quietly I was there at his wish. She listened very coldly, and answered nothing could alter the past—not even a thorough reformation on his part. I saw a figure coming up the street that I felt sure was Grahame, and I understood her coldness. Carew saw it too, I saw the fire of rivalry, of love, spring into his eyes as a few quick, passionate words fell from him. I thought Nelly had learnt the secret from his hasty words, but she too was watching the advancing figure, and Carew's wild words seemed unheeded. I drew him away with difficulty, angry and ungrateful at my interference. But once in my room his mood changed; he sank into a chair

"It's better so, I'll leave to-morrow. I can never forget what you have done for me; and one thing more, tell Nelly two days after I am gone.'

That night he slept in my room, and left next morning by the early coach. I saw him off. He grasped my hand in parting as he thanked me, over and over, and asked me if ever I should find myself in the old country to visit Cardorn—and he meant it too.

The two days gone I went to find Nelly. I told her I had an important message for her, so she got the table-maid to take her place, and led the way to the empty sitting-room: closing the door she sat down and waited quietly. My mission was certainly not a pleasant one, but I stumbled somehow through it. She listened without a word, but a white look passed over the pretty face that was studying the table-cover so intently. She raised her head once.

"You prevented him from telling me; I know he wanted to," she said quietly, but with a curious dilation of her black eyes.

I felt a coward as I looked on the pale, downcast face. I had certainly prevented him. Was it regret for a grand career? Was it love that had whitened the pretty face? Twice missed — first £30,000, then a title. What woman ever lost two such golden opportunities in the short space of a week! A sudden wave of unreasoning pity passed over me, and I broke into clumsy half-apologies, half-hopes; it would make no difference, that she would not mind, that she would be my friend. I had scarcely finished my headlong speech when the girl had risen and stood before me. A change had passed over her face; it was flushed with passion. As my voice ceased she broke into perfect storm of anger. The regret, the disappointment, or whatever passion lent its vivid coloring to the girl's face, found its vent in the bitter invective, she poured out. The hate against me that had smouldered so long found an outlet at last. I must confess I never could face an angry woman, and I turned to fly. I fumbled with the door, and Nelly followed me. Never had I felt in such a humiliating position. My offer of friendship was treated with scorn. The dropping of her h's in her fury took little from the force of her outbreak. At last I opened the door and fairly fled. Never did I wish to see the face of Nelly Wilson again.

I severed my connection with Jacobs and Anderson next day, and left Waruinga by the first coach. As the coach drove past the hotel I saw Nelly on the verandah and Grahame beside her; a mocking smile lit up her face as we swept on. I have never seen her since. Does she ever speak of her one-time lover, the Earl of Cardorn? Trust Nelly for that. Neither have I visited England, nor am likely to. I don't suppose the Earl would care to be reminded of a very unpleasant episode in his life, but I certainly wonder whether he has told the Lady Muriel of his engagement with Nelly Wilson, the pretty barmaid of Waruinga.

CRAIG ELLACHIE

FOOTBALL

We are growing old and stiff, boys! The youngsters take our place,
And don the brave old colours that we wore;
With a calm contemptuous pity on each cheeky youthful face,
They tell us that our football days are o'er.
Yes! Our football days are over; it is useless to deplore,
Those days when "goal" and "try" could still enthrall,
Yet some tingling fierce excitement of the contest thrills once more,
At the cheery football watchword "on the Ball."

It is strange how memory wakens, at the sound of some old phrase,
What pictures rise at the catchwords of familiar football lore;
It is "Rally well up forwards" "Now then boys! Put on the pace,"
Or "collar low" the smart "back" to the fore.
When the "barrackers" hoarse voices mingling rise in one fierce roar,
As the swaying active figures rise and fall,
What to them our blows or tumbles, what though every bone is sore,
At the cheery football watchword "On the Ball."

Then to fail at "kick" or "passing" was a deeply felt disgrace,
And football fame was more than golden store;
The hero of the hour is he who wins a race,
Or "pots a goal" or adds a point unto the score.
Yes! Our football days are over, the golden days of yore,
When in careless opening manhood we held youth's festival,
And yet grim time, a moment, seems our lost youth to restore,
At the cheery football watchword "On the Ball."

ENVOI!
Old boys! The brave old comrades, leal and loyal to the core,
Would we could now those football days recall;
We'd meet once more together round the leather as before,
At the cheery football watchword "On the Ball."

Craig Ellachie

POETRY AND TRIFLES.

ORIGINAL POETRY.

" NO MORE SEA."

A strange superstition which exists in many parts of the earth among the dwellers by the sea is that the souls of the dying wait for and depart with the ebbing tide.

> My life's going out with the tide, laddie,
>   It ebbs with the tide ebb slow ;
> And the dawn's coming bright o'er the sea, laddie,
>   It has come, but to see me go.
> Repeat but the words once again, laddie,
>   Faintly your voice sounds to me,
> But they ring in my heart evermore, laddie,
>   " For there shall be no more sea."
>
> The sea-voice has ruled all my life, laddie,
>   It echoed my childish cry ;
> A girl and a wife I was here, laddie,
>   And here I am now to die.
> One by one it has called all I love, laddie,
>   Husband and children and friends;
> And I'm glad that the call's come for me, laddie,
>   Glad that it all now ends.
>
> And the winds and the wild waves cry, laddie,
>   And the fierce storms come and go,
> But the dear dark head of my love, laddie,
>   Lies down in the depths below.

CRAIG ELLACHIE

And the smiling waves hide deep, laddie,
   My boys with their eyes of blue;
The "flag half-mast" coming back, laddie,
   Was ever the first I knew.

How the old dead voices call, laddie,
   In the cry of the stormy wind;
In the roar of the waves I recall, laddie,
   Memories of days behind.
Oh heart-break and days of fear, laddie,
   Sorrow and midnight tears ;
With the pulse of the great sea hearty, laddie,
   Has my heart beat for seventy years.

Ah well is the flow of the tide, laddie,
   But the ebbing tide is best;
When the long, long years are done, laddie,
   The tired heart turns to rest.
I shall meet the love of my youth, laddie,
   With my bonnie laddies three ;
Will he think of the blythe young lass, laddie,
   When the old wife he will see ?

I thought that the call had come, laddie,
   When the midnight hour struck low,
But flowing then was the tide, laddie,
   And my soul with the ebb must go.
The morn's glowing bright o'er the sea, laddie,
   Like the glorious years to be ;
Farewell to life's passion and tears, laddie,
   " For there shall be no more sea."

                        CRAIG ELLACHIE

THE TWO SHIPS

The clouds of the sunset strange beauty unfold,
A glory of crimson, and purple, and gold;
But the glow dies away into dusk, into night
Till the stars quench their beams in the moon's mystic light.
So still is the air and so still is the sea
That the moon seems the Flower of the Silence to be.

All voices are mute, and the low hollow swell
Of the waves does not mar, it but adds to the spell
Of this hour, seen in dreams by the camp fires afar,
When kind sleep had covered the red field of war;
When the grim campaign's over, the land is in sight,
All hands that were parted shall clasp close tonight.

A few more swift leagues, and across the white foam
The war worn shall rest in the sweet peace of home.
Behind the dark hull, in the wake of its flight
There glides a dim shape, in the shimmering light;
Like mist in the dawning, like foam of the seas,
Like rime in the sunlight, it wavers and flees,

Elusive and faint as the fabric of dreams,
White, white in the moonlight, a spectre ship gleams;
Line for line, spar for spar, are the vessels as one,
Yet unseen by the living, the dead follows on.
The moon, through its decks, in the waves as they flow,
Sees her face pure and cold in the ocean below;

And forms, spirit-pale, pace the decks side by side,
With wistful eyes turned o'er the waters so wide
To catch the first glimpse of the land they love best,
The land that they seek, who, exiled, could not rest,
For Country they fought, for her honour they strove,
Now their spirits come back to the land that they love.

CRAIG ELLACHIE

Though deep are the graves past the sundering sea,
Love stronger than death, can the spirit set free.
The living! The living may clasp hand in hand!
Shall the dead not return to their own native land?
Glad music, wild music, beats out on the air!
The quay is ablaze with the torches' bright glare.

Oh! Smiling and weeping, in joy keen to pain,
The loved and the longed-for are greeted again!
The eyes of the mother are fixed on her boy,
Her worn face is radiant, illumined with joy;
And the father's grey head is held higher with pride,
As he scans the bronzed face of the son by his side;

While fair faces smile through a raillery of tears,
That past are all partings, forgotten all fears;
But silent and sad so the desolate yearn,
Whose brimming eyes dwell on each soldier's return.
Oh! Tumult of welcome that mocks but their pain!
Oh! Passion of heartbreak! They come not again,

The stalwart! The noble! The light of their eyes!
Ah! Far, far, their graves under alien skies.
Oh! Veil of the flesh that holds ever between!
The dead have returned; but unheard and unseen,
They pass through the midst, with the breath of a sigh,
Their greeting is born on the wind passing by.

But a sweet sudden sense of their nearness has filled
The hearts that long grieved; and the music that thrilled
With their anguish of sorrow, now throbs with their pride,
In those who for Country have battled and died;
Who the gift of all gifts on her altar has laid,
The one, the supreme, the best sacrifice made.

Death comes unto all, to the coward, the slave,
Who seeks life, shall lose it, who loses, shalt save.
Thus the music beats out, in its rise and its fall,
"Who died for their Country they die not at all,
The living! The living may clasp hand in hand,
But the dead heroes are part of their own native land!"

THE VALLEY OF THE CHILDREN,

      Past the mists of Long Ago,
      There's a Valley that we know,
Pleasant vale of Morning Glory, where the Happy Peoples are;

      And the stars of their kind skies,
      Are the love-lit mother-eyes,
Shining ever down upon them, where the Happy Peoples are.

      But a stairway quaint and strange,
      Leads up to a snow-capped range,
Past the Uplands wide and weary, where the Grown-up Peoples are.

      We can scarcely see through tears,
      Those first sunny steps of years,
Though the steps below are golden, while the steps above are grey
(Ah! The heads below are golden, while the heads above are grey)

      There is sorrow, there is care,
      In the Uplands stern and bare,
Little People, little People, wherefore hasten up the stair?

      Oh! The faces rosy fair!
      Oh! The heads of sunlit, hair!
Like a radiant cloud of sunrise, floating up the wondrous stair,

      Oh! The childish laughter sweet!
      Oh! The music of their feet!
Ah! Our hearts beat back an echo, to the music of their feet!

CRAIG ELLACHIE

Oh!   The winsome little faces!
Oh!   The thousand nameless graces!
Like the early dew they vanish, in the noonday glare and heat.

Tender loving hearts grow cold,
Eyes grow hard   with greed of gold,
As the stairway winds and broadens, in the noonday glare and heat.
(Ah! The mem'ry of the valley in the noonday glare and heat!)

CRAIG   ELLACHIE.

A BALLADE OF CONVICT DAYS.

From out the mists of days that were
Grim sombre faces glance again,
Whose dim eyes veil their hearts' despair,
Whose fierce brows bear the brand of Cain;
Oh, sunny Land ! thy skies were vain,
Thus shadowed o'er with alien crimes;
For life was death, and death was gain,
Those dark and distant Convict Times.

Whene'er with showers and keener air,
The first strange sultry seasons' wane,
Did thoughts fly backward unaware
To childish homes beyond the main?
Did dear dead voices wake again,
Or echoes of old hallowed chimes,
And mingle with the falling rain,
Those dark and distant Convict Times?

Ah ! many a dash for freedom there,
The quiet stars watched o'er many a plain,
And many a creek and wild waste bare,
The secrets of dark dooms retain;
But Ceres followed with her train,
With fruits and flowers of far off climes,
And hid for us in smiling grain
Those dark and distant Convict Times.

      Envoi.
Yet, hapless Pioneers! your pain
Wakes but to mock at idle rhymes;
Let silence fall—forget we'd fain
Those dark and distant Convict Times.

CRAIG ELLACHIE.

CRAIG ELLACHIE

ORIGINAL POETRY.

BALLADE OF REGRET.

"'Give me power the world to sway,"
The young man cries, with a glowing eye,
"To feel on my brows the victor's bay,
Love and Fame, when the blood runs high."
"Not thine, O Youth!"   The Fates reply,
"But a life that is commonplace, weak and tame
Though thy ardent hopes the years see die,
In a hundred years 'twill be all the same."

What of the dreams of the yesterday,
Maid! with the sweet face sad and shy,
The lover has loved and ridden away,
And the rue of life for the wine, you try.
Your story was told to the sea and the sky,
When Œnone called false Paris' name,
Bear it in silence nor reason why,
In a hundred years 'twill be all the same.

Green are the graves on our life's pathway,
Where we bury our hopes as the years roll by,
Never December turns back to May,
Dead, in the dead past, for ever they lie.
"Give us our daily bread," we cry.
And the soul asks more than the lips can frame,
If Death can give, what life must deny
In a hundred years 'twill be all the same.

ENVOY:

Stranger: I warn thee, Time flits by,
Snatch at Love's roses, or laurel of Fame,
Brief life, summed up in a smile and a sigh,
In a hundred years 'twill be all the same!

CRAIG ELLACHIE

OMAR'S WISH.

Omar Khayyam, the astronomer-poet of Persia, shortly before his death, said to one of his pupils, "My wish is that my tomb shall be where the north wind may scatter roses on it."

The words of Omah dying
Haunt like the quaint refrain
Of some old ballad sighing,
Its notes of wistful pain.

"When deaf to all Life's calling,
I find Death's quiet place,
May soft rose leaves come falling
Upon my sleeping face.

Like touch of loving fingers,
A childish memory keeps,
Or mother-kiss that lingers
On sleeping baby lips.

The silent perfumed showers
Shall lull me to my rest
Till I forget the hours
Wherein I've been unblest.

Nor Joy shall I remember,
Nor young love that was mine,
When faint rose perfumes tender
Wake in the moonbeam's shine.

Nor friendship's true devotion,
Nor foes relentless strife,
Shall reach me, no emotion
Of this glad, mad, sad life.

CRAIG ELLACHIE

The north wind of the mountains
Upon its snow-pure breath,
Shall bear from rose-kissed fountains
The slumber song of Death.

And I shall lie, forgetting
All that I toiled to know,
Among the roses, letting
The seasons come and go.

Above the poet, grasses
Their slender banners wave,
The North wind as it passes
Strews rose leaves on his grave.

CRAIG ELLACHIE.

LOSS OF THE "VICTORIA."

'Tis in vain wild sceptics tell us, that the hero breed is dead
Still, the brave man dares to follow, where past heroes dared to tread.
This the age, they say of science, this the reign and power of gold,
Only time for sordid striving, since the world has grown so old.

New survival of the fittest, leaves no time for deeds of glory,
Yet a thrill passed through the nations, as they learned "Victoria's" story;
Though "each door is barred with gold and opens but to golden keys",
Still the world's cold pulse beats quicker, as it hears of deeds like these.

Life is sweet e'en to the saddest, 'tis an fearful thing to die,
To enter on the great unknown, to solve life's awful mystery;
Yet in wild din of the battle, or the tempest's furious crash
Men have died in mad excitement, hardly felt death's pang at last.

But the blue sky smiled above them, the calm blue sea below,
Not the strife of deadly foemen, a friend's hand dealt the blow,
Who can paint the fearful picture on the lost "Victoria's" deck
As the mighty warship, reeling, swiftly sinks a living wreck.

Not the wild rush of the coward, mad with impotent despair.
Not a sound of craven weeping, smote the peaceful noon-tide air,
Ah! those swiftly flying moments, fraught with all a nation's woe,
As brave men fulfill their duty, passing quietly to and fro.

CRAIG ELLACHIE

To and fro with faces steady, only Duty's call to hear,
Though their grave beneath the waters, every heart beat brings more near,
Death is waiting, they are ready, let the story still be told
Britain's sons can die with honour, now as in brave days of old.

Down, far down, beneath the blue waves, softly lies each sailor's pillow,
While in deep strange music o'er them sounds the ever restless billow,
And sad friends, amid their sorrow proudly still shall tell the story
Of those heroes, death undaunted, Britain's loss and Britain's glory.

CRAIG ELLACHIE.

THE COLONIST'S RETURN.

Across the seas at last I came
  My ain dear land to see,
  The land I dreamed of many a time,
Beyond the Southern sea.

The land I left full forty years
  To win the Australian gold,
  And toiling 'neath a burning sun,
Has found me worn and old.

Ah! Mine old friends have left their place,
  Their children fill them now.
  The old kirkyard shows many a grave,
Loved names of long ago.

The hills alane, keep still the same,
  The burn rins to the sea.
  But mine old friends, my dear old friends
On earth I'll never see.

Though back again 'tis all in vain,
  I scan each well-known scene.
  The light of other days has gone,
The village of my dream.

CRAIG ELLACHIE

The old spot canna bring me back
  The happy boyish days.
  I canna take the life I left,
Their ways are not my ways.

The toilsome life, the hard-earned wage,
  The dreamy plodding strife,
  How changed indeed from memory's tale
Is this, the real life.

I wander sadly by the burn,
  Or down the sunny brae.
  Or to the schoolhouse once more take
The old remembered way.

A ghost among these living men,
  An alien far apart.
  The change is not in hill or glen,
'Tis in the old man's heart.

To childhood's haunts I dared return,
  By life's long conflict worn,
  A stranger, and a foreigner,
In the land where I was born.

CRAIG ELLACHIE,

ORIGINAL POETRY

GLADSTONE

As o'er the throbbing wires the tidings sped,
  While rose the Pole Star, or while set the Cross,
  Bound by one boding pang of common loss,
A hushed world waited by one dying bed.

An old, old man lay dying hour by hour,
  For *him* the World forgot its golden gain;
  Its great heart beat to one dull pulse of pain,
And futile Love and Pity learnt Death's power.

Through long, long years, seeing the good afar,
  Steering through troubled seas the ship of State,
  Unflinchingly, as one who conquers Fate,
He held his course, by Freedom's sacred star.

And when through mists of Tyranny and Pain,
  From some poor helpless storm-tost sinking bark,
  A cry for help rang o'er the waters dark,
His kindly ear ne'er heard the cry in vain.

Wearing the silver crown of honourable years,
  He, like another Grecian Nestor wise
  Who spins youth's efforts with his watchful eyes,
Still marked the helm his hand no longer steers.

Now! storm clouds loom upon our skies, and list!
  How faint and far across the rolling foam,
  But near and nearer War's fierce echoes come.
Oh Gallant Captain! how shall thou be missed.

CRAIG ELLACHIE

Where shall we find again thy peer on earth?
Oh dauntless heart! that ne'er knew shame or fear,
Oh steadfast eyes! so eagle-keen and clear,
Our world is poorer for thy vanished worth.

The People's King! enthroned by right divine,
True Hero thou! of vital primal mould,
Towering o'er all, as Saul in days of old,
A world lay at thy feet to call it thine.

Oh King uncrowned! what titles dare belong
To thee, who scorning still, all lower fame,
Disdain'st but to earn and bear the name
Of "Grand Old Man" upon the people's tongue.

Calm, thou could'st lay thy work aside—and then
Leaving behind for aye, Earth sordid seeming,
Waking to life, beyond hope's utmost dreaming,
Did'st meet Death Angel with a quiet "Amen."

       CRAIG ELLACHIE.
Rockhampton.

BACKGROUND TO THIS PUBLICATION

A second *nom de plume* that Isabel used was MacDonald Grant. This was her mother's maiden name – a name of which they were inordinately proud and which was often used by the females as a Christian name for their boys. Isabel had an older brother named Kenneth Macdonald Grant who helped keep her and the other younger children at school after the death of their father. He was himself well educated and later became a Minister in the Queensland Parliament.

Isabel's maternal grandparents were very devout folk from Glenurquhart in the highlands of Scotland. John MacDonald, her grandfather, started his working life as a weaver but by strength of will and hard work became a successful merchant. Besides his commitment to The Free Church of Scotland he also educated all his family, including the girls, to a high standard.

Kenneth MacDonald, Isabel's uncle, was the most visibly successful member of his generation. He gained his M.A and D.D from Aberdeen University. He was an educator and author as was Isabel. Kenneth was a lecturer at Duff College, Calcutta, described in 1866 as "the largest educational institute in Asia." He wrote text books on mathematics and English which were used for study for the entrance exam for the Calcutta University. By 1901 he had 149 works published of religious or educational interest and was an examiner for the B.A. degree. After retirement he spent the remaining twenty years of his life in India as a missionary for the United Free Church. His biography was written by Sir James MacPhail in 1905.

The following story is written under this name and was published in the Christmas supplement of The Queenslander in December 1903

The Queenslander was a weekly newspaper, first published by Thomas Blachett Stephens in 1866 to attract the regional market. It was a synopsis of Brisbane's daily newspaper *The Courier Mail* owned by Stephens. Its first editor Angus Mackay added items to interest the agriculturalists and pastoralists and a good supply of light reading. This formula had already proved exceedingly successful for the weekly versions of southern metropolitan newspapers and was to prove so again in the far flung regions of Queensland. Australian literary rates were high and the paper filled a need to provide entertainment and contact with the wider world.

By the1880s *The Queenslander* introduced photo engraving for pictorial journalism and by the 1890s the more difficult half-tone illustration. In 1903 it pioneered colour printing in Queensland.

Noteworthy figures associated with *The Queenslander* were Marcus Clarke (For the Term of His Natural Life) who contributed fiction, W.H.Thraill an editor and an outstanding figure in the journalism of his day and a full time female journalist Mary Hannay Foot. Mary had a book of poems "Where the pelican builds and other poems" to her name when she was asked to join the staff in 1887.

The Queenslander continued as a successful and influential weekly and published its first annual in 1930. However by the end of the 1930s the popularity of these weekly newspapers collapsed. Leisurely attitudes had been replaced by a modern urgency not satisfied by infrequent doses of news. The effects of the motor vehicle and wireless had broken the isolation of the bush and the imminent threat of war further precipitated their decline.

THE COLLECTED PUBLISHED WORKS OF ISABEL GRANT

THE QUEENSLANDER CHRISTMAS SUPPLEMENT, DECEMBER 12, 1903

An Amateur Providence.

—:o:—

By MACDONALD GRANT

The dinner was spoiling, but still we waited.

"I do think Fred might have more consideration," I said crossly. "He will not be ready to go with us, and he promised faithfully to be home early."

We seldom get a good company up here, and we were looking forward so much to the first night of "The Belle of New York."

"Something may have happened," Mary suggested—"some extra work at the last moment. The manager of a big affair like the works cannot always call his time his own, you know."

" All very well, but a promise is a promise even if it is made to a wife," I snapped; "and your first opera too, Mary. I'll give Fred a piece of my mind."

"Oh, do not bother about me," Mary said easily. " Besides, couldn't we go by ourselves if he did not come."

"We could," I said shortly; "but half the pleasure of a thing is gone if there is a fuss about it; anyhow what is the use of a husband unless he is at hand when you want him?"

Mary laughed. She has a pretty laugh; in spite of myself the next moment I joined her, and my vexation half melted away.

Mary Torrance and I have been friends since she came, a small rosy-cheeked new-chum, to my class at school. The other girls began to tease her about her funny Irish way of talking, and her short curly hair like a boy's. I was two years older than Mary, and a big girl for my age. I took a fancy to the little thing, and I soon let the girls understand that if they wished to plague her they would have to reckon with me. Before long I had good reason to be glad that I had Mary for a friend. I was slow with my lessons, and I believe I would have never reached the upper class if she had not been beside me to push me on. She was the cleverest little thing, and never seemed so happy as when she was helping somebody. We had the most idiotic sums in this class, "Cubed Roots" – I wake sometimes at night now, and I'm grubbing at them again. The teacher was a tall, thin woman, with a cold eye and a sarcastic smile that used to wither up the dull girls, though she had quite a different expression of countenance for clever girls like Mary. It was no use showing me the rule; it went clean out of my head as soon as I wiped the sum off my slate; for between my dread of the teacher's sarcasm, and my fear of the girls' ridicule, no sooner was there a Cube Root on the blackboard than my mind became a perfect blank. But Mary was beside me, my good angel: she used to pass along the slate to me, I would copy the root and the last line, and nobody was a penny the worse.

I left school at 17, and I was just 18 when I got married; in fact, I only put my hair up to go to church with Fred. It was a splendid match, everybody said; for Fred Warren was the catch of the place. I might be only a schoolgirl, but I could hold my own in looks with the best of them: and I guess Fred has found out that he has got a wife who understands how to dispose to the best advantage of the "root of all evil," and knows what roots are suitable for the table, if cube roots were beyond her.

I do not deny that I was always a "duffer" at lessons; but, though I say it myself, I had plenty of common sense--- what we girls used to call "savee."

Poor Mary! Two years after my marriage she was a penniless orphan. I offered to give her a home; Fred was willing, and it would have been a great pleasure to me to have Mary in my nice big house; but she would not hear of it. She came to me, indeed, for a month, and I believe every one in the house adored her, from baby to the Kanaka who did the gardening, but then, in spite of all my coaxing – the independent, obstinate girl—she left us to take up governessing on a Western station. She wrote regularly at first; but I am a bad correspondent—I am ashamed of my writing, to tell the truth—and letters became fewer between us; though I always made a point of sending each year an invitation for the holidays.

Seven years went past before she accepted; then only, I believe, because her health broke down, and the doctors ordered six months' rest from teaching.

She seemed so surprised and touched at our welcome, that I could not but think that they had not been too good to little Mary at the station. She is just the kind of willing, soft-spoken creature that gets imposed on, and carries every burden without a word, till she breaks under the strain.

Not that Mary complained; that was never her way. If she had nothing good to say about a person, she was silent; and as she said very little about her life as governess, I formed my own conclusions; but I determined that she would have a good time in the six months I had her to myself. This was partly the reason I felt so vexed at Fred's delay, for I do love, myself, being early at the theatre, and watching each group come sailing in, the ladies smiling with the smile that says plainer than words, "I am the best dressed woman in the house to-night." I wanted Mary to see the crowd before the opera began, so that we might enjoy the fun together. She is so quick to catch the amusing side of things, and makes such a pleasant companion at all times, that I do not wonder, they were loth at the station to let her go.

We had got ready before dinner; Mary was in a soft white silk with cloudy lace, and I was in blue satin-it suits my colouring. Mary had been singing at the piano while we waited, till I broke in with my remarks on Fred's want of consideration, and she had laughed at my definition of the use of a husband. As she turned round in her merry coaxing way, and looked at my cross face, all at once the thought came over me with almost a shock – "What a pretty little thing she is!"

We made a curious contrast, for I am big, fair, and, lately, growing rather plumper than I like. She is so small and slight; she looks like a child beside me; her boots and gloves would nearly fit my little Dottie. Her eyes are blue; sometimes they look almost purple. But I fancy that dark look is caused by her lashes, which are thick and curiously long. Her hair is black; it used to be a regular mat of curls; but since she has put it up some of it, in spite of hairpins, will keep tumbling down in little curling rings round her brow and ears. Her features are clear, but not sharp; though I must say she has a funny little pointed chin. To-night, in her white dress, with the bright colour that comes back when she is excited, and the wide shining look in her eyes, I seemed to see her in a new light. The longer I looked the prettier she seemed to grow, and the more I wondered at my previous blindness. Perhaps I had got so used to compliments on my own looks that I did not realize there could be beauty in a style so much the opposite.

Mary caught my steady gaze, and she blushed. That is another of her ways – she reddens as easily as a sensitive boy. But on the other hand she can turn so cold and dignified that even I am almost afraid of her in those moods.

"A penny for your thoughts," she said, and wheeled round on the music stool.

"I was wondering," I said in my blunt out-spokenness, "why you never married; for you really are not at all bad looking, Mary."

She rose and gave me a mock bow.

"Thank you, Betty; 'nobody axed me, sir, she said.' "

"What a story, Mary! I think better of the taste of the bush boys than to believe that."

As I expected, the sudden blush answered me. She laughed a little.

"Oh! Well, I'll modify the quotation. 'Nobody axed me' that I cared to accept."

"Not seen any one in those seven years you could care for! Nonsense! Men are pretty much alike; six of one, and half a dozen of the other. If Fred hadn't asked me, do you think I would not have seen some one else I'd have cared for before now? Perhaps you think I'd have pined away in the single blessedness, or died of a broken heart? Not much."

"No one could see you without admiring you," Mary said, quite seriously; "but it is different with me.

Honestly, Betty, no one asked me that I could really care enough for to marry. I am happy as I am; so, because you are happy as you are, you must not begin to worry over me. I don't think I'll ever marry."

I sniffed; I could not help it.

"I notice," I remarked, "since you have been here, that there seems to be a general wakening up of the boys around. What picnics, dances, and tennis parties have been given lately to us; and I do not fancy that I am the attraction. I am sure Dick Langley did not get up his picnic to the mountains to please me, for he knows I hate climbing, though he insisted on my coming. I remember too, the fuss he made about taking our photos. He took care to put you in the center; no doubt he wished to show the rest of us whom he wanted most to please. And now I think of that day; after all poor Dick's pains you were about as cordial as an iceberg to him, and gave all your best smiles and talk to that silly little Bobby Trent, with his atrocious puns, and his stupid jokes. Why! Bobby does not get a pound a week, and Langley's billet at the Works is pretty much, except in name, the same as Fred's. Bobby has a fat little wooden face, while Dick, everyone admits, is a tall, good-looking fellow. I do not care for those dark serious faces myself; I prefer something a little more frank and jolly; but it is your style, I know, so you need not shake your head. Then, where is the enlargement of the photo I heard him promise to make, especially for you, when he gave the rest of us a scrubby little copy. I have been longing to see it; did you get it?"

I rushed this all out in a stream; firm now that I had started on the subject, I meant to rouse the foolish girl to a sense of her opportunities. I did not see any reason why she should go back, and waste her sweetness on the desert air of the drought-stricken West, when I felt certain that Dick Langley was only waiting a chance to ask her to be his wife.

The two families, Mary's and Dick's, had come out from home in the same boat, but after the first year in Queensland they had separated. When Mary came to visit me, and found Dick Fred's assistant at the Works, it was the first time they had met since those early years. I keep my eyes fairly well open, and I soon noticed Dick's partiality; but Mary is such a self-contained young woman that I had not the remotest idea whether she guessed the truth or not.

"Did you get that photo?" I repeated provokingly; then something in the silence startled me, and I glanced quickly at Mary. The colour had ebbed out of her face, and she looked strangely at me, with a piteous half-smile quivering on her lips, like a little child grieved by one whom she had trusted; and suddenly the truth flashed on my slow brain—I could have beaten myself for my stupidity. She shook her head, and turned again to the piano.

"I beg your pardon, Mary," I cried remorsefully. "I always was a blundering fool; but I can't bear to see you act so senselessly – snubbing an old friend, and encouraging twopenny-halfpenny whipper-snappers who mean nothing and dance attendance on every pretty girl they meet."

I felt a bit nervous, but my love for her overcame my fear, and sharpened my tongue. If she put on her cold, distant manner now, I must, of course, apologise and leave the subject alone; but I knew I could never again summon up enough courage to open the conversation.

Perhaps Mary saw that I meant well, in spite of my clumsiness; for she forgave me the pain I had caused, for the sake of the old friendship. She looked up from her music with the sweetest look in her eyes.

"There is no need to ask my pardon, Betty; and I will not let you call yourself a blundering fool either. You have been the dearest, kindest friend to me; and, to show you that I really understand what you mean, and love you for your care of me, I'll tell you something, but you must forget it afterwards; at any rate we will never speak of it again."

I looked at her, so small and delicate, yet so reserved and strong in herself, and admired her over again, with an added love for the effort in one naturally so reticent.

"It is quite true – I don't mind you knowing it – I do care for Dick Langley. I think I have cared for him since I was a little child of ten and he was a big, kind boy of fourteen. I can't tell you how glad I was, when, after all these years, we met again, and I began to fancy he had not forgotten me, any more than I had forgotten him. I think somehow it was my old remembrance of him that made other men unsatisfactory; for there is no one like Dick, so good, so honest, so kind and true. But, after all, nothing will come of it – nothing. I shall go back to the station, at the close of the holidays, and there it all ends. I am not like you, Betty; I cannot show my real self to those I love most. They must break the ice, for I cannot. I cannot help myself; it is part of my nature. Dick is shy and backward, for all his grave and masterful manner, and I have made him think that I do not like him. It is not his way to win a woman's heart by storm, or by sheer persistency. We both belong to the melancholy Celtic type. He could no more lay himself open to certain rebuff than I could give what is termed encouragement. With all the others I can laugh and joke and be my natural self; as soon as Dick comes in sight I become so constrained and reserved that it is no wonder when he sees me at ease with others and stiff with himself that he fancies I find no pleasure in his society. If only he would speak it would be different; but as it is, it is a perfect deadlock; and, being what we both are, so it will remain."

"But," I protested, "surely there is a medium between encouragement and downright snubbing."

Mary smiled a little ruefully, but her colour had come back, and she seemed more herself, able now to laugh good-humouredly at our somewhat emotional outburst.

"I can't help it; it was born with me, I suppose – a fatal 'thirst' in my nature, Betty."

"All very well," I broke in; "but in the meantime that sharp Nellie Struthers, with her bold, black eyes and her saucy speeches, will snap him up under your very nose. She must be included in every party, for it wouldn't do to offend her father. She has none of your scruples, my lady; she is clever enough to entangle a man when she has made up her mind to hook him, and Langley is exactly the chivalrous fool to be caught by a scheming woman, and be miserable ever after. If that is the prospect to please you, you had better keep up your contrary ways. I'd like to shake a little common sense into you; you both need it badly, in spite of your cleverness." Just then the tinkle of the telephone bell caught my ear. A presentiment, only too soon verified, seized me.

"I bet that is Fred, telephoning that he can't get away from the Works," I said. "Wait a bit, Mary, I'll run to the study, and give him a few plain truths, or my name is not Betty Warren."

I went to the telephone, and took up the receiver. I always think the voice sounds strange and unreal through the telephone; here and there only a familiar tone comes out. At first I felt sure it was Fred who was calling me up; but I could not make out what he said. "Dick Langley is speaking," I heard at last. "Is that Mrs. Warren?"

A wild idea flashed upon my mind, so overpowering that it seemed the direct prompting of Providence. I had left Mary in the drawing–room; here was my chance to do for her what she could not do for herself. I would give Dick a little delicate encouragement that could not even offend my Puritan friend, and yet might get rid of the awkwardness between the lovers.

"No this is Mary Torrance," I said. And my voice shook guiltily.

There was silence for a minute, then the reply came;

"Tell Mrs. Warren, please, that Fred has been unexpectedly called away, and asks her and you to excuse him to-night; he will not be home till eleven. He was very sorry about the opera, and wondered whether I might call for you in a cab, about half-past seven, and take his place."

I could tell by the tone that he was a little nervous, though the two miles of distance, no doubt, gave him some confidence.

"That will do very nicely," I said demurely. "I am longing to go; just think, it will be my first opera. Am I not a bush-wacker?"

I jumped when I heard him say; "Did you recognise my voice at once?"

"Yeth," I said in a flurry. When Mary is excited, she really does lisp, though she never will admit it. "Did you know mine?"

"Yes, I'd know it among a thousand," he said; and though I felt relieved, I nearly spoilt everything by bursting into one of my hearty laughs. But I smothered it in time, remembering if I wished to help my friend, it was now or never.

"Anyone else in the office?" I asked.

"No one but me; it is after office hours, and I have had something to finish. Are you alone?"

"Yeth," I said promptly. I was delighted to have a solid fact to rest upon at last.

"Why didn't you," I said shyly, "let me see the photo, you promised?"

This seemed a good beginning. I waited to see how he would reply.

"You never asked for it. I've had it ready for two weeks, but you did not seem to think it worth while asking for!"

"Oh," I said softly, "I thought it was you who had forgotten. I'd love to see it."

"I'll bring it with me tonight." He spoke quickly, and with more assurance. I smiled at the subtle difference in tone, as he continued: "What makes you so queer and strange lately, Mary? You are nice to all the boys but me."

"How queer?" I asked innocently, "What do you mean?"

"Not like you used to be long ago, when we were boy and girl together. We were real friends then, Mary."

"We are no longer boy and girl," I said sweetly and mournfully. I seemed to feel sad and romantic, just like Mary; I was surprised to find how well I could enter into the situation.

"No, we are man and woman now," he said, with a queer shake in his voice.

Things began to get interesting. I was quite enjoying myself, but I must hasten matters a little.

"I wonder you are not afraid to come to the house. You seem to be. I suppose it is Mrs. Warren that has scared you, for you never come. It couldn't be a little thing like me."

"Couldn't it, though? That's all you know. But between ourselves, I fancy your friend Mrs. Warren is a bit of a tartar."

"Indeed she is not!" I said indignantly.

"Yes, that is right in you; stand up for her. I admire a woman who is true to her friends; but, all the same, Fred Warren was not game to tell her himself that he could not come. He asked me to do the telling; and that speaks volumes."

"Oho!" I said to myself. "Thank you for nothing Dick Langley. That explains your elaborate politeness to me, does it? But I can't afford to lose my temper, and spoil Mary's chances."

"How do I look in the photo?" I said, after waiting a moment to get my voice to the proper pitch for the part I was playing.

"Like a darling, as you are," was the quick reply.

"Oh!" I said faintly. Dick evidently did not lose much time once he had made a start. I began to feel a little alarmed.

"I must tell you now," he continued, "when I can't see you to frighten me into silence. Somehow I can never screw my courage to the point in your presence, for you are so stiff and cold, I am afraid to begin."

And then such a torrent of hot words came pouring out, that I wondered the wire did not melt. I was ashamed and confused, but I kept my head, and accepted him hurriedly. Then a thought struck me: I would make things safe for Mary.

"You will see me tonight? I cannot believe it is really true till you tell me again. Don't take any notice if I am stiff and cold at first- I can't help it, it is my foolish way: for Mary Torrance cares for no one but Dick Langley, and she loves him with all her heart."

I rang off sharply: I would let well alone now. In spite of my conscience pricking me. I turned away from the telephone with a laugh on my lips.

A sound of bitter sobbing came from somewhere behind me. I jumped with fright. Mary lay half kneeling against the couch, her pretty head buried in the cushion, her whole attitude heart-broken. I held my breath, my head went round. What had I done in my blundering self confidence? Had I hurt my poor Mary, who had never shown me but kindness since first I saw her dear face?

"Mary!" I said in a whisper. She never moved, but sobbed on.

I looked at her miserably: she would not raise her head. I remembered never to have seen her cry before, except when her parents died: she was not given to easy tears, as some girls are. I could stand it no longer. I burst out crying myself, ran to the couch, and caught her up in my arms as if she had been my own Dottie.

For a moment or two we sobbed together; then Mary's kind heart could not bear another's grief; she raised her little hand and tried to dry my eyes.

"Did you hear it all?" I whispered.

"Yes." She said, holding her head against my shoulder, and keeping her face away. "I followed you from the drawing-room. I meant to tease you afterwards over the scolding you were to give Fred. I hid behind the curtains, and you never saw me. I never dreamt of what was coming; and I could only listen helplessly, after you began. How could you, Betty? How could you?"

"I only meant it in kindness," I said feebly. How weak my excuse sounded now! "I was morally certain the man loved you, and this seemed such a heavenly chance of putting things straight between you. You know I wouldn't hurt you for the world, Mary."

"Oh! Why did I tell you," she cried. "I could bite my tongue out that I could so far forget myself and my whole nature as to speak as I did. I am punished truly, but I trusted you, Betty. It is all finished now; I can never look him in the face again, never! I'll go back to the station to-morrow; I'm better; I've had a long holiday; I know they will be glad to get me back again. But! Everything is spoilt, even my pleasure in this happy time. Oh! Betty, I can't bear to think of it; he will believe me so bold and forward."

"How could he?" I said, plucking up a little spirit. "I said nothing bold or forward, I am sure." She scarcely listened.

"Or he will think I joined you in a plot to laugh at him. Fancy a man proposing to the wrong woman by telephone! He is a proud man, Dick, and he will never forgive either of us." She broke down again.

"He need never know, for I asked him to do it over again." I could not help giving a watery smile to myself over my hedging. "I'll never breath a word of it, and you can accept him properly yourself, so why need it ever come to his ears?"

Mary raised her head, the tears were still wet on her pale cheeks.

"I love Dick," she said proudly. "I'm not ashamed to repeat it; but I will not win him dishonestly. He must be told the truth, but I will never look him in the face again." I stroked the soft hair gently, and repented bitterly of my foolish meddling. I would give a great deal to undo the wrong, and I felt I could not rest till I had succeeded; but I knew how difficult to deal with are these proud sensitive natures. At last I resolved what to do, it was my only chance. I drew the slender little figure more closely into my arms.

"Listen, Mary, and try to forgive me I'll tell Dick all about it; I'll abase myself in the dust; I'll eat humble pie; I'll say anything and everything to appease him; but if I do, you must promise to give him at least the chance of saying a word to you before he goes."

Mary would not promise; but I coaxed and cried, and cried and coaxed, till at last she yielded.

I shivered when the maid ushered Dick Langley into the drawing-room, and he glanced quickly round, surprised to find me alone. His fine dark face was alive with a wonderful new brightness; he looked the very picture of a handsome happy lover.

All his shyness and backwardness had vanished; he even moved with a different step. I trembled at the sudden change that I saw coming, as I began my halting explanation.

And well I might, for he had the hot temper of his race; but after the first plunge the worst was over.

Indeed, I almost thought that there was some shamefaced gratitude behind his indignation. At any rate he had burned the bridge behind him, and must now go on; there could be no drawing back. It was with a light heart at length that I brought Mary in, and swept out of the room to see about our forgotten dinner.

The three of us went to the opera, and as I glanced now and then from one radiant face to the other, I began to think that though, of course, honesty is the best policy, some ultra-fastidious people are not the worse of a less scrupulous friend to come to their assistance at times. As I sat there, smiling, I almost felt like a new kind of Providence, helping those who cannot help themselves; but my experience would not tempt me a second time to try so risky an experiment.

ISABEL'S ACKNOWLEDGED WORKS

The following works have all been published under Isabel's own name. They begin with two poems which have been clipped from newspapers, but have not been dated or identified. The third poem was selected by the judges in London for publication in "a handsome volume" on the coronation of the King (George VII). It was published in 1902.

The remaining short stories are arranged chronologically with the first publication from 1904 and the last from 1925.

These stories have been found in publications from Sydney, Brisbane, Rockhampton, Gympie and London in the form of newspapers, periodicals and books. Her best work has naturally been accepted by the more prestigious publications. In this category is "A Prospector's Christmas Dinner" from *The Lone Hand*.

The Central Queensland Teachers' Association in 1908 thought enough of her paper on the Bronte family to have it printed in booklet form for private circulation.

Isabel has used the Australian vernacular to some effect as well as Irish and Scottish accents. Her very young children also speak believably and without over-sentimentality, well shown in her short story "*The Making of Men*."

She appears to favour some place names and surnames as they recur over several of the stories. Two slightly unusual surnames can be traced to children in her classes in Rockhampton: Neddrie and Sumner. "Araluen" appears to be a favoured house name.

Isabel wrote most productively from 1890 to 1910. She remained constant to the style of this time so that while still being published into the 1920s her stories were becoming somewhat old-fashioned for the younger reader unhampered by the constraints of a Victorian upbringing.

Isabel's style is in the story telling form, playful and optimistic with interesting plots. Her characters are deftly drawn initially but it was not an era to develop characters in depth so their thoughts are suggested not exposed

A second novel and several radio and stage plays are not included in this collection as there is no evidence of these having been published or performed.

ISABEL GRANT

ORIGINAL POETRY.

THE TWO TIDES.

A sullen sea, a somber sky,
A restless creeping tide,
A faint, pale quivering starlight shed
Upon the waters wide;
There came to me as still I gazed
Across the dark'ning blue,
A simile as old as Time,
As old, yet ever new.

Resistlessly, resistlessly,
The ebbing waters flow;
And ceaselessly – ah! ceaselessly!
The Life-tides come and go.
Tide follows tide, tide follows tide,
Wave unto wave makes chime,
The steadfast shores of Time.
Beneath the quiet eternal stars,

Beside the ageless sea,
How brief and frail seems human life,
As life by life is broken on
How slight a thing to be.
Oh! human grief and joy and pain,
Oh! human hopes and fears,
What are ye, but as wind-blown foam,
On that dark tide of years?

Great Spirit, moving through all time
Upon the waters deep,
Grant that Love's star may rise for us,
Before we fall asleep
Before our lives, like broken waves,
Lie spent   upon the shore,
Oh! let that star shine to the verge,
For we return   no more!

ISABEL GRANT.

Written at 'Tintilla' Pialba

ISABEL GRANT

MISS GRANT'S POEM.

Ah !. June's sweet roses bloom again,
As in the days of old ;
But the stately head is silvered now,
That then was sunny gold.

The Noble Lady on the throne,
Does she look back again,
And see herself the timid girl
Who feared so much to reign ?

That strange June morning long ago,
Does she remember now,
Or the tender eyes that wept to find
A crown for that young brow ?

The happy years in passing saw
The fair young queenly bride,
The happy wife, the mother true,
The nation's hope and pride.

The sad years came, they saw her too,
Pale in her darkened home,
Where he whose true heart loved her most,
Ah ! never more could come.

The war-red years they came and went,
Years bright in British glory.
Wild Russian plains and ragged steeps,
Ye know Crimea's story!

Let Lucknow's graves and Cawpore's mounds
Their thrilling tales unfold.
While Havelock, Campbell, Gordon's names
Can ne'er in love grow old.

Yet; let us trust that past for us
Is glory's war-red page;
That higher pride in nobler deeds
Will bless our later age.

That gentler manners, freer laws,
Have taught our race since then
A something more of " peace on earth,"
And more " goodwill to men."

There's wars to wage 'gainst want and sin,
To make our wisest ponder,
Whilst science soars, with growing wings,
From wonder unto wonder.

The poet's rule, the reign of books,
Is dawning now for men,
When wars shall cease, the sword be sheathed,
And honoured high the pen.

From sweetest girlhood to old age,
Those sixty years have run,
And clear shines forth a peerless life,
A noble record won.

From East and West, from North and South,
Where Britain's sons have sped,
They join to-day, and homage pay,
That queenly good grey head.

ISABEL GRANT

The following item appeared in The Morning Bulletin
on September 29th. 1902

"THE EMPIRE'S GREETING."

A ROCKHAMPTON ODE

About the beginning of the year the publishers of the magazine "Good Words" offered three prizes for the best odes on the coronation of the King. The competition was wonderfully popular, compositions reaching the publishers from all parts of the Empire, until in all 1084 were received. The prizes were awarded to – First, the Rev. Lachlan Maclean Watt, Alloa, Scotland; second, the Rev. S. Cornish, Watkins, Kington, England; and third, Mr. Wood, Bromley Park, England, and Lucy Eveline Smith, Dunedin, New Zealand, equal. The publishers have now issued a handsome volume under the title "The Empire's Greeting," in which they give these four odes and sixty-nine others which have been selected because of their superior merit, seventy-two out of the 1084 have thus been deemed worthy of publication. Among the number is the following ode by Miss Grant, "Corrimony," The Range, Rockhampton:-

Oh! Rose-crowned month of blossom! Come, your perfumed splendour bring
And make a royal road unto the crowning of our King;

Oh! Golden sunshine! Gleam adown from blue and laughing skies,
And mirror back the happy light within the peoples' eyes;
Oh! Whisp'ring winds! Awake, and bear across the summer sea
The echoes from a hundred shores of love and loyalty.

When dawns the first faint flush of morn upon the looked-for day,
ERE yet the dewy tears of night have flushed in smiles away,
When, blushing like a waiting bride, the fair, sweet world awaits
The tarrying of the chariot wheels before the sunrise gates,
In that calm breathing hush before the earliest bird has stirred.
One well might dream strange dreams, and well might mystic tones be heard,
And scarce one starts, O King, to see, from out the morn mists fine,
The phantom monarchs of thy name of England's Royal line,
From Saxon Edward, Saint and King, with cloistered look and high,
To him whose boyish hand had laid the regal sceptre by;
They felt the stir of throbbing life thrill all the land they loved,
And rose a spectre hand to learn what their long peace had moved,
Ah, see their mail-clad leader comes, a shadowy form, and yet
By that keen glance one still might know the eye Plantagenet,
The eye that flashed at Crécy's name, the glory of Poitiers,
How would it light to know aright, the long triumphing years.
To him who held the ocean walls no barrier to his sway,
How small would seem his Gallic dream of conquest at this day.
Could he but know, that from our lands the old-time feuds are gone,
That warring Saxon, Norman, Celt are blended into one;
Could he but see that side by side, on many a hard-fought field,
Like brothers for the motherland, their common love is sealed,
Could he but mark our Empire bounds, from Ganges' flowing tide,
To Niagara's rushing flood, and Murray's waters wide,
But hear the call of deep to deep, till from the Southern Seas
The voice of kinship sweeps across the farthest Hebrides,
Would he not cry, O King, to thee, among his long dead peers,
"Behold! The priceless heritage of all the strenuous years!
Oh brother! Guard this sacred charge bought with our peoples' blood,
They spared not heart, nor brain, nor nerve, to make our purpose good
In furious fight, or harder far, in weary homesick toil
They won through famine-stricken years now kingdoms for our spoil.
This day, O King! From all thy lands thy people look to thee,
Look thou unto thy King above, while millions bend the knee."

Oh! Thistle, Rose and Shamrock, joined this many a year agone,
Bring now from over seas, to greet the Lady on the Throne,

ISABEL GRANT

The Maple Leaf from Canada, with changing radiant light,
The Silver Fern from Maori Land, the Cape Heath glowing bright,
The Indian sacred Lily fair, the Austral Wattle's gold,
Ah! Blood-red dews of loyalty gleaming petals hold!

Our Princess-Queen! No stranger thou! But fondly loved and known,
Since first in all thy girlish charms our hearts were made thine own,
The years slipped by, the glad, the grave, but Time relenting passed,
And would not touch the loveliness, but yet new graces cast
In that sweet face, for the fair head that now a crown must bear,
The crowns of wife and motherhood had known full well to wear,
Our King and Queen! The noble dream of Britain's ancient king,
The stainless Arthur, may ye not until fulfillment bring
A Court and people pledged to right, to lofty purpose bound
A goodly fellowship of knights, a glorious Table Round,
Who shall make true the hope that lies in every earnest heart?
"Our nation in life's onward march may net no laggard's part?"
Our King and Queen! The people turn their eyes unto the throne,
Show us the path and let us see, our goals, our aims are one;
Like him, who all "his blameless life," the bond of brotherhood
Kept with his poor, and her who "wrought her people lasting good"
Through all her long illustrious reign, until Victoria's name
A symbol seemed of Britain's truth, her honour and her fame.

There's war to wage 'gainst want and sin, there's work for eager hands,
As great a need for knightly deed as ever in our lands,
While little children cry for bread, while toiling mothers weep,
While rank to rank, and class to mass, their angry factions keep.
Oh Britons! On this joyous day let us unite, and make
A newer Table Round of knights to fight for Britain's sake!
To win our spurs 'gainst Want and Crime, 'gainst Ignorance and Sin,
Until with "Peace, goodwill to men," we bring the glad years in,
Until to every wind of heaven our glorious flag unfurled,
Shall lead, in freedom's holy-name, the Thought of all the world!

A STOLEN GAME

Background to the Publication

Isobel's story "The Stolen Game" was "written for the Gympie Times" and published in December 1904.

The history of the Gympie Times is illustrative of the endeavours of men with a Passion to Publish.

Publishing is a business and the first newspaper on a rich gold field will reap the just rewards. First, however, there is a large expenditure of effort and money. The considerable risk of capital ventured on an unknown field, the physical hardships and the gathering and energizing of adventurous and skilled men speak more of a passion than a business speculation. High adventure, a high risk gamble and a vehicle in which one can have a say and guide and influence an emerging community – these are the foundations of a passion.

The Gympie Times emerged in an era of expansion in the newspaper industry. The telegraph had linked Adelaide to Melbourne, Sydney and Brisbane by 1861, wood pulp was cheaper and printing equipment more readily available.

It is still remarkable that within four months of James Nash's discovery of gold at Nashville, later renamed Gympie, the field's first newspaper was published. This journalistic venture was undertaken by the owners of the Queensland Times who had heavy, awkward printing and type equipment hauled overland from their base in Ipswich to Gympie. The trip was made in during a hot summer through unexplored, uncleared country by horse teams.

Conditions did not become easier. The first edition was published under extreme hardship in February 1868 during a flood which invaded their office building!

With all this in the forefront of his mind the first editorial writer Herbert Rogers proclaims - "We shall urge the extension of this goldfield by the best obtainable communication of all kinds, postal, telegraphic, and by teams, insisting especially on making good roads available in all weathers. We shall jealously, but in no captious spirit watch the administration of justice whether peripatic or in court – advocate the maintenance of an efficient body of police, encourage all benevolent and religious efforts and discourage rowdyism and vice." Passion indeed.

Hand compositing where each letter is hand set, was practiced in Gympie until 1902 when a new type setting machine the lino-type was installed. Isabel's story was published just 2 years later. Gympie then was still principally a gold mining town as can be seen in this advertisement from the same paper.

MINING EXCHANGE HOTEL,

G. A. MOESSINGER, Proprietor

(late of Kilkivan Hotel, Kilkivan)

Commercial Travellers House.   Telephone No. 14.

Most Comfortable and Up-to-date Hotel on the Field

The Gympie Times Saturday December 24th. 1904

The "Nashville Times and Mary River Mining Gazette" became "The Gympie Times and Mary River Mining Gazette" eventually reducing to The Gympie Times to reflect the change of emphasis from mining. It has also changed shape from tabloid to broadsheet to tabloid again. The venture which began in 1868 has ended in success and the paper as a daily publication continues to serve Gympie and the Cooloola District.

Isabel wrote two short stories for the Gympie Times. This one was published in 1904 and the second "A Tale of a Turkey" was published in 1910. Both stories were published when Gympie was still a thriving gold producer. Gympie's gold mining continued until the 1920's Both have fairly robust plots, no doubt pitched to engage the taste of a mining population– which she understood well from her connection to Mount Morgan.

The Gympie Times

SATURDAY, DECEMBER 24, 1904.

'A Stolen Game.'

[Written for the 'Gympie Times,' by Isabel Grant.]

THE hoarse scream of the "hooter" tore through the clear air and before its last echoes died, the brown slopes leading to the township were dotted with the figures of the miners and labourers returning from work, at the change of the "shift."

The homeward track for many of them ran by the side of the creek that flowed sluggishly by its discoloured banks and stole past the "Works" as if sullenly resenting the pollution of its scanty waters. The path dipped down into a long narrow gully, fringed with a dense tangled growth of shrubs and grasses which formed a natural hedge, and screened the golf links behind from the passers-by.

Few of the workers, however, had much interest now in the game or cared to go out of their way to watch any of the players. When golf had first come to Bundamurra, two years before; the sight of a couple of men on the links would draw a crowd at once; but the novelty have by this time died away, and the players were left for the most part undisturbed to their enjoyment of the pastime. "Golf" was essentially the "Bosses'" game, and the men were willing to leave it to them; the younger ones with the half-contemptuous pity of footballers, or football supporters, the older ones with the cynical toleration of those whose hard lives leave no margin for sport, as a serious occupation for grown men with families to support, and wives to obey, in the matter of wood chopping, or gardening.

The game was over; the two opponents handed their clubs to their caddies, and turned to leave the links. It was only a practice-match, but in spite of this, there was a sore feeling in William Simpson's mind, and he was aware that Jack Neddrie, though he was decently quiet, was triumphant nevertheless, over such a fine victory. Three holes! Against Simpson the Bundamurra champion; it was no wonder Neddrie could with difficulty conceal his exultation.

The caddies followed at some distance behind.

"Laugh!" cried Jimmy Scouter, with a splutter – Jimmy was Neddrie's caddy. "I thought I should have died to see old Billy busting himself to catch my man and all for nothing. He lost his temper, and went right to pieces, when he landed in the bunker, before the last hole. Crikey! To see him make a jab at the ball and land it in the creek! I wouldn't have missed it for a pound, and there was my boss saying 'Hard luck! Simpson, my word! Hard luck!' when it was all he could do to keep his face straight."

"You wait till Saturday," retorted Davie Holden, Simpson's caddy and champion. "I bet you what you like Simpson will lick Neddrie into a cocked hat, he'll make him smile on the other side of his mouth then. My boss is off to-day, but you wait till Saturday."

"Huh!" was the scornful reply. "Neddrie is growing better every day, he has caught up Simpson now, there is no fear for the match. I'll give you a straight tip for the championship of Bundamurra if you like." His small freckled face was aglow with pride, and the joy of tantalizing his companion.

"Keep your tips till you are asked for them: they are too valuable to be given away on the cheap," said Davie sourly, and, unheeding the courteous retort of his enemy, he withdrew with his bag of clubs to the lonely little house beside the links where he lived with his widowed mother. Neddrie turned round at the click of the gate, and taking his golf bag dismissed the other caddie, while he and Simpson went towards the "Bosses' " quarters.

William Simpson, until the arrival of Jack Neddrie, six months before, had had the distinction of being the only unmarried boss at the Works. Though Simpson had no intention, as he would have said, of surrendering his liberty, yet, in his own way he fully appreciated his position, and enjoyed the fact that he was the catch of the township, the despair of the girls, the hopeless mark to which the married ladies brought up their sisters from other towns to try their skill. His heart, which had sustained many a desperate siege, was a tough organ now; no ordinary assault could carry it. Without being actually selfish, he was a self-pleasing man and enjoyed to the full, his life of bachelor ease and adulation.

When Neddrie appeared all this was changed. Simpson no longer reigned alone; a younger rival had come to share the throne with him. Neddrie was a bright, handsome, lively young fellow; a lady's man; one who understood the fine shades in the art of flirtation, and besides his charms, Simpson's attractions sank into insignificance; he was no longer the only eligible bachelor, and he was made aware of this in a hundred subtle ways.

When Neddrie came to Bundamurra he knew nothing of golf, and Simpson, who was champion of the club, undertook to initiate him into the mysteries of the game. Now, the pupil bade fair to outstrip the teacher. But Simpson had still more solid reason for jealousy; though nominally Neddrie's superior in the mine, it might at any time happen that their positions would be reversed, and it was the fear of such a possibility that added a sting of apprehension to his growing jealousy.

"Your luck was dead out this afternoon," Neddrie said, as the two men reached the quarters, Simpson flushed; then he laughed.

"I am afraid my temper spoiled my game," he said with an effort.

"Oh, better luck to-morrow. Shall you come down and have a practice? I think the others are coming. I know some of the ladies are."

"I don't know, I'll see," Simpson said rather coldly; but Neddrie went on "Have you chosen your partner yet for the mixed foursomes? They are coming off first in the afternoon, aren't they? I am going to get a bit of practice in with mine, just to see what form she will show before the match comes off. If you have your partner we might have a try to-morrow."

"Who is your partner?" asked Simpson quickly. It was Neddrie's time to flush, but he said easily:

"Oh, I've asked Miss Robinson, and she has promised to be my partner."

Miss Robinson, Miss Stella Robinson, the best player in the club, in fact the only decent lady player they had got, it was just like Neddrie to snap her up, as soon as it had been decided to have mixed foursomes. Miss Robinson, whose sister was Mrs.Hillier, the wife of the manager, was popularly supposed to have come up to Bundamurra to secure "Bill" Simpson, and though he had no intention of fulfilling the gossip, Simpson was distinctly aggrieved at such rapid appropriation on Neddrie's part. Miss Stella Robinson was a society girl, smart, witty, distinctly good-looking, and very amusing company in a flippant empty way; but Simpson, who was no fool, did not approve of her style, nor was he attracted by her beauty. As a golfer, however, he admired her, and it annoyed him to think that he had not been quick enough to secure her before Neddrie. Next Saturday was the great day of the golfing season. All society and some who were not in society in Bundamurra would be there. Visitors were expected from the neighbouring city, and altogether if Neddrie won, it would be a public victory, as his rival bitterly acknowledged to himself. Simpson dissembled, however, he would not give Neddrie the satisfaction of observing his chagrin.

"No I have not yet asked my lady," he said quietly, "there is no need to rush it."

"Not for you," said Neddrie with a laugh. "But what about the rest of the poor beggars? Though it is from scratch, you could win with any lady who would be lucky enough to get you, if you are in your usual form. But what about the others, eh?"

There might have been a spice of malice in Neddrie's words, but he had no idea of the sudden passion of anger that his laughing speech roused in his rival's breast.

Simpson did not reply, but turned to his own rooms.

"Hang the conceited ass," he thought. "I'd give something to take him down on Saturday, but if my form is the same as to-day's, I've got Buckley's show of downing him. The mixed foursomes comes off first, he says; well, if I lose my game, my nerve will be gone for the medal play, that's certain; and he has snapped up Miss Robinson; the selfish beast, when he knows there is not another in the giggling, bungling crew, I'd care to ask."

In the whirl of angry thoughts, Miss Robinson for the first time seemed desirable, and a half-formed resolve to cut out Neddrie if he were really paying her attentions, formed in Simpson's mind, as he began to dress for dinner; but a remembrance of her cold blue eyes made him thoughtful, and cooled his ardour.

If Simpson took his defeat hardly, his small caddie suffered no less, for his pride in his master's prowess was cruelly wounded. His small face was set gloomily, as he entered his home and put down the golf bag. Kate Holden had finished her music lessons for the day and as she prepared the evening meal, she watched Davie curiously. He did not speak, but after a few minutes got out the clubs again and began to clean them, with a face of such sad pre-occupation, that his mother smiled to herself. Davie was like his dead father, he had no sense of humour, he took life very seriously. Kate had found life a hard thing, but she had not yet learned to take it seriously. She laughed at it, instead, with a fearless hopefulness, that should have caused the fates to relent to her undaunted cheerfulness. But so far the fates had been blind, and suffered Kate to toil on wearily, through discouragement, through hardship, even now and then through actual want. She had tried to earn a living as a music teacher in the neighbouring city, but only certified teachers could hope to receive any support there, and after seven years of struggling, she had come to Bundamurra where the musical standard was less exacting and people were willing to have their children taught by one who, if she had no musical diplomas to exhibit, yet asked such moderate fees, that lay within the means of most of them.

But it was uphill work, and even Davie's little wage as caddie was a help to the household.

Kate had rented the small house beside the links, for the rent was within her means, and her choice seemed doubly fortunate when Mr. Simpson engaged Davie as his permanent caddie. At first Kate thought only of the extra shilling or two, but before long she became interested in the game. She coaxed Davie, in spite of his conscientious scruples to let her try the clubs in their own paddock, until under his instructions she became so expert in the game that nothing would content her but she must play on the links.

In spite of Davie's protests she had several times taken the clubs, and on the first hint of daylight played the whole round to her own satisfaction and her son's terrified upbraidings of conscience. There was little chance, however, of discovery, the links were hidden from the township, and few people were likely to be abroad before sunrise. So Kate had many a happy round in the misty dawn, and rapidly improved in her play.

Davie, in spite of his misgivings, could not help being interested in his mother's progress, and he gave her all the hints he could, as to her play. An expert from the south came up to instruct the golf club in the beginning of the season. Davie's observant eyes and retentive memory gave Kate the benefit of the teaching; it was no wonder she improved rapidly under her stern little tutor, for he would be satisfied with nothing short of excellence, and she was never weary of striving to reach it. At the end of the second year, she was no mean player, as Davie was forced to acknowledge, but it became less and less easy for her to obtain the clubs from him; and now this very night, as he remorsefully polished the clubs, Davie was resolving to be more faithful to his trust. His conscience had been roused, as his poor master turned to him after coming so hopelessly to grief over the bunker that afternoon, and said half suspiciously, half irritably, "You are careful with the clubs aren't you Davie? You don't knock them about do you? Somehow I don't like the feel of this brassey, it seems different in some way," and Davie hastened to declare that he was very careful of them, while he inwardly determined not to let his mother handle them again.

Simpson had now and again, of late, experienced an uneasy sensation about his clubs. He could have scarcely have put the feeling into words, and only a real golfer could understand or sympathize with it, but on taking up a club he received a curious impression that some one had been playing with it since his last game. It was as though the insensate wood sought to communicate with its master, to impart to him the faithlessness of his caddie.

Something foreign pervaded each club, especially his pet ones, until he had made a stroke or two with them, when it completely dissipated, to return again with its intangible suggestion the next time he played. Without becoming actually suspicious, he had become uncomfortable, and inclined to be watchful as Davie dimly comprehended.

ISABEL GRANT

Kate saw the cloud hanging over her son's face, and she knew it was no time to coax him into lending the clubs, but she had set her heart on trying them on the morrow. She was anxious to see what her score would be like compared with that of the players on the following Saturday. Once before, she had played a few days preceding the match, and had done the round in 99; no bad record for a woman; in fact she had come close to Neddrie's score.

"Davie, would you like me to help you?" Kate Holden smiled at her son, but he looked up, with an air of seeing through her offer, and of being on his guard that amused, and provoked her, as he declined her offer, briefly. "I'd sooner do them myself; I don't want anyone else to touch them." His small pale face was unyielding in expression, the curl of whitish-yellow hair on the top of his head had an air of aggressive virtue.

Kate smiled, and said no more then, but began to prepare a supper such as Davie's heart loved. Davie was a good boy, but he was only ten, and his appetite was his vulnerable point. After supper she returned to the assault, and poor Davie succumbed. He would allow her to take out the clubs in the morning, if she would promise never to ask for them again, and to this Kate consented.

"It shall be the last time," she said with a sigh, "but I should like just to see what I can do before the match comes off."

She thought of the fashionably dressed women who would appear at the links on Saturday, who came, most of them, because it was the "swell" thing just now in Bundamurra, not because they really cared for the game at all, while to her who longed for it, the privilege was denied. But Kate was a true golf enthusiast, and loved the game for its own sake.

It was no marvel she was a good player, she was physically well equipped, being tall, strong, and supple, but more than all, her whole heart was in the game. She was only twenty-eight, but she had had no play-time yet in her life, she had always to fend for herself, to toil and work for others.

This taste of golf was the only thing she had ever had of the round of tennis, croquet, and all the pleasant games that fall to the lot of other girls. To the monotonous drudgery of her daily work, golf came to absorb her thoughts; and she looked forward every week to the one spare afternoon, the Saturday, when she could watch the game on the links in the intervals of her household work.

She knew the good and bad points of each golfer, and when Davie came home they criticised the various players and discriminated between strokes in a way that would have made the subjects of the criticism open their eyes. Kate was still so young, and Davie so wise for his years, that the pair were more like comrades than ordinary mother and son. Kate had the sweet wholesome nature that can enjoy the sight of another's unshared happiness; but the thought floated mistily through her mind sometimes, that things do not seem quite fairly distributed, that she had more than her share of hard work, with very little of play, and that little only to be obtained clandestinely; while others had lives that seemed all play and no work.

Like the bat in Aesop's fable, Kate Holden belonged to neither world, was not in society, for she was only a poor music teacher, neither did she belong to the world of the people who sent their children to her to be taught. She had no women friends, though she was of a friendly nature, but with her son and her golf, she was happy, and did not know how solitary she really was.

When supper was over Kate coaxed an unwilling consent out of her boy, but she felt half repentant, and sorry for her victory, as she saw how troubled his small face looked after yielding.

"You need not come with me," she said with some compunction. "I'll not need you I'll be careful of the clubs, and only take one ball."

"Of course I'll go," said Davie shortly, "but we must be back before six."

Kate agreed at once, and Davie retired to his own room very doubtful as to the morrow, but confident that his mother could not again ask him for the clubs, or if she did that he would be firm and refuse to lend them.

After dinner, Simpson went out for a walk; the unsatisfactory mood in which Neddrie had left him, made him anxious to be alone.

It was needless for him to try and hide from himself how strong had grown his jealousy of Neddrie. He felt that he would give much to beat him, even if it were only for this once. He saw again the irrepressible gleam in his rival's eye, as he "foozled" his last hole, the mocking condolence of his sympathy, the anticipatory smile of triumph as he announced that Miss Robinson was to be his partner for next Saturday. It really spoke something for Simpson's self-control that he had not given vent to his irritation before he parted with Neddrie. Perhaps if he had, it would not have such power to move him. By suppressing it, and brooding over his defeat, he worked himself into a fever of jealous resentment, and as he walked rapidly along the hill, his irritation found solace in his lonely brooding.

He passed the manager's house, and he glanced into the lighted drawing-room where he would be a welcome guest, he knew. But a second glance showed him Jack Neddrie's tall figure, and the next moment Jack's ringing laugh came to his ears, followed by Miss Robinson's quieter merriment.

"Conceited puppy," cried Simpson, and plunged back into the darkness. H tramped for about an hour, then he retraced his steps.

When he reached his own room he sat down moodily, then rose and went to the mirror. He looked at it long and earnestly, with growing dis-satisfaction. There was no denying it, his figure was losing the slimness of early manhood, his hair was perceptibly thinning on the crown, the lines around his eyes and mouth were deepening, he was growing old! He could not blink the fact.

ISABEL GRANT

Beside his own discontented face he saw a younger, handsomer one, alert, happy, instinct with vitality, the blue eyes shining out of the triumphant face. He turned away sharply.

"You are an old fool, Bill, an old fool," he thought bitterly, and caught up a magazine.

It was late when he retired to rest; the air was hot and sultry. He could not sleep. He tossed from side to side, but his tired brain refused to rest. The petty annoyance of the day seemed to have got on his nerves; in spite of every effort he found himself going over the links again in imagination, and once more playing the game he had lost so ignominiously to Neddrie. He tried to banish the subject, but it refused to be driven away. He despised himself for allowing such a small thing to upset his equanimity, but in vain; and at last he realized that sleep was clearly impossible. He lay still with hot tired eyes, and resigned himself to the inevitable. The house was quiet, no one else seemed awake, and the long hours passed, until through the open window the first pink glow of approaching dawn tinged the eastern sky.

"Hang it all," thought Simpson at last in desperation. "I'll just get up and take a walk to cool me down before I have to begin the day." He set out or the creek, and soon found himself from sheer habit on the way to the links.

He swung along, his weariness and vexation forgotten. The exhilaration of the morning air entered his blood, and he felt fresh again in spite of the wasted night.

As he came up the path from the creek, he was surprised to hear at such an hour the sound of voices on the links. He paused and listened. A woman's voice in an encouraging tone, and a young boy's doleful and half frightened was born to his ears. The boy's voice seemed strangely familiar; and, peeping cautiously through the bushes that bordered the cutting Simpson saw that the early visitors to the links were Davie Holden, and a woman, who was probably his mother.

Davie carried the bag of clubs, and the woman stepped briskly beside him swinging Simpson's most cherished driver in her hand. She moved with a jaunty step; a flush on her pretty face, a sparkle in her clear dark eyes. Could she have seen the red angry countenance glaring at her through the bushes, she would not, so light-heartedly, have ordered Davie to tee the ball for her.

Some subtle instinct of childhood seemed to apprise the boy of danger. He glanced timidly about him, his hands were damp, his face was pale, he sighed at intervals; altogether he was not a cheerful companion, but his depression had no effect on his mother. He teed the ball with gloomy disapproval.

"You'll only be sorry, mother. You can't expect to play well," he said solemnly.

In the clear air his boyish treble came distinctly to the listener.

"The little hypocrite!" Simpson breathed heavily. In spite of a character for easy good-nature, the Boss was a passionate man; and his blood rose, as he watched the preparations, and recalled his vague suspicions. He was not only angry at the liberty taken with his clubs, he was hurt at the revelation of Davie's perfidy.

Simpson had taken a great fancy to his little caddie. There was such innate refinement in Davie's manner, such a quiet conscientious tone about him, that unconsciously to himself the boss had come to rely on his small retainer, and at times even went so far as to form plans for his future benefit. It was a great blow to his liking to find that the lad was unworthy of his confidence, and his anger doubled at the thought of how he had been fooled by his innocent childish appearance. He would wait, however, and let the culprits prove the whole extent of their crime.

Kate laughed fearlessly, a merry audacious peal.

The laugh was almost her instant undoing, for the sound of it so maddened Simpson, that he was on the point of scrambling up, and confronting them, when something in the woman's attitude as she 'addressed' the ball, gave him pause. There was in it the indefinable touch that distinguishes the golfer from the amateur.

Here was no clumsy bungler with his precious clubs, but a woman who knew, and meant business. His anger was not lessened, but his curiosity was aroused; holding himself in reserve, he resolved to watch in silence. The club was held in the proper grip, not in a woman's helpless way; the body was rigid, yet swung through on a steel pivot, as the arms came round in the easy circular swing that meant a perfect stroke. The ball rose like a bird and whizzed through the air. Simpson rubbed his eyes, and wondered whether after all he was not dreaming.

"Not half a bad shot, Davie!" Kate cried out in honest pride.

"Pooh! Mr. Simpson drives it twice as far," said Davie doggedly.

"The hypocrite! The little hypocrite!" the boss muttered under his breath, but he was pleased; his brow grew a shade less dark and threatening.

"I can beat Mr. Simpson at putting, anyhow," Kate said sharply.

"Putting is a woman's game!" said Davie in such a repressive tone that the listener almost betrayed himself by laughing outright. He could not help being tickled by the woman's pride in her play, in contrast to the chilling disapprobation of the boy. With the first awakening of his sense of humour, his anger began to evaporate, and it was with something of good humoured amusement he resolved to follow up the game behind the shelter of the cutting.

He crept along the gully, carefully keeping out of sight, yet never getting out of earshot, and watched the play while he listened to the simple talk of the pair. By piecing together what he overheard he began to understand the whole story, and something akin to pity stirred in his naturally kind heart, beneath the outer crust of self-pleasing that the years had given.

Everybody knew everybody else's business in Bundamurra. And though he had never met the woman before, he

ISABEL GRANT

had heard of her, and the hard struggle she had to be independent and support her little home. No wonder she threw her whole heart into the stolen game, when it provided the only brightness of the long monotonous days. Besides, one who could play in the style of Mrs. Holden ought not to be judged by ordinary standards, even if it came to feloniously using another person's clubs. Last of all Kate was an uncommonly pretty woman, looking her best too, in the soft freshness of the dawn, and much can be forgiven to a pretty woman that cannot be tolerated in her plainer sister.

Davie hurried on after the ball, and his mother followed him; she would not lose a moment, nor waste the precious time in remorse, as her son seemed to think was her bounden duty to do. She ought, he felt, to assume a little of the virtue even if she had it not. He feared that such light-heartedness was sheer tempting of Providence, but his manifest uneasiness failed to communicate itself to the headstrong woman. There was no hesitation, no wavering in her play; every stroke was a distinct joy; she drank recklessly of the cup of pleasure. When she reached the first hole, the Boss saw that she had indeed spoken truly, her putting was magnificent. She came to the green, and stood still for a moment, her black eyes glancing from the ball to the hole, then her decision was taken—a quick dexterous turn of the wrist and the trick was done, the ball was in the hole.

"You are in form this morning, mother," Davie said with grudging admiration.

"Aren't I just," Kate cried exultantly, "why every club knows it is my last chance, and does its level best."

The Boss smiled, he knew the feeling when the clubs conspire to achieve success.

"The last time!" Davie teed the ball again, but paused to improve the occasion, - the relations between the son and mother seemed comically reversed.

"So you say, but you'll try to get round me to lend them, just the same. But I have your promise and I'll keep mine. This is the very last time no fear; I'll see to that. All the same mother, it is hard luck you can't play on the Links on Saturday like the other women. None of them can hold a candle to you, not even Miss Robinson."

"Do you really think so, Davie?" said his mother wistfully.

Simpson did not smile now, the appeal touched him, the little drama had its pathetic as well as its humorous side.

"When you are in form like this morning," said Davie, magnanimously, "you stand a good show of beating Mr. Neddrie, and you are really not so very far behind Mr. Simpson, that is, when he is not at his very best."

"Oh Davie," Kate could only gasp out, as she addressed the ball.

"The smug young prig!" thought Simpson, but he was not displeased with the slur to Neddrie's play, and the compliment to his own. Simpson could see as the game went on that his probable play on Saturday was the "Bogey" that Mrs. Holden was trying to beat, and he could not help feeling flattered.

"My word," he thought, "she does not come far short of it either. Miss Robinson is not in the same street with her. I can hardly believe the woman learned from Davie's instructions and from watching our play. What a nerve, what a figure, and by Jove! What a pair of black eyes!"

At length the player drew near the hazard where the onlooker had come to grief under Neddrie's unfeeling eyes the day before. It was a cunning hazard—a stony piece of ground, a clump of tussock, a treacherous patch of sand, and beyond it the danger of the creek—the worst spot on the links. A keen eye, a steady nerve might ensure a good lift, but the least hesitation over the stroke, and the hole was lost. Simpson had a theory of his own with regard to playing this hazard, but only when in good form did it come off. The least wasn't of self-confidence at the crucial moment was fatal. This hazard was the testing point of many a cracked-up reputation. It was the joy of Bundamurra golfers to get a cocksure Southern player to this spot, and watch him lose his temper as he attempted to negotiate the innocent seeming bunker, and found himself in "grief." The course came close to the cutting at this spot, and Simpson watched eagerly, as he peered through the sheltering hedge.

Kate approached the hazard with the calm assurance of perfect form. Fate could not harm her this morning, for this once, the worst bunker was impotent. She paused and took a serious, dispassionate survey of the hazard, she did not fear that she would make a mistake, but she knew that she had reached the critical point in the round.

Davie in silence handed her a brassey and drew back anxiously, his pale face puckered into nervous lines as Kate deliberately addressed the ball.

Simpson forgot everything except the stroke, and how he had foozled away his chance yesterday. He pushed through the bushes and cried out excitedly—

"Try a cut, try a cut, for Heaven's sake, try a cut."

Davie gave a faint shriek, then froze into horror-stricken immobility. The club dropped from Kate's hands, and she turned round with a startled echo of Davie's cry on her lips. But the next instant she recovered herself. She was not lacking in courage; she had her pleasure, now she stood ready to pay the price. But in spite of her resolution, her heart beat fast, the colour died out of her face, her dark eyes faltered, and she knew that she was trembling visibly, as she watched the Boss approach.

The signs of her mortification and fear were not lost on Simpson, who at first had been too startled by his own impulsive outburst, to collect his thoughts sufficiently to decide on his course of procedure. But as he slowly advanced on the guilty pair, a generous purpose crystallized. The thought of a triumph over Neddrie night have come to reinforce his natural kindness of heart, perhaps the woman's beauty might have had a little influence over the decision, but what he said was :-

"I must complement you on your grand play, Mrs. Holden, and I want to ask you a favour, if you will allow me to do so on such a slight acquaintance."

Davie's hair sank down on his head, and he breathed more easily. The thunderbolt might not fall after all.

Kate did not speak, a burning blush spread over her face.

"I want you to allow me, if you will be so kind, to give in your name as my partner on Saturday for the mixed foursomes."

"As his partner! Could it be Mr. Simpson, the great Mr. Simpson, the champion golf player of Bundamurra who was speaking?" Mother and son looked at each other with a world of incredulity in their eyes.

There was a long talk, a great deal of explanation, shame-faced apologies given and brushed aside, but at last Kate consented; she allowed herself the wonderful happiness of being persuaded to do what she had always longed hopelessly to have the chance of doing.

"What do you say to a practice this morning, just to see how we get on together?" Simpson said at last. "We could get in two or three practices in the early mornings like this before Saturday; that is, if you do not mind."

Kate did not mind, and they made the round.

On Saturday Simpson and his partner won the mixed foursomes by two holes; and in the flush of this success, he went to the medal play, coming out again as Bundamurra's champion, Neddrie being a close second.

Mrs. Holden's wonderful play formed quite the sensation of the afternoon. The ladies of the club were patronisingly kind, or contemptuously uncivil according to their natures, to the humble music-teacher so suddenly admitted within the pale of fashionable Bundamurra society, but Kate was too happy to be critical or self-conscious.

And before another Christmas had come round, Kate Simpson, as wife of one of the bosses, was quite able to hold her own in more things than golf.

---------:o:---------

THE MAKING OF MEN

Background to the publication

 This work presents a mystery as all identification on Isabel's original newspaper copy has been removed. A few clues suggest its date of publication to have been in the first decade of the twentieth century.
 The first clue lies in the name of the illustrator James Muir Auld (1879 – 1942) who was born in Sydney and trained as a painter and illustrator at Ashfield Technical College at evening classes. Later he trained at the SAS after resigning his clerical job to paint full time. From 1902 he contributed illustrations to the Sydney Mail and the Bulletin. He spent 1909 to 1911 in England studying painting. During this time he could have sent illustrations back to Sydney newspapers as did Norman Lindsay. When he returned to Sydney he started work in advertising but continued painting - still-life, portraits and *plein-air* landscapes. He won the WYNNE PRIZE in 1935. It seems reasonable to assume from his history that this paper was published between 1902 and 1911.
 Another clue is an article on the reverse side of Isabel's story written by Julian Ashton about Sydney through an Artist's Eyes. This is illustrated with photographs of young girls gowned very much in the style of the early 1900's. The surrounding graphics give a strong art nouveau impression which was also popular in these years.
 It is on the superior smooth paper used from the 1890's by the better class of weekly paper and by the early 1900's for dailies.
 Isabel shows her complete understanding and delight in very young school children in this story. She has used humour so the tale has lost little of its appeal over the intervening years. The brief sketch of Mrs. Wilson, the principal character's "Muvver," is masterly. Only in the attitude to discipline does the story show its age, but even there Isabel's natural kindness and sense of justice keeps the story pleasant and lighthearted.

THE MAKING OF MEN

By
ISABEL GRANT

HAD you asked any boy in the fourth division of the first Kindergarten who was the cleverest boy in the class he would unhesitatingly have answered "Phil Herricks." Had you further inquired as to who was the dunce, you would as promptly have been told "Bob Wilson." Not only so, but while Phil was far and away the best-mannered pupil, Bob's preeminence was just as noticeable in the opposite direction—he was distinctly the "bad boy" of the class. It was quite curious how marked was the contrast between them. Bob was slow, painfully slow, his "fingers were all thumbs," his capacity for learning was small, for mischief, great.

Phil was exceptionally gifted, with a natural bent for intellectual work, so that while as fond of fun as any six-year-old could be, he found school work too interesting to allow of time or desire to transgress rules. Held up, as it was perhaps inevitable that such a boy should be, as a model of manners, morals, and attainments, Phil was in a fair way of developing into a prig of the first water, and Bob loved the "best boy" as we all love our shining examples.

"I should feel sorry for poor Bob," Miss Creswell sighed one day, as she looked at the sullen little figure in the "punishment" corner." He is so shockingly dull, so sadly handicapped in life's race, if he were not such a perfect plague with his idling and mischief that his naughtiness wears out all my sympathy. He seems an almost hopeless case. I haven't seen the sign of a single redeeming quality

Now, this morning, just because I sent Phil along to show him how to do his copy, Bob turned and struck the poor boy out of pure spite. Simply, in fact, because I praised Phil's writing and asked him to emulate it.

"The same feeling, probably, that prompted Cain to turn on Abel. Ah! Well, I daresay human nature is not materially altered since the first two small boys strove together," and, with a smile and a sigh, Miss Creswell turned to see to her other pupils.

Bob stood in the corner, glowering vindictively at class and teacher, his little heart one flame of anger and impotent longing for revenge.

He hated them all, especially Phil, whose "smartee writin'" was the primary cause, he felt, of his woes that morning. To get even with Phil, that was the burden of his childish aspirations.

Miss Creswell detained the small culprit for a minute or two after recess and in a few quiet words strove to show him the meanness of his conduct. The other children with frank curiosity hung about outside waiting for the exit of Bob; but their enjoyment was short-lived, for, with his little face one smear of tears and grime, Bob hurried past them and was speeding out of the gate, and down the street, before they quite realised what was happening.

"He's going home, and he never asked teacher," cried a horrified voice. To leave the grounds during the playtime was expressly forbidden.

"P'raps he's gone to fetch his muvver," hazarded one small tot, and at the possibility all the eyes grew wide with awed expectancy; for Bob, when in trouble, often threatened that he would bring his mother up to the school. She would "pay teacher out," Bob was wont at such times to declare, and, as most of them knew Mrs. Wilson – a big, loud-voiced, virago type of woman, who lived not far from the school – they considered that Miss Creswell's chances in an encounter would be but small.

Bob did not stop running till he reached his home; but when he got there, instead of going at once to find his mother, he cautiously reconnoitered.

For in spite of his boasting of "muvver's" intervention on his behalf, in his inmost heart he was somewhat doubtful about obtaining her championship. It was not always safe to bring home a tale of woe; a hasty and hearty "hidin'" might be the result, as likely as not. "Muvver" was a bit uncertain at times.

He crept through the house, and saw his mother, as slatternly as when he left in the morning (not, indeed, that the boy observed critically what was the normal condition of things), gossiping over the back fence with a neighbour.

He suddenly felt he was hungry, and, keeping a wary eye on the back fence he foraged at large.

The smears of jam .and honey did not improve his appearance, but, like his mother, he was not troubled with fastidiousness, and browsed away happily among the shelves.

As his hunger became appeased his anger died away, and when by a lucky chance he came upon a basket of early peaches set aside for cooking. Robert felt himself again, and decided not to evoke "muvver's" championship.

Cramming every pocket and stuffing his sailor jacket with the peaches until he resembled a small barrel, he crept quietly out of the house, and hurried back to school.

When he reached the school gate he found a crowd of children waiting eagerly for his return. Seeing him unaccompanied, they felt as disappointed as might their elders when defrauded of an expected sensation, but there was something in Bob's eye that aroused their curiosity, and they held their peace.

As he walked through their midst, Bob's heart swelled with blissful knowledge that as soon as they knew what he possessed they would be eaten up with envy.

Unregenerate Bob had many faults, but meanness was not one of them; he fully intended to share those peaches with his playmates—but not at once. They had smiled at his humiliation; they had crowded to watch his disgraceful exit—he did not forget that. For a little while he would harrow up their feelings by displaying his booty before their covetous eyes; then, when he had extracted the full flavour out of that sensation, he would turn benefactor, and thus win their gratitude.

Not that the small boy's thoughts had any such definite conscious sequence; they were, of course, chaotic and childish. But, nevertheless, Bob understood and appreciated the possibilities of the situation. He took out a peach and began to eat it. The peach, in spite of its beautiful bloom, was hard and unripe; but the little ones did not know that.

Their mouths watered; the first peach of the season, they thought, and they eyed Bob in silence. The small plutocrat patted himself all round. "I've heaps of 'em," he said, addressing no one in particular.

Every eye shone, every face showed that the public opinion of Bob Wilson had undergone a rapid, but radical, change.

They gathered about him like flies round a honey-pot. "Here's free marbles," cried Freddie White, with a prompt seizing of the occasion that excited the envy and emulation of his companions. There were quick fumblings in tiny pockets; abstruse calculations in many pairs of eyes.

Freddy White was little and fat, a wee roly-poly of a boy but he had the instincts of a born financier—some day he would make a successful broker. He hustled the boys aside, keen to arrange "a deal." Bob hesitated, however. New possibilities were dawning upon him; he declined to trade in a hurry.

"I'll do your thums," lisped an eager voice.

"I'll write you're topy," capped another breathlessly.

"My big bruvver's dot a knife. I'll det him to lend it to you," volunteered Joe Sellars, the smallest boy in the class, and he added, frankly, "I like peaches."

"I'll div you all some; I've dot enough," said Bob magnanimously and he basked as happily as older folk have done in the sunshine of material prosperity.

"I'll div every single one some," he continued, glancing around with a lordly air. Then he caught sight of the "best boy," "all 'cept Phil. Herricks; he's a sneak, ain't he?" A few voices assented uncertainly; but Bob was satisfied.

"I don't want your nasty peaches. I wouldn't eat one of 'em," burst out Phil, hotly, but his eyes belied his proud speech, and no one believed him.

Like the knell of doom, the clang of the school bell sounded through the air. "Give's them now," cried the children pressing round, but, unwilling to part so quickly with the tangible reason of his sudden, popularity, Bob shook his head and hurried to the line.

"I wonder what the boys in the middle of the class are shoving for?" thought Miss Creswell, whose suspicions began to be further aroused as she saw how persistent yet careful were the endeavours of the children in her charge to get next to Bob Wilson as they marched into school.

She caught sight of one boy holding up to Bob a tattered but, as she knew, cherished collection of cigarette pictures, another suggestively displaying a lump of chewing-gum — popular currency.

"Bribery, or is it barter?" speculated Miss Creswell. "I wonder what mischief that young monkey Bob is up to now. He has something contraband, I'm certain." But she said nothing till the class was formed in a circle for the lesson; Then she said quietly; "Come here, Bob."

A thrill of apprehension passed through the class as Bob went slowly up

"I'LL DIV YOU ALL SOME; I'VE GOT ENOUGH," SAID BOB, MAGNANIMOUSLY

to the table and stood beside Miss Cresswell.

How they trembled for the hidden treasure! They held their breath, and glued their eyes on the hapless Bob. Something unusual in the boy's appearance struck the teacher, and she drew him towards her.

"What's this?" she cried, as she felt the swollen jacket. She drew out a handful of peaches. A deep sigh, the breath of a dying hope, floated in the air when Miss Creswell shook the last peach out of the little sailor jacket.

"Where did you get those peaches, Bob?"

"Home, teacher," was the unwilling reply.

"Did your mother give them to you?"

There was no evading Miss Creswell's eye. Bob squirmed unhappily.

"I see you took them without leave. Your mother indeed, would not be likely to give them to you, for they are unripe and fit only for cooking. Now, what have you to say for yourself?"

Bob had nothing to say, so wisely held his tongue. Miss Creswell piled the fruit into a basket that was on the table, then looked thoughtfully at the crestfallen boy.

"I think, as you took them from your own home, I'd better send them back there, and leave the matter for your mother to deal with. Come here, Phil Herricks; I can trust you, I know. You take these peaches back to Bob's mother, and tell why I sent you."

Full of pride in his commission, Phil stepped out of the class. He felt it served Bob, naughty Bob, right, to lose those precious peaches that he had so ruthlessly declared Phil should not share. What a naughty boy he was, to be sure! And Phil's heart swelled with Pharisaical pride as he contrasted his own superiority with the other's unrighteousness.

Forty covetous eyes followed the small erect figure to the door, and sadly, almost to tears, returned to the lesson books—now so flat, stale, and unprofitable.

As Phil walked down the street he gazed hard at the fruit. Some of the peaches were faintly pink and yellow, they were certainly tempting to the view.

"Teacher said they weren't ripe, but they look ripe," he meditated, poking a small forefinger at the nearest peach.

"Feels soft, I b'lieve;" he took it up and squeezed it.

"'Taint quite ripe, but it's neely ripe;" he sat down on the grassy footpath and took the basket on his knees. "Teacher said they weren't ripe, and weren't fit for eating, but if they're ripe they're fit for eating," the young sophist argued to himself, as he dallied with the temptation.

"I'll just take a teeny, weeny bit, anyway, to see if this one's ripe; it looks all right;" he lifted another peach, and looked at it longingly. The paragon of the Kindergarten was after all only a little human boy, and alas for perfection, he fell!

ISABEL GRANT

The peach was not ripe, but it disappeared; another followed, and another. With a start he pulled himself together. What had he done? How many had he eaten? Did not the heap look sadly shrunken?

He rose to his feet and at an unsteady run made for Bob's house. Opening the latchless gate he crept up the untidy steps. The door was open, and he knocked timidly at it.

"Heh!" cried a big voice that nearly made him jump out of his skin.

"Heh, sonny; and what is ut ye may be after wanting?"

With downcast eyes, Phil explained his errand. The woman, giving a short laugh, took the basket from his trembling hands.

"So that's ut, is it, the young monkey! takin' them peaches when me back was turned. He badly needs a 'hidin', so he does, and I daresay he'll get it too. But howsomedever, boys 'ull be boys and shake things when they gets the chance. I should have planted them; that's the only way to keep things in this house. Them peaches wasn't worth your teacher bothering herself over, but tell her I take it very kind of her to be sending them back. I'm obliged to her, mind you tell her that."

Phil promised and turned away.

"Wait a bit, sonny! I'll get some stewed peaches for your trouble."

The fiery Mrs. Wilson, in spite of a temper, was the soul of good nature when not roused.

" No, thank you, no, thank you," cried Phil, and to the woman's surprise he tore down the steps and away.

Phil took his place in the class, but he could not settle to his work. His awakened conscience would not let him rest. Too late, he saw his conduct in the ill light which his teacher would regard it.

What had Phil Herricks, " the best boy in the class," done? He had stolen those peaches, he knew it now. He was a thief, a wicked thief, and policemen came to put thieves in prison. Oh dear! oh dear; he wished he'd never seen a peach.

He looked at the blackboard, but the figures of the sums danced before his eyes, and he could not get them down correctly.

Feverishly he rubbed his slate and recopied the work, to find that he again made mistakes.

Bob, knitting his brows over his sums, was at length attracted by Phil's restlessness, and, having looked, his whole attention was absorbed; he stared as if fascinated. He appeared, indeed, unable to look away.

Phil felt the stare, and glancing furtively up caught Bob's fixed gaze. The black eyes seemed to burn into him, he writhed under their malevolent intentness. He took his sponge and cleaned his slate once more. When he looked up again, there was Bob staring as hard as ever.

"What in the world is the matter with you, Phil! No a single sum

THE COLLECTED PUBLISHED WORKS OF ISABEL GRANT

WITH DOWNCAST EYES PHIL EXPLAINED HIS ERRAND

finished yet." Miss Creswell's voice made him start apprehensively. She looked at the flushed disturbed face Phil dared not lift his eyes to face the battery of inquisitive glances Bob was staring harder than any; there was a touch or grimness in his keen detective regard.

His expression grew every moment more concentrated, he commenced to breathe hard; an uncanny light leaped into his black eyes. Some intuition, self knowledge perhaps, gave his slow brain the clue.

He bounded to his feet crimson with indignation.

"Teacher! Teacher! Phil's been an' ate all the peaches! I knewed it! I knewed it. He scoffed dem all. They wasn't his peaches neither." He ended in a roar of anger and baffled longing.

"Be quiet, Bob! "Miss Creswell's voice broke upon the storm; but before she could say another word the sound of heart-breaking sobs filled the room, and Phil Herricks had flung himself across the desk in such agony of childish abasement as the teacher felt, with a pang, proclaimed the truth of Bob's accusation.

For a few moments there was no sound in the room but Phil's piteous weeping.

"Come here, Phil Herricks." Miss Creswell's voice was low, but the boy, struggling with his sobs, came slowly to the table.

"Did you eat those peaches I sent you to take to Mrs. Wilson's?"

In a shame-faced whisper, Phil confessed that he had.

"All of them?" asked Miss Creswell, in a horrified voice.

"No, please, teacher."

"How many?" The tear-filled eyes were truthful. "I dunno, teacher!"

"Oh, dear!"' thought the worried girl; "unripe peaches, too! I hope they won't do him any harm.

What dreadful little creatures boys are, to be sure! I must go home with him and explain about it to his mother."

"Go and stand in the corner," she said I am disappointed in you, and ashamed, too. I trusted Phil Herricks."

Phil stumbled blindly out and literally turned to the wall and wept." Not loud bull roars, as Bob would lave given in his case, but low pitiful sobs that told of child's utter abandonment to the present grief. Bob Wilson sat in his place, but he only pretended to work. His triumphant eyes wandered from the class to the culprit and back to the teacher with self satisfied vindictiveness as who should say, "Look, teacher, that's what your best boy has done ! "

" Serves him jolly well glad," he whispered to himself. But by-and-bye his pleasure began to ooze curiously away.

It was queer, yet every glance at his unhappy classmate n the corner gave him less and less satisfaction.

"He shouldn't have tooked my peaches," he argued to himself, "Hope teacher will div him what for," but somehow he did not really hope that at all; in spite of his efforts to spur his flagging appetite for revenge he new he was weakening.

Phil Herricks, abased and humbled, Phil sobbing hopelessly in the corner, did not seem the same Phil as the immaculate "best boy " of the class, whom it would be a pleasure to see get taken down.

The low sobs began to hurt him, an unwonted something—the first faint stirring of the seed of pity and sweet compassion moved in his hard little heart.

School was dismissed, and Miss Creswell sitting down at her table wondered how wisest to deal with the small culprit.

A shuffling at the door, caught her ear, and she turned her head quickly. Bob Wilson was peering in with a hang-dog look on his chubby freckled face.

"Little wretch!" she thought angrily; "he is just sneaking round to gloat over poor Phil. "What brutes boys are!" Aloud she called out sharply. "Do you want anything? Come here if you do."

Bob came slowly up to the table, dragging his feet so clumsily that the tired and exasperated girl felt it would be a genuine relief to break the rules and box his ears. Well!" she said shortly.

"Please, teacher," the big black eyes were raised to hers, half-sheepishly, half-defiantly. "Please, teacher them was my peaches, an' I don't mind 'bout them now; please, teacher, don't div the cane to Phil." A sudden dimness veiled the girl's eyes as she put one hand under Bob's chin, and gazed earnestly at the hard little face.

"I was wrong, quite wrong," ran the happy burden of her lightened thoughts. "And, oh, how glad I am to know it. He did not come to gloat over his playmate's misfortune; he came to intercede. After all, there is nobility in the stunted mind I despaired of. I'll never lose hope for the worst again. Poor, wee, handicapped Bob, you'll make a fine man some day."

Then a second thought occurred to her. "I wonder how far his magnanimity will go. I believe I'll test it."

"Somebody stole those peaches, you know," said Miss Creswell, and her voice was grave. "Somebody will have to be punished? If you don't want Phil to be, are you willing to take his punishment and let him go free?"

The girl waited in silence reading the conflict in the unwontedly thoughtful face. Had she asked too much? After all he was but six years old, a little natural savage, the uncivilized primitive man, the true barbarian. Bob looked up, the conflict was over—his heavy figure, seemed somehow to straighten, a light flashed into the big black eyes, as setting his lips half-nervously together, he held out a small grimy hand.

Miss Creswell smiled bewilderingly down on the tense-set face.

"Wait a bit, Bob!" Then she raised her voice. "Come here, Phil."

Hiding his tear-stained countenance with one crooked elbow, Phil came slowly up to the table.

"Bob now says he is willing to take your punishment. What do you think? Shall I punish Bob, and let you go free? Shall I?" How anxiously Miss Creswell looked at the young face. Surely when

Bob, poor, stupid, handicapped Bob, could rise to such a height, Phil would not be lacking in honour!

"Which shall it be, Phil, you or Bob?"' Like his companion, Phil gave no answer in words. Words, after all, are not the truest vehicle of thought. Our best thoughts are those that are never uttered. With the tears still wet on his dark lashes, Phil looked up simply into his teacher's face arid held out his tiny hand.

To the surprise of both boys, Miss Creswell gave a quick, happy laugh, and patted the two heads, while she said in a curious tone, "No, Phil; no, Bob; there won't be any caning this morning. You can both run away and get your hats. I think somehow you have learned a lesson you will never forget."

Hand in hand, with their gleefulness decorously suppressed till they got out of sight, the boys scampered away.

They gave a subdued whoop when they found themselves outside, but their faint wonder at the incomprehensibility of grown-ups was dissipated before they reached the gate in the sweet buoyancy of childhood.

They had learned their lesson, nevertheless, all the surer for their very unconsciousness.

THE COLLECTED PUBLISHED WORKS OF ISABEL GRANT

PADDY'S LOVE STORY

Background to the publication

PADDY'S LOVE STORY was published in Britain in the "Family Pocket Stories" (No. 282). It is, as its name suggests, a pocket sized booklet of about 46 pages containing three short stories. Isabel's is the first story, the second is called "Only Jerry!" written by Annie Haynes and the third by B. Dempster called "The Prodigal's Return." These two stories are of a similar sentimental vein but they are set in England not Australia. The book was published by Penny Magazine of Fiction in London for The Family Library of Short Stories. This series was first published in 1904

Unfortunately the front cover and date and all publishing details are missing.

Because of its cheap mass produced nature this publication would have a very temporary life span. As one of the advertisements mentions May 1st.1906 I think we can confidently assume that it would have had to be published close to this date to keep the buying public confident they were reading the current (i.e. desirable) copy.

The publishing details above are from a Sanford University web site which holds one of the publications in a collection called Dime Novels and Penny Dreadfuls. While not strictly belonging to this category which were based on real and imagined crimes and murders (blood stories), it was one of the numerous publications issued to the new prospering middle class which, with its ever growing rates of literacy, emerged in Victorian times.

The success of Dickens' Papers in 1836-7 provided, in part, the impetus to publish cheap, entertaining reading, and the greatly increased mechanization of printing supplied the ability to provide it. When W.H. Smith opened his first Railway bookstall in England these publications proved a runaway success to the growing traveling and reading public.

These pages have been left as much as possible in their original layout and style. The punctuation has been faithfully copied to emphasize the fashion of long periods with punctuation used to give cadence.

To set the story in the context of its publication and time I start with several of the advertisement pages from the booklet.

IMPORTANT NOTICE.

NEXT WEEK'S

Family Pocket Stories

(No. 283)

Will contain TWO CAPITAL COMPLETE STORIES—

"A TWENTIETH-CENTURY KNIGHT."

"JANE."

At all Newsagents and Railway Bookstalls.   PRICE ONE PENNY.

After Reading **FAMILY POCKET STORIES**, read

This **Week's**	And This **Week's**
FAMILY HERALD SUPPLEMENT	**HAPPY HOUR STORIES**
(No. 1436)	(No. 320)
A Long Complete Novel, entitled	A Long Complete Novel entitled
A YOUTH AND A MAID.	"BY RIGHT OF LOVE ALONE."
By the Author of "A Modern Anthony," See.	*By a* Popular *Author.*
PRICE ONE PENNY.	IN HANDY BOOK FORM, PRICE ONE PENNY.

IF YOU SUFFER

FROM

HEADACHES.	PALPITATION,
INSOMNIA,	INDIGESTION,
LANGUOR,	BILIOUSNESS,
ACIDITY,	CONSTIPATION,

A course of MOTHER SEIGEL'S SYRUP will quickly sot you right. It is a purely vegetable compound, acting directly on the stomach, liver, and kidneys. It promotes healthy digestion, expels impurities from the system, enriches the blood, and imparts health and tone to every part of the body.

MOTHER SEIGEL'S SYRUP

Thousands of people are **every** year cured of stomach and liver disorders by MOTHER SEIGEL'S SYRUP, and testify in letters that MOTHER SEIGEL'S SYRUP possesses curative and strengthening properties which they have not found in any other medicine. "My tongue was thickly coated and a nasty sick feeling quite spoiled my appetite, I had pains after food and wind, so that I could not sleep, I lost flesh and finally broke out in abscesses, but MOTHER SEIGEL'S SYRUP quite cured me."—Charles Johnson, Alkborough, near Doncaster, May 1st, 1906.

WILL CURE YOU.

ISABEL GRANT

All Rights Reserved.

PADDY'S LOVE STORY.

S TRTCTLY speaking, it was not Paddy's love story at all; for Paddy, otherwise Reginald Francis Desmond, was only a schoolboy of fourteen, but he had so much to do with the development of the story that it was natural he should assume proprietary rights in it.

Boys of fourteen do not as a rule have love affairs of their own, neither do they take much interest in those of others; and in the ordinary course of events, Paddy, being just a simple, healthy-minded schoolboy, would have been oblivious if a dozen love-affairs were going on under his very eyes.

But this was now the third month that he had lain a prisoner with his left thigh in plaster-of-Paris. From the window of the pretty house at Potts Point, Paddy could see across the dancing blue waves of the most beautiful harbour in the world, the forests of masts, the bewildering mass of houses; and he knew just where, behind all this, his schoolmates were going through their studies, or at the welcome recess showing their prowess in the school sports.

How he longed to be back among them—not for the sake of study, for Paddy was no bookworm—but to be able to pit himself against his fellows in the football-field, for the season was now at its height and he had been selected as one of the half-backs at its commencement.

Paddy had only to shut his eyes, and he was back among the boys; he could hear again the shouts and cheers that hailed the marvelous run that ended in the terrible accident. He could see himself slipping through the startled ranks of his opponents, feel the spring of the turf under his flying feet; he could hear the panting breath of his pursuers—then came the stumble just at the goal-post, the crash, the sharp pang, and he could recall no more!

He did not see the boys disentangle themselves from the mass at the goal-post, nor their scared faces as they rose and drew back from the crushed heap that they knew was Paddy, but whose white face, with the black lashes lying so strangely on the deeper shadows beneath them, sent a shuddering sense of fear into their boyish hearts. No.282.

B

Paddy woke to find one side of his body stiffly encased in splints, and he became aware of a dull, sickening pain throbbing in every nerve.

His mother's anxious face came before him.

"Did our team win?" he asked in a tone whose weakness gave him a curious sense of surprise.

To his further surprise, his mother—his sensible, matter-of-fact mother—burst into tears, and it was Dan's grave face that bent over him.

"Yes, Paddy—ten to three; but never mind about that now. How do you feel—better, eh?" Dan's keen gray eyes looked a little dim.

"Yes," said Paddy doubtfully. "What is up with me, Dan? Did I come a cropper?"

"You did, old man; a beastly cropper!"

Dan gave a half-smile at Mrs.Desmond.

"What is up with me—have I broken my leg? I thought I felt it crack against the goal-post."

"Yes--, a pretty bad break. The doctor calls it a compound fracture. I'm afraid you are in for a great deal of pain Paddy, but you'll be a brave chap, and grin and bear it, won't you?"

"Did I get a try?" the boy asked eagerly, as if nothing else mattered.

Again his friend smiled.

"Yes; the referee counted it a. try. The ball was right under you, and you were half over the line. So you scored the first try— the first blood of the season"

"Hooray!" cried Paddy feebly. Then a strange darkness swallowed him.

The next two weeks were scarcely more than the memory of a feverish nightmare to the boy, but after the first dreadful fortnight, though he chafed a little at his helplessness, he did not make a bad patient on the whole.

He developed an unsuspected love for reading, and Dan Gresham's library was at his disposal.

Dan's taste was somewhat old-fashioned, but Paddy found no fault with it.

He devoured Thackeray, Dickens, Cooper, Lytton, Lever, and Scott, with whom he rode to the lists, bore off the fair lady, fought, loved and triumphed in the dear immortal way.

The days, he found, were scarcely long enough for his reading. The first glint of dawn saw the book brought out from under his pillow, and it was not until his mother, refusing to listen to further entreaties, turned off the gas, that his hot eyes could relinquish the enthralling pages.

Mrs. Desmond was delighted that her poor boy should have such a solace, but when one day Paddy complained of a pain in his head and eyes, she wondered whether this incessant reading might not be harmful. She mentioned the matter to the Doctor, making light of it, for, indeed, she did not imagine there was cause for alarm.

Doctor French looked sharply at the boy.

"Does he read much?" he asked.

"Read?" said Mrs. Desmond. "He is never done reading."

"Indeed! Let me look at your eyes," Doctor French said in a dry tone, but something in his intent look alarmed the mother.

Paddy's eyes—the beautiful blue Irish eyes of his dead father! Surely, thought Mrs. Desmond, there was nothing wrong with them.

"Here, turn your head more this way."

The Doctor stepped back and swiftly drew up the window curtain, letting a sudden flood of sunlight upon the bed.

Paddy sank back, his eyes contracted, the tears rushed into them and scalded his cheek.

Doctor French nodded his head.

"Hurts, does it? Never mind. I want to have a good look at them. I've left my bag in the dog-cart. I'll be back again," he said, and left the room.

He returned a minute later, and began a severe examination of the boy's eyes. Paddy bore the pain without flinching, but his mother winced as she saw each involuntary sign of suffering.

"That will do now, my boy," the Doctor said at length. "I'm sorry I hurt you. But I had to make sure."

"Oh, it is all right. I suppose it is all in the day's work?" said Paddy, his straight, honest glance meeting the Doctor's. "But there is nothing really the matter with my eyes, is there, Doctor?"

Doctor French did not reply at once, but turned to Mrs. Desmond, and Paddy, getting no answer to his query, took up his book again. The Doctor wheeled sharply at the movement, and laid his hand gently on the book, with a pitying look.

"No more of that, my boy ; you must positively give up reading altogether for a year at least. Then I shall see how the eyes are doing."

Paddy looked blank.

"Give up reading !" he cried.

"Entirely; and besides that you must have a pair of dark glasses at once, to wear during the day time, until the nerves get a thorough rest. I'll examine them again in a week, and I'll know better what to say by then."

He left the room, followed by Mrs. Desmond, and to her he spoke decidedly on the danger that threatened the boy's eyes.

"With care—very great care," he said finally—"we may save them, but he must give them rest."

When Mrs. Desmond returned to Paddy's room, she found him again buried in "Ivanhoe."

"Paddy," she cried sharply, "didn't you hear what Doctor French said ? Give me the book at once!"

Paddy surrendered the book without a word, and listened while his mother explained to him the gravity of the situation. He agreed to give up reading, though he wondered how he could endure to lie there without his beloved books. A few days' trial made plain to him the hardship of the new order of things.

He kept his promise. Indeed, his mother saw that temptation was put out of his reach, but he found the time pass very slowly. His brain, stimulated by the steady course of reading, had become so abnormally active and so accustomed to the stimulation of the imagination, that he was almost like a drunkard forced into sobriety.

His temper gave way under the strain; he worried himself nearly into a fever, and the household into revolt.

Mrs. Desmond was an affectionate mother, but she was a very busy one, and perhaps she was not altogether wise in her treatment of him. She alternately fretted and petted him.

Besides her large household of "paying guests," she often attended auction sales and bought on commission for some of her fashionable friends, so she had not much spare time on her hands now that added to these was the care of a captious invalid. The time seemed almost as long in passing to her as to the boy.

* * * * * * * *

Fourteen years before, when Paddy was a baby of three months, his father, a rising barrister, was killed in a trap accident. In his inconsequent Irish way, Charles Desmond had omitted to insure his life, and his widow was left practically penniless.

Fortunately, the house "Araluan," a beautiful villa in one of the most fashionable of the suburbs of Sydney, was her own. It was well-furnished, and the widow resolved to take in boarders. She had no relatives in Sydney, but a great many friends, who at once rallied round her, and volunteered their help. Refusing all offers of assistance, however, she advertised for "paying guests," as the Society phrase went; and almost from the first she succeeded.

She was a shrewd woman, and understood what a factor towards success was the reputation of being exclusive; so she kept up her fashionable circle of acquaintances, and made it a favour to admit any whom they might recommend to "Araluan."

Titled tourists occasionally took her rooms, and it soon became the hallmark of "swelldom" for Sydney visitors to speak of being one of Mrs. Desmond's guests.

One guest only made no pretensions to fashionable greatness, and lived his quiet unostentatious life just as he had done when he first came.

Daniel Gresham was a barrister, and had been a friend of Charlie Desmond. He was, if not quite briefless, still struggling with the first difficulties of his profession when Charles was killed, but he was the first to come to "Araluan" as a paying guest, though only he knew how scarce was money with him then.

He understood what a hard fight was before the plucky little woman in her gallant attempt to be independent and support her boy. No one rejoiced more than he when success crowned the venture.

It was a hard battle. A woman could not easily manage a large household and lead the life of a society woman at the same time. Mary did both, but she knew that the price she was paying for her success was her youth and beauty. She paid it, if not gladly, at least cheerfully and with a brave heart.

Dan was a great stand-by; always ready with advice if asked; never proffering it unsolicited.

The same accident that had made Mary a widow darkened Dan's life; the girl who was to have been his wife had been out driving with the Desmonds, and since that fatal day she had never left the couch to which she had been carried.

Mary knew this to be the secret sorrow of Dan's life, and though they seldom spoke of poor Helen, she respected his faithfulness and admired his loyal steadfastness.

But if there was one person in "Araluan" who gave Dan whole-hearted affection it was Paddy. Since he had been able to toddle he attached himself to Dan, and the friendship between the two, in spite of the disparity in age, was both strong and tender.

Dan had taken him to school, and in all the small troubles of his life Dan was his confidant and companion. It was Dan's strong arms that bore him from the football-field that dreadful afternoon, and it was Dan now, in his forced inactivity, who was never too tired or too engrossed in business to find time to chat with the poor boy over the events of the day or the gossip of the school, which by some strange means reached the busy barrister.

When the fiat went forth, and reading was given up, it was Dan who seemed to understand best of all how hard a fellow finds it to be patient when he is tied to one spot for all the dreary days, and Dan who did his best to mitigate the weariness of the captivity.

Paddy knew that the great case "Lewis and Co. versus Tucker and Cranston" was on, and that Dan was up most of the night studying the intricacies of the case; yet no sign of anxiety was suffered to appear in Dan's manner as he talked to his young friend; no impatience spoke in the slow steady voice that soothed the irritable restlessness away. No wonder Paddy loved him, and was at his best in his society. Dan, however, was absent most of the day. and none of the boy's attendants could make up for his absence, none understood him as Dan did, not even his mother; the irritation the boy suppressed in his friend's company was often vented in his absence.

The boy fretted himself into such a state that at length the Doctor suggested moving his couch to the dining-room, in the hope that the stir of busy life there would rouse him from his feverish irritability.

Dan hailed the suggestion with joy, and bought at once a wonderful spring couch on wheels that could be moved from room to room with ease.

But, although he appreciated the change, Paddy was still an unhappy, petulant, spoiled boy and a great trial to his mother. Unfortunately, in spite of his love for books, Paddy could not endure to be read to unless Dan or Violet Sunners, a young guest in the house, were the readers, for other voices seemed to get on the boy's nerves and annoy instead of pleasing him.

It was no wonder that Mrs. Desmond was nearly distracted, for, besides her invalid, she had every room occupied, and had moreover undertaken several commissions for her friends.

* * * * * * * *

One morning Mrs. Desmond went to find her housekeeper.

"Anne," she said half-hesitatingly," are you very busy just now?"

"So—so," said Anne doubtfully. She was devoted to her mistress, but dreaded the request she guessed was coming. "Is there anything you wanted me for, Mrs. Desmond?"

"I must go in to the Ewing's sale. I promised to get that cabinet for Mrs. Forsythe"—she had no secrets from her faithful servant—"but my boy seemed so upset this morning that I do not like leaving him. He was quite feverish yesterday. Could you manage to spend an hour or so with him till Miss Sunners comes back from the city. She promised to play chess with him."

Mrs. Desmond's tone was apologetic; she knew Anne was not fond of attendance in the sick-room. Paddy's tongue, when his temper was awry, had a rough edge to it. He seemed to take a perverse pleasure in teasing Anne, whom he really liked, little as he showed it.

"A good spanking would do him a world of good," was on the tip of honest Anne's tongue, but she knew her mistress too well to say it. A short sigh heaved her bosom as she put down her work, and she promised to go at once to Master Reginald's room.

"Ho, Nancy! So you're put on duty?" said Paddy, with a wicked glint in his eyes. "Good morning! The top of the morning to you! Glad to see you! Hurry up and amuse me. I knew mother was going to fetch you."

"Amuse you!" cried Anne indignantly. "'Tis the baby we've got for sure."

Paddy winced, but retorted at once—

"That is what mother sent for you to come to me, and you cannot deny it. So hurry up, show your paces, trot out your fun. This is a dull hole. I am ready to be amused."

ISABEL GRANT

Anne looked at him in silent exasperation; then, in spite of her anger, she noted the thin pinched face, the frail white hands, and her good heart softened with pity.

"'Oh. Master Reginald, 'tis right you are! Sure 'tisn't natural for a slip of a lad like you to be here from day to day while your mates run and play at their own sweet will."

"Shut up," cried Paddy fiercely. "Shut up, I say."

Anne rose indignantly.

"Your mother wouldn't believe that you would speak like that to me that nursed you in my arms when you were a baby, indeed she wouldn't."

"I beg your pardon, Anne," said Paddy awkwardly, but still with a frank manliness. "I did not mean to cheek you, but"—he hesitated —"I'd just as soon you didn't pity me."

Anne was instantly appeased.

"As Mr. Gresham says, an apology is sufficient between gentlemen." she said, and Paddy joined in her laugh.

But, rack her brains as she would, Anne found nothing of interest to her patient. He refused her offer to read, she could not play chess, and every topic fell lifeless.

There was almost friction between them again, when some happy instinct made Anne touch on the one subject that could hold his attention. She spoke of Mr. Gresham and saw at once that anything concerning him would not weary Paddy.

The frown left the pale face as the blue eyes with new life in them grew intent on the speaker.

"Yes, 'tis sure of it I am," Anne said with conviction. "Miss Sunners is dead shook on Mr. Gresham, but that is all she will have of it. Though he cares for her too: how could he help it— the pretty trusting thing, browbeaten and ill-treated by them as ought to put her first, more shame to them."

"But why do you say that is all she will have of it?" asked Paddy.

"Why, don't you know, Master Reginald, that Mr. Gresham is engaged to Miss Helen Leigh this fifteen years back, and is like to be fifteen more? Wasn't she hurt cruel in her back the day your father was killed?"

"Tell me all about it," said Paddy eagerly.

"I thought you knew it long ago, Master Reginald. Didn't your ma tell you?"

"I know about my father," said Paddy gravely, "but I never remember hearing of Miss Helen Leigh."

"She was a school-friend of your mother's—just a year or two younger—and she came to stay with us when you were about three months old. She has a pretty house out Randwick way, where she lives with her father. Mr. Gresham and she got engaged, and that was how he first came to "Araluan." I was minding you at home the afternoon she went out driving with your pa and ma. I was wondering what was keeping them, when, they brought the master home. Oh, my poor, poor mistress! Oh, the black, black day!"

Anne stopped and unaffectedly wiped her eyes. Paddy looked away and she went on.

"Well, you know, when it was all over, my mistress made up her mind to keep boarders, and I made up my mind to stick by the poor forlorn creature.'Tisn't through the want of offers I haven't left her since; but that's neither here nor there"—Paddy looked up with a quizzical glance, but Anne did not see it. "'Tis of Miss Leigh and Mr. Gresham I was talking. She lies there a helpless cripple, and never a week passes, rain or shine, but he is out twice to see her. Faithfulness itself, I call it! I heard he wanted to marry her, that it is asking over and over to marry he is, cripple and all as she is, but she will not hear of it. Fourteen years, and in all that time I don't believe his eyes ever turned to look at another woman's face till now; and my name is not Anne Regan, if his heart will not be torn in two soon, between his old love and the pretty little English girl that has been this six months at "Araluan." At first, mind you, I believe he was just nice to her, not because of her beauty, but because that step-mother seemed so unkind to her."

Paddy drew a long breath.

"What is she like, this Miss Helen Leigh?" he asked. "Oh, 'twas the dark girl she was, my own colouring belike, and our figures were somewhat of the same build, too. But fourteen years make many a change. She is not a girl of twenty years— nor is Anne Regan, more's the pity, a scone o' yesterday's baking, as Jennie McGregor says," and Annie gave a hearty laugh.

Paddy did not even smile. He took the matter gravely. He looked seriously at Anne; at the broad, almost shapeless, figure; at the black eyes twinkling above the fat cheeks; at the skimpy, dark hair sprinkled with gray, tightly drawn into a hard knot at the back of the head, and he naturally pictured Helen Leigh as resembling her.

Another picture rose before him, and. he saw Violet Sunners in all the glow of her young loveliness. The wild rose beauty of the face, the charm of the shy blue eyes, the gleam of the golden hair, the grace of the supple, girlishly rounded figure were lost on Paddy; but even he, who almost scorned a girl even between the covers of a book, confessed that he found Violet a pleasant object of vision; and it hurt him when by contrast he saw the other woman to whom Dan, his beloved Dan, was tied, this stout, hard-featured cripple, who had his friend's bond.

Anne was elated at the interest with which her story was received, and when at length she was called away by a housemaid, she left him with a complacent sense of being appreciated.

Paddy's heart was stirred to its depths by the narration; his passionate love for his friend made him, boy and all, as he was, understand it. He had never imagined that old Dan, as he called him in his affectionate way, could be the hero of such a sad little romance.

He lay still and thought over it, until, with a start, the luncheon-bell warned him of the lapse of time.

"I don't quite believe it all," was the conclusion he came to. "But I'll watch and judge for myself."

The guests filed leisurely into the dining-room, and Paddy's eyes under the black glasses were fixed at once on the English girl's pretty face. Violet's voice was seldom heard; not so that of her step-mother, whose devotion to her slender little hypochondriac husband was counterbalanced by her indifference to her step-daughter.

Lady Sunners had successively and successfully married off four of Violet's sisters, and she found it hard to pardon the youthful selfishness and disregard of her parents' wishes that prevented Violet from accepting a splendid settlement that had been offered to her before they left England. True, the man was older than Sir George himself, and a widower for the second time, but none the less Lady Sunners could not forgive the girl for her refusal, nor forget that it was this that had forced her to take the girl with them when Sir George was ordered abroad for a health trip. In the English nursery there were three little girls and two boys, whom their fond mother was obliged to leave to the care of hirelings, while their father and she set out for Australia in search of the ideal climate that would suit Sir George's peculiar case: the care of a young and beautiful girl added, Lady Sunners felt, no little to her worries.

There was not much outward friction, but much latent antagonism between the two women, though it was bridged over for the present by a common anxiety concerning the health of Sir George; for his illness had taken an unexpected turn when they arrived in Sydney, and the doctor called in had warned them that it would be extremely dangerous to the baronet if they were to continue their tour.

Sir George did not concern himself about the relations between his wife and his daughter. His whole mind was absorbed in the study of his own ailments. He lived from one doctor's visit to the next, in brooding over what he had managed to extract from him; nothing less than the rise or fall of a degree in his temperature could rouse him into excitement.

A thin, pale, meagre slip of a man, Sir George had outlived one handsome robust woman, and might even survive his present masterful partner. Between a father absorbed in himself and a stepmother absorbed in him Violet could expect small consideration. She looked for none, and was thankful if Lady Sunners's hostility to her found no outward expression.

In her loneliness in a strange land, and among such careless relatives, it was natural that Mr. Gresham's kindness should appeal to the girl. She liked the frank, steady, unembarrassed friendliness with which he treated her. It was the first time that she had met a man of Dan's type, and she compared him mentally with young men she had met in society at home—to Dan's advantage. He neither put her on a pedestal nor appeared to imagine that he must bring down his conversation to her level. He talked, instead, to her, with a simple comradeship that the girl found both pleasant and stimulating. She grew to depend upon his companionship and in it lost her sense of loneliness.

When she saw his big figure coming up the path, she forgot her father's querulous complaints, her step-mother's sharp tongue, and was strangely happy. The girl did not acknowledge, even to herself, how largely this new friendship bulked in her life.

Paddy, too, was a great resource, and though at first Violet sought the sick-room as a refuge from her step-mother, yet before long she grew fond of Paddy for his own sake, as well as because of their common interest in Dan.

Lady Sunners, who was grateful for Mrs. Desmond's kind consideration to her invalid, made no objection when Violet began to devote herself to Paddy. If the girl were in the sick-room, she was not up to mischief, thought the lady; for, and this was one of Violet's grievances, she did not trust her, and was ready to believe the worst of her on the slightest provocation. Lady Sunners, in her own way, was a good-natured, well-meaning woman, hut she could not bestow any kindness on one who dared to oppose her. Violet's refusal of a good settlement had embittered her against her; a girl so lost to her own interests as to refuse a rich man because she did not wish to marry him was outside the pale of her ladyship's consideration.

* * * * * * * *

When lunch was over, Violet came to Paddy's couch and challenged him to a game of chess.

She won, for Paddy's mind was still dwelling upon Anne's story. They played another, with the same result, then Paddy, with an effort, threw off his preoccupation, pulled himself together and retrieved the situation.

His final resolve at the close of the second game had been—"I'll just see for myself, I'll make quite sure. I'll watch them together." Then a doubt troubled him, and he mused—

"I wonder how you find out in real life if people are in love? Do they show it so that you can be pretty certain? I wish I had taken a bit more notice of love-affairs in books when I was allowed to read. It is too late now."

Violet, seeing Paddy did not seem to care for chess, suggested at the end of the fourth game that he might like her to go on with the book she had been reading to him the day before, and Paddy signified his assent.

The book was "Handy Andy." To Violet's surprise, Paddy could scarcely raise a smile at the most exuberant humour of the comic chapters, while, contrary to his wont, his interest was unmistakable when she came to a sentimental chapter. He did not say, as was sometimes his habit on such occasions.—"You can skip that," or "I'd just as soon you let that slide, and go on with the sensible part."

But Violet's wonder was brought to a close by the unwelcome sound of her stepmother's voice, as the large figure of the lady came into the room and appeared to fill it.

"Violet, you must go to the city at once. Your father's last prescription was not made up. He wanted the medicine just now, and it was not there. So hurry. Don't lose time."

Lady Sunners left the room, after pausing to say—"Are you better, my boy, this morning?"

"Yes, thank you," said Paddy, in a weak voice. He was very much afraid of the baronet's wife, and not at all desirous of obtaining her notice.

Violet rose to go, but there was not the usual petulant remonstrance from Paddy, and she wondered afresh.

Left to himself, the boy tried to recall all that he had ever read in books about love-making. He could not remember much that was likely to be of service to him at this juncture; for his habit had been to slur over any love-scenes in his eagerness to get on with the story. In his downright way he had denounced them as "rot," and considered them a waste of good material. Still, after a while, he found his memory retained enough to furnish him with a working hypothesis in conducting the present case.

Lovers, it seemed, gazed at each other, and ignored the rest of the company; they blushed and stammered when addressed; they went—the phrase was Paddy's—"off their feed"; they treasured trifles belonging to the loved one; each was easily alarmed concerning the safety of the other; in a word, they acted unlike the usual sensible people about them.

With all this data as a standard by which to test the genuineness of love, Paddy felt that he could watch his couple with a fair hope of arriving at a just conclusion.

When Mrs. Desmond returned home late in the afternoon she was delighted to find Paddy neither restless nor unhappy. He lay whistling gaily to himself as he idly gazed about him. Not a murmur, not a. complaint, escaped him. It almost seemed to the mother that an indefinable change had taken place in him; and while she marveled she rejoiced, though with trembling.

She went in to dinner with a relieved mind, and gave herself up to the pleasant conversation of the table.

The dinner was a disappointment to Paddy; from his couch he could see most of the guests, and, as far as he could judge, Violet and Dan both appeared to take a healthy interest in their food. So one of his tests had failed. They were sitting side by side, but that had been their position since the Sunners had arrived, and, though he saw that they spoke, they did not seem to gaze exclusively at each other at all. In fact, Violet seemed to avoid Dan's eyes, but Paddy was not expert enough to consider that a symptom. So he was reluctantly compelled to eliminate another test.

Now and then the conversation became general, and there was always a lull when Dan's deep, full tones were heard. Sometimes a laugh followed, or Dan's own hearty laugh answered some good-humoured hit; but there was nothing in the talk to dispose Paddy to think that either Dan or Violet was suffering from love.

After dinner most of the guests left the room. Some of the gentlemen went out for the evening; the ladies found comfortable seats on the cool flower-scented verandahs; but a few remained in the pleasant dining-hall. Dan sat beside Paddy's couch, while Sir George and Lady Sunners took their places under the best light and examined a medical journal.

Violet went to the pianoforte and began to play some simple, tender old melodies. Mrs. Desmond, seeing that all her guests were comfortable, left the room to consult with Anne.

"Did you have a good day?" asked Dan softly, lest he should interrupt the music.

"Oh, all right!" said Paddy in an off-hand tone. "Violet played chess with me; we had four games and finished level. Then she read 'Handy Andy' till her mother hunted her off. She's a first-rater—ain't she, Dan?"

Behind the dark glasses the boy's glance was keen, though he was inwardly trembling at the temerity of his first attempt to find out how Dan regarded the girl.

"Who? Lady Sunners?" asked Dan imperturbably, and the quiver of a smile touched his firm lips.

"No, Violet, I mean," said Paddy, chagrined at another failure.

"Then I suppose you are too tired to play a game or two with me?" said Dan.

"Stuff!" was Paddy's elegant reply. "Get the board; I'm your man."

The game began, and Dan gave himself up to it in the whole-hearted manner with which he did everything, but Paddy was drawn two ways. A game of chess with Dan was a pure delight, but how could he throw himself into it and keep at the same time a wary eye on the golden head bending over the pianoforte, and on Dan's conduct also?

Sometimes Dan paused to think over a move, and then Paddy's eyes were free. The melody rippling from the slim white fingers grew softer and softer, and Violet's eyes wandered to the two friends, dwelling, it seemed to the boy, unconsciously long on Dan's bent head. She could not see the eager eyes that were watching her behind the dark glasses, detecting again and again the shy exploring glances; if she had, she might have been more careful.

Paddy wondered that Dan could be unconscious of them, as the night went on; but at length, as he watched, the eyes of the two fairly met, a flush spread over Violet's face, and Paddy was almost sure that Dan blushed too.

He could not be quite sure, for he had lowered his own eyes in embarrassment at the first hint of mutual consciousness, and before he recovered himself Dan sprang up and declared it was time for bed. He wheeled Paddy's couch out of the room before the astonished boy had recovered himself sufficiently to remonstrate.

ISABEL GRANT

The next day passed, and the next, until a week had gone, and still Paddy was in a state of uncertainty, though he was daily coming nearer to a conclusion. His interest in the quest grew with the lapse of time; he was living in a story a hundred times more enthralling than any written one. He forgot his weariness, his pain, his irritation, in his absorption in Dan's love-story.

*   *   *   *   *   *   *   *

It was no wonder that Mary Desmond said to herself at times that the boy was changed, that his very disposition was altering.

But it was Paddy's love for Dan that was at the bottom of the change. It was this that came to the aid of his boyish faculties, sharpened and quickened them. There is no teacher like love and Paddy was learning rapidly under that tuition.

Then the inaction that chained the body without touching the mind forced it to find food for its occupation, otherwise the fretted brain would have worn out the fragile body.

In spite of discouragement, Paddy persevered, and daily it grew more apparent to him that Anne had made no mistake—at least, in the case of Violet.

He laid small traps, and she invariably fell into them; indeed, she walked into them, as Paddy said to himself, with her eyes open. It became the boy's chief business to devise plots against her.

They were talking one bright sunny morning on the verandah, to which she had wheeled his couch. She sat on a low chair beside him and sorted papers for Sir George.

Paddy looked at her in silence, and saw, as he often did, the older woman, the dark, elderly, forbidding cripple, beside the fresh young beauty.

Violet's face was as sweet as the roses swinging behind it in the garden, her shy, kind eyes were as blue as the violets she had picked and put in a little glass beside his couch, and yet it was to the other woman that Dan, his splendid Dan, was bound!

Fourteen years! Paddy's whole lifetime! If he had Dan's legal knowledge he might have quoted the Statute of Limitations and applied it to a love-affair too.

The thought of it, at least, was in his heart as he dumbly protested against the further sacrifice that might involve the lovely girl beside him. Surely Dan had given enough time to Helen Leigh, and might consider himself free now?

"Talking of names"—Paddy had skilfully brought the talk round to this very point—he was preparing a trap for the unsuspecting girl—"Don't you think some names are hideous?"

"Indeed. I do." said Violet innocently. "I call it a crime to burden a poor helpless child with such a name as Bridget, Maria, Jeremiah, and Abraham."

"And Daniel." said Paddy guilelessly—but his glance was keen; he was growing clever. A flush rose to the girl's face.

"Yes," she said with an effort. "Daniel is rather horrid, but Dan is not so bad somehow."

"No, I rather like Dan myself for a name," said Paddy in a matter-of-fact tone, "at least, when it finishes Dan Gresham, like our Dan's, don't you?"

The girl assented hurriedly, but rose at once, saying she must bring the papers to her father.

"I guess she'd do more than blush if she had any idea that I simply led up to names, just to see if she wouldn't say that Dan wasn't a bad name after all. For my part I don't see anything in a name. I'd just as soon—sooner indeed, be called Paddy, as Reginald Francis"—there was a world of contempt in Paddy's mind — "but girls are different, they like pretty-sounding names."

That evening Paddy mentioned casually to Dan that Violet had given him the flowers, and after dinner he saw Dan unobtrusively possess himself of them. Paddy smiled again, and said mentally— "Score one again, my boy." It was not often that he scored against Dan, and he was proportionately exultant.

It was no wonder that Paddy rapidly improved. He had no time for fretting, and the broken limb was suffered to knit in peace. The plaster was removed and he was promoted to crutches. Still the play went on before his eyes, and still a tantalising uncertainty hung over the affair.

Mrs. Desmond was too busy with household cares; and except Anne, who did not count, and Paddy, who kept the secret to himself with a reticence partly natural, partly due to his love for Dan, none seemed to have eyes to notice the situation.

Soon Paddy was able to move about, though slowly, from room to room; and one afternoon, as Violet sat on one of the verandah-chairs, she heard the pathetic tap, tap, of the boy's crutches coming towards her. She rose at once to help him. His couch was now generally on the verandah. Waving aside her proffered help, he managed to seat himself upon the couch, and Violet took her place beside it.

"What had Doctor French to say to-day?" she asked.

"He says I am getting on capitally. He does not think there will be any permanent lameness after all. The bones have set nicely, all owing to the good patient I've been."

"And what about the eyes?" she asked.

'They are first rate too. I shan't have to wear those wretched glasses much longer. I say, what are you doing? Fixing up the flowers for mother? Well, you are a jolly, good-natured girl."

Violet laughed and threw a rose at the boy's head. She was very fond of Paddy, and never saw through his constant trap-laying. Paddy cleverly caught the floral gift and threw it back, so that it caught in her bright hair.

Violet tried to disentangle it, but failed.

ISABEL GRANT

"There you stupid boy, you will have to take it out," she said, with an assumption of anger that delighted Paddy.

He obeyed, nothing loth, taking more time than was necessary, but finding a curious pleasure in the touch of the soft clinging tendrils. But even while he was thus employed the idea of another trap occurred to him. He would give Violet a scare about Dan, and see how she acted.

"How could I forget?" be began in a tone, whose mock horror the girl did not detect. "Did you hear what Doctor French was saying?"

"No. What?" asked Violet, vaguely disturbed by something in the boy's tone.

"About Dan Gresham," Paddy went on. "He was crossing the street to get one tram, another tram was coming behind, and----" He stopped dramatically. He was really a fine actor when his sham distress was changed into real consternation.

The flowers had fallen from the girl's hand, her lips were parted, the pretty colour had left her face, her piteous eyes were fixed on the boy to meet only the blank stare of the dark glasses.

A strange smothered cry broke from her, and Paddy's heart throbbed in sympathy, but he instantly cried out in a shame-faced attempt at a laugh.

"Dan got into the first tram, and went to the office as usual!" For an instant the slender figure swayed helplessly against the side of the couch, and then the pretty golden head fell against it. Paddy slipped from the couch and was beside her. "Here, oh, I say, Violet, look up! I never meant it; it was all a stupid joke!"

There was stillness, and in that moment Paddy received a measure of punishment for his cruel experiment. Then the girl recovered herself, drew herself up, the colour returned to her face, and Paddy breathed again. Half-afraid lest she had betrayed her secret, Violet gathered her girlish dignity round her as a garment of defence, though she said to herself—"I do not believe Paddy would notice anything. He is only a boy." Aloud she said—"I think I will go into my room. I feel the heat. It makes me giddy—indeed, it makes me quite faint sometimes, and you startled me with your stupid joke. I will take the flowers in first, though." She was striving to speak at ease, to regain command of herself, but her face was still white, when she left him, and Paddy felt miserably guilty. But, sad to remark, in spite of his compunction, he was triumphant.

"What did I say? Violet must be properly in love with Dan, else why did she go flop when she thought he was killed. I wonder what it is like to be in love!" and Paddy felt again the thrill of the soft hair that had clung to his awkward fingers.

A day or two after this incident Violet was in the city doing some commissions for Lady Sunners, and Paddy, whose remorse over his heartlessness was passing into oblivion, conceived the idea of trying the same trick on Dan, if he came to "Araluan" before Violet returned. What had proved so effective with the one, might answer for the other too.

He perched himself on the top step of the verandah stairs, and waited till Dan's tall figure came to the gate.

As Dan mounted the stairs, Paddy called out in a tone of mingled grief and horror—

"Oh, Dan, did you hear what happened to Violet to-day?"

Dan halted and looked up anxiously.

"She was just hurrying up to one tram at Circular Quay when another came behind, and---" He stopped and shuddered realistically. Paddy had neither time nor opportunity to make observations. It seemed to him that a whirlwind seized him, crutches and all.

He found himself on his couch a few seconds later, gasping out— "It was a joke—a joke, Dan. Violet got into the first tram," when he stopped, frightened by the blaze in Dan's gray eyes. He crouched back and whispered—"I only meant it for a joke."

"Paddy!" Dan's grave voice had a new tone in it for the sobered boy. "I thought you were a gentleman, and I do not think that is a joke for a gentleman. No gentleman would lay a trap to wound another's feelings, or joke about such a thing as death."

"I'll never do it again, Dan, honour bright!" said Paddy. "I beg your pardon."

Dan in his youth had been plain, his features were rugged, his figure awkward. But no one would have called him plain now, neither would they have been justified in calling him handsome. "Distinguished-looking" was, perhaps, the best term to apply to him. The awkwardness had left his strong, tall figure, and thought had moulded the features into strength and harmony. The man's character was plainly written on the calm thoughtful face—there was something better than beauty in it. The keen, deep-set, observant gray eyes could look sternly through the flimsy veil of pretence to the miserable reality behind; or they could soften into pity for a child or a woman; flash into anger at injustice, or gleam with the twinkle of humour. For Gresham had a quick appreciation of the comic side of things— indeed, his witty sallies or good-humoured sarcasms often relieved the tedium of a dull case at Court.

But in spite of his kindliness, he was a reserved man. Few understood him as Paddy did, or were admitted into so close an intimacy as he; yet Paddy feared as well as loved his friend.

* * * * * * * *

Paddy slept away his repentance, and his remorse was gradually being forgotten, while he devoted himself as steadily as ever to the solution of the problem.

He saw what no one else appeared to see—how unhappy Violet was at times, how feverishly gay at others.

ISABEL GRANT

Day by day the watcher became more heart-sore as he saw more clearly, with a strange unyouthful clearness of perception, that these two were growing more to each other, and that Violet at least did not attempt to hide her love.

Paddy's grudge against the cripple who stood thus in the way and doomed them to unhappiness grew daily stronger, and at last a bold project came into his mind; no less than that he should call in person on Miss Leigh, explain the situation to her, and see whether his persuasions might not induce her to release Dan; for he, Paddy well knew, was too honourable to seek release himself, even if he found out, which Paddy did not quite believe he had done, that Violet loved him.

The Doctor, about a week before this, had ordered drives in the open air for Paddy, and he had been out, either with his mother or with Violet, or alone, each day since then.

It would be no difficult matter to secure a morning to himself, and go to Randwick. He laid his plans and was successful.

The address he managed to secure from Anne, and he set out with some trepidation, but with a brave heart.

He was painfully conscious of a sudden sinking of the heart as the cab, driven along the smiling country road, was stopped at a large white house in the midst of a garden.

He could not mistake the house. "Hillside" was plainly written on the gate. In an irresolute voice he told the cabman to wait.

He mounted the white stone steps and touched a shining brass knob. Almost immediately a trim housemaid stood before him.

He gave his name, and asked to see Miss Leigh. The girl took him into a wide hall and left him while she went to her mistress. She returned in a few minutes.

"Come this way, please," she said, and Paddy, with a beating heart, followed her. He hated the sound of his crutches on the polished floor, and wished, when too late, that he had never resolved to see Miss Leigh.

A door was opened, and he was shown into a large sunny room. It seemed to him that there were flowers everywhere. At first he imagined the room was empty, but a soft voice from a windowed recess called out—

"Come right up here, Paddy. I'm Helen Leigh." And Paddy stumbled forward.

The light, subdued by golden-tinted curtains, fell upon a couch, on which a woman was lying with her face turned to meet the boy,

The picture of the coarse-featured, stout, uncomely cripple vanished, and Paddy saw the real woman, no more like Anne than Anne was like Violet. In the golden light it seemed to Paddy that it was a spirit that lay there, so frail was the mortal frame that enclosed it.

"Why, she is only a girl after all!" thought the bewildered boy; and, indeed, the years had been kind to poor Helen

The soft, dark hair waved in a youthful way about the beautiful face, that Time had pitifully forborne to touch, the lips were curved in a smile, but it was in the eyes, the sweet, dark-brown eyes, that the tragedy of the broken life was written.

Such strange, sad eyes they were. Paddy, with touch of poetry of his Celtic blood, thought of brown pansies after a storm

Fourteen years, and the lips still kept their smiles! Paddy remembered the ill-tempered period of his own captivity, and was dumb.

"Take the seat near me, and we can have a talk. You are Paddy, aren't you—Dan's Paddy? You won't mind me calling you by his name for you?" Helen said with a laugh.

Paddy nodded, and took the seat. He felt incapable of uttering a word.

"You wanted specially to see me?"

Paddy reddened, and half rose. He could never speak of it now—of that he was assured.

Helen saw the look of fright in the boy's face, but she saw also that he had really come with a purpose, which his courage now failed to carry out, and she was determined to get from him what it was. First, however, she would set the boy at ease, that he might lose his fear.

Dan had so often spoken of Paddy that Helen seemed to know him quite well. She would have recognised him anywhere without the crutches or without having heard the name, she felt sure. She knew by heart the clear-cut, honest little face, with its wonderful blue eyes and long black lashes, and for Dan's sake she loved it.

So she spoke of his accident, and of what had led to it. She knew that Paddy had scored the first try of his team for the season in fact, she appeared to know all about him.

Insensibly the boy's constraint wore away.

"Now, Paddy, tell me what it was you came to say," Helen said at length, and once more dumbness fell on her visitor. "Was it about Dan?" A faint pallor touched her fair face.

Paddy fidgeted, but made no reply.

"Is he ill?" Helen's tone was urgent. "Is anything the matter with him?"

"No, he is all right," was the blunt reply, but a flush came over the boy's ingenuous countenance, and Helen noted it.

"It is something about him you came to tell me," she said quickly. "You want to tell me something about him."

"I don't want to say anything about him," said Paddy.

"But you did—you came with that very purpose, and I think it is very unkind not to tell me now." Her lips quivered.

"But I don't want to tell you now," said Paddy desperately, his, soft heart touched by the quivering lips. "I'd far sooner not. It was all a mistake. Please do not make me tell you."

ISABEL GRANT

His tone was beseeching, but Helen would not be entreated.

"Paddy please; I ask it as a favour. Tell me, Paddy."

"You won't like it when I tell you," cried the boy, driven to his wit's end.

"That will be my look-out, you will not be to blame." Helen answered steadily. "I insist on hearing what, you came to say," and with the courage of despair Paddy told his story.

He dared not look at Helen. He stared out from the window to where a spray of pink roses swung to and fro in the morning wind. His voice grew hoarse and almost ended in a sob, but at length the tale was told.

There was silence, but he could not recall his miserable gaze from the flaunting roses in the sunshine.

He thought he heard the sound of weeping, yet he dared not look round. He wished the floor would open and swallow him—a stupid, interfering, cruel, blundering boy, as he felt himself to be.

"Paddy." The soft whisper caught his ear, and he turned round. The brown eyes had a strange expression, sad and hurt, yet behind it all an exaltation of gladness. "Paddy, I'm glad you told that story—glad and yet sorry, but more glad than sorry. I've something to tell you too—something I've been grieving all day to think that I must tell my poor Dan. The Doctor was here yesterday, and he told me that when another week is gone I shall be gone too. Don't look so frightened, Paddy; it is something I've been suspecting for a long time, but which until yesterday I was not quite sure of. I told father about an hour ago, and he has gone out to try and walk away his sorrow. He takes it very hardly, poor father! Wouldn't you think, Paddy, that in fourteen years he would be weary of waiting on his crippled daughter; that the long attendance would have worn out his love?"

She smiled at the boy, and there was no bitterness in her smile, but Paddy felt a rush of tears in his eyes.

"Yet his love never failed. He feels it as much now as when I was brought home a wreck fourteen years before. Father is old, and that is my consolation. He will not be lonely long, and what you tell me about Dan takes away my last anxiety. My death will not leave him desolate. What is she like, this pretty Violet Sunners, Paddy?"

Paddy could not answer.

Helen went on with the same strange, smiling calmness—

"Does Dan care for her so much, you think, Paddy?"

"I think," said Paddy, with an effort, "that Violet likes him better than he likes her."

"How old is she?" asked Helen, after a. pause.

"Nineteen or twenty—I am not sure," replied Paddy with wonder in his clear gaze.

"Nineteen," Helen repeated softly; "what a desirable age! I was just nineteen when I met Dan." She lay still for a few moments, then she spoke as if she had forgotten the boy's presence. "So she loves him, this sweet English girl? Poor Violet—happy Violet! who is to make my Dan a happy wife—a kind, true-hearted girl, well-born, well-bred, fresh, unspoiled; giving him her whole girlish heart, I am sure. Her parents are going to stay another six months in Sydney; by that time Dan will have got over the first sharpness of his grief. No, I do not believe he loves her best; I feel that I am first still in his faithful heart, as I have been these fourteen years. Not unhappy years now, as I look back to them; but after I am gone, this young girl who loves him will comfort him and be to him what I could never be."

She looked up with a start to find the blue eyes fixed wistfully upon her.

"Cheer up, Paddy!" she said, with her strange, sweet laugh. "Do not look so mournful. You have done me good and not harm, and good to your friend too. I am far happier now than I was when you came in. It was a shock at first, but I'm past the borderland. I have no jealousy now of the girl who is to be Dan's wife."

She held out a shadowy hand, and Paddy grasped it.

"This visit shall be our secret, Paddy," Helen said, keeping the boy's hand in her own. "Dan might not quite understand, and might blame you unjustly, for you meant it for the best. I know exactly how you meant it. Be just as loyal to your friends through life, Paddy—just as honest and brave. Keep that kind, true heart of yours, and some day, when you are a man, find a sweet girl who will be worthy of it. That is a strange way to speak to a schoolboy, isn't it, Paddy?" Again the low laugh was heard. "But we understand each other. We share a secret. I shall carry mine with me, and you will keep yours. Good-bye, Paddy! I am afraid father might return, and I do not want him to know of your visit. Still, I'm glad we've met; that Dan's friend is my friend too. Good-bye;"

The tender voice ceased, and Paddy, like one in a dream, returned the pressure of the frail fingers, and turned suddenly away, ashamed, boy-like, of the tears that rushed to his eyes.

He could not remember the homeward journey. His thoughts were still in that strange sunny sick-room.

*   *   *   *   *   *   *   *

"So Miss Leigh is dead?' Anne said to Paddy three days later. "Just as well, for she could never be anything but a cripple, and now that leaves Mr. Gresham free to take up with pretty Miss Sunner, who is longing for him."

Paddy turned impatiently away, but Anne continued—

"You take my word for it. Mr. Gresham can't but see it; and how that bullying step-mother treats her, while the poor shiftless medicine-chest of a father lets her be down-trodden! Mr. Gresham pities her, and pity is next door to love, especially with a kind-hearted man like him who was always ready to befriend the oppressed

ISABEL GRANT

or the helpless. You take my word for it, a wedding will take place from "Araluan" before the six months are out!"

The way Master Reginald "flew" at her, as Anne expressed it, gave her quite a turn; but time, nevertheless, proved Anne a true prophet.

Lady Sunners was able to return to England freed from her step-daughter, and could congratulate herself on having another successful marriage to her credit.

Paddy, his lameness gone, is back again at school, apparently the same thoughtless, harum-scarum schoolboy as of old. But in spite of his roughness and care-free buoyancy, there is a change in Paddy; he can never be quite the same boy as before the accident. There is a tender spot in his heart for Dan's first love. He sometimes hears the sweet, low voice again, the echo of a silvery laugh comes back to him, and he remembers the secret that lies between him and the brave heart that carried its own into the silent grave,

ISABEL GRANT.

THE COLLECTED PUBLISHED WORKS OF ISABEL GRANT

THE PROSPECTOR'S CHRISTMAS DINNER

BACKGROUND TO THE PUBLICATION

The Prospector's Christmas Dinner appeared in *The Lone Hand* monthly magazine in January 1910 with illustrations by D. H. Souter. One can easily imagine that the nucleus of this idea came to Isabel from an amalgam of the stories her father, William, would have treasured and retold to his family about his adventurous youth, when as an eager nineteen year old he landed in Melbourne to find that a huge gold rush had just begun.

Kit Taylor in his book *A history of the Lone Hand with Indexes* calls *The Lone Hand* "a magnificent experiment of Australian enterprise." Its inception can be attributed to Norman Lindsay the artist and illustrator, Frank Fox (later Sir Frank Fox) the sub-editor of *The Sydney Bulletin* newspaper and J.F. Archibald who had just resigned the editorship of *The Bulletin*. It first appeared in February 1907 published by *the Sydney bulletin* and the 50,000 copies sold out in three days. It was designed to give scope to the growing pool of high ranking Australian artists and writers who were being forced overseas to further their talents.

The title of the magazine was Archibald's concept. He wanted to celebrate Australia and being Australian by showing the typical Australian male as enterprising and independent and had Norman Lindsay design the first cover showing a "lone hand" mining prospector. Lindsay's smiling, virile young man in the mining garb of the day did just that.

The Lone Hand was closely modeled on *The Strand* magazine in Britain with 60% articles and 40% fiction and the same proportion of stories, verse, illustrations and cartoons. Archibald, however, had long been a disciple of American story techniques so he looked for stories that were less sentimental and verbose or padded with descriptions. This was the time of Commonwealth and a pride in

Australia. It was a time when we had formed an identity based on acceptance and rejection of the culture of Britain and were in expectation of progress on the world stage. He therefore started the magazine with the idea of satisfying a world demand for factual information on Australian people, places and opportunity. It was to have a fully Australian content, unheard of before then.

Over its fourteen years of publication this ideal was diluted but it did provide the literati with a quality magazine showcasing some of our most famous artists and writers. Besides Norman Lindsay just a few of the other very well known Australians to contribute were: - Henry Lawson, Mary Gilmore, Banjo Paterson, A.H. Davis, C.J Dennis and Miles Franklin.

D. H. Souter, the illustrator for Isabel's story, was a contemporary of May Gibbs, and like her did fantasy sketches in the same genre. He was born in Aberdeen in 1862 and arrived in Australia in 1886 working for Sydney printing firms and drawing for the *Bulletin*. He was a painter, cartoonist, illustrator, writer and stage director. He embraced the Art Nouveau style and used a trademark cat which dotted his cartoon drawings and even metamorphosed into "cataroos" --- Kangaroo shaped cats. He was co-editor of *Art and Architecture* from 1904-11. He was a well known artist of the time and is claimed as an Australian artist of note. He died in Sydney in 1935.

Before the start of the story I have included pages from the publication in which it appears showing advertisements, promotions for forthcoming issues and the contents page. I believe this sets the scene for the era and her style.

THE COLLECTED PUBLISHED WORKS OF ISABEL GRANT

The Lone Hand

JANUARY 1, 1910 Vol. VI. No. 33.

CONTENTS FOR JANUARY.

page

Cover— The Koala—*(Painted by Norman Lindsay)*

Frontispiece—
The Australian Yachting Girl—*(Painted by Percy F. S. Spence)* - . -Facing- 233

Color Plates-
Illustration to "Sir Henry Brown Hayes "—*(Painted by Norman Lindsay)* - Facing 241
The Brown Girl of the Beaches—*(Painted by J. J. Hilder)* - - - Facing 257
Illustration to "A Promising Pupil"—*(Painted by Alek Sass)* - - - Facing 321

Pictures—
The Australian Girl—*(As seen by C. Wheeler, At. Stainforth, Florence Rodway, Percy F. S. Spence, Ruby Lindsay, Norman Lindsay, Alek Sass, D. H. Souter and G. H. Dancey .* - - - **281-289**

Serials—
African Game Trails—*(Illustrated by Photographs)* - -Theodore Roosevelt 268
Galahad Jones—*(Pictures by Norman Lindsay)* - -Arthur H. Adams 290

Articles- Sir Henry Brown Hayes: A Stormy Petrel- *(Illustrations, in tint, and colored plate by Norman Lindsay)* - - - - - - Chas. H. Bertie 236
Australia's Amphibians—*(Illustrated with Special Photographs and colored plate by J.J. Hilder)* ....- Egbert T. Russell 252

The Stage: Calve—*(With Photographs)* ....J. M. C. 338
   The Drama of Ideas - - - - - Leon Brodzky 342
Some Remarkable Habits of the Australian Case-Moth—*(Illustrated by Photographs)* Edmund Jarvis 335

Art and Letters: In Adam Lindsay Gordon's Country - - G. K. Soward 347

Stories—
In Moonlit Waves—*(Illustrations by D. H. Souter)* - - - C. A. Jeffries 247
Dorothea Greene's Letters - - - - - - Eve Lyn 303
Morning Glory—*(Illustrations by Norman Lindsay)* - Randolph Bedford 306
A Promising Pupil—*(Illustrations and colored plate by Alek Sass)* - - T. Carnett 316
The Prospector's Christmas Dinner—*(Illustrations by D. H. Souter)* - Isabel Grant 322
Etella of the Pangurangs—*(Illustrations by G. H. Dancey)* - - W. Sabelberg 330

Verse-
The Christ-Child Day in Australia—*(Decorations, in tint, by Alek Sass)* Ethel Turner 233
At the Ford—*(Illustration by F. P. Mahony)* - - - - D. Hirst 266
The Green, Green Hill - - - - - Mary Gilmore 321
Judgment.. . - Harry Sullivan 346

Departments—
The Dictates of Fashion - - ... - - xxxiii
The Judicious Thief.. xlii

ISABEL GRANT

THE NEXT

ILLUSTRATION BY N. LINDSAY
To "THE SWINGING GAFF"

The Sham OF *Amateurism*

To the sport-loving public the most interesting article in "The Lone Hand" for February will be the sham of Amateurism. In this striking article the writer exposes the pretences of amateurism that are to be found everywhere in the domain of sport. The public will be shocked to learn the true-blue, unsullied "amateur" does not exist.

Norman Lindsay— his Works and Aims.

For the general public the comprehensive study of Norman Lindsay's artistic development will, perhaps, prove of greater Interest. The article is written in non-technical style, interspersed with characteristic anecdotes of Lindsay in his youth, and illustrated with rare drawings done by Lindsay from the age of fourteen onward. The examples of his work from his fourteenth to his seventeenth year will come as a revelation of his graphic power. This intimate article is the first authoritative "explanation" of Norman Lindsay's mental outlook and artistic aim; and those of the general public who do not like the Norman Lindsay Woman" will find out the reason for their dislike.

The Panama Canal

A timely Informative article deals with the digging of the Panama Ditch. The writer is an Australian, who was for two

THE COLLECTED PUBLISHED WORKS OF ISABEL GRANT

LONE HAND

years employed on the colossal excavation works. The article shows by a magnificent series of photographs the modern machinery used and the vastness
of the undertaking.

Hunter-Naturalist.

"African Game Trails" deals with a different species of African game. Only two animals of each species is slain —for the trip is made to secure specimens of African fauna.

The SnaKe Season.

February is the snake season. In an article entitled " Snakes and Snakebite,' the writer tells some facts about the reptiles that will be news to the average Australian.

Fiction for the Hot Weather

issue. There will be stories of widely different appeal, ranging from the gaiety of Stories will bulk largely in this heat-wave "Kodak's" "Emotional Ghost" to the grim tragedy in "The Swinging Gaff." This story— one of the finest sea-stories ever written— is by a new writer, Eleanor Mordaunt; and its Illustrations, by Norman Lindsay, give it added strength.

NORMAN LINDSAY IN HIS STUDENT YEARS SKETCH BY LIONEL LINDSAY

"KODAK"

The Editor

THE MAGNIFICENT AUSTRALIAN Inter-State Mail Steamship Services

Three Regular Sailings Weekly

from MELBOURNE, SYDNEY, and BRISBANE To QUEENSLAND PORTS and VICE VERSA.

S.S. KAROOLA.

TWO REGULAR SAILINGS WEEKLY from SYDNEY, MELBOURNE, and ADELAIDE to WEST AUSTRALIAN PORTS and VICE VERSA.

Also other regular intermediate Passenger and Cargo Services between all Ports.

S.S. KYARRA.

For full particulars of Fares & Freights apply

Adelaide S.S. Co. Ld.
A.U.S.N. Co. Ld.
Howard Smith Co. Ld.
Huddart Parker & Co. Propy. Ld.
M'Ilwraith, M'Eacharn & Co. Propy. Ld.

S.S. COOMA.

THE "ABBOTT"
Australian Filter

PRICES from ...

12/6 to £30.

THE "ABBOTT" FILTER has been approved by the Boards of Health, and is installed in the leading Aerated Water Factories, Steamship Cos., Government Offices, and homes throughout the Commonwealth of Australia.

Catalogues from the Manufacturers.

N. GUTHRIDGE LTD.,

263 George Street, Sydney; 486 Collins Street, Melbourne.

CONSULT US ON ALL MATTERS OF FILTRATION.

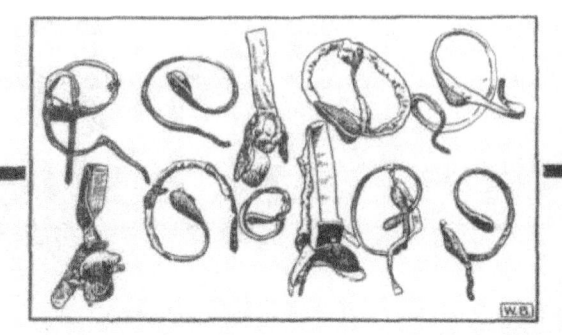

Trusses Are Useless!

No truss in existence can cure rupture. It may occasionally give slight relief, but more often not it increases the irritation, and leads to more serious troubles. We show a few of the many torturing trusses that have been discarded in favor of the Dr. J. A. Sherman Treatment—a method which has lifted thousands from the darkness of despair into the broad sunlight of health and happiness.

The truss can never do any good,

But the Sherman Method Will Cure Your Rupture.

Read this convincing extract from a letter recently written by a Sydney lady, who for 17 years vainly tried to be relieved of this awful affliction:

Mr. A. W. MARTIN.

Dear Sir,—From the very first day I started your treatment I had relief, and before six weeks had passed the tissues were healing, and in less than three months I was so well that I accompanied my husband on an eight-mile tramp across hilly roads. I have steadily gained weight, and am now the picture of health.

(Name supplied on request.)

CONSULTATIONS ARE FREE.

Will you come in and see further proof of the efficacy of this wonderful treatment? We can show conclusive evidence of its success, and will tell you exactly what can be done. If you cannot possibly arrange a visit, write for two books with details and testimonials. Just fill in the coupon and post it.

Mr. A. W. MARTIN,
Dept. L, Gibbs' Chambers, Moore Street, Sydney.
Please send me your two Books on Rupture.

M..

....

....

HOURS:—Daily (Sundays excepted), 10 a.m. to 12 noon; 2 p.m. to 5 p.m. Saturdays, 10 a.m. to 12 noon. Extra hours:—Friday Evenings, 7 to 9.

A. W. MARTIN, Sole Controller of the DR. J. A. SHERMAN METHOD,

Dept. L, Gibbs' Chambers, 7 MOORE STREET, near the G.P.O., SYDNEY.

THE PROSPECTOR'S CHRISTMAS DINNER

By Isabel Grant

"MY word! Mac, she does smell first rate; but aren't you lettin' her get a little too brown on this side?" said Jim Larman, pointing with the stem of his pipe to the fat turkey that hung before the camp fire on a bush spit, ingeniously contrived out of three sticks and a piece of wire. Duncan McGregor, a huge man, with "New Chum" written large over his flushed face, was engaged in cooking the Christmas dinner for the camp.

The other two members of the prospecting party, as they lay and smoked in the shade behind the tents, were too full of languorous enjoyment even to raise their heads from the grass to watch the progress of the coming feast. Unfortunately for Larman, his place of shade commanded a view of the fire, and thus his complete enjoyment was spoiled by some twinges of compunction at the sight of the cook's perspiring face. With a natural desire to pass on the irritation he called out,

"Frank Carter, you lazy beggar! Wasn't this week your turn for cookin'? What do you mean by sneakin' out of it, and imposin' on Mac's good nature like this?"

"That uss ahl right; that uss ahl right," said Mac soothingly, while the wave of the pewter spoon that had been employed to baste the turkey seemed to dismiss further speech on the matter. Frank Carter raised himself to a sitting position, and spoke in an aggrieved boyish tone.

ISABEL GRANT

"Oh, hang it, Jim I don't want to impose on Mac's good nature any more than you do; but seeing that this was Christmas week, and that I'm such a poor hand at the cooking, I thought I'd ask Mac to take my turn for once in a way."

"Once in a way!" retorted Larman scornfully. "I like that. Seem Mac's always on the job. Last week was his own turn, and the week before Joe got him to take it for him on some excuse or another. It's not the fair thing boys; especially when you remember it's Mac's first summer out here."

Carl Jorgensen, or "Joe," as his mates called him, now sat up, and, taking the pipe from his mouth, he drawled out, with a twinkle in his light-blue Danish eyes, "And the week before, Jim Larman, it was your turn, and you coaxed Mac to take it for you."

"That uss ahl right," interposed Mac. His English was rather scanty, though he could be fluent enough in his native Gaelic. "Cooking ahlwehs wass easy to me; ass far back ass I can mind I wass a coot hahnd at it. Ahnd then, ass I wass telling you, I worked mah passage out here, under a second kissin who was cook on a pig steamboat; so what uss ferry hard for you uss shist play to me. Put, perhaps, ut wass more petter ass Jim sehs, so I'll feenish thus week ahnd then we'll take our turns apout ass pefore."

"As before," said Carter with a grin, "that will suit me down to the ground."

Larman suddenly grew serious. "Anyhow, boys, we can't expect to have Mac cook for us much longer. If his luck keeps up he'll be marrying Molly Ryan, and leaving us in the lurch."

Mac tried to hide his bashful red face by peering into the big pot, where the plum pudding, the culminating triumph of the feast, was bobbing briskly up and down. Molly Ryan, servant maid with Pattison, the chief grocer of Neumurra, was, as her name might seem to imply, of Irish extraction. She had come out to Australia with her parents in her early teens, and had been in service ever since. She was now a bright, pretty girl of twenty, and the faintest touch of soft Kerry brogue remained on her witty tongue.

In woman-deserted Neumurra even a plain girl has a choice of suitors; and Mac's courage in joining the train of such a popular girl as Molly Ryan, if it did not command success, at least deserved it. His mates laughed at the mere idea of Molly's accepting the raw new-chum; but Mac's big, simple heart held a trembling hope of ultimate success.

It was now nine months since the four men had agreed to join forces and leave wage-earning at Neumurra, the great gold-mining center, for prospecting among the creeks and gullies some, five or six miles from the mine. The little company shared expenses, but each man's find was his own. Except Mac, who did remarkably well, the others met only fair success. Duncan McGregor was a curious contrast to his companions.

He almost seemed to belong to another species, so big, dark-skinned and clumsy was he beside their fair, clean-limbed suppleness. The loss of an eye gave a sinister cast to features that were strong to the verge of harshness. But it was a curiously feminine soul that inhabited the huge body. Feminine in its love of pleasing, its delight in approbation; more feminine still in a quaint, Martha-like carefulness about little things, which sat oddly on such a giant. For ten years a shepherd on the bare braes of Lochaber; the sole support and nurse of a widowed, bed-ridden mother, Duncan, in the tiny "but and ben," had become trained in woman's ways, and confirmed in incongruous traits that made him at once the laughing stock and the admiring wonder of the men who had been fortunate enough to persuade him to join them in their mining venture.

Order was Mac's first law. The hollow, lightning-blasted trunk behind the tents he had converted, with the help of a couple of fruit cases, into a tidy pantry. On newspaper-decorated shelves he kept, in neatly labelled tins, necessaries for cooking; and it was as much as their lives were worth, according to Carter, to disturb the spick and span arrangement of these shelves.

The sun poured down from a grey-blue, cloudless sky, the heat waves danced about the hollows, over the stringy-bark where the soil was poor, over the silver-leaved ironbark and the bloodwood of the richer country.

Through the heat-haze the Nulla Ranges glimmered in misty blue; while down the gully, from the grasses, tree-ferns, mahogany, ti-tree and native hops, mingling shades of brown, olive, grey and golden greens melted in the sunshine.

But when, at Mac's call, the prospectors rose to take their places on their accustomed logs, they had no eyes to spare for the marvellous beauty of the scene; Their gaze was fixed instead

In blandest after-dinner mood, the men once more resumed their pipes."

on a picture with more instant appeal to hungry men— amber-brown turkey and cream and russet potatoes, ruddy pumpkin, green cabbage and greener peas providing color enough for any possible aesthetic craving.

In blandest after-dinner mood, the men once more resumed their pipes.

"I've always heard, the better the cook the worse the cook's temper," said Larman; "but Mac, here, don't bear that out. Another sort of chap, instead of cookin' a bonser dinner like this would have turned rusty at the mean way the lot of us had been imposin' on him ; and if he didn't strike would have done some trick or other to bring us to our bearin's."

"Another sort of chap," laughed Frank," would have given us cold poison, and not hot brandy sauce for our pudding.

Mac echoed the laugh, as he sat down with his now cold portion of turkey.

" 'Deed, then," he said, smiling like a benevolent Cyclops, "ahnd I could hef poishoned the lot of you ef I hed the mind, for I got some arsenic ass I passed the new chemist's last night, I hef enough poishon, mebbe, to poishon a clachan."

"It was strychnine, not arsenic, we talked of gettin'; not that I suppose it matters. One poison is as good as another for dingoes," said Larman.

"Well! well!" replied Mac serenely. "So it wass not the arsenic you wanted efter ahl; put ut would pe a peety to waste ut, for 'deed I had some trouble to get ut. I wull not use ut on the beasties tull efter the New Year, whatefer, for I do not like the notion of kulling anything —not even Anna Maria," and he chuckled.

"Poor Anna Maria," said Frank. "Then New Year's night will be positively her last."

Almost the only drawback to the prospecting camp was the attentions of some dingoes, which, though generally too cowardly to venture near enough to steal, made night hideous with their howls. One of their number, distinguished by a whitish ruff along the back and by a lugubrious and peevish persistency of howl, had been named "Anna Maria."

"I hope you took care where you put the stuff," remarked Jorgensen uneasily. "I know too much about poisons to believe in being careless."

"Oh yuss, I wass ferry careful. I looked efter ut ass soon ass I cot hom. The pepper wass not too strong; so I pit the arsenic into an empty tun I hed by me, ahnd I pit the tun aweh in a hole in the tree apove mah top shelf. I'll show you where ut uss when I hef hed mah denner; put you may hef your smock in peace now, there uss no call to pe fashing apout ut."

A choking gasp from Frank Carter drew all eyes towards him. He staggered to his feet, his eyes dilated, his face paled, even to his boyish lips. He tried to speak, but no words would come; the others waited in anxious wonder. When at last he spoke the words came in a breathless rush, but the voice was the toneless voice of an automaton.

"I was looking about for something to put my stuff in this morning, as I'd found a hole in my bag; and I came across a tin above the shelves. There was a white powder in it, and I thought it was an extra supply of something Mac had got in. I looked through the things in the tins on the shelves, and the cream o' tartar one looked exactly the same; so I emptied the powder into it.

Mac was down at the creek washing up, but I wasn't going to say a word anyway about it till he missed the tin; then I meant to chaff him about finding something out of its place in his old-maid contraption. I watched him take down that very tin for the plum pudding."

"He tried to speak, but no words would come."

ISABEL GRANT

With a Gaelic guttural of horror Mac, who like the rest had been listening in hypnotized silence, dashed down his plate and rushed to his beloved shelves. He came back wringing his hands and crying out in his mother-tongue.

"With a broken Gaelic phrase Mac was gone."

In his fear and horror his English had departed from him. They gathered round him, the three men, and looked at him speechlessly. A few minutes before they had been boys, their eyes alight with the joy of life, their faces full of frank, physical satisfaction of the care-free, blessed abandon of youth; now they turned on each other, the drawn, ashen faces of old men stricken with death.

Jorgenson turned a distorted face to McGregor, and screamed, "You paid us out right enough, you knew what you were about; you took good care not to taste any yourself," but Lahman sharply.

"Don't be a fool, Joe! Mac's not to blame; as for Frank, he'll pay dearly enough for his monkey tricks. We're too far out from Neumurra to try to walk there; so, as we've only got one horse, Mac had better take it and bring Dr. Francis out to us."

With a sudden lightening of his woe-begone visage Mac hurried away. He returned in a few minutes on horseback. Frank came to meet him. "Here," he said, "take this paper. I've written down all about it in case, you know. We've signed it, too; now no one can blame you;" and his cold hand met Mac's hot clasp convulsively. Larman's face was white, but his voice was steady. "Yes, we thought it just as well to put it in put it in writing. Now, don't you worry, old man, but ride - ride like --!"
Jorgensen came up, too, and held out a shaking hand. ."I never meant it, Mac. So long."

With a broken Gaelic phrase Mac was gone. The Highlander was no lightweight, as poor Darkie found to his cost when, in a lather of foam and sweat, Mac tied him up to Dr. Francis' gate. Straight to the surgery rushed Mac. He had not noticed the doorbell, though he made up for the omission by the pounding his heavy fists gave the wall.

Dr. Francis came hurrying into the room, and regarded his formidable-looking visitor with an eye of half-humorous apprehension. "Thankyou, that will do," he said quietly. "Now tell me what it is I can do for you."

Mac heard the sound and turned at once. Unaware in his perturbation of mind that he spoke in Gaelic, he dashed into his story. "Is he a mad Russian, or what?" wondered the doctor. " 'Vodka' is about the only Russian word I know; I'll try him in French." He tried him in French, in halting German; he assayed a phrase of Italian and of Spanish, but met only a look of pitiful bewilderment, as Mac gazed hopelessly at him and wondered by what means he could make this strange doctor understand. Willy Nilly, he must bring him back to the gully.

Suddenly the idea of appealing for help to a polyglot dipsomaniac in the "works" close by occurred to the doctor, and he turned to leave the room.

To his horrified astonishment he found himself lifted in a pair of giant arms and borne to the door, sown the steps, out to the gate. Helpless as a child and choking with indignation, Dr. Francis, who was no coward, resisted violently, and, managing to get his arms round the gate-post, cling to it like grim death.

"No, no!" he shouted, now thoroughly alarmed.

"Yuss, yuss!" shouted Duncan in reply, following the doctor's lead, and dropping into English, with the same unconsciousness as he had used Gaelic. "You must come; three men poishoned! Thus pepper wull tell you ahl apout ut;" and, settling the doctor on his feet, he thrust Carter's paper into his hand.

Dr. Francis was quick witted; one breathless glance put him in possession of the situation.

"Why didn't you speak English at once, you fool?" he cried; "losing time like this over your absurd gibberish!"

"I wass speaking the English; I hef the English ferry well. It wass not me wass losing time ofer gupperish," retorted Mac. indignantly

"Arsenic, did you say? H'm! h'm! only chance, an over-dose. I'll get. Dr.Hickson to come with me. You go up to Pattison, the grocer, and borrow his light spring-cart. It will do to bring them up to the hospital if there's a chance—in any case to bring them up—you under- stand."

Yuss, I under-stand," said Mac heavily, and departed on his mission. He would probably see his sweetheart; but the thought brought him now no joy.

It was Molly who came at his knock
She was alone in the kitchen, and to her perforce he had to explain his errand.

Mac began his story like a criminal awaiting Before he had finished it he but for his anxiety over his mates, the happiest man in Neumurra, and even his anxiety was almost submerged in the wave of joy that overwhelmed him.

"It was Molly who came to his knock."

Molly went to tell the story to her master, and then came with Mac while he harnessed up the horse that Mr. Pattison had lent to replace poor, spent Darkie.

"Wasn't the arsenic colored black with charcoal?" she asked. She had once been in service with a chemist, and, as her way was, had picked up a good deal of useful information. She had, besides, more wisdom in her little finger than Mac possessed in his whole great body; and an idea had just occurred to her.

"No, white; shist like the cream o' tartar poor Carter thought ut wass," said Mac.

"Then," said Molly, triumphantly; "that new chemist is in for a bad time; and it's myself will go round to tell him so. He has broken the law, and he'll be had up for manslaughter."

"Ahnd what coot wull that pe to mah poor mates?" said Mac.

" 'Deed mah wumman, when I think of them --- the best a mahn efer had—ef ut wass not for you I'd put a pullet through mah own brains."

"Don't be a fool, Duncan; you've none too many to spare," said Molly.

But Mac carried away with him the remembrance of a smile that atoned for the words.

Molly was as good as her promise

"A furious thumping roused the chemist."

half an hour later, she was at the shop.

A furious thumping roused the chemist, who was putting in Christmas in a tiny room behind the shop, and sent him hurrying to the counter, to find a pretty girl pounding on the floor with a stub-headed umbrella; The girl, not observing his entrance, continued her exercise.,

"If you've quite finished"— the chemist's tone was affable, and he gave a twirl to a

weedy moustache, for the girl was undeniably pretty—" I'd like to know what I can do for you."

The girl turned round with most disconcerting self-possession. "Oh, you would, would you? Then please tell me what you mean by selling a man arsenic without coloring it to prevent accidents. The chemist started, but looked at the girl with fresh admiration. "See here," he said frankly, "I don't know how you happen to know; for the man came in late last night, and he told me he was going straight back to the bush; but I'll tell you all about it. The fellow—a regular Goliath he was—came in and asked for arsenic. He said he wanted it to put some Anna Maria out of the way; then he got confused, and explained he was going to poison dingoes. I couldn't make out all he said, he spoke so queerly; but, anyway, he was a touchy kind of man. I pity Anna Maria if she is his wife; he looked as if he'd run amok at the least opposition. I don't mind owning I didn't want to provoke him."

"Coward!" Snapped Molly

"He didn't say his name was Howard," said the chemist with simplicity. "In fact, he gave it as Duncan McGregor, and he looked it! A big, black, murdering Scotchman. Well, I didn't feel like getting my face smashed up by a raging lunatic; neither did I want to have the responsibility of giving poison to him and I couldn't put him off; so I made up a packet of cream o' tartar - it looks exactly like arsenic, I may tell you—called it arsenic. I didn't bother to color it of course "
But at the word the girl took to her heels and ran out of the shop.

Mr. and Mrs. Pattison, who were preparing to go for an afternoon drive, were scandalized by the sight of their maid tearing madly towards the house. Molly told her curious tale to the couple.

"What do you say, Bessie," said Pattison to his wife, " to driving to the gully and putting those poor chaps out of their misery ? We might take Molly along, too; she can get into the back seat; I reckon she deserves to be in at the death. Cream o' tartar ! Two doctors ! Ha, ha !"

The buggy was soon speeding towards the gully. Half way there it was met the spring-cart driven by a dejected Highlander, while two sober-faced doctors rode one on each side of it. Carter, Larman and Jorgensen lay prone on the floor of the buggy, their ghastly faces and hollow eyes those of men in the last extremity.

Dr. Francis drew up to the buggy. "Sad case, all round," he said in a low tone. "I'm afraid it's all up with these poor fellows; though, if they can only hold out till we reach the hospital, we'll have another go at them." Pattison, leaning forward, said a few words; Dr. Francis stared at him incredulously. . Meanwhile Molly slipped down from the back seat and ran up to the cart.

"Duncan! "'she cried, and the laughter brimmed over from her blue eyes." It was real cream o' tartar, not arsenic, that blessed fool of a chemist gave you last night."

Mac's Homeric roar of joyous' relief was followed by a whoop from the cart, as the three invalids sat up and gazed around.

122

"They had every symptom of arsenic poisoning," objected Dr. Francis.

"I'm afraid," said Carter sheepishly, " that's owing, to Jorgensen. He told us every symptom we ought to have; and, by Jove, we had them all! I know I did."

"The power of the imagination—" began Dr.Hickson; but his further wisdom was drowned in a wild burst of laughter. Again, and again, and yet again, the chorus rang out, till, the kookaburras in the scrub hard by fled in envious disgust.

"We'd better get back to the camp," said Larman at length, preparing to get down from the cart.

"No, you don't," cried Carter, pulling him back. "We'll drive in state to Neumurra; and then Mac and I will shout you all the best spread the Grand Hotel can set out. I'm ready for a square feed, I can tell you."

" Yuss, yuss; that will be shist right. I would like fine to hef a bite mahself," said Mac.

And a look from Mary told the mates that Mac had cooked his last dinner.

ISABEL GRANT

The Gympie Times AND MARY RIVER MINING GAZETTE

SATURDAY, 17th DECEMBER, 1910.

A Tale of a Turkey.

(Written for the "Gympie Times.")

"Did you ever meet Bob Jones? He was transferred down your way, and being in your branch of business, I thought you might know him. A little fair chap he was, inclined to be stout - stuttered a bit, and went in for writing poetry and that sort of thing for the papers. He married Judd Williams' daughter."

"You don't mean to tell me Jonesy's married Judd Williams' daughter! My word! She'll bring him a pile! For all he looked simple, Jonesy knew how many beans made five most days in the week. I remember his saying it was as easy to fall in love with a rich girl as a poor one, and a jolly sight easier to take up house-keeping with her afterwards. He stuck to his principles all right. Jonesy had the knack of falling on his feet and getting the best out of things; but too much luck like that isn't healthy. Bet you ten to one the wife is the boss."

"Did he ever tell you the trick a number of us played on him with a turkey? I laugh yet when I think of it—but hold on! I'll let you have the yarn."

"Six of us young fellows, who were pretty chummy at the time, got the idea of camping out for the Christmas holidays. We figured it out, and reckoned we could have three times the fun, with about a third of the cost, in batching for ourselves, as in boarding.

We hired a couple of tents, bought some groceries, pots, and dishes, not too many—it saved cleaning up—and off we set for Rialto.

Pretty well the whole town was down at the sea-side that year, every house was taken, the hotels and boarding-houses were chock-a-block; and, with a good many others camping out besides ourselves, the place was fairly lively.

We chose a bit of scrub just behind Carrington's. You know Carrington's place, "Seaview," that big house with latticed verandahs facing the Bay, at Kissing Point, the show place of Rialto.

Well, we pitched just down from it in the scrub. We were, all six of us, Roberts, Campbell, Hardy, Fleming, Jones, and I, by way of being struck on Florrie Carrington, or on her cousin, Amy Lyons, who had been brought up with her, so you can guess why that bit of scrub was the most suitable spot we could find to camp in.

It was the fashion with most of the young fellows of the town to be after Florrie or Amy; they were the belles of every assembly, and as they were full of fun and mischief it was always "room for one more" with them, so to speak. They could always spare a smile for another boy in their train, and were quite prepared to lead him a dance if the spirit moved them.

Florrie was a dashing, handsome girl, with a well set up figure, and pair of big black eyes that could do fair execution, I can tell you.

Amy was a little, soft, fluffy fair-haired thing, not exactly pretty, but she had a way with her that most fellows would find hard to resist. They were both real popular girls, and they deserved to be, for better girls it would be hard to find. No nonsense about them, ready for every bit of fun going, and straight as a die with it all.

Of course we knew that Powell, the manager of the Union Bank, was right bower with Florrie, and that Greenfell, an English Johnnie, a jackaroo, who used to come down pretty well every week from Glenlevat station, was considered booked for Amy, but there was no engagement yet, and so we let on, each of us, to be great with the girls, making a great blow about any little sign of notice taken of us. We weren't more than lads then, and what could you expect. We made the most of every chance word or smile that came our way. None of us were badly gone. Perhaps we knew we hadn't the ghost of a chance, or perhaps it was because, like measles, love doesn't do so much damage when you get it young; but anyhow it didn't affect our appetites, or take away from our sleep; it just gave a spice to things generally.

I remember (and very likely the others were just as big fools) I used to think, from one little thing or another, Florrie had a ticket or two on me, but I wasn't earning in those days much more than would have kept her in gloves, much less dresses, so I had sense enough to keep my head shut, but not enough to quit fooling round her neighbourhood, and advertising my lunacy.

Well, it didn't take us long to pitch our tents and get ready for a high old time. We had it too! Boating, fishing, swimming, pretty well living on the water, until it was time to go to the railway station to watch the evening train come in.

It was the great event of the day to meet that train. All the folks, more or less, turned out. The girls in big sun bonnets, that made it hard sometimes to tell one from another (but that was all in the game). The boys with hats perched back from their sunburnt faces.

This was flirtation time at Rialto, and you can bet none of us missed the chance of a word or two with the "Seaview" girls if we could any way manage to secure it, before the train arrived, or by walking back, if we got the show, with them to their house.

The second day we came, we heard (the girls did not tell us, it was common report), that the Carringtons were giving a great dinner on Christmas day; but 1 suppose none of us were significantly big guns, for we weren't invited. We hardly expected it, yet we were disappointed, for we were, we thought, on friendly enough terms to be invited. Each of us fancied, most likely, that if he had been alone, he might have been asked, but understood that Mrs. Carrington could not see her way to take in the whole camp, so had had to refuse the girls' requests for an invitation.

Powell and Greenfell, who were staying at the swell hotel were going, of course, and some other toffs were coming down from town. There was a good deal of talk over the affair at Rialto, for it was rumoured to be going to be something out of the ordinary.

We heard on the day before Christmas that Florrie and Amy had gone up to town, and wouldn't be back till Christmas morning, when some of their guests would be coming down with them.

I suppose that's why we went out for a longer day's fishing, but we paid pretty dearly for going out so far, for in the afternoon the wind freshened, and we were driven across the Bay, and what with the high seas, and a couple of squalls, we had a narrow shave of ever seeing land again. We were none of us great shakes with a boat, and it was about two in the morning when we got back to our tents, wet to the skin, and aching in every bone. We didn't get up with the sun, I promise you, and when we did begin to stir, nobody felt inclined to tackle getting the breakfast ready.

We had plenty of fresh fish, but it seemed too much like hard work cleaning them, in spite of our hunger.

However, after a bit, Jonesy volunteered to turn cook. That was just like him. He was born good natured, and hadn't been able to get it out of his system.

For shame's sake, Fleming went to give him a hand, and I was pleased to see it, for I had been feeling it was fair up to one of us to help him, but didn't somehow want to be that one.

The rest of us went for a bathe to take the stiffness out of our bones, while breakfast was preparing, easing our consciences, or what did duty for them, by telling the two cooks we'd wash up after breakfast. As nobody was allowed more than a tin plate, a mug, a knife and a fork, we hadn't taken much of a burden, either, on our shoulders by our generous promise.

After breakfast Jonesy and Fleming went off for their bathe, and we lay on the grass smoking and talking, having got the washing-up done in a couple of winks.

Most of us kept our eyes on "Seaview," not that there was much to be seen just then, seeing the girls were away, but still we liked to look at the house—you understand—you've been there yourself.

Carrington's two servant maids passed, on their way for their dip. The little plump one giggled as she went by, but the tall red-headed cook gave us a scowl, as if she believed we were up to no good smoking and idling there.

Presently Mrs. Carrington came down the back verandah steps carrying a huge turkey, which she hung on a hook under the house, probably to keep it fresh for the great dinner.

The turkey was stuffed, it did really look tempting, even though not cooked, and our mouths watered.

'By jove! What a whopper!' Hardy sat up and pointed with his cigarette to the thing. 'That's going to be the crowning glory of the feast! Yum-yum, I shouldn't mind sampling him. Bet you he weighs twenty pounds!'

None of us took him up, the turkey was certainly a magnificent bird, and it didn't want much imagination to fancy how he'd taste when done to a turn. Fish seemed to pall on us at the mere sight of that appetising bird.

Hardie turned round, there was something queer in his eyes.

'What a lark to take the gobbler and give ma a fright.'

'Oh shut up Hardie, you make me tired!' said Campbell.

We thought of course, though we knew Hardie of old, that he was joking. But no, pretty soon we saw he was in dead earnest; and the more we got on to him to give up the idea the more set he became on carrying it out.

He rose to his feet, and put his cigarette on a log, and looked at us with a grin.

'Of course, I'll put him back all in good time for the dinner, I just want to give the old lady a bit of a new sensation. Won't her eyes pretty near drop out of her head when she finds her big turkey gone, but the joy of finding him afterwards will more than make up for the fright. I reckon ma will be thinking she'd better invest in a pair of specs when she finds her gobbler back on his hook, after she had imagined him gone for good,' and he laughed heartily, taking not the slightest notice of what the rest of us said.

He was a beggar for a lark, Dick Hardy, and no matter how heavily he paid for one piece of mischief, he was just as keen on the next. Still, we hardly believed he'd be dare-devil enough to go up to the house in broad daylight, and take the turkey from its hook; but that was what he did a few minutes later, and he came back to our half-scared group without anyone interfering with, or appearing to notice him.

He threw the turkey on one of the stretchers, and laid himself down just where he had been, before the Plan came into his mad head. He lifted his cigarette calmly from the log, and lit up as if nothing had happened, while the rest of us were on the jump with nervousness, and couldn't enjoy a decent smoke.

About half an hour went by. A good many people passed and re-passed, but in all that time no sign of life came from "Seaview."

Presently the servant girls returned and began to bustle about the kitchen. Then soon after Mrs. Carrington came out to the back door, and slowly, for she was a stout woman, went down the steps with a couple of ducks in her hand.

She stopped, as if shot, and we could almost see the shocked astonishment in the very set of her back.

'Mary! Susan!' she called out, 'which of you took up the turkey. I left it purposely here in the coolness. The kitchen is too hot; bring it down at once.'

The girls came out and leant over the verandah rails, then ran down the steps protesting neither had touched the blessed bird.

Then there was a hullabaloo, if you like. Every one of the three speaking at once.

'I seen some blacks coming up this way as we went to our bathe. They must have took it,' was the plump little girl's theory.

My word I was glad when I heard her say that! But next minute I felt worse than ever when I saw Mr. Carrington, followed, to our astonishment, by Florrie and Amy, walk out on the back verandah, and hurry down the steps. The girls must have returned by the last night's train after all. Hardy hadn't reckoned on that. I looked at him to see how he took it, and he did seem a shade less cocksure of his lark turning out all right.

Mrs. Carrington with the servant girls helping her, told the terrible news, and we could see Mr. Carrington was upset too when he heard it.

He was a thin, tall, precise sort of man, what they call one of the old school, for his manners were of a politeness we younger men don't seem to have much use for (which, I suppose, isn't anything to our credit). But for all his politeness he wasn't the kind of man it was healthy to make angry—not by a long chalk.

Mrs. Carrington began nodding her head towards the piece of scrub where we were camped, and we didn't need to hear what she was saying to understand she was urging her husband to go down to us, and make some enquiries.

There, now Dick, see what you've let yourself and us, too, in for?' said Roberts angrily, 'I shouldn't mind so much, only they'll lump us all together, and think us as big fools or knaves as you. I guess your joke won't appeal to them much. Likely enough they'll think we were hungry, and put the whole thing down to low thieving. I've no patience with your tomfoolery.'

'Keep your hair on, the game isn't lost yet. You've no nerve, Roberts. I don't wonder you make such a shocking bad player. Can't you see the girls have put the old folks off the notion that high-toned chaps like us could have anything to do with the disappearance of the turkey. You wait a bit, and you'll see the whole lot go inside to discuss what they had better do, to cover up the unexpected loss to the dinner, for the girls will persuade Ma to make the best of a bad job.'

'Perhaps to send for the police,' said Roberts in his glum way.

'Now, now, my son, you must try to get out of that bad habit of looking on the dark side. See here at me I'm not worrying. I know it will be alright. You've no judgment. Send for the police indeed! What a morbid imagination you've got! I can't fancy anyone in "Seaview," certainly not those charming young ladies having the cold bloodedness to think of sending for the police on Christmas Day. Not even pa would agree to such a thing. They would just grin and bear it! Mark my words and be easy in your mind. Besides the cream of the joke is to come.'

Hardy was right so far, the excited group went up the steps and into the house, though it was an even toss whether or not Carrington wasn't getting ready to carry out Roberts' suggestion.

Hardy lay back and laughed, till Campbell came up and slapped him on the back to prevent his choking.

'If you don't stop acting the laughing-jackass, and don't at once tell us what further mischief you are planning, I won't be answerable for the consequences,' I said, and I got up too.

Dick knew, I was as good as, or even better than my word, so he began to explain without further loss of time.

'When Jonesy comes back from his dip—and by the by, he is taking so long, I must enquire into it—(not but it's all the better for my plan), I'm going to wait till he is togged up to the nines to go over to the station, for I know he'll want to be an extra swell to-day, then I'll get him to go to Mrs. Carrington, and hand her the turkey, asking her with our compliments to cook it along with her bird. I'll tell Jonesy it was a Christmas present to us from my uncle the Hon. Peter Mulholland, and it is the dead spit, down to the stuffing, of the one that Mrs. Carrington is going to cook for her big dinner. Then the fun will begin, or I'm no prophet.'

We burst out into yells of laughing, though we tried to smother them on the grass. The lovely cheek of this last development was too much for us, and then the thought of little Bobby marching up with the turkey, and requesting the angry owner to cook it for him, was too tempting, we hadn't the heart to put Hardy off his mischief.

Before long, Jonesy and Fleming returned, and were well chaffed by us as to what had kept them, then Fleming joined us on the grass, and Jonesy went in, as we expected, to do himself up, 'regardless.'

We told the joke to Fleming, and he nearly took a fit.

When Jonesy came out, he was a sight for sore eyes—cream flannel suit, Panama hat, lavender tie, and tan boots. As Campbell said, he did us all proud.

Then Hardy sailed in, buttering the little chap up, and telling him he was just the one to send to ask a favour, for no woman could resist him when got up in that style and while Jonesy was grinning foolishly, and we could hardly keep our faces straight, he went to the other tent and returned with the big turkey, giving his explanation, and declaring that we all thought Jonesy would be the proper one to send on the mission to Mrs. Carrington.

Jonesy was so flattered that he never made the least bones about going. In fact we could see he was quite uplifted at the thought that the rest of us recognised that he was the best man for a delicate job like this.

He took the turkey from Hardy, as pleased as punch.

'Well, I don't mind having a shot at the old lady, as we're by way of being good pals, Mrs. Carrington and I, but I reckon I'm due to get my pick of this turkey when it is cooked.'

That about finished us, but Hardy, without turning a hair, agreed to see to this matter, and off Jonesy set, holding the turkey very carefully away from his nice clean suit.

Fleming gave a choke almost before the fellow's back was turned, but a well-aimed kick from Hardy changed it into a cough.

As soon as Jonesy got far enough on his way, the rest of us had our laugh out, but we didn't let ourselves go, as we were longing to do—it wouldn't be safe.

'All the same, it's rough on Bob,' I said.

'Oh, be a sport, be a sport,' Hardy snapped out in disgust, so I shut up. After all, it was more his funeral than mine.

The hurry-scurry and confusion at "Seaview" had by this time quieted down. The back door was shut, and we could not see how events were progressing inside.

Jonesy walked up the paddock briskly, more slowly towards the steps, and having mounted them, he hesitated a little before he knocked at the door. Rehearsing his speech, we thought.

The red haired girl opened the door, then gave a screech.

Mrs. Carrington came running along the hall. The sight of her face must have frightened Jonesy, for he went back a step or two. The air was so clear every sound reached us. 'P—p—p- please Mrs. C— r—-arrigton, the b—oys send their c—c—ompliments, and wish to know if you'd be s—so k—ind as to c—c—ook this t—t—urkey of theirs with yours.'

We could imagine the smile with which Jonesy got out this polite message.

Mrs. Carrington went purple. 'Your turkey with mine! The impudence of the pack of you! Why, this is my turkey! I stuffed it myself. I'd know it in a hundred.'

Jonesy at once fired off an explanation, but between fright and anger he couldn't get a sentence straight; he stuttered and spluttered, and nearly tied himself into a knot in his efforts to make Mrs. Carrington understand that this turkey was rightfully ours, though it might be the "dead s—s—spit of the one Mrs. Carrington laid claim to." Between Mrs. Carrington gasping with indignation and Jonesy gamely but vainly trying to make himself clear, it was as funny as a pantomime. But pretty soon the red-haired girl, hovering behind her mistress, lost all patience, and swooping down grabbed Jonesy round the middle, dragged him, turkey and all, into the kitchen, and shut the door.

This was more than we had bargained for. We didn't feel at all too good. The business-like clutch of those big red arms sent a cold shiver down our backs. Even Hardy was put out, and went a bit white, to tell the truth.

'Now then, Smartee! There'll be something to pay. What are you going to do I'd like to know?' said Roberts, glaring at him.

But before Hardy could open his mouth, we heard a hail from the road on our right, and there were two chaps we knew, Turner and Crossland, coming over to us. They had got a loan of Geddes' motor launch, and were going out to the islands for the day. They invited us to join them, and Hardy jumped at the offer. I could see he was jolly glad of the excuse—any decent excuse to get away from the place just then, and I won't say the rest of us were much behind in accepting the invitation, either.

I did say to him, 'What about Jonesy? Hadn't we better go up to the house and straighten things out for him. He won't like us going off like this.'

But Hardy said he was quite easy in his mind. 'Jonesy's all right. He has plenty of savee, for all his simple ways, and once he gets going, he won't let his stuttering stand in the way of explaining matters. I know little Bob. I bet by this time he's bursting over the joke himself, or perhaps he's cleared out round the front to the railway station to have the laugh against us. He'll guess we were flabbergasted to see him made a sort of prisoner of. Bet you anything he has sneaked ahead of us, and taken the girls off by himself.' That was Hardy all over. Trouble rolled off him like water off a duck's back, but nevertheless his remark sounded fairly reasonable, or perhaps I was only too glad to believe it so for I said no more, and off we set.

It was a splendid day, especially the first part of it, with the sea a bit choppy, but only just enough to be pleasant, and on our way over we were full of spirits—animal spirits I mean, none of us went in for the other kind—but presently we began to get a bit quiet, and to find little to say, and then somehow or other our pleasure in the outing was gone, and we grew as melancholy as owls.

The wind rose when we reached the open sea, and the boat began to pitch about. We were taken with a touch of sea-sickness, every one of us, and I put it down, not to the rough sea, for it had been much rougher the day before, and not one of us had gone down to it, but to our feeling so dumpish.

I don't know how the others felt, but for my own part I was longing to get back to land and see what had become of poor Bob. I thought of his good nature, of his simple ways, and how the rest of us put upon him, till I felt "as mean as a bandicoot on a burnt-out ridge." Hardy's idea that the poor chap was laughing over the joke, seemed too thin, now. I couldn't forget the way those big red arms had closed round the little chap, nor the sight of Mrs. Carrington's face; besides, I knew Mr. Carrington wasn't the kind of man to provoke for the fun of the thing.

Crossland and Turner must have wondered what had come over us, but we kept mum, and didn't let on there was anything on our minds.

We tried to laugh and joke and carry on in our usual style, but there was no heart in our fun.

Coming back, a cold drizzle set in, and five more miserable specimens than the chaps that left the motor launch it would be hard to find. Crossland and Turner didn't come ashore, as they meant to go up the river to town. I think they were glad to be quit of us; and as for us, we were jolly glad to leave the boat.

We crawled up from the beach, and when we reached the top of the first sand hill, we could see that Carrington's house was lighted up in every window. As we drew closer to it, we saw the French lights of the dining room were fastened back, and the whole table was open to our sight. It did look splendid, with all the silver, cut glass, and flowers. The hum of talk and laughter, the brisk clatter of knives and forks, came so distinctly to our ears as we stood out there cold and hungry, that it made us feel bluer than ever.

'Great Scot' ! Roberts made a grab at me, and with that we all gave a start, for there, before our eyes, sitting between Florrie and Amy, and tucking in for all he was worth, was Jonesy.

'Hold me up, my legs do fail me, if he isn't passing up his plate for another helping of turkey, ' said Hardy, and he fell back against Flemming.

We nearly fainted. There, sure enough was Bob Jones, his face one big smile, having the time of his life between talking to those two pretty girls, and tucking into the great spread like a kid at a Sunday school picnic.

It was too much. There were no words left in us. We made for our tents in silence, thinking, every one of us, of the afternoon's repentance we had wasted over the lucky chap. Jonesy. Jonesy! who was at Carrington's great dinner in all his glory, for he had got into his dress suit, which he had sneaked down on the chance of his going to the dances. We had chyacked him enough about bringing it, but I suppose he didn't mind that now, sitting up there like a wedding cake, as he talked first to one girl then to the other, but we felt we could have murdered him.

The only satisfaction we got from the whole thing, and that wasn't much, was by keeping strictly to the agreement we made before turning in, and that was not to allow Jonesy the joy of telling us about the affair.

It wasn't so very late when he returned, but we were all too sound asleep to be wakened by his utmost efforts.

He was full of it, and it must have hurt him somewhat to have to keep it to himself, when he was bursting to tell all about it; but that was nothing to his sufferings next morning, when we had no time for him or his great yarn.

He got it off his chest somehow or other before we went back to town, but his pleasure in it was a poor mean thing to what it would have been had he been allowed to tell his story as he wanted, when it was in its first flush. In spite of our policy of indifference and interruption, we managed to get a fair idea of what had occurred, however, and this was the gist of it.

When Hardy took the turkey, he imagined, and so did we, that no one saw him. But this was not the case. Florrie and Amy, resting before the affair in their hammocks, behind the latticed verandah, were watching him, scarcely able at first to believe their eyes, but soon dropping to its being a joke, and then being real tricks themselves, keeping mum and waiting further developments, they let events take their course.

When the wild scurry over the lost turkey had quietened down, they went back to their hammocks to see what was next on the cards, for they guessed we were up to mischief, and soon their patience was rewarded.

Mr. Carrington came round the verandah and found them laughing fit to kill themselves over the way red-haired Susan had snavelled Jonesy.

On his enquiring what had amused them so, they told him all they knew about it. Mr. Carrington didn't think much of the joke at first, but the girls talked him over and presently he was laughing as heartily at the trick as themselves.

He went with them to the kitchen just in time to save Jonesy's best suit, for Susan was preparing to dust him over her pots and pans. Jonesy's stuttering indignation must have been as good as a play, and his attempts at an explanation when he was rescued must have been nearly as funny, for Mr. Carrington was so tickled at the whole thing that he invited Jonesy on the spot to come to the dinner and taste the turkey.

Not only that, but Mrs. Carrington, who was really one of the kindest women alive, proposed to invite the rest of us also. 'The more the merrier,' she said. 'There's lashings to eat, and plenty of room. After all, boys will be boys.

ISABEL GRANT

We have had a good hearty laugh, which is better than medicine any day in the week, and no harm is done. The turkey is none the worse, so let them all come.'

He was a forgiving chap, Jonesy, or perhaps we mightn't have believed him when he said he was disappointed to find us gone, but I don't think Hardy has quite forgiven him yet when the little chap insisted on describing that dinner in detail, especially when he tried to explain to us the exact flavour of the turkey stuffing.

I know it wasn't safe to mention turkey for many a long day to some of the campers-out."

ISABEL GRANT.

PHARAOH'S DAUGHTER

[By ISABEL GRANT.] .

Moses Gordon moved leisurely down the crowded railway carriage to where, by an open window, he saw an obliging acquaintance signaling that he could make room for him.

The square-built, clumsy figure, the heavy, clean-shaven, expressionless face, were evidently well-known to the other occupants of the carriage ; but only a curt nod, a muttered word or two, replied to their greetings ; and even the amiable neighbour received merely a few perfunctory remarks before Moses Gordon opened his paper and buried himself in its columns, with an air that did not invite further attempts at conversation. It was plain the millionaire was in no mood for talk this afternoon, though, indeed, at any time, the minor amenities of life had little place in Moses Gordon's scheme of things. The bell rang, and a slim young fellow carrying a sleeping infant, and supporting a pale, slender pretty girl came hurrying past the window. It was Moses Gordon the second, who appeared to be intending to travel by the same train. A few quick glances turned to the father, to see if he had observed the passers-by, but it was evident he had not noticed them, for his head was steadily bent over his paper.

The rupture between Moses Gordon and his son, though now over a year old, was still a matter of interest to the good folk of Williamsborough.

ISABEL GRANT

A silent, undemonstrative man, Moses Gordon had been a fond and devoted parent to his motherless boy. It was patent to everybody that outside his business nothing else mattered to the old man save his son. Nothing was too good for him, no wish was denied. In spite of all the indulgence, however, "Don" (the schoolboy nickname clung) turned out a fine, manly unaffected fellow, a son of whom any father might well be proud. Then like a thunderbolt from a clear sky came the break between them, and Don., obtaining a position as clerk at one of the wholesale houses, married Edith Douglas, a girl whose father had once won a lawsuit against old Gordon, which had been an occasion of bad blood between them ever since. Don had married against his father's direct prohibition, knowing all that it entailed; henceforward he was to be to him a stranger. This, it was said, was the old man's threat.

It seemed hard to think of the son struggling along on a bare pittance, with a delicate wife, scarcely fit to cope with housekeeping cares; while the father heaped up his useless balance at the bank; more especially, when, after the baby's arrival, the mother's health gave way almost entirely ; but there appeared little hope of any reconciliation. Don and his father passed each other daily without one look of recognition, one face growing thinner and paler, the other more stern and implacable with each encounter.

Unconscious of, and, in fact, indifferent to any speculation among his fellow passengers concerning his private affairs, Moses read perseveringly on, until the fading light forced him to relinquish his paper, when with an unmistakable intention to avoid conversation, he leant forward, and stared with intent but unseeing eyes at the monotonous grey-green country through which they were passing. Besides the ordinary taciturnity which belonged to Gordon, and which, since the quarrel with his son, had become noticeably intensified, he had today received a shock, and was in no humour for the small give and take of railway chat.

For a few weeks he had been feeling out of sorts and to-day when with some reluctance he had gone to consult his doctor, he had been bluntly informed that his heart was affected, that he must practically withdraw himself from business cares, and be much in the open air. Meanwhile, he was ordered to leave the city for at least a month to go to some- place where he could have mountain or sea air. At the end of that time, the doctor would make a further examination. With three or four hours of hard work, Gordon was able to leave his business affairs in charge of his head clerk, Garvey, a new member comparatively of his staff. In fact, he had only come to him since his son's departure ; but he had come rapidly to the front, being an energetic and pushing fellow. Then having arranged with his housekeeper for a month's absence, he was in time to catch the half-past five train to Dayton, the new watering-place. Gordon chose Dayton because he found out that a coach left it every morning at half past six for the Tableland, where there had long been in existence several small farming districts, mostly settled by Germans.

As Meryla, the nearest of the so-called townships on the Tableland, was only twelve miles distant from Dayton, while it was some two thousand feet above sea-level, Moses calculated that not only could he follow out the doctor's prescription and enjoy both mountain and sea-air by boarding at some Meryla farm house ; but by hiring a trap and going round among the farmers, he might make some good deals in the way of corn or general produce, thus combining benefit to his health with profit to his business.

For, in spite of what the doctor had said, Moses could not dissociate himself from his business or contemplate withdrawing from it, even partially.

No German princeling ever felt more pride in the hereditary honours of his house than did the self-made man in the business he had built up. Indeed, now this his son had left him, it was his one object in life; almost, he felt, his sole purpose of being. To meditate giving it up dissolving into nothingness the work of his lifetime, was more bitter than death. Once he had looked forward, in the natural order of things, to allowing his son to join him in the business; but that was out of the question now and for ever. Perhaps, for he seemed a capable, shrewd, resourceful fellow, he might see how Garvey shaped during the month; and if well, then take him into partnership, stipulating, however, when the time came for himself to leave the business altogether, that it must be continued still under the old name. It would not be the thing he had dreamed of but it would be something.

Amid all his confused musings there ran through the old man's mind a kind of indignant surprise that Fate should have played him so scurvy a trick; for if things had only gone as he had planned, the old firm need not lack succession. Don, and his son after him, could have upheld the honour and continued the name that he himself had made respected by high and low.

But Don himself, and that very morning of all others, had given the final blow to any chance of reconciliation. As it happened, they met face to face on the steps of the Post Office, and whether it was that the doctor's words had weakened his resolution, making him feel how much it would mean to him to have his own son by his side, or whether the sight of Don's thinness and careworn pallor startled him, Moses, after an instant's hesitation, spoke to the young man and held out his hand.

What a light came into the lad's eyes at the moment, how pleased he seemed! And yet what real feeling could he have for his father, when in telling him of the little son that had come, he had admitted that instead of calling it Moses, as by rights he should have done, he had called it Douglas.

Douglas! the name of the man who was his own father's enemy! It was bad enough that he had allowed his wife to show this slight to the name his father had made honoured; but to give the preference to her own father's, knowing the feeling between them – it was unforgivable! "Call him what you like," he told Don. "But since you've chosen to name him after that low trickster Douglas, not a penny of my money comes him or to any of the Douglas breed. Be sure of that!" The lad's pride – and somehow he was not sorry to see it – was as quick as his own.

"Wait at least," he had cried passionately, "till any of us ask for your money before you throw it in our teeth. I'm man enough, I hope, to be able to support my own." And so, once more, they had parted in anger.

With a start, the old man woke up out of his bitter musings to find the tickets were being collected, and a few minutes later they were at Dayton. It was not the petty economies of a rich man, but Moses' natural independent character which made him carry his slim portmanteau himself and set off at a brisk walk to the Queen's Hotel, which, though further along the beach, away from the station was the best hotel at the little watering-place. It resulted, however in his missing his son, who drove with his wife and child to the same hotel, and so arrived there before him. As Edith was wearied out with her journey, Don ordered supper to be brought to their room, and thus it came to pass that though father and son were actually occupying adjacent rooms that night, neither was aware of the fact. By the time Don had roused himself to begin a new day, the active old man was well on his way to Meryla.

Yet, strangely enough; or, perhaps because cause of the unconscious close neighbourhood, the young man's dreams that night had been all of his father and his boyish, days under his care.

With something of remorseful tenderness the son recalled the past and thought how lonely his father must be in the old house, with only the deaf old housekeeper to speak to, and he wished, from the bottom of his heart, that the unhappy estrangement were at an end.

With an effort he threw off his melancholy thoughts and went out on the verandah.

The hotel was built almost on the beach; on two sides of it the primeval scrub came down to mingle with the yellow sand of the shore. There was no fence round the building except at the back, where there was a rough enclosure for horses. It looked delightfully quiet and secluded, an ideal spot for a holiday. He longed to be able to afford to let Edith and the baby stay for a few weeks; it would be just the thing to set her up.

However, it was no good wishing, they must make the best of the four days at their disposal. For the first thing, he would take Edith a walk along that tempting looking path under the sea pines, where the undried dews were yet sparkling beneath the shady avenue-like line of trees.

But it was not till after lunch that Edith could be persuaded to go out, and even then she demurred against leaving baby Douglas, who was sleeping soundly in the improvised cot, which, truth to tell, was but one half of his mother's dress-basket.

"Seeing that Baby sleeps on an average three or four hours at a stretch, and that even a brass band at his head wouldn't wake him till he chooses, I can't understand why you need have any scruples as to leaving him for a half-hour. I can easily get one of the girls to keep an eye on the room," said her husband, vexed to think of the precious hours wasted, as he felt them to be, indoors.

Hereupon, an old lady, knitting in a rocking-chair just outside their door, volunteered to look after the child till their return. She came into the room.

"Yes, that dress-basket is just the thing,' she said; " it is really handy; I see not many mothers making use of them nowa-days. Put a cloth over it to keep away the flies, and place it here beside me in the cool shade. I won't move from this spot till you come back," and she smiled indulgently at the amusing over-care of a young mother.

They accepted the offer and prepared to go out.

"Good-bye, little Moses," said Don, laughing at the vexed look on his wife's face.

"I'm sure Baby ought to be thankful he has had a mother who refused to handicap him with such an ugly name," said Edith, with a smile of satisfaction at the little sleeping face.

Don bit his lip, but he was generous enough to forbear to say how much the name had already cost him, and might cost its small possessor. He turned to the old lady and said lightly.

"You won't mind doing the Miriam act then, will you? Keep a sharp lookout that no Pharaoh's daughter comes sneaking round our little ark of bulrushes."

"Eh, what? said the old lady, somewhat mystified; then she laughed heartily. "Oh, I see! I see! and, indeed, the little basket here, with the cloth over it, isn't unlike the pictures I used to look at in Sunday school. The Miriam act doesn't call for too much exertion from an old body." She twinkled all over her cheery face. "I think I can promise to fulfill my part."

But an anxious pucker was on Edith's pretty face, and she lingered irresolutely on the verandah.

"Come along, Edith, and don't be silly," said Don, laughing "Nobody is at all likely to want to steal him. It's only a foolish joke of mine. Money wouldn't buy him from us, you know; but no one else would take him as a gift."

The old lady gazed after the handsome young couple, then with a reminiscent sigh she resumed her knitting.

* * * * * * *

A stout man, plainly a German settler, occupied the box seat along with Moses Gordon that morning; the inside passengers were two girls; one fair, plump, and German-looking: the other small, dark, and vivacious. The fair girl was Amelia Hoffmann, the other was her friend, Emily Arnold. Both were teachers bent on enjoying their Easter vacation. The fair-haired Amelia, so the driver, in the course of a one-sided conversation, informed Moses, was the niece of a Mrs. Brockhaus, a farmer's wife in Meryla. Mrs. Brockhaus occasionally took in boarders, her husband probably (this in answer to a question) had a horse and trap that might be hired.

Coach-drivers have chances of gleaning out-of-the-way bits of information, which a smart business man might find useful. Moses encouraged the man's natural garrulity; though it went rather against the grain for him to simulate geniality. The coach made its first halt at the Brockhaus farmhouse. Moses took down his portmanteau and followed the two girls, having decided to make Meryla his headquarters if he were pleased with the accommodation offering.

A stout, blonde woman, a typical German frau, came hurrying to the gate, a troop of lint-locked, chubby youngsters at her heels. The fair-haired Amelia was enveloped in a German embrace, her friend welcomed; then Moses was able to make his own arrangements, and fortunately found everything just to his mind.

The sound of excited voices broke up his conference with the farmer's wife. It appeared that a basket belonging to Miss Arnold must have been left behind at Dayton.

"I put it out with the rest of the luggage," the girl protested almost tearfully, while the driver was equally positive he had taken all the luggage waiting for him. Mrs. Brockhaus left Moses and hastened to reassure her visitor.

"Nein, nein, Mit Arnold, do not be worrying yourtelf. Gurt haf to town dis morning to go mit some botatoes and bumpkins. She vill at de hotel your basket get."

In answer to a queer look from her niece, Mrs. Brockhaus explained volubly to the slightly amused Moses and the anxious girl that Gurt was her stepdaughter, her right hand with the house and farm. She was not quite "all as other volks," some thought, but that was how you took her. Explain quietly what you wanted done, make her comprehend it, and Gurt would see the thing was carried out. She might be "allmight's slow," but she was sure.

Old Louis Brockhaus came across the paddocks while the discussion was going on, and Moses went with him to have a look at the trap that was to be given to him.

The dogcart was rough but serviceable, the hire fairly moderate. Moses returned to the house satisfied.

As he came across the yard, a large covered-in cart drew up to the back door, and an unwieldy looking young woman with a broad, ruddy face, its expression simple to the verge of idiocy, but with a calm bovine look of goodness and kindness that redeemed its vacancy, jumped down from the seat. The girl, for she was little older, was more than commonly strong, as the ease with which she tossed into the body of the cart sundry heavy-looking bags testified, and Moses at once guessed that this was Gurt the stepdaughter under discussion.

At this moment the two teachers ran out to speak to her, one of them holding the half of a dress-basket the better to explain what was a-missing. Gurt nodded, smiled, and apparently quite grasping her mission, drove at length out of the yard followed by the reiterated directions of the worried owner of the basket.

Moses went up to the room assigned to him, and feeling drowsy after his early morning drive, did not wake till the summons came for the excellent mid-day meal provided, when he found himself eating with a better appetite than he had enjoyed for many a day.

Scarcely had they left the big, bare dining-room when the sound of an approaching vehicle was heard, and presently the big, white covered-in cart was seen coming into the yard.

The girls ran out, followed by Mrs. Brockhaus with her husband and her chubby brood, while even Moses yielded so far to the general excitement as to saunter out on the verandah.

"Got it, Gurt ?" shouted Amelia, as the cart came within hearing distance.

Gurt nodded, her broad face one glow of pleased benevolence.

"Ja! ja!" she shouted back." Ja, ja. I haf gott him! Ja wohl!" and she laughed with pure delight.

"Thank goodness !" ejaculated Miss Arnold." I am glad. I don't know what I'd have done without it."

"I could have lent you anything you needed," said her friend, but the young girl hardly heeded her, in her eagerness to make sure that her property was actually there.

"Where is it ?" she cried as the cart drew up at the low verandah.

Gurt laughed happily, and springing down from her seat, lumbered to the back of the cart.

She pushed up the calico, cover and leaning forward, lifted out something in her arms.

"Oh," cried the disconcerted girl watching her, acute disappointment in her voice. "That isn't my basket at all! That's only the half of a dress-basket, anyway, with a cloth over it."

Gurt deposited her burden on the ground, hurt bewilderment on every line of her good, simple face."

"I gott hims like as you vas toldt me. Ja, just so, on de verandah, und de basket was dere all as retty."

Amelia stepped up and pulled the white cloth from the basket, then with a hysterical scream she dropped, it again.. Gurt followed her example, throwing up her hands, aghast, she cried "Gott in himmel!" and sank down on the verandah steps.

Miss Arnold leant over and looked into the mysterious package.

"A baby!" she shrieked, half laughing and half-crying. "You wicked, wicked girl! What do you mean by stealing a baby?"

Gurt's mouth opened, but no words came, and with a fresh howl the poor girl abandoned herself once more to her grief.

"It's no use scolding or trying to hustle Gurt," broke in Amelia." She'll only go clean dotty if you do. Leave her to auntie; she knows how to manage her."

Mrs. Brockhaus sat down beside the bobbing creature and patted the big heaving shoulders. Quietly and cautiously, as one deals with a very frightened child, she drew out the story of the unlucky journey.

Gurt did her usual errands in Dayton, then having finished them she drove along the beach road to the Queen's Hotel. There was no need to go in and inquire as to the missing basket, for she saw it as soon as she came near the house. There it was, exactly like the one Amelia showed her in plain view on the verandah; so she just went and took it straight, and put it in the cart. There was an old woman was sleeping in a chair near it, but she did not think there need to waken her, so she came away and drove as fast as she could home. Poor Gurt, clumping up the little track with her big foolish face, she as little recalled the daughter of Old Nile as did the stout elderly lady sleeping at her post the dark-eyed Hebrew maid of Biblical story. Her's not to reason why. Gurt followed, at all events, what she believed to be her instructions. It was not her way, as she protested to her stepmother with tears, to spy into any of the parcels, many as she had carried. The baby had not uttered a cry, and until Amelia had lifted the cloth, Gurt had no suspicions of the contraband she harboured.

Mrs. Brockhaus looked at her husband, but he only shook his head forlornly and turned to Moses as thought to say "Here is a brain fitted to deal with a problem too intricate for us."

"After the girl has had something to eat," said Gordon, answering the unspoken appeal "let her take the infant at once back to its parents."

But, with a passionate burst of her native German, Gurt asserted she would die sooner than face the mother.

Old Louis, his face blanching with fear lest the terrible stranger should order him to drive the cart to Dayton, shuffled off in a panic to the back of the yard, muttering something about the impossibility of his being able to leave the farm that day. At this moment, the child., the innocent cause of all the excitement, opened his big blue eyes upon the group. Moses gave a start; but no one observed it, all were gazing at the soft baby face with its wide eyes of wonder.

A pang of indescribable love and longing came into the old man's heart, as, for one brief moment, he seemed to be looking into the eyes of his long dead wife.

The momentary likeness vanished, the little face began to pucker, the lower lip to droop dolefully, as, in the touching language of the old Book, when another such castaway found itself among strangers, "Behold the babe wept."

What woman, princess, or peasant could resist such an appeal? Mrs. Brockhaus snatched up the forlorn mite to her motherly bosom with soft German phrases of endearment.

Old Louis, not many minutes after with chuckling self-congratulation was ordered to get ready the dogcart, for the formidable old man who was, marvellous to relate, going to drive to Dayton himself with the child to return it to its probably irate parents. The two young girls offered to accompany Gordon to the township, but he refused, curtly enough.

"No, thank you. I can strap the basket to the seat beside me quite easily. I'll be back inside of four hours and I'll bring your basket with me, Miss Arnold. I've no doubt that you thought you brought it out, but, like most women, you were too excited to make sure and left the basket in your room."

The girl hardly knew whether to resent the blunt speech, or thank the man for his kindness. As matters afterwards turned out, the cynical prophecy came actually true, to the young teacher's mingled discomfiture and satisfaction.

Moses set out for Dayton, the child once more asleep in its basket beside him. He was half-shamefaced, half-amused in his grim saturnine way at his own unusual burst of amiability, while acknowledging in his inmost heart that it had been the mere hint of a likeness to a beloved lost face that had caused him to take upon himself the business of restoring the child to its parents, for in spite of the fugitive resemblance to his wife's face, the old man had not the slightest suspicion that it was his son's child that he was carrying back to Dayton. The strongest influence in Moses Gordon's life had been, and was still after all the sundering years, his love for his wife.

Had she lived he would have been a different man. His love, deepening and broadening in the sunshine of domestic happiness. would have kept him from the corroding pursuit of wealth as a means in itself. The love for his son had done much, but since the breach had come between them it seemed that the very love itself, denied its outlet, had by its intensity driven him to business still more as to something that, if it did not compensate, would make him forget his loss. So that, and he was dimly aware of it himself, his very nature was growing harder and more narrow every day.

As he drove along with the sleeping child beside him there came to him, with prick of shame, the recognition of the fact that he had been getting out of the way for some time of doing kindnesses from which he could expect to reap no reward. That, in truth, among his fellows, he was little more than a money-making machine.

Farm after farm was passed, each looking so cosy and comfortable with its tilled fields, its fruit gardens, its sunburnt youngsters running out to cheer at the passing vehicle, that there seemed to the solitary man to breathe out an air of peace and quiet and simple home happiness from every humble dwelling.

The warm afternoon sunshine was around him, but he felt suddenly cold. A chill feeling of desolation, of impending forlorn, childless old age clutched at his heart. He had cut himself off from his son, and there was no one to take his place. When the time came for him to step aside from the business – his life-work, the very apple of his eye – strangers must come in and reap the reward of his toil.

"Oh, if only Mary had lived, how different things would have been!" was the burden of his bitter regrets.

For the first time he asked himself, had he been unjustly hard on Mary's boy?

If the mother had lived would she not have pleaded in her gentle way with him to allow his son the same liberty he had once claimed for himself?

He seemed to see again the faithful loving eyes, to hear the low, sweet voice, till like a flood tide sweeping into long dry watercourses, purifying and revivifying in its flow, the softer emotions of the soul crept along half-obliterated brain paths, and brought into life thoughts buried for many sordid years.

In a dream, the old man urged on his horse, and at length the last hill was reached. Dayton was before him.

* * * * *

When Don and Edith returned from their quiet and pleasant walk through the natural avenue that bordered the beach, and then back along the sands, some three-quarters of an hour had elapsed.

As they drew near to the hotel they could perceive the old lady in her rocking-chair on the verandah.

"I don't see Baby's basket," cried Edith, quickening her languid steps, an intangible sense of uneasiness beginning to assail her. "Of course, you can't, from here, the chair hides it," said Don with a smile, lengthening his own pace to keep up with his wife's hurried rate.

Edith's quick walk became a run, as the whole front verandah came into view, and no basket was visible beside the chair. She rushed breathlessly up the steps, followed, in still protesting amusement, which yet had behind it the first faint stirrings of foreboding, by her husband.

"Where's my baby? What have you done with my baby?" she cried, shaking the chair of the old lady with hands that trembled between weakness and terror.

The old lady opened her eyes and stared in a dazed way at the two white faces fronting hers; then her glance fell on the vacant space where the basket had rested and she sprang to her feet with a strange inarticulate cry.

The next moment the landlord and landlady, followed by several servants and many of the boarders, had rushed to see what was the matter, and the verandah was the scene of the wildest confusion.

But nothing could be discovered to elucidate the mystery. No one had seen or heard anything. How the child could have vanished baffled anyone to explain. But, as poor Edith was borne fainting to her room, and the old lady led tottering and weeping to hers, the men of the place formed themselves into search parties to scour the surrounding country.

The moments of merciful oblivion were brief. Edith woke to find the compassionate landlady chafing her hands. In spite of the woman's protests, the poor girl insisted on getting up and joining in the search.

"I should go mad," she cried wildly, "if I stayed here, waiting for news."

Scarcely conscious that her limbs were trembling, her head dizzy with the shoe she ran down the steps, and without an instant's hesitation, took the road the led to the Tableland. Along this road she hurried, sometimes running, sometimes having to stop to get her breath. Only she fainted when passing through a bit of scrub, and lay, she knew not how long unconscious. As she recovered she saw dog-cart on the brow of the hill just ahead of her. Her heart gave a bound.

"Perhaps, the man has seen, or heard something; at any rate he'll give me lift, for I'm sure no one could be so inhuman as to deny a mother looking for her lost baby."

Soon the trap came plainly into sight a solitary man driving a chestnut horse.

But what was that on the seat beside the driver?

With an exultant cry of gladness breaking from her, Edith ran up the slope weakness and weariness forgotten as she saw that the strange object was indeed her own basket.

The man now observed her approach and, as he whipped up the horse to the sooner to her, the dogcart lurch suddenly and the wail of a baby came Edith's ears.

"My baby! oh, my baby!" she cried and ran the quicker for very joy. Soon she was beside the trap and climbing with man's help into the front seat.

She snatched the little one from the basket, covering its face and hands with kisses, murmuring the while broken words of tenderness and thankfulness. Moses did know that his own eyes were moist when at last he ventured to ask the absorbed mother if they would drive on to Dayton.

For the first time Edith really looked him, and then she recognised who it was for Moses Gordon's was a familiar face in all Williamsborough, though she herself was a stranger to him.

The rugged face looked strangely gentle the deep-set eyes sad and kind.

All her fear melted from her; she forgot that here was the man, who had harshly cast off his own son; she saw only the man who had restored her baby to her empty arms.

She fixed her eyes upon his face, and for a moment hesitated lest her effort at conciliation be rejected; but something she saw there gave her courage to make the venture.

"Father," she said, and her soft voice did not falter, though her pale pretty face flushed with her beating heart. "This is Don's son. Come with us and let him thank you. "The keen grey eyes met the brown ones and measured the gentle sympathy that shone out from them, then the man nodded his head.

"Yes," he said slowly, "we will go to Don together. Perhaps, I can help him in the future to look – to look after you both - my daughter and my grandson."

THE COLLECTED PUBLISHED WORKS OF ISABEL GRANT

ST. GEORGE AND THE DRAGON

BACKGROUND TO THE PUBLICATION

"ST. George and the Dragon" was published in The Sydney Mail on 4th. January 1922.

The Sydney Mail began in 1860 as a cheap condensed version of Fairfax's Sydney Morning Herald. It ceased close to the commencement of WW11 in December 1938.

Most of the nineteenth century Australian newspapers had their weekly edition. These proved popular in remote areas, with circulation in the case of the Sydney Mail reaching 10,000 by 1865 which exceeded that of its parent the Herald. The popularity can be attributed to the fact that newspapers provided information and entertainment in a country bereft of easy recreation. With a literacy rate of 78 percent in 1846 for both men and women reading was a valued form of leisure time activity.

The New South Wales Premier, Sir Henry Parkes, called the press "the greatest, the cheapest and most effective educator of all" (SMH 20th. March 1869). His Government backed this policy of educating the population by providing free postage of newspapers to the country. Towns-folk, squatters and their shepherds and stockmen received their weekly link to the outside world at an affordable rate of thripence (three pence) per copy.

Because of increasing popularity in the bush the weeklies expanded their range to cover country, agricultural, pastoral and mining news. Later they included sports news. In 1871 they introduced women's interests which were enhanced by illustrations. By the 1890s The Sydney Mail was a very attractive, high quality magazine with a good reputation with a quality smooth paper liftout of 16 pages with photographs.

One of the prime uses of these feature weeklies was to publish books in serial form. They provided a short interesting read, encouraged subscribers to continue buying the papers and as a valuable offshoot gave budding authors the chance to let their works be seen in print. Rolf Bolderwood's "Robbery under arms" was first published in The Sydney Mail in 1880. Many other talented Australians including A. B. Paterson, Kenneth Slessor and Mary Gilmore also owe their exposure to the press.

The character of newspapers changed after World War 1. It was essential for dailies to have access to the Australian news Service and a good cable service but the weeklies needed little or no news. The Sydney Mail became newsless in 1919 but remained a quality magazine with the contents change to entertainment and brief pithy journalism the beginning of the modern format.

In this story Isabel addresses the problem of readjustment faced by a serviceman returning to his family from five years overseas in the Great War. She deals with it in the way she knows best by putting it into a domestic setting and including a child. As always she has a happy ending. She has no moral or political comments to make and touches but lightly on the horror of war. The touch of humour and the human situation make it an agreeable read.

The accepted authority of a husband over his family is a key element for her plot. This attitude, which still persisted as servicemen returned from WW11, will either enrage or amuse today's reader. The sub title is also a challenge to current thinking being much too authoritarian to be acceptable.

THE COLLECTED PUBLISHED WORKS OF ISABEL GRANT

THE SYDNEY MAIL, JANUARY 4, 1922 —Page 20

Saint George and the Dragon

A Story for Children with a Lesson for Parents

By Isabel Grant

FIVE-YEAR-OLD Georgie Selwyn swung slowly under the big bauhinia tree, and paid no heed to the bees that were humming deliciously among the lavender blossoms overhead. If you had chanced to be passing by, and had noted the wistful droop of the sensitive lips, the questioning appeal in a pair of limpid grey eyes, you would have felt like stopping and trying to put right whatever it was that was troubling the child. But had you seen Georgie a week ago, before the hair, now so closely cropped round the small well-set head, had lost its riotous glory of golden curls, you would have had hard work not to pick him up in your arms and run away with him to find the place where little boys never grow up, but stay, like Peter Pan, small and lovable for ever. The question perplexing Georgie Selwyn this afternoon was: "How can a coward" – that's what his own splendid Daddy called him – "grow so brave that he will not be afraid of anything, not even of a dragon like the one on the picture of St. George which Mother gave him on his birthday?" Georgie loved this picture, not only because Mother had told him all about his namesake, but because, before he ever saw his Daddy—for he had been born just after Captain Selwyn went off to the war—Mother often said to him that there was a resemblance between the face of St. George and his Daddy, as,

indeed, Georgie could now see for himself since the "welcome home." A week yesterday Mother and he had been so busy. The whole house was as clean as a new pin; not a weed could you find in any garden bed, and to make quite certain that the flowers would be looking their freshest Mother and he went round with watering-can and wearisome dipper just before going to the station, though dressed in their best and fresh as the roses by the front verandah, both of them—Mother in a pretty white frock, Georgie in a cream serge sailor suit, his golden curls bobbing up and down and blowing in front of his eyes under his sailor hat. Mother was only a slip of a girl, and she was generally rather pale; but to-day her cheeks were as rosy as her boy's, and her eyes were as bright—though they were not grey, like those of Georgie and his father, but brown as pansies, with something a tiny bit sad in them even when she smiled, as she was doing now, and gave back laughing replies to the excited happy questions of the boy.

They reached the station in good time, and then— oh! the rapture of having not only a Daddy like other boys in the kindergarten, who were always bragging at what "my Daddy can do," but a tall, handsome Daddy with a Military Cross on the Captain's uniform, which had been a private's when Mary Selwyn saw it last.

ISABEL GRANT

"Were there ever three happier beings in the whole wide borders of Australia?

"Hullo, Mary! I thought, you said it was a boy; why, this is a girl!" was the perfectly dreadful remark Captain Selwyn made coming home in the cab, and he pulled one of the long yellow curls.

He could not be expected to know that the words would hurt so; but how he laughed when as soon as they were in the house Georgie disappeared, and was found in front of the wardrobe mirror in the bedroom just as the last of the curls was falling to the floor.

Mother caught up the shining mass to her as if it were something dear and alive. Her eyes were full of tears.

Georgie looked from her to his laughing father, half-sorry. half-exultant, and waited for what would happen; but Captain Selwyn settled the matter by asking for the scissors to finish the job decently, saying, with another laugh, that he was glad to find that Georgie was a boy, and not, after all, a girl.

What a happy time followed, with Daddy at home for good, especially as Captain Selwyn, instead of going back at once to the billet the honourable firm, which had so pledged its word, had kept open for him all these years, decided to take a month's holiday, putting the whole place, house and garden, to rights before returning to his work in the office. Georgie trotted after him everywhere, adoring him as only a five-year-old can adore somebody big and strong, as well as kind, of his own sex. A word of praise from Daddy was enough to turn him into a small incarnation of perpetual motion all day.

For a whole perfect week not a cloud was in the sky; then something happened which blotted out the sunshine.

One morning Daddy set to work on the small room which opened out of the front bedroom. He put up two long shelves for Georgie's own picture books, and two wide ones lower down, for his toys; hung a few prints, including St. George and the Dragon, on the nursery walls; and altogether made quite a bright, pretty nursery. Last of all he brought from the next room Georgie's cot, which had always been close beside the big bed.

Georgie could not remember a night when Mother did not lie in her bed and lean over to him, now telling him a story, now having a talk about the days' happenings, and now singing some child song or nursery rhyme, till, as his eyes grew heavy, she gave him his good-night kiss, while he took a last sleepy glance up at the face bending over him, watchful and tender in the subdued light, and went a-sailing with Winkum, Blinkum, and Nod to the sleep land.

"There you are, young man," said Daddy, briskly; "I am going to turn you into a real proper boy, with a real proper room of your own. Won't that be fine?"

Of course, Georgie said it would, and he said it stoutly, too; but it somehow gave him a queer lonesome feeling to see that cot standing by itself in the room, and as the day wore on he began to be thoughtful and have doubts, which he brought to Mother, who assured him that it would be quit all right; she would be with him till he fell asleep, just as before. Moreover, she would be slipping in every now and then during the night to make sure that he was covered, for he had a trick of throwing off the Mother were not on the alert.

But Daddy, it transpired, had ideas somewhat differing from those of mother and son.

"Right-oh, young man," he said, when he had kissed him goodnight; "Mother will tuck you into your cot and leave you to go to sleep."

"Georgie's doubts were beginning to change into fears. Did Daddy really mean that Mother was to leave him "straight away," that there was to be no little talk, no story, no soft lullaby? It looked like it. With his throat feeling tight and "hurty"

Georgie said his prayers and climbed into his cot.

Mother's own eyes were a little strained as she tucked him snugly into the blankets.

Daddy marched in, very tall and resolute, and took the light saying, "Now, then, Mother, come with me. You have had Georgie for a baby long enough. I want to make a boy of him now."

"You're taking away the light, Dadsie!" cried Georgie.

"Of course I am. You are five years old. It is ridiculous to, think of your needing a light. I was far younger when I had to do without a light in my room. Indeed, I don't remember our ever being left with a lamp burning. Mother heard us say our prayers, tucked us in, kissed us, and"—he laughed—"I believe we were asleep before she reached the door with the light."

"But I'm shy of the dark," the quaint plea came out, shakingly. Captain Selwyn laughed his big, jolly laugh. "Boys have no right to be shy of the dark. Are you sure it's not a girl you are, after all?"

"I'm a weally truly boy, all wight, Daddy; but I never did go to sleep all by myself in the black dark— "

"Time you learned, then. Come Mary!"

There was no gainsaying that tone, Mother's kiss was a long one. "Georgie will shut his eyes tight and go sleep; Mother will only be in the next room."

Obediently Georgie shut his eyes. Presently he heard Mother's step in the front bedroom. She was humming softly as she placed the lamp on the washstand, so that it shone right into his snuggery. He opened his eyes, the queer, scary feeling all gone as he listened to the familiar tune. Almost he was stepping into the slumber boat direct for the Land of Nod when Daddy called out in a tone, quite new to his son

"What are you doing there, Mary?"

"I'm tidying this top drawer," was the reply,

"Isn't this a curious time to be tidying drawers?"

There was a silence; then the sharp command, "Come here Mary!" and Mother's step was heard.

"You left the light: bring it at once." Silence again: then, very slowly, Mother walked along the hall, the lamp in her hand, her head well up.

Georgie heard the sound of voices, but he could not make out what was being said. "You are doing wrong, Will, her brown eyes had a strange glow in them, as if a hidden fire were alight behind them. "You are going too fast. It would be much better to get the boy used to sleeping like this by degrees, not all in one jump. You say you were always made to go to sleep in the dark, but you forget you had an older brother in the same bed with you to take away the sense of loneliness, and, besides, you had got used to it while you were an infant. I do not know what you were at 5, but I do know that Georgie's both imaginative and highly strung. He is just at the age when a fright might do him a great deal of harm. Since he was born he has never gone to sleep without me, and here you have not only taken me away, but actually made the poor wee man go to sleep in the dark. It is not right, Will. I don't want to go against you, but I must tell you that you are making a mistake."

Captain Selwyn's face was white, too, but it was with anger. He was naturally soft-hearted and reasonable, but he was doing the right thing, and he had been so long used to taking charge of men whose obedience must be prompt and unquestioning that insensibly the habit of command had grown upon him, and, instead of conceding to his wife an equal right with himself to decide matters for their child's welfare, he felt as if her opposition was what he would have termed rank insubordination in one of his men.

"You have made a spoilt baby of him long enough. It's time he learned to be a boy, if you don't want him to turn out a coward," he said.

"Perhaps I have spoilt him a little; he was all I had for five long years, and he was such a darling kiddie I almost grudged to see him grow out of babyhood; but he isn't a coward, Will – truly, he isn't. You'll be surprised to find how manly he is in some things. It's pretty to see how he tries to take care of me when we go out together. He won't let me cross a street till he first looks up and down to make sure it is quite safe." She finished with a touch of pride.

A scream of terror rang through the house. Without waiting for the light, Mary flew to the room.

"What is it Mother's treasure?" she cried, gathering a shivering figure unto her arms.

"The big dark is coming down on me. It was all black and furry, with wings and claws!" sobbed Georgie.

Captain Selwyn stalked into the room carrying the light.

"What's all this shindy about?" he asked, in his unfamiliar tone.

Mother interposed: "Georgie is not used to the dark. He is asleep other nights before I take the light away. He will get over it by-and-bye, but just now he is nervous, you see, and imagines things."

THE COLLECTED PUBLISHED WORKS OF ISABEL GRANT

Captain Selwyn coldly ignored the explanation, and went up to the bed" I will not have a coward for my son! Do you hear, George?"

"Yes Daddy," was the sobbing reply.

"Well, then, go to sleep at once, and without a light, too, if you don't want a good whipping. You'll have to learn to sleep alone."

"Not to-night, Will. I'm going to stay here with the child. You may take the light." Mary's tone was final.

Without a word Captain Selwyn turned on his heel and left the room. Half an hour passed, and still the soft murmur of voices went on. An hour, and sleep was evidently not yet come. Nine o'clock sounded, and there was silence; but Mary did not return, and the frown deepened on the young man's face. Ten o'clock! With a lowering brow he took the light and went to the bedroom.

Mother and child were asleep. The dark head and the fair cropped one lay on the pillow. The boy's two hands were clasped round the arm thrown over him. Mary's slight body lay stiff and huddled beside the cot. Utter weariness spoke from her pale face.

Captain Selwyn shaded the light and gazed long at the two faces, whose pure, delicate features looked in sleep so strangely similar.

"Mary!" he said, softly. "Mary!"

Startled, she wake and, flushing, scrambled to her feet; but as she moved the child caught at her hand with the spent sob of past grief, and she bent over him. Across the sleeping boy her eyes met those of her husband, and Captain Selwyn was again a tiny lad waking from the crisis of a fever, to find his mother, who had nursed him through weeks of delirium almost single-handed, bending over him. The look in her tired yet untiring eyes was the same which now met him in Mary's brown ones. Ah, that look! How many times had he not seen it in. the terrible war years, as the troops of refugees, French or Belgian, passed the lines; and the women, gaunt and spent, still battled on for the sake of the wasted babe at the breast, the toddlers, skin and bone, clinging to the tattered skirts. Motherhood! — tenderness and courage incarnate! Late into the night husband and wife talked together, understanding each other as they had never done before.

Next morning Mrs. Fenwick, the doctor's wife from over the way, motoring to the bay, came to borrow Georgie for his playmate, Mick, like himself an only child of a soldier father

Mary was relieved, for a perceptible constraint had arisen between Will and his boy, who, shamefaced and diffident, no longer trotted after his Daddy, but kept in the background, as if feeling that he had lost favour. The two would be better apart till they had readjusted relations. Moreover, the little fellow was pale and heavy eyed; a romp on the beach with the sea-breezes and merry little Mick would work wonders.

At 4 in the afternoon a flushed and excited small boy returned, eager to tell all about his happy day.

After hearing his stock of news, Mary, who was lying down with a headache, sent Georgie to play in the garden till Daddy returned from town, which might be at any minute.

Childlike, Georgie had put his trouble behind him the moment he heard about the expedition to the seaside; but no sooner was he left to himself in listless loneliness than the bother began.

The bees humming so distractingly in the blossom-laden tree from which his swing was hung could not make their cheerful music reach ears which were hearing only, in the new strange tone which seemed to put one so far away, "I will not have a coward for my son!"

He trotted back into the house but Mother was asleep; so, sadly he crept into his own room, seeing again the lonesome-looking cot. St. George, over the head of the bed, gazed steadily, disapprovingly, away as if, like Daddy, he too had never been a boy who was "shy of the dark," but had always been brave. There was no comfort to be got out of staring at him, even though he seemed to look more like Daddy than ever. If he had a little boy, he would probably say, too, "I will not have a coward for my son."

How? How could a boy who was a coward become brave? Was there any wonderful, splendid thing to be done which could make Georgie fit to be the son of such a wonderful, splendid Daddy?

There seemed no answer to these questions, and disconsolately Georgie wandered into the tool-shed to look at the new gardening tools which Daddy had bought.

All at once he grew rigid, and stared into the darkest corner." It was not easy to see clearly, for the shed, which was overhung by a big weeping fig-tree, was a dim place even in the morning, while of an afternoon it was quite dusky; but there, between two brown bags of the sort used for the horse's chaff, was something which Georgie knew at once for a black snake.

For a minute or two he stood transfixed,-incapable even of moving or screaming; then a queer feeling ran through him and braced his slackened muscles.

Here was his chance to do something tremendously brave! With every-nerve strung to its utmost tension, he flew to the wood-shed and: returned with the new axe, its blade keen and shining. Yes, there lay the creature; it had not moved. The head was, luckily; under the bag; probably it was asleep, and might not see or hear him. With his hearts thumping against his side, Georgie swung his axe over his shoulder and brought it down, the sharp edge cutting right into the earth beneath.

Not daring to as much as glance at what the gory result of his stroke might be, Georgie flung the axe from him and dashed out of the shed, only to see his father at the gate.

He flew to him, and the next moment was in his father's arms, telling his story as best he could for his nervous excitement.

"I did kill a big, big black snake in the tool-shed! I did, I did, Daddy; like St. George killed the dragon, only I did kill it wiv an axe! Now you won't need to have a coward for a son, Daddy, no more— 'cause I ain't a coward now!" Stuttering with his hurry to tell it all in one burst, Georgie, half-laughing and half-crying, clung to his father and looked into his startled eyes with pride.

Captain Selwyn's bronzed face whitened under its tan as he put the boy gently on the ground. "Sit here, Georgie. "Don't move, and don't call out too loud. Mother must not be frightened. I'll go and find out, if you have really killed the snake."

With hasty steps he made for the shed and peered in, before cautiously stepping forward. He saw first the axe, where it had fallen from a small nerveless, hand, then something between two hessian bags. Then he sat down weakly on the bench and shook with noiseless laughter.

The new hose, which had only come that forenoon; and which he had left in the corner, was minus its nozzle, which, hidden beneath one of the bags, had been neatly severed. In the dim light it was no wonder that the little chap, who knew nothing of the coming of the thing, should have taken it for what, indeed, it looked remarkably like—a black snake. Only a comparatively short portion of the pipe was visible, and this looked very snakelike indeed. Captain Selwyn took up the severed piece and laughed helplessly, soundlessly; but his eyes were very tender. He could feel again in his arms the small excited morsel. It had cost the boy something to do the deed, and why had he done it? Was it not to prove that he—poor wee man! - in spite of being "shy of the dark," was no coward? Captain Selwyn's thoughts went back to his own first baptism of fire. Man though he was, and after all those months of disciplined preparation, he had to confess to himself, though he had successfully hidden it from his mates, who, perhaps, were having the same battle to fight, that it had been fear, cold, deadly, paralysing fear, - which filled his heart as the shrapnel whined and screamed above his head, and winged death flew past the lines.

The time came when danger had a thrill, a spur, for him, when a fierce and awful joy leaped in his pulses which made personal fear a thing to be laughed at; but this came only when familiarity and immunity had given him a fatalistic security. Yet here had he been demanding from a child of five, faced with new and terrifying circumstances, what he would not have expected of a man meeting the unknown; forgetting that courage, like every living thing, must grow from small to great, as knowledge proceeds from the known and familiar to the unknown. Mary was right; he had been trying to go too fast. He would adopt her methods, assured that there could not be much coward blood in the tiny frame which held so virile a spirit.

"Is it quite dead, Dadsie?" There was tremble in the voice.

"Quite dead." Will Selwyn's reply was not devoid of a telltale shake.

"And I did it my vewy own self!" Oh, the pride there!

"You did it. You certainly did it, my son," returned the father, hastily pushing the pipe into one of the bags, for he had made up his mind not to undeceive the small exultant hero, but to put the hose out of sight for the time being, till he could contrive a way of bringing it into use without the boy suspecting how it had figured in his great adventure.

"Is there vewy much blood?"

The Captain started and choked, but he had the makings of a diplomat. "Not as much as I expected. You stay where you are till I wash away what there is."

Captain- Selwyn managed to find his wife when ostensibly going to fill the watering-can, and to tell her the story; so that by the time Georgie came to narrate his Iliad Mary was quite prepared, to be duly impressed and admiring.

When Georgie is old enough to enjoy the humour of the situation they may tell him how mild a dragon, he encountered in his first knightly essay; but for the present they will not destroy the pride which restored boyish self-respect and made the lad feel he would yet become the brave son of a brave father.

THE COLLECTED PUBLISHED WORKS OF ISABEL GRANT

THE POINT OF VIEW

BACKGROUND TO THE PUBLICATION

"The Point of View" was published in *The Sydney Mail* on 21st. June 1922.

The Sydney Mail had a fine reputation from its beginning as a solid in depth read to its later magazine style. Although the effects of Motion Pictures and the magazine section of the Sunday papers reduced the circulation by the 1920s it was still a respected and sort after publication. Short stories provided a staple and it is to Isabel's credit that her work was accepted.

From the works that have been discovered Isabel appears to have two time groupings for her published work. The first prolific period was from 1892 to 1910 during which one of her novels was published and the second period starts about 1922.

These stories appear in a second grouping which probably came about by the re-emergence to writing after a break of twelve years for her new status of wife and motherhood.

The early life experiences of guiding and advising children, and in her words "struggling, ambitious years of mutual help and study" which saw "fatherless children" (Isabel and her siblings) rise to positions as heads of School and Firm are now deep-seated in the fifty year old Isabel's repertoire.

In this story she uses sober, established personalities for her principal characters. Both this and the previous story show that she has become a little pontifical and we can view her perspective of the 1920s with her use of phrases like –"the cowboy-hero parts in those American pictures," and her "face was covered with paint and powder." She remains true to the Victorian ideals of her upbringing and is showing a certain distain for changes in society.

ISABEL GRANT

THE POINT OF VIEW
By Isabel Grant

The western mail was an hour late; but John Mowbray, waiting in grim patience for his sister, did not leave the platform.

"At last, Nell," he said, as the train steamed in and he saw her preparing to leave the carriage. "At long last!"

"Only these two suitcases. I'm sorry but before your letter came I had promised to meet Miss Ives in Sydney on the 23rd. If I disappoint her she may forego the trip to New Zealand the doctor ordered. So I can't stay longer.

No more was said till the two, so curiously alike, though the dark features which looked merely strong and handsome in the man seemed hard in the sister, took their places in the car, which Mowbray himself drove.

"I asked Anne to make a point of going out with Del this afternoon, so that I could come alone to meet you. I'm bothered, Nell and want your help."

"You know it's yours for the asking," was the quiet reply: but the smile of rare sweetness which accompanied the words was one to redeem any face from charge of plainness.

"If I did not know that, is it likely I'd have broken so selfishly into your hard-earned holiday? You and I have pulled together too long not to rely on one another now," he said and in the silence that fell the thoughts of both flew back on the long, struggling, ambitious years of mutual help and study which found John head of the old, respected firm of William Barnes into which he had entered as an office boy; and Helen developed from pupil-teacher to Mistress of Arts and the moving spirit of the large school for girls in the bracing heights of Southern Queensland. The widowed mother, tenderly cared for by both for many years, was now at rest in God's Acre beyond the city, where she had seen her fatherless children rise to positions of trust and influence.

"I'm in no hurry, John; so drive slowly along and take your time," said Miss Mowbray at length, breaking the silence. "Is it Dell?"

"Yes, it's Del," almost groaned the man. "It's Del, our only child, and she is going in a fair way to break her mother's heart and mine. You know yourself, Nell, what it meant to us both, but especially to Anne, when, five years after the last of her two babies died, Del was given to us. To say the mother was wrapped in her is to put it mildly. Her whole life seemed to center in the child's. If Del sneezed, or refused her food, or came out in a rash, the doctor must be in the house post haste. To tell the truth, I used to wonder how she lived through the times of measles and whooping-cough, and the rest of those numerous childish ailments. In fact, I really believe that if you had not managed to persuade Anne, when the kiddie was 11, to give her to you for those six years, Del, instead of being the healthy well-grown girl she is now, would have been a neurotic with all her mother's worrying and coddling.

The six years worked wonders for Ann too. Once she was convinced her treasure was really safe with you, she became again the Anne of our early married life. She grew interested in outside things, and enjoyed a concert or a picture show, or whatever came along, and, upon my word, you might take them for a pair of sisters." He paused, but it was unnecessary for the sister who knew him so well to say a word, and he continued.

"You remember Jack Barnes, the only boy among four girls in the Barnes family? I took him on – he was just 16 when his father died- as an articled clerk."

"I remember him well; but I think I recall him best as a fine boy of 10, with such pleasant manners and nice dark eyes. He seemed so fond of Del. I can see him now, a gentlemanly laddie, making himself a perfect slave to the child. She was then a tiny fairy of 5." The head-mistress laughed, with a touch of shamefacedness. "Do you know, I was thinking in my own mind, and hoping, too, that the handsome little pair would one day make a match of it, John."

A deep furrow ploughed itself in the man's forehead; his lips took a set, half cynical, half sad. "So we plan, and dream dreams, and Fate steps in. 'The moving finger writes.' Well to go on, Mr. Barnes, shrewd business man though he was, got taken in over those mines at Randoona- you've heard of them. Trying to retrieve his losses, he speculated, and got in deeper. I firmly believe it was worrying over things that brought on the stroke which carried him off. When everything was settled there wasn't much beside the house and the insurance left the widow. I don't think there was any merit in my articling Jack without taking a premium, and giving him help with his studies, or securing a good position in the Treasury for the second daughter; but the poor woman was more than grateful

Last year I took Jack into partnership, and then the firm was back to its old name, only with Mowbray first. Jack is my right hand; a fine lad he is. Indeed, I question if I could be fonder of him if he were my own son. Anne thinks the world of him too. You know, Jack has had the run of our house since he was a nipper, and Del's greatest chum is Eunice Barnes; so you can guess how delighted I was when Jack told me that, as his affairs were on a firm footing and his mother comfortably provided for, with the girls all earning good salaries, besides what Jack can allow (for Randoona had at length turned into a paying concern), he hoped one day to be my son in reality.

Ann was just as delighted, but nevertheless, she stipulated that Jack should wait until Del was 20. She had missed the child so all those years she was away with you, and was so happy to have her once again, that she was in no hurry to resign her to a husband. For my part, too, I felt like keeping Del a child a bit longer. However, we talked it over with Jack, who agreed, though very reluctantly, to continue for a year more in his 'big brother' capacity, coming and going in the house as he had always done. Del was so young, and, as far as we knew, Jack seemed her chosen boy friend. You can imagine, then, how I took a request from her three weeks this very day that I should consent to her engagement to some Dave Logan, a tram-driver on our line."

Miss Mowbray gave an exclamation of shocked surprise, and her brother continued in the same hard tone:-

"I asked Del where she had met the fellow, and she told me quite openly that she had been interested in him ever since he had, six months ago, come onto our line. He looks so exactly like that – what's his name? who takes the cowboy-hero parts in those American pictures – that she used to take the front seat when she could going to or from town, just to have a good chance to look at him. But after the day he saved her life (the child had told me of it and I thanked the man myself!) by catching her as the car swerved unexpectedly in turning a sharp curve, they had become friendly. She never met him elsewhere, but the acquaintance ripened, and when the man proposed the romantic creature imagined she had only to ask us to receive our consent! All her life hitherto, I suppose, we had scarcely denied her anything she asked; but Del, as you know, Nell, was never a troublesome child – high-spirited and impulsive she was, but generous, and led easily by love. Now her very nature appears changed; she declares if we do not consent she will die sooner than give him up. It's not the fellow's position, Nell, though, naturally, when I have known the hard struggles and pinch of poverty, I hoped I'd be able to spare my child what I'd gone through. Many decent chaps are drivers, no doubt – there's your old Sunday-school pupil, Ned Freeman. I got him the job on the same line, and a fine little fellow he is, too; he supports an invalid mother, and a sister who attends to her. He had been a motor-car driver, but the pay was too uncertain. If it had been little Ned, even though he is somewhat illiterate, I might have given in. But this Logan (I put a detective on his tracts) is a low brute. I say the words advisedly, Nell.

There's a girl he goes with, whom if he had a spark of decency in him he would marry. We've tried to show Del what it means to have her life joined to such a man – Del, who has been brought up to the refinements of things – but we might as well talk to the wind. She thinks we are prejudiced, that we are purse-proud and tyrannical. She declares she will not believe a word against him. Yesterday we had a regular scene; but it comes to this; if we don't give our consent, she'll run away and marry him. He plays on her simple, generous nature, the low blackguard. Do you think I'm going to stand by and see my child commit suicide? Not if I have to lock her up and feed her on bread and water."

The veins stood out on the forehead; the grey eyes had grown bloodshot, the nails in the knotted hands that grasped the wheel were digging into the palms, the voice had sunk to a menacing growl. Miss Mowbray laid a gentle hand on the tense arm.

"That's not the way to manage Del, John. In spite of all her surface sweetness and gentleness, she has your own will – yes, and your temper, too. You can lead Del, but you can't drive her."

"What in heaven's name can I do that we haven't done? Ann has wept and begged; I have coaxed and bribed – yes I offered a trip to Europe! I've threatened and stormed; but you know the mule Del can be once she gets her back up. As a last resort, I've selfishly broken into your hard-earned holiday, knowing how much influence you used to have with the girl; and here you are."

"And here I am," said his sister cheerily. "Well now I know my ground, I'll see what I can do. Don't give up hope, John; I have enough faith in Del, whose instincts are sound, whose heart is still that of a romantic child, to believe she will come to her senses in the end."

"What if she comes to them too late?' was the low reply.

"Don't drive her to it, John. Keep a light rein on such a tender young mouth, and don't rush things. This phase, in which the purely physical attracts, is one most girls pass through. I can remember the time when I thought the sun rose and set on a certain big footballer." The rare smile broke out, lighting up the fine, clever face wonderfully. "Yes, I did, John. I used to think as I watched him sprinting across the field in his jersey that he was a very Hercules of grace and strength. I never wanted to meet or speak to him; it was enough for me to look at him. The phase passes off as harmlessly and naturally as do measles, as a rule; but this fellow, you see, happened, unluckily, to do Del a service and to make her acquaintance while the glamour still remained, and he has taken advantage of it. Del fancies he is her ideal hero that she sees portrayed on the screen come to actual life. Now, John, we're almost at Barina. No cold looks, no mention of the banned lover. Give me at least a week to work my magic."

Miss Mowbray had had a hot bath, and was dressed in a pretty rest gown sipping iced coffee in the cool lounge room, when Anne and Del, looking like the pair of sisters Mr. Mowbray had compared them to, came home. Mrs. Mowbray was a graceful, slender woman, retaining yet much of the beauty of clear blue eyes, peach-bloom complexion and golden hair which Del possessed in the flowerlike loveliness of youth and perfect health. They looked a contrast to the dark Mowbrays; but a keen observer might have noted that the young girl's mouth for all its pretty sweetness, and the formation of her chin for all its pretty roundness, were those of her father over again.

The aunt caught a hint of defiance in the air with which the girl greeted them both; but as she ignored it, and steadfastly maintained an attitude of pleased interest, while John, though with a touch of constraint, sought to second her efforts, the girl with feminine flexibility accepted the happy keynote of the meeting, and a stranger coming in would not have guessed what heartache, despair, and sullen anger lay behind the light, bantering conversation.

Having discovered from her brother that Logan was on duty in the forenoon, Miss Mowbray made a visit to an old friend the excuse for going into town next morning alone. She was fortunate enough to strike the tram on which the man was employed, and she placed herself where she could give him a keen scrutiny unobserved.

"I don't wonder Del was impressed. The man is the flapper's cowboy hero to the life, except that his mouth has a look the other does not possess. No, John is right; in spite of that splendid, stalwart body, those very fine dark eyes, and those handsome features, I would not like to entrust Del to one whose face shows such unmistakably bad lines as does yours, Dave Logan. Coming back I'll try, like Del, to get the front seat, and see what I think of you at closer quarters," she finally decided.

Her friend, however, declined to let her go till the afternoon, and Miss Mowbray was thinking to herself this meant further delay in any plan she might form when she cane to the stand and found an empty tram, with Ned Freeman, her old pupil, standing at the front. She came up at once, and, finding the tram would be leaving in five minutes, she thought she would take the front seat in it, and ask Freeman a few questions about Logan.

After some kind inquiries concerning his mother, sister and self, she broached the subject, and at once the young fellow told he was glad she had asked him, because he had been making up his mind for the last week or two to speak to Mr. Mowbray, but had hesitated, not wishing to appear to be telling tales upon Miss Del.

"Tell me all you know, Ned," she said, as through her mind came the thought of how often we fondly imagine that our trouble is our own secret, when as a matter of fact it is shared by those we little dream have knowledge of it. Substantially what Freeman told her agreed with the tale John had given.

"I don't like to be running down one of our chaps, Miss Mowbray," he said in conclusion, "but Logan is a bad egg. If Miss Del once seen him the way I do at Bennet's every second Saturday goin' home, she'd be done with him, sure."

As he was asked to explain further, he continued: - "Bennet's is the big refreshment rooms beside the railway station at Rassenden, in the flat below there's some good tennis courts, an' some of the town boys come there reg'lar to play, an' up to Bennet's for afternoon tea, as Bennet's make a specialty of their catering for that class; but it's since the horse races started at Rassenden the crowds have started to come there. I most always take a look in on my way home – we live at Rassenden you know – an' buy mother some scones, an' there's hardly a second Saturday I don't see Logan at a table shouting his tart afternoon tea. He's lucky with bettin', an' likes to flash the money about – speshul if he has had a glass, for he's the sort can't take an' leave the licker; he must go the whole hog, an' turn himself into a lunatic. He never goes 'cept when he has the weekend off, for he don't want to lose his billet, an' he knows he wouldn't be fit to drive the next mornin' when he's been on a bender."

"Have you forgotten how to handle a car, and could you get off next Saturday afternoon to take Miss Del and me out in Mr. Mowbray's?" asked Miss Mowbray, and a slow flush crept up her sallow cheek.

The young fellow looked at her in surprise, which turned to grinning comprehension.

"I'm off duty every Saturday at 3.30; but the Mowbrays go to their house at the Bay every week-end at this time of year. Mr. Jack Barnes is pretty often at Rassenden for tennis, an' he don't go when the Mowbrays stay home."

"They will be staying home this weekend. Now, Ned, not a word to anyone, but give me the number. I will ring you next Saturday midday to make arrangements."

Freeman gave the desired information; then, as more passengers took their places, he went to his station, and Miss Mowbray sat down, her old pupil following her quiet, decided movements with humorous admiration.

Beyond asking her brother to hold secret the fact that next Saturday he was to take his wife to town in the tram, leaving the car to his sister and Del, Miss Mowbray kept her own counsel. She had no mind to allow Logan to gather a hint that the family were remaining in town. In the meantime she set herself to regain the old friendly relations with her niece.

Ned Freeman was easily secured, and at a quarter to 4 he was at the door in irreproachable chauffeur's livery to take the pair for a drive round the town.

"Where could we get a nice cup of tea?" asked Miss Mowbray as she saw the car drawing near the railway lines, and the chauffeur replied respectfully, hiding the smile that lurked round his boyish lips, "There's a refreshment room just round here, Miss Mowbray, where they keep very nice afternoon tea."

As they glanced round, seeking to find an unoccupied table, more than one eye in the crowded room turned to look again at the tall distinguished woman in the well-cut tailor-made costume of navy blue, wearing the garnered beauty of the years in her fine intellectual face, and the pretty girl beside her in the simple yet most effective white muslin, whose knot of Bride roses in her girdle was not more sweet and fair than her own young countenance.

A raucous voice behind made both women turn suddenly. Miss Mowbray's heart gave a leap and seemed to stop beating, for there, with a heavily over-dressed – or, rather, under-dressed – girl, whose pretty, shrewish face was covered with paint and powder, sat Dave Logan. He was flushed, his eyes were vacuous, and it was plain he was the worse for drink.

"Now then, Trix, none of your tricks!" He burst into a laugh at his own wit, "I gave you fair an' square your share of the last book. Not one scrummy more do you git outer me. I don't mind takin' you to the Tiv. To-night, but I bar luxuries. Bust me if I don't!"

Miss Mowbray heard a choking gasp, and turned to see Del, her face as white as the dress she wore, staring at the pair with eyes of frozen horror.

"Hush, you fool! The waiter will be puttin' you out. This ain't the place to make a row. Look at the folks about."

"My troubles!" The maudlin laugh rang out. "They all know Dave Logan! His money is as good as the best. Shut up yourself, Trix!"

He looked up; his wandering glance lighted upon Del, and he rose to his feet. What he meant to do or say the

"My troubles!" The maudlin laugh rang out.

aunt did not wait to ascertain, for the moment he stood up, as if the spell that bound her snapped, Del darted through the throng and was gone.

Along the path to the station the girl fled blindly, heedless of where she went so long as she was out of hearing of that voice, out of sight of the fallen idol. A pair of arms seized her, and she shrieked aloud, till she found herself drawn to the shelter of an empty waiting-room. Jack Barnes had led her to a seat, and asked her in a voice of the keenest anxiety what ailed her, what had frightened her. Miss Mowbray, coming upon the scene at that moment, was able to explain that the girl had had a fright from a drunken man when at Bennet's for afternoon tea.

"Since the races have started Bennet's is no place for ladies on a Saturday afternoon, Miss Mowbray. It is much too crowded. We chaps come up for tea from the courts, of course; but I shouldn't like my mother or sisters to drop in for tea then. It's right enough on other days," said Jack in a tone of annoyance. "Is your car outside? I'll put you both in," he added; but when Del caught his arm, with a whispered "Don't go, Jack – don't leave us!" his face lighted up, and he said briskly, "Wait a couple of shakes till I get my things and excuse myself. Then if you've no objection, I'll come along."

Del was still pale when the car reached Barina, but she seconded her aunt's invitation to the young solicitor to come in and spend the evening with them, which he consented very readily to do after he had rung up and told his mother. Some music followed the early tea, and then the young people went out on the moonlit verandah, while the others remained to play an uninspiring game of dummy bridge.

That night, as Miss Mowbray had turned off the electric light and prepared to retire, the door was gently pushed open, and a pair of soft arms were thrown round her neck. Then Del, as if a schoolgirl again, was sobbing into the ears of the woman who had so tenderly and wisely guided the most difficult years of her life the story of Dave Logan.

"I've told it all to Jack," she finished, with a deep-drawn breath; "and, Aunty, he told me something, too. I wonder he could when he understands how silly I have been; but he did, and though, I could not answer the way he wished – if ever I can – he says he is quite sure now he will win. At any rate, he is going to keep on asking me till I'll have to give in."

The hysterical laugh that closed the sentence was half a sob; but as the older woman kissed the quivering lips and dismissed the sweet penitent she did not lie awake long to worry over the situation. Rather she fell into the sound sleep which ought to follow "something attempted" something done," which had well earned the "night's repose."

———◆———

ISABEL GRANT

A WHITE CARNATION

BACKGROUND TO THE PUBLICATION

This story accepted for holiday reading by *The Queenslander* was serialized over 5 episodes from December 22nd 1923 until January 19th. 1924

It was aimed at a female audience - slow moving and concentrating on the style, emotions and interaction of the characters. There is very little humour and much intense "feeling." As usual her plot rolls gently and continuously forward encouraging the reader to continue to a conclusion. Again as usual the ending seems truncated. She seldom seems to build up to an ending. One often gains the impression that she has a lot more story to tell but that the required number of words for the publication was suddenly reached and the editor has cut to an end.

Isabel has dwelt at length on the working conditions of nurses which she appeared to know intimately and their social interaction during breaks makes very believable reading.

The accepted ultimate goal of marriage and home duties even for this professional group of women sets it sharply into its era and shows Isabel to be comfortable with the precepts. Here is no angry woman pushing for equality and release from irksome restraints which ultimately dooms it to be left in its era. However one could say that is true even for classics (think of Dickens and Mark Twain) which have been discarded by the general reader for novels with modern speech and mores.

This story is the only one of the collection to be edited. Uncharacteristically Isabel beloboured points or themes in a way that seemed to be padding. It could have been a shorter story reworked to a size needed for five long episodes. The words are all her own only repetitions have been removed.

A WHITE CARNATION.

By ISABEL GRANT

It was an afternoon in mid June; and the slack hour, if any could be so designated, in Dr. Penfield's busy private hospital, St. Veronica. Afternoon tea had been carried round to such patients as were able to partake of it. Matron Ware, a slender woman in her early thirties, with that indefinable air of distinction which birth and breeding impart, was sitting in the dining-room enjoying, along with five of her six nurses the brief refreshing interval from duty. Matron Ware's rule was characterized by a somewhat unusual touch of comradeship. Nevertheless, there was a perceptible easing of tension, a loosening of tongues, when she excused herself to make ready to go out.

The conversation, however, beyond an occasional grumble over work imposed, or a glancing reference to a special case, dealt with ordinary girl themes. Mrs. Walsingham, the leader of what was considered the first set in the town, had given a big society dance the previous night, which Larry, one of their number, had attended.

A few doors away, a fine type of bush manhood was stoically counting out the hours left him by the dread friend cancer. In the women's side, about midday, a baby, white as a snowdrift, perfect in feature as a tiny doll, instead of being red and wrinkled, had opened star-blue eyes, and closed them again for ever. At this very moment one of their number was watching every fluctuation of temperature, every alteration of heartbeat, in a promising boy who was nearing the crisis of double pneumonia. A stranger, listening to the merry talk might have thought the chattering group callous, unwomanly creatures lacking the natural softness of their sex. The stranger, however, would be wrong; the nurses, one and all, were just ordinary girls; they had merely acquired that film over their feelings which doctors, nurses and such as are brought continually into contact with suffering must acquire, if they are not to render themselves liable to be obsessed by the pain of the world.

As in most hospitals, the girls of St. Veronica addressed each other by contractions of their surnames. Thus the nurses Larrigan, Robertson, Nimmo, Pattison, Thompson, and Martin were accustomed to answer among themselves to the names of Larry, Rob, Nim, Patty (or Pat), Tom, and Martie respectively. In the few minutes of freedom left after the departure of the matron, Larry, the senior nurse, who bore the title of "sister," and the organised wit of the staff, held the floor, relating amid the bursts of laughter which generally marked any tale of hers, everything interesting or amusing she could recollect about the Walsingham dance.

Larry was a mixture of nationalities, in which Irish, perhaps, predominated, though the brilliantly red hair, the saucy, freckled face and the Danish blue eyes did not belong to any recognised type of Irish beauty. Larry, indeed, was not beautiful. If you took her features in detail, she had not, apart from her bright eyes, a single good one. But, for all that, Larry was irresistible to the boys. It might have been her hair - red, we are now being told, is the colour most attractive. Helen of Troy, Mary Queen of Scots, Cleopatra, and various other disquieting beauties of the past boasted tresses of Titian hue. Then, again, Larry's attraction might have been her sparkling eyes, or the touch of coaxing blarney which in spite of her Australian birth, had given Larry a witty tongue. Whatever the reason for her popularity, Larry was always sure of a " boy" to fetch and carry for her, to spend his substance upon extravagant boxes of chocolates, or in dance or theatre tickets; or, failing all else, upon the inevitable "pictures"; to write her amorous epistles, and generally endure, for a time at least, her teasing, flirting propensities. True, Larry's "boys" seldom reigned long. Either they tired of her, or she grew weary of them. They were changed so often that, as an old aunt warned the girl, there was danger that she might be one of those foolish virgins who go through a wood picking up and throwing down stick after stick till in the end they emerge on the further side with empty arms or a crooked stick.

Larry, however only laughed at the well meant advice, and proceeded along the primrose path of dalliance, careless of a future reft of matrimonial chances. Just as a burst of laughter broke in upon her recital of the events of the dance, a cry was heard from the children's ward. "I want! I want! I want!" The insistent wail gathered force, and Larry, irritated by the interruption, cried out, sharply, "There's that little devil of a Mickey Freeney, started on his everlasting howl. You're on duty there, Mim, so cut along for all you're worth, before he sets all the other kids on the go."

The nurse addressed, a short, square built girl with a swarthy complexion and an air of lazy good-nature, which patients found amusing or exasperating, nodded calmly, and was continuing to nibble at her cake and sip her tea, when the Sister bore down on her like a cyclone, and drove her from the room without ceremony. "Come back if you can get the wretch quiet, or take your tea there; but, for the love of the Saints don't leave Micky howling. He'll have the whole place by the ears in a shake, and then where will we be?"

Quite unoffended – for who could take offence at Larry? – Mim leisurely departed, while the other continued, "It's all very well to laugh at Mickey, but if you were on night duty, as I've been this last week, you'd bless him. He seems to know when he can be most aggravatingly annoying, and has discovered that the best time in the night is from 2 to 3 in the morning. You know yourselves girls, that that's the worst hour in the whole 24. If a case is dicky ten to one the change comes along about then. If Micky's sounds dreary in the day, it's absolutely eerie at that unholy hour in the morning. The minute I hear him start, I tear off before he has time to rouse the hospital."

"Poor wee beggar!" said Rob, a tall girl with fine eyes and a good complexion, who could, if she desired, dispute belle-ship with Larry. Rob's interests lay rather in the line of golf and music than dances. The man who would win clever, high-spirited Rob must have something more to recommend his wooing than dexterity in jazz, or ability in turning compliments.

"Poor wee beggar!" mimicked Larry. "Wicked little devil, you mean."

"No, no, Larry. You'd be one big 'I want,' perhaps, if you'd been neglected by a drunken father and mother like wee Micky, so that at three years old your body was feebler and more shrunken than an infant in a Chinese famine. It's splendid of Dr. Pen to treat the child free of charge; but he ought to have gone further, and set the police on the parents. That sort don't deserve to have children; but, as a matter of fact, they seem to have many more than decent couples, and leave the poor kiddies to drag themselves up anyhow. It makes my blood boil just to look at the starved wee body."

"Perhaps you'd like to adopt Micky?' suggested Larry, slyly.

Rob shuddered. "I'm afraid the philanthropic instinct has been left out of me. To tell the truth, it's all I can do to touch the tiny bag of bones. He looks a hundred; and did you ever see such a face in a child? It's a cross between that of a monkey and the Irishman of caricature.

"Do you insult my Hibernian blood?" cried Larry, fixing her slim singers in the upper part of Rob's arm, with a pinch none of the girls could either imitate or endure.

"I take it back; I take it back! Let go, you Spanish inquisitor!" cried Rob. " It is time for me to go and relieve Martie, if her tea is not going to be stone cold."

"Curious how the sense of duty woke with the pinch. Well, cut along, and send Miss Prunes-and Prisms to me. She has been looking a bit pale of late. I think I must try to rouse her up."

"If you imagine your teasing rouses her up, you are much mistaken, Larry. It only sends her further into her shell," was the quick retort.

"I don't know that it's any worse to give Martie a bit of good-natured teasing than to leave her alone in the superior way you do."

"I don't pretend to be superior. If I leave the girl alone, it's because she seems to want to be left to herself. I've stopped asking her to go anywhere, for she's invariably refused."

"Well, you have a good look at her, and see if you don't agree with me that she's thinner and paler than the girl who came here nine months ago. It's my belief she takes things too hard. She was nursing Ferris last week, and when he went out to it, poor chap, I thought Martie would have fainted at the last, when the whole family were sobbing there, even though they were one and all strangers to her. Martie must learn, like the rest of us, not to give herself up to her cases so. If they have to go; it does no good to anybody for the nurse to get so upset too. I'm going to kid Martie she has a secret admirer. The girl wants to be taken out of herself, and I'll see if I can't manage it."

Rob, however, with a shrug of her shoulders, did not wait to hear more.

"Martie has not one, but two secret admirers," said Patty, a little bit of Dresden china with an air of fragility which was distinctly misleading. If any one, in hospital phrase, "cracked up" after a hard day, it was not slenderly-built Pat, whose muscles were of wrought steel. Without being exactly pretty, this nurse, with her sweet expression, her clear, fresh colour, and the gold glasses which her short-sightedness required, that seemed somehow to add to the general effect of twinkling brightness, was a pleasant object to contemplate. Her daintiness and deftness made her a general favourite with patients, and there was no better nurse for nervous cases. Though not yet engaged, she approached nearer to being so than any of the staff, having a very definite "understanding" with one of the officials in the Post Office. Unlike Larry, who was always off with the old love and on with the new, Pat had been faithful to Herbert Merivale since they had been boy and girl in the same Sunday school. As soon as Herbert got his next rise, the engagement would be announced; for the sensible couple did not approve of long engagements, and secure in each other's loyalty, were content to wait.

"Martie with two admirers! Why, I thought she was too shy to look at one," cried Larry in genuine astonishment.

Patty smiled. "Well if you're really keen on finding out who they are; I'll tell you. The first is Micky Freeney. Half his fretfulness to-day is because Martie has been taken off the children's ward and put on special duty with Bert Inwood. Martie's got a way with the children; and they all adore her, but Micky positively worships her. The other" – Pat's eyes twinkled behind the glasses – "is Old Simpson."

"I might have guessed it. Martie seems to get on better with the old folk and the babies than with any of the rest. Grannie Christ thought the world of her," said Tom, who was tall and very strongly built. Tom herself believed she was hopelessly plain, but an artist would have found, if not beauty, nobility in the rugged face, shapeliness in the contours of the long limbs, the deep bosomed figure. Tom was a silent girl, a nurse of unusual capacity, but self-distrustful, and slow at making friends.

"It's Simpson's candid opinion," went on Pat, doing her best to reproduce in her fresh young voice the querulous tones of four score, "that Nurse Martin is the pick of the bunch at St. Veronica. She seems, anyhow, the only one to pay much attention to his bell, though he's seen three nurses on the run together past his door to that of

Mr. Burton, the bachelor bank manager. Matron has her work cut out to keep chasing the nurse out of that room, though she is not above liking a chat with him herself; but once old Jock Simpson is fixed up for the day, he may ring his bell to smithereens before he gets a hurry out of a single nurse, unless its Nurse Martin. He's a good mind to speak to doctor about it."

"Speak to doctor, indeed!" said Tom, roused out of her ordinary composure. "What next? Mr. Burton is an operation case, and, of course, must have constant attention. Mr. Simpson only needs a bit of good food, and the rest. It's real kind of Dr. Pen. To take the old chap in and treat him gratis, and I think it's most ungrateful of Mr. Simpson to grumble at the attention he gets. I'm sure he is well looked after."

"There's no need to fire up, Tom," said Larry with lazy malice. "I don't suppose you answer Jim Burton's bell more than three times out of four."

A deep flush overspread the dark face. Kate Thompson and Jim Burton were friends of many years. If there was more than friendship in poor Tom's feelings, that was her own secret; but doubtless it was hard for her, who had been put in charge of the case, to see Larry, who was in attendance at the dressings, subjecting Jim, to her witching blarney and the artillery of her eyes.

Before Tom, however, could bring out the angry words plainly trembling on her lips, Patty, the peacemaker, interposed; "Well, I've told you Martie's two admirers, so don't say she has none."

"Three years old and eighty! Give me something nearer my age, thankyou. Fancy poor old Simpson jealous, though, because we find Jim Burton more interesting. Tell me when does masculine vanity die?" queried Larry of the world at large.

Meanwhile, the girl who had formed the subject of her companion's discussion had reluctantly allowed herself to be relieved for afternoon tea. Matron had told her she fancied the sick boy would reach the crisis of his illness in the next few hours and already Martie's anxious eyes fancied she had detected a faint improvement. The feeling come over her, which all nurses know at times, that they cannot bear to resign a critical case lest the almost invisible bettering should have a check. Often a nurse will stay by a bedside till she is almost dropping sooner than let her patient be disturbed by a change in attendance. The feeling may not be so unreasonable as it sounds. One reads, nowadays, of such marvels of wireless and mental telepathy that the question of whether there may not emanate from the heart of sympathy viewless waves of vitality to reinforce the flagging energies of the life that is fighting inch by inch with the dread Enemy.

Be this as it may, Martie, who had not reasoned out the matter at all felt she did not want to go from that room. Rob, however, in her common-sense way, made short work of the probationer's reluctance.

"Of course, you will go and have tea with the others; and, mind now, no hurrying back. I'm off for the rest of the day; and as they won't be coming for me from home till later on, I'd as soon stay here as not." Rob's eyes followed the slim, graceful figure thoughtfully. Yes, Larry, who was essentially level-headed on all points but one, was right; Martie was not looking well. She had lost flesh and colour, as well as changed indefinably from the rosy-cheeked bush girl who had come to St. Veronica. She had at first, been quite open in her talks, unlike the guarded way she seemed to have gradually acquired. From her first artless confidences they had learned that she was an orphan, brought up by her maternal grandmother, who, as a widow of a railway official, had been given a small railway station where trains seldom stopped, except to take in or put out cream cans.

The girl was fond of reading, and had read everything her granny possessed in the way of literature, which meant nothing later than the works of mid-Victorian poets and novelists. These she apparently knew by heart. Their language was her own. Of modern slang she was so amusingly ignorant that the other nurses loved to puzzle her by employing it, and Larry; who enjoyed nothing more than shocking the newcomer, would at times, just to see the big grey eyes open in astonishment, use the occasional swear in an off-hand way.

But all at once – with curious suddenness, towards the end of the first month, Martie's whole manner underwent a change. Her outspokenness ceased; she began to retire into her shell until by insensible degrees, as she quietly repelled each advance to greater intimacy, she was left, as the Scot puts it, "to gang her ain gait" by most of the staff, though Larry still kept up her teasing, which Martie either ignored or learned to parry as best she might.

The other nurses, having passed their examinations and gained the two necessary certificates, had more time for social pleasure than had the probationer; but, as she was quick and intelligent, it could not be the study which was affecting her health. Neither was the work she was called upon to do unduly hard. Nurses nowadays, as Larry declared, hardly knew they were living, under an award which made nine hours the maximum, and assured two free days every fortnight, as well as giving even a beginner a decent wage compared to their sisters of an older day, who worked, when a rush came, in poorly staffed hospitals twenty hours a day, and that for a mere song.

Rob's conscience was pricking her as she thus cogitated over Martie's case, and thought that it needed frivolous Larry to awaken her to the fact that the girl was not happy. Teasing, Larry might imagine, would brighten Martie up. Rob, feeling mutely reproached by the hint of forlornness, decided in her own mind that she would no longer allow herself to be repulsed, but make and effort to get within the barriers of the girl's reserve. As a beginning she resolved to try and induce Martie to come with her for the motor car drive which her home folk had arranged for that very evening.

Unconscious, however of Rob's good resolutions, Martie made her way to the dining-room, where the thought of the sick boy kept coming between her and the merry talk of her of her companions, spoiling the flavour of the tea, and taking all taste away from the dainty coffee sandwich-cake which was cook's treat of a Wednesday afternoon.

(To be continued)

"THE QUEENSLANDER"
DECEMBER 29th. 1923.

Sometimes, Martie wondered whether she had done right to leave, even though it had been granny's own wish to have her take up what they so grandiloquently called "a nursing career." Certainly, the work was entirely different from their vague and romantic notions of what it would be, and how she, who had been the smartest girl in the little State school along the line, would acquit herself at it. Far from proving the brilliantly capable nurse her ambitious dreams had pictured, she had found herself a very raw recruit indeed. She found herself increasingly held back by her ignorance, her awkwardness, as compared with the trained deftness of the other nurses, and learning more and more the hospital axiom that the best of intentions cannot take the place of exact knowledge. Moreover, though she did not distress granny by admitting it, she feared herself that she had indeed made a mistake in choosing this work; she never seemed like the rest, to be able to keep her cases and her personal concerns in different mind compartments. There were some aspects of her profession, too, which revolted her, some that terrified her.

She could never, for instance, get over her horror of the operating room. The sheer whiteness of the theatre walls and furniture, the cold glitter of the glass operating table, the shining instruments the dishes, the very smell of the anaesethetics and antiseptics made her shudder, and, though she did not faint now, even when asked to hand the sterilized instruments to the doctor, her very blood ran cold, while she was in the room. She shivered if she passed it in the darkness, and she could no more "enthuse" as the American says over an operation, or criticise its various details, and glow with admiration over the magnificent surgery as some of the others did, than she could enjoy a concert if she had an anxious case in charge.

But it was not alone on the professional side of her life at St. Veronica that the probationer was dubious whether she had done wisely to leave the old home. She had looked forward to finding what she had missed since her school days, the companionship of other girls. Granny was the dearest of grandmothers and mothers in one; but the youth tingling in Marty's veins called to youth for mateship, and seemed to have met all it asked in the nurses of St. Veronica, so kind, so jolly, and so willing to be on friendly terms. Three weeks went past, and an incident happened which spoilt the entire newcomer's pleasure in her life at the busy, up-to-date hospital.

On this morning the matron was not quite finished with a lecture which she was giving Martie on sterilisation when it was time for morning tea, and finding the supply of towels had run short, she directed the girl where to get them from the linen room, which adjoined that in which the rest of the staff were having tea, though it opened upon another verandah, along which Martie came from the sterilisation room.

Through a grating overhead she could hear the cheerful rattle of cups and saucers, the voices of the girls, and smiling in sympathy with the frequent bursts of laughter, she inclined herself to listen; only to stiffen with a sudden realisation that she herself formed the subject of the merriment.

"Yes." said Larry, in her ringing tones —little dreaming that Martie was not otherwise than safe with matron for some time yet "our little Pro. is not quite pleased with us. She does not approve of the way we bob our hair. It seems to her silly for grown-up women to try to look like school girls. She can't fancy her dear granny wearing skirts up to her knees, yet she's seen a lady who must be every bit as old, with a frock too short for a school girl. Neither does Martie consider it nice of us to use so much slang. It grieves her to note that we have apparently only one word, and that an expression she was accustomed to hear applied to decaying matter, used for whatever fails to please, from a cake to a game of tennis. 'Bonce' as the term employed for what we approved of was almost as objectionable; while what dear granny would say if she knew they actually at times used a swear or two she really did not know."

The merry laughing voice went on till it was stopped in the stilted phraseology which Martie recognised as an imitation of her way of speaking, by a perfect gale of merriment, and the listener woke to the fact that she was overhearing something not meant for her ears. With blazing cheeks, and a heavy chest, she grabbed up her bundle and fled.

How she managed to assume a semblance of intelligent interest in the rest of the lecture she hardly knew; but at last, she was sent to rejoin the others. Had she dared she would have asked to be excused; but she could not trust herself to utter even the few words necessary to voice her request, and made her way to the dining-room with a beating heart.

As Rob kindly poured her out a fresh cup of hot tea, and Patty began to cut some thin bread to be buttered, she felt like crying out: "You are nothing but a lot of hypocrites making fun of me behind my back, and pretending to be nice to my face. I'll never, never be friends with one of you again," However, she had sufficient self-control to keep back the burning words, and briefly thanking the two girls, she subsided into a corner, where the others, fancying she must had a trying time at the lecture, left her to recover her usual happy serenity.

It was a pity, since the sensitive girl had been so unlucky as to hear so much, she had not heard more, and found Larry admit, when the laughter was over, that the whole thing, where it was not pure imagination, was exaggeration of guileless replies to her own artfully guileful queries. Then ignoring all remonstrance, she had continued gleefully: "But the new Pro.'s a real Prunes-and-Prisms miss, and thinks we are shocking. She just about dropped the other day, when I rapped a wee swear word at her."

"Why did you, then? You're the only one of us that does use 'a wee swear word,' as you call it, and you know it's merely for effect, too," said Tom indignantly.

"It amuses me to see the kid open those big eyes of hers," was all that Larry condescended to give by way pf explanation, however; and the others, knowing her so well, knowing how little real malice there was in the girl's fun, said no more.

Martie herself, in time, learned to understand this, and to know how much genuine kindness there was in every member of the staff; but in the meantime the mischief was done and the shy girl had grown self-conscious, and nervous of her life and associates, unable to do herself justice with doctors or matron, afraid to be her natural self with patients, unless they were so old or so young that Larry could not tease her as she did the other girls about being specially attentive to interesting masculine ones. Worst of all, the incident, slight as it was, had spoilt the other nurses, who really were willing to be friendly, for Martie. She declined invitations which would have done much to brighten the dull monotony of work and studies; for some of the girls, like Pat and Rob had homes in the town, and would have been pleased to take her there. But as each invitation was steadily declined, the girl was left at last to herself, and found her vacations from duty limited to a visit to a childless old couple named Macgregor who had been friends of her granny, and had promised to look after her, to going to church or solitary walks. As the first sharpness of her mortification began to blunt, and Martie grew to understand things more, she recognised that she had been making something like a mountain out of a molehill, had begun to laugh with the others at Larry's nonsense and even to venture on a smart retort to her teasing. But by this time her own attitude had been accepted, and no one seemed to notice how solitary she really was, so she threw herself into her work and her study, finding scope for the repressed warmth of her young heart among the children or the old folk, who were grateful for a little extra attention. She had been very pleased to be put on such a case as this very serious one of a boy with double pneumonia and she made up her mind that if any watchfulness or care on her part could pull the lad through, Bert should not lack it. As she sat now among the other girls at afternoon tea, she took, as usual, but a small share in the conversation, for her thoughts were back with her patient, and no sooner was her last morsel swallowed than she rose to return.

"What's your hurry? Don't you think Rob is able to take your place?" asked Larry.

"Of course, Rob is a far better nurse than I am," said Martie with a shamefaced laugh; and the senior nurse continued, not unkindly, "well, sit down, then, stupid, and take your full time off. Matron means you to have it.

See here, I've a bit of news for you. What will you say if I tell you 'somebody' is very interested in you? Isn't that the correct ladylike way of putting it?"

Martie stared at her superior in absolute astonishment. This was indeed a new line for Larry to take in her teasing; but, as she glanced quickly up, she fancied she caught a significant look pass between the three girls, and, at once on her guard, replied composedly, "I suppose I ought to say that was very kind of 'somebody.'"

"He looked everywhere for you last night at the Walsingham dance, and wondered, as he had heard some of us were invited, whether you would be there," said Larry, her blue eyes clear as a child's.

"I hope you told him I was not asked and do not dance," said Martie in the same composed tone.

Tom broke into a short laugh, and a glint of annoyance came into Larry's blue eyes. She was not going to be "bested" by a pro. in a duel of wits.

'It's a pity you don't make up your mind to learn, with Miss Bligh's class so handy. You could spare one night from your study and find the dancing might help to shake off the dumpiness that seems getting hold of you lately I wonder who needs brightening up more than us poor devils of nurses? But, leaving the dancing alone, I'm asking you about this admirer of yours. I don't treat the girls like you. I share my boy's chocs. and tell them all about him. Why do you keep your admirer so dark, pray?"

"I've no difficulty in keeping my admirer, as you are pleased to call him, dark," said Martie, roused at last, "seeing I don't know a single young man in the town."

This was exactly what Larry wanted, and assumed a shocked expression

"You don't know a single young man in the town! Don't tell me you are carrying on with a married man?"

"What utter nonsense and drivel you do talk!" burst out Martie, hardly knowing whether to be angry or amused.

"What's the utter nonsense and drivel?" asked Matron Ware, appearing at the door way. "It surely can't be Nurse Martin I hear using such strong terms?"

"I'm just trying to persuade her that she ought to learn dancing," said Larry, with cheerful mendacity. "We think she has been looking pale of late, and that the lessons would brighten her up."

"A capital idea. I'll be meeting Miss Bligh this afternoon at Walsingham's and I'll see if she can manage to take on another pupil. I know her classes are pretty full up, but still - she might be willing to make room for one more. Let me see, Wednesday is your night off and you go to Miss Bligh's, don't you, Nurse Pattison?" Matron, for one who appeared to notice little of what went on among her staff, was curiously cognisant of their doings. "Well, we shall try if we can't contrive to let you off the same evening, Nurse Martin and you could go together. You'd like me to arrange with Miss Bligh, wouldn't you?" Somewhat bewildered at having her affairs settled in such a summary fashion, Martie assented, and Matron went on kindly: "I like my girls to have a happy time off duty. All work, and no play makes Jill as dull as Jack, and we don't want any dull girls at St. Veronica." Miss Ware understood, as one who had been through the mill, without getting soured or hardened in the process, that those who devote their lives to the sick and suffering ought to have plenty of ordinary human happiness to keep their natures sweet and wholesome. After a few minutes' chat with her girls, and a discussion over the programme of work in her absence with the senior nurse, matron left the room.

"There, what did I tell you? Even matron backed me up, and agreed that it would be good for you to take on dancing. I wouldn't be surprised, either, if 'Somebody" doesn't turn up at Miss Bligh's, once he knows you've joined, Martie."

"I think 'Somebody' is a masculine 'Mrs. Harris,' " said Martie , blushing at her own daring, and escaping before she could see how "Sister" took the retort. Larry, indeed to whom Dickens was a sealed book, looked questioningly at the others. "What does she mean? A masculine Mrs. Harris?"

"She means there's no such person," said Tom, not unpleased to see Larry for once nonplussed. "Give it up, Larry; you never raised a hair. Martie is so used to your teasing that she takes no notice of it."

"She did bite, I tell you. Didn't you see the way she coloured up?"

"Not a bite," said Patsy. "She blushed at her own cheek. Martie colours up at anything, you know. I never saw such a girl for blushing."

"Well at any rate, I managed to wake her up. She looked twice as bright as when she came in. As for her bit of cheek, as you called it, I was rather pleased to hear it, for it's a good symptom. Shows she's beginning to sit up and take notice. My medicine is having some effect, you see."

Martie, meanwhile, had returned to her post, and if Larry had said she looked wakened up when she left the dining-room, she would have been still better pleased to note how, when the sick boy glanced up with a faint, but unmistakable smile of welcome, before he lapsed again into the solemn absorption of mind and body in the grim life and death contest, how bright the face of the probationer grew. What Martie, indeed, needed was a little appreciation, something to make her feel that she was not a mere cog in a machine; and a glow of real happiness surged through her heart at the thought that here at least was someone who was glad to see her again, even though she was not so wise or so capable as the older nurse.

To her joy, as the afternoon wore on she found that her inexperience had not been mistaken; there really was a change for the better, and doctor, when he came to see the patient just before dusk, confirmed the impression, and actually complimented her upon her careful watch of pulse and temperature.

It was thus a happier-faced Martie than St. Veronica had seen for months who came off duty, was met by Rob with the invitation for the motor car drive, and accepted it with none of her usual hesitation.

When Martie, after a long, delightful spin in the clear, cool starlight returned to the hospital, she had somehow got into terms of happier intimacy with Rob than she had yet known. At last—at last, was the thought with which sleep came to Martie that night.

How long she slept she did not know, but she woke with a start. Listening, she could hear the sound of careful footsteps and opening of doors. She sat up in bed, and saw that the theatre was alight. "A case come in so urgent that it must be operated upon at once;" she thought, and snuggled down into the warm bedclothes with the comforting feeling that the matter was not her concern; she was neither the nurse on night duty, nor the one detailed this month for such sudden emergencies.

Presently, she could hear the whirr of an engine which she recognised as the ambulance car. "I wonder if it's a case from the country?" she pondered. Through her mind rushed many a heartrending incident of such hurried arrivals of the ambulance cars - needs so imperative that attention dare not wait for daylight! It would be cold work getting everything ready on a night like this. Martie shivered to think of moving about the operating room under the austere, brightness of the electric light, and she pulled the blankets up to her, wishing that she dared to call out to one of the other girls. Listening to hear if by some lucky chance any of them were awake, she caught a faint, weird cry, which made the very hair rise on her head. What could it be? Trembling and shivering, Martie seemed to listen in every nerve and at last, with a sigh of relief she disentangled from the sound the pitiful, "I want! I want! I want!" Of the tiny deformed lad in the children's ward.

Someone must go to him, for if he were left many minutes more he would have the other children wakened up and most likely the adult patients as well. Larry, of course, was on night duty, and therefore responsible; but the chances were that she had been called away to assist at the operation, for there was not one of the nurses, not even matron herself, equal to Larry in a sudden emergency. Nim, on duty with the pneumonia case, was furthest from the children's ward; and, moreover, might not be able to leave her patient. No one else appeared to be disturbed by Micky's wailing.

Reluctantly - for she felt in anything but heroic trim - Martie crept out of bed, and donned warm gown and slippers, when, like a breath of cold wind, the thought came to her that to reach the child she must pass by the room they were accustomed to call the "morgue." It really was only a spare room, but having been occasionally used, when a country patient had died, to hold the body awaiting burial it had a sinister association. But again the mournful cry came to her ears, and, with her heart beating like a hammer against her side, the girl fled along the verandahs till she gained the children's ward, and, with unsteady fingers, turned on the electric light. The moment her eyes fell on the tiny pinched face she forgot her nervous tremor, for, inexperienced as she was, she could see that a change had passed over the lad. She could read in the sunken eyes, in the livid blue-greyness of the cheeks, that his need was urgent; without losing a minute, or giving one thought to the morgue, she fled back along the verandahs till at the entrance to the theatre she stumbled across matron.

Miss Ware listened to what Martie had to say. Then, after giving some directions to Larry, she hurried back with the girl to the children's ward. When everything was done that could be done to relieve the child, she asked Martie if she would mind being left in charge of the case. Neither Nim nor Larry could be spared and it seemed a pity to wake any of the others.

She did not say, though she thought it, that no earthly skill would now avail; the sands of the little neglected life were running out fast. The child might last for a few days more; that would be all. He was more comfortable now, but he seemed to be sinking into a stupor.

For about an hour wee Micky lay still; then, as the change to greater chill which heralds the turn of the night arrived, he stirred with the icy breath of the cold air which often wakens them, and opened his eyes. As his wandering glance fell upon Martie, his favourite attendant, his features lightened into the nearest approach to a smile which Martie had ever seen. Her own heart warmed to the love in the child's face.

"What a wicked girl I've been!" She thought, "grumbling about being out of everything, when first Bert and then poor wee Micky have shown they care for my nursing. Perhaps I've been making myself miserable over other things at St. Veronica, with as little reason as for thinking I'm a complete failure as a nurse."

"What is it now Micky boy?" she said aloud; for there was so pitiful a question in the sunken eyes that she longed to be able to reach the cause of it.

"I want! I Want!" The old cry the only words beyond a half-articulate jumble or a muttered "Yes" or "No" which had been all the child had uttered since his arrival three weeks ago, scarcely rose above a whisper now. "What is it you want, Micky - poor, wee Micky. Tell me and I'll try to get it for you," said the girl, tears smarting in her own eyes.

For answer the wasted creature raised his arms and stretched them towards her. Some instinct told the girl that what poor Micky wanted was something of the mothering his hapless years had missed. Lowering the front of the cot she took the shivering body in her arms.

"Go to sleep Micky boy," she said softly and obediently the eyes closed. Soon the regular breathing showed that the child slept. Martie grew first cramped then numb but she held her place. Presently and almost unaware, sleep came upon her.

As the dawn was beginning to struggle with the electric light, Dr. Penfold and Matron Ware, spent but triumphant, stood silent at the door of the children's ward.

On the pillow of the nearest cot two heads lay together: the girl's face in sharp contrast to the waxen pallor of the child upon which death had stamped a beauty which life had never seen. Martie woke and tried to rise, but it was not till matron and doctor half led, half carried her to a seat that she realised her tiny charge was dead. The next moment she was shaken with sobbing. Dr. Penfield left the room until Miss Ware told him the girl was herself again, when he returned and asked her a few questions about the occurrence. Finally he came and sat down beside herself and matron.

"I think Nurse Martin has been getting a little thin and pale lately. See that she keeps to her room for the rest of the day and does not take up duty till Friday. You've had a bit of a chill and a shock, young woman" he added talking to Martie directly "so take things easy for a bit. We don't expect our nurses to do night duty after a hard day, you know, but I'm very pleased you were able to do a little for that poor forsaken piece of humanity."

Matron hurried her to her room and helped her in such a kind sisterly way that the feeling of awe with which she had hitherto regarded her head seemed changed to one of affection. Having forced her to drink a cup of hot milk, which she had made ready for her, matron drew down the window blinds and left the room.

Martie believed the milk must have been "doped," for scarcely had a curious thought that the taking away of her old nervous fears of doctor and matron was a gift from poor wee dead Micky crossed her drowsy brain, than she was fast asleep.

(To be continued.)

"THE QUEENSLANDER"

JANUARY 5th. 1924

A week had passed, and Matron Ware was in her sitting-room discussing with the trembling, happy parents of Bert Inwood the possibility of his being permitted to be taken to the seaside to complete his convalescence. The nurses were gathered together for afternoon tea and, as matron was absent, were enjoying the utmost liberty of speech.

Martie's first lesson in dancing was the subject under discussion, and it was not Larry alone who was giving the girl much good-natured teasing, which the probationer received in a give and take way which would have been impossible to her a week ago. Martie, from the time she woke late in the afternoon of the day the tiny lad died, and received visit after visit from the girls, began to feel that she was at last not outside the pale.

On Friday afternoon Rob and she had gone shopping and from the few yards of cream Japanese silk she bought they had between them fashioned a pretty little frock, which would be just the thing, Rob assured her, for the dancing class. As Rob was an authority on dressmaking Martie was comfortably settled about her appearance, at least, at the lessons.

"Why, I look exactly like the rest of you," was her delighted comment when the dress was finished and tried on. Rob smiled, for she understood that 'the rest of you' was Martie's unconscious standard of smartness; but she did not say – that if Martie would only look as bright and animated at the lessons as she did now, none of them could hold a candle to her. Perhaps the thought struck Larry too, this afternoon, that the hitherto despised neophyte was turning into an uncommonly pretty girl, and may have given a touch of the Alexander-like dislike to having a rival near his throne to the tones of the senior nurse, as she asked Martie whether she had heard any more of her "admirer."

"Not since you last spoke of him," said the girl with some spirit.

"Aren't you expecting him to be at the dancing to-night?" continued Larry.

"I never thought any more about him," said Martie, reddening; for she felt that all eyes were on her and something of her old diffidence returned.

"Well, take it from me that 'somebody's' sure to come to 'Araluen.' "

"Of course somebody – a good many somebodies – are sure to come to Miss Bligh's classes; they always do, or where would the girls' partners be?" said Rob and her tone was not a pleased one.

"But I'm referring to some very special 'somebody,' " went on Larry, quite unabashed. "You see," she drawled, "I happened to mention to him Martie was going to join and he more than hinted he was following suit. What do you think of that, Martie?"

"I think you've a very vivid imagination," said Martie stoutly, and Rob threw her a smile of approval.

"Very well then," said Larry, nettled, as she caught the interchange of glances, "perhaps you'll believe me when I say he actually went so far as to arrange to wear something by which you might recognize him." Her bright eyes travelled round the room, and rested on a bowl of white carnations. The flowers, which had come all the way from a certain railway garden, were Martie's shy gift to her mates. Their clove-spice fragrance filled the room.

"I was to tell you," Larry continued with a sneer on her pretty lips, "that he is going to wear a white carnation in his buttonhole. Now Martie keep your eyes well open for the man who comes in wearing a white carnation!"

"I won't do any such thing. I'm going to try and learn dancing in the shortest time I can, and not trouble my head about anything else," replied Martie stoutly.

"Quite right. Don't let Larry spoil your pleasure with her teasing," said Rob, as she linked her arm in the girl's and drew her away.

"Look here Larry," said Tom after the other two had gone, " tackle us if you feel in the humour for teasing, but leave the poor kid alone. She is looking forward so to these lessons and you know how shy she is; you will make her so self-conscious she will be quite miserable. It's a shame!"

"I like that!" cried Larry indignantly. "Here I am doing my best to liven the girl up, and you accuse me of trying to spoil her pleasure. Martie's pretty in a way, but she's so stiff and bashful she's predestined to be an absolute frost. I really believe she's afraid of being nice to any man under sixty for fear he should imagine she's trying to catch him."

"What rubbish!" retorted Tom. " It's just the child's shyness, though I don't suppose you will believe it; for no one can accuse you of being afraid to be nice to any interesting masculine patients."

Larry, who always respected a courageous opponent, was in no whit offended at this and laughed heartily as she left the room to attend to duties elsewhere.

At a quarter to eight o'clock that evening, a placid Patty and a very excited Martie went down the garden path of St. Veronica to meet at the gate a tall, heavily built young man, whom Patty introduced as Mr. Merivale.

Herbert Merivale was handsome in a dark solid way. His mind, like his body, seemed built on steady foundations. His conversation ran along certain grooves of settled thought. It was plain that a grievance with his chief at the Post Office, to which his talk soon drifted after a few perfunctory, courteous remarks, was a long-standing one.

Martie, apparently forgotten by the pair, was left to her own happy thoughts. To the bush-bred girl it was quite an event. Larry had been so persistent that Martie could not but wonder whether there was any truth in the teasing. "But even if there is 'somebody' he will not continue long to be interested in such a foolishly shy girl as I have grown to be. Oh dear! I wish I could get rid of my shyness. I'm sure to freeze up like an icicle when I'm introduced."

But here Martie's doleful reflections were brought to an end, for as they reached a pair of handsome white gates Patty and Herbert seemed to realise they had a companion and told her they were now at 'Araluen.'

Before they left St. Veronica Martie had learned from the other nurses the history of the Bligh family which had been among the wealthiest in the town. Tessa, a beautiful girl of 18, was away with an aunt in Sydney and the mother had with her only Dick, a boy of 13, when the crash came. After the father's death from a stroke it was found that he had been speculating wildly in mining and when his affairs were straightened up there remained but the beautiful house. This too would have gone but the creditors refused to take it from the widow.

Tessa, recalled from Sydney, soon proved that she had grit and ability as well as good looks, for she set to work by teaching in the big hall, which had been the scene of many a select gathering of friends, the new dances she had learned down South. In another year Dick was found a position in a bank and things grew easier, till with the outbreak of the great war the lad enlisted, and Tessa was obliged to take in boarders. On Dick's return and his reinstatement in his office, Tessa resumed the dancing lessons. Four years later, between Dick's salary and Tessa's earnings the mother was able to pay back the last installment of the debt.

This year Miss Bligh had engaged an assistant. It seemed that the whole town had gone mad over jazz.

When the girl was introduced to her new teacher she did not wonder that all the town wished to become pupils. Martie fell in love with Miss Bligh the moment she saw her. Never had she seen such a beautiful girl. It was hard to believe that she was 35. Tessa's grandmother who had been an Italian, had given the warmth to the colouring, the depth to the blue-black rippling hair. Martie decided that Miss Bligh's manner was just as fascinating as her appearance. Her voice, a deep contralto, was music itself. She could but wonder that such a beautiful girl had never married.

Martie's wonder had been shared by many of Miss Bligh's friends as the years passed by and saw her apparently heart-whole in spite of the many aspirants. Jim Ware, who had been one of Tessa's train when she was little more than a school girl and who had recently returned form America, wither he had gone about six months before the death of Mr. Bligh, could have given a guess to the reason. Jim an electrical engineer now in charge of the city engineering , had no more to say on the matter, however, than Tessa. It might have been observed by the curious that few evenings at Araluen passed without the long, lean figure with the humorous eyes being seen in the hall chatting for a few minutes to the teacher, or having the occasional dance, no one seemed to attach much importance to the renewal of so old a friendship.

"Come here Len," said Miss Bligh when she had chatted for a few minutes to her new pupil, and a young man who seemed to be hovering round waiting till she was free, came eagerly up. "Let me introduce you to Miss Martin. She is a stranger in the town and has only lately begun to learn nursing at St. Veronica so you must help me to give her a pleasant time at the lessons. You're my first assistant, aren't you?"

"Rather!" was the emphatic rejoinder. But Mr. Ashton after a few preoccupied remarks followed Miss Bligh to the piano and began speaking in a low tone to her.

Patty, who was a perfect encyclopedia of information, then told Martie that Len Ashton was really a most important person at these classes. He was the son of old Bill Ashton, who was reported to be almost worth a million. Len, at present kept to a clerkship in one of his father's many businesses, would no doubt, as his only son, come in for most of the old man's wealth. He was a favourite among the girls, but one person only counted for Len and kept him these three years faithful to the study of dancing. Of course, Miss Bligh was years and years older than Len; but then he was such an undoubted "catch" you never could tell. So far, beyond allowing him to do more work for her at the time of her annual ball than he did at his father's office she could not be said to show him any special favour.

At this point Herbert, who had been listening in visibly growing impatience interrupted to tell Martie that, in his opinion, Len Ashton was nothing but an empty headed conceited puppy, spoilt by a pack of silly girls.

Somewhat astonished at such ascerbity in the excellent Herbert, Martie listened while Patty smoothed down the ruffled feathers. Marty might have forgiven Herbert had she understood that Len generally asked Patty when disappointed in an "open" with Miss Bligh. It was hard for poor Herbert, who had about as much idea of dancing as a rhinoceros, to watch her trip round in the arms of Len, who might sing in his lordly way the words of the ragtime in which they were dancing, "Hold me just a little closer, closer, closer," or "Give me a cosy corner and an armchair for two," or the like.

Martie, however, was more interested in watching the gay scene, so the pair dropped into talk more personal and intimate.

With secret dismay, the shy newcomer glanced from the girls in their pretty frocks apparently self-possessed and happy, running over with laughter and teasing chaff to one another or to their boy companions. The latter seemed inclined to keep together as if for mutual protection, but still looking superciliously sure of themselves and their value as partners, for the masculine element was in a decided minority.

Not one of the boys wore a buttonhole, much less a white carnation, and though Martie had known all along it was only some of Larry's nonsense, she was relieved, for she did not feel at all attracted to any of the lads. Certainly Len Ashton, with his bored indifference, had not impressed her.

Martie was not long left to her survey of the hall, for the lessons now began, and all the pupils formed into two lines and proceeded to follow, with varying grace and dexterity, Miss Bligh's instructions. Martie was made happy at the close of the lesson when Miss Bligh took her round the hall herself to show her how the step was danced with a partner, to be told that it would not take her long to be a good dancer, as she had the first requisite of success, an idea of rhythm.

Martie, by the time four of five lessons had been given, and her teacher had taken her a few more times as a partner, admitted to Patty she was glad she had come and was enjoying herself very much.

The first "open" dance was announced and Len Ashton was seen making his way to their corner. Herbert glowered at the approach, then frowned in a puzzled way, for it was in front of Martie, not Patty, that he stood and asked for the pleasure of the next dance.

"It's the Maxina, the last one we've had," Len volunteered, as blushing at being thus singled out, Martie accepted his arm.

She would have been less flattered and fluttered had she heard a conversation which had just taken place between Len and Miss Bligh.

"Will you do me a favour?" Tessa's eyes were dangerous when they pleaded.

"Try me!" was the ardent reply; but the flush on the fair boyish face died away as she said:-

"I'd be so pleased if you would ask that pretty little Miss Martin, my new pupil, for the open dance. I'm going to give the Maxina over again. It's easy, and she seemed to be getting nicely into it. You see, I promised Miss Ware to get her on as fast as I could, as she can only let her off for one night. I know I said I'd have the fist "open" with you tonight, but I've changed my mind."

"You promised faithfully!" was the sulky reply.

"Did I? Well we're having two "opens" tonight and I'll dance the next with you – unless anything unforeseen happens," said Tessa, lightly.

"Unless Mr. Ware turns up." Blurted the boy, his instinctive jealousy blazing up; but before the flash which came into the dark eyes he was humbly apologizing. Miss Bligh, however, declined to be appeased, and dismissed him in cold displeasure.

It was therefore with inward anger, though with outward grace, that Len sought Miss Martin. While he did not actually propose to vent his disappointment and chagrin upon his partner, he was certainly not in the humour to be patient with the gaucheries of a "tug" as the phrase went.

(To be continued.)

THE QUEENSLANDER 12TH. JANUARY 1924

After the first thrill of gratified vanity at being thus sought out for an open dance by the exclusive Len had subsided, it began to dawn upon Martie that her cavalier was not enjoying the dance. The moment this disturbing thought struck her all her self confidence fled. No longer seeking to follow subjects of discussion, her whole mind became centred upon her steps, with the result that everything she had learned escaped her. In vain she strove to get into step. Once the rhythm of the step miraculously returned to her, but at the next corner she lost step and eager to regain it gave a hop. This brought the sharp heel of her white shoe right upon Len's toe.

A spasm of uncontrollable agony for a moment contorted his face, but by the next her had recovered himself and was gallantly laughing away her apologies. Oh! How Martie longed to be able to sit down! It was only her miserable shyness which kept her from asking him to spare them both the torture. It was with intense relief that at last she heard the music stop.

Len took her back to her seat, but he did not offer as most of the other boys did to sit down beside his partner and enter into conversation. No! He seemed glad to be gone; though he was not a whit more happy than was his poor little partner.

She discovered that she had managed to wrench the button almost off her new kid shoe. It was hanging by a single thread. If she was clumsy with a tight-fitting shoe, what would she be like with a button missing?

Patty, however, took the mishap very coolly. "Oh! That's nothing," she said, smiling at the worried face. "It's always happening. See the doors there, at the end of the hall, the one on the right is for the girls. You will find a table with pins, needles, thread, everything you may need. Slip along. Sew on the button. Lucky you did not lose it."

Thankfully Martie followed the advice. It took her some time to find a needle which would fit the strong thread she had picked out to hold the button fast. As she sewed it on she heard from the other side of the curtain Miss Bligh say in a laughing tone.

"Thanks awfully, Len, for dancing with Miss Martin as I asked you. How did you get on? She is so daintily light, I'm sure you did splendidly."

"Don't be cruel, Miss Bligh. Of course you saw us, and, like the others, were killing yourself laughing. I'd never have gone through with it if I had not promised you. Daintily light indeed! She landed on my toe and I thought it was a hippopotamus!"

Miss Bligh's rich laughter came to the ear of the girl who, unwittingly and unwillingly was again an eavesdropper. She looked around; there was no exit form the recess except by the curtain.

"Did she land on your pet corn? Oh! My poor Len. Did you swear?"

"Did I what? Of course I told her it was nothing and I believe I about saved her from bursting into tears. But, apart from the fact that she could not dance a step, the girl hasn't two ideas in her head. I hope I'll never meet a duller partner."

Behind the curtain Martie's little white teeth had met with a vicious snap: "Hippopotamus indeed! I wish now I could have come down with both feet on your pet corns. If ever I get the chance, I will, too."

"Why Len," cried Miss Bligh, in an altered tone, "I think you're mistaken there. I found the girl most intelligent and charming. You must have frightened her. I told you she was shy, you know. Wait a bit till Miss Martin learns the steps and gets over her shyness. You'll see if you won't find plenty of the boys eager to secure her for a partner. I'm no prophet, but I venture to say you'll be as keen as the rest in a couple of months."

"Will I? Like smoke!" was the sulky reply, and the speakers moved away.

Martie slowly finished sewing on the button, and, though much of the hurt feeling had vanished in her teacher's kind remarks, her wrath against Len Ashton had by no means abated. And to think she had actually plumed herself upon being asked when Len only did it as a favour to Miss Bligh! Mentally anathematizing herself for a credulous fool, Martie put on the offending shoe and came out. She was thankful to observe that her return was apparently unnoticed by either Miss Bligh, who was talking to a tall, thin man at the verandah door, or Len. The dancers had taken their places in two lines on the floor. Martie slipped into her place beside Patty and congratulated herself on getting back so unobtrusively.

Len Ashton pretended to be occupied with the portfolio of music while he kept a jealous scrutiny on the pair in the doorway. Could he have heard their conversation he would have learned how vain were his hopes. Not that he could have blamed her; she had never allowed him to make love to her and had always treated him as the younger brother she sometimes called him.

"Any news yet?" Tessa's dark eyes were anxious, though her face still kept its smile for any observers who might chance to be watching her and Ware.

"The very best, old girl. I've got the appointment in my pocket, so to speak." He slapped it triumphantly. "Who says my time in America was wasted? Behold now, the general manager of the new electric works. I'll have tramway lines cutting this little old town from end to end before you can say knife." His joy in his success was good to see. A spark appeared in the dark eyes watching him. "When can all this foolery be given up?" continued the man with an impatient wave towards the hall.

"Not till the end of the season; I must play fair with my pupils."

Ware grunted discontentedly. "After all these years to be kept waiting now!"

"After all these years! Whose fault was it they were so long? You could go wandering the wide world over and never come back to find what had become of Tessa, that you professed to love."

"Let the dead past alone Tessa. Let it alone. I was a hot-headed young fool. I heard you were carrying on with Ned Stringer, and you wouldn't deny it when I asked, so we quarreled. Ned was transferred to Sydney, you went down to visit your aunt there, and that was enough for me. Our firm were sending two men to America to study electrical engineering. I was given the chance to be one, so I took it. Somehow when my time was up the wanderlust got hold of me. The years slipped by and I scarcely seemed to notice them. I came across an advertisement for a city engineer in my old town and while the fit of homesickness the old names gave me lasted, I sent along my application, and back I trotted to the old shop. I never wrote home in all that time, more shame to me. I never heard of your father's death."

"Forget it all, Jim," said the girl in a low tone for his voice had been gathering passion with every hurried sentence. "Forget it all; we were both young and foolish, I should have written. Never mind, the future is ours. Listen Jim; mother and Dick, too, until he is married, will have a home with us?"

"The whole bag and baggage, Tess." The man's voice shook. "I'm too happy to know I've a position and a home to offer the one girl I always loved. But how have you contrived to keep so young? Look at me; I might be double your age."

Tessa smiled, but her eyes were misty. "Somehow I knew you would come back to me, so I couldn't grow old. But we've had enough sentiment. Tell me, who is to take your place?"

"My present assistant, a young chap but smart as they make 'em. Mark Treloar is his name. I liked his credentials and picked him myself. He comes from Newcastle but he belongs to the district. All this is on the strict Q.T. It won't come out for a month or more. I like Mark he's straight and he's clever too, but a bit raw and bashful. Tell you what Tess, it would do him the world of good to have a couple of sessions here before you knock off. What say if I bring him?"

"Are you and Connie in a matrimonial conspiracy by any chance?" Tessa's laughter was infectious and Ware joined in though he said in a puzzled way, "A conspiracy? What are you driving at?"

"Well Connie asked me last week to take as a pupil, one of her new nurses, a shy bush girl, who needed to be taken out of herself a bit; and here you come with your bashful bush lad."

"I didn't say he was a bush lad, but I believe he did come from the bush. He looks it too; he's a big strapping lad. What say we do try a bit of match making?"

"I'm not going to begin match-making at my time of life," was the laughing reply, "but if you want you can bring your man next Wednesday and I'll introduce him to Miss Martin. That's her , the pretty little thing third form the end."

"There's only one pretty girl for grizzled old Jim Ware, as there was only one for the same Jim Ware when he was a brumby of sixteen," said the man in such a dangerously sentimental way that Tessa decided it was wiser to return to her teaching without more ado.

Half an hour later Patty and Martie were on their way homewards, the latter congratulating herself that the first evening was safely over. She did not tell them what she had overheard. The Martie of nine months ago would have blurted out the story, but Martie, who had been taught reticence in St. Veronica, kept the incident to herself.

Next morning, matron, who had been up all night in the women's ward, was sleeping in her room, so the rest of the staff had a fine opportunity to ask questions. Patty was the chief speaker; Martie said as little as possible.

"So you had the first 'open' with Len Ashton. What did you think of him?" asked Larry in some curiosity.

"I didn't think much of him. I didn't care for the way he had his hair all streaked back from his forehead, and as long as some of the girls wore theirs," said Martie indifferently.

"I suppose he wasn't by any chance wearing a white carnation?" continue d Larry with a touch of acid in her tone.

"He was not!" Said Martie with such sudden heat that a laugh went round the room. Luckily the conversation drifted away from the subject of the dancing lessons and Martie breathed a sigh of relief.

Next Wednesday evening, as Patty and she passed along the hall in St. Veronica, Larry popped her head out of a room and said in a mysterious whisper, "Carnations are still blooming in the gardens, and 'somebody' may present you with one to-night." Larry smiled wickedly to see how the angry flush rushed up.

At the gate the faithful Herbert was waiting with two packets of sweets, one of which he presented to Martie. The kindly thought touched the girl and her vexation at Larry's teasing died away.

The night was a cold one and the three stepped briskly along the moonlit street. "Araluen" was soon reached and the lessons began.

Martie felt more at home now and being less excited got on better with the step. When the first 'open' dance was given Len found Miss Bligh could not be persuaded try it with him. He made a bee-line for the corner, but it was not Martie he bore away this time but Patty, leaving her gloomily resigned Herbert to turn to her companion and ask whether she would attempt to dance with him. "I don't mind telling you," he admitted with melancholy candour, that I'm such a frightful dancer I never seem able to turn round without getting tangled in some other couple unless my partner can do the steering. You see it takes me all my time to manage my feet."

"I don't think it would be at all wise of us to try to go round the room together," said Martie, unable to keep back her smiles. "You hurry up and see if you can't get a good dancer. I don't mind a bit looking on." "You're sure you won't mind being left here?"

"I'd far sooner watch, the dance looks such a queer one," she said.

"Well, if you really don't think it unkind leaving you, I'll see if I can't strike a decent dancer to get in some practice," said Herbert. Martie assured the good-hearted fellow that she really was pleased to be a spectator. It was a pleasure to sit there and watch the gay scene. The wonderful agility of both men and girls filled her with admiration. Among them all there were none to compare with Patty and Len who seemed to skim the floor like swallows

(To be concluded)

THE QUEENSLANDER
19TH. JANUARY 1924

Lost in her interest of the kaleidoscope panorama, Martie failed to notice that two men had entered the hall and were standing near the piano talking to Miss Bligh. One was Mr. Ware, the other a tall fresh faced young fellow, whose crisp brown hair was not brushed back in the American style, which most of the boys affected, but was dressed in the old-fashioned way, parted on one side, and who wore a white carnation in his button-hole.

Mark Treloar, the youngest of seven sons, had shown so decided a taste for mechanics that he had been taken from the dairy farm to the foundry in Bundamurra. Now at twenty five he was fit, so Ware asserted, to occupy the position of city engineer when he would vacate it.

Mark had not climbed so far on the ladder of success by holding up lamp posts or by frequenting bars; but his work and studies had not been barren of sport as sundry rowing, cricket and football lists of teams could show.

On the social side of things alone Mark had made no excursion and was as tongue tied and bashful at twenty five as he had been at fifteen. His chief was everything that Mark admired, so when Ware suggested that Mark should take dancing lessons, though more than dubious, he consented to think about the idea. Thinking about it, however made the advice seem nothing short of appalling.

Go to "Araluen", the fashionable gathering of those who fancied they formed the elite of the younger set! Meet terrifyingly up-to-date girls who would laugh at his raw ignorance! He begged to be excused. Ware insisted; pointed out the advantage of learning from the best teacher and the benefit it would be to make pleasant friendships, till, more to please him than any wish on his own part, Mark agreed to come.

Mark still boarded with motherly Mrs. Coomber, to whose care his father had confided him when he had begun work in the foundry. As was natural the kind woman was quite interested in the lessons. She brushed and pressed the dark serge suit for the occasion and when the young fellow was leaving she presented him, as the final touch of smartness, a white carnation for his buttonhole.

Mark was a bit doubtful about the flower. He was not accustomed to "sport" buttonholes, but Mrs. Coomber assured him it was the correct thing for a dance. "My half always wore a button'ole w'en 'e went hout to a darnce. All the toffs uster be speshul fond of a white carnation too."

Tentatively then, Mark allowed the finishing touch to be given and set out to meet Ware. He was detained for a while as some unexpected work had cropped up for the older man, and it was nearly nine when they set off.

Ware smiled inwardly as his humorous glance travelled over the shining new dancing pumps, the well pressed suit and finally the buttonhole. The charming fashion of wearing a flower in their coats seemed to have died out among the young bloods of this later day. He could remember that at Mark's age he would have felt that his appearance lacked something if his coat was bare of the single choice bloom. Oh Youth! Youth!

With a jerk Jim Ware pulled himself up to find that they were at the gates and a minute later Tessa was welcoming them both. After a few minutes conversation Tessa suggested that she should introduce him to another beginner like himself.

"Miss Martin comes from the bush though more recently than Mr. Ware tells me you have done. I'm sure you ought to have many things in common," and before Mark quite knew how it had happened he found himself walking along the verandah to be introduced to a strange young lady.

Martie was absorbed in watching Herbert who had contrived to tangle himself and his partner and it was with quite a start she heard herself addressed.

What was her absolute astonishment to find Miss Bligh waiting to introduce to her a good looking young man, just now wearing an expression of acute embarrassment and a white carnation in his button-hole!

There really was "Somebody." Would he shortly present her with the carnation to prove his identity? What would she do? What could she say? Before she could collect her scattered faculties, Miss Bligh had gone and the stranger had seated himself beside her. A stolen glance told her that Mr. Treloar had no immediate intention of doing anything. He looked very far from comfortable, but she decided that she preferred his diffidence to the alarming self assurance of the rest of the boys in the hall.

Presently he ventured to remark that it was a warm evening and Martie, equally flurried, assented, though, as a matter of fact, the night was rather on the cold side. With this exchange of sentiments the courage of both seemed exhausted and they stared in silence at the dancers.

As Mark's eye travelled round the room he noted that he was the only man in the room sporting a button-hole. With the super sensitiveness of youth Mark felt the modest flower gradually assume the proportions of a cabbage. Why oh why had he allowed Mrs. Coomber to make him look an ass? How could he rid himself of his foppish adornment? He wished the girl would rise and go away. Surely he was not supposed to ask her to try the outlandish gymnastics they seemed to be indulging in on the polished floor of the hall! Beads of perspiration rose on his forehead at the bare thought.

Presently the girl turned her head quite away and seemed absorbed in following the gyrations of a couple at the very end of the hall. Now was his chance. He would rid himself of his absurd decoration and feel less conspicuous.

Stealthily his hand moved up to his buttonhole. He managed to draw the blossom, with its piece of maidenhair fern, free. In another minute he would have stowed both in his pocket; but at the slight movement the provoking girl turned round and stared full in his face as he held the carnation suspended in mid air.

"Oh, thankyou!" cried the astonishing creature. "Thankyou. I just love carnations. They are granny's favourite flowers. You should see our garden at Noomdulla," then with a blush she took the flower from him and began luxuriously sniffing it.

To say that Mark was taken aback was to put his sensations mildly; but his relief at getting quit of the carnation was at least equal to his astonishment. For the first time he really looked at the girl. He saw that she was an uncommonly pretty one. Shy too. She seemed half afraid to meet his eyes. The thought gave him courage. Here was no self assured self sufficient creature who would look him up and down with cool appraising glances. She seemed indeed, more nervous than he was. He recalled Miss Bligh had told him that Miss Martin was a bush girl who was being trained as a nurse. He liked the way she had done her hair. It might not be so hard to enter into conversation with her; on the contrary it might be distinctly pleasant.

Before many minutes were over the two were chatting away like old friends. It was simply astonishing the number of things they seemed to have in common. Their reading appeared to have run along similar lines; their ignorance of the Terpsichorean art was yet another bond of sympathy. Before they realized it they were telling each other of their work; Martie confiding her nervousness over an approaching examination and Mark imparting more to her of his past history and his love of engineering than he had confessed to his own mother.

When Patty and Herbert found way back to the corner, they were introduced to Martie's new friend and all seemed to take an instant liking to one another.

At the next lesson when the lines were formed and instruction and practice began it seemed natural for Mark and Martie to glance at each other when anything amusing occurred. When the lesson was over the four took the homeward way together. On parting the boys arranged to call in company next Wednesday, thus establishing a precedent for the time of the lessons.

It was not only on Wednesday evenings, as time flew by, that Mark met little Martie; but it was the only one, and then merely because he came with Herbert Merivale, that he was permitted to wait outside the gates of St. Veronica.

At other times, so fearful was the probationer lest any of the staff gather an inkling of what was going on, their trysting place was the next corner where a big Moreton Bay fig shaded the end of the police barracks. That big fig, if it could speak, could unfold many a tale of meeting lovers.

It saw Mark place the ring on the small hand. It heard Mark's remonstrances because shy little, sly little Martie refused to wear the ring except when they were alone together.

It was not surprising, so well had the pair kept their secret, that it came as a shock to St. Veronica when it was learned that Martie had passed her examination with credit and that she was resigning to get married.

"So you've gone and caught the new city engineer! Still waters run deep," was Larry's characteristic remark.

"I did not catch him, for I never fished for him," said Martie sturdily.

"What about 'Somebody' and the white carnation?" asked Larry. Martie began to laugh in a queer, helpless way which she refused to explain.

Mark, to be sure, had been told the story of the carnation and declared that whatever their garden would miss, it would not be white carnations.

Granny, who was coming to live with them, knew the little comedy too. Both of them understood why the bridal bouquet was composed of these clove-scented white blooms and maidenhair. The nurses imagined it was not more than a curious coincidence.

THE COLLECTED PUBLISHED WORKS OF ISABEL GRANT
AT THE SIGN OF THE THERMOMETER
BACKGROUND TO THE PUBLICATION

As with every other story she wrote *At the sign of the thermometer* has a happy ending. However the greater part of this story is frankly maudlin. At fifty five Isabel is facing old age and the trials of a teenage daughter at the same time. Her only child was born into the very rapidly changing societal structure of the early 20th. Century. It was unfortunate for Isabel that she had such a difference of age with her child at this time in history. Isabel was brought up in the Victorian era to be compliant to and respectful of authority. By 1920 the social mores and the strict upbringing of the Victorian era were an anathema.

The story deals with the difference between a "modern girl neither bold nor shy – frankly casual" and an older female relative who "at the same age would have been more ceremonious." It seems likely that her characters spring from her pressing concerns at home. She has the heroine self sacrificing, self effacing and with utterances like "Forgive me Molly it is wrong of me to sadden your bright youth" frankly tedious.

The story uses much of her known history in the settings and shows her perceptions of herself so is very interesting for a family history researcher. Also historically interesting is the use of the terms like "an unprincipled scamp sent to Australia on remittance." "Remittance men" being the troublesome sons of wealthy or aristocratic families packed off to the furthest part of the Empire with a carefully dribbled remittance that would keep them from poverty but unable to return home.

The Queenslander was the weekly edition of *The Courier Mail* and started in 1866. Like every other weekly newspaper it was suffering from the competition of the Pictures and other women's' magazines. However it was still a popular read and did not stop publication until just before World War II.

AT THE SIGN OF THE THERMOMETER

III!.—DOWN THE LONG AVENUE.

By ISABEL GRANT,

Constance Ware, lying weary, open eyed, waiting for the dawn, in the pretty boarding-house bedroom which she shared with her niece, looked very different from the girl (for she was little more in spite of the responsible position which she held) that the nurses of St. Veronica a year ago, called matron. A sad and trying time Constance had had in interval since she had left the hospital to nurse her mother in whom the dreaded modern scourge of cancer had developed. After giving the best that was in her, for ten anxious months, to save the beloved life, the girl herself had been attacked by a low, weakening fever, from which she emerged a wreck of her former self.

There were few names better known and respected in the district than that of Ware. The grandparents, who were among the first pioneers, had a large family even for those days of numerous olive branches, their sons and daughters had married among the descendants of other pioneers so that in Bundamurra alone Constance had several namesake cousins, as well as many brothers and sisters. The family was a sincerely attached one, but friends sometimes said laughingly; that Constance, being the youngest, was the worst, for she put her

Mother in the place other girls kept for sweethearts, seeing that in spite of various good offers, she declined to accept any. They did not know, most of them with what reason, Constance clung to the tried, loyal love or that the attitude of smiling indifference to masculine attention had its roots in a cruel lesson on masculine perfidy, which the girl had received, when in her early teens. More than usually bright, pretty, and accomplished, Constance was a general favourite; and. no one was surprised when after a visit to the station of a squatter uncle, the girl returned engaged to a jackeroo, the Hon. Allan Gordon, youngest son of the Scotch Earl of Dunoon. Allan was some years older than Constance, dark, strikingly attractive in manner, and he did not attempt to hide his infatuation. When he appeared as a chosen lover on a visit to her home, Constance was considered singularly fortunate by all her friends except her old minister, who, in the curious way coincidences occur in real life, came from the same district in Scotland where the estates of the Gordon family lay, and who had an indistinct recollection of having read in a letter received a few years earlier, an account of secret marriage contracted by the Hon. Allan, who was said to be, despite good looks and charming manners an unprincipled scamp, and, for this reason had been sent to Australia on a remittance. Resolved to make sure, the doctor wrote home for proofs, which arrived a week before the wedding day. Unable to deny his guilt, the lover fled the country, while Constance went off for a visit to an aunt in Sydney, while the secret of the rupture was kept in the family. Six years passed, during which Constance, who had studied for the nursing profession, paid occasional visits home, till at his urgent request she agreed to accept Dr. Penfield's offer of the matronship at St. Veronica.

Returning thus to her native town, Constance went into society again and was as popular as ever, if not more so; for the beauty that her early girlhood had promised had now ripened, while beyond that she was in herself an interesting woman. Her attitude, however, towards masculine attentions was a baffling one. While she evidently enjoyed them she gave no encouragement to suitors. In fact, as she frankly admitted, she had "no time" to be bothered with men, beyond seeing that her nurses tended to them at St. Veronica; her mother was all the sweetheart she cared to have. To tell the truth, the girl at heart was afraid again to trust her happiness to a man's keeping. The old wound indeed, had healed, but, as a burnt child dreads the fire, so Constance Ware could never forget the humiliation of her first adventure. Her love for Allan Gordon might have been largely a young girl's romantic fancy, but his falsity had cut her to the quick, her natural young dignity had been outraged, her innocent faith destroyed and she was firmly of the resolve that never again would she put it in a man's power to hurt her as her perfidious handsome early lover had done. Her own innate wholesomeness and her mother's influence had prevented her nature from becoming warped like Larry's; and it was with genuine kindliness that she repressed in the bud any attempt of her many men friends to become lovers, but after the death of her dearly loved mother and the long illness which followed it Constance seemed a changed creature. Her old happy serenity was gone: nothing sufficed to rouse her out of her sad lassitude and it was only after the united persuasions of her brothers and sisters, now all comfortably married, that she could be induced to accompany her favourite niece, her namesake god-child, for a holiday to the Blue Mountains to see if fresh scenes and faces could wean her from her sorrow, and restore her health.

As Constance, this morning, waking long before daylight, tossed wearily on her pillow, she wondered, with a faint stirring of hope weather the of the boarding house, "Beulah," was an omen of good; whether here, indeed she might find renewed strength of mind and body.

The health-giving mountain air stole into the room, but she felt no desire to go out and see the beauty of hill or valley, or famous waterfall. All she asked was to be left alone, to lie quiet for ever, away from the world of busy happiness and women. The feeling, she knew, was chiefly physical, due to the long exhaustion of her powers in nursing, followed by the drain of her own illness. No doubt, in time, her bodily health would return, but her life was empty of all interest. Her mother had been its center, without her it had no meaning. She was not needed anywhere; her place in the hospital had been filled; fond as her sisters and brothers were of her, most of their thoughts were necessarily absorbed by their own personal affairs, their homes and families.

As her musings reached this stage the first ray of sunrise entering the room touched the sleeping face of the girl on the opposite bed, and showed the soft dusky hair, the heavy lashes, the smooth rounded cheeks, the sweet smiling mouth. Half bitterly Constance recalled that people declared the girl was her living image. Perhaps Molly, as they called her to avoid the confusion of names was not unlike in appearance to what she had been at the same age; but there was little similarity in natures. She had certainly not been the calmly self-possessed individual her niece was. Molly was essentially a modern girl. Neither bold nor shy, was good chums "cobbers," or "pals," as they phrased it, with her boyfriends; frankly casual, where Constance at the same age would have been more ceremonious. It was the way of the younger set, of course; quite right and proper, she supposed. Lying idly thus watching the girl, Constance smiled, for an old incident of her youth recalled itself, and she thought how very differently Molly – practical Molly – would have acted had she been in her case. It happened at a young folks' dance, and a certain red-haired young fellow, an engineer who had lately come to the town and had in his shy way paid her some attentions, was there. Harry Thurlow, that was his name, was sitting beside her chatting, for they had danced the last dance together. The next was announced, and

Harry remarked that a polka was his favourite. Whether he was going to summon up sufficient courage to ask her to try this also with him –a rather marked thing for those days – or not, she never discovered, for at this moment Billy Higson, son of the richest man in the place, a boy whose proprietary ways used to annoy her, came up in his bouncing manner and asked if she were engaged. Too diffident to reply in the affirmative, for Harry had not actually asked her, she allowed herself to be carried off, followed, or so she imagined, by the mute reproach of a pair of honest blue eyes. She did not see him again, for she left for the visit to the west, where she met Allan Gordon; but she heard that Harry, about the same time, had secured an engineer's position on a boat. Now Molly, in a case like this, would probably have told Billy that Harry and she had "half a mind" to try this dance and so have pleased the one admirer without offending the other.

"What in the world brought such a silly, old, forgotten incident to my mind?" She wondered, unable to keep from smiling at her thoughts.

At this moment the sunshine touched Molly's lashes, and the girl opened her eyes.

"Oh, what a glorious morning!" cried the girl, springing from the bed with the vigour of youth and perfect health. "How do you feel Auntie? You look better already. What say to a cold bath, a smart walk, and then a big breakfast?"

Constance shivered.

"Carry out your programme, Molly; but don't expect me to be too enterprising yet a while. To tell the truth" – in spite of herself, her lip quivered – "I don't feel like quitting my room. You have a good time, dear, and leave me to gather courage to meet the world again. Just now, all I ask is to be allowed to lie here and hide away from everything. I'm out of tune with life, I'm afraid."

Before she had finished speaking, a pair of warm arms were round her neck, soft lips were kidding her thin cheek, and a perfumed cloud of dark hair fell over the pillow. "Don't, don't dear, dear auntie! It would only grieve grandma to have you sorrow so hopelessly. For her sake, and for all of us who love you, try to get better, try to see that you have still something to live for."

"Forgive me, Molly; it is wrong of me to sadden your bright youth." The older woman with an effort threw off her mood of depression and, wiping her eyes, pointed out the pretty path between pine avenue. "See there, isn't that beautiful—the long sunlit avenue leading to the valley below where the mist is just beginning to rise? Do you remember an old song, Down the Long Avenue; I used to hear it as a girl, and I always pictured some such avenue as this, when I read in an old fairy tale of Prince Charming riding the long avenue to meet the Princess. Dear, dear, how far away those happy days seem!"

"Plenty more happy days to come, auntie. One would think to hear you talk you were nearer seventy than forty."

ISABEL GRANT

I suppose thirty-three seems near enough to the sere and yellow leaf to justify me in feeling my life story is ended," was the quiet reply; upon which Molly laughed, and declared she had read "the thirties" was a woman's most fascinating age.

Soon after the girl was up, and had had her cold shower, followed by a short walk. She took good care, however before she went for her own breakfast, that a dainty tray was carried to her aunt's room; and she felt rewarded when on returning, she found her lying on a couch by the window looking better and brighter. . She sat down beside her, and having a natural gift for mimicry, she entertained the invalid by an amusing description of her numerous fellow boarders. It was astonishing how much Molly's keen eyes had seen, how much her clever brain had recorded, and before Constance quite realised how it had happened she was laughing herself.

The plump man, who enjoyed his food, "with a staccato accent"; the serious spectacled tourists bent on improving their minds, even at meal time; the dark, vivacious woman, so evidently the "Merry Widow" type; the tall, reserved man with "something distinguished in his appearance," who seemed inclined to be shy, for though once or twice Molly had caught his eyes covertly on her, he had glanced away the moment she looked in his direction; the jolly, "real dinkum, - nice," boys and girls, on holiday bent, who had asked her to join in the tennis carried on at the fine courts Beulah boasted— Molly had them all reproduced so faithfully that Constance could almost see them. She would not, however, allow the young girl to spend the morning shut up with her, but insisted upon her joining the tennis players. With a good book, she was quite happy, she assured Molly; and at last, though unwillingly the girl went to join her young companions, coming back every now and then to see to her aunt's comfort or amuse her by telling how the play had gone.

So the days passed, and it was not till the fourth that Molly was able to coax her aunt to come downstairs, and go for a walk, along the pretty avenue which seemed to have captured her fancy. It was a beautiful afternoon, and Constance did not feel the exertion too much for her. She had, indeed been growing stronger every day, as the touch of colour, the slight filling out of the cheeks, the soft, yet clear lustre of the dark eyes attested. The air of fragility which still dung to her made her look younger than her years; though she only smiled sadly when Molly told her that they were being taken for sisters.

As Constance did not feel like trying the ascent without a rest, the two sat down on the rustic seat, thoughtfully placed at the end of the avenue. A moment later Molly said softly:

"Here comes my distinguished stranger, who hasn't yet made friends, though I fancy he'd like to. Now you're with me, it would be quite proper, wouldn't it?" she added teasingly.

"Hush, Molly,"" said her aunt sharply, for the man was but a few paces up the hill. "I hope you've been careful, seeing I was not able to chaperon you."

"Careful ? I've been Early Victorian discretion itself; but surely it is admissible to look up when one sees a Prince Charming coming down the long avenue?" said Molly wickedly, and smiled as she noted the pleased way the fellow boarder raised his hat. But. what was her astonishment when her aunt, who was evidently included in the salute, instead of giving the cold repressive glance Molly half expected, rose with a flush from her seat, and, extending her hand, cried in tones of unmistakable pleasure:

"Surely, it's never you, Mr. Thurlow.?"

"Well, of all the delightful things!" was the reply, which evinced equal joy. "To think of meeting you here! Now 1 understand the likeness in the young lady that puzzled me, so that I'm afraid she sometimes found me rude enough to stare at her. I didn't know you' had a younger sister. To tell the truth, I've never heard anything of the Wares since, just before I accepted the position at Buenos Aires, I saw in the paper you had married Billy Higson.

"I did not marry Billy. It was my cousin and namesake who did," said Constance, while Molly, quite forgotten by the two old friends, drew back, and. with a queer smile on her face, pretended to be searching for pine cones in the grass.

"Billy wanted you, I know," continued Thurlow.

"Did he?" was the indifferent answer. "Well, he soon consoled himself. But tell me about yourself."

"Surely you've not been so misguided as they tell me I have been, to remain single." "Just as misguided," said Thurlow laughing with a touch of constraint. "I'm too slow I'm afraid, too shy; never got over the old failing you see. I meant to come back to Bundamurra after I was through my time and passed my final, but somehow I didn't get up before I left for America, and it was only a year ago I came back, on being offered a specially tempting appointment in Sydney. This is my month on leave; but I was thinking, before I met you, of cutting it short, I've been here a week, and find it rather dull. I'm slow at making friends, as you may remember, and I fancy the other boarders think me a stiff old stick, but now I've been lucky enough to meet you I think I'll see the time out."

"That will be very nice," said Molly, coming up. "A gentleman in a party is one of the most useful things going; it will take a lot of trouble off my shoulders."

"Molly, Molly!" cried Constance reprovingly; but she seemed as pleased as the girl to add to the party. The Harry Thurlow she remembered had, been a lanky, shy, awkward boy; the man was evidently still somewhat diffident, but he had enormously improved in looks and manner. He was now distinguished-looking, and carried himself with the quiet self-confidence which told its own story of the man who had made good in life. A man's man, essentially, one who had travelled, had seen and done things which broaden the mental landscape, but, all the more attractive for that, little as he seemed to realise it, to women. Constance at first felt inclined to ask him whether there must have been telepathy in the fact that on walking the first morning at Beulah, her thoughts should have flown to the incident of the dance with Billy Higson; but on second thoughts she decided not to refer to the thing—it might create a false impression. She and Harry for the year he had been working in Bundamurra, had been good friends, no more on her side, at least, though perhaps had she not left for the station and met Allan, her dawning partiality might have turned to love. Now she felt she would prefer to meet him on the simple ground of old friendship, and to continue on the same plane.

So it came to pass that Thurlow, much to his gratification, became a member of the little party, and was no longer a solitary unit in the company of pleasure seekers. He and Molly formed stiff combination at tennis, which it seemed had been his chief relaxation abroad, while to Constance in her weakness, he was kindly thoughtful as a brother. As her strength came back, he arranged expeditions, taking all the care of each upon his own shoulders, and being ever solicitious that her energies should not be unduly taxed.

It was a happy time, the happiest, Constance told herself, that she had known since early girlhood. The colour came back to her cheeks, her eyes lost their shadows, and she could not but realise that it was natural enough that strangers should take Molly and her for sisters, as they continually did.

But in the third week an incident occurred which spoilt for Constance all pleasure in the expeditions. Their little company of three had joined another party of tourists on a visit to Leura Falls, and the older woman, feeling it unwise to attempt the interminable steps, stopped not far from the top in a little ferny hollow to await the return of the more adventurous spirits, among whom were Harry and Molly. The latter were late ascending, and Constance waited, a strange ache in her heart, for it was seldom she was left so long alone, and the others had all come back some time before. At last she caught sight of the truants. Molly's sparkling face was raised to Thurlow's; he was bending down in an attitude which was suggestively loverlike. and, as their laughing voices, ringing with what seemed to her jealous ears such mutual happiness came up the slope, the listener woke, in the fierce sudden pang that rent her heart, to a realisation of the cruel truth that she, who believed herself immune from love, had given her all to a man's keeping. It was no use trying to deceive herself; she loved Harry Thurlow with all the fervour of a nature which did not love lightly.

As soon as they saw her, the pair hurried up, all apologies for keeping her waiting, through their desire to go down to the last step. Unconscious Molly was eager in her inquiries about her aunt, who submitted to her pretty petting only by putting the strongest restraint on herself. She almost felt as if she hated the girl for her fresh young charm, which, though all unconsciously had stolen the affections of the only man whom she since the days of her bitter disillusionment, had felt she could trust. What an irony of Fate it was that one who might have been her lover in the old. days, had she given him the least encouragement, should now have won her love but bestowed his elsewhere! She had often met some such situation in fiction, but that did not render it any the less hard to endure when it came to herself.

Pleading a headache she retired early and, while there floated up to her room . the sound of Molly's clear voice in the usual concert organised by the musical set among the boarders, she fought a battle with herself. When the girl, flushed and happy, came up to the bed-room, Constance had won the victory and could return the good-night kiss without bitterness. What more natural than that Harry should have been attracted by such sweet, fresh, innocent charm? As natural as that Thurlow, the distinguished, travelled, kindly man should have captured a young girl's romantic fancy. As for attempting to trade upon the old friendliness, or in the slightest degree, seeking to enter into competition with Molly, to regain what she believed she had once possessed—Harry's love—the idea was repugnant to her. Even more than in her girlhood, her innate sense of dignity demanded that she should be the pursued, not the pursuer. Therefore for the remainder of the time, without doing it in any marked degree, Constance withdrew into herself, and left the two alone.

Whether Harry resented this, or was relieved by it, she could not tell. He was not the masterful type. The Hon. Allan, when he wanted to secure her society, simply overruled every objection, and, willy-nilly, contrived to make her inclination yield to his ardent persuasion. Harry, on the contrary, quietly accepted her decisions, and took Molly on many expedition when she refused to make one of the large parties that the boarders, now like a big family group, got up. True, he was as tenderly solicitous as ever for her comfort and never left her at Beulah without seeing that she was supplied with plenty of good books. It was seldom, too, he returned without bringing her some momento of his outing. But in spite of all his kindness, it cost Constance many a pang to note that he seemed content with Molly as a companion, and took her excuses as a matter of course.

It was now nearly the end of the holiday, and one afternoon, left, as so often happened now, alone, Constance's long constraint was growing intolerable. She could no longer pretend to be interested in the novel whose pages she so idly turned. Nature, long stifled in her woman's heart, was exacting payment with usury. In spite of her pride, in spite of her resolution, the numb aching pain of unreturned love, of unavailing regret, was too much to be borne longer without relief. She could not endure to sit quietly there and pretend to be absorbed in the empty pages. She must get out and fight down this climbing sorrow. A long solitary walk might give her strength, a chance to get the better of the weakness that was now overcoming her.

The sun was drawing to the western horizon when she came to the foot of the avenue and sat down to rest at the spot where she and Molly had first spoken to Harry. The slanting rays of the sun filtering through the network of branches made the same flickering car-. pet of shade and shine that had caught her eye on the morning she had wakened in Beulah, and her thoughts had so curiously turned to her old friend. And now, even with the recollection, she saw the tall spare figure, so instinct with life and virility, coming down the path— "down the long avenue" she had told Molly the old childish fancy of the Princess waiting while Prince Charming rode down the long avenue to meet her. It was again the irony of fate—for it seemed to her there was something new and-purposeful in the man's very gait—if Harry was coming to tell her, as Molly's chaperon, that the girl had accepted him.

Harry's face did indeed look paler, his voice was hardly steady, as he greeted her, and stammered something about Molly saying since they had not found her at Beulah when they returned from Medlow, the most likely spot was her favourite pine avenue.

Constance's heart gave a sudden throb and seemed to stop beating for a moment then went on with dull, heavy thuds, as she said, with outward composure:

"Was there something you wanted to tell me?" Inwardly she was saying to herself "I know, only too well, what it is. Out with it, before I betray myself."

"Yes, there's something"—he hesitated, and flushed—"but I'm such a slow, tongue-tied chap. I find it hard to say all I want to. That was always my fault, as you may remember. Too slow! Why, I can look back and see many a thing I lost when a smarter chap would have got it. Do you know it comes back to me now how, through that very reason, I let Billy Higson do me out of a certain second dance with you long ago. I don't suppose you remember, though."

"I remember," said Constance quietly, wondering how much longer the man would take in coming to the point, and telling her that Molly had accepted him. He did not look exactly the happy lover, but perhaps he was dreading the interview with her. Had he guessed even remotely, that she had learned to care for him? Was he attempting to make some excuse to her for transferring his old allegiance? The bare suggestion was whip to her pride. She must make him understand that she did not consider herself to have a shadow of claim upon him, that, indeed, she quite understood and approved of his love for Molly.

"I'm sorry I kept you both waiting, but I can guess what you are going to tell me. Molly sent you to look for me, didn't she?"

"She didn't exactly send me, though she said if I went down the long avenue I'd be likely to find you." Constance winced; the old phrase had lost its music in her ears, but not all her pride could force her to meet the man's eyes; her face was pale and set in cold lines of endurance, though her lips smiled as she said, trying to be cordial:

"Molly is the dearest girl I wish you both every happiness."

"Both!" stammered Thurlow. "Molly and I, do you mean? We're 'good pals', as she calls it, but surely you know, you must know that her attraction for me has been only her likeness to you, her affection for you. It was she who told me, in spite of the way you've been snubbing me of late, declining to join us, and so forth, that there might be hope for me. She suggested from the start how things were with me. What I said about taking the American billet when I thought Billy Higson had been the lucky man was enough for, quick-sighted Molly." The man stopped his headlong speech, for emotion had choked him. The pent-up love of all the long years was too impassioned for utterance.

"Molly took a great deal upon herself" began Constance, but her eyes, and her fluttering breath, betrayed her.

Shy and backward Harry Thurlow might be, but he was no fool; and the moment he realised that his faithful love was returned, he caught the girl in his arms, masterful as ever the Hon. Allan had been.

An hour later, from their secluded rustic seat under the big pine, the pair caught sight of a figure in white coming down the path.

"Bless you, my children!" cried Molly saucily, "You're nothing but a. couple of Babes in the Wood, compared to a worldly-wise woman like me. Why, I engineered the whole affair, saw it from the very start, made auntie jealous by appropriating you, 'pal o' mine,' and finally sent Prince Charming down the long avenue to meet the Princess, for I knew that was the secret magic charm to get her consent!"

"Respect the grey hairs of your uncle," cried Harry, all his old shyness apparently gone for ever.

"Grey hairs—where are they?" laughed the girl. "Your hair is red—quite the fashionable colour just now. I hope you haven't a temper; most red-haired folks have. I pity poor auntie." but there was nothing in Constance's radiant face to call pity, and Molly smiled slyly as she hurried on ahead.

ISABEL GRANT

THE BRONTE FAMILY.

A PAPER BY MISS GRANT.

Read before the Central Queensland Teachers' Association and reprinted, for private circulation, from "The Morning Bulletin" at the request of the Association.

Rockhampton, Queensland:
PRINTED AT "THE MORNING BULLETIN" OFFICE, EAST STREET.
1908.

THE COLLECTED PUBLISHED WORKS OF ISABEL GRANT

THE BRONTE FAMILY.

In one year ten thousand tourists visited the small parish of Haworth, which lies on the confines of a moor in the West Riding of Yorkshire, England. There is little in the monotonous, sombre-hued scenery of Haworth, in its bare stone houses, its great ugly mills to attract the sightseer. It was but the charm of the Bronte name that had brought these strangers from different parts of the globe to this insignificant village, to wander through the poor parsonage garden, to gaze over the bleak, wide-spreading moor, to visit the old church, to stand with quiet reverent eyes before a mouldering tombstone, and read the names engraved there? Little, while they lived their brief, strenuous, troubled lives, did the quiet sleepers below dream, that sixty years after their death, the literary world would be still writing about, still speculating on, still fascinated by the life story of the Bronte family.

Though Yorkshire is proud to lay claim to these writers, it obtained that honour only through adoption, when in 1820 Patrick Bronte, the newly-appointed incumbent of the parish of Haworth, brought to the plain stone parsonage, his delicate wife and six young children, the eldest of whom was not yet seven. As one might expect, the parents of the Brontes were not commonplace people; the tenacity of purpose, the cool reasoning powers and restrained Celtic fire, the tragic and consuming passion of resentment against life's unequal handicap, came to the children; by direct inheritance. The father's protest against life was a dumb one, he bequeathed what he could not utter. Patrick Bronte was a tall, stately man with a fine, well-set head, and a keen, dark face. Even in extreme old age, he was a remarkable looking man; in youth he had been considered very handsome, and had made many conquests. Born in Ahaderg, County Down, Ireland, Patrick had nine brothers and sisters with whom to share the meagre fare of the home. At sixteen the ambitious boy began to teach school in his native village; succeeding at this, he was able to go to Cambridge and obtain his degrees there. He was appointed Curate at Withersfield, thence he went to Deus-bury, where a tragic love affair brought his residence to an abrupt close. His next curacy was Hartshead, where he met, fell in love with, and married Maria Bramwell, daughter of a prosperous Penzance merchant.

In person, Maria was small and slender. Without actual prettiness, she had a sweet, refined, and engaging appearance. A few of her letters, which have been preserved, show her to have possessed the literary gift. She is said to have been most closely resembled in her children by Charlotte, the third daughter. When the family removed to Haworth, the poor mother's health was even then, though none knew it, failing with an internal cancer, and in the cold cheerless north —so different from the milder climate to which she had been accustomed—she drooped daily. Little more than a year passed by, and the children were motherless.

The sister-in-law came to take charge of the desolate household. Miss Bramwell was a good, conscientious woman, and anxious to do her best, but she failed to understand her charges. Few, indeed, could have understood them, for they were strange children, with quaint old-fashioned manners, and reserved self-effacing natures. They were quiet and obedient, and gave no trouble. Already they had learned to look after themselves, to keep out of the way, to make, with scanty materials, their own pleasure. Hand in hand, with Maria the eldest—a little mother at seven—in charge of them, they wandered out to the moors that they grew to love with a livelong passion ; or they busied themselves with queer literary pursuits in the little room that from the first was called the "children's study."—never the nursery, though the eldest student was little more than a baby in years. Their father seldom appeared among them, his health necessitating careful dieting, he dined alone; he seems, in fact, to have had little to do with their bringing up. Mr. Bronte, "the pistol firing ogre" as some writers have unjustly termed him, has been accused of selfishness and indifference towards his children; this, however, does not appear to be altogether true, for he won their respect and affection. But it is clear he was self-absorbed to a degree that made him almost a stranger to his children, and deepened in them the reserve that was partly, no doubt, their natural inheritance. Helstone, the grim taciturn rector in "Shirley" is considered by many to be a portrait of Mr. Bronte, and, though Charlotte declared another clergyman was the original of the character, it must be admitted that the description is too curiously applicable, and the character drawing is too cleverly done to be a haphazard sketch.

No common children truly, were these amazing Bronte youngsters who took to literature almost from their cradles—as naturally indeed as a sea-bird takes to the water. "Maria" (at seven) says a biographer, "would shut herself up in the 'children's study' with a newspaper, and be able to tell one everything when she came out, debates in Parliament "(poor Maria!)" and I don't know what not."

It seems hard to credit that this could be true of a child of such tender years; but her father says that long before she died, at the age of eleven, he could converse with her on any of the leading topics of the day with as much pleasure as with a grown-up person. If this child's early promise were sustained, as in the case of the younger sisters by ultimate, or even partial fulfillment, what has the world not lost in the premature death of Maria Bronte?

In 1823, a school for clergymen's daughters was established at Cowan Bridge, a small hamlet on the coach road between Leeds and Kendall. Thither, in 1824, Mr. Bronte sent the two elder children, Maria and Elizabeth, to be followed, later on in the year, by Charlotte and Emily. Cowan Bridge, identified as the Lowood of "Jane Eyre" was an unfortunate choice for the delicate, home-loving girls. Charlotte Bronte's description of the school may be somewhat coloured by her indignation against the place, and the harsh system that cost the lives of her two sisters; but it is probably substantially correct, for a child's memory, where a deep impression has been burnt in, is generally to be trusted. If she had known that Lowood would have been so immediately recognised as Cowan Bridge, Charlotte afterwards acknowledged to a friend that she would not have written so freely.

"Helen Burns," says Mrs. Gaskell in her biography, "is as exact a transcript of Maria Bramwell as Charlotte's wonderful power of reproducing character could give. Her heart, to the latest day on which we met, still beat with unavailing indignation at the worrying and cruelty to which her gentle, patient sister was subjected."

The school was in an unhealthy, foggy situation, the compulsory walk to the distant church was exposed and cold, the food was prepared in neither a cleanly nor a nourishing way, and it was no wonder that, when typhus fever attacked the school, the ill-fed pupils went down to it. Though none of the Brontes took the fever, the causes which induced the epidemic were to blame for the deaths of the two elder girls.

Charlotte and Emily, recalled in the term following their sisters' deaths, now pursued their Studies in their own home under the superintendence of their aunt. Miss Bramwell taught them her own small accomplishments; but she did more than this, she made each of the girls an expert needlewoman, and an efficient cook and housekeeper. These years at home were the brightest and happiest in the children's lives.

The days were filled with useful household labour or with study; but when the evenings drew on, the time was given to the children for themselves, and they employed it in true Bronte fashion. Safe from interruption, or reproof, in their stronghold, the "children's study," they wrote, acted plays, edited magazines, issued romances, poems, and essays, without number, held spirited discussions on the politics of the day, or argued hotly over their favourite historical heroes. Charlotte's was Wellington; Emily's Napoleon; Anne's Hannibal, and Bramwell's Caesar—and what unchildish incursions into the world of history, does not this youthful choice imply? Bramwell, the idolised brother, took no small part in all this stir of busy intellectual life. Miss Bramwell, who was inclined to be somewhat strict and severe with the girls, had always an excuse for her favourite Bramwell, whose manners had none of the shyness of his sisters, but were characterised by the frank geniality of his Irish blood, and a kind of natural gallantry.

ISABEL GRANT

Mr. Bronte did not send his son to school, as he believed himself capable of being his tutor, and good schools cost money. Bramwell was a quick and brilliant pupil, as intent on learning as his father was in imparting instruction. Lessons were never a task to him; but Mr. Bronte did not know that when the hours of study were over, and while the girls were busy over their household duties, Bramwell stole away and mingled with the village boys in amusements— innocent enough at the first—that led finally to his undoing. Bramwell's remarkable powers of conversation and entertainment grew to be a matter of importance to the landlord of "The Black Bull," when a chance traveler felt dull or solitary over his liquor; but of this no hint was allowed to reach the parsonage, and in those happy early days Bramwell seemed everything that partial affection could desire. The dark tragedy of the future was as yet hidden behind the kindly curtain of the years, and Bramwell, the affectionate, merry boy, with his power of winning love, his impetuous and interesting personality, was the hope of the household, his sisters' pride and joy, the centre of all their fondest hopes. Little did they dream that he would be their anguish, their heartbreak in the years to come, that with all his magnificent promises blasted, he should sink into a drunkard's grave.

But that sad future was mercifully held from them. The shadow of the past sorrow was lifted, for childish hearts are buoyant; and the grey old parsonage was alive with the ardent young life within its walls. The rain might sweep across the open moors, driving in fierce gusts against the bleak house, sweeping over the tombstones that crowded up almost to the parsonage windows, the snow might cover the whole outside world in a freezing mantle of whiteness, the sleet might come stinging to the close shut doors; but within the walls was warmth, and hope, and budding promise, and the dreaming of young dreams.

As they gather round the fire—often their only light—in the "children's study," let us conjure up a picture of that eager youthful group. In the firelight glow we see Charlotte's slight, fragile figure, her soft, thick, brown hair, her wonderful eyes—the only strictly beautiful feature in her pale sensitive face. Wonderful eyes indeed, they must have been! Mrs. Gaskell tells us "their visual expression was a quiet listening intelligence, till now and then on some just occasion for interest or wholesome indignation, a light would shine out, as if some spiritual lamp had been kindled behind those expressive orbs."

A sudden blaze of the firelight lights up Bramwell's red head, his massive forehead, his fine well-cut features, his handsome, intellectual face; but it shows too, lines of weakness in the beautifully-shaped mouth, weakness also in the slightly retreating chin. But the face is very attractive, it is instinct with vitality, and promise, and the gay confidence of youth. Emily draws back into the shadows. A strange reserved nature belongs to this girl. She does not resemble either Charlotte or Bramwell in appearance; taller and more strongly built than they, she possesses more actual beauty, but less simple human charm. Indeed, she seems a being from an older world, who has strayed into this one by mischance. "A daughter of the Titans'," she has been termed, and truly there is something primitive, almost pagan, about Emily. In "Shirley," that passionate idealisation of the sister who, she says, was "dearer than life itself," Charlotte draws a picture of Emily. "Pantheress! Beautiful forest born! Wily, tameless, peerless nature! . . How evanescent, fugitive, fitful, she looks; slim and swift as a northern streamer! with her noiseless step, her pale cheek, her eye full of night and lightning . spirit-like, a thing made of an element! The child of a breeze and a flame, the daughter of ray and of raindrop! A thing never to be overtaken arrested or fixed!"

"Emily," says Mr. Heger, "had a, head for logic, a capability of argument unusual in a man, rare indeed in a woman. She should have been a man, a great navigator, a great historian, so keen were her powers of analysis, so vivid her touch in reconstructing the past." Liberty was the breath of Emily's nostrils; a strong, indomitable, incomprehensible character was hidden in this slight girlish body. She loved the moors with so passionate a fervour that she pined and sickened away from them. She was peculiarly fond of animals, indeed, Charlotte says "Emily never showed a regard for any human creature, all her love was reserved for animals."

Mrs. Gaskell tells a story which at once illustrates Emily's love for animals, and her masculine strength and doggedness of will. The dog "Tartar" mentioned in "Shirley" was a portrait of "Keeper," a savage bull dog, Emily's especial favourite, and shadow. "Keeper's household fault," says Mrs. Gaskell, "was this. He loved to steal upstairs and stretch his square tawny limbs on the comfortable beds, covered with delicate white counterpanes. But the cleanliness of the parsonage was perfect, and this habit of Keeper's was so objectionable, that Emily, in reply to Tabby's remonstrance's, declared that if he were found again transgressing, she herself, in defiance of warning and his well-known ferocity of nature, would beat him so severely that he would never offend again. In the gathering dusk of an autumn evening Tabby came half triumphantly, half tremblingly, but in great wrath, to say that Keeper was lying on the best bed in drowsy voluptuousness. Charlotte saw Emily's whitening face and set mouth, but dared not speak to interfere. No one dared when Emily's eyes glowed in that manner out of the paleness of her face, and when her lips were compressed into stone. She went upstairs and Tabby and Charlotte stood in the gloomy passage below, full of the dark shadows of the coming night. Downstairs came Emily, dragging after her the unwilling Keeper, his hind legs set in a heavy attitude of resistance, held by the "scruff of his neck," but growling low and savagely all the time. The watchers would fain have spoken; but durst not, for fear of taking off Emily's attention, and causing her for a moment to avert her head from the enraged brute..

She let him go, planted in a dark corner at the bottom of the stairs ; no time was there to fetch stick or rod, for fear of the strangling clutch on her throat—her bare clenched fist struck against his fierce red eyes, before he had time to make his spring, and in the language of the turf, she "punished" him till his eyes swelled up, and the half-blind half-stupefied beast was led to his accustomed lair to have his swollen head fomented and cared for by the very Emily herself.

The generous dog owed her no grudge, he loved her dearly ever after. He walked first among the mourners to her funeral, he moaned for nights at the door of her empty room, and never, so to speak, rejoiced dog-fashion, after her death. Let us somehow hope, in half Indian creed, that he follows Emily now, and when he rests, sleeps on some soft white bed of dreams, unpunished when he wakes to the life of the land of shadows.

Some verses which she wrote will give us another glimpse of this austere, baffling, self-sufficing nature :—

"Riches I hold in light esteem,
And love I laugh to scorn;
The lust of fame was but a dream,
That vanished with the morn.
And if I pray, the only prayer,
That moves my lips for me,
Is 'Leave the heart that now I bear,
And give me liberty.'
Yes! As my swift days near their goal 'Tis all that I implore;
In life and death a shameless soul With courage to endure."

Verily it was no ordinary soul that belonged to this poet maiden of the wide Yorkshire moors, but a virile, unconquerable thing. She has been well termed the Sphinx of Literature, the Wonderful Vestal icy pure as Artemis.

But, leaving this curiously fascinating character, and returning to our fireside picture, we can see now the youngest of the four, the tenderly cared-for, much beloved little one. Anne's soft, sweet face discloses little of the genius so plainly to be read in the faces of the others ; yet power, too, though of a less striking type, shows in her tender timid face. Beside the brilliant lustre of her sister's intellects, Anne's milder radiance shines less brightly, but there is strength and sweetness, and a shy grace about the gentle, ill-fated girl. Can we not almost see the four young faces now, lit with the boundless enthusiasm of youth as they confide in each other their hopes and ambitions for the future?

The eager talk by the fireside was occasionally interrupted, we are told, by the sharp tongue of Tabby, the rawboned Yorkshire woman who served the family with such life-long devotion, and whose energetic figure in the quaint North Country costume must have added piquancy to the parsonage picture. If Tabby found fault, however, it was often but to hide her inordinate pride in her nurslings, for no one else dare decry them in her sturdy presence.

This happy home-life was broken in 1831 by the girls being sent to school at Roe Head. Miss Wilson, the Principal, became a firm friend of Charlotte's, and was her chief adviser in after years. It was while visiting another school friend that Charlotte saw the scenes afterwards described with such faithfulness in "Shirley." A busy year or two of study followed, but Emily, who fretted into actual sickness in her exile from her beloved moors, was recalled home, while Charlotte remained at Roe Head as Governess-pupil. In spite of Miss Wooler's kindness, and her own firm determination to continue in her work, Charlotte was at length obliged by ill-health to follow Emily to Haworth. Unable to understand children, she found the drudgery of teaching unsupportable. But nevertheless she abandoned her life at Roe Head with great reluctance.

Soon after Charlotte's return, she and her brother sent some of their poems with letters requesting advice to Southey and Wordsworth, The answers, when they came, were not encouraging, it was plain neither of the poets thought the young writers would be well advised in following literature.

Now however, Bramwell was seized with the idea of being an artist, and was anxious to obtain academy training in London, perhaps, too, he wished to get away from the restraints of the home, into the freer life of a great city. An art training meant money, and of that there was little to spare in the parsonage: but in order to help her brother, Charlotte volunteered as a governess, and the boy was sent to the academy. This year Charlotte received and refused an offer of marriage—the first of four that were destined to be laid before her. The suitor, according to some biographers, was the original of St. John, in "Jane Eyre." Charlotte respected, and admired, but did not love him. Still the stress of hard times was felt in the parsonage, and as Emily so plainly could not bear transplanting, Anne resolved to adopt the career of a governess also, and so lessen the burden on her father's shoulders.

Of all positions, that of governess was least suited to such dispositions as the Brontes. The semi-servitude of the life, the anomalousness of the position were unbearable galling to their independent natures. A governess, like the bat in "Æsop's Fables," hovers between two worlds, and belongs to neither. The Bronte girls realised with Dante, "how hard a thing it is to climb other people's stairs." Charlotte says somewhat bitterly "I used to think that I should like to be in the stir of grand folks' society, but I have had enough of it; it is dreary work to look on and listen." How deeply, the iron had entered into her soul, every one of her books testify. "Jane Eyre" and " Lucy Snow" reveal how inexpressibly distasteful was the life to her, while "Agnes Grey" tells how Anne too re-belled in heart against it. The whole training of the girls, their very natures, in. fact, unfitted them for the position of governesses. After a few years' trial of the life. Charlotte and Anne found they must give it up, if they valued their health. The prospects of the family looked very dark. Bramwell had returned to Haworth, having failed to make any headway as an artist, and though he became a railway booking clerk, his salary was very small. Mr. Bronte's health began to fail, and it was plain something needed to be done to relieve the strain on the home resources.

ISABEL GRANT

The idea, of keeping a private school where the three girls could work together seemed to promise a little hope. Miss Wooler, of Roe. Head, being consulted, wrote to them and proposed, as she was retiring from teaching, to resign her school into their hands. This seemed a solution of their difficulties: but on considering the matter, the girls recognised that to carry on the school in the same manner as Miss Wooler had done, it was imperative that they should acquire some further accomplishments, and to do this they must study on the Continent.

Their aunt being persuaded to embark one hundred pounds of her savings in the education scheme, Charlotte and Emily entered as pupils Madame Heger's Pensionnat in the Rue de Isabelle, Brussels. In spite of their shyness and insular reserve, the girls enjoyed their stay in Brussels. Emily indeed sighed for her moors; but her strong will and her determination to acquire those needed accomplishments conquered her home sick-ness and nerved her to endure her exile. But the foreign studies were brought to a close before the end of the year by the sudden death of their aunt. They hurried back to Haworth, bringing with them an offer from M. Heger to their. father that one, or both, should return to the pensionnat as governess pupil. Impelled by her irresistible desire for study, yet feeling that her duty required her to remain in the home, now darkened by the loss of the aunt, by the fear of Mr. Bronte's failing health, and the unsatisfactory conduct of Bramwell, Charlotte, though with many misgivings, returned to Brussels and remained there for two years.

This Brussels life she has portrayed with curious fidelity in "Villette," and "'Lucy Snow" is undoubtedly but a portrait of the authoress herself, "Paul Emanuel" and "Madame Beck" of that novel have been identified as Monsieur and Madame Heger, and therefore some critics have imagined that "Lucy Snow" was in love with "Paul Emanuel," it must necessarily follow that Charlotte was infatuated with her instructor.

No doubt Charlotte must have felt the attraction of a character in affinity with her own, must have appreciated the contact of a mind she could reverence and respect. Perhaps, too, she may have wondered at times over the curious adjustments of life which could give to a selfish, narrow-minded, inquisitive, treacherous woman like Madame Beck, the love of a noble, intellectual man, and offer to herself but the love of commonplace men; yet that the romance of "Villette" is not the story of Charlotte's own life, her womanly and innate reticence and modesty render impossible.

When in 1884 Charlotte returned to Haworth, it was to make all arrangements for beginning the new school. Owing to their father's precarious health, the girls gave up the idea of Roe Head, and decided to teach in the parsonage, so that they might remain with him. Additions were made to the building, friends promised help and interest; everything seemed favourable; but after waiting some time and no pupils appearing, they abandoned the undertaking, reluctantly, but decisively.

One day, about this time, Charlotte accidentally came across a collection of Emily's poems, and on examining them, she perceived them to be, as she says in the preface to "Wuthering Heights condensed, "terse, vigorous, genuine." To my ear they had a peculiar music, wild, melancholy, elevating. It took hours," she continues, "to reconcile Emily to the discovery I had made, and days to persuade her that such poems merited publication."

Seeing that the discovery had been made, Anne now quietly produced some verses that she had written ; Charlotte brought out hers ; and the sisters, collecting the best of their poems, sent them to a London publisher. On remitting £31 10s., Messrs. Smith, Elder, and Co., agreed to issue the poems of Currer, Ellis, and Acton Bell, for such were the names the girls had chosen. Reluctant to assume admittedly masculine names, yet anxious that their sex should remain a secret, they took the midway course of adopting those which might be either masculine or feminine. The poems, which were supposed to be the work of three brothers, attracted little attention. The Athenaeum, in whose verdict Charlotte heartily coincided, awarded the palm of originality to Ellis Bell.

The sisters saw that there was no money to be made out of poetry ; and money they must manage to make, or else return to the hateful governessing. They could not remain at home a burden, on their father. Moreover, his health was growing so uncertain, that they knew they ought to be prepared to rely on themselves. It looked as if they must fall back on governessing, but they resolved to make a gallant fight for their independence before they gave in. Undismayed by the meagre results of their first venture on the sea of literature, they pluckily prepared for another attempt. They set to work, each on a novel. Charlotte wrote the "Professor," Emily "Wuthering Heights," and Anne "Agnes Grey."

A minister's household, especially in a poor parish, is no idle one, and the girls had not much spare time. During the day they attended to their several duties, and only wrote when these had been faithfully discharged; but when night came on they gathered as of old in the "children's study." There they read over what had been written during the day, and discussed, compared, and criticised to their heart's content.

It was to these busy, yet happy days, that poor Charlotte looked back with such bitter regret and longing when her comrades had left her. In the preface to "Shirley" out of the depths of her loneliness, she writes: "The two human beings who understood me best, and whom I understood, are gone. I have some that love me yet, and whom I love, without expecting, or having a right to expect, that they shall understand me."

The novels were written and sent to London. Many a weary journey they made before they met with a publisher. Finally "Wuthering Heights" and "Agnes Grey" were accepted, while intimation was sent to Currer Bell that a work in three volumes from his pen might be considered. Mr. Smith, of Smith, Elder, and Co., publishers, mentions as curiously illustrative alike of Charlotte's name, simplicity and blunt honesty, that the "Professor," when it reached his office, had on its brown paper cover the addresses of all the publishers to whom it had been previously sent. The addresses were not obliterated, but merely scored through, so that Smith at once perceived the names of the houses to which the unlucky parcel had gone without success.

While the girls were thus bravely daring Fortune, Bramwell, who in the meantime had lost his position in the railway, now returned to the home. The sisters wondered at the indefinable change that had come over their beloved brother, the transformation of the high-spirited, ambitious boy into the moody, dissatisfied, irritable man; but their love as yet, and their ignorance of the world blinded their eyes, and they still hoped great things from Bramwell.

After a short stay at home, Bramwell was given another chance, he secured the position of tutor in the same family that Anne had been governess; but before long he was sent home in disgrace, so deep, that his father and sisters dared not question its extent. As day by day he lounged about the parsonage, or sought for distraction his boon companions in the village, they hid their anguish from one another, and tried to believe that the unfortunate boy would yet retrieve himself. These were dark days at Haworth, and a darker shadow fell when Mr. Bronte was threatened with blindness. Cataract attacked his eyes, and his only chance lay in an operation.

Charlotte accompanied him to Manchester, where the operation was to be performed. It was when in attendance upon her father, while yet smarting under the non-success of her first novel, while filled with anxious forebodings over her brother, and the future of the household should Mr. Bronte not regain his sight, that the brave girl began "Jane Eyre". Charlotte had once told her sisters that they were wrong—even morally wrong—-in making their heroines beautiful, as a matter of course. They replied that it was impossible to make a heroine interesting on any other terms.

"I will prove to you," she said, "that you are wrong. I will show you a heroine as small and plain as myself, who shall be as interesting as any of yours. Hence 'Jane Eyre,'" she said, in telling the anecdote, "but she is not myself further than that."

"Jane Eyre" was at once accepted by the publisher; it was a sudden and marvellous success. Written almost at white heat, it swept like a flame through the reading world. It was translated into most of the European languages, and placed upon the stage in many lands.

Lewes—the foremost critic of the day— gave it unstinted praise. "Almost all," he writes, "that we require in a novelist is there, perception of character, and power of delineating it, picturesqueness, passion, and knowledge of life" The intensest curiosity was everywhere felt, as to the identity of the writer, but the secret was jealously kept to the home. Emily and

Anne, now that the book had proved such a success, urged Charlotte to tell their father about it

It says much for Mr. Bronte's unsympathetic isolation that he should have remained so long unaware of the ferment of literary activity that had been going on around him. But Mr. Bronte, though no doubt an affectionate parent at heart, was too absorbed in his own concerns ever to mingle freely in the home life of his children.

Charlotte at last yielded to her sisters' solicitation, and agreed to break to him the great news. "Papa, I've been writing a book."

"Have you, my dear?"

"Yes, and I want you to read it."

"I'm afraid it will try my eyes too much." (Though the operation had been successful, Mr. Bronte was cautioned to be careful with his eyes.)

"But it is not in manuscript; it is printed."

"My dear, you've never thought of the expense it will be. It will almost sure to be a loss, for how can you get a book sold? No one knows your name!"

"But, papa, I don't think it will be a loss; no more will you if you will just let me read you a review or two, and tell you all about it."

"So," continues Mrs. Gaskell, "she sat down and read some of the reviews to her father, and then, giving him the copy of "Jane Eyre" she had intended for him, she left him to read it.

"When he came in to tea he said 'Girls, do you know Charlotte has been writing a book, and it is much better than likely.'"

Stern old Stoic! Seeking to hide his pride in his wonderful child! It is said that after his death it was found that he had collected all the criticisms he could obtain about his daughters' books, dated them, and kept them for his own private reading.

The mistake, wilful or otherwise, of an American publisher in advertising the forthcoming edition of Anne's book "The Tenant of Wildfell Hall," as by the author of "Jane Eyre," led to Charlotte and Anne deciding to go to London to disabuse the mind of Charlotte's publishers, or the "Bells" having any complicity in the error, and also to prove to them that there were really two writers, and not one. For a rumour was circulated that these books were the work of one person at different periods, and the publisher referred to this report.

The two girls travelled to London, and in their utter simplicity went, where they knew their father had once gone, to stay at the Chapter Coffee House, Paternoster Row—a place frequented solely by men. There was, in fact, only one woman servant in the establishment. From there they proceeded to Smith, Elder, and Co.'s publishing house, and to the amazement of the publisher, introduced themselves as the authors of the much-talked-of books.

Smith tells how, on taking his wife next day to visit the celebrated authors at the Chapter Coffee House, he found the two timid girls clinging together on the most remote window seat, and gazing down, half-fascinated, half-terrified, at the turmoil of the London streets. Though the kindly publisher and his wife endeavoured to persuade the girls to prolong their stay in the city and enjoy its sights, they refused to stay. Their mission was accomplished, their separate identities established.

They dared not remain long away, for their anxiety would not suffer them to rest away from the home that Bramwell's disgraceful conduct rendered so full of misery, and ceaseless care.

And now, before his sister's pitiful, and sometimes indignant eyes, there passed the last acts of poor Bramwell's sordid tragedy. Opium had been added to drink, and rapidly, steadily, with inexorable sureness, the unhappy young man hurried to his doom. For some time before his death he had frightful attacks of delirium tremens. He slept in his father's room, and he would often declare that one or the other would be dead by the morning;

The parsonage stood in such a lonely exposed position on the edge of the wild moorland that Mr. Bronte was accustomed from his first residence there, to load a pistol every evening in readiness for any lawless character that might venture to attack the house. It was the rumour among the parishioners of this habit of Mr. Bronte that has given rise to so many absurd tales of his eccentricities. In the morning the pistol was discharged, to be loaded afresh in the evening. He still kept up his old habit, though his son now shared his room, for he thought it would not be wise to make any alteration on that account, or allow Bramwell to think that he took notice of his ravings. The trembling sisters, sick with fright, would lie awake the long hours of darkness, waiting with straining ears and fainting hearts for the report of a pistol in the stillness of the night, till their worn-out nerves gave way, and they slept the sleep of utter exhaustion. In the morning Bramwell would saunter out, and say foolishly "The poor old man and I had a terrible night of it. He does his best, poor old man! But it is all over with me." And so the cruel months dragged on, in nerve racking, heart torturing suspense.

Without a doubt the premature deaths of these wonderfully-gifted girls (their marvellous genius blasted before it had come to its perfect flower) were due to their home life blighted by the cruel and shameful suffering that Bramwell caused them, to the long and intolerable strain of those anxious wakeful nights.

Well might Charlotte say, referring to Thackeray's lecture on Fielding—"I was present at Thackeray's lecture on 'Fielding'; the hour spent in listening to it was a painful hour. Had Thackeray owned a son grown, or growing up; and a son, brilliant but reckless, would he have spoken in that light way of courses that lead to disgrace and the grave? I believe if only once the prospect of a promising life blasted in the outset by wild ways had passed under his eyes, he never could have spoken with such levity of what led to its piteous destruction."

In October, 1848, the brief faulty life was over. At the last Bramwell seemed to awake out of his long madness. He realised what he had lost, and gathered all his powers to meet death with a brave heart. With something of Emily's fortitude he insisted on meeting death standing. Poor, hapless, misguided Bramwell! With his fine powers, his ambitions, his warm impulsive nature, to have come to such an end! He might have done great things, he accomplished nothing!

Charlotte, writing to a friend, says "Till the last hour comes, we never know how we can pity and forgive a near relative. All his vices were, and are, nothing to us now, we remember only his woes." Emily, who clung to her miserable brother to the last, with the reward that he basely tried to deprive her of literary fame, now worn out by the long struggle, was seized by the illness from which she never rallied, though with characteristic courage she fought against it.

A flippant and rather cruel criticism appeared about this period in the "North American Review." "What a bad set the Bells must be," says Charlotte, mocking at their critic. "What appalling books they write. To-day, as Emily appeared a little easier, I thought the "Review" would amuse her, so I read it aloud to her and Anne. As I sat between them at our quiet, but now somewhat melancholy fireside, I studied the two ferocious authors. Ellis, the 'man of uncommon talents, but dogged, brutal, and morose,' sat leaning back in his easy chair, drawing his impeded breath as best he could, and looking, alas! piteously pale and wasted. It is not his wont to laugh, but he smiled half-amused, half in scorn, as he listened. Acton was sewing; no emotion ever stirs him to loquacity; so he only smiled too; dropping at the same time a single word of calm amazement to hear his character so darkly portrayed. I wonder what the reviewer would have thought of his own sagacity could he have beheld the pair as I did."

In the preface of "Wuthering Heights"—that strange, inexplicable, yet fascinating book of Emily's, a weird prose poem —"knarled and knotty as a root of heath" —Charlotte speaks of this last illness of her much beloved sister," Never in her life had she lingered over any task that lay before her, and she did not linger now. She sank rapidly. She made haste to leave us. Yet, while physically she perished, mentally she grew stronger than we had yet known her. Day by day,, when I saw with what a front she met suffering, I looked on her with an anguish, of wonder and love. I have seen nothing like it, but indeed, I have never seen her parallel in anything; stronger than a man, simpler than a child, her nature stood alone.

"The awful point was that while full of ruth for others, on herself she had no pity; the spirit was inexorable to the flesh; from the trembling hand, the un-nerved limbs, the faded eyes, the same service was exacted as they had rendered in health. To stand by and witness this, and not dare to remonstrate, was a pain no words can render."

" Many a time," says Mrs. Gaskell, "did Charlotte and Anne drop their sewing, or cease their writing, to listen with wrung hearts to the failing step, the laboured breathing, the frequent pauses, while their sister climbed the short staircase; yet they dared not notice what they observed with pangs of suffering even greater than hers. They dared not notice it in words; far less by the caressing assistance of a helping hand." They sat still and silent, looking on, poor girls! with the yearning helplessness of love.

When too late, Emily, who had steadily declined until then, allowed a doctor to be called in—he could do nothing. To the very last her inflexible spirit which burns through those last lines she wrote, refused to surrender. Beaten, but unsubdued, she waited for death.

No coward soul is mine,

No trembler in the world's storm-troubled sphere;

I see Heaven's glories shine,

And faith shines equal, arming me from fear.

Oh God, within my breast,

Almighty, ever present deity!

Life—that in me has rest,

As I—undying life—have power in thee!

Vain are the thousand creeds,

That move men's hearts; unutterably vain!

Worthless as withered reeds

Or idlest froth, amid the boundless main!

To waken doubt in one

Holding so fast by thine infinity,

So surely anchored on

The steadfast rock of immortality.

There is no room for death,

Nor atom that his might could render void ;

Thou—Thou art Being and Breath, And what thou art may never be destroyed."

The great solitary spirit was soon at rest.

Anne followed; in the same path with a slower step and a meek patience that equalled her sister's austere fortitude. Six months after Emily, in quiet and Christian hope, the gentle girl passed away. Her last verses contain some lines of wistful and touching pathos.

"I hoped that with the brave and strong

My portioned task might lie,

To toil amid the busy throng

With purpose pure and high.

But God has fixed another part,

And he has fixed it well,

I said so with my bleeding heart,

When first the anguish fell.

Much of Anne's verses will live in popular hymnology, while her two books, though unassuming like their author, contain evidence of uncommon powers of quiet observation and reflection that the years might have brought to brilliant maturity. Her second book "The Tenant of Wildfell Hall" was a conscientious, though mistaken, attempt to portray the sad deterioration of a fine character through drink. With her brother's career before her eyes, she deemed it a matter of duty to undertake and carry through this distasteful task. Anne's nature was so shy and retiring that she remains a more shadowy personality than either of her sisters, but that she had a distinct individuality, and genius of her own, her writings abundantly witness.

Charlotte had begun her new novel "Shirley" some time before Emily's last illness, and it was with difficulty that she could bring herself to finish it.

THE COLLECTED PUBLISHED WORKS OF ISABEL GRANT

Begun under the stimulus of success, and with the helpful criticism of the other two girls, it is perhaps the happiest of her two books. It is an idealisation of Emily, and now that both the cherished sisters were gone, it was almost too great an effort for Charlotte to continue the story. But there was a strain of Spartan endurance in the Bronte blood—the book was finished, and sent to the publisher.

In this time of depression and sorrow, a most vindictive and uncalled for notice appeared in the "Quarterly Review." Speaking of "Jane Eyre" the critic (writing too, under the shield of anonymity), had the hardihood to say of an unknown writer: "She must be one of those who, for some sufficient reason, has long forfeited the society of her own sex."

That Charlotte suffered under adverse criticism goes without saying. In her simple country judgment, she placed an altogether too high value on a review appearing in a magazine of any standing. The criticism carried with her the weight of the paper in which it appeared. Mrs. Smith, the wife of her publisher, with whom she was once spending a short London holiday, tells how one morning, not finding "The Times" as usual, Charlotte guessed that it must contain an unfavourable notice of "Shirley," and that her hostess had purposely hidden it. She therefore, insisted on seeing it, and taking the paper, sat down to read it, sheltering herself behind the large sheets. Her kind friend could not help being aware that tears were stealing down the girl's pale face, and dropping on her lap as she, read.

Wounded, though she was, however, Charlotte's first thought was for others, she hoped the unfavourable notice would not check the sale of the book, and so injure her publishers.

But fame was coming for the lonely girl. "Shirley" was an immediate success, and curiosity as to the authorship was raised to fever-heat, when through the shrewd guess of an old Haworth man, who had gone to Liverpool, the secret was disclosed to the world. Letters and congratulations from enthusiastic admirers poured in, invitations came from titled personages. Strangers filled the little Haworth Church for the chance of a glimpse of the author of "Jane Eyre"; the sales of her books increased so rapidly, that there was no further cause for anxiety over money matters in the parsonage ; but Charlotte, shrinking from notice, and almost morbidly fond of solitude, refused the invitations, and busied herself as of old about her household duties.

Fame, she told herself, had come too late. Those who would have rejoiced with her in her triumph, who would have shared it with her, were no more. Her father, though he felt pride in his daughter's success, could not break now through his life-long habit of isolation and reserve, and become a real companion to her. and she sat alone, poor girl, in the long evenings in the "children's study;" and. as the firelight flickered over the room, empty now but of memories, she .must .have realised too keenly:

"How dreary 'tis for women to sit still, on winter nights, by solitary fires, and hear the nations praising them far off."

Her health began to fail, and she yielded to her father's solicitations, and paid a visit to London. In spite of her modest and retiring disposition, she had to submit to be lionised. The most intellectual men and women of the day were eager to become acquainted with her. A meeting was arranged between her and Thackeray—the idol of her girlhood. Charlotte was too nervous to do herself justice, but Thackeray was keen-eyed enough to read the real character behind the sensitive backwardness. "I remember," he said afterwards, the trembling little frame, the little hand, the great honest eyes. An unflinching honesty seemed to be characteristic of her. She gave me the impression of being a very pure and high-minded person. A quiet and holy reverence for truth seemed to be with her always."

While in London Charlotte attended Thackeray's lecture on " Fielding," and great was her dismay at the close of the address to find as she turned to leave the hall that a large body of the audience through whom the whisper had gone round, that the quiet little girl to whom Thackeray had come down to speak, was the author of "Jane Eyre," formed in two lines to stare at her as she walked to the door of the hall. She was glad to leave London and all the wearisome lionising, and retire to her quiet home at Haworth. In 1853 she wrote "Villette," her last, and most critics agree, her best book. It was received with the same acclaim as the two former novels.

In 1854 she married the Rev. Arthur Nicholls, who had proposed and been refused some time before.

In 1855 a severe cold brought on a low fever, which gained rapidly on her. She became weaker and weaker, sinking into delirium. "Wakening," says Mrs. Gaskell, "from this stupor of intelligence, she saw her husbands woebegone face, and caught the sound of some murmured words of prayer that God would spare her. 'Oh, she whispered forth, 'l am not going to die, am I?

He will not separate us, we have been so happy.'" A few hours later the sad tolling of the bell told the Haworth parishioners that the last of the wonderful Bronte sisters was no more.

More than fifty years have passed away, and yet new books are still being written about the Bronte's.

Clement Shorter, the great critic, who has written one of the best, says of Charlotte—"Were all her works destroyed, and nothing but her letters preserved to us, we should still owe abundant reverence and gratitude to the author of "Jane Eyre." Our literature has produced few greater writers, and fewer still so brave and true to high ideals."

The poet Swinburne writes: "In the eyes of Englishmen yet unborn, no one will be found to have left a nobler memorial than the unforgotten life and the imperishable works of Charlotte Bronte."

THE COLLECTED PUBLISHED WORKS OF ISABEL GRANT

THE FURNACE OF GOLD

BACKGROUND TO THE PUBLICATION

This, one of the two known novels by Isabel, was serialized by *The Sydney Morning Herald* in 1905 when she was thirty-five. She was single and her church, her job as a teacher and her family were still the main influences of her life.

The setting is spectacularly local, with the gold mining town setting based on Mt. Morgan of the 1890's. Her brother was a private building contractor in Mt. Morgan but his wife's father provided an entrée into mine life and the chlorination plant at the mine which he had designed and built. For a woman of that time she displays an unexpectedly deep knowledge of that process and gold-mining generally. To have access to this knowledge Isabel could thank her socio-economic level, (middle-class Australian), her education level and the equality inherent in her Scottish background. She would have faced many, many restrictions but luckily she could expect the men-folk of her extended family to allow her interest in their work and to indulge that interest. She seems to have been entranced by the power and scale of the mine and uses it skillfully as the setting for both primary and secondary plots. The graphic scene she paints of the "opening of the furnace" at night-time was also enjoyed by her great-nephew, Hugh Grant, fifty years later.

She was undoubtedly an astute listener and observer as the setting and characters are believably drawn. It is regrettable that the required sentimentality for the era has taken this work out of popular regard. Those who do read it will get not only the story but an authentic glimpse of life in Edwardian Australia and for history buffs that is a treat.

The following paragraph introduced Isabel's novel under the heading "Our New Story."

> "We begin next Saturday the publication of a story called "The Furnace for Gold; a Tale of a Mining Community," by Isabel Grant. The interest of this work is entirely Australian, and in this regard it should challenge sympathetic consideration. But

THE FURNACE FOR GOLD

if it had been written about silver mines in South America, if every person of the drama were a foreigner, and if the writer were in no sense connected with Australia, there would still remain the fact that "The Furnace for Gold" is a capital story, full of human interest, capitally told. The scene is laid in the neighbourhood of Neummurra, a somewhat primitive township in Queensland. We are introduced to a number of interesting people of various grades in society, each with one well-defined aim in view, and each crossed, as happens in real life, by the counter tendencies of their neighbours' ambitions. There is a rivalry between two women which warps the view of each as to the character of the other, a rivalry which is built up and maintained in facts distorted and in absolute mistakes. There is the excitement of a mining township going on all the time, men opposing and helping each other in the race for wealth. The story of the action of the drama is touched with a fine vein of poetry; but our author does not give way to sentiment. "The Furnace for Gold" is a strong story, and none the less compelling in its grip on the reader because other finer things than royal metal are tried in the furnace. By a clever arrangement of her figures the author manages always to present some new point of interest, each point to be afterwards absorbed in the purposes of the general plot. We have fun and pathos in their natural combination, and the sad is alternated by the pleasant, as in real life. "The Furnace for Gold" is a distinct

acquisition to Australian literature, and
great things may be hoped of the author."

The novel takes up the second half of the book and is presented as the finale. It was first published in this form in 1905 but was reworked as "The Furnace" and submitted to publishers Robertson and Mullens Ltd. in Melbourne and Curtis Brown Ltd. in New York in 1947. The New York response is not known but the reply from Melbourne asks for the author to resubmit in twelve months time as they "are finding it impossible to get production of new publications at present owing to the scarcity of paper and the labour in both printing and binding factories." Isabel was seventy-seven years old then and may not have had the energy or good health to pursue this.

A second novel and several radio and stage plays are not included in this collection as it was to be limited to published works and while it is probable some were used I have found no evidence yet of these having been published or performed.

The publication of Isobel's novel started on Saturday 18th. February 1905 and runs every day until Saturday 15th. April 1905. It is a long book and she was able to develop her scenes and characters slowly and carefully, as seemed to be her preference.

To set the mood for the time of publication I have reproduced the banner and some information from the front page of the 27th. February 1905 edition of *The Sydney Morning Herald*. This edition contains the end of Chapter VII and the first half of Chapter VIII.

THE FURNACE FOR GOLD

The Sydney Morning Herald.

PRICE ONE PENNY.

No. 20897   SYDNEY, MONDAY, FEBRUARY 27, 1905   12 PAGES

[For Notices of Births, Marriages, Deaths, &c., See Page 8.]

SUMMARY.

The Japanese on the Sha-ho are gradually closing in on General Kuropatkin's left flank.

Lieutenant-General Saktaroff reports that the Japanese have renewed the attack on Tain-chen-shan, and have turned one position.

A first Japanese attack on Beresneff Hill, Tain-chen-shan, was repulsed, after desperate fighting.

The attack was renewed, and superior numbers forced the Russians to abandon the base of the hill.

General Kuropatkin, fearing that he will be outflanked, is heavily reinforcing General Lajervitch commanding the first Russian army.

Japanese state that Cossacks or Chinese brigands in Russian pay tried to wreck a bridge at Hal-cheng.

General Kuropatkin has telegraphed his Government that 20 Japanese torpedo boats and warships are proceeding to Vladivostok.

There are 44,400 Russian prisoners in Japan, including 616 officers.

The Simplon tunnel, connecting Italy and Switzerland, was completed on Friday.

The finding of the International Commission on the Dogger Bank Outrage is that Admiral Roxhdestvensky was responsible for the order to fire.

The firing, the commission holds, was unjustifiable since the trawlers were regularly lighted, and their attitude was not hostile.

Joel Taylor, aged 46, lately residing at Aberdeen, Queensland, committed suicide at Ellis Coffee Palace yesterday.

Mr. Franki, manager of Mort's Dock, at the annual picnic on Saturday strongly advocated the manufacturing of iron and steel in the State.

Mr. H. O. White of Havilah, a prominent pastoralist and sportsman, died at Hobart on Friday evening

---

SHIPPING

P. and O. COMPANY'S
ROYAL MAIL STEAMERS.
For MARSEILLES, PLYMOUTH, and LONDON.
FIRST AND SECOND SALOON ONLY.

Steamer.	Tons.	Commander	Sydney noon.
Oceana	6,610	E. Street	Mar.1
Marmora	10,500	G. Langbome	Mar.16
China	7,912	G. Wright RNR	Mar.29

Via Hobart; a twin-screw.
PASSAGE MONEY TO LONDON
£38 to £75.
Return, ---£63 and £112
Return tickets available for 24 months.   E. TRELAWNY.
68 Pitt St. Superintendent in Australia

N. D. L.

IMPERIAL MAIL STEAMSHIPS.
THREE-WEEKLY SERVICE
TO LONDON AND CONTINENT
Via COLOMBO, SUEZ, NAPLES, GENOA, SOUTHAMPTON, ANTWERP, and BREMAN

steamer.	tons.	Commander.	Sydney,	Adelaide
			1.30.	
Fredrich	10,605	Maass		Feb.25
Bremen	11,570	Nierich	Mar.11	Mar.18
Seytlitz	7942	Dewere	April 29	May 6
Oldenburg	5006.	Troitsch.	May 27	June 3

Twin-screw Steamers.
leaving Melbourne Tuesday after Sydney.

FARES TO LONDON:

	Single	Return
First Saloon	£65 to £75	£112
Second Saloon	£38 to £43	£63
Third class	£15 to £17	£27

Saloon Return Tickets now available for Two years.
ROUND THE WORLD, £130, with £20 Atlantic birth
REDUCED FARES THROUGH TO NEW YORK, VIA SUEZ.

To CHINA AND JAPAN.
REGULAR FOUR-WEEKLY SERVICE, calling at BRISBANE, NEW BRITAIN, and NEW GUINEA, for HONG KONG, KOBE, and YOKOHAMA, connecting at Hong Kong with the FORTNIGHTLY EXPRESS MAIL SERVICE of the N.D.L. from Japan and China to Europe.

PRINZ WALDEMAR (Twin Screw) March 18
PRINZ SIGISMUND (Twin Screw) Apr. 13
WILEHAD (Twin Screw) ... May 13
Fares to Hong Kong:—1., £33; 11,..£23; 111, £15; Deck £9.
Linen washed on board at moderate prices, Civility and cleanliness leading features.
             LOHMANN and Co.,
General Agents, 7 and 9 Bridge St. Sydney.

David Jones and Co.
Opp. G.P.O.
Last Two Days
MIDSUMMER SALE
In order to secure the reductions during the sale orders must reach us not later than to-morrow (Tuesday)

SEARLE'S BULBS
Are full of life
You'll find the best Bulbs at Searle's. If we could procure better we would. But we can't – nor can anyone else.

THE FURNACE OF GOLD

―――――:o:―――――

A TALE OF A MINING COMMUNITY.

"The fining pot is for silver, and the furnace for gold; but the Lord trieth the heart."—Proverbs XVII, 8.

BY ISABEL GRANT.

All Rights Reserved.

CHAPTER 1.

HIS WORSHIP THE MAYOR.

The sudden tropical storm was over; and, as the sun broke through the fast retreating clouds, Neummurra clothed its crude bareness in a garment of evanescent loveliness. A soft mist stole up the valley and hid the scarred hillside; a vivid greenness touched the scanty grass and the thick scrub by the creek; strange warm tones of red and brown appeared in the mounds of "tailings;" the tents, new-washed by the shower, gleamed whitely along the slopes; even the ugly little iron or wooden houses of the township were for the moment transformed in the mellow glow of the storm-tinged sunset.

But Anne Hetherington, as she came out on her verandah and gazed anxiously towards the main street of Neummurra, had no eye for the beauty of the scene.

At the sound of her footsteps on the wet boards a slight rustle came from below the boards, and a small boy, with a square-built figure, a bullet head, and a secretive, pallid face, began cautiously to ascend the steps, while contriving to keep out of the woman's sight behind the passion vine that clustered over the railings.

His dark eyes glittered with intense curiosity as he kept watch, for Tommy Ratten had been puzzling his brains for some time over the erratic movements of his mistress.

She had seemed unable to settle herself below stairs, even during the storm, but had been hurrying at intervals to the window that commanded the best view of the township, and tantalising her small helper all the afternoon by her evident excitement.

Tommy was a State Orphan, bound out for a small weekly sum; and in the three days since he had entered her service Anne had only noticed that he was very small for his twelve years, and seemed imbued with a spirit of insatiable curiosity.

Except that, as she expressed herself, it gave her a turn to find her every movement under the observation of a pair of inscrutable black eyes, she had no fault to find with the boy, who was ready and willing in his obedience to every order.

As she peered over the edge of the creeper, her eyes narrowed, a thousand fine lines drew themselves on her sharp, eager face, and the expression of tense anxiety was involuntarily reproduced on the small, unchildlike countenance of the watcher.

At last her patience was rewarded. The mists cleared away, and she saw that the large door at the end of her husband's store was closed. It was the preconcerted signal. If John were chosen Mayor, he had promised to close the door at the back of his store. Anne gave a triumphant laugh, and cried out, "Dave's bested, after all his blow! Dave has gone down!" It was twenty-five years since David Morgan had jilted his cousin, but some memory of that day was in Anne's triumphant laugh at this moment.

It was evidently as an afterthought that she added, a minute later, "and John is Mayor of Neummurra."

She had uttered the words aloud, but was unconscious how much of self-betrayal there was in them till, as she swung round in her joyful excitement, she caught sight of the intent eyes of Tommy, who, excited also, inadvertently raised his bullet head into view.

"Go down to the kitchen this minute; what business have you up here?" she cried out angrily. The boy cowered at her sharp tone, but his excuse was ready. His orphanage training had made him glib in excuses. His command of feature was strange in one so young.

"Please, I only came up to ask you could I chop some more wood." Tommy seemed to have a passion for chopping wood; every spare moment found him, to his mistress's amusement, out at the wood-heap, wielding an axe nearly as tall as himself.

She burst out laughing, and her momentary vexation vanished.

"Of course not, Tommy; you have got enough in the kitchen to last a week; besides the wood in the yard is wet."

Tommy vanished, but Anne was uneasily aware that some amusement seemed to lurk behind the demureness of his dark eyes, and a faint flush touched her sallow cheek.

She waited for a few minutes debating some question with herself, then with one last glance towards the store she went down the steps and entered the lower part of the dwelling.

"The rain is quite over," she thought, "and I promised to give Pen that setting of Longhorns. I may as well run over now, before John or Jim comes home."

She was unwilling to admit, even to herself, that she wished to go over to her cousin's cottage to enjoy a sight of David's discomfiture, but nevertheless this unacknowledged motive had more to do with her visit than her promise to Pen.

The two cottages were built on the slope of one of the many little hills of Neummurra and were but a few hundred yards apart.

She went up the paddock, collected the eggs, and made ready to go, finding a certain satisfaction in Tommy's look of baffled curiosity as he watched the preparations.

As she opened the gate, a bent, misshapen figure stood before her. It was "Dummy" as the township named the poor, deaf mute, who was, despite his affliction, general messenger for Neummurra.

The wretched, uncouth creature seemed scarcely human, with his distorted face, grotesque gestures, and guttural cries; but Anne was used to him and showed no repulsion at his appearance.

He had a letter in his hand, and he gave it to her, with a quick gesture of explanation.

It was from Mrs. Marlow, the wife of the Boss of the Lower Works. When Anne read it she beckoned Dummy to follow her into the kitchen. The poor fellow had been caught in the storm, and looked intensely miserable. His face brightened as he shuffled after her into the warm room, and, fixing his sodden hat on one shaking knee, he sat down expectantly.

At the first sight of him Tommy fled precipitately into his own little room, which opened on the kitchen.

"Tommy, come here, and put on a better fire; I'm going to warm up some of the soup for Dummy," Anne called out.

Tommy shrunk out of his hiding place, and, making a wide detour to avoid the stranger, dashed at the wood-box and then retreated again. His eyes were starting out of their sockets with horror; his broad face was white with fear. Anne looked after him with swift and slightly amused comprehension, then followed him into the room, to find him under the bed-clothes.

"He won't hurt you, stupid boy," she said laughing; "He is quite harmless, poor old Dummy." But Tommy was not to be reassured, and clung to the protecting blankets.

Anne waited to give Dummy a good meal then she let him go, and brought Tommy out of his room, but it was plain he bad received a shock. Anne could not help laughing, for she had a keen sense of humour, but she was a kindly woman, and did her best to set Tommy's mind at rest before she set out for her cousin's place.

"Dave will not find it easy to tell his girls that he has lost," she reflected, as at length she walked along the narrow track; "he was never the kind of man to enjoy climbing down."

Penelope and Daphne Morgan were at the gate looking towards the town as Anne drew near.

In spite of herself a thrill of unwilling admiration passed through Anne as she glanced up and saw them. They were well named— Penelope in her rich, dark beauty, Daphne in her fair loveliness—"The Rose and the Lily of Neummurra."

With a mother's quick instinct, Anne guessed that her son James was by no means indifferent to Penelope, and this did not tend to increase her affection for the girl, whom she had never cordially liked, and was now almost growing to hate.

Pen caught sight of her visitor some little time before Anne was aware that the girls were at the gate. "There is Cousin Anne," she said, in a soft tone to Daphne, "what ever is bringing her up here on such a day? She has got a basket on her arm."

THE FURNACE FOR GOLD

"I expect it is the setting of Leghorns she promised," said Daphne, equably; "the rain is gone now, and the roads are nearly dry. What is there strange about her coming up Pen?" Daphne could not always follow her sister's moods.

"I could bet anything," cried Pen, her colour rising with a touch of her hot temper, "that she has got word that father is defeated and is coming up to gloat over us."

"Pen!" cried Daphne in a shocked tone, then her disappointment overcoming her surprise, she added with keen regret in her fresh young voice, "Do you think father is not Mayor after all?"

"I'm sure of it." Pen declared, "I can see it to the set of Anne's bonnet, in the spring of her step. Just watch her picking her way so daintily up the track, and tell me if Lady Mayoress is not written all over her in large capitals,"

"Hush she will hear you!" Implored Daphne.

"Let her," laughed Pen. "There is no love lost between Cousin Anne and me. I am sure I scarcely know why, either. She likes you, Daph, I believe, and perhaps Lew, too; but as for father and me, well, least said soonest mended. "

"Don't, Pen," said Daphne, "Cousin Anne is really kind. I am sure it is just an idea of yours that she is not as fond of you as of me."

Pen gave a short laugh. "Keep believing, Daph, I would not spoil your innocent belief for the world, but I must say you are not very observant."

It was characteristic of the girls that Daphne, who had taken her cousin's part, should feel embarrassed in greeting her, while saucy Pen welcomed her with such gay good humour that even her sister was almost deceived. Anne received Pen's pretty graceful thanks with cynical composure, but there was real affection in the glance she cast at Daphne's gentle, disturbed face. The younger girl seemed a little weary, after her day's work, as her cousin noted anxiously.

Pen was housekeeper for her father. Daphne was an assistant teacher at the State School of the township.

Anne remained in the garden chatting with the girls till she saw what appeared to be David Morgan coming along the road.

"Is that David?" she asked innocently and Pen turned sharply, adroitly interposing between Anne and the newcomer. Pen's wit was quick, her intuition marvellous, where she either loved or hated, and she did both with the same ardour.

"The old cat" she thought "I was right; she has just come out to spy out the nakedness of the pain. She simply wants to crow over poor father in the first freshness of his disappointment."

But she was too late. Anne had seen David, noted exultantly the beaten set of the shoulders, the discouraged droop of the whole figure, the reluctant, dragging step.

As soon as David reached the gate and caught sight of his cousin he pulled himself together. His face cleared, his shoulders straightened, his bent head was held erect, as he walked smartly towards the group. "Hullo, Anne." he called out; "you are venturesome. I am afraid another storm is on the road."

"Oh, I just ran over to bring some eggs I promised Pen. I must be on my way back now," she replied.

"Don't hurry away," said David politely. "It is not so often we have the pleasure of seeing you."

"I must be off," said Anne, but she made no effort to go. The storm was discussed thoroughly, and still Anne showed no sign of moving. David began to fidget, his brown eyes snapped, a sign not too reassuring to his daughters, but still Anne lingered, and blandly ignored his impatience.

There was, as is often the case, a greater likeness between the cousins than is sometimes seen between brother and sister

The slight, wiry figures, the sharp features, the bright eyes, and the sallow faces, were curiously alike. But the resemblance went deeper than mere externals; it extended to the mind. There was so close kinship of nature between the cousins, that each felt what the other thought. Their thoughts at times met each other, and fought, even while their tongues spoke peace.

Anne in her strange way was enjoying herself now, and David knew it, resented it, but was reluctant to take steps to rid himself of her presence, lest she should consider it tantamount to a confession of weakness. Just as David's patience neared its limit, a quick step sounded on the path, and Llewellyn Morgan appeared at the gate.

Anne prepared for instant flight. However brave she was against the others, she had, with all her liking for him, a wholesale dread of Lew, and his sharp tongue.

"Now, now, Cousin Anne I can't allow this, you know, hurrying away as soon as I come in sight. Surely you can spare me a minute," and Lew's long, angular frame blocked up the path, as he looked down on them all with a twinkle in his eyes that recognized the relief of his father's and sisters' expression and the slightly dubious look of Anne, who indeed began to feel for the first time that she had not acted wisely or kindly in forcing her society on poor David, in the first keenness of his defeat.

There was in Lew's smile a curious hardness that made Anne suspect that he had penetrated her motive in coming there, and she discretely resolved to escape from the danger of an encounter with him.

Lew Morgan possessed none of his sisters' beauty; he prided himself, so he said, on his ugliness; but there was something very likeable for all that about his broad, hairless, clever face. The features were inclined to be harsh and the expression cynical, but on the whole the type was one which is often found in a humorist; and when one listened to Lew's racy talk, with it's quaint turns of native humour, of a frankness at times little short of appalling, one forgot the plain face, and the thin, spare, "lamp-post" figure.

Anne murmured something about the lateness of the hour.

"Now, a minute or two will not

make any difference," said Lew with assumed gravity. "What do you think of the news? Of course John has sent you word and you wished to carry our congratulations to him."

But Anne had shaken hands with her cousins, and was outside the gate before Lew could proceed any further. Wisely ignoring his remarks, she hurried away, glad to escape so lightly.

"So you went down Dad," said Lew. "Never mind, better luck next time." "I withdrew my name," said David sharply.

"There has been too much of this opposing of John and me lately, and as I am running against him for the presidentship of the hospital. I decided to withdraw from the Mayorship."

"That's where you made the mistake, Dad," said Lew. "You shouldn't have funked the contest after all the fuss and talk you've done"

"Talk sense!" said David angrily, but Daphne's soft voice broke in with an account of the storm at the school, and David was glad to leave the discussion alone.

CHAPTER 11.

A NIGHT ALARM.

John Hetherington was a silent man, but he could not quite hide from his wife and son his elation over his new honours.

"So, you are the Mayor of Neummurra," said Jim with a smile. "I think Neummurra is to be congratulated on its wise choice. I was not sure before that there was too much wisdom in our city fathers."

"Dave Morgan's opinion and yours will not agree on that point," laughed Anne.

"Was the voting equal John?"

"There was no opposition," said John, "David Morgan guessed he had a poor chance I suppose, for he withdrew his name, and all the aldermen voted for me."

"What a poor-spirited fellow," said Anne indignantly. "He was not game to face the election, and so wanted to shirk it, and gain praise at the same time."

"What was the place all locked up for, when we came home?" said John., unwilling yet to discuss the subject of the Mayorship. He posed a little, now, even before his own family, wishing to impress on them his indifference to his victory. He would soon unbend, however, and tell them the whole history of the afternoon, but just at first he was too conscious of his new distinction to be quite his honest, natural self.

Anne began to laugh, as she remembered the fright Dummy had given Tommy. She was a capital story-teller and a clover mimic in her own way, and as she described the scare of the small boy, both her listeners laughed heartily.

"My word, though!" said Anne, a little excited with the way in which her story was received, and willing to amuse John still further. "It was as good as a play to see David coming home this afternoon. If ever a man looked sour and sore, that man was David Morgan, when he caught sight of me in his garden. If looks could hurt, 'tis I who would be sore to-night."

Jim looked up hastily. "Oh, Mother," he said in a vexed tone, and Anne could have bitten her tongue, that she had foolishly allowed the fact of her visit to her cousins to escape her. "I wish you had not gone over there this afternoon, when you knew father had won. You night have thought it would be awkward for David to meet you in a friendly manner, when his disappointment was fresh in his mind."

There was an undercurrent of something deeper than vexation in her, son's tone and Anne recognised it.

"It is just Penelope he is thinking of," Anna thought jealously. "His father and mother are second to Penelope, of course," aloud, she said in a soothing tone.

"I promised Penelope I'd give her a setting of Leghorns, and 1 had just the right number to-day, so 1 ran over with them. She was awfully pleased to get them." Jim's face cleared, and he gave his mother a grateful glance, which the diplomatic woman did not meet.

"So you and Dave will be rivals again, this time to see who will be President of the Hospital," she said, anxious to change the subject.

"Oh, I'm going to withdraw my name. I shall not stand against poor Dave twice in one week," said John.

Anne laughed meaningfully. "He will not like that, you know. He would sooner give you a good beating."

"Then if he does not like it, he can lump it," said John in a satisfied tone. "I did not like him doing the same thing this afternoon."

"It is queer how often you and Dave seem pitted against each other," said Jim uneasily. "Since I came back from Melbourne, and that is two years now, it almost seems as if you two were enemies, instead of friends."

John looked slightly annoyed. "To hear some of the folks talk one would imaging Dave and I were like cat and dog, just because we have rival stores, I suppose. I bear Dave no ill-will and I am sure he wishes me well, unless I interfere with his business; but it would be hard to make some people believe that. Not that he treated me too well when we dissolved partnership; but let bygones be bygones."

"Neummurra is a gossipy, scandal-mongering little hole," said Jim hotly, "I never appreciated it properly till I lived in a big city like Melbourne. Our township here is not big enough to allow of folks minding their own business – and what makes them so small minded is they are always getting their minds crushed squeezing them into other people's business."

"Oh, I wouldn't go as far as to say that," said John quietly. "It is a pleasant, hearty little place; and if people take too much notice of other people's affairs it is all in the way of friendliness and goodwill, you take my word for it."

"Is it indeed?" said Jim quickly. "The place is just eaten up with curiosity and gossip. Neummurra spells simply the mine and its bosses. It is not a good thing for a place to owe its very

THE FURNACE FOR GOLD

existence to any one thing as Neummurra does. You know yourself that if the gold were to give out this town would tumble down like a pack of cards. And what have the people to talk about but just the mine and their own small concerns? Don't they know everyone's affairs better than the people themselves? Can't any old woman of either sex tell you of an engagement before the young man or woman have thought of it themselves? Is it any wonder with all the busy tongues that they are turning you and Dave from rivals in business to enemies in reality?"

"My goodness, James," said Anne, uneasily, "you do speak sharply. You never used to find fault with Neummurra before and you have lived here since you were a child, till you went to Grammar School and then to Melbourne University."

Jim looked a little ashamed of his outburst.

"Oh, well Mother, when a fellow has spent a few years in the south among men of wider interests and broader sympathies Neummurra strikes him as somewhat cramped and narrow."

Anne felt sure it was not the lack of interest in higher things among the people, but the gradual change in the relations between the two households that had provoked her son's heated speech. He was feeling how little more than kin how little less than kind the cousins were becoming, but she was too wise to provoke further discussion. Jim went out shortly after this to see Marlowe, his boss. When he had gone John allowed himself to be drawn out on the subject of elections. He listened with amused complacency to Anne's graphic description of David's chagrin; and now that her son's disapproving face was absent, she allowed herself more latitude for she knew that at heart John was pleased to have beaten David and of hearing of his discomfiture.

When Jim returned he found the house in darkness. He came upstairs and passed his parents' door as quietly as he could, but Anne could never sleep in comfort till she heard her son's step in his room, though she had no fears if he came home late, for Jim; in spite of his fun-loving disposition, was steadiness itself, and had no delight in low pleasures. With the sound of his closing door there seemed to Anne to come a strange patter of feet up the backstairs, followed by a whimpering cry in the passage. She listened intently, but all was still for a few moments, then a terrified yell broke the stillness of the night

"Oh, the Dummy! The Dummy! He is after me. Let me in, Mr. Jim; let me in." Her husband sprang up and opened the door.

"Is that you, Tommy?" he shouted, and a faint voice sobbed out, "Yes, sir, it's me," and John followed the voice.

In the moonlight that streamed in through the window in the passage he saw a small huddled shape on the matting.

"What is the matter?" he said, in alarm; and Jim also came hurrying out of his room with a light.

"Oh, the Dummy! The Dummy!"

shrieked Tommy in an ecstasy of terror. "He opened the door just now, and came into the house; I ran upstairs, and he followed me."

John took the light from Jim, and, followed by the trembling boy, they searched thoroughly below stairs.

"It must have been my coming that frightened him, poor chappie," said Jim at last, as they found nothing.

"I'll poor chappie him," said John angrily, "waking us all up in such a fright. Off you go to bed." He pushed Tommy into his room, and closed the door.

The two men returned to their rooms, and Jim had scarcely lain down, when he heard the sound of heavy breathing coming from under his door. Hr rose and silently opened it to find as he expected that Tommy was crouching outside.

He lifted the small figure, and carried it downstairs.

Tommy allowed himself to be placed into his bed, but Jim could feel that he was shivering as if with an ague, though he uttered no sound.

A wave of pity for the poor little creature passed through Jim's heart. He was very tired and sleepy, and the night was inclined to be chilly, but he could not leave the boy in such a state of fear.

"Look here Tommy." He said softly, "you lie down quietly and try to go to sleep. I shall stay here until you are asleep. I shall not light a lamp, for my father would see the light, and he would not be pleased, but I'll lift up the blinds and the moon will shine clear into the room. Now, little chap, I'm going to explain to you all about Dummy, so that you will see what a kind, simple man he is, and you will never be afraid of him again. Besides, it was I you heard coming up the stairs. Dummy never comes out at night. He looks after the horses at the "Three Crowns, and sleeps there too."

Then, in a few, quiet, soothing words he explained how good-hearted and kindly poor Dummy was, in spite of his severe affliction.

"Now, Tommy, you will never be afraid of him again, will you?"

Tommy shook his head, but his small grimy fingers tightened on Jim's strong, firm hand. The dark eyes were losing their look of fear, and the small face regaining its usual solid composure, but there was a hysterical tendency yet in the laboured breathing.

Jim could see that sleep was still far from Tommy, but he gave no sign of impatience; he let his hand remain in the hot clasp, and went on talking in an easy, cheerful manner.

He did not know what a large loyalty, what a warm, unwanted feeling of gratitude were welling up in the small, neglected heart, that had met, in the twelve years of its State Orphanhood, so little of the natural tenderness that should be birthright of every child. The clasp of the strong yet gentle hand meant something that had been wanting in poor Tommy Ratton's life until now.

The moonlight flooded the narrow room, and in clear radiance Jim's handsome, frank, honest face took on a new and higher beauty. The broad forehead, the well-shaped head, and the grey-blue, observant eyes gave token of intellect. But something better than either intellect or beauty stamped the thoughtful face-the impress of a nature both good and kindly. A brown moustache hid the rather wide mouth, which had a humorous curve that made the whole face very attractive and human. Anne's fiery ardour and John's calm, phlegmatic temperament were blended in their son into a nature evenly poised, yet free from selfishness; generous, yet not easily carried away; tenacious, yet neither passionate nor irritable.

The keen sense of humor was a direct heritage from his mother. Jim's laugh was the essence of his wholesome nature. To hear and not join in his merriment was almost impossible to the average listener.

Two hours passed silently by and still the moonlight lighted up the dark head and the brown; but at last Tommy slept, and Jim stole up, stiff and cold, to his own room.

Next day David Morgan was elected president of the hospital, and his hurt pride was healed.

Neummurra, as Jim said, took a lively interest in affairs of its people, and there was a great deal of talk over the two elections. Shut out from the rest of the world with only a ramshackle old coach to connect it by a daily journey with Walsingham, the nearest town, it was no wonder that Neummurra was fain to magnify each petty happening into a topic for monotonous days. Even a dispute between two miners, or a disagreement between neighbours, was carried over the township, and discussed in every detail, and from every aspect, before the day of its occurrence was over.

But with all the gossip, and in spite of all the scandal-mongering, there were a simple, natural kindness, a mutual helpfulness, and an honest independence in Neummurra that do not invariably distinguish great cities. Scattered here and there throughout Australia, you will find many such isolated townships as Neummurra, self-centered, one-ideal; but jovial, generous, hearty, outspoken, and boisterous as only a mining township can be.

CHAPTER 111.

A WOMAN SCORNED.

It was understood in Neummurra, as has been pointed out, that David Morgan and John Hetherington, owners of the two largest stores in the township, were rivals, and there was a good deal of truth in the supposition.

They had been partners in business at first, but soon separated, with a little sorry feeling on both sides, and started opposition stores. Anne perhaps was not entirely innocent of a share in the friction that had grown between the partners.

David Morgan and Anne Thomas were cousins once removed, and had been brought up together. Though Australian by birth, they were of welsh blood. Anne's parents were dead, but from David's she had received the care of a daughter.

As the cousins grew up it was tacitly understood that they were engaged to be married. They were fond of each other and Anne at least was pleased with the proposed arrangement.

The death of the parents postponed the marriage, but at length the wedding day was actually fixed; all was made ready; the guests were invited; the bridal feast was prepared; when David, to the shocked surprise of their friends, brought home as his wife a beautiful girl, Lucy Agnew, whom he had seen and fallen in love with on a trip to the next town, whether he had gone in the way of business, for David was at that time a commercial traveler for a mercantile firm in Brisbane.

There was no scene; Anne received the news in apparent composure and indifference; six weeks later she married John Hetherington, who had long been a silent admirer of hers.

But in her own fiery way Anne had loved her cousin, and she could not forgive his desertion, nor the cruel and cowardly blow he had dealt with her pride. Had David explained the matter to her, she felt, bitterly, she could have borne to have lost him as a lover, while she could still keep him as a friend. But he had put her to open shame before her friends and neighbours, and this she could neither forgive nor forget; even now when the old love was long dead, when she had been a happy wife and mother for more than twenty years, the memory of it still rankled.

David congratulated himself on the quiet manner in which Anne had received his defection, but he could never forget that he had humiliated her, nor bring himself after all these years to feel at ease in her society. John Hetherington believed that Anne cared for him, as indeed she soon learned to do, giving his faithful heart the affection it deserved. Then Neummurra, the new mine, was opened, and the two men left Brisbane to take up a store there. The venture was a fortunate one, and for seven years they worked together in apparent friendliness until the death of David's wife.

Strangely enough, Anne had never felt either jealousy or ill will towards Lucy; she knew it was no fault of the beautiful, gentle girl that David had proved false to his promise. Neither by look nor word did Anne hint to her the truth.

Lucy was a romantic, affectionate woman, and she idealized her busy, scheming, hot-tempered husband until the day of her death.

The names of the children-Llewellyn, Penelope and Daphne and her sweetness and beauty were the only legacies she had to leave them.

For a while, in pity for his passionate grief, Anne's feeling of vindictive jealousy died away. She was rich in the love of her husband and son, and could afford to bury the old grudge at last.

But in this very affection for her son some feeling of jealousy began to revive in Anne's heart.

Jim, after passing through the Grammar School and University with

THE FURNACE FOR GOLD

honours, came back to his home, and, instead of entering any of the learned professions as his talents fitted him, and his parents wished, he took up the study of metallurgy and, worst of all, chose to work in Neummurra, as he had done for the last two years, a common workman in the mine. In that time he had worked with the miners, the dry crushers, the vat-men, the smelters, and among the men in the assay room.

It was a great blow to Anne's pride, the more so as Lew, who had never appeared to possess half Jim's cleverness, was getting on rapidly in the largest bank in the township.

It was gall and wormwood to her mother pride to see her handsome son in the clothes of a common working man, his hands and face grimed with the red grey dust of the works; while Lew passed by in his trim black suit and immaculate linen.

Jim laughed at her distress, and declared he meant to know every bit of the working of a gold mine from practical experience before he put his scientific studies to use, and set out to become a rich man. When he became a millionaire he would turn into an exquisite, he told her.

The other cause of the renewal of Anne's jealousy was the fear that had arisen in her mind since her son's return that his old boyish partially for Penelope was growing into something deeper. Not that anyone less sharp than Anne could have suspected that this was the case, for Jim had never enrolled himself openly among the little army of lovers of the "Rose of Neummurra" and the cousinly intercourse between the households gave no indication of any lovemaking; but Anne was not deceived.

In her exclusive love she would have disliked any girl her son might chose, but the mere fact that it was Pen, the daughter of the man who had jilted her, was sufficient to rouse her enmity.

And that Pen seemed to care nothing for Jim, but teased and laughed at him, was no mitigation of her offence in Anne's eyes, rather than reverse. That Pen should dare to scorn her boy was the thought that gave the sting to her jealous anger; ever since his return the girl seemed to have nothing but cruel and saucy speeches for her cousin, especially if Anne were present.

Pen could not understand her own anger at the metamorphosis of the handsome student into the rough workman. She could not see how, with all the professions open to him, Jim could be content to come back and work in the mine with men who had not, most of them, a tithe of his education. There were among the miners many men of good birth and breeding; one of the dry-crushers was reported to be a baronet, one of the smelters had a doctor's Diploma; but these men were broken-down dipsomaniacs, she reflected. Jim did not drink, yet he degraded himself, as she thought, by working with his inferiors; and as Pen was not by any means a silent girl, she expressed her views to Jim and his mother with unblushing candour.

It was a wonder that with all the

admiration Pen received, and with her own knowledge of her beauty that the girl was not spoiled, but her nature was too wholesome and honest to be corrupted by flattery. In spite of Anne's disapproval, she was after all neither vain nor selfish, but simply a genuine fresh-hearted girl, pleased with herself, and friendly to all the world.

She was a general favourite, notwithstanding her quick temper and her sharp tongue. She was never afraid to utter her mind, and her frankness was rarely resented. For if Pen's tongue was sharp, her heart was kind and her tact wonderful. Her smile of fearless goodwill that brought into play half a dozen dimples would have been enough to convert Timon of Athens himself, even if her merry wit had no effect on his misanthropy. In short, admitting a hundred faults, Pen was charming; and, except from Lew, who by virtue of his two years' seniority, endeavored to keep her in order, the "Rose of Neummurra" received only the petting and the delightful admiration of the whole township; Anne, of course, also excepted.

It was more, perhaps, to complete the phrase that Daphne was styled the "Lily" of Neummurra, for as a matter of fact she was not considered nearly as pretty as her sister.

Her features were fine and delicate, her eyes of a clear blue, and her hair was soft and wavy, and "yellow, like ripe corn;" but the fire and brilliancy, the sparkle put the softer, fairer tints into the shade.

While Pen's easy pleasant manners made her so general a favourite, Daphne's shyness was considered haughty reserve; and her gentle diffidence, pride. Daphne was a far cleverer girl than Pen, though few suspected this, for the younger sister was lacking in self-confidence.

She was too sensitive to do herself justice with strangers, and was at her best in her own home, or with those who understood her shy nature. While Pen was a finished woman of the world at twenty-one, Daphne at nineteen was in many things a very child.

The bond between the sisters was very close and tender. Daphne looked up to and admired her sister; while Pen was more influenced by Daphne's opinions, and gave more weight to her quiet counsel, than one would have supposed possible to see them together

CHAPTER IV.

A VICE - REGAL VISITOR

The day was unusually hot for the time of the year.

David Morgan threw himself on a verandah chair and wiped his heated face, while Pen brought him a cooling drink. There was a certain subdued elation in his manner which struck his daughters, and they telegraphed this impression to each other with their eyebrows behind their father's back.

David looked at his two pretty girls with a benevolent eye. "The Governor has set out this week", he said, "on a tour through the colony. We've sent him an invitation to visit Neummurra." The girls were silent, they could see

THE FURNACE FOR GOLD

there was more to follow, but Lew called out from the garden below, where he was pruning some rose trees.

"So Neummurra is at last to be recognised by Vice-Royalty?" Lew had two hobbies, gardening and boating, and he pursued them in every leisure moment. He had built for himself a small boat, which he named the "Waratah", and in which he occasionally took his sisters for a sail or row on the lagoon above the Works.

"The hospital is badly needing funds," said David impressively, ignoring Lew's flippant remark, "so we decided today to give a ball in aid of it, and in honour of the Governor, when he comes."

Pen gave a shriek of delight, Daphne looked slightly alarmed. "Nobody of importance ever came before to Neummurra," said Pen. "We won't know ourselves with a real live Governor. Is any one else coming with him?"

Her father smiled at her glowing face. "I have not heard definitely," he said, "except that Lady Thurston is not with him; she has just gone to England. Oh! By-the-bye, I did hear that Mr. Buxton is coming with the vice-regal party."

"Old Billy Buxton!" said Lew, disrespectfully. "It is a long time since he favoured us with a visit, though he does get so much of his money from the mine. It must be three years since he was here last. I shouldn't think dancing would be much in his line at his time of life, an old fossilised bachelor like him."

"That's all you know," said David sharply. "I do not call myself an old man, and Buxton's younger by a good three years than I am." Lew bent his lank figure over a rose bush and made no reply.

"Will the Governor care for dancing, do you think? Is he young, Dad?" Pen could scarcely wait for the answer. "Oh, the Governor always dances at these affairs, I believe. Very likely you will have a dance with him yourself," said David.

"Me!" cried Pen ungrammatically, but joyfully; then she added thoughtfully, "I wonder who will have the first dance with him?" "The first dance?" David looked at her in some surprise. "I don't know, I expect the first one he picks out. You'll have your chance with the rest, my girl."

"No, Dad," said Lew, coming up the steps. He guessed the thought that was flushing Pen's cheek. "The Governor does not pick out his partners, like an ordinary man. His programme, or at least part of it, is fixed up beforehand, and the arrangement is intimated to the Governor by the aide-de-camp. I've heard fellows at the bank speak of it."

"Oh, Indeed!" said David slightingly. "I think my way is better. Why should the Governor not have his show like any other man to choose a pretty young girl, instead perhaps of having some old frump shunted on him?" Lew smiled in a superior way. "It is not the thing, Dad," he said. "The first dance, at any rate, is always arranged for: after that there may not be the same formality, but it is an understood thing that the lady belonging to the gentleman of the first importance in the place, is to be the Governor's partner in the first dance. But I do not think." he smiled still more broadly, "that this time the Governor need be put off, with an old frump. At a hospital ball the president's daughter would naturally expect the first dance."

Pen jumped up in her excitement. "Dad, do you hear? I'm to have the first dance with his Excellency. Oh, won't the other girls expire with envy?" "What about Daphne?" asked Lew mischievously, "will she expire with envy, would she not like to dance with the Governor?" Daphne looked at him in horror. "I'd die of fright at the mere idea," she said in such a heartfelt tone that the others laughed. "Let Pen have him. I do not care for dancing anyway; Pen will not be frightened of him.

"I should think not." said Pen, "I'd like to see the man, Governor or commoner, that I should be afraid of. But, dad, what sort of a man is our Governor; what is he interested in? I'd like to know, if I am to be his partner."

"Listen to the girl!" cried Lew, choking with laughter, "If she isn't thinking of making a conquest of the governor himself, well, for pure native conceit, Pen, I never met your equal."

A spark of temper flew to Pen's eyes; but as she caught her brother's amused and understanding glance, she smiled in some confusion. "Oh, never mind him, Pen!" said David. "He is chockfull of vanity himself. You must wait and see whether or not the Governor accepts out invitation, and if so, you can get ready your prettiest speeches to please him. We will leave all discussion of the matter till then," and rising slowly he went into his room.

A week later the Governor's courteous acceptance of the invitation threw Neummurra into ferment. Ordinary topics dropped out of sight, and nothing was talked of but the approaching visit. The Governor was to arrive on Thursday morning and leave on Friday at midday, so he would not have much time to spare to see the mining township.

An entertainment committee was formed, of which both David Morgan and John Heatherington were members, and a most elaborate programme was drawn up.

The main street, as much as there was of it, was to be decorated with floral arches, and with the aid of the volunteers, the band, the friendly societies, and the scholars of the State School, it was hoped a fitting welcome could be given.

Loyal and ardent addresses were prepared, and those who were chosen to read them began to rehearse their speeches, in the bosom of their families. The entertainment committee decided to give, not only a ball but a concert, as local talent was ambitious of vice-regal recognition.

The name of "The Citizens' and Hospital Concert and Ball" was adopted; the concert was to be given first, then the hall was to be cleared for dancing. The tickets sold rapidly and the committee were full of enthusiasm and nervousness. Now there arose,

THE FURNACE FOR GOLD

especially among the women, much speculation as to who should have the honour of being selected as the Governor's partner for the first dance, seeing that two seemed to have equal claims to the distinction.

If the ball was purely a hospital ball, then Pen Morgan, the president's daughter, was entitled to the honour of being the Governor's partner; if, however, it was to be a citizens' ball, then Anne Heatherington, as wife of the Mayor of the town, should undoubtedly be chosen.

It was a very nice point to decide. Who should arbitrate between the conflicting claims? Once more Morgan and Heatherington seemed fated to be rivals; the decision was awaited with keen interest by Neummurra. Anne heard the gossip of the women, and, listening to their discussions, her jealousy was stirred into new life. To yield the honour to Pen, or see John allow David to snatch it from her, would be more, she felt, than she could tamely endure.

John was by nature easy-going, slow to move, but hard to stop once his obstinacy was aroused; and if he could only be brought to see that David was trying to deprive him of a right, no one could be more dogged or tenacious of his dues than he.

But Anne was half ashamed to speak openly, and half afraid of showing Jim her dislike of Pen, if she broached the subject. However fate seemed working for her. In the committee meetings John began to resent the fact that David, who was too fond of usurping all control, seemed to imagine his ideas were the only ones worth carrying out.

It was David who did most of the speaking. The secretary, Fred Norrie, the bank manager, appeared to look to him for direction, and though the rest of the committee were satisfied to have it so, the Mayor began to feel that he must assert himself and put the president of the Hospital in his proper place.

The difficulty concerning the first dance had been well discussed over the town before it came to John's ears, but at last he heard it across the store counter, and he was indignant at the bare idea that a young girl should be chosen before his wife, the Lady Mayoress.

CHAPTER V.

THE LOST BANKNOTE.

"Here, Anne!" said John one evening as he came home from the store, "is some money for you. See you get yourself a dress that will do credit to us, as you must be the Governor's partner for the first dance. If you need any more, you can let me know. We may as well do the thing properly, if we do it at all."

Anne could scarcely believe her eyes when she saw that it was a £10 note which John placed in her hand. She was wondering whether she would be able to coax any money from him for a new gown. For, as Anne admitted to herself if John had a fault, it was that he was a little near. He parted with even necessary sums for the household, reluctantly, while few things aroused his placid temper to irritation more quickly than any sign of extravagance or carelessness with money. But there was nothing sordid in John's constant endeavours to save, for there was nothing selfish in it. It was all for his son that he hoarded and scraped, and taxed his slow brain with fresh scheme for money-making. It was a great disappointment to him that Jim had not chosen one of the learned professions, but he had not given up hope that he might still take up one of them; and it was against this day that he tried to lay by a good sum in the bank. It was for this that he kept so tight a hold on the purse-strings; for this that he bore with being considered mean and miserly. John knew that he was misunderstood, and resented it in his dumb way, but kept his own counsel.

Jim was quite ignorant of the motive that impelled his father to those petty economies which he had noticed since his return home. It was a pity that John did not drop a hint of his reasons; it would have taken away Jim's sense of vicarious shame over many a small restriction, as well as Anne's soreness at the grudging way in which he now doled out the housekeeping money. Indeed, out of his own scanty pay, Jim often contrived to provide his mother with some harmless luxuries as well as helping considerably with the ordinary expenses of the house. It was he who had insisted on giving her the little help-boy, making himself responsible for the wages.

No wonder then that Anne was delighted with the money, as well as with this assurance that John considered that she was to be the Governor's partner. She had been afraid to say much to him on the matter, especially in the presence of her son. She feared to meet the surprise of his clear eyes; but she was almost ashamed to think how largely this very matter bulked in her thoughts.

She would not have cared to show either her husband or her son how eagerly she was looking forward to the chance of taking precedence of all her neighbours, and especially of Pen: for now it seemed to her as if all her old anger against David returned, to add force to the bitterness of a new jealousy of Pen. But when John gave her the ten-pound note she felt more assured that she would be chosen before Pen. She had even thoughts of making a trip to Walsingham, to secure more fashionable material, and have the dress made up by the city dressmaker, and she went to bed with her head full that night of ideas of new costumes.

Next day when Jim came home for his lunch at noon, Anne met him with such a white, frightened face, that he was much alarmed. "What ever is the matter, mother?" he asked anxiously.

"I don't want father to know, and he will be here in a minute," said Anne almost in a whisper, "but I've lost the ten-pound note he gave me, and I don't know what in the world I'll do." There were great dark circles under her eyes; she looked worn and drawn.

Jim broke into a laugh of relief. "Is

THE FURNACE FOR GOLD

that all?" He said, "you gave me quite a start. I thought something dreadful must have happened."

"All!" cried Anne sharply; "It is bad enough. I am afraid to tell him. He will be so angry, but I have not a penny to spare from my housekeeping money, and I don't know where to turn. I was sure I put it carefully away last night, but I've looked high and low to-day and I can't find it. My head is fairly turning between searching about and the worry of it altogether and as for Tommy"—her lips twisted with an uncertain smile—"I'm certain he will suffer from suppressed curiosity." Jim looked at her, and he saw that though she was putting some restraint on herself Anne was fairly sick with weariness and anxiety.

"Don't say anything about it now. I see father is coming. Have a good rest after we go, and think quietly where you put the note. Then when I come home this afternoon, if you have not found it, I'll hunt too. I wouldn't be a bit surprised it hasn't blown out into the yard. Anyhow I'll do my best to find it."

Anne said no more then, but when her husband and son were gone, she could not rest, but once more began her feverish searching. At last she gave up in despair, and as she realised that she must tell her husband, she trembled at the thought of his displeasure. John had a bitter tongue when he was roused, and nothing roused him more effectually than a thing like this, she knew. She sat down hopelessly on a couch in her bedroom, when her eyes caught the dress she had been wearing the day before. She wondered in a listless way whether by any chance she could have overlooked the dress in her searching.

She tried the pocket mechanically, and brought out a crumpled roll of paper. She unrolled it with a beating heart and found that it was the missing note. She almost wept in her joyful relief, as she hastened to lock it up in her drawer. It was with a light heart, though still a little ill that she set about preparing the evening meal.

Husband and son came in together. Jim gave a quick glance at his mother, but not caring to speak on the matter in front of John, she shook her head gravely. Jim misunderstood her, and believed the money was still lost, since his mother looked so pale and wan. He went out quickly to the back of the house, and, as Anne watched him from the kitchen window, she saw him searching carefully by the woodheap. She ran out to him; he turned with a guilty start at her approach and held out a note to her. "See if this is it, mother," he said quickly, "the note you lost."

His honest face was flushed, but a deeper colour glowed in Anne's cheek as she caught his arm. "Oh, James, James, how could you! That is your own money; you went and got it out of the bank this afternoon. I can see through you. I found the note that father gave me in the pocket of my old pink dress after you left. Your ten-pound notes are scarce enough, you stupid boy, without throwing them away like that." Her hand tightened on her son's arm, as she looked up with swimming eyes to his face.

Jim laughed with a little embarrassment, but he smiled down at his mother with a curious mixture of amusement, defiance, and tenderness. "What in the world is keeping the two of you at the woodheap?" John shouted from the back door, and Tommy's face, flattened against the kitchen window, was imploring for an explanation also.

Anne's eyes followed her handsome son with a wonderful pride and an unusual softness in their depths, as she hastened in to her impatient husband.

CHAPTER VI

THREE WHO LOOKED ON.

"We are going to hold the final committee meeting to-night, in the Oldfellows' Hall," said David, as he rose to go out on Wednesday night. "I think everything is pretty well settled, though. What about the school children, Daphne? Does Mr. Andrews think he will have them ready for us to-morrow?"

"Oh, yes, I think so," said Daphne. "If they do not know the National Anthem I am sure it will not be for want of practicing. I hear it in my dreams at night; it is beginning to amount to a nightmare. We have got such a beautiful address ready. It is on white satin. Mr. Burgess, the chairman of our school committee is to read it." "How many more addresses is the Governor to have to listen to?" said Lew, scornfully. I sincerely pity the poor chap. In fact, I do not think I shall take on his billet, if I get the sack from the bank, 'Uneasy lies the head that has addresses chucked at it.' Fancy going on a tour through the colony and being obliged to listen politely and reply politely to half a dozen addresses from every twopenny-half-penny township."

David stopped on the threshold to give a withering look at his son. Like the rest of Neummurra David took the Governor's visit very seriously, and he was indignant at his son's levity. But though he paused for a speech that should be cutting enough to silence Lew, he had to content himself with a look, for Pen rushed up, and, seizing his arm, dragged him again into the room.

"Dad," she cried eagerly, "are you going to decide to-night about the first dance? Not that I mind much, one way or the other, but it would be much better to know for certain before to-morrow. Perhaps it had better be cousin Anne, for she is the Mayor's wife. I don't care one way or the other."

A laugh from Lew cut short her speech. "Well for my part I know this, the ball began as a hospital ball, it is to be in aid of the hospital funds, and as president of the hospital I believe I am entitled to say that my daughter shall be the Governor's partner in the first dance," said David, dogmatically, and he looked his pretty daughter in the eye.

"Good for you, Dad. Stick to that," said Lew, "but what about it being called a 'citizens' ball? Isn't the Mayor the first citizen? Isn't his wife the first citizeness? And ought she not then to be the Governor's partner in the first dance? Pen looked at her brother in ill-disguised anxiety.

"That is altogether outside my contention," said David shortly. "I look upon it entirely as a hospital ball."

A gleam of fun shot from Lew's eyes, but the melancholy look in Pen's face restrained him, for Lew was both fond and proud of his lovely sisters in spite of his teasing. "How do the papers speak of the ball?" He said. "I heard that the 'Standard' calls it 'Hospital and Citizens' concert and ball' the 'Echo' 'Citizens' and Hospital Concert and Ball' - but David slammed the door and went down the steps.

Neummurra had two papers; each published once a week, and each, as most natural, taking in any question opposite sides. The "Standard" upheld David Morgan, while the "Echo" was the champion of the Mayor in any municipal dispute.

"I promised Jim Heatherington to give him a look-in tonight," said Lew to his sisters. "I expect I shall be a bit late, so ask Gwenny not to lock me out," and the two girls were left alone. "Come and sit on the verandah, Daph," said Pen, as soon as Lew had gone, and Daphne consented.

The Oddfellows' Hall was a gaunt wooden structure, about a hundred yards down the slope from the Morgan's house. The light from the window at the back of the hall shone upon the girls as they sat chatting together.

The night was dark and close. The only sound that could be heard was the noisy music of a concertina from one of the tents along the creek. The lights from the township gleamed through the darkness, like stars in the distance.

"Daphne," Pen said, as a short silence had fallen between them, "will you do something for me."

"What is it?" said Daphne slowly. It had been a trying day at school; the excitement of preparation for the vice-regal welcome had got upon the nerves of teachers and scholars alike, and she was loath to leave her comfortable seat. Just to take a run down to the hall. It will only take a minute. Do, there's a dear! "What for?" said Daphne, her blue eyes opening wide in languid surprise. "Just to take a little peep into that tempting window down there, to see what father and the rest of the committee are doing."

"Not for the world," cried Daphne, in a shocked tone. "I thought you despised eavesdropping, Pen. My goodness! What an idea!" "This wouldn't be eavesdropping." said Pen indignantly. "There is nothing private in the meeting; the public are not excluded, and the secretary sends a report of the meeting to the papers." "It wouldn't be nice; father wouldn't like it, nor Lew," objected Daphne. "Wait till father comes home, and you will know who is to have the first dance, for I suppose that is what is worrying you."

"Yes, it is," said Pen frankly. "But Daph, we would only be a minute; besides it would be such fun. We could kneel on the bank and look in quite easily, and nobody would be a penny the worse. I am just dying to see father and cousin John having a set-to. Do come!" she spoke quickly, so that

Daphne might have no time to raise further objections. The idea had occurred with such tempting suddenness that impetuous Pen was on fire to carry it out. Daphne demurred, and tried to persuade her sister to give up the expedition, but finally she yielded to the artful coaxing.

"Let us slip on dark dresses, and then no one can possible see us," said Pen. The few moments delay made her somewhat doubtful about pursuing her plan, but she kept her misgivings to herself, and the two girls hurried down the hill.

The hall being, like many other buildings in Neummurra, placed on wooden piles, and on a slope, rested at the back almost on the ground, while in front a flight of several steps led up to the entrance. A narrow ledge, or bank of earth, bordered with stunted bushes, ran along the windows at the rear, and beneath the ledge was a small waterhole which municipality often spoke of filling up, but still left to be the delight of the small boys of the neighborhood.

Pen and Daphne crept up the bank, and, kneeling cautiously there, found their heads were just a little above the bottom of a window. Pen's scruples vanished as she looked with dancing eyes into the room, and saw the members of the committee gathered round a small table beneath her.

"Look, Daph," she whispered, "there's father and cousin John sitting together as amiably as you please. Let me see if I can make out the rest. Yes, there's Mr. Neddrie, the secretary, – isn't he a superfine old dandy – and there's Graves, and Dinny Finucane, how his bald head shines in the light; Good old Dinny! Doesn't he look an ideal butcher?"

"Hush," whispered Daphne in an agony of nervousness, she had none of Pen's love for queer adventures. Daphne had a great sense of personal dignity, and could not endure the thought of anything that might compromise it. She wished too late, she had not yielded so easily. "Kneel down further Pen; further yet," she implored; "you can still hear and see all you want to." and she drew her sister towards her.

The two pretty heads, the dark and the golden, were bent together for a moment, then Pen gave a stifled giggle.

"They can't possibly see us," she said softly "in among these bushes. Anyway I don't care a button if they do." Her eyes flashed back a laughing defiance at her sister, but nevertheless she kept herself out of view; and before long Daphne too gained sufficient courage to look into the room.

The proceedings seemed at first dull enough, for the committee busied themselves over papers, but Pen saw, or fancied she saw, there was an air of tenseness about her father and her cousin, that was having a disturbing effect on the others.

Neddrie, the secretary, was popularly supposed to be a man versed in all the etiquette of society, and therefore he had been appointed Master of Ceremonies for the ball. He was a great favourite in Neummurra, especially among the ladies, in spite of, perhaps because of, his persistent bachelorhood, but he seemed to-night, for a wonder, ill at ease. His round, rosy, good natured face was puckered into lines of worry. He felt the electricity in the mental atmosphere, and dreaded every moment that the storm was about to break.

He hated a scene above all things, and feared from the elaborate politeness of Morgan and Hetherington that they were preparing for one now. He was not ignorant of the friction between the two men, and wondered if they actually so far forgot themselves as to dispute about the right of deciding which lady should be the Governor's partner, what he would be expected to do in such an awkward position. He hoped that the meeting might pass off without either of the men referring to the dance. Ordinarily a man of tact and resource, Neddrie to-night, from nervousness, was not quite master of himself. The two strong, obstinate natures oppressed him by sheer animal magnetism.

"The pig-headed, ignorant boors!" he thought while he tried to smile conciliatingly from one set face to the other. "They are both spoiling for a fight. How ridiculous," he commented internally, "but how confoundedly provoking to a man of peace." Jack Graves, the chemist, whose name belied his jolly face, was a man of infinite jest, and the mere prospect of a fight gave a delighted sparkle to his small grey eyes; while "Dinny," as Neummurra was fond of calling its stout prosperous butcher, was Irishman enough at any time to glory in "a bit av a shindy." The fat creases deepened along his nose, and he winked joyfully at his boon companion, Graves, to draw his attention to Neddrie's uneasiness at the nearness of the explosion between the president and the Mayor. These two had all the enjoyment to themselves. The other members of the committee were serious enough in all conscience.

CHAPTER VII.

THE UNEXPECTED HAPPENS

The meeting grew steadily duller. Pen became tired of hearing about addresses, speeches, banquets, and all the petty details of the arrangements. A faint sound behind her caught her ear.

"Daphne," she said huskily, "there is someone coming up the bank after us." The two girls waited, holding their breath and dreading they scarcely knew what. A dark figure crept slowly towards them, and at length with a heavy sigh crouched among the bushes.

"It is cousin Anne". I know that sigh," breathed Pen. "Fancy the proper Mayoress stealing up to listen at the window, like our common selves. Oh, what a fall was here, my countrymen."

"Do be quiet," entreated Daphne. "Do not let her know we are here. She will feel so ashamed." "Let her!" retorted Pen. "So Anne's curiosity and anxiety got the better of her propriety. I suppose she stole out, and left Lew and Jim together. Cousin Anne!" she said in a thrilling whisper, "Cousin Anne! Do you see anyone coming?"

Anne – for it was indeed she – nearly fell off the bank in the violent start she gave. "Who is there?" she quavered.

"It is just Pen and Daphne," came back the laughing whisper, and Anne came closer, angry yet relieved. I just slipped down to see if John would be much longer," she said – apologetically. "The boys were busy over some new fad of Lew's about his boat. They are in the kitchen heating some irons on the fire."

"Oh! Indeed!" said Pen politely. "We've been here quite a while. I wanted to know how they were going to decide about the first dance, so I made Daph come with me. She is feeling mean, because she says it isn't nice to peep in at windows and listen to conversations without being asked; but" she continued blandly, "I do not mind; I really did so want to know whether they say I am to be the Governor's partner or not."

Anne's face burned in the darkness. She felt the challenge of the girl's tone and tried to return a biting answer, but her anger and jealousy choked her speech. Daphne felt her cousin's slight form tremble with passion, and she broke in hastily. "We had better not speak, had we? For though the three of us are in for it now, we do not wish to let Neummurra know of our escapade?" Her soft voice broke a little, and Pen remorsefully squeezed her sister's arm, and kept silent. The three women turned their attention to the room below. "Well, I think that finishes our business for this evening. We have arranged for everything now, haven't we?" Neddrie's smooth voice was speaking and for a moment Pen feared that she had missed what she had specifically come to hear, but she saw that her father rose quickly to his feet.

"Quite so, quite so, Mr. Neddrie; anything that we may not have seen to we leave in your hands, and we could not leave it in better." A murmur of assent came from the others. "Just one little matter occurs to me now, however," he paused for a minute, and the eyes of Dinny and Graves met – appreciatively. "Have you arranged for the first dance? The Governor is, I believe, to dance with my daughter as I am the president of the hospital ball, but what about the other couples in the first set? I suppose you will arrange every one? You know most about such matters."

"Oh, certainly, certainly," said Neddrie nervously. "Well, I'll see to everything, gentlemen; we need not spend any further time over discussion tonight." But John Hetherington's deep voice broke upon the flurried speech. "Is it a hospital ball?" he inquired ponderously. "I was under the impression that it was a citizens' ball."

"Oh, certainly, certainly," said Neddrie, mechanically, "you will find it so printed in the programmes." "Hospital and citizens' ball." snapped David. "Citizens' and hospital ball," said John fiercely.

"Oh, certainly, certainly," said the un-nerved secretary.

An impartial onlooker, had there been any deserving that description there, would have been amused to see the deadly earnestness of the men over a matter seemingly so trivial. But at Neummurra no matter was trivial on which a dispute might turn. "I think you will find that I am correct," and John thrust the "Echo's" printed advertisement into Neddrie's hand.

The secretary took up the paper with a proprietary smile at Morgan, which faded away before the lowering glance it encountered. A reddish light appeared in David's eyes; there was no sign of yielding there, and the secretary looked hopelessly at the "Echo."

"The Governor generally dances two square dances; perhaps we might – arrange –" he began feebly. But Morgan broke in with a harsh laugh. "For two first dances?" Neddrie reddened, and the speaker went on. "Here is the 'Standard' " he drew a paper from his pocket; "I happened to bring it with me, as my friend here brought the "Echo" – a delighted chuckle from Dinny – "and I found it printed 'Hospital and Citizens' Ball.' " Dinny's fat shoulders heaved. He felt grateful enough to both papers at that moment to double their circulation if he could.

"Suppose," said Neddrie tentatively, "that we decide that Mrs. Carson, our manager's wife, shall be the Governor's partner. I could see her and find out if she would be agreeable. As neither the president not the Mayor can agree about the matter I suggest that they allow the manager's wife to be chosen for the first dance." Graves and Finucane looked disappointedly at each other; Then an idea occurred to Graves.

"What about letting the aide-de-camp arrange it when he comes?" he asked, innocently.

The secretary looked at him in horror, and Dinny smiled broadly.

"The matter is not worth discussing," said David, ignoring the suggestion. "In fact, I cannot understand that that can be any question in the matter. If this is to be a hospital ball, the president's daughter has a right to the first dance." "It is first of all a citizens' ball, as any fool could see," said Hetherington, his temper giving way as he saw that Morgan was determined not to give in.

"Any 'fool' might," retorted David pointedly, "but perhaps the rest of us are not qualified." John glared back speechlessly, and Dinny, who was a good-hearted fellow In spite of his mischievous nature, called out—"I propose we have an innovation at Neummurra, bhoys! Let us give the Governor a free hand, and not bind him down to any wan partner. Why should not his Ex. have a chance to look round the ballroom, and choose out the purtiest girl for himself?"

Anne, on the bank above, gave a sudden dismayed start, and leaned forward in her excitement. "Take care," whispered Pen, drawing her back from the window; "do you want them to look up and see you?" but her voice quivered with irrepressible laughter. All Anne's pent-up jealousy and resentment broke into sudden flame. She caught the restraining hand, and pushed the girl fiercely from her.

The next instant with a stifled shriek, she found herself following Pen down the crumbling edge of the bank, and tumbling headlong into the pool below.

The waterhole was not deep, scarcely waist-high, but full of black mud and clammy weeds. A cold fear gripped Anne's breast, for Pen had made no sound since she struck her. As she struggled to her feet, and found her way to the bank, she knocked against a stooping figure. "Is that you Pen?" she said, trembling, "I am so sorry, I did not mean to push you down."

"Yes, its Pen," said the girl softly; "I am all right, only muddy. Of course it was an accident. Where is Daphne?" Daphne rushed up in a rapture of thankfulness, and tried to catch hold of her sister.

"Hands off, Daph, I'm all over mud." Pen's teeth were chattering, but a laugh bubbled to her lips. "Let's run for our lives, for I'm afraid we must have made some sound, and if they find us like this we'll never hear the end of it." The creak of an opening door gave point to her words. A shaft of light followed their flight, but they made good their escape up the hill into the darkness. Pen had to stop at intervals to laugh hysterically, and at last Anne lost all patience. Her animosity was coming back, now that her remorse had lessoned and her sense of shamed discomfort increased.

"I'm off home; take my advice and run for it, too. Goodnight," she said shortly, and turned away. Anne slipped in quietly at the back of her house, and stole into the bathroom. She could hear the voices of the young men from the kitchen. Lew was speaking, she found after a few minutes. "Tell you what, Jim," he said. "I believe that little beggar of a Tommy of yours has got his nose glued to a crack of the door there. I see a pair of black eyes through the slit." "Nonsense," said Jim, and Anne heard a shuffle and a cry. "Why, you are right, Lew. What is up with you, Tommy? Have you been here listening at the door all the time?" "No!" Tommy protested; "but I heard someone coming into the bathroom, and I got frightened." "Go to bed and don't be silly," said Jim.

Anne shivered lest he should try to verify Tommy's statement; but the two young men went on with their experiments, and she managed to change quietly and get away to her own room. She came down soon after, but found that they had not observed her absence. Meantime Gwenny, the old servant at Morgan's, as she sat dozing before the fire, was startled to hear a sudden rush of feet through the passage. She called out in alarm, but Pen's voice reassured her. "It is all right, Gwen. I'm just going to take a bath, we have been for a walk, and I feel so hot."

Pen closed the bathroom door, lit a candle, and fell in a heap on the floor." Daphne bent over her in sudden terror, which turned to indignation as she saw that her sister was only helpless with laughter. "Oh, Daph," gasped Pen, "this will be the death of me! Fancy Anne in this plight! To think of us both there in the waterhole, mud from head to foot, and groping, groping our way to the bank! If they had come out of the hall and found us, I should have died on the spot. I'm sure I should, Oh dear! Oh dear!" and she fell over again.

Daphne looked at her severely. It was at times like this when it seemed as if she were the elder sister, and not frivolous Pen.

"It will not look to you so very funny tomorrow. You'll have your work cut out to get these things clean without letting Gwenny see them. If Jack Graves has caught sight of you it will not be long before the whole yarn is over Neummurra, and I do not suppose Jim Heatherington will think it quite such a laughing matter as you do, that everybody is making fun of his mother and you." Pen's laughter died away, and a strange expression appeared for a moment in the lovely dark eyes, as she soberly drew off her muddy shoes.

CHAPTER VIII
THE GOVERNOR ARRIVES.

Thursday morning dawned clear, bright, and cloudless. "A perfect day," sighed Pen as she woke up with the sun, none the worse for her adventure. "I wonder how things were finally arranged. I must ask father." She looked remorsefully at her sleeping sister for a moment, then dressed and stole quietly from the room. The fair face, even in sleep, seemed weary.

At breakfast time David appeared with an irritable expression on his face. "Nothing was right," he averred, and grumbled through the entire meal. Daphne was in a depressed mood, and Lew, too, appeared out of sorts. Pen alone seemed to suit her spirits to the sunshine outside.

"Did you have a nice meeting, Dad? So, have you settled about the first dance?" she said anxiously, and flashed a merry glance at Daphne's flushed, disturbed face. "I am longing to hear all about it, Dad, do tell me before you go."

David gave a grunt, but Pen met his ill-humour with a charming smile and half unwillingly he allowed himself to be coaxed into a better temper. "Oh! same kind of meeting as usual." he said reluctantly "There is not much variety about a committee meeting," Pen's fine eyebrows lifted imperceptibly, as she met her sister's glance. "But about the first dance. Well, I can scarcely say it is settled yet. They decided to leave it to the aide-de-camp, in spite of Neddrie's protest. Three names are to be submitted"—he looked at Pen thoughtfully –"Your own, cousin Anne's, and Mrs. Carson's"

Lew gave a deep laugh. "I suggest the three of you fight it out, or draw for it, or something like that," he said considerately. "Don't be a fool!" cried his father angrily, and the young man continued his breakfast in silence. David looked irritably at the impassive face for a few moments, ready to be annoyed, and eager to resent annoyance; but Lew did not look up, and seemed resolved to give no opportunity for reproof.

"'Queer thing, though, broke up the meeting," David went on in a few moments, more amiably, as he found that Lew had no thought of interrupting him with irreverent remarks. "Just as we were discussing this very matter we heard what sounded like a woman's shriek, and Graves declared he heard a splash in the waterhole behind the Hall. We waited a few minutes, but heard no more. Then we went out with a light, but found nothing, so we decided it must have been a bird in the bushes. But somehow we could not settle down to anything after that, so the meeting broke up. I stayed a bit later down town talking with Dinny Finucane and Graves over the Governor's visit."

Pen's bright colour had ebbed a little, but her saucy laugh rang out. "So you really cannot tell me whether or not I am to have the honour of dancing with the Governor?" "You can smile at the aide-de-camp when you see him, perhaps it may have some effect," said David with grim pleasantry, and he rose to go to work, followed soon after by Lew and Daphne.

As Daphne reached the school gate, the postman handed her the letters for the school. Among them was one in a long, official envelope. As Daphne went into the master's room and handed him the bundle of letters a curious feeling came over her, a sudden and inexplicable presentiment. "Is it a transfer for me?" she said, scarcely conscious that she was uttering her thought aloud.

Mr. Andrews glanced at the girl, but did not speak. He opened the official letter first and scanned its contents.

"You are right," he said gravely. "It is a transfer for you. You are transferred to Bundamango. How in the world did you know it was for you, or that it was a transfer at all?"

"I didn't know," Daphne could scarcely frame the words, "only as I handed the letter to you something told me it was a transfer for me."

"I am very sorry to lose you," said Mr. Andrews. "Will you go, do you think? Bundamango is a long way from here, and only a very small bush school, I believe."

Daphne's face paled and her hands shook as she tried to fold up the paper, but she looked up calmly.

"Yes, I shall go, I expect. But, Mr. Andrews," she hesitated, "do you mind my keeping all about this transfer to myself till tomorrow? I do not want the others to know today, it would spoil all the fun and Pen is looking forward so much to the ball. I'll tell them tomorrow if you would be so kind as to keep it from the other teachers to-day. No one saw me with the letters, I think."

Mr. Andrews was reputed somewhat hard and severe, though just, but he had a kind heart in spite of his gruff manners, and he was genuinely attached to the young teacher whom he had trained since she was a child. He looked at the earnest, troubled face. There were, he could see, unsuspected reserves of quiet strength in the girl's character. Most lady teachers, his experience told him, made a scene on an occasion like this, and few would have had so much consideration for others as Daphne evinced.

"Why, yes, if you wish it. But it gives you one day less to stay at home and get ready. I think you are a plucky girl, Daphne, and I know the children

THE FURNACE FOR GOLD

will be heart-broken at losing you."

The tears rushed to the girl's eyes, but she drove them back, and, thanking him gravely, she left the room to get her class in line for marching.

The Neummurra scholars were soon on their way to the pavilion erected for his Excellency. A large body of the parents escorted them there, for a half-holiday had been given to all workers in honour of the vice-regal visit. In the afternoon they were to return to their duty, as the Governor had expressed a wish to see the working of the mine. Lew Morgan, among the spectators, was inwardly tickled, though his serious face gave little signs of this, by the absorbed air of importance of the officials, and those who were to present addresses.

Everybody in the town, from infants in arms to the oldest (though he was not very old) inhabitant, was gathered around the gaily festooned pavilion, and as the four-in-hand drove up, the children, with the hearty assistance of the band, broke into the National Anthem. The men uncovered their heads, showed their honest, sun-browned, jovial faces, and cheered vociferously. It was an inspiring scene!

"King Billy." the millionaire who owned most of the mine, and who was a prime favourite in the township, looked at the crowd from his position beside the Governor, with a heart swelling with pride in Neummurra, his own kingdom.

When Sir George Thurston stepped forward to speak it was seen that he was a tall, soldierly man, on the sunny side of middle age, with a pleasant, smiling face, and kind grey eyes.

He spoke briefly, but though not an orator, there was something manly and attractive in his direct, honest, style of speaking. The children were to be given a holiday on the morrow, he said.

The children and the grown people cheered heartily at the conclusion of his speech, and everybody seemed happy.

But, as one after another, the men who had been selected stepped forward, presented their addresses, and received a reply, a blank-ness of boredom began to settle on most of the faces. Whatever he may have felt, however, his Excellency contrived to look pleased and interested until the whole long-winded function drew to a close; but the air with which he at last sank back against the cushions of the buggy, as he stepped into it again, was in itself a confession of weariness. For the vice-regal party had been driving all the morning over a dusty road, and now while the addresses were being read the sun beat mercilessly down on the hollow, and the heat waves danced over the grasses. The children in spite of their excitement, grew weary, and the miners looked hopelessly at each other until the last address was safely got rid of. The Governor's fatigue had but short respite, however, for the indefatigable entertainment committee had prepared a programme that would occupy every moment of his stay in Neummurra

As soon as lunch was over, Sir George was given to understand that the hospital was awaiting the honour of a visit; and that as an address would be presented by the president, he would be expected to make a speech in reply

Nestfield, the local member, and Colville, the Minister for Mines, who had accompanied the Governor, looked at each other in dismay; it seemed to them the badgered Governor must have exhausted his vocabulary, but no expression save one of pleased expectation, could be read on the face of Sir George Thurston.

After the hospital visit, the committee had arranged with the manager to have the Vice-regal party shown over the mine, and shortly after three o'clock they came up the hill.

Daniel Marlowe, "the boss of the Lower Works," held in his hand a test tube with solution, and as he poured into it some sulphate of iron, he stared fixedly at the mixture, but his thoughts were not on his occupation The men working in the shed stole sly glances at the moody face, and wondered "what had put the Boss out." A few of them guessed the reason, for they had noticed that Buxton had passed the sheds with the Governor, and gone straight to the upper works without a glance for Marlowe, who was standing at the entrance, and they knew that it was the boast of Marlowe that Buxton's first visit to Neummurra was always to his old mate. William Buxton and Daniel Marlowe had been mates at school, and again in a shipping office in Sydney.

At Buxton's persuasions, Marlowe had left the office and gone prospecting with him. After a few unlucky year they had separated, Marlowe returning to Sydney, and Buxton going to North Queensland.

Buxton at first had a hard struggle, but before long he had made a little money, and began to speculate in mining shares.

He was strangely fortunate, and was becoming moderately wealthy, when chance threw in his way the original owners of Neummurra. He made a trip to the mine, and soon saw that the opportunity of his lifetime had come. When a company was floated he bought as many shares as he could, and by the time slower-witted investors were beginning to make inquiries after shares Buxton was practically the chief shareholder. In a few more years he had bought out three of the five original shareholders, and was made chairman of the directors of the "Neummurra Gold-mining Company Limited."

Some people called the millionaire a scheming rogue, but the miners recognised in "King Billy," as they called him, a straight dealing man, with a contempt for humbug, and they respected him. In defiance of adverse reports on a trip south, after his appointment as chairman of directors, he met his old mate in Sydney, and persuaded him once more to leave the office, where he was still struggling on a small salary. A position, was found for him at the mine, and as year after year passed by and Marlowe grew to understand the work, he was promoted step by step, until at last he was "Boss of the Lower Sheds," with but one man above him— the manager of the mine.

In this steady promotion Dan

recognised the influence of his old mate, but though he was grateful to him, be felt in his own mind that all this was no more than his due. Were they not mates? And had it not been share and share alike in the old days? If he had been lucky enough to drop into such a good thing as this Neummurra mine, would not his first impulse have been to share his good fortune with his mate? It was true, Buxton had done a great deal for him; but in doing this Dan felt be had not actually parted with a penny of his own money. His patronage had cost him nothing.

Two years ago, on the removal of the last manager, Dan had expected that this position, the last step on his career of promotion, would be given to him. But Buxton was then in England, and the directors had appointed Carson, a southern man. As soon as Carson was appointed manager a deep sense of injustice rankled in Dan's heart. He had grown to expect the position as his right, and he felt that a wrong had been done him when he was passed over. Like many another man, Dan reasoned from such a narrow personal standpoint that he could not see the other side of the question at all.

He seldom spoke to Carson, and ignored as much as he dared his authority. But apart from this mental twist, though not at all clever, he was a painstaking, conscientious worker, a sensible man, and a good master; kind, considerate, yet firm to his employees, and a prime favourite with them. Truth to tell, Buxton, who understood the idiosyncrasies of his old friend quite well, was perfectly aware that he had expected to have been made manager, and had timed his visit to England purposely to be out of the way until a new manager was appointed.

Marlowe had been a good clerk, but though he succeeded fairly well as "Boss" of the lower works, with the familiar routine of duties, he had neither the scientific training nor the natural bent that would have fitted him for the position of manager. It was, however, with no thought of either slighting or avoiding Dan that Buxton passed by the lower works, and took the Vice-regal party up to the cuttings. The millionaire considered himself the host for the afternoon, and wished the Governor to enjoy his visit to the mine: so on the advice of the manager they set out at once for the top.

As for Marlowe, Buxton forgot altogether about him, in the confusion of the moment, and it was only as he followed the manager up the hill that he remembered him. It was too late to go back then, and, besides, he was curious to see what kind of a man Carson was, for this was the first time he had met him. The manager was a tall, spare man, with fair, scanty hair streaked with grey, and a tone and manner that would have suited a professor or schoolmaster. He seemed to enjoy his work, and led the Governor from place to place, explaining and describing with great gusto. Buxton watched him with some inward amusement. Carson was not much liked by the men, who believed that he wished to stand well with the directors by cutting down their wages, and who besides resented a number of petty restrictions that he had instituted; but Buxton could see that he was a capable man, if rather fond of the sound of his own voice. "Very little tact, and obstinate if opposed," was the millionaire's verdict as he listened to the flow of the new manager's eloquence, and he felt that he was not greatly attracted by him. "Good heavens!" he thought to himself about an hour later. "Does the man want to kill us outright, making us tramp all over the place at this rate? His voice will drive me crazy," and Buxton, who was heavily built, toiled after the Governor, and mopped his streaming face at intervals.

The manager was too absorbed to notice that there was any flagging in the courtesy of the visitors, and too unobservant to see their weariness. The tired men followed him through tunnels, over ridges, down shafts and across "benches" till their faces grew purple and blotched with heat.

"We shall go down now to the Lower Shed." said Carson at last, as he looked round the hill to see whether anything of interest could have escaped his vigilant eye. "His Excellency will, no doubt, like to observe the process of extraction and smelting of the gold; I think there is nothing up here we have left without seeing."

"Nothing, I am sure," said Sir George fervently, "but I am afraid we are trespassing too much on your kindness."

"Not at all, not at all; it has been a pleasure to me, I assure you," said Carson, much gratified. Captain Langely, the aide-de-camp, turned his handsome, melancholy face towards the speaker, with such a sulky air of injury that Buxton. who himself felt on the verge of apoplexy, could not refrain from smiling. Carson's satisfaction and his visitors' patience were almost too much for the millionaire's sense of the ridiculous.

"Here are my wife and daughter, with some afternoon tea." Carson said, as they turned down the hill, and at that moment his victims felt that they could forgive him, even the tunnels. The two ladies, in cool, white dresses, stood at a pretty little table, under a clump of gum trees, and the exhausted sight-seers, sank down gratefully on the grass, without further invitation. Captain Langely's face brightened at the sight of the young lady, and he soon began to show himself in a more amiable light than he had hitherto done.

CHAPTER IX.

AN UNFORTUNATE MISHAP.

With some reluctance the Vice-Regal party rose from the grass at the manager's suggestion and began the descent towards the lower works. The cuttings, with their vertical walls, composed of varying red and yellow stone, the narrow tramways of the upper portion of the mine, were left behind, and the heterogeneous mass of buildings known as the "lower works" lay at their feet. The cloud of smoke and dust which hung over the sheds and the constant steady hum of machinery

THE FURNACE FOR GOLD

gave evidence of the busy work within.

The strangers followed the manager down a succession of narrow steps, eyeing with some curiosity the dusty hoppers, the "dry-crushers," the greasy barrels, the vats, engines, dryers, rolls, screens, and all the mysterious machinery for crushing, chlorinating, and precipitating the gold.

The workers looked up and grinned a friendly but embarrassed welcome to their distinguished visitors, then went on with their duties as the manager had previously ordered. "I think you will find this the most interesting step of all" began Carson, when from the opening in the flooring above a dense greenish vapour fell upon the little group, which instantly broke up in disorder each man staggering, coughing, choking his way to the pure air outside. Nestfield stumbled and fell, but Buxton and Colville dragged him out between them. His Excellency followed quickly. Carson was the first to get out. Captain Langely who had been lingering in the rear with the ladies, alone escaped.

"What—what is this?" stuttered Sir George leaning weakly against the side of the shed. Nestfield sank down on the grass and gasped for breath. "Chlorination fumes" panted Carson. "Someone must have taken the lid off a barrel." He stopped abruptly as Buxton gave him a warning glance. "An accident must have happened, I can see," said Buxton smoothly. "The fumes will soon be gone—will they not Carson?"

The millionaire's fresh colour had faded but his eyes were steely bright with anger. He seldom allowed himself to lose his temper, but he lost it now, though he managed to hide his wrath.

"It was not less than a deliberate insult," he considered, "that such a thing should have been permitted to occur at such a moment." He did not believe that it was an accident. He knew too much to think this was the case, but it suited his purpose to say so to the Governor. Sir George received the explanation in all good faith, and made light of the discomfort he had suffered.

"We shall be right in a few minutes," he said. "Do not let a little thing like this disturb you." Nestfield gave an inarticulate groan, and Buxton said quickly, "Will your Excellency excuse Carson and me if we leave you for a few minutes to see if the air is clear again so you may continue your inspection of the works?"

The Governor seemed pleased at the respite, and with the rest of the Vice-Regal party sat down on the grass and gratefully inhaled the fresh air of the hillside. The manager and Buxton waited for a few minutes with the others, then went back to the shed.

"Where's Marlowe?" Said Buxton sharply. "What sort of oversight is this you keep, Carson? I wouldn't have had such a blackguardly thing happen for the yearly dividends. Come along and see if we can catch the rascals." Carson was annoyed at the tone, and said resentfully. "There is Marlowe coming up from the smelting room, you can ask him about it. He is in charge of the lower works." Buxton was too angry to greet his old friend in his ordinary manner. He began at once to speak of the mishap. The three men went up the steps to the second story of the shed.

As soon as they reached the top they saw that the coverings were off three of the barrels just above the opening of the flooring. A group of men with scared faces were at the far end of the shed. Buxton looked grimly from them to Carson and Marlowe. "You had better see what they know," he said at last.

The manager's anger rose, too, and he resolved to punish Buxton. "I'll see to this matter." he said coldly, "but there is no need to delay his Excellency over it, as the shed is clear of the gas, Marlowe will be able to explain the process to him as well as I could." There was something of spiteful satisfaction in thus leaving Buxton and his guests to Marlowe, for Carson knew that, at the best of times, the boss of the lower sheds was an unready man, who could not be depended upon in an emergency to do either justice to himself or his subject: and from the nervous twitching of his face now he could see that he was upset by the way in which Buxton had taken the unfortunate contretemps. It was plain there was no love lost between the manager and the boss. Buxton turned on his heel and went down the steps; Marlowe followed in silence.

The millionaire thought to himself—"The man is in the right. I had better go back to the Governor. I wish I had not rushed away from the others, but my temper got the better of me. Most likely they were too upset to think anything of my leaving them. I do not want Sir George to suppose that the men of Neummurra are curs enough to invite him here, and then play such a cowardly trick on him. I've heard of them trying to pay off a spite in this way before. I wonder did they have it "In" for Carson or me? Perhaps, after all, it was an accident, though it is hard to credit it."

The visitors were chatting together, evidently quite recovered, but somewhat at a loss at being thus left to themselves. "Those barrels are not too safe at times," said Buxton, "but it is unfortunate that your Excellency, should have been here when they proved their untrustworthiness. I cannot tell you how sorry I am it should have occurred.

"Not at all," responded his Excellency politely. "I confess I was a bit startled, and the fumes were rather unpleasant, but I am all right again, and so is Nestfield, who came off worse than any of us." The member for Neummurra gave a some-what sickly smile as he corroborated the Governor's remark. Buxton introduced Marlowe and said, "The shed is quite clear of fumes now, so if your Excellency would really care to follow the process Mr. Marlowe will be pleased to give us all the information on the subject. I think he can promise you a pleasant and safe time among the gold."

Dan felt the implied reproof in Buxton's tone, and resented it, but he led the way into the shed. He had some misgivings as to his ability to make a guide that would satisfy Buxton;

256

THE FURNACE FOR GOLD

especially as he knew that, from sheer nervousness, he was not likely to do himself justice now.

Dan understood his work, but he could not put that knowledge into words. Before he had gone half-way down the shed, he could tell by his old friend's face that he was growing impatient and his nervousness increased. "How long do you expect the mine to last? Have you formed any estimate? Is it keeping up to the same mark as at first?" asked Sir George at last.

"We have not been having such good returns lately," said Dan, awkwardly. "We have been meeting a lot of poor stone this good bit back."

"The same stone with less gold in it, or different ore altogether?" asked Sir George, smoothing on his palm the fine dust, just ready for the furnace, that Marlowe had brought to show him the last stage in the dry-crushing process.

"The ore is changing all the while," said Marlowe, then hesitated, and looked at Buxton. "Mostly we have the best returns from the red stone, or the peacock stone." "What stone have you been putting through this month?" asked Buxton, tormented with the slow, tongue-tied way in which Marlowe spoke.

"Mostly white and yellow Ironstone. You can see by the colour," said Marlowe stiffly. He was a poor cicerone, and the Governor, who in spite of his weariness, could not help being interested in the wonderful chlorination process, wished that Carson had not left, though he was too kindhearted to show this to Marlowe by any sign of dissatisfaction.

Buxton guessed it, however, and looked round with some irritation in the hope of seeing the manager appear; and Marlowe, who read his old friend so well, was quite aware of his angry impatience, yet felt too nervous to launch into any long explanation lest he should make some mistake. Just at this moment Jim Hetherington came in search of the boss, and hesitated at seeing him so occupied.

Jim had not heard of the mishap with the gas, but a few minutes before, on looking out of the window of the assay-room, he had seen Schultz, one of the shift men in the chlorination-shed, running down the steps at the back and then hiding behind a disused barrel outside. In agonies of silent amusement.

The man slipped out of sight as he came towards the shed, and Jim was wondering over his mysterious behavior as he went to find Marlowe. He guessed the fellow must have been playing a trick, but there was something diabolical in his still merriment. As Jim came up to the group he could not but observe the irritated expression on the millionaire's face, and the nervous, uncomfortable look of Marlowe. Jim was very fond of Dan, who indeed had been almost a father to him; and knowing his weak points he hoped he was not in a difficulty now. Since his childhood, and after the death of his own son, little Johnnie Marlowe, Dan had made a pet of Jim. It was he who had urged him to try for the Grammar

257

School scholarship, and had gloried most in his success. Jim's very handwriting was a monument of Dan's interest, for he had striven to give him his own solitary accomplishment, his fair, clerkly style of writing.

Jim had come back to study mining, chiefly because he would be under his old friend: and though, since his return, he found that Dan had his limitations, it had made no difference to his respect and affection.

"Can you give me some idea of the assay you have made in the stone lately? I am really interested in metallurgy, though I know very little of the subject. I should like to ascertain what has been making the difference that you speak of," said the Governor; and as Marlowe only looked at him hopelessly, he turned to the young fellow who had just come in. The bright, intelligent face had attracted his notice, and he asked him the question involuntarily. Jim flushed at being addressed, but answered at once, glad, as he thought, to be able to get Dan out of a difficulty. "We have been meeting lately alternating patches of silicious ferruginous, and kaolinic sinter, mostly of low grade, and a good deal of iron pyrites, what the miners call 'mundic.' In fact, a rather larger amount of refactory ore has been put through this last month than all the rest of the year, but we have not been getting quite our assay value even out of the stuff we have treated; perhaps a change in the treatment might give a better result."

Every eye was on the speaker. Mrs. Carson and her daughter stared in undisguised amazement at hearing one of the men speaking in such a way; one who, though a little abashed at their notice, was yet perfectly self-possessed.

Jim was in workman's dress, his shirt sleeves were rolled back, from his muscular arms, his face was covered with red dust of the works, yet there was something in his look that caught Clara Carson's eye. "He is quite handsome," was her inward comment. Buxton turned his watchful eyes on the young man. "Been here long?" be said; and Jim returned, as laconically, "Since I was a boy."

Sir George smiled slightly. "Have you been working long in the mine?" "I have been two years at the works," said Jim, briefly. And where were you before that?" said Buxton.

"I was at the Melbourne University," said Jim reluctantly. Nestfield broke in: "I thought 1 knew the face, too. Aren't you Jim Heatherington, the Neummurra lad who passed the scholarship for the Grammar School and afterwards won an exhibition?"

The red dust could not hide the flush that rose to the young man's cheek as he assented. "How is it," asked the millionaire, bluntly, "that they did not make a lawyer, or doctor, or something like that of you?"

"I suppose, because I did not wish to take up any of those professions," said Jim; "I had a fancy for metallurgy; so, as my home is at Neummurra. I thought I would find out all I could about the business here, and then perhaps go over for a bit in America, where they seem in

THE FURNACE FOR GOLD

advance of us with gold extracting methods."

"Quite right." Said Sir George, looking thoughtfully at him, "I am very food of metallurgy myself. It is a fascinating study. Jim was so entirely free from self-consciousness that after the first shyness was over he willingly agreed to Buxton's suggestion that he should act as guide to the party for the rest of the time. Buxton was so delighted at finding a competent and ready guide that it scarcely occurred to him to think that Marlowe would resent being thus summarily superseded.

Sir George, as the millionaire's guest, was prevented from expressing any personal feeling, and Jim, who knew nothing of what had transpired, in all innocence was quite pleased to act as guide. He did not guess the storm of jealousy and anger that was working in Marlowe's breast as he saw him taking his place. Jim's sturdy independence made him soon feel at ease with the strangers, and as he possessed a natural gift of talk and a fund of humour that unconsciously played round even the dry technicalities of the works.

It was soon a very interested and amused party that gathered round him. The Governor forgot his weariness and went from vat to vat, examined tubes, tested solutions, and followed each step of the extraction and precipitation of gold, until finally to the smelting room the beautiful glowing blocks showed the initials of the company in sunk letters on the bottom.

It was growing dusk before the Governor declared himself ready to return to the township. He thanked Jim, and so did the other visitors. Jim went back to the shed a little excited at so much notice.

Sir George stood at the door of the smelting room and touched the millionaire's arm" If you are hard up for a manager, I should recommend you to try that young Heatherington."

"You are about right. I am going to take the first chance of having a talk with the young fellow," said Buxton, when to his annoyance he saw that Miss Carson was behind him.

He stood still and the Governor passed on. "I say Miss Carson," said Buxton in his peculiar way. "Take my advice and capture that young man if he is still at large. He will be worth something one of these days; besides, he is a handsome young man, as you must have noticed."

Clara gave him an indignant look, and turned away, reddening in spite of her indignation, for the millionaire had but uttered the thought that had sprung into her mind as she heard the Governor's words.

"Horrid, vulgar, rude old man" she thought furiously as she hurried to rejoin her mother. It angered her that he should have dared to refer to it, but the fact was that the young man had made a considerable impression in the heart of the manager's daughter. Clara was a stickler for position and that he was a university man made, she felt, a wonderful difference. He was not a common workman; probably he was the future manager.

Buxton smiled grimly to himself at

259

the young girl's air of offence. "I meant to pay her out for overhearing what was not meant for her," he thought, "but I believe I struck home too. I remember now that young miss seemed as much interested in the processes as the Governor himself, and perhaps that was owing to the handsome instructor. A shallow empty headed creature, she looks to me! The young chap is miles too good for her, and I would be sorry to put her on his tracks, for I took quite a fancy to him. He seems to have a fine head on his shoulders. I must see what his ideas for altering our present treatment are; there might be something in them."

Carson was at the gates as Buxton reached them, and was receiving with smiling gratification the thanks and compliments of his Excellency.

Buxton excused himself from returning with the Governor, as he wished to remain at the works. "Well, did you find out who did the trick with the barrels?" he asked of the manager.

'No, the men stick together and profess entire ignorance. They may know something and refuse to betray their mates, but after spending all that time over it I am no wiser than I was at first. No one will admit to being near those barrels at the time the thing happened, and though it is scarcely possible that it was an accident, it would be a hard matter to convict anyone of it."

Buxton had recovered his good humour. It was seldom he lost it; indeed, his perfect command over his temper was no little factor in his supremacy over other men.

"Never mind now, there is no use crying over spilt milk. What is done is done, and if we make a fuss over it now, it will only help to deepen the bad impression; so if I were you, I'd let it alone, Carson."

The manager looked at him doubtfully. This was very different from the despotic manner in which the director had ordered him about at the time of the accident.

"I'll tell you what, Carson," said Buxton, pleasantly, "I'd like you to send over that young fellow Heatherington to the office. I wish to see him for a few minutes."

"Certainly!" said Carson, in some surprise; and without another word, the millionaire turned away.

"A queer fellow, blunt and abrupt sometimes, but as sweet as honey, when it suits him," was the manager's comment, as he went towards the Lower Works, and sort a messenger to find Heatherington. "What is in the wind now?"

Jim went to the office of the boardroom and had a long conversation with Buxton.

The young fellow had formed a theory for dealing with the tailings and slime, also with the refractory ores, that, if successful. would mean greatly increased returns from the mine; and though Buxton made no promises he seemed very interested in the idea, and anxious to hear all about Jim's experiments.

It was nearly dark when Buxton left the mine.

THE FURNACE FOR GOLD

CHAPTER X,

THE BALL

The night was pitch dark as the Governor's carriage drove past the works, on the way to the Oddfellows' Hall, where the ball was to be held.

Just as the vehicle came opposite the Lower Shed the mouths of the furnaces opened to allow of the charges being stirred with the "rabbles."

"Stop a moment," Sir George called out to the coachman, and the carriage came to a standstill in the red light of the open doors.

"By Jove, Buxton, look at that!" cried Sir George excitedly. "Isn't that a sight that Doro would have reveled in. 'Pon my word, it is cruelly suggestive of Dante's Inferno." Buxton laughed, but he, with the rest of the Vice-Regal party, leaned forward to watch the scene.

The open mouth of the furnace, the blazing fury of the glowing ore, the grim faces of the men, with their sinewy forms, half nude to the waist, the flashing lights, and the strong, dark shadows made altogether a wonderful play of sombre colouring.

"It seems to me," Captain Langely's even, expressionless voice seemed to heighten the effect of the words he spoke; "that what with a temperature like they are having in there, what with the recurrent enjoyment of the fumes we encountered this afternoon, and the dust which they have always with them, as their lungs must testify, those fellows in there ought to get a fair share of the gold they work for."

A frown gathered on Buxton's face as he stared thoughtfully into the shed, then he shrugged his huge shoulders.

"Poor wretches; indeed they do not get it. I should not care at this day to earn my bread under their conditions, though I've done it as hardly in my time. However, as we are on our way to a ball, we needn't stop now to discuss the labour problem in the mine need we?" The aide-de-camp made no reply, and the coachman drove on. The Hall was almost filled when the Governor and his party were shown into the seats reserved for them.

Anne with her husband and son, sat just behind the strangers. Anne's usually pale face was flushed, her eyes shone, she looked almost young and pretty. She was uncomfortably conscious of the stiffness of her grand new dress, and nervous, yet pleased, at the thought of dancing with the aristocratic man, who sat so quietly in front of her, unaware as yet of what was awaiting him.

The Morgans were but a seat behind their cousins. "Doesn't he look nice? He appears different somehow from the Neummurra men, yet he seems dressed like an ordinary man," Pen whispered to Daphne, "and that is the aide-de-camp, I expect. I wonder what makes him look so sad," but Daphne did not answer. Pen leaned over to her father. "Is it settled yet who is to have the first dance?"

"Hush!" said David shortly. "No, nothing is settled yet. You will know after the concert is over." Pen's face fell, but it cleared the next moment. How could a girl, conscious that every glance was repeating the flattering tale that her mirror had told, be otherwise than happy in the intoxication knowledge of her own loveliness.

Neummurra girls have seldom much colour, but Pen's cheeks were like roses, and her wonderful eyes, lighted up by the glow, sparkled like stars on a frosty night. In the brilliancy of Pen's beauty, Daphne seemed strangely pale and wan; yet with her sweet blue eyes and her shining golden hair, she was as perfect in her way as her sister in hers.

Never before had the title of "the Rose and the Lily of Neummurra" seemed so apt, thought many a man with a thrill almost of pain as his glance lingered on the beautiful pair that night.

It had been a long, trying day for the Governor, and in spite of his air of polite attention he could not prevent himself from feeling tired and growing paler and paler as each item of the concert programme was gone conscientiously through, and many an encore added by the hearty, honest, and happy audience. At last it was over and when the performers had been presented to the Governor, and had each received a few appreciative words, the crowd began to assume an air of alertness.

The decision must be shortly made, and the claimants for the honour of the first dance were aware of the glances of their neighbours, even while they endeavoured to look calmly indifferent and unconscious.

The M.C. came forward, and led the Governor towards the platform, where he could be with his friends in a recess until the hall was cleared of chairs and made ready for the dance.

For a few minutes a scene of wild confusion ensued, as a hundred willing hands seized chairs, and carried them to the verandah, which was curtained in for a refreshment room.

Then gradually order was formed out of chaos and the ladies took their places on the row of chairs that had been left to line the walls. There was a hush of suspense, none of the young men cared to advance into the ballroom and secure their partners until the Governor appeared. They hung in eager groups at the doorways, or leant in at the window sills, and took observations on the positions of favourites, so as to enable them to make a beeline for them on the first opportunity.

There was none of the lackadaisical attitude of southern men about the honest young fellows of Neummurra; they knew they were here only wallflowers among the sterner sex; and the point of ambition with them was to see which would be first to secure the prettiest girls for the dances; the laggards must be content with the less popular girls.

Mrs. Carson, with her daughter Clara, sat in state at the upper end of the hall, and looked around with a condescending air.

There was always at the Neummurra balls a distinct understanding that the upper end was reserved for the aristocracy; or, as they called them, the "silver-tails." You could gauge the social status of anyone by observing their nearness to, or distance from, the upper end of the ballroom. Anne sat stiffly beside her cousins, and endeavored to seem at ease; while Pen, in spite of every effort, was excited and a little strained. The three ladies were doing their best to appear oblivious of the interest with which the crowd were, observing them, but without much success. A group of men appeared at a doorway.

"The entertainment committee," whisper went round the ball. They seemed somewhat nonplussed, and hesitated on the threshold.

"Go in, Neddrie, you explain; aren't you MC?" Dinny's rolling voice was plainly audible.

"Ladies and gentlemen," began the secretary in a low tone. "Speak up," someone called out from the doorway, and a laugh followed.

"Ladies and gentlemen," he repeated in a louder tone. "His Excellency has asked me to thank you most heartily for the splendid reception you have given him. He will not soon forget Neummurra" ("I bet he doesn't" whispered Lew Morgan to Jim Hetherington as the two young men stood together at a window), and also for the charming concert, which he has so much enjoyed listening to. But he asks me to convey to you his regret that owing to indisposition, he feels himself unable to remain for the ball. The coach will be leaving early in the morning. In order to catch the boat at Walsingham, so he will not have another opportunity of meeting with you on this trip, but he hopes, another time, to be able to make a longer stay with you."

A murmur of applause followed the speech, Neddrie bowed, and withdrew.

The crowd looked blankly at each other for a moment, and then with one accord at the three claimants while a subdued ripple of irrepressible amusement ran along the walls, and broke into open laughter on the verandah.

Mrs. Carson faced the inquiring eyes with a cold stare. Anne bent down for a minute, and smoothed her pretty dress. If her colour was a little dashed when she looked up, her sharp black eyes defied criticism, while Pen, after the first dismayed gasp at the announcement glanced at her discomfited rivals, the humour of the situation overcame her chagrin, and she began to laugh helplessly.

Lew caught Neddrie's arm as he would have passed him on the verandah. "I say", he said innocently, "what frightened the Governor away. He isn't simply dead beat with addresses – nine and the concert – is he?" Neddrie glanced at his young clerk, but overlooked his impudence, in his own annoyance and longing for comfort.

"You can thank your father and John Hetherington for the obstinacy that made it impossible or me to do otherwise than explain to the aide-de-camp that there were three ladies waiting for the first dance," he said, angrily.

"And how did the Governor take it when Captain Langley explained the situation?" asked Lew guilelessly.

"He came striding up to me", burst out the angry MC "and he said 'three women are waiting now, God bless my soul, do you really expect me to choose between them. I really must beg to be excused.' Then he asked me to say he did not feel well and must leave early in the morning. He really was tired to death. I believe Carson took him all over the mine. Nestfield says he will be even with him yet for it. He desired me to express his thanks and make his excuses as well as I could. The aide-de-camp left with him but the rest of the party is remaining for the ball" and the secretary moved away leaving Lew leaning against the supporting post of the verandah in silent laughter.

Anne's eyes contracted as she saw her son rush eagerly up to Pen and ask for her programme. Anne could not hear what he said but the look in his eyes and the laughing response of Pen's gave her a pang. Yet the words were harmless enough.

"Now the governor is out of the way I wonder if I may ask for the first dance" Jim said and Pen answered with a half pout that was contradicted by a dimple in her rosy cheek.

"Why, yes. If you think there is something special about the first dance? But I shall not give you more than one."

"The last one, too. Just to finish off the thing in style," Jim suggested, but was almost pushed aside by a small army of impatient aspirants.

"Here, you, Hetherington, you don't think you own the ballroom do you? Let the rest of us get a show." But Jim held his ground doggedly, till he received a smiling nod of ascent from Pen then he turned to Daphne.

"I do not want to dance tonight Jim," Daphne said in a low tone. "I want to go home but I'll wait till the first dance is over as I do not wish Pen to know I'm going."

Jim and Daphne had always been friends; the other girl guessed, though she had never spoken of it, that he loved her sister, and she believed Pen, in spite of her flirtations, loved him in return.

"Never mind me Jim; go and fill your programme," she said, and turned to speak to Anne. Her cousin's sharp eyes saw the strained look in the colourless face. "What's up child? Are you sick?" she asked anxiously.

"I want to go home, if I can get away without Pen seeing me. I cannot keep up any longer," said Daphne, faintly. "Do you think we could slip away?" "Of course we can. I'll just leave word with John to tell your father by-and-by and we can leave without anyone else being the wiser. They are all too busy over themselves to spare a thought for us."

No sooner said than done, Anne and her companion were soon walking up the hill in the cool, fresh, night air and Daphne told about her transfer. They did not see, in their absorption, a small dark figure flittering before them, nor did Anne ever find out that Tommy had followed her to the ball and home again.

THE FURNACE FOR GOLD

Anne wished, as she had often futilely wished before, that Jim had only chosen Daphne – sweet gentle Daphne – instead of the willful, daring, spoilt, flighty Penelope.

Anne was genuinely fond of Daphne. The jealousy that flamed in her breast at the mere thought of Pen had no place towards Daphne. She felt that she could welcome her as a daughter, yet with the contrariness of human nature, Jim must fix his affections on saucy Pen.

For Anne felt assured of her son's feelings, in spite of the fact that Jim was seldom seen with Pen, who it was patent to Neummurra had only to pick and choose among all the eligibles and ineligibles of the township who were all at her pretty feet.

"I'd like to see you for a few minutes, when you can spare them to me," Buxton said to Jim at the close of the first dance, as the young man passed on to the verandah with Pen on his arm.

"Don't let me keep you, Jim; I can sit down," said the girl, quickly. She knew the millionaire by sight, and her instinct told her he meant well by Jim.

Her soft, rich voice caught Buxton's ear and he looked at her. It was seldom that a woman's face got more than a passing glance from him, but Pen's glorious beauty compelled his attention.

"No, no; not now, later on!" he said, after a pause, that rocked the young man's angry resentment. Again his eyes wandered over the lovely face, and the tall lissome figure, girlish, yet rounded, with subtle gracious curves of young womanhood.

"Allow me," Dinny Finucan's voice behind them was suggestive of too early an acquaintance with the refreshment table "to introduce the 'King' to the 'Rose' of Neummurra. Miss Morgan was to have been his Excellency's partner. If Sir George had not left too early to enjoy the felicity."

Jim's brow grew dark, but he could not prevent the introduction, nor avoid seeing the open admiration in the millionaire's eyes. Pen may have seen it, too, but did not look ill-pleased. Jim knew that love of admiration was one of her weak points, but he was angry nevertheless.

"Oh, Mr. Finucane", she said with a merry smile, "how cruel of you to remind me that his Excellency wouldn't care to dance with me. To think how carefully I was studying up my part so as to be able to talk to our Queen's representative in case I was selected, and all for nothing, you see."

The two men joined in her laugh, but Jim was gloomily silent.

"I'm sure the Governor would have been only too pleased to dance with you, but the honest truth is, the man was fagged to death. He would have been delighted to bow his allegiance to the queen of the district, the Rose of Neummurra!" said Buxton with a bow.

No one was more surprised at Buxton's heavy attempt at gallantry than the man himself. Pen laughed outright, but there was a delighted spark in her eyes as she bowed a smiling acknowledgement of the compliment, and then suffered herself to be drawn away, by her impatient partner.

Buxton, with his hands clasped behind him, and his great head bent forward, gazed after the pair for a few moments; then he turned abruptly to where he saw Mr. Carson leaning against a verandah post.

The manager hated all social functions. A ball was to him purgatory, and only the united entreaties of his wife and daughter, and the presence of the Vice-Regal visitors, had induced him to attend to-night. His face brightened at the sight of Buxton; he had forgiven him for the afternoon, and was besides worldly-wise enough to appreciate the power of "King Billy" in the directorate.

"The very man I wanted to see," Buxton began; "I have promised Sir George to go with him to Walsingham, and I have no idea when I may return to Neummurra. There are one or two things I want to speak about to you. I fancy I see a way to increase our returns." Carson's face brightened still further. The meetings of the directors had not been so pleasant of late, the dividends had not been satisfactory, and the shareholders were growing discontented.

"Is Marlowe here, by-the-way? I haven't seen him," asked Buxton.

The feeling of the manager for the boss of the lower works was not too friendly, Buxton could see, as the reply came coldly: "Marlowe? No, I can't say I've seen him. I do not believe he is here. I saw his wife and daughter, but not the old man." Buxton winced. Marlowe was so very slightly his senior that the speech stung him. He gave no sign of his annoyance, however; his grey eyes smiled as frankly as ever as he continued the conversation without giving a sign that he was commenting inwardly, "Tactless fool! And that's the kind of man they appointed in my absence! I do not wonder now that he is not getting on too well with the men; he is the kind of man that would rasp anybody." Aloud he said:

"I am sorry that I have not been able to see so much of my old friend this time as I generally do. You know Marlowe and I were schoolmates. I hoped to see him to-night, as my time is so very short." Too late the manager remembered having heard, though he had not believed, that Marlowe had a friendship with Buxton. "He is a most estimable man, I respect him highly," he said hastily.

The shadow of a smile appeared for an instant in the grey eyes, and vanished.

"I want to speak to you about that young fellow in the lower works, Hetherington; he seems altogether a most remarkable young man. I suppose you heard how much the Governor was taken with him. I had a talk with him after you sent him up to me, and I have made up my mind to give his ideas a trial. I shall lay the matter before the company myself, so you need not be in the least anxious about it. But I want you to give him a free hand in the lower works. Let him have as many men and as much help as he requires, and let him see what he can do in the way of getting clean concentrates out of the tailing and slime. He may wish to try some

THE FURNACE FOR GOLD

experiments in the chlorination process with those new refractory ores as well."

"Do you mean he is to be made a boss, or foreman, or what?" asked Carson, stiffly and Buxton detected the latent antagonism in the tone. "Oh, never mind what you call him; that will be decided at a director's meeting," said Buxton; "just let him understand that he is given an absolute free hand, and has the run of the place, smelting and assay department and so forth."

Carson lifted his eyebrows significantly, but Buxton continued. "I do not think he is the kind of man to betray any trust reposed to him, if I am any judge of character. You see it is only by keeping abreast of the latest knowledge that we can hope to hold Neummurra in the first place as a gold-producing mine. This young fellow is fresh from college, and well up in metallurgy. If the ore changes, well, our methods must change, that's all. Look at America. Why, men are making millions out of tailings that were thrown away as sheer waste."

"Certainly I shall do what you wish," said Carson, as the rapid flow of words ceased, but his expression showed how distasteful the proposition was to him. "I am thinking thoughts that you will be putting young Hetherington into somewhat an anomalous position. So lately a workman, then a boss, yet not a boss. It will be rather a difficult place for him."

"I fancy young Hetherington will manage," said Buxton. "And how will Marlowe take it?" asked Carson maliciously.

With the frank air of taking one into his confidence that was one of Buxton's most effective weapons, he said, "That is just the point on which I wanted specially to consult with you, Carson. I would not hurt my old mate's feelings for the world, and I am afraid he may not quite like this new move. However, we are bound to consider the shareholders and what is best for the mine. I cannot manage to see Dan about it myself, since the Governor has got my promise to go with him, but I feel sure I can leave it quite safely in your hands."

The Manager smiled in a pleased manner, and the millionaire continued: "Make him understand that no slight is intended to him in this experiment. I feel confident you will be able to make him see the matter from our standpoint. Dan is touchy, I know, but he is sterling. I have a great regard for him, and only that I am pushed for time I would not trouble you."

"I quite understand", said Carson, "and you can rely on my doing my best. The situation calls for a great deal of tact, but I think I can promise it will be used," Buxton's lip twitched, and he gave a queer side-glance. "Do you wish the changes to be made at a pace?"

"Yes straightaway; it is the end of the month, and I see no sense in wasting time. Take the morning to explain to Marlowe, and make the change in the afternoon. I see young Hetherington coming this way. I'll just have a few words with him."

Jim was surprised to find his arm taken by the millionaire, who drew him to the seat at the end of the verandah, and at once laid before him the proposed changes.

At first Jim was too astonished to realize his good fortune, but he soon recovered his equilibrium, and though his pulses tingled and his face flushed, he managed to bear himself quietly and modestly. The two men spoke long and earnestly, parting at the close of their conversation with mutual respect and liking.

Jim forgot all about his incipient jealousy in his joyful exultation. "They may say he is an unscrupulous rascal," he thought his eyes following the millionaire's strong face and figure, "but I do not believe it. He struck me as a clever man, but a straight one, too. I do not blame him for walking over the fools who get in his road. I like the 'sizing-up' glance of those sharp; green eyes, the set of that square head, low down on the broad shoulders, the strong, healthy look of his face, even the way he shuts that big mouth of his over those strong, white, cruel looking teeth. That is the kind of man to crush difficulties out of his path; to let nothing stand in the way of his desires. I wonder do all the millionaires look like him. He is the first I have seen, perhaps he is – really the millionaire type – our modern equivalent of the warrior conqueror of the olden time." And Jim, a little shamefacedly laughed at his own enthusiasm.

He was in the first flush of his gratitude but a few minutes later his admiration suffered a perceptible shock, as he saw Pen being taken to the supper room on the arm of the same indomitable millionaire.

CHAPTER XI.

DAPHNE GOES TO BUNDAMANGO

There was great distress in the Morgan household when they awoke after the dissipation of the great ball to the news of Daphne's transfer. Pen had wondered at her sister's disappearance but had been satisfied with cousin John's explanation that she had gone home with Anne, who was tired. Neummurra girls troubled little over chaperons, and Anne's absence did not disturb Pen. Pen knew that Daphne did not care for dancing, and would be glad of any excuse to leave the ball, so she felt no anxiety, but enjoyed herself to the top of her bent. But now she reproached herself bitterly for her heedless selfishness, as contrasted with Daphne's unselfish behavior. The sisters were fondly attached, and had not been separated from their birth until now. It seemed to Pen that half of herself would be gone when Daphne left Neummurra.

But Daphne, in spite of her sister's entreaties and her own regret, held steadily to her engagement. Lew gave his frank opinion as to the foolishness of remaining in the Department of Public Instruction that removed thus callously young girls from their homes to forsaken spots of the Never-Never.

"Chuck up the whole blessed concern," he said. "Who'd be a teacher if he could help it, even in a civilized community like Neummurra but at an end of the earth like Bundamango? Before I'd teach the young idea to shoot there, I'd shoot the young idea."

Daphne gave a transient smile. "I can't send in my resignation now, for I know this year has not been a good one at the store; father was only saying so the other day. Since the wages went down at the mine, the profits went down at the store. He could not afford to keep two grown-up daughters at home; not to speak of Gwenny's wages. Pen does the housekeeping, but I am no good at that, even if I were needed. I shall try it until Christmas anyway; it will only be a few months; and then if I find it too bad I'll resign and come home; perhaps I could find some music pupils."

David said little, but it was clear he agreed with Daphne. "No, I am afraid you must stick to your teaching, my girl," he said that night at the tea table. "I cannot see my way clear to ask you to resign, unless," he looked at his eldest daughter somewhat grimly, "Pen can make up her mind to quit fooling with a dozen fellows, pick out one steady one, and marry him out of hand."

"Oh, Dad," cried Pen, looking at him with her lovely laughing eyes, "I did not think you wanted so badly as that to get rid of me. I'm sure there is not one of those same young fellows I'd leave you for."

"Stuff and nonsense," growled David, but he was pleased at the speech. Pen could wind him round her fingers, and she knew it.

Lew glanced up quickly. "Pen is waiting for an unmarried Governor. It was no good trying her attractions on Sir George Thurston, even if she had had the chance, for he has got a wife," Pen ran up and boxed his ears.

"Yes, a Governor, or," he paused, "a millionaire," but the flash in the brown eyes warned him to beware what he said, and he changed the conversation calmly. "What a beastly day we are having, it hasn't not stopped raining, ever since I got up. The skies are sympathizing with us in losing you Daph." But a glance at his sisters' faces showed that this subject, too, had better be abandoned, and he again changed the conversation with much diplomacy to the new ward at the hospital, in which David was deeply interested, and on which he held forth for some time.

The rain was still falling on Monday morning when Daphne took a sad leave-taking of her family, and a crowd of tearful scholars, who had gathered at the coach to bid her farewell. The pretty gold brooch she wore at her breast was a present from the teachers and the children; and as the coach drove away amid cheers and farewells, Daphne, with tearful eyes, leant back and waved her handkerchief to the group until she was carried out of their sight.

The girl's pale face turned through the driving rain to the familiar scenes, rich in so many associations of childhood, girlhood and opening womanhood, until when Sandy Rift was crossed, and the winding creek was lost to sight. Neummurra, crude, bare, but beloved Neummurra, was quite hidden from her eyes; then Daphne felt that she was leaving something of her old self behind her.

Now, at last, irresponsible youth was over, and the serious business of life begun, thought the girl, as her serious eyes turned to the path before her.

A few more months and she would be out of her teens – it seemed a great age. She was going away from the home care, and shelter, among strangers, but in spite of the regret that troubled the girl's tender heart, some thrill of excitement at thus going into the world, and braving single-handed its unknown dangers, set her heart beating with the thought of the mysterious unknown future.

In spite of the quiet reserved manner that was so often mistaken for pride, and that made her seem older than her years, Daphne was indeed but a child yet; and the forming ideas that thronged her brain as the coach bore her rapidly away from her old home were little more than the innocent romantic dreams of a child.

Daphne had never had a lover; the youths who gathered round pretty Pen read Daphne's clear candid eyes aright, saw the child there, and left her alone. Daphne's nature was one to develop slowly, and the vague feeling that something of herself was being left at Neummurra, that the future with its possibilities was before her, was the first stirring of conscious womanhood.

The rain fell steadily, remorselessly, all through the four days journey, which was by coach, by boat, by train and by coach again, to Bundamango. Daphne began to lose a little of her shyness at this constant intercourse with strangers, but the journey, except to her excited youthful fancy, was uneventful, until she reached the last part of the second coach journey. Daphne and an old woman were the only passengers inside the coach. The old woman, who informed Daphne that her name was Mrs. Hogan, and that she was Mike Hogan a settler's wife, was stout and an excellent talker, in a racy Irish way, that enchanted the young girl.

Three men were in the box-seat with the driver. The country through which they passed was flooded, the creeks were up. Now and again the coach was in water half way up the wheels and Daphne trembled for her precious dresses in her traveling box.

But when the Niragin Creek was reached it was found to be more flooded than any other they had passed. It received its supplies from the Nira Range and though in the drought season it was but a succession of water holes, it was now running a banker: a swollen, roaring torrent. The bed was a treacherous one, full of hollows and matted weeds.

"I do not quite know what to do", the driver said as he drew rein, and looked at the swirling yellow waters. "I have never crossed the Nira in flood before; I am a bit new to this part of the country. I don't reckon it is deep; it isn't that, but this here Nira is the most awkward creek along my road. The current is strong, and the holes in her are so deep in places, too, so full of blessed, ugly, old weeds that the coach

THE FURNACE FOR GOLD

might be overturned before you could say Jack Robinson. Yous are all right, you chaps, I expect yous can swim, but it is the women inside that bother me. They'd be smothered before we'd have a chance to right the coach."

The three men looked at each other and then at the red, weather-beaten face of the driver in silence. They had nothing to suggest, and the prospect of a swim in those muddy waters was not alluring. The driver turned round to explain the situation to the inside passengers, when he saw two riders with a led horse approaching the creek. "The very 'dentical!" he cried joyfully; then, as an afterthought, "If I can get them to see things in my light."

The riders came up, and the driver explained matters to them, asking for their assistance.

"If yous would be so good" – "mates" he was going to say, but at a glance at the younger man he altered it to "gents" – "as to help these ladies across, seeing you've got a spare horse, I'd be much obliged. I am afraid to risk taking them in the coach. There is only two ladies inside, so perhaps you wouldn't mind obliging."

The riders appeared to hesitate for a moment. Mrs. Hogan put her head out of the protecting tarpaulin and said briskly: "It's myself can ride, bhoys, if you'll let me having the spare horse. I'd sooner any day of my life face a danger than run the chance of being smothered up in here like a pig in a poke. There won't be any need to lead a horse for me. I'm a bit heavy, gentlemen" she wiped the rain unconcernedly off her broad, good-natured, capable face, "but I'm used to riding. I know this creek as well as any man in the district. It won't be the first time I've crossed it in a flood. I offer myself as a leader, bhoys. Follow me and I'll lead you to safety." Her jolly laugh was infectious.

Behind the homely Irish face the riders caught a glimpse of another, and a very different one, Daphne's beautiful face lit up the gloomy interior of the coach. A change so instantaneous as to be ridiculous, if there were anyone quick enough to notice, came over the strangers.

"Of course we can, with pleasure" the younger man spoke first, "the spare horse is yours" – he gave a charming inclination of a shapely head towards the old lady. "Joe can lead it, or, if you prefer, we shall accept you as leader, and if the young lady will allow me, I shall be very pleased to take her up in front of me on my horse. He is very strong and surefooted, and we can follow you over the creek."

Daphne flushed rosily, and glanced doubtfully at the stranger. She had never looked more beautiful than she did at this moment in her pretty embarrassment, for the sordid surroundings heightened the effect of her delicate beauty.

The other rider muttered in his beard, "Oh! A fine, unselfish chap, upon my word! I like your division of partners. I am told off to look after the old woman, while you reserve the young beauty for yourself," but he brought up the spare horse, assisted plucky Mrs. Hogan to mount, and set off with her, with no sign of malice in his sharp brown face.

Daphne stood hesitating on the step of the coach, while the rain beat pitilessly on her soft cheeks, and the roar of the torrent sounded in her ears. Had she been Pen, the adventure would have been quite to her mind, but being shy Daphne, it seemed to her a most bold and daring thing to allow herself to be placed in front of this handsome stranger and carried on his horse across the creek.

But as none of the others appeared to see anything unusual in the situation, Daphne's very shyness made it impossible for her to protest, and when the young man again repeated his proposal, in a quiet and respectful manner, she nodded consent, and the next instant, with her sweet young face aflame she felt herself lifted in a pair of strong arms and placed on the horse's back. The same strong arms came round her in order to hold the reins, and thus the eventful little journey began.

Now and then the horse stumbled slightly and Daphne's wildly beating heart was in her mouth; but the rider was both patient and skillful and the creek was safely crossed.

"We had better wait for the coach," the young man said, and he made no attempt to lift her down, but reined the horse and began to talk to his companion with an easy self-possessed manner that quite overcame her shyness. Daphne's usual diffidence vanished; something in the stranger seemed to set her at ease, yet her innate reserve through all the pleasant conversation was like a delicate veil thrown between them, heightening the subtle witchery of the moment that held such possibilities of romance for them both.

Now and then at some witty turn in the young man's speech he found the blue eyes raised swiftly with laughing comprehension in their depths to his own; but most of the time he could only see the pure oval of a softly flushing cheek and a small ear peeping out from the tendrils of wind-blown golden hair.

He may have wished to protract the charming episode; but soon the coach, after nearly fulfilling the driver's prophecy reached the bank in safety, and he was obliged to hand over his pretty charge to the guardianship of Mrs. Hogan.

Daphne did not acknowledge to herself how poignant was her sense of regret as the strangers bade farewell and rode away. But she felt, without being able to understand it that the coach ride was now but flat, stale and unprofitable, and that her erstwhile agreeable companion was after all but a wearisome old woman with an untiring tongue. Daphne listened to her as before but her simple interest in the talk was gone. She saw the merry eyes, the bewildering smile, the handsome face of the stranger instead of Mrs. Hogan's friendly face, and instead of her Irish voice she heard another one, a deep manly voice with strange inflections, that would echo in her ears for many a long day.

Bundamango school proved a great

THE FURNACE FOR GOLD

surprise to the young teacher. She had expected a rough lot of children, and a poor bush school master, instead of this she found the children intelligent and well-mannered, far ahead of those she had been accustomed to teach; while the head master, Mr. Willgrade, was a polished and intellectual man.

Years afterwards Daphne acknowledged how much she owed to those few months at Bundamango. She often wondered that a man of Mr. Willgrade's stamp should be content to be buried in the bush, while others with half his ability were in charge of large city schools. But she grew to understand that he was not the man to bombard the department with petitions for promotion nor stoop to secure political influence to obtain his rights.

Once appointed to Bundamango, he worked contentedly there, and did the best he could with the uncouth bush children in his charge.

A month of hot, scorching days followed Daphne's arrival, and the country that she had first seen running over with water, now looked as if a spark would set it in a blaze, for the long grass became yellow and inflammable as tinder. Soon fires appeared on the hills in the distance. Daphne often watched the Nira Ranges, smoky in the day time, and flames at night, and the settlers around, trembling for their homesteads, kept watch day and night, lest the enemy take them unawares. The elder boys were detained from school to help their parents.

Three days of intense heat, with an acrid dryness in the air, followed the appearance of fire on the ranges.

On the third afternoon a shout from one of the girls startled the school. "Teacher! Teacher! The fire is coming our way, it is coming near our paddocks". Mr. Willgrade hurried to the door; the danger was imminent, his practiced glance assured him,

"You are right, Maggie," he said quietly. "Just run in and tell Mrs. Willgrade. Say it is all right. Now then, boys, if you will be so kind as to help me, we shall do our best to keep the fire from our school. Ted and Jack bring in the boys' horses and my cow to the paddock. The rest of the boys come with me, get the bags and we shall make "fire fight fire" as we did last year. We shall get up a little fire of our own, and send it off to tell the big fire we don't want it today."

While Mr. Willgrade spoke in this brisk way, he took from the recess the empty sacks kept ready for such an emergency. His small lieutenants soon wetted these and, armed with them, they joined their master in fighting the fire.

Flames shot up in all directions and for a few moments, Daphne, in spite of her faith in Mr. Willgrade, grew alarmed; but the quiet composure of Mrs. Willgrade, who came out with her baby boy in her arms, made her ashamed to show her fears. The gallant little bush boys worked like heroes; those who had no wet bags got braches of trees and used them, while the girls nearly wept at being kept from the fun.

The flames were beaten back till the

school house was surrounded by a charred circle on every side but the one towards the approaching fire. While the battle was still going on, a solitary rider galloped up, took a bag from the smallest boy and joined the gallant little regiment. He had seen from the highroad the danger of the little school. With the hearty free-masonry of the bush, Willgrade accepted the stranger's help, with a simple nod of acknowledgment.

Daphne gave a start of surprise, a thrill passed through her, as the thought flashed upon her mind that the strange helper was the man who had carried her on his horse across the swollen Nira Creek.

The stranger's face was soon grimy with smoke, and wet with heat, but when at last the fight was over the school was saved, and Willgrade brought him up to the house, Daphne saw that she had made no mistake, it was really the knight of the flooded creek. She drew back into the schoolroom, and retreated out of sight, in spite of her desire to speak to him,

The girl's cheek burned, as she wondered whether he would remember her, and a vague melancholy filled her, when she heard the stranger refusing to stay for longer than a wash and a cup of tea. Daphne heard the well-remembered voice saying, "I must hurry and get to Wooni Station before dark, thank you, so I cannot remain, though I should like to. I'll just wait a few minutes till the grass between here and the road has cooled down a bit," and he went into the house with Mrs.

Willgrade; half an hour later he mounted his steed, and Daphne saw with an indescribable pang that he was really going away.

Still, though longing to speak to him again, she lacked the courage to appear, and only watched him from the schoolroom window. The horse was restive, plunging and rearing as he stepped on the hot stubble. "He will be thrown! Oh, he will be thrown!" cried the girl to herself and the next instant her prophecy came true. The horse's foot plunged into a small fiery hole and with a snort of terror, the poor creature bucked so suddenly that he threw his rider over his head on the charred earth, where he lay motionless.

Mr. Willgrade was on the spot a moment after, and, lifting the limp figure in his arms he bore it to the schoolroom. Daphne ran up with a blanched face. "Here, Miss Morgan, hold his head, while I find out if he is hurt. Run away all of you like good children round the back," for the pupils came crowding in after him, but they obeyed the order at once, and left the room. A faint flush rose to the girl's face as she did as she was told and supported the handsome head on her knee.

He was so helpless, who had been so willing to help others. "I think he is only stunned, no bones broken," the master said, at last, rising to his fee, and going to the door to see if his wife was coming.

Daphne gave a sign of relief.

"Oh, I am so glad," she whispered, and, as though stirred by the sound of the sweet, low voice, the stranger opened his eyes and looked up to the girl's face.

It was a strange look, for the man's eyes, though yet with scarce consciousness in their depths, held the wide blue eyes in a long, compelling gaze. Mr. Willgrade's voice broke the spell. "Why, he is conscious," he said, coming back from the verandah. Daphne flushed all over her sensitive face, and the stranger rose, unsteadily to his feet. He was bruised and shaken but not otherwise hurt. "Oh, I'm all right," he said, though in a broken tone. "Did I come a cropper after all?" Daphne nodded.

"You must make up your mind to stay with us now," said the master, "You are not fit to go on. Do give us the pleasure of putting you up for the night at least." The young man's eyes were longing but he shook his head and thanking them earnestly, he said he must continue his journey.

"If it depended on myself I would remain with pleasure, but it does not. I must go. I have promised, but I am more than sorry to go," and so, in spite of the persuasions of husband and wife, he refused to remain. He spoke for a few moments to Daphne, but her class was now waiting for her, and she had to return to her duty. She could scarcely believe that the little interlude was not a dream. The dream pervaded many a waking hour. In the letter she wrote home after her arrival, she touched lightly on her adventure at the flooded creek, but did not say that one of the riders was young and handsome. And strangely enough, when she described the fight with the fire, she forebore to mention that the stranger who helped them had thus the second time come to her assistance, but Daphne's letters were like herself, full of fine reserves.

Sometimes in her walks in the lonely bush, an old rhyme rang in her head and haunted her with its obscure meaning:

"If the old saw do not borrow,
Fire is love, and water sorrow."

CHAPTER XII.

JIM LOSES AN OLD FRIEND

Jim Hetherington went to the works on Friday morning with a confused sense of elation and trepidation. .The thought uppermost in his mind was that now, at last, he saw before him some prospect of making a home for Pen. He had never wavered in his boyish allegiance; though, with the quiet steadiness that was part of his nature, he had kept to the determination he had made on leaving college; that he would not speak to her of marriage until he could show David Morgan that he was able to support a wife. Few young men in Neummurra would have been deterred by such scruples as influenced Jim, most of them, indeed, rushed into matrimony, as soon as they left off receiving boys wages and were indifferent to the fact that their wives, with such a small weekly sum coming into the households, must needs turn into drudges. As Jim looked at pretty Pen, he resolved to wait till he had a home that would be worthy of her. He had little doubt of her, in spite of her flirtations. Pen was fond of admiration; but her heart was true, he said to himself. They had been childish sweethearts, and the promises they had made then were binding now, or so he believed.

He was always ready, if Pen needed him, but he did not wish to give the gossips of Neummurra a chance to couple their names together so he had of late avoided his old friend, though not in a marked way. As he walked into the shed, he pictured Pen's surprise when he broke to her the delightful news that now he was a "boss" himself; he knew nothing could give her greater pleasure, and while he went to the second floor to wait for Carson, he smiled to himself at the thought of her joy.

He saw no sign of either the manager or the boss, so he began to work at his usual duty of attending to the solution, until he was formally put in charge of the new experiments. One of the men told him that Carson had been through the shed about 10 minutes previously, in search of Marlowe.

Carson was told the boss had gone into the smelting room, and he followed him thither. "I want to speak to you for a minute," he said, as he found him, and when Marlowe rose and came towards him it seemed to the manager that he had never before realized what a giant the man was. There was a sullen, wooden look on the face, too, that gave his self-confidence a sudden check; he began to wish that Buxton had not entrusted him with so delicate a mission.

"If you want me, I am ready now; I was just having a look at this crucible," said Marlowe shortly. "Oh! Do not let me disturb you. I know how busy you are, but I just wished to ask your advice about a little matter." Carson smiled at the expressionless face, and Marlowe thought of something he had overheard on of the dry-crushers saying.

"He means something nasty for you when he smiles, but if he 'palavers' you, look out for trouble," and some intuition warned him that the manager's business with him that morning boded no good to him. "That young chap was quite the professor yesterday, I believe," Carson said, hoping to find some easy way of broaching the subject.

"What young chap?" asked Marlowe gruffly. "Oh young Hetherington, I think his name is," Carson appeared to recollect as if by an effort. "I heard he had had quite a brilliant course at the University." The light eyes under the dark level brown flashed one glance at him, then the grizzled head was bent again.

"It wouldn't be a bad idea," went on Carson, somewhat disheartened at his reception, "to see if he couldn't use his smartness to help on the mine. The directors are looking rather sour over the returns, and it is quite true we are not getting the assay value of the ore, not even a fair working percentage. You know that as well as I do. Perhaps you could suggest something."

"What is he driving at?" was Dan's

thought; a sudden idea entered his brain, and held him passive while he followed it through all the windings of Carson's talk. "Has Billy said anything to him about Jim? Is he to be put in charge of the Lower Works?" was the gist of the idea that had seized him.

He kept silent and Carson's patience was nearing its limit, as he saw that Marlowe was resolved to give him no help. "You know, so much depends on the next few months, if the dividends grow smaller we shall find our pockets will suffer, too," he said.

Still Marlowe maintained his provoking silence. "We might let the young fellow have a chance to see what his talk is worth; give him an opportunity of treating some of the ore," he continued, looking at Marlowe, who stared into the crucible with a provoking air of aloofness.

"Mr. Buxton spoke up on the matter to me at the ball," he said, and stopped, half-startled at the curious gleam that came into the light eyes. Dan's glance dropped the next instant; he had got the clue he was seeking. The black lashes lay on the sallow cheeks. He waited dumbly for what was to follow. Carson hesitated; the man's look had not been reassuring, but nevertheless he would fulfill his promise, and use, as he had said to Buxton, tact in dealing with the situation.

"He wants us to allow Hetherington a free hand, as he puts it, in the works, so that he can be at liberty to carry out any experiments he may need, in treating the new stone or the tailings. That is what Buxton explained to me, and he said he would put the matter before the directors."

Dan's heart began to beat in loud, heavy throbs. He wondered whether Carson could hear it.

Billy had turned against him at last. The claims of mateship were no longer binding on the millionaire, who had not had even the courage to say straight out, man to man, that Dan's place in the works was to be filled up he must needs get Carson to break the truth to him. Dan felt he could have borne it if Billy had come to him and told him candidly that he had no further use for him; but to humiliate him by getting Carson to do his dirty work for him - it was too much.

Poor Dan's thoughts whirled in this sickening circle, as the manager's smooth voice flowed on. But his dark face gave no sign of the storm that was rising, and Carson went on more hopefully. "Mr. Buxton told me particularly that it was to make no difference to you; your position as boss was not to be interfered with."

"Eh, what?" Dan said, stupidly.

"He has the greatest regard for you." Carson felt that at length his tact was having a chance. "He said you and he were very old friends; indeed, he repeated twice over how anxious he was not to hurt your feelings. I assured him how much I valued your services."

Dan looked up at him, but the slow scorn in his eyes escaped the manager's notice.

"However, I know Hetherington is quite a favorite of yours; I heard it said that he is like a son to you. You will be as glad as if you were really his father to think what a fair prospect lies before him now that Buxton seems inclined to take him up."

Dan's eyes flashed their disturbing glance once more, but even while he tried to bring his tongue to speech a picture of the past rose before him. He stood by the door of the smelting-room on a Saturday afternoon some seventeen years before, and the Dummy came rushing clumsily towards him. Dan had always been good to the poor creature, who had repaid him by an affectionate doglike fidelity. He knew by the man's face that something terrible had happened and he remember with a vague fear that his little Johnnie and Jim Hetherington had been playing round the works that afternoon and that the two little lads had gone up the hill towards the new cuttings.

Dummy rushed towards this spot, and Dan hurried after him.

A truck with two children in it was rushing down the narrow tramway. How the accident happened he could never tell, but the truck slipped off the rails and rolled into a hollow as the two men drew near. For one paralyzing moment the father's heart stood still, and he was rooted to the spot, while the Dummy rushed to the cutting with uncouth cries.

Dan looked over the edge of the broken ridge. The two children lay in front of him, side by side, and clear of the truck. One was motionless, and one began to rise. As he looked Dummy pushed him gently away, while he climbed down the sloping sides of the opening. Dan fell on his knees and covered his eyes until Dummy returned. He knew at once as he looked at the Dummy's face that on himself the blow had fallen, knew it as surely as when he carried his little dead son home to his mother. One child had fallen on soft earth, one on a heap of broken ore. How bitterly his heart had swelled as he bore off his sad burden, and little Jim ran sobbing by his side, for Jim was not even stunned by the fall that had killed his little playmate.

One taken and one left! How fierce a grudge he bore at that moment to the one who had been left; and after all the years in which he had grown to love the boy, had worked for him and gloried in his triumphs the old bitter resentment revived, as Carson said, "He has taken a son's place with you."

"He has, my God! He has!" The words burst from him involuntarily; his strong hands clenched themselves.

At that moment he felt in his arms the little light body of his dead son, and again the fierce sense of the injustice of the punishment caught him by the throat but his iron will crushed back the recollection, as he realized the inquisitiveness of the glance that the manager cast upon him. Dan was an ignorant, obstinate old man, but his pride came to the aid of his slow faculties. He would not show how keenly he felt the slight that Buxton had given him, nor betray his jealousy of Jim Hetherington. With a mighty effort he pulled himself together and said carelessly, "Right you are. If you and Buxton are pleased, and it is for the

THE FURNACE FOR GOLD

good of the company it is no affair of mine. I have known Jim Hetherington long enough to understand what is in him, and I don't doubt he'll manager all right. Like enough he will be filling both our shoes in another 12 months."

In spite of his anger, Dan's eyes brightened with satisfaction at the start the manager gave, and the sickly smile with which he tried to hid his discomfiture. "You had better tell Hetherington of his new billet at once, so that no time need be lost," he continued suavely.

"Buxton has left that in your hands, too, didn't he?" The manager's muttered reply was lost as he turned away. There was some excitement and comment among the men when they learned of the change, but the promotion was a popular one, for Jim was well liked by them.

In spite of his University training, he had not put on any airs with his mates, and he had, to a marked degree the power of attracting goodwill and affection. This was less due to his hearty, laughing way, and his witty tongue, than to his innate and unaffected kindliness and honesty. He was a Neummurra boy, and the men of Neummurra were proud of him.

There were friendly congratulations from nearly all his old mates. Dan alone seemed to stand aloof, and Jim wondered at his coldness. He did not in the least suspect what a strain it was on Dan to assume even the semblance of congratulations with him. It was late in the day before he came up to the young man.

"It is a good chance for you; I hope you'll make something of it," he said, coldly. And Jim thought:

"He is anxious for me to do my best. Just like old Dan; he pretends to doubt me, to put me on my mettle, as he used to do when I was a boy." "I'll do my best, Uncle Dan, never fear; but won't Ellie be pleased," he said aloud.

"Ellie will be pleased, I don't doubt it," was the constrained reply, and the first chill of misgiving touched Jim's enthusiasm. "I'll see you after my shift; you'll be going home my way," Dan said, turning abruptly away.

"Did Dan mean that he would keep his congratulations till then?" wondered the young man, or was there not a hidden threat in his words. Ridiculous as the supposition seemed, Jim could not quite divest himself of the latter impression, though he tried to reason it out of his mind.

Dan's face was lowering as he went about the day's work. It was scarcely a sudden thing after all, this feeling against Jim that now took possession of him.

Under the stimulus of his jealous anger against Buxton it became almost an obsession, but nevertheless the feeling had been growing for months, and Jim's promotion had simply brought it to a head. For in the learned young University man Dan began to lost sight of the small boy he had patronized, and now saw only a possible supplanter.

Many a father experiences something of the same feeling when he realizes that his own powers are failing, and that his son, a cleverer man, perhaps, than he, is awaiting for his shoes. It is the natural antagonism of age towards superseding youth.

"Step down from the throne, and let me prove that I can fill it better than you," is the challenge the old king reads in the eyes of his heir; and this is what Dan had been vaguely feeling since Jim had been working under him.

While Dan followed him, yesterday, as he went round the works with the Vice-Regal party, and listened to the fresh, young voice explaining each step in the process, he felt instinctively that Buxton was comparing the two guides to Jim's advantage; and that even the old friendship was unable to bear the strain of the contrast.

"The boss seems thirsty to-day," Karl Schultz looked up with a sneer to Hetherington, and jerked his head towards the bridge across the creek. "What's that you say?" Jim said. He disliked the man intensely; he could scarcely have said why.

Schultz repeated his words with a snarl. "That is the third time he has been to the 'Three Crowns' this afternoon. Wonder what has put him out?" "It is a hot day," Jim said, but without conviction. He felt an undefined uneasiness.

Dan was not a drinking man; in fact, he seldom touched liquor, but at rare periods he was seized with a craving for drink; and while the craving lasted he became an altered being. He did not give way like most men and became an absolute drunkard. He was able to attend to his daily work, and appear none the worse for his steady drinking. But it was at home that they found the difference. The usually affectionate man became morose and harsh. His poor wife and daughter often feared for his reason and their own safety in his fits of savage brooding, at those times of drinking bouts Jim Hetherington had been the only one who had any influence over him then, and it had always been a habit of his, when a boy, to haunt Dan's steps when he was, in Neummurra phrase, "on the drink".

"I do hope poor Dan is not going to give trouble again. I am afraid it is coming on. I'll have to give Ellie a hand. There he goes again," said Jim to himself some time later. No one would have guessed from Dan's manner that he had taken what would have been enough to make an ordinary man helplessly drunk, but Jim could read the signs in the feverish brightness of the eyes and the flush on the dark face.

"Time is up; I'm ready if you are," he called cheerfully to him. "Yes, come along; I want you," Dan's voice was quite clear and steady, but Jim felt there was something unwanted in the look with which his old friend regarded him.

The two men walked on for some time in silence. For once in his life Jim was at a loss for talk. They left behind them the tents of the men "batching it" in mining parlance, and turned up the little hill, on which the house of the boss stood by itself.

"There is no one now to hear us, so I'll free my mind of what I've been bottling up all day," said Dan at last.

"That's right, out with it, Uncle

THE FURNACE FOR GOLD

Dan," said Jim, with a laugh.

Perhaps the sound of the old boyish name gave the heeded spur to Dan's anger. "Uncle Dan! Uncle Dan!," he sneered; "It was not Uncle Dan on Thursday when you tried to shame me before that fine crown, my lad."

Jim halted, and looked at Marlowe in blank astonishment; but he only gave a wild laugh, and went on fiercely.

"Oh yes, precious little Uncle Dan about you then. It was 'look at me gentlemen, listen to me, the fine University scholar, the man who knows assaying; don't mind the old fool standing there with his mouth open, he does not know gold from iron pyrites, vulgar mundle. He knows nothing. I can boss the whole show. Mr. Buxton put any slight you like on your old mate; he is a useless fossil now and it is a long time since you and he were prospecting together. Don't mind old Marlowe; he is a back number. I'm the new edition. He taught me most of what I know that is any good to me now, but never mind for that. You could not tell his writing from mine; they are both copperplate. I owe that to Marlowe but never mind for that. Get Carson to tell him to make way for me; I'm the coming man. I may sneak and toady to Buxton and work behind the back of the man who treated me like a son, but never mind for that!"

Marlowe's voice broke with passion, and he had to stop against his will. Jim could scarcely believe his ears as the storm of indignation burst upon him.

"He is drunk," he tried to reason with himself, though he well knew that the drink was not to blame for all the outbreak. Dan must really feel that he had a grievance against his old favourite, yet Jim's conscience was so perfectly clear that he could not understand how Dan could have made himself believe such a monstrous thing. How could his promotion injure him? Surely Dan knew he would sooner leave Neummurra than do him harm?

"You'll think differently in the morning. You know well Dan, that I'll never forget how much I owe you. There's no thought of supplanting you in my mind, nor in Buxton's either, I could swear".

Dan laughed brutally, "Just so, just so," he sneered. "I'll be up after tea to talk it over with Ellie," Jim said, determined not to quarrel.

"You'll not darken my door again Jim Hetherington. See Ellie, indeed! Yes, it was always 'Ellie, do this; Ellie do that; Ellie hear this lesson' with you. I've seen through your selfishness, let me tell you. She has been a slave to you since you led poor little Johnnie to his death down the cutting."

"Dan!" cried Jim in horror; "don't say that. Johnnie was older than I, and he was only seven. I grieved for him enough, but it was his plan, not mine, to go into the trucks; we could not know a rail was loose. It was no fault of mine that my poor little playfellow was killed."

"I've seen enough, I tell you, of you and your ways," Dan went on, unheeding. "I won't have you coming near Ellie. Never a week when you were away but Ellie wrote you a letter, and when you were a schoolboy here it was the same thing, nothing too good for Jim."

"Ellie is as dear to me as a sister could be," Jim said; and it was with a full heart that the words were spoken. A harsh reply rushed to Dan's lips but Ellie's little pale face came before him. If he had guessed something of Ellie's heart, it was Ellie's secret, and even in his drunkenness he had enough manliness to hide it.

"You've won your point, Jim Hetherington, though I'd scorn to stoop like you did for it. I wash my hands of you for the future. Take your way, I'll take mine. I feel now what you robbed me of when I lost little Johnnie for it is through you that I've lost my old mate."

Jim's temper was a good one, but it gave way at last, without one backward look he broke angrily away, and walked swiftly down the hill. It was only thus that he could prevent himself from uttering his wrath. But after supper his heart, naturally kind and soft, relented. He could not rest at enmity with his old friend, and he went up to see whether or not he could talk him out of his absurd ideas.

Ellie came to meet him. She was only a tiny girl, but a great spirit dwelt in her small frame and shone out of her steadfast eyes. They were strange eyes, those of Ellie's light in colour like Dan's but with a blueness in their depths that is rarely seen except in a child's eyes.

She was not pretty, little Ellie, but there was something attractive about her; what it was it would be hard to define. Her face cleared when she saw her visitor.

"Oh, Jim," she said anxiously, "father has broken out again." "That's what I came to see you about," Jim said, wondering how much Dan had told her. "You'll take care of him, I know," said Ellie "that is one comfort. It is a long time since he touched the drink. Not since you went to the Grammar school. Mother says he only started taking it when Johnnie died."

"Did he say much?" asked Jim.

"Not a word to us. That is his way, you remember, when he gets like this. At home has not a word to say. He just had tea and went out. We are waiting for him to come home now. Do you know what has happened to upset him?" Jim explained a little of what he thought was the cause of Dan's outbreak. He was so sure of Ellie's sympathy that he told her all about his promotion, and his sore heart was comforted by her loving congratulations. If Jim had eyes to see, had he only vanity enough to notice, little Ellie's secret shone out of her tender blue eyes that night. But he was blind and saw nothing.

"Won't you come in and see mother?" said Ellie at last. "I had better not. To tell the truth Ellie, your father said I was not to darken his door again," and he told her about the quarrel making as light of it as possible. "He will forget about it before morning I expect," he concluded, " and we shall be as good friends as ever."

"I don't know about that; father is

THE FURNACE FOR GOLD

obstinate when he takes a set on a person, but it would be the first time he ever turned against you. He looks upon you almost as if you were his own son."

"And that is what I feel myself; why, if I had a real sister I could not care for her more than I do for you, Ellie." The girl said good night abruptly, and went inside. Jim turned away, wondering what could have annoyed his little friend.

CHAPTER XIII.

MARLOWE'S FALL

On leaving his home Marlowe turned towards the works. He looked in, and had a glass at the Three Crowns, but this made no perceptible difference in his gait. It was not often he appeared at the sheds at night, unless there was extra pressure of work at the end of the month; but Randall, the boss of the "night shift" though somewhat surprised was glad to see him, for Dan was an obliging fellow, always willing to lend a hand.

"I think we might as well burn-off to-night," he said. "I sent the charcoal down to the smelter. Schultz and Innis are down there with it. If you are not in a hurry, perhaps you wouldn't mind giving them an eye for half an hour. I'll be down there. I just want to see about charging these barrels."

Dan nodded, and went slowly along towards the smelting department. A lantern was swinging from a beam on the verandah; but the dull glow from the windows it was evident the reverberatory furnaces were alight. Dan came heavily along, but in the soft sand that reached to the door of the smelter his footsteps made no sound. A sudden freakish fancy to startle the men by his unexpected presence entered his drink-bemused mind. He leant for a moment against the door and pushed it gently backward. A curious scene disclosed itself for one flashing second.

The two men were bending over the charcoal, which was ready to be burnt off and which contained 90 per cent of gold. They had between them a small canvas bag, and were filling it rapidly. Dan looked at the two with drunken gravity for a moment, then his presence was observed. He did not move a muscle as Innis fell limply against a table and Schultz looked round, as if in search for some weapon of offence. The different manner in which the two men bore discovery amused him. The limp, crouching attitude was as characteristic of Innis as the prompt fierce search for something to strike with was the natural action of the stronger man. Dan continued looking at the two men with the curious pondering gravity of a drunken man and they returned his gaze in silence. Schultz soon saw that the Boss was not quite himself and with the recklessness of desperation he resolved to try whether he could take advantage of his master's condition by a bold semblance of indifference.

"Looks queer don't it, Boss," he said quietly; while his companion drew back his white face, lest Marlowe should strike them both. Something in the bolder villain took Dan's erratic fancy.

"You may thank your stars it was not Randall who caught you," he said gravely. "Where is Randall?" asked Schultz boldly and his frightened companion groveled closer to the ground. "Oh, Randall," said Dan, who appeared to find nothing strange in the daring question, "He'll be back in half an hour; he is seeing about charging some fresh barrels."

Schultz looked at his master with an unmoved face, while his mind, like a trapped animal in a cage, was darting round and trying each suggestion as a probably chance of escape and rejecting each as unpractical. To rush up on the Boss and overpower him would make a scene that would call round them the men in the next room, not to mention that Marlowe, even though drunk, was more than match for them both. Suddenly there flashed upon his mind the remembrance of young Hetherington's promotion, which he felt firmly convinced was the cause of Marlowe's outbreak.

"Say, Boss," he hinted, deferentially, "I don't think you have been treated on the square putting young Hetherington on as boss without as much as asking your leave."

It was a chance hit, but it stuck home and he could see in the flash of the light eyes.

For a moment or two Dan's common sense almost prevailed over the drink, as he looked at the mean face and listened to the palpably false voice; but his anger against Buxton and Hetherington swept away his reason. The jealousy and resentment that had been raging all day in his heart burst from him in an irresistible desire for sympathy.

"That's it. That's what I complain about. What right have they to put anyone over my head as long as I'm Boss of the Shed? We were mates, Bill Buxton and I, since we were boys at school; but it was a dirty trick he played me at last." "A low-down, dirty, crawling trick," said Schultz, his small eyes wavering between the door and the drunken man. He did not know how soon Randall might return.

"When we were mates, fossicking," continued Dan with pitiful volubility, "it was what is mine is yours, Dan, what is yours is mine. We shared honestly, starve or feast, till we chucked prospecting up, and I went back to the office. If it had been my luck to have struck Neummurra, it's not a Boss I'd have made Bill; no, I would have shared my fortune fair and square, as we always shared whatever we got in the old days. If I had my rights it would be half of the gold of Neummurra that would be my share." He paused breathlessly, there was something unnatural even to them in this fluency in a man naturally reserved.

"Certain sure, Boss, it's because we think Buxton's treated you shabbily that we didn't mind helping ourselves to some of the gold they stole. Innis and me are not the only ones, by a long chalk, that tries to get even with the company when they gets a chance. It's a poor return we have from them

THE FURNACE FOR GOLD

anyway. We work in the dust, and our lungs are gone before we are forty; or a dose of the gas gets through us and we are wrecks for life. Poor pay for cruel hard work." Dan seemed to ponder the point, but it was only seeming, his poor sodden brain was incapable of proper thought.

"Have you been long at this game," he said, nodding at the charcoal, "stealing the gold, I mean." Innis fell back against the support. "Just a month or two, Boss; we haven't been here long, you know," Schultz answered, "It's only now and then we get a chance like this."

"How do you dispose of it. I thought Neummurra gold would be recognized anywhere?" asked Dan. "We've got a mate who is supposed to be a fossicker; he is up the creek. He alloys it for us, so it looks like alluvial gold, and takes it off to Walsingham where he can sell it, and have no questions asked."

Innis leant forward and furtively plucked the sleeve of his companion. His white lips trembled over his chattering teeth. Schultz pushed away the trembling wretch. He was telling the exact truth; no other plan had occurred to him. He must gain time and keep the Boss occupied.

But Dan's mind had wandered back to his grievance. "Jim Hetherington! Jim Hetherington!" he said harshly. "It is going to be a wonderful thing he will show us all. Gold out of the tallings, no less! He expects to have twice the gold to send away this month!"

"He'll have this much less; but what is that," said Schultz, "the little we got won't make any difference.

Dan only looked at him in silence.

Schultz was a clever man, if he had devoted half his talents to something useful, instead of perverting them to base ends, as he had done all his life, he might have risen high, and obtained fairly the money he coveted. An idea almost preposterous even to himself, yet perhaps worth attempting with his drunken master, now flashed upon his brain. It would at any rate give them a little more time, and if Marlowe rose to the bait, enable them to obtain such a hold on him that it would not be likely he would "round" on them afterwards.

Schultz, in his career of crime, had seen many a strange thing done by a drunken man.

His plan, improbably as it seemed, even to himself was to work on Marlowe's evident anger against Hetherington. To see whether to spite the latter, he would join them in the gold stealing. If only he could coax the Boss to take some gold to-night, before Randall arrived, it would close his mouth when he became sober and he would, for his own sake, allow them to escape.

"Tell you what Boss," he said keeping his eyes on the flushed face of the listener with a steady intentness that seemed as if it would force the wish upon the other by sheer strength of will, 'I'd get even with them both, by taking a little of what is your own. What's to prevent you taking some of the gold itself, there's some in there waiting to be put in the moulds. There's no one to say a word against you, and you'd make

Hetherington's dividends look small at the end of the month. I can fancy the sour looks of Hetherington, Carson, and Buxton if the new treatment turned out a failure."

Dan stared fascinated as the speaker went cautiously on; fanning the jealous anger, raising the latent cupidity, tempting by every art, the poor, tempest-fussed, bewildered soul of Marlowe. By the same infernal cunning he had won over Innis, a weak creature with a shallow, covetous mind, and Achmann, a good-matured, easily-led fellow, whom he had persuaded to leave the works and pose as a fossicker, that he might act as their agent in retorting and alloying the stolen gold. He had only been a few months at Neummurra, coming up from the South with a record that would not bear much investigation; already he had contrived to corrupt two hitherto, honest men, and as the Boss listened, Schultz felt confident he was succeeding with him.

In his angry vehemence Dan had given to Schultz the hint on what to speak. He played on the two chords of jealous anger and revengeful desire; till at last to his relief he found that Marlowe was willing to consider his proposals. The chance of triumphing at one blow over Buxton and Jim was too tempting to poor Dan.

As soon as he consented Schultz rapidly sketched a plan, but with something of his old obstinacy preferred his own way.

He would share the stolen gold in the proportion agreed upon by Schultz, one-third for the men and two-thirds for himself, but he would not hear of giving the gold to Achmann to dispose of, nor explain his own plans with regard to it. It must suffice for them that he would take entire charge of it, decide how much could be taken at one time, and give them their share when he considered fitting.

Shultz could scarcely believe in his escape, and the easy victory he had obtained. The only thing that disturbed him was the doubt whether Marlow sober could be trusted to the same extent as Marlowe drunk.. If only the gold were taken to-night the Boss would find his hands tied, and himself, whether he would or not, bound to his fellow-conspirators. He could not get them punished afterwards without implicating himself. Having disposed of the subject, Shultz was quite willing to return the charcoal, and to set to work under the direction of the Boss in putting it into the furnace.

This done, Marlowe went into the next room and took away from the safe a small, rough, spongy lump or two of solid gold from the heap waiting, with what was burnt off to-night to be fused again in plumbago crucibles and poured out into the moulds to be cast into ingots on the morrow. Dan came back and showed them what he had taken.

The covetous eyes of Innis flickered with desire, his lips twitched, and his small thin body seemed to expand at the sight of the gold. He sighed unconsciously as he watched Marlowe dispose of it, and it was very reluctantly that he allowed Shultz to push him back to the furnace, as Marlowe carefully

THE FURNACE FOR GOLD

and methodically secured the safe and the door.

The manager and the bosses of the sheds had each a key to the smelting-room but when the gold had been put in the moulds, the ingots, after a tally had been kept, were removed to another safe with two keys that could not be used except in combination. One key was in charge of the manager, Marlowe had the other. They could only open the safe together.

Strangely enough at this time the same precautions were not used for the rough gold; and as for the charcoal, which was practically 90 per cent gold, it was brought in open cases from the vats to the smelter, often under the sole charge of the man who carried it.

This has been altered of late years. The charcoal is brought to the furnace in locked cases, and the chances of stealing are practically eliminated.

It was about an hour later when Randall arrived. He apologized for his delay but thanked Marlowe for his assistance. Dan gave a sleepy reply, for the drink was beginning at last to show its effects, and he turned to go home.

"The Boss seems a bit upset to-day over young Hetherington's promotion," ventured Shultz, anxious to find whether Randall saw anything unusual in Marlowe.

"Think so?" said Randall sarcastically. "I suppose you are paid to think about matters that don't concern you. I want neither talk nor loafing, so you need not try them on."

Randall, like Jim, had an instinctive, but what he believed to be an unreasonable antipathy to Shultz, whom he had always found a willing, obedient worker.

At the snub Shultz became silently attentive to his duties, and Randall felt that he had been unnecessarily sharp.

CHAPTER XIV.

A WOMAN'S WAY

Marlowe awoke next morning with a confused sense of trouble. Gradually a hazy remembrance of the previous night's occurrences returned to him, but he could scarcely believe that it was not a ghastly dream.

His anger against Buxton and Jim still burned steadily, but remorse at his own crime lay upon his mind with a dull heavy weight.

He went to the sitting-room and opened a drawer in his bookcase. There lay the gold wrapped in his handkerchief. He must not leave it there. The mere sight of the glittering mass roused a strange desire to retain it. Dan's cupidity awoke. There was an old tin box in a lumber room at the back; he would put the gold in it, and bury it in the garden at night, until he could see how to deal with it.

As for the two men, he was undetermined as to his attitude towards them. Dan had been an honest man until now, and not all his sophistry could blind him to the fact that taking the gold was stealing, in the barest and ugliest sense. He ate his breakfast in moody silence, and set out immediately after for the mine.

But a visit to the "Three Crowns" altered his way of thinking; his remorse fled, his action seemed now perfectly justifiable and legitimate. Jim came up to speak to him as he entered the Shed, but Dan deliberately walked past him with level brows.

Jim's spirit rose against the injustice of the treatment; he would make no further effort at reconciliation; the next overture must be from Dan. And having decided thus, he forced his mind to leave the subject. He was young and hopeful; busy with his new duties, he contrived to put all thought of Dan into the background.

He was kept later than usual, but as soon as he was free he hurried home, for he meant to get over to see Pen that night. He had not spoken to her since the ball and he knew she would be hurt at hearing from others of his promotion. But as he came up the path the sound of a girl's voice reached him, and he saw to his surprise Miss Clara Carson sitting on the verandah with his mother.

The girl looked very pretty in a white dress, and she coloured a little as he came up to them. Her fair rosy face, blue eyes, bright hair, and plump rounded figure showed to great advantage against Anne's sallow face and pinched little form. There was a pleased smile in Anne's dark eyes.

"Miss Carson came down to see me this afternoon," she said, "and she has taken a fancy to my crochet, so I have been showing her the stitch. It is so late now that I've been trying to persuade her to stay to tea and you will see her home. Father is in there; we were just waiting for you to sit down."

With inward unwillingness, for he was eager to be able to get away as soon as possible, Jim joined in his mother's solicitations. Clara refused, she could not think of staying. But finally, in her pretty, affected little manner, she allowed herself to be persuaded.

"I told mother I might be staying for tea with Ellie Marlowe, so they will not be expecting me home," she said at last. Jim had no patience with her airs, though no one could have guessed it from his manner.

"Why couldn't the girl have said so at first?" he thought, "without all this shilly-shallying. I'm glad Pen has none of that foolish nonsense about her." Pen's honest face came before him, and her merry natural voice sounded in his ear. John Hetherington surveyed the young lady from under his grizzled, bushy eyebrows, and his verdict was not favourable.

"A mass of affection. What's her idea in coming and sweetening mother, as she must have been doing all the afternoon. She has known us for some time but she never before seemed to think us worth cultivating. What's in the wind now?" His old eyes twinkled as he looked at his comely son. Jim was now a boss, even perhaps worthy of a thought from the manager's daughter.

But John after all was a gentleman, and let none of his cynical amusement in the situation appear; not even to Anne, who seemed in a state of gratified pride at the graciousness of

THE FURNACE FOR GOLD

Miss Carson.

After tea Anne suggested that Miss Carson might care to see Jim's prizes and medals that he had won at the Grammar School and the University.

"Nonsense, mother," said Jim, "Miss Carson might not care to see them. You shouldn't bore your visitors by making them look at my prizes. Miss Carson would rather not look at them I am sure."

"But indeed, indeed I would; I'm not clever myself, but I adore cleverness in others." Therein Miss Clara did herself an injustice, for she was a very clever girl, and if she had had but enough common sense to throw off her absurd affections, might have been a very fascinating one. In spire of Jim's remonstrances, the prizes were brought, and Clara went into ecstasies over each.

The young man's patience was beginning to fail him; he thought of Pen, and wondered whether she had heard the news. It was almost impossible for her not to, and here, this girl was keeping him chained to her side, while she rhapsodized over his bygone successes, and taxed his patience almost to the limit.

The time slipped by, and still Clara gave no sign of going. Jim relapsed into monosyllables, and at last his mother, seeing the flag of mutiny in his eyes, came to his assistance.

"You'll come down again some other afternoon, and I'll show the other stitches," she said. Clara thanked her warmly, and promised to come, but she understood the hint, rose and put on her hat.

"They'd make a fine couple, wouldn't they?" Anne said, as the door closed on Jim and Clara.

"Humph!" grunted John, and buried himself in a paper. "The girl has him in her eye," went on Anne, as she carefully collected the prizes and put them away. "A girl can't look at Jim but you think she is after him; there's not such another lad in Neummurra to your thinking" Anne laughed, "Nor to yours either, John. You take my word for it, she likes Jim. I could see it in her face, though she tried to hide it."

"Hide it!" John laughed heartily. "That's all she will get for it; you take my word for it. Jim wasn't taken by her at all; so she needn't go wasting her sweetness over his mother, for he is not the man to let his mother do his courting for him."

Anne's smile faded. She knew in her inmost heart that Jim loved Penelope Morgan, and that his was no fickle nature, to swerve from its allegiance at a new attraction. Jim did not belong to the type of man who would allow himself to be made love to, or who is flattered by the hint of a girl's preference. Rather the exact opposite. The base idea that any woman could forget her modesty, and seek, instead of waiting to be sought, would be almost enough to send him from her with a feeling not far from loathing. But it takes many types to make this world of men, and some are not averse from a pretty girl's advances.

Anne knew better than to rouse Jim's dislike to the girl by hinting at such a possibility, though she felt certain in her own mind that Clara had taken a fancy to him, and she built a new and airy castle as she saw the pair leave the house in pleasant conversation.

Jim forced himself to listen and to reply cheerfully to Clara as they went up the hill together. He was amused or would have been amused another time, to listen while she tried to impress him with her love for rather abstruse reading, though she kept protesting that she was not clever. What did Jim care whether she "adored" to use her own phrase, Huxley or Spencer, or whether she found Kent difficult of comprehension. He heard her, it is true; but he was listening at the same time to Pen's voice with the ring of anger in it, scolding him for not telling them about his promotion at once, for allowing a day to have passed before coming to see his cousins with such wonderful news.

Clara exerted herself to the utmost to be entertaining to her companion, and flattered herself that she was succeeding, when he listened with polite interest, through which Clara was not quick enough to see the bored expression. She was quite tired when he left her at her father's door, but satisfied that she had begun well in her desire to cultivate Jim's friendship. She did not know that when Jim was with Pen it was he who did the entertaining, and Pen who, like a queen, allowed herself to be pleased or otherwise with his efforts.

If poor Clara would only place herself on a pedestal in like fashion, and allow the young men to exert themselves to please her, they would find her as charming as they voted her boring, for, in truth, the Manager's daughter was not a favourite with the simple swains of Neummurra as she was dimly aware, without understanding why.

Jim almost ran along the slope to the Morgan's cottage.

Gwennie opened the door, and informed him that they were all out; she did not know where, but fancied that Penelope and Llewellyn had gone to spend the evening with Ellie Marlowe.

Jim scarcely waiting to say goodnight so sharp was his disappointment. He would not venture a visit to Dan's house after his recent prohibition and therefore he returned moodily back. But he could not be moody for long. When he thought over his new prospects he forgot the petty annoyance of the day, and his face was as clear as ever as he entered his own house. He would not wear his heart on his sleeve, even under his mother's eye.

"Tommy was in a fine to do over the visitor," Anne said as he sat down. "He kept peeping at her from the passage. That boy's curiosity will be the death of him some day." "Oh, it is not much of a fault," laughed Jim. "He's a good little chap otherwise, isn't he?"

"Oh, he'll do," Anne said, and began to talk over the changes at the works. She was anxious to hear how Jim had got on, and he gratified her by giving her a long account of the eventful day.

Jim was able to see Pen next

evening, but his apologies were badly received.

"You had time to see Ellie, she told me," Pen said sharply; and as Jim could not speak of the quarrel with Dan he could not explain his tardiness. "I know what kept you last night; we couldn't expect you to come over to see us when you have to escort the manager's daughter home," said Pen with a snap of her pretty teeth.

"I couldn't help her coming," began Jim, and stopped.

"Who is blaming you? Why, it is a great honour, I assure you," and she looked him coldly in the face.

"Now Pen, don't lets quarrel over nothing," cried Jim.

"Quarrel – who wants to quarrel with you? I'm sure we are all delighted to hear of our cousin's good fortune;" and this was all the satisfaction he received.

CHAPTER XV.

A YOUNG HYPOCRITE.

The following day was Sunday, and Jim wondered whether he would go over to Morgan's and get Lew to go out for a walk with him. It was possible Pen might be persuaded to join

Little Tommy was hurrying through his dressing for Sunday School, for Anne insisted on seeing that the little orphan had every chance of improvement.

"You'll come straight back home, Tommy," she said, as the little fellow stood waiting for her inspection before going.

"Yes Mrs. Hetherington," said Tommy; "some boys stay and play marbles after Sunday school."

"You won't, will you, Tommy?" said Anne, earnestly.

"No, indeed, I know better. I wouldn't play on Sunday for anything; it is wicked. I know what the Bible says: 'Six days shalt thou labour and do all thy work,' said Tommy, with much unction, repeated the fourth Commandment, his small face shining with virtuous complacency.

Anne was highly pleased. "That's a real good boy, Tommy. Here is an apple for you, and Tommy went to the door. "Come here, you young shaver," said John, looking up from his book. "I think you are a smug young hypocrite, I always distrust anyone who makes an uncalled-for profession of piety," he said to Anne, as she followed Tommy, who came unwillingly and stood before his master.

"Let me have a good look at you." A suspicious bulkiness in the little sailor Jacket caught John's eye. He touched it, and it felt hard. "What's this?" repeated John, and Anne gasped in horror.

"Marbles." muttered Tommy. "And what's the card for?" "It's for playing with", said Tommy, raising his head with some pride. "I made it myself, ten boys put marbles on, then we have a marble in the middle. The boy who hits the centre marble gets six."

"Who gets the rest?" asked John, with interest. "I do, because it's my card; and if nobody hits the centre marble, I get the lot," he finished, triumphantly.

"Well, of all the young scoundrels. This is a complete gambling machine, Anne, and your hypocritical young hopeful is fleecing his companions. You wouldn't play on Sunday, indeed, you young Pharisee! I wonder what you will come to."

Tommy was clearly indifferent to his future, but as Jim appeared his aspect changed, his face fell, his black eyes filled with tears, what might have been a blush of shame reached even to the back of his ears. If there was one person who held the key to the door that might unlock the possibilities in Tommy's neglected nature, it was Jim. His affection for his handsome young master was scarcely more than that of a faithful dog as yet, but it held the germs of higher things.

Jim was told the story, and the sight of his reproachful face was too much for Tommy. "I'll never do it again; you can burn the whole blessed thing," he sobbed.

"Give it to me, father," Jim said quietly. "Now, Tommy, come with me, and burn the card yourself. If you want to play marbles, play them fairly, and don't be a little swindler. The marbles can stay on this shelf for a week, then I'll give them back to you."

Tommy sniffed, but obeyed, and afterwards departed mournfully, to Sunday School.

As soon as he had gone, Jim burst out laughing. "The little financier," he said, who would have thought it of him? Don't worry over him, mother, he is only a boy; perhaps with all your teachings of morals and manners, he will grow up a fine man some day, and thank you for your training."

Anne's face did not brighten. Tommy's duplicity had given her a shock. Suddenly she heard her name called.

"Mrs. Hetherington, Mrs. Hetherington! Hullo, I say, Mrs. Hetherington. Here's the lady what was here the other day," shouted Tommy from the gate. Anne looked out and saw Miss Carson. "Run away this minute," she said, as the boy lingered in his usual inquisitive way. Be off with you," and she motioned him away.

Tommy held his ground with provoking obstinacy, and favoured the young lady with a hard stare, which she pretended not to observe.

"I'm off too, mother, I'll just run out by the back. I promised to see Lew Morgan," said Jim hurriedly. "You'll do no such thing. The girl has seen you, and it would be downright rudeness to rush off like that. Besides. I don't expect she will stay long." Anna spoke insistently, but in an angry whisper; the while, her face was breaking into smiles to greet the manager's daughter.

"If Jim had any sense of what was for his own good he would be only too pleased to show attention to Miss Carson," she thought bitterly. She knew well that Lew Morgan was merely an excuse for getting a chance of seeing Pen. But though he was her son she held him in some respect, and did not venture to express such thoughts in words. It was enough that he paid

THE FURNACE FOR GOLD

attention to her wish and waited for the visitor.

"I just ran down," began Clara Carson as soon as the greetings were over, "with some news about my brother. We got a letter yesterday. He is coming home for a month or two. He was ill, he says, but is now all right again, and is going to take a long holiday. He spoke of you," she looked at Jim. "He saw your name in one of our letters lately, and wants to know whether you are the 'Plugger' Hetherington that he used to know in the 'Varsity. He says that if that is so he will be delighted to see an old chum."

"What is your brother's name?" asked Jim. "Lynnton, but we always call him Lynne," was the smiling reply."

"Lynn Carson," cried Jim eagerly, "Is he your brother?" There was such frank surprise in his tone that Clara reddened with a vexation that she did not choose to show. "We are not much alike. Lynn is dark and I am fair," she said easily.

"I shall be glad to see him. It is five years since he left us. He went off to Queensland to an uncle, I heard, and was taking up the law with him, studying for the Bar," said Jim.

"He has passed all his examinations as a barrister. He is Judge Rutherford's Associate." Clara said, with some pride. Anne smiled. She was pleased to hear that this young barrister claimed friendship with her son, but she could not quite forget her own and John's displeasure that Jim had not chosen the law himself.

"We wanted Jim to be a barrister too," she could not help saying.

"It is quite an old story mother," Jim said, laughing. "Besides, I might not have passed my examinations, you know." "What nonsense! Weren't you an exhibition boy?" said Clara, and her eyes said plainly, "What examination could be too hard for you?"

Jim laughed again, but he did not resent the flattering implication. "When is your brother coming?" asked Anne, glad to see that Jim was interested at last, and apparently forgetting his promise to Lew Morgan.

"At the end of the month," the girl answered, "and he says he is not at all an invalid, but is ready for all the fun and gaieties Neummurra can show him. He is used to balls, picnics, and parties, and, hopes he will not find our town a dull hole." A jealous misgiving crept into Jim's mind, as he recalled the Lynne Carson of 'Varsity days.

"Adonis" the boys used to call him. He had the bold, striking style of good looks that is apparent to the most casual glance; and by his mates was looked up to and admired, even then, as a lady-killer of note. He made a point of knowing every pretty girl in the city, and was considered the authority on the subject of beauty. When any new theatrical company came to Melbourne Lynne's judgment on each actress was waited for eagerly by his companions. There was no appeal against the decision of "Adonis."

Lynne was always supposed to be chronically in love, the course of his love affairs being as a rule brief. The last pretty face swept out of his heart the last but one. With it all, however, he had not the slightest trace of affection. He was, as Jim remembered him, but a handsome, laughter-loving boy, spoilt a little by too much admiration from the other sex.

Though Lynne spoke of Jim as an old chum, strictly speaking there had never been any great friendliness between them, except the ordinary comradeship of common studies and common liking for sport. Jim's nature was too reserved to admit many into close affection, and the lovemaking of Lynne was too opposed to Jim's ideas to allow the lads to become very congenial. But they had been pleasant companions, and retained yet the liking of their student days.

As these memories dashed quickly through Jim's mind, a faint doubt stirred in him at the thought of Pen. What would she think of Lynne, with his southern airs, his fascinating manner, and again, what impression would the Rose of Neummurra make on beauty-loving Lynne? He wished he had been able to have a definite promise from Pen, and he would not care who came to Neummurra.

The more he thought of Lynne, the more unsettled he became. He was rapidly losing his feeling of security, and blamed himself for the backwardness that had allowed the time to slip by, had kept him from securing Pen before this new and possible aspirant entered the lists.

He wished that it would occur to Clara to take her departure, but it was late in the afternoon before she made any movement to go.

She chattered about her brother all the way home, and did not notice that Jim's attention began to wander. He could scarcely tell the girl that he wished her to hasten her steps especially as she seemed so pleased with herself and with him, but he felt that he owed her a grudge, when he realised, as he turned to go home, that it was too late now to think of calling over for Lew Morgan.

CHAPTER XVI.

ADONIS APPEARS

The month drew to an end, the fateful month of Jim's experiments; the gold escort came to Neummurra to carry away the monthly amount of gold. The returns were made up, but the quantity obtained was so very little in advance of the returns of the previous month, that Jim could scarcely credit the tally, but was obliged to confess that it was correct. The manager was annoyed, but he wore the expression of one who had expected no more. The directors could scarcely blame him for a change that Buxton had ordered him to make.

He had not much faith in Hetherington's new-fangled ideas, and events had shown the justice of his doubt, he thought, as he watched with Marlowe the escort ride away from the office.

Dan Marlowe said little, as he listened with apparent indifference to

THE FURNACE FOR GOLD

Carson's remarks, but in spite of his anger against Jim he felt some stirring of remorse at the sight of the young man's downcast face. He resolved that for the next month at least he would not tamper with the gold as he had done three times, since the night he had caught Shultz and Innis stealing the charcoal, for he had neither returned the gold, got rid of the men, nor set himself free from the strange power that Shultz had obtained over him that first night.

But however firmly he determined now, he knew in his inmost heart that when Shultz tempted him again, his resolution might fail. It was strange how completely poor Dan had succumbed to Shultz's evil influence. He had been a man who prided himself on his force of character, on the strength of his will, and now he knew that his force was powerless, his strength, weakness, before the malign and secret coercion of this man, one of the workmen under him, and one whom he should be able to dismiss if he chose on the morrow, but who, he knew, laughed in his sleeve at the mere thought of such a possibility. Shultz was well aware that the boss was afraid of him. Since the night when in his passion of jealousy and anger he had condoned their theft and allowed himself to be persuaded to join in the plunder, he had lost his proper ascendancy over him, and was helpless against their encroachments.

It was Shultz who was the mastermind; the craven Innis lived from hour to hour in fear, waiting for the day of reckoning, and Achmann, who still continued to work the creek in the hills for free gold, though he no longer received the charcoal amalgam from them, trembled at the thought that his secret was known to one of the bosses.

But Shultz gloried in his power, and boasted to his companions of its extent. Dan's anger against Jim was dying away, but he showed no signs of this. He never spoke to him, except when absolute necessity required it; and Jim grew hopeless of any ultimate reconciliation.

He knew Dan, thought outwardly careful, was still drinking, and, though his iron frame showed little sign of any deterioration his sullen taciturnity became more marked at home, and at the works. The new born taint of cupidity, too, was growing; Marlowe began to feel that he would find it hard to bring himself to part with the gold he had stolen.

"Old Dan doesn't look the same man; I wonder what's come over him these days," the workmen remarked to each other, and Jim wondered how much longer this unnatural state of things could last.

He would not have believed at one time that Dan could continue to treat his old favourite so coldly, and being a warm hearted young fellow he grieved over his friend's defection.

The low return of gold on this first month of his experiment with the new treatment was a great blow to Jim. He could not understand how it was possible that such a thing could occur. He worried himself with assaying, and calculating that seemed to prove that the free concentrates alone treated should have sent the yield up considerably not to speak of the ordinary stuff, that should realise a fair percentage of the assay value. He was bitterly disappointed, but not hopeless. Next month would prove that he was right, and meantime he was doing his best, working overtime and sparing neither himself nor the men, in his determination to succeed. He was not one to bring his worries home, but that night Anne could see that something was disturbing him. She was wise enough to leave him alone; if he wished to give her his confidence he would do so, without being teased for it. She wondered whether he was grieving over Pen, as he had not been up to the cottage for some time. Jim had not yet had the longed-for conversation with Pen, though he had met her several times during the month.

She had seemed different somehow, and the right moment to speak never appeared to arrive. When he saw her, she was with others, or, if alone, in one of her provoking moods, when it seemed impossible to speak of sentiment lest she should turn himself and his love into ridicule.

Now that his experiments at the works were so unsuccessful, and his future so doubtful, he wondered whether he was justified in asking Pen to be his wife, and he resolved to wait another month. But the thought that perhaps after all she did not care for him came to him at times, especially since he had heard of Lynne's approaching visit, and in spite of his strong will it made his resolution waver. If he got a good chance, he almost resolved to speak and end his misery.

The day after the escort left he heard that the manager's son had arrived, and in the afternoon Lynne came down to the works. He was not much altered, a little paler, but as handsome as ever. Jim wondered what Pen would think of the stranger, as he noticed the fashionable cut of his clothes and the assured ease of his manner.

"So here is where I meet you," Lynne said, looking round with an amused smile at the busy scene. "I wondered whether the Jim Hetherington my sister wrote about was old 'Plugger'. Who'd have thought of your taking to mining?"

Jim laughed at the quizzical look in Lynne's face. "Oh, I like it, thought it wouldn't suit your superfineness, I'll admit."

"The dad has got a fair billet here, and the climate suits mother and Clara," said Lynne, ignoring the reference to himself, "But what sort of a place is Neummurra anyway?"

"Oh, the usual run of mining townships you've been in them before, surely?" said Jim.

"No, they never came much in my way any more than their gold came into my pocket."

"Why, I understood you were a plutocrat in the way of barristers," said Jim.

"Behold me," Lynne threw out his white hands dramatically, "an almost briefless barrister, talented, I'll admit, but not yet appreciated, a mere Judge's

Associate."

"Stuff and nonsense," said Jim, laughing, "Come now, how are you getting on at the bar?"

"Fairly well," said Lynne, "I've been Rutherford's Associate (good old boy Rutherford) but I am now on my own. I've had a case or two, and really think I'm getting up a fair connection. Things are a bit dull down south just now, and as I have not been too well lately, I thought I'd take a run up and see the old people. Fancy my luck in striking you here, old fellow."

"Not much luck in that," said Jim, but he could not help feeling pleased, though he knew how easy it was for Lynne to say pleasant things.

"Any pretty girls around here?" asked Lynne.

"What? About the works? I'm afraid not. We have no girl miners here," replied Jim, purposely obtuse; but his thoughts flew to Pen, and he wished that he could feel sure that the handsome barrister would not try to steal her away.

And yet, as the two men stood together one might have considered the advantage in good looks lay with Jim, in spite of his working clothes and his face touched with the red-grey dust of the crushers. His fine head, with its crisp brown waves of hair, topped the sleek dark head of his friend, and in some indefinable way his personality, too, gave the impression of being higher than that of the other. But both were good-looking men in the first flush of manhood.

"I see you won't give me any help in that line," said Lynne, seeing that Jim refused to be drawn on the subject of the young ladies of Neummurra. "I expect you've grown into quite a woman hater. I always prophesised you would, you old Diogenes."

"And you are still as great lady killer as ever," said Jim, "Old Adonis," with a laugh. "A bit more fastidious than in the old days, my boy. It takes an uncommonly pretty girl to set my heart beating in these degenerate times."

"A bit blasé," said Jim with a grin, "feeling old age creeping on now you've turned your quarter of a century?"

"You've struck it," said Lynne, but here comes a rum-looking beggar. Who is the gloomy chap, Jim?"

"This is Mr. Marlowe, the boss of the works," said Jim.

"I can't say very much for his looks," said Lynne. "What is he scowling at? Does he think I'm wasting your time? Or planning to abstract some of the gold? I'll be off."

Jim did not try to detain him. He watched the slim, retreating figure with a certain wistful, yet half affectionate, envy. There was an all-conquering air about the young fellow that seemed a pledge and guarantee of success. Jim felt strangely depressed as he went about his work.

CHAPTER XVII.

THE POWER OF BEAUTY

"I've got an invitation for you," his

mother said to Jim about a week later, "The Carsons are giving a party and have invited you. Miss Carson was here this afternoon, but she could not stay." "When is the party to be?" asked Jim. "I don't think I'll go. I'm not much in the party line you know."

"It is on Friday, in two days, of course you'll go," said Anne, "The first time you are asked, too." Then while she pretended to busy herself at the table, she added, "The Morgans are to be asked, the first time for them, too, though the Carson's met them soon after they came here," She saw with a quiet, side glance how the blood rushed to her son's face and she said angrily to herself, "He thinks of nothing but Pen. I bet I'll hear no more of refusing the invitation, now that he knows Pen is likely to be there."

Nor did she, and Friday night saw Jim, in spite of his diffidence and some trepidation, entering the manager's house.

As he looked into the room there seemed to him to be a great many ladies, but there were really only some half dozen or so. It was the effect of their massed light dresses that gave an impression of a great number.

"Your friend, Mr. Buxton, the great and only millionaire, the Mogul of Neummurra, is here and father told me how much he thinks of you," said the laughing voice of Lynne in Jim's ear, as he stood in the doorway. "He came up to see dad, and was coaxed somehow to stay for dinner. Clara managed after that to inveigle him into the drawing room and the sight of pretty Miss Morgan did the rest. He shows no sign of wishing to go away, does he? He is said to be a woman-hater but you wouldn't believe it to see him talking to her, would you?"

Jim's heart began to beat quickly. All his shyness vanished. He entered the room and having greeted his hostess and her daughter, took a seat and looked anxiously for Pen.

He soon saw her, and waited till he caught her eye. She gave him a slight recognition and then turned to her companion again, Jim watched them in silence for a few minutes half wondering whether a new and formidable rival had entered the field.

Buxton's face looked unusually serene and satisfied as he continued his conversation with the beautiful girl. Now and then his great laugh rang out and sounded strangely against the subdued tone of the voices of the others, who turned at such times, and gazed curiously at the millionaire and his companion.

Jim wondered, jealously, what she found to interest her in an old man and he remembered he had not liked the way in which the millionaire had looked at Pen on the night of the ball, though he had forgotten all about it until he saw him again gazing at Pen with a look of frank admiration. Jim found that Ellie Marlowe was seated beside him and Jim thought she looked uncommonly well. He told her so in his open, brotherly way.

"Do you think so," Ellie said, a deeper colour tinging her cheek, "but look at Pen. Isn't she lovely?" She

THE FURNACE FOR GOLD

added this involuntarily as her eyes followed Jim's eyes.

"Isn't she," said Jim fervently. "There is not a girl in Neummurra can hold a candle to her."

"That's straight anyway," said Ellie sharply but she laughed the next moment for Ellie also had a keen sense of humour. "I am glad it was to me you said that and not to Miss Carson. The young barrister seems to think the same as you do, Jim about Pen. He has been trying for some time to get a chance of speaking to her but old King Billy is too smart for him. He keeps Pen to himself. Just look at his majesty doing the agreeable to a pretty girl, like an ordinary man."

"Who are those girls on the other side of the room?" asked Jim, turning his eyes with effort from Pen's bright face. Those girls in white."

"Do you mean to say you don't know the Misses Koulson?" asked Ellie with mock horror. "The daughters of Reginald Koulson, the latest, the most aristocratic director of the mine? Why not to know them argues yourself unknown."

"Oh well let it," said Jim indifferently. "I suppose they are up visiting Neummurra now their dad has an interest in the mine."

"You've hit it. They are only here on a very short visit. They are 'doing' Neummurra, just as they have done Europe, Japan, America and all the other places they have visited. They are just up from Sydney now. They are examples of the absolutely correct in the latest Southern style. They are the guests of the night, let me tell you; we are very 'small potatoes' we other folk. The party was got up in their honour, I hear, and if young Mr. Carson does not turn some of his fascinating attentions to them instead of pretty Miss Pen, I fancy his mother and sister will give him a rather bad time. The Misses Koulson are now going to give us some music, I see – latest Sydney effects."

Jim smiled faintly. These little waspish speeches were not natural in Ellie, though he could not help being amused by them.

The ladies in question, while neither plain nor old, were yet neither young nor strikingly attractive, in spite of their fashionable style. As they rose to go to the piano the chair next to Pen was left vacant, and Lynne quickly slipped into it. The next moment Clara as unostentatiously, got him up from it, and sent him to the piano to turn over the music for the ladies.

Her manoeuvres afforded a quiet but intense amusement to Ellie Marlowe, who perfectly understood Clara's tactics.

Mr. Neddrie, who was one of the guests cleverly, secured the coveted position next to Pen and under cover of the brilliant but mechanical music there began a duel between him and Buxton as to which should secure the most of Pen's attention.

Buxton was put on his mettle, and determined to monopolise the conversation. There was something in the fresh, charming girl that appealed to him very strongly. No woman had ever interested him in the same way before and seeing that she seemed contented with his society, he pursued his advantage with the same grim masterfulness that gave him his ascendancy over his fellow shareholders at the mine.

Pen had come with her brother to the Carson's with much inward perturbation. It was as Anne had said, the first time either the Morgans or Hetheringtons had been invited to the manager's house.

Pen had met Clara soon after the family had arrived at the mine, but the intimacy had not gone any further than mere acquaintances. The manager's and storekeeper's daughters were in two very different sets, Pen did not care for the patronizing attitude of Miss Carson, who in her turn was somewhat prejudiced against the girl, whom she had heard spoken of as the "Rose of Neummurra". But Clara had set her heart on inviting Jim Hetherington to the party, and while her mother consented at once, her father had insisted on the Morgans being invited at the same time, both families being in the same position and also being related, he knew.

Clara was not averse to appearing with her new friends, the fashionable Koulsons, before Pen, and overawing her in her simplicity, by her grandeur and patronising kindness. She meant to show the storekeeper's daughter how great was the condescension that had allowed her to receive the invitation.

Pen had not been two minutes in the house before she was perfectly aware of Clara's attitude. She wished she had not come, as she received the limp handshake of Mrs. Carson, and met the calmly superior bow of the Misses Koulson. She appreciated, in one swift glance the fashionable perfection of their attire and felt how countried her simple creamy muslin made by her own hands looked beside the wonderful city costumes of the visitors.

She was glad to sink into a retired seat and forget her dress, in looking at the strangers. She felt out of place; even little Ellie Marlowe, as the daughter of a boss, had an assured position in that aristocratic party; while she was being decidedly shown that her social standing was merely that of a shopkeeper's daughter. A Thackeray could find material for a new "Book of Snobs" in many an Australian bush township, it is to be feared. She felt defiant and miserable, yet was too proud to show the pain she suffered, the unaccustomed sense of being looked down upon.

But, indeed, the despised dress, made by her own clever fingers, just suited the beautiful, brilliant face, and the tall lissome, girlish figure; its very simplicity accentuated her native loveliness.

Excitement had deepened the rose on her cheek, and touched with strange glamour the depths of her starry eyes, while the hint of shyness, of diffidence in her manner, was the one charm that needed to render her irresistible.

Clara anathematized her own folly in bringing the dangerous beauty near her brother, as she saw that, at the first glance at her, he appeared to forget his duty to his other guests. Before her appearance he had been getting up a flirtation with the younger Miss Koulson, but since Pen arrived he had eyes, apparently, for no one else in the room. If wishes could have been slain, poor Pen would have suffered that night every time that Clara's eyes fell on her pretty face.

Mr. Buxton, as Lynne had explained to Jim, had been coaxed with some difficulty to come into the drawing room. Immediately he caught sight of the obnoxious girl he took the seat Lynne was obliged to vacate for him, and ignored all the rest of the company to devote himself to Pen. And Clara had coaxed the millionaire into the room to please the elder Miss Koulson! She would know better next time she thought. Never again would the upstart shopkeeper's daughter have a chance to disturb the harmony of their evenings, if Clara could help it. To add to her chagrin, she soon began to understand, with the subtle instinct of a jealous woman, that though he had not spoken to her, Jim Hetherington, too, was far from indifferent to Pen. She saw the glances that, in spite of his will, indeed half unconsciously Jim kept directing to the recess, where before the night was over Pen held quite a little court of her own. Clara's manoeuvres from time to time withdrew one or another of the courtiers, but still, in spite of her cleverness they came hovering back to the siren queen in the corner.

Besides Lynne, Buxton and Neddrie, Allitson and Payne, two of the younger assayers, Frankcombe, one of the cleverest draughtsmen of the company and Burnand, the only unmarried boss of the mine, gathered round Pen, and basked in her smiles.

It was not in human nature to avoid a feeling of triumph and as the evening wore on Pen's trepidation vanished, and she began to enjoy herself, though with an angry sense of retaliation against Clara's patronage. Mr. Buxton had been the first to sit down beside her, and as it was in his pleasant conversation that she had begun to forget the provoking airs of Mrs. Carson and Clara, Pen felt very grateful to him.

She knew he was considered the most important man in Neummurra, and wondered at the kindness that could trouble him to set such an unimportant individual as she at her ease. She appreciated the compliment he paid her in talking as though she were a woman of intellect, not a pretty child. He must be a kind old man, she thought, for fifty seemed very old to twenty, and she would never forget how good he was to her, while she was still smarting under the supercilious glances of the fashionable strangers and the discourteous treatment of her hostess. So Pen enjoyed her little triumph, and smiled with simple happiness on her cavaliers.

Every moment, it seemed to poor Jim, Pen's beauty grew, the number of men round her increased, her charms displayed themselves, her merry laughs, her dimples, her witty replies, she opened like a flower to the light, and she received admiration as naturally as does a flower.

How could he dare to enter the lists with such a crowd against him? He thought, as at last, in spite of the warning flash of Clara's eyes, he saw Lynne bear Pen in triumph to the supper table.

Little Ellie had gone with Lew Morgan a few minutes before, and Jim found himself, he hardly knew how, with Clara on his arm, finding a place at the table beside them.

The meal seemed to drag out somehow. Jim could scarcely have told what he had eaten, when he once more found himself back in the drawing room.

Clara was saying "The Misses Koulsons are such nice girls. My brother has known them some time. They are quite old friends of his." She looked with some natural exasperation at her distant partner.

Jim answered vaguely. He was watching Lynne talking to Pen, at the other end of the room. Clara turned from him and bit her lip in annoyance. "Oh follow your eyes," she felt inclined to say, but remarked instead, "I think Miss Morgan is a connection of yours, isn't she?" She was determined to secure his attention.

"Pen? Oh, yes we are distant cousins," said Jim, who, indeed, with mingled anxiety and jealous anger, was not quite master of himself.

"Too distant to suit your taste, I suppose," said Clara pertly.

Jim did not answer, and, provoked at his silence. Clara said, "I'm afraid your cousin is a bit of a flirt. I must tell her that my brother Lynne is an incorrigible one, too." Her voice had grown shrill. "Hetherington!" Jim turned with relief, as a pair of large hands was placed on his shoulders, "I want to have a talk with you by and by."

"Don't let me detain you," said Clara, irritably; "I am going over to speak to Avis Koulson."

Buxton lowered himself cautiously into the seat she vacated.

"I'm always a bit afraid of these gimcrack chairs," he said with a smile, "I have no wish to amuse the company by measuring my length on the carpet."

Jim, apart from his incipient jealousy, and also from his feeling of gratitude for the influence he had exerted in his favour, had a curious sense of attraction towards the millionaire; there was, in spite of Jim's transparent integrity, and the unscrupulous audacity of Buxton, a strange affinity between them. They mutually enjoyed each other's society.

"There is the making of a vixenish woman about that girl," Buxton said in a low tone, with a slight inclination of his head towards Clara. "Not the sort I'd ever speculate in. There's a girl here worth the whole roomful of them, though – frank, witty and unspoiled, in spite of her beauty. You know who I mean – the girl I was talking to most of the night." And something almost resembling a blush appeared on the strong, fresh coloured face.

"You mean my cousin, Miss Morgan?" said Jim quietly.

"You cousin, hey?" said Buxton,

thoughtfully; "so the beauty is your cousin?" He drummed idly with his fingers on the arms of the chair, then gave a short nod. "But it is not about her I wanted to speak to you. Carson tells me the escort did not take very much ore than the usual away this time."

A shadow gathered in Jim's clear eyes; he spoke with some effort.

"No, and I cannot understand it at all. I've put a good lot of the tallings through and the slime from the barrels that used to be thrown away in the creek, as well as a fair amount of refractory ore, and instead of us having a very big return the difference is rather slight. It has been very disappointing. I'll be putting still more through this month, and I hope we shall do better then."

"Now, don't you be worrying about that my boy." Said Buxton with a kind smile. "I suppose they've been striking very poor refractory ore in the cuttings, so that your lot could not bring up the rest."

"Oh, I don't know about that; the average assay value is not altered," said Jim uncomfortably.

"I hope not. I do not want the mine to peg out quite yet. I haven't got all I want out of it – not by a long chalk. But anyway, I'll see you through and I believe you'll come out on top. Carson has been at me to put a stop to your experiments, and return to the old ways. But between you and me, Carson is a fool."

Jim looked round hastily, and Buxton's great laugh rolled out.

"There's none of them round. The missus and Miss Clara are fussing over their pets, the Koulsons; the young barrister is flirting with your pretty cousin and Carson has vanished again. He has no great opinion of you, but I needn't repeat what I think of Carson, I believe in you, and said before I'll see you through. I shall probably take a run up again in a month or two. I am only going as far as Sydney this summer."

The hearty confidence of Buxton touched Jim very closely. He thanked him, and took fresh courage.

As the visitors prepared to go Jim resolved to see Pen home; but as he stepped forward to join her on leaving the house he found that, in spite of his efforts, he must share the privilege with several others. Ellie Marlowe and Lew came together, but following Pen were Payne, Burnand and Allison, and they were by no means disposed to efface themselves for Jim's benefit. The whole group set off. Pen guarded on every side by her attentive cavaliers, to the disgust of disappointed Jim.

CHAPTER XVIII.

THE MANOEUVRES OF CLARA CARSON.

"Did you have a nice time?" asked Anne wistfully on the morning after the party. Jim was somewhat heavy-eyed and quiet at breakfast.

"Very nice; great swells there; a good deal of fine music; and a splendid supper." He said briefly; but Anne was not satisfied until she had coaxed out of him a better account of the affair.

"Fancy Mr. Buxton being there! What has come over him?" she said, with great curiosity in her tone. "He came up to talk over the mine with Carson, I believe, and they asked him to stay," said Jim.

"But I thought he couldn't bear parties; that he was a real woman-hater," she said. Neummurra gossip had not spared a single peculiarity of the millionaire. "He didn't look like it last night," said Jim shortly.

"No," cried Anne, with interest; "Was he paying attention to anyone? Who was it?" her black eyes glittered. "He was talking a great deal to Pen," said Jim flushing, and wishing he had left the subject alone.

"Oh, I daresay; she is forward enough to push herself to the front; trust her for that; she would only be too pleased to take him if he offered himself," said Anne bitterly. To think that Pen should have attracted Buxton's notice was not an agreeable idea, but she managed, with an effort, to restrain any further expression of antagonism.

"I hear the great ladies, the Misses Koulson, are staying with the Carsons." she said. "I expect Lynne Carson was very attentive to them. It was Koulson that got Mr. Carson his appointment, so I've heard." "I don't think Lynne bothered much over them," said Jim wearily.

"Was he another of Pen's admirers?" Anne could not forbear saying, though she saw that Jim winced at her remark. "It looked like it," he said curtly. "I'm off, mother; you'll hear all of it from Ellie Marlow. She told me she would be down seeing you today."

Anne sighed as her glance followed her son down the hill. Poor little Ellie, she had guessed her secret long ago, her mother eyes had pierced the thin disguise of Ellie's friendship, but she was too fond of her to allow a hint of it to escape, and she knew Jim was free enough from vanity to suspect nothing, even had his whole mind not been centered on Pen. "That girl is a regular firebrand," thought Anne, "she will set the Carsons in a fine blaze if the young barrister falls in love with her." Ellie Marlowe came in the afternoon, and some time later Clara Carson arrived.

"I just ran in for a minute," said the latter. "Lynne came down with me to see the Koulson girls off by the coach, he will be here in a minute; he wanted to see your son." Clara's face was wreathed in friendly smiles.

"Oh, Jim will be here directly," said Anne, "come in and sit down in the coolness." "Lynne just ran into the shop of Graves, the chemist, and told me to go on, he would soon catch me up," said Clara, as she followed Anne up the stairs.

Ellie came on the verandah and the three women stood for a moment looking down the road. "Who are these two coming up this way?" Ellie said. "It looks to me like Pen Morgan and your brother."

"What!" cried Clara. "Where did you say they were?" Anne shaded her thin, eager face with her slender, brown hand, an enigmatical smile flickering

304

over her delicate face.

"That is Pen right enough," she said. "I expect she has been up the town shopping, and your brother met her. He looks a fine fellow, I'll say that for him. He walks well too," and she gave an approving glance at the young man who did not appear in any hurry to rejoin his sister, but passed the gate with Pen and went on.

"I call that cool, when he knows I am waiting for him," said Clara angrily. "I believe he saw her in the shop, and just sent me on." "I wouldn't be surprised," said Anne. "Young men will be up to tricks, you know, when they may want their sisters out of the way." Clara gave an annoyed glance at Anne, who only smiled slightly, and left the two girls together.

"Here's Jim," said Ellie brightly. Clara turned quickly, "So he is; he is nearly at the gate. I hope Lynne will look round and see him." But Lynne did not look round, and Jim had joined the girls for some time before it occurred to Lynne that he had told Clara that he was anxious to see him.

"I have only about a month's holiday," Lynne said in his easy way after greeting them, "and I think it would be so nice if we could manage to get up a few picnics to the beauty spots of Neummurra."

"There aren't any," said Clara. "Neummurra is just a bare, ugly mining township." "There's the creek; we could explore it, and gather ferns, or there's the lagoon; we could get up some boating parties. I saw some boats on it, I think, yesterday."

The lagoon was the name given to the large basin of water that was filled by the Neummurra Creek, about half a mile above the works.

"Lew Morgan has a very nice boat," ventured Ellie timidly, and Lynne's charming smile was her reward. "Then we'll get him to join us, and lend it. He and his sister seem very pleasant company." Clara laughed mirthlessly but did not venture to protest.

"You could come, couldn't you, Miss Marlowe and help a lonely fellow to pass his holiday pleasantly?" said Lynne coaxingly. Ellie agreed with enthusiasm; very little pleasure came her way; she was glad at the prospect of some, and delighted with the young barrister's amiability.

"Jim, our old Diogenes, here; you'll join us, too. We shall need some one to keep us in order. Say you'll come, old man," said Lynne. "I'm afraid I can't get away," said Jim, wryly. "I am not having a holiday you know, though I have every Saturday afternoon off. I shall join you then with pleasure, but I cannot promise for anything else."

He had a vision of the holiday party, with Lynne and Pen as the central figures, and it was not a pleasant vision to him. "Every Saturday afternoon then, remember, you belong to us. I am going to get up a regular programme of enjoyment. We will explore Neummurra, mine and all, before my time is up," said Lynne enthusiastically.

"I thought you came home in the character of an invalid," said Jim in a dry tone. A shade passed over Lynne's handsome face; some feeling quivered on his lips and softened his dark eyes. "So the mater imagines," he said. "But I'm really quite well again. I only need to pick up my strength a bit that is all. Well, Clara we must be going. Are you coming our way, Miss Marlowe, we might have the pleasure of your company in that case?"

Ellie assented with a soft, blushing smile.

"You old fraud, you should not try to steal every heart," said Jim with an undertone to Lynne, as the two girls descended the steps of the verandah together. "Same old humbug, Lynne! Same old imposter!" "Same old Adam, you mean. How can I help myself?" was the reply, as Lynne hastened smiling away.

Jim watched the trio with envious eyes. He felt that he was somehow left out of the pleasures natural to his years, and his feeling was deepened as the days passed on. He heard now and again of the expeditions that were planned by Lynne, and could not prevent some pangs of jealousy at the thought of them. It seemed hard to think that he must give Lynne so clear a field for winning Pen away from him, if, as Jim feared, such was the young barrister's intention.

The first Saturday afternoon Lynne decided they should see over the works, and Jim should act as their guide. Jim would have enjoyed this much better if it had not been taken as a matter of course that his chief duty was to explain everything to Clara, and that here his duty ended. That young lady cleverly managed to make the others understand that Jim must be considered her property and the party seemed naturally to divide itself into three groups. Pen and Lynne, Lew and Ellie, Clara and Jim. Jim's clumsy open endeavours to effect a change of partners had no chance when opposed by the dexterous maneuvering of the brother and sister. Let him try ever so cleverly he could not manage to secure Pen for himself. Lynne was always on the watch, it seemed to him, or if not, Clara had him off, willy-nilly to show her something or other that she professed to be longing to see.

The second Saturday Jim was detained at the works and he could not get away to join the others. He chafed at the delay but the manager took no heed of his impatience, as he waited in his deliberate manner while Jim undertook some assaying for him.

The assayers had received their Saturday half holiday, and Jim was leaving the works, when Carson came down and asked him to assay some ore for him. It might as well wait till Monday, but such an idea did not seem to occur to Carson, and Jim, knowing that the manager was prejudiced against him, thought it better to oblige him even at the risk of losing the afternoon in Pen's company.

It was too late to think of going with the picnickers when at last he was set free. "I dare say it is just as well," Jim thought, "if Pen cares for me, all the attentions of Lynne will not make any difference. If she does not really love me, I may as well know the truth first at last. At any rate, I can give her a chance to know her own mind. She is perfectly free." The bitterness of this thought was that perhaps it was his own foolish tardiness that left her so free. "If he wins her, he is as good as I and has just as much right, if it comes to that. I can take my gruel, I hope, as well as any other man. I can surely as I've been fool enough for these two years, be patient for one month more. But I know Lynne of old, and I doubt if he could keep true, even to Pen, suppose he wins her love. Light come, light go it used to be with him, and I question if he is much altered now. As for me, there never was but one girl in the world for me, and there never will be another if I lose Pen."

CHAPTER XIX.

PEN'S ENGAGEMENT

Jim came home from the works in a mood of strange weariness and depression. A curious premonition of impending trouble oppressed him. Anne sighed as he passed through the dining room, she missed the cheery boy he used to be, his merry whistle, his ready laugh, even his little teasing ways. These seemed changing rapidly into the quiet soberness of manhood.

John came in a few minutes later and said hastily,

"Miss Carson is just coming in."

Anne bustled to the front, while Tommy slipped out from the kitchen, and peered inquisitively from behind the dining-room door. Jim joined his father and mother, as they waited for Miss Carson.

"I thought I'd run down and tell you the news," she said somewhat breathlessly, "I knew you'd be interested. You are the first outside our family to be told."

"Out with it, lass," said John bluntly, then he drew to the rear again. He saw that for some reason or another Jim and Anne seemed unable to speak. Their instinct too truly told them already the importance of Clara's news.

"Why the first engagement in our family," said Clara shrilly.

Her eyes were fixed on Jim's face, and she noted mechanically that the fresh colour was pulling even under the dust of the Works. And as she watched she suddenly realized that she wished to hurt him, to do something to him, to pay him out for the dull pain that was stealing into her own heart.

"Yes, Lynne is engaged to Pen Morgan. I expect they will be married – after the new year."

"How does your mother like it?" asked Anne with apparent simplicity, "or yourself? I used to think he'd fancy one of your friends the Koulson girls." There was a touch of maliciousness in her question. "Oh mothers and sisters have never much to say in a boy's marriage," said Clara tartly. "Pen is a pretty girl and a nice girl enough; I think she will make him a good wife."

With an effort that seemed to leave him numb, Jim threw the oppression from him.

"Lynne is a good hearted fellow; I know he'll be kind to her," he said.

"Yes and she'll take my advice," said

Clara, "She is not the first girl, by a round dozen, that Lynne has fancied himself in love with, though this is the first time he was engaged."

"That's a fine character for a sister to give," John's deep voice startled them all. "Pen is a fine, honest lass. I'd be very sorry if the man she gives her heart to is too fickle to keep it. But better for her to find out before marriage then after." He came forward and his tall form towered over the shrinking girl.

"I must be going home," said Clara abashed for the moment, and Jim silently followed her out. There was little said between them as they mounted the hill together. Jim did not appear to know how silent he was and Clara thought viciously of Pen, yet lacked the courage to refer to the engagement again. She was glad when they parted at her father's gate.

Marlowe passed Jim as he turned homewards. The elder man's heart smote him, as he saw the haggard young face. He thought Jim was worrying over the shortage of gold. Last night, in spite of his resolution, Dan had allowed Shultz again to triumph.

Some gold had been once more abstracted; Dan had taken it home, and hidden it with the rest. He would not own even to himself how strong a hold the gold was beginning to take of him, but his power to resist his tempter was steadily declining as the amount stolen increased and the gold remained in his possession. On one point he was firm, and not all Shultz's cleverness could move him. He would not let any of them handle the gold, and he himself alone knew where he hid it. He would give, he promised to each of them an equitable share in the spoils, but he must have his own way in the disposal of it. Shultz tried persuasion and bullying but to no purpose; Dan grew only more obstinate. "I'll see it is sent South, all in good time, and you will have your fair share I tell you, if you let me alone. I know what I'm doing and if you get your share in sovereigns or notes you can be well satisfied. I've got it all down on paper, weighed to the last pennyweight; I'll take my fair proportion, and I'll give you yours."

Shultz, afraid that his victim should revolt, hurried to express his satisfaction.

And now as Dan passed his old pupil, he renewed the vow to get rid of Shultz, and give poor Jim an opportunity to show the company that he had earned his promotion. But he promised himself also that Shultz should not get a chance of handling the gold already taken.

But Jim did not see him; he walked past him without being aware of his presence. The blow Clara had given him seemed to have deadened all his faculties. He felt no anger either against Pen or against Lynne, that might come later; all that he was conscious of now was an overwhelming sense of unavailing regret; a dim, irretrievable feeling of loss. The evil that he vaguely dreaded, as soon as he had heard that Lynne was coming to Neummurra, had fallen upon him, and it seemed to him more than he could bear. That Lynne

THE FURNACE FOR GOLD

should possess Pen; Lynne! Who had flirted with so many while he had been ever faithful seemed cruelly unjust. In his absence, the father and mother spoke of the engagement, and agreed not to discuss it in Jim's presence, so that when he returned there was no occasion for him to brace himself to bear their talk about Pen.

The mother's heart was wrung as she saw how great was the effort with which he tried to make a pretence of eating, and of joining in their conversation, but she gave no sign of observing any difference.

She talked brightly and easily, with a woman's power of hiding her feelings; but it was a relief to her though she could scarcely conceal her anxiety when Jim rose after supper and said he was going out for a walk. "Of course I trust him," she told herself, "but I wish he were safe asleep tonight. He is not the kind to do himself a mischief, nor her either, poor, foolish girl, who doesn't know pure gold when she sees it. But I believe he set his heart on her since he came from college, and before that too. My poor boy! I wish, indeed, he was a little lad again, running up to me with his small trophies. Don't I remember him such a pretty boy, with his fair curly hair and his blue eyes! My poor Jim; he has got beyond his mother's comforting now," and her eyes filled involuntarily, while she thought again, with vindictive resentment, of Pen, who had caused all the trouble.

It was late before the father and mother went to rest, and though she lay silently in the darkness, she did not fall asleep till with a sigh of relief she heard Jim's step on the verandah, and knew that her fears were needless.

Jim had gone for a very long walk beside the creek, he tramped for miles in the darkness, careless as to where he went, and only returned home when he was wearied to the point of exhaustion. But in the darkness and silence of the lonely bush he had fought and conquered himself.

"What's this I hear?" cried Lew next day as he came home from work. "You might have had the decency to tell me yourself instead of letting me hear it as gossip at the bank. Are you engaged to Lynne Carson?" Pen held up a finger with a sparkling ring.

"What have you to say against it?" she said quickly.

"Oh, its your own affair," said Lew, disgustedly, "but it beats me how you could choose a little dandy, like Lynne Carson, when you could have had a manly fellow like Jim Hetherington."

That was hardly fair; Lynne was about five foot eight but Lew was too angry to be just.

"Jim Hetherington does not want me," said Pen. "Why he has scarcely spoken to me lately. I am not likely to throw myself at his feet, and Lynne is not a little dandy either."

"Good reason why," said Lew, brushing away the side issue, "where was the good of him trying to push in while you let Lynne Carson monopolise you all the time. Jim says like this 'Pen knows me well enough to understand that I care for her, I'll just give her a chance to see whether she has the sense to recognise a good man when she sees him. I'll let Lynne have the field for a month, then Pen can decide between us. I know she is a terrible flirt, but I gave her the credit of having enough sense to understand why I am drawing back'."

Pen looked at Lew with startled eyes.

"Did Jim say that to you?" she cried. "No, but I could bet anything that's how he put the matter to himself. You know he has always cared for you."

"How could I know?" said Pen quickly. "He never spoke of it to me. We have been great chums but then of course we are cousins. He never said he cared for me."

"Not in words, but if I guessed it, I can't understand how you could be so dense. However you've made your choice now. I suppose Jim will get over it. I think you are a little fool, myself."

"You are not very kind about my engagement." said Pen, faintly.

"I'm a bit disappointed, that's all; but of course as I said before, it is really your own affair. I do not pretend to influence you but Jim is my friend, and I am sorry for him. I've nothing to say against Lynne Carson, he seems a pleasant enough fellow, clever too but he is not a patch on Jim."

"Oh you think there's nobody like Jim," said the girl peevishly.

"Not many, I'll admit, and there are a good few in Neummurra of my own way of thinking," said Lew, honestly. "But look here, Pen I'll give you my candid opinion. I think you and Lynne are too much alike in disposition to suit each other. You are both too fond of admiration, both too fond of talking, and," but here he broke off abruptly and as Pen looked at him with serious intentness he went on with a laugh, "I'm glad I'm not a sentimental chap myself. I don't bother the girls and they don't bother me. We are mutually indifferent to each other, thank goodness! I see through their little tricks and that does not suit the sweet creatures so we leave each other alone."

"Wait," said Pen, with a curious laugh, "your turn will come some day, Lew."

"Never," said Lew firmly.

"They'll see most who live longest," she said quietly, "though you are two years older, Lew, than I, you're only a boy, after all."

Lew walked out into the garden whistling superciliously and Pen went to the kitchen to speak to Gwenny.

David Morgan was delighted at his daughter's engagement, and his simple pleasure in her prospective good fortune was a source of comfort to Pen, who, after the first flush of excitement subsided, began to feel some misgivings. Lew's words influenced her more than she knew. For though she fancied she was very wise and experienced, she was but a child after all, a pretty child who was still ignorant of her own heart. She did not know how much of her feeling for Lynne was gratified vanity and desire to outshine her companions.

THE FURNACE FOR GOLD

CHAPTER XX.

MYSTERIOUS SHORTAGE OF GOLD.

"You see I've kept my word, I'm back at the end of the month, and expect we'll have a better show this time." Buxton's loud voice startled Jim as he was bending over a truck that had just brought up some tailings from one of the mounds at the foot of the hill.

"I hope so, sir; I don't see why we shouldn't," Jim said. "I have not heard the exact amount though; I have not been round yet this morning; the escorts are not there, are they?"

"They are coming up now," said Buxton "Here is Carson. His face is not what we might call too cheerful, is it? Where is Marlowe?"

Jim's heart sank. He guessed there was bad news for him. He replied gravely, "Mr. Marlowe is down in the assay department. They are weighing the gold again, before it is made up for the escort."

"What is up?" asked Buxton, as Carson drew near. "The number of ingots is the same as last month. We've a few ounces over, that's all." Was the gloomy answer.

"What is that you are saying?" said Buxton roughly, glancing from the manager to the pale, shocked face of the young man. Carson repeated his speech, and added "I thought perhaps you might care to come and see for yourself, before we hand it over to Warren. He is here with the escort."

Buxton's face flushed darkly and he swore under his breath. "Come along, Jim," he said, "There is some funny business about this. I want to get to the bottom of it, and when I do" he stopped and looked fixedly at the ground.

"I wanted to see you a moment if you could spare me the time. I wished to ask your advice about something," asked Carson, half hesitantly. He was displeased that Buxton should invite Jim to accompany him down, because he himself had no faith in the young man, and he resented the friendly interest that Buxton seemed to take in him. Further, what he wished to consult with Buxton was the advisability of getting rid of Hetherington all together. The shortage in the gold, compared with the amount treated, had only occurred since his promotion, and there was little doubt in Carson's mind that it would cease on his dismissal. He could scarcely be said to suspect Jim of stealing the gold, but he could not overlook the coincidence of the drop in the returns and Jim's promotion to power.

"I shall see you again about anything you want to consult me," said Buxton curtly. "Just now the point is the shortage in the yield for the month. It is not the amount we are losing, that is not much, though still even a few ounces make some difference. It is the mysterious way the thing has come about. Of course we have not been getting this last two years anything like what we used to get before, but a sudden drop like this especially when we thought we were in a fair way to make up our deficiency; that is the kind

311

of thing that I cannot understand. You've no light to throw on the subject?" He turned to Jim, who shook his head.

Carson looked as if he could have managed to see through the darkness of the mystery, if he tried, but without a glance at him Buxton hurried to the smelting department.

A few minutes later he came out with Carson, and the two men went to the office. Buxton's face was set in hard lines, his eyes were impenetrable. "There's something fishy about this business. It's no use showing me those books. There's the gold for the month; there's the assay value of the ore put through each treatment. So many vats, so much put through, that tells me nothing I do not know already. I want to know where the leakage is. Can you account for it? Surely every precaution is taken. Who are responsible for the stuff once it leaves the charcoal filters?"

"Marlowe, Todd, Randall and myself," said Carson, "and of course Hetherington looks after the stuff he himself is treating until he brings it to the smelting department. I hope you are not beginning to suspect there is any tampering with the gold."

"Have I said anything about suspecting anybody?" said Buxton sharply.

"Your words might bear that interpretation," said Carson, as sharply, "If you are reflecting on me as manager, I am willing to submit to any inquiry and I'm sure neither Todd, Randall, Marlowe - " he hesitated, "nor Hetherington need fear the fullest investigation."

"Tut! Tut! Man who is accusing you? Who is suspecting you?" said Buxton feeling for the first time something approaching liking for the manager. "I only want you to keep your eyes open. You'll admit yourself that things are queer. I fancy our next directors meeting will be a lively one. But what did you want to consult me about?"

It was somewhat difficult for Carson to express his suspicions of Hetherington, and, indeed, at the first word against his favourite Buxton's manner altered completely.

"You are mistaken," he said coldly. "It is not there you will put your finger on the weak spot. We've gone over every step in his treatment of the tailings and the slime, and I can see for myself that he understands the matter fully, and that his process ought to be thousands in our pockets if it can be carried out thoroughly. Of course, he is little more than experimenting now, but that little ought to have made a difference. As for suspecting him, I'd as soon suspect yourself, or my old friend Marlowe, who looks as gloomy as yourself over the shortage."

Carson received the compliment dubiously; but he saw it was useless to try to convince the millionaire that Hetherington was otherwise than perfect, and, though still keeping to his own opinion, the manager resolved to await further developments.

Buxton returned to the smelter to look for Dan Marlowe. He found him just leaving the room, with two

THE FURNACE FOR GOLD

workmen beside him,

"Busy Dan?" asked Buxton, "I wanted to see you for a minute."

"Not particularly," was the quick reply. The workmen at once turned away, and left the two friends together.

It was strange that Buxton saw no difference in Dan, or, seeing it, did not suspect something. In spite of every effort at self-control, Dan's voice shook, and his eyes fell before Buxton's friendly glance.

To look at the two men – Buxton, healthy, alert and cheerful, and Marlowe, worn, lined and broken – no one would think there was but two years' difference between their ages. The last two months had aged Dan more than ten years should have done.

But Buxton observed nothing strange in Marlowe's manner except a constraint that he feared was due to his own neglect of him. He resolved to overcome it, and get back tot the former friendly footing. After the passing reference to the trouble of the gold, he began to recall the past with such kindly remembrance that insensibly Dan forgot the present, his guilt fears, his sleepless remorse, and was once more the Dan Marlowe of the happy-go-lucky prospecting days.

When the 'hooter' went for the change of shifts Buxton rose to go.

"I'm sorry I can't come to your place tonight," he said, "but I promised Carson I'd have dinner with him, but I'll be up tomorrow to have a chat with Mary and Ellie. You seem a bit off-colour Dan; pulled down. I fancy. I think I'll have to give Mary a talking to for letting you overwork yourself."

It was with difficult that Dan responded, but he managed to reply in his usual way.

As soon as Buxton had gone Dan sank down on the lid of a filter, and drew his hand across his wet brow. The strain of the last few minutes had been terrible; he felt weak and despairing.

"That settles it," he said to himself; "I'll meddle no more with the cursed gold; but what am I to do with those men?" and Shultz's face came before him, threatening, yet furtively terrified. He rose heavily and went down the shed.

Dan thought long and earnestly over the situation, but when the next shift was over he was no nearer a solution of the difficulty. He left the works, and went slowly down the path towards the creek. Shultz and he seemed to stand upon the ends of a see-saw. Neither could move without endangering the other. He could not denounce the thieves while he himself was compromised. Neither dared they appeal against him for the possession of the gold which still lay hidden, though they knew it not, in the old tin box in Marlowe's house. Dan had given them to understand that the gold had been sent south to be alloyed and sold. Innis and Achmann would be almost willing to leave Neummurra without any of the booty, but Shultz, though he distrusted Marlowe, was fiercely determined to receive his share of the stolen gold.

Dan dare not tell Shultz to leave the mine. He read daily in the man's small, narrow eyes a threat that kept him from even hinting at dismissal. And such was the ascendancy that Shultz had succeeded in obtaining over him, at the end of the second month that Marlowe actually trembled at the thought of telling him that he had resolved to take no more gold. He wished in his despair that some accident, some turn of fate's wheel, would set him free from his tempter. Only in this possibility could he see any way out of the toils. If only Shultz would die suddenly; his guilty secret and his cruel power with him was the hopeless burden of Dan's thoughts. As he stood there for a few moments at the bar of the "Three Crowns" he drank down that wish with the fiery liquid. To have Shultz out of the way, and then find some means of restoring the gold, he asked no more than that. He felt sure that he could bring himself to return the gold.

In front of him a man was hurrying up the hill. "That is Jim Hetherington," he thought. "What is he doing up my way?" And a sudden suspicion entered his mind.

Suppose Jim had found out about the gold and was going to search the house for it. No idea was too preposterous for Dan's guilty conscience and overstrained nerves at that moment. He dashed out of the hotel and strode up the hill.

Jim had left work a little earlier than he usually did. He felt so downhearted and miserable that he longed for sympathy. He would not grieve his mother, in her pride over his elevation, by letting her know how small now appeared his prospects of succeeding in the experiments.

"I'll run up and have a talk with little Ellie," he resolved. "Dan will be an hour or two yet, and I have not been up since he forbade me the house, the day I took up my new work."

Jim felt secure of Ellie's interest and sympathy.

"She guesses about Pen," he thought, "though I've never said a word to her. I'm sure she knows. I'm having a fair share of hard luck since I've got my promotion. It seems everything comes together. I lose Pen, I'll be losing my billet, I expect; and Carson's manner almost seemed to hint that I've a chance of losing my character, though I can't see where he can get such an idea from."

Jim's hand was on the garden gate, when he heard heavy steps behind him.

"Go home, Jim Hetherington," Dan's voice, hoarse and deep with anger, sounded behind him. "Won't one telling do you? I ordered you not to darken my door again."

Jim turned with a smile, half nervous, half apologetic.

"I only just came up to ask Ellie," he said but he stopped shocked at the sight of his passionate face.

Dan's anger overcame his judgment, his insane jealousy returned in all its power, and with it came fear, that swept from his drink inflamed brain the last vestige of reason. He caught Jim's arm and swung him roughly aside. His words were scarcely coherent, when at last he managed to speak.

"How dare you come prying and peeping about my place when you think you've got me out of the way?"

For a moment the hot blood surged up the young man's face, as he stumbled backwards from the fierce thrust. Then a girl's voice; piteous and horror-stricken stayed the return blow that he was preparing to give.

"Father! Father! What is it, Jim? What is the matter?" Jim looked up and saw Ellie's white face; and pity swallowed up his anger. His poor little playmate! How much had she seen?

"It is nothing; just a word we've been having. Good-bye Ellie, your father will tell you when he is himself again. I won't try to come up here after this till you ask me Uncle Dan. I don't know what the quarrel is that you are trying to pick with me. But when you ask me to come back, perhaps you'll tell me then. Fair and honest, Ellie, I do not know what the trouble is, but I will not add to your burden by entering upon a quarrel with your father. I'm off."

Another pale face peeped behind Ellie's. "Come along in, Jim. Dan, tell Jim to come in; there is no quarrel here against you. Come in, and let us talk it over." But Dan did not raise his sullen face; and with a long look at him, Jim glanced up at the weeping women.

"Good-bye Aunt Mary! Good-bye Ellie!" he said huskily and turned away.

He felt sick and faint as he walked down the hill. This mysterious grudge of Dan's was but an additional weight to the burden of care he had to carry.

The road from the boss's house was a lonely one, and as he walked along Jim allowed himself the luxury of dwelling on his troubles.

Life did seem hard just then to poor Jim, he felt himself hemmed in, thwarted and beaten down, on every side. Friendship and love had both failed him, and even his honest pride in his work seemed on the point of being taken away from him.

With his love for Pen tugging at every fiber, with each day proving to him that it was impossible for him to tear her image out of his heart, this business worry and Marlowe's cruel estrangement, came to render him almost desperate.

But when he thought of his father and mother, and the grief any hint of Carson's suspicions or Dan's attention, would cause them, he determined to keep his troubles to himself.

As soon as he came to the town, especially when he reached his own home, he must assume a cheerfulness, whether he possessed it or not. He fancied that Anne did not observe his depression; he did not know that she merely suffered him to receive that impression, lest he should be hurt by knowing that she, too, was grieving with him.

Lew Morgan was sitting on a log on the hillside. He was waiting for Lynne Carson, who had gone up to his home for his fishing rod. The two young men were going to the lagoon.

He looked up at Jim's approach. Jim in his sad absorption did not see him, but the haggard face gave Lew a curious sensation.

"Poor Jim! What a terrible change," he thought. "He looks a complete wreck. And that, I suppose, is Pen's work. A fine fellow like Jim, just breaking his heart over a girl. I wouldn't have believed it possible, but there is no mistaking the look in poor Jim's face. Preserve me from ever caring for a girl like that!" and Lew's own face grew sad and thoughtful.

Lew came so quietly up the steps of the back verandah that Pen, who was sitting on the front verandah, did not notice his approach. She sat with some lace lying idly in her hands, while she gazed sadly towards the white rolling volume of smoke that rose from the chlorination furnaces. There was something so dejected in her air that Lew did not speak, but watched her intently, while he thought of Jim's haggard face that had so shocked him an hour before.

While he looked, a tear gathered under the dark eyelashes, and stole down the girl's cheek, but she seemed unconscious of it in her mournful reverie. Lew could not stand it any longer; he stumbled against a verandah chair, and called out "Hullo! Where is everybody? Isn't tea ready yet? I'm hungry as a hawk!"

Pen sprang up, the sadness vanishing, as if by magic. "Whatever kept you, Lew? We've had tea an hour ago." "I promised Lynne that I'd look him up this afternoon. You know he is going on Monday, and he wanted to arrange for a specially nice Saturday for the last of our expeditions."

"And what have you settled on?" asked Pen indifferently. "We'll see tonight; he is coming over. What do you say if I'll run up and ask Ellie Marlowe to come down and discuss it with us." "Very well," said Pen. "Come in now and have your tea."

"Perhaps I'd better run round first and see whether Jim Hetherington will care to come with us," said Lew, keeping his eyes upon his sister.

CHAPTER XXI.

LEW'S EXPERIMENT.

Pen bent to pour out a cup of tea, but she could not hide from him the hot colour that rushed into her face.

"Why need you bother this time?" she said, constrainedly. "He always comes with us if he can get away from the works," She would not meet her brother's glances.

"I'll look him up, anyway," said Lew. He had found out what he wanted to know, Lew now felt certain, in his own mind, that the engagement with Lynne was a mistake, and that Pen was beginning to realize it. She had been thinking of Jim and regretting her foolish choice, he believed, when she gazed so sadly towards the works.

He knew her too well to speak, however, and he quickly changed the subject. While he walked towards Marlowe's place he thought over the situation carefully, and after much deliberation formed a plan which he felt confident ought to set matters right. His thoughts ran as follows:-

"Here are Pen and Jim, both unhappy; and I do not think Lynne cares so very much after all; he is just the sort to run after every pretty girl he sees. He is simply a bit struck, no more, that's my firm belief. With him there is none of the life and death business that there is about poor old Jim. If the thing is allowed to go on it will simply mean three being unhappy, for I do not envy the man who is tied to Pen, unless he has her heart. Pen's temper would drive him silly in a month, if she feels she has made a mistake. Why, see already how changed she is in these few days. If only Jim could discover that Pen really cares for him, he would never give her up, but unless it comes out by accident he will never find out. Pen is too proud to admit she has made a mistake."

Lew determined to provide the accident.

"I'll take them out on Saturday night, in my boat, on the lagoon. It will be moonlight. Then, when we are in the middle of the lagoon I will give them a fright, and see if that does not bring out the truth. I've always heard that danger will bring the real feelings of a man or woman to the surface."

Lew had a natural knack for building; the little "Waratah" was a triumph of his mechanical skill and ingenuity, and with it he believed he could contrive, with sufficient naturalness, to provide the necessary stimulus to self-betrayal.

"I'll manage it, I think; no real danger of course, but enough of the imitation article to scare the truth even out of Pen. Let me see. There'll be six of us. Pen and Lynne, Jim and Clara, Ellie and myself, a tight fit for the Waratah but I think she can do it. I'll fix up one of the planks so that at the fateful moment I can just let in enough water to make them think we are sinking. I'll arrange for Pen and Jim to be together, by hook or by crook, and in her fear Pen will turn to him for help, and the trick is done. I must not lose any time; this is the last chance I shall have of Lynne, for he is going on Monday."

Lew felt very proud of his scheme, as he elaborated it, and settled the details satisfactorily in his own mind. "There's nothing the fear of sudden death for getting rid of shams or so I've always read," was the conclusion of his deliberation, as he knocked at the door of Marlowe's house.

"Yes, Ellie is in," said Mrs. Marlowe, to reply to his inquiry. "Dan is reading the paper, and I think I'll go down with you myself, too, as I want to see your father about the hospital." Mrs. Marlowe was one of the ladies of the hospital committee, and arrangements were being made just now for a systematic canvass of the town in aid of the funds of the institution.

"Will you come with us, Dan?" she said, turning to her husband, who had not looked up from his paper during the colloquy with Lew. "No; I'm not going out tonight," came the gruff reply.

Mary sighed inaudibly, but it was her simple creed to take no notice of any ill temper on her husband's part. When Dan had been drinking she never scolded him; she let her forbearance make its impression, and she had her reward when he regained his senses.

"Then," she said with a pleasant

smile, "I'll leave you to mind the house. See you do not get into any mischief when I'm away. Come along, Ellie."

Dan waited in moody meditation for some time after they had gone. Then he took up the lamp and went into his study.

He was a methodical man, even in his demoralization, just as he had been when he was a model clerk, and he arranged some shelves of specimen ores, sorted his papers and consulted a book of reference, before he touched the iron box with the gold.

When Lew came for Ellie, and Mary proposed to accompany them, Dan could scarcely believe his good fortune. He had been forming and rejecting plan after plan for getting rid of them since supper, and now, without any volition on his part, he had the house to himself. The fright he had received from seeing Jim going to the house that afternoon shook him yet. While the gold lay thus carelessly, though locked in the box, he felt he could no longer bear to leave the place. He would always be afraid now, lest its presence might be somehow suspected.

This room was his special sanctum. Mary was not supposed even to dust it, but he knew that she had a woman in periodically to scrub out the room, and then the box might be moved.

Its weight, compared to its small size, might cause surprise. At any moment the secret might be suspected and discovered. Dan locked the door on the inside, saw that the curtain covered the window completely, and, drawing the box from a dark little recess he knelt down beside it and opened it.

At the sight of the glittering pieces a spasm contorted his face. Could he endure to part with the beautiful gold, to allow Shultz to share in it, even to restore it to the company? For in spite of his twinges of conscience, there had grown up in his mind a strange attraction for the yellow gold. The fascination that a miser feels for his glittering heaps had begun to affect Dan.

He bent over the box and shivered as if with an ague. There is a strange uncanny power, a malevolent spirit, as it were, sleeping in a mass of gold, thought the man, as he knelt and feasted his eyes upon it; it meant so much – that glittering heap. Could he but keep it; or better still, could he but change it into shining sovereigns, how much it would mean to him? His brain swam with the thought of actual unchallenged possession.

At that moment he regarded Buxton no longer as the injured friend, but as the ungrateful mate who had refused to share his prize with him; and Jim, his old pupil, the recollection of his miserable face but added fuel to his angry satisfaction in his failure to succeed with his experiments.

"I must put it out of sight," he muttered at last. "It is not safe in the room. There's not a soul about now, and our home is all by itself. I'll dig a hole in the garden and put the box in it. I shall not take any more. What's here'll do for me, but Shultz and his mates will not get any of it. It belongs to me. I've the best right to it, and I'll stick to it. It will be safe here till I can find means to get it away. I must think of some method of getting rid of those men."

The Dan Marlowe, whose confused brain plotted and schemed to conceal the stolen gold was a strangely different man from the simple, kindly boss of but three short months ago.

If one who knew him in his happier mood could have seen his face as he dug feverishly into the sandy soil to make a hole large enough to hide the box, it would have been a sad revelation of human weakness. When he had finished he smoothed over all trace of his work. He brought out the lantern and examined the ground carefully.

"We'll be having a storm directly, after all this heat," he said to himself, "so the grass will soon cover it. I'll just mark the tree nearest to it, then I shan't forget the spot."

He came back from his study and took some papers from a drawer. He picked out a thin slip and read it over carefully.

In this slip he had written out in his methodical way the exact amount of gold he had taken, with the dates of each theft. He had meant to show this to Shultz but now decided that he would not do so. He folded up the paper. It was against his clerkly training to destroy it, and he carefully replaced it in the drawer, turned the key, and left the room with a satisfied step.

When his wife and daughter return he was, as they had left him, reading, or pretending to read, at the dining table.

Lew succeeded in the scheme, at least so far as securing his passengers for his boating trip, though he had some difficulty in getting Jim to come.

The lagoon from which the township was supplied with water was about half a mile from the works. It was a large body of water, wide but not very deep, being scarcely more than 10ft., for the most part, though here and there it had hollows that were supposed to be much deeper. Neummurra Creek ran through it and good fishing could be obtained in it. Ducks and wild fowl haunted its banks, and afforded shooting to the youths of the town. A few of the young fellows, like Lew, had boats, but they were not often used, being stored up for a good part of the year under an open shed. But when the lagoon was full after the wet season boating was often indulged in.

The afternoon passed very pleasantly. If Jim or Pen were unhappy, they contrived to hide it. Towards sunset Lew landed his party and all set about getting ready a picnic tea. The time passed quickly, too quickly for poor Jim, who felt a pleasure, painful yet sweet, in the fleeting moments.

"There is a nice breeze rising," said Lew, as the picnickers lounged in lazy comfort on the grass, "so I think we shall be able to have a sail round the lagoon when the moon gets up. I'm tired of rowing, and I expect you fellows are too."

"Rather," said Lynne, "besides, I've helped the girls make the tea." The laughter of the girls was a mocking comment on this remark.

"Helped us," said Pen. "Why, what did you do?" Lynne looked at her reproachfully, "Ask Miss Marlowe what I did." "It is no use asking me," laughed Ellie, "for I never saw you do any thing, except help yourself to something to eat. Now Jim here did work. He made the fire, boiled the billy and looked after everybody, didn't he, Pen?"

Pen started a little, her pretty face had drooped under her big hat. "What did you say, Ellie?" she said guiltily.

"She said what we all say – that Mr. Hetherington did most of the work," said Clara, turning her smiling blue eyes upon Jim, who, however, did not look up from his occupation of pulling up tufts of the coarse grass of the bank. Lew looked at the two abstracted faces.

"Come, I like that," he cried with disgust, "who rowed you up most of the way, who went to the bother of arranging this affair answer me that!"

For an answer Lynne threw an orange at his head, and a scrimmage took place between the two young men, to the amusement of the others, but behind Lew's apparent merriment he was keenly observant.

"I do not believe Lynne is properly in love with Pen. Why he tries to flirt with Ellie, and he is only a week engaged. Not that Ellie takes much notice of him, I'll do her that much justice. It is my firm belief those three girls are in love with Jim. Clara is, for she is making a dead set at him. Pen cannot meet his eyes and upon my word I fancy little Ellie is fond of him too. What is the attraction in Jim, not his looks alone, for Lynne's a handsome fellow in a way, though he misses Jim's inches," and Lew tried to examine his friend critically but he soon gave up in despair.

"He is good looking enough," was the conclusion he arrived at in a few minutes, "but it is not that alone, nor his cleverness either, though Jim is a brainy man; nor his manner, for it is too reserved. I think the attraction is in Jim's smile; it has something so kind about it somehow, or perhaps it is the steady look in his blue eyes. Jim has such clear, frank, honest eyes."

"A penny for your thoughts!" cried Lynne in his ear. "Too valuable try me in gold," said Lew.

"I've none to spare," said Lynne, "Jim here is going to be the millionaire with his new treatment, ask him."

"No good asking me," said Jim quietly. "You are not getting on too well, are you?" said Clara sympathetically, "I heard father say something or other about your experiments not answering so far."

Pen looked up eagerly and so did Ellie, but Jim only said, with something of an effort. "Oh! Things are just at the start yet, we can't say how they will be for some time yet."

"There's the moon, we may as well be packing up," said Lew, "we do not know how long this breeze will last."

"It looks a jolly little vessel to hold six of us," said Lynne, as the party were ready to embark, "Are you sure you have no designs on our lives? Remember. I'm not insured, and I do not believe the rest are. I thought it was

THE FURNACE FOR GOLD

a pretty tight fit coming up, but we were rowing then. You'll be careful with the sail, there is a bit of a gale rising."

"Lynne," cried Clara sharply, "do not say such a thing. It is enough to spoil our nerves to suggest it." Lew's laugh rang out heartily while he endeavoured to arrange his party to suit his plans.

Jim was to steer, so Lew tried to get Pen placed next to him but before he could do it Clara stepped into the seat and as was natural, Lynne and his fiancé took the other end of the oars, in case he might need to use them.

"We'll go round the bank and then cut for the other side," he said, eyeing his party with much disfavour. Fate seemed bent on thwarting his well-meant endeavours. Still he could only try his best against unfavourable circumstances. Under his foot was a small, cleverly-secured piece of board. By using his foot as a lever, he could displace it long enough to ship sufficient water to give the impression that the boat was filling, then with another movement he could fix the board back into place.

They were in the middle of the lagoon, when Ellie gave a faint exclamation.

"The boat is leaking, Lew; you'd better row back to the bank. Look!" – she put down her hand and brought it up, dripping with water – "It is coming in fast!" she added.

"What!" shrieked Clara, standing up and looking wildly around, "is the water coming in?" "Sit down and do not be a fool," shouted her brother angrily, but his voice was drowned in another hysterical scream from the terrified girl.

She stood up again, and crying "Jim! Jim! Save me!" threw herself into his arms. At that moment a gust of wind caught the sail.

How it happened they could not have explained, but the next instant the frail little bark was overturned, and all of them were struggling in the lagoon.

With the rush of water over his head Lew realized that he could scarcely swim at all; in fact, he had but the most rudimentary idea of the art. As he got to the surface, however, he struck out, and looked round him anxiously for the others. Lynne was bearing Pen with him to the bank and Jim was just behind, with Clara clinging desperately to him. Her shriek came to his ears at the same moment, but with one flash of contemptuous anger, he dismissed her from his mind, while he turned round to look for one girl who was missing.

Where was little Ellie, who had no one to look after her? As he swung round he saw a little dark head at some distance to the right. "Ellie," he cried, and she turned at his voice.

Her eyes, blue with a strange blueness in the bright moonlight, seemed starting out of her white face in terror; then she sank out of sight.

"Ellie! Ellie!" Lew shouted and struck out desperately for the spot where she had disappeared.

In the midst of all his agony of remorseful distress, there came to Lew, as he gazed wildly at the quiet water, the sudden consciousness, the absolute certainty of his love for little Ellie. A passing wonder at his own blindness hovered in the background of his distracting whirl of ideas, but all his forces were concentrated in the effort to save the girl if he could from the consequences of his mad experiment.

After what seemed an eternity, but which in reality was but a few seconds, Ellie rose to the surface near him, and Lew caught her in his arms. She clung to him and he said, almost beyond himself with the joy of his relief.

"Hold on, Ellie darling, and I'll save you yet."

But Lew reckoned without knowing how hard it would be to support himself, let alone hold up Ellie, with the weight of their heavy clothes dragging them down.

The girl did not speak, but she seemed able to retain her grasp on his arm, and Lew found that, though he had got no nearer the shore, he could manage to keep both their heads above water. He looked round for help.

"Hullo! Can't you get out? I'll come and help you," shouted Jim from the bank. He was soon alongside, and took Ellie in his arms. Lew following him slowly as he brought Ellie to the bank, and saw that she was able to walk towards the others.

Pen was bending over Clara, who lay white and still on the grass. "Is she dead?" Lew whispered fearfully. "No, she has only fainted," Pen answered, and at the words, to Lew's unspeakable joy, Clara's eyes opened, and she tried to rise. A weight seemed lifted from Lew's remorseful heart.

"Don't move yet a bit," said Pen gently. "Do you feel alright?" But Clara only shook her head, as she looked piteously at her companions. "Come now, Clara, you are feeling better, aren't you?" said Lynne cheerfully. "How do you feel, you other two. All right, Pen, I see. What about you, Miss Marlowe?"

"I feel a little queer," Ellie said in a choked voice, "but I guess it is all the water I've swallowed. Oh, I am thankful! What a merciful escape!" Her lips quivered. "Now then, Ellie," Jim spoke in quite his old way, "no breaking down now after being so plucky. The point is how are we to get home."

"I can walk, anyway," said Pen, rising, "but oh, how heavy my clothes feel. I weigh a ton I'm sure. Do you feel that you could move, Ellie?"

"I think so, though I feel a bit shaky. It is not far from here to my place, and it is still nearer to Clara's."

"What about you Clara?" asked Lynne. "I think the sooner we get home the better. I can carry you if it comes to that, but I do not think we had better get any conveyance or the news will be all over Neummurra by morning. There is no one likely to meet us if we go round by the scrub."

"What about us?" said Pen. "It is hardly possible that we shall escape notice." Then the comical side of the affair struck her, and she began to laugh; the others joined her for a minute.

"Lynne is right; it is a warm night, but the sooner each of us gets off our wet things the better," said Jim briskly.

THE FURNACE FOR GOLD

"If Miss Carson needs to be carried I'll come along and help." It was with a little effort that Jim added this, for though he had dismissed from his mind the girl's appeal to him at the moment of the capsize, as an hysterical outburst yet it had left him with an uncomfortable feeling.

"Not at all, Jim, thank you," said Lynne. "I think Clara feels quite herself again, so we shall get home all right. But if Miss Marlowe will pardon me, I think the first thing you should do would be to see that she gets safely home. You don't seem fit to look after yourself tonight." He continued kindly. "As for Pen, Lew will see to her, and she will not mind my going home with my sister."

"Why should I mind?" said Pen, half indignantly. "Go home, of course; it shows your good sense, but really I think Jim had better go with you. You know the hill is so steep, and Clara looks so white. I think it would be as well if the two of you went; Lew and I can pass Ellie's door, so that will be alright."

As she rose to her feet, her hair came tumbling down over her shoulders; such a darkly gleaming, rippling mass it was in the moonlight. Jim's eyes fell on it, but he resolutely turned them away the next moment.

"Do not trouble to come with us, Mr. Hetherington," said Clara in a weak voice. "You had better go home and get into dry clothes as soon as you can," but when Jim said bluntly that he was in no hurry, she ceased her half-hearted protestations.

Jim felt with an almost angry regret that he had lost the walk homeward with Pen, to which he had been looking forward to all afternoon. It would make no difference, he thought bitterly and probably they might not speak to each other, but at least for a few minutes more he would be able to listen to the dear voice, and steal glances at her face in the kindly moonlight; for a few minutes more he could cheat himself into forgetting that she was promised to Lynne.

Pen might have wished that Clara's feeble protest had been neglected, so that Jim might accompany them home, but if she regretted this she knew that she herself had brought it about.

The Waratah now came towards the bank, and Lew ran out and drew her up it.

"The moon is taking pity on us and going under a cloud," he said. "Let us trust she will have the good sense to keep there." He was glad to think the darkness hid his poor Waratah also.

"Wouldn't Neummurra be delighted to hear all about our adventure? We will not give them the pleasure, if we can help it," Lynne said. "Goodnight and run home, like good children."

Pen's high spirits were subdued, and she walked beside her brother and Ellie in silence. Lew tried to talk, but his accustomed self-confidence had left him. He was still feeling overwrought from the combined effects of his remorseful fear and the surprising self-revelation of his love for little Ellie. He found it impossible to speak as usual, and as Ellie seemed nervously shaken, the three hurried along in a somewhat constrained fashion. Luckily for them, clouds continued to obscure the moon, and when they left Ellie at her own home Lew and Pen ran down the hill and along the lower slope.

The managed to get into their house without attracting any attention; fortunately also, Gwenny was not in.

"Lew," Pen said as she stood for a minute in the darkness, "how in the world did it happen? Fancy Clara being so foolish; it was all her fault wasn't it?"

"That we upset," said Lew, "I should think so," but to himself he added, "I'll take jolly good care to be down the lagoon before sunrise to see how the Waratah is, and that she does not tell tales on me. I'll have to fix her up before anyone else has a chance to inspect her," aloud he said as he lighted a candle, and looked at Pen with some anxiety.

"You must hurry to bed, now you are warm with running, and I do not think you will be any the worse for your dip. Would you like me to get you a hot drink, or anything?"

"I'm all right thanks," said Pen, and indeed her glowing face attested her words. "You hurry to bed yourself. I do not think either of us is soft enough to take harm from a wetting on a night like this."

Still Lew looked anxious, and it was only after some difficulty that she persuaded him that he need have no fears for her health. She did not know and Lew felt he could not tell her, with what remorse he regarded his beautiful sister, as he knew that, with the best motives for the world, he had brought her into needless danger.

"No more experiments for me," was his reflection when he got to his own room. "I'll interfere no more in love affairs. I've only done harm. I believe, for I'm sure that affected little Clara has set her fancy on Jim, and means to follow up her ridiculous behaviour tonight. I pity him, for I'm jolly certain he cannot endure her. I must have been off my head, there is no other explanation, when I could try such a mad thing as I did with my poor little Waratah. My intellect is clearly tottering, but I think it is still equal to cover up the traces of my share in the accident. He lighted his lamp, and gazed solemnly at his reflection in the mirror on his dressing table.

"You have got a precious ugly phiz!" he said, as his reflections gazed solemnly back at him. Then a slow flush spread over the broad, hairless face, and Lew became aware that he was blushing.

"Did she hear me, how much did Ellie understand?" he wondered, and a strange new softness curved the firm lips. "I know she does not care for me, all she thinks of is Jim, but" he blew out the light with an air of finality, "I'll win her yet, my little Ellie."

CHAPTER XXII.

THE MANAGER EMPLOYS A DETECTIVE.

Mr. Carson was closeted with Trent,

THE FURNACE FOR GOLD

the detective in his office at Walshingham.

"No, it would be no good my going up, sir, I am too well known; and I take it you do not want to let the faintest suspicion escape until you've got matters well in hand." Trent was speaking earnestly.

He was a long, lean, dark-faced man, with such strongly marked features, and with a figure of such conspicuous length, that one might be inclined to wonder at his choice of a profession.

Carson looked at him thoughtfully. "You think you are pretty well known in Neummurra?"

"So well known that it would not be very easy for me to pass myself off as a workman in the mine. My occupation here is seldom of a kind that renders any disguise necessary, but for the business you want it is essential that the man be a complete stranger."

"What would you advise me to do? I've laid the facts of the case pretty plainly before you, in my own mind there is but one explanation of the shortage of the gold."

"A young fellow was in my office yesterday," said Trent. "He is a detective, so he says, though I'll frankly confess I never heard his name before, and I do not think much of him, judging from appearances, but he happened to call in, seeing us on his way north. He is out of a billet, and would no doubt be glad to serve you. I'll find out if he is still in town and send him on to you."

Carson thanked him and shortly withdrew.

The following day the young man appeared at the manager's office. Carson, who was not a quick observer, and who had been rather prejudiced against him by Trent's report, was agreeably surprised with him. He gave his name as Frederick Michael, and he seemed about 25 years of age, though his face belonged to that fair, colourless, indefinite type where it is rather difficult to guess the age. He might be anything between 20 and 40. His deferential air pleased Carson who often complained that the men of Neummurra were too independent for his taste.

"I shall put you on in the lower chlorination shed, for the first week, at any rate," Carson said, after he had imparted to him his views on the position of affairs. "I'll speak to Marlowe about it." "Excuse me," said Michael, politely, "but might I suggest that you give no hint as to anything concerning the detective business. I should prefer, if you do not think otherwise, to keep that a secret between ourselves."

"Certainly, certainly," said Carson quickly. "I particularly wish to keep it a secret. I have no desire to let it be known why you are really here. I expect you will be able to manage the work you'll be given to do."

"I shall not take long to get into the way of it," said Michael, "though if I occasionally slip round to give an eye to anything that seems suspicious I am afraid I'll be likely to get into trouble with the bosses."

"I'll fix them up. If you are in any

difficulty refer them to me, but do not needlessly give any handle for fault-finding," said Carson. "I can promise that," said Michael, "You may trust me to throw dust in their eyes, if it is only dust from the hopper."

Carson unbent so far as to smile at the sally, then he looked steadily at the detective.

"You might find it worth your while to give some attention to the new treatment under the care of Mr. Hetherington. I'll put you on his shift before long. Go down now, and tell someone to show you where you have to work; I shall speak to Marlowe."

Michael returned the look with one as steady, though an understanding gleam came into his oblique eyes as the manager turned away.

"You mean, I see, to insinuate that this Hetherington needs watching," he thought. "Well I'll keep your hint in mind."

The new workman was before long accepted by his mates as a pleasant companion. He had a hearty word for all, and it was soon found that he was not averse to "shouting" on the way to or from the works.

But Marlowe, the boss, seemed to take a curious dislike to him, and seldom lost a chance of finding fault with him. His obsequious manner irritated Dan, and though not the slightest suspicion of the real nature of the stranger's employment entered his mind, yet some instinct caused him the dread the glance of those small, sharp, brown eyes.

Dan was not alone in his antipathy towards the stranger. Jim, too, soon conceived an active dislike of him.

Several times when the shift was over, Jim found him hanging around the large vats that had been constructed for the new treatment, instead of the barrels that had before this been used for the chlorination process. Once Jim came upon him unlocking and lifting the lid of a vat to peer down into the mixture.

"What do you want there?" Jim shouted sharply.

"No harm, boss, I was only taking a look. It is mighty interesting," Michael said with a smile that was meant to be ingratiating, but which unaccountably irritated Jim.

Another time he found him stirring up some clean concentrates that he had just left, and the same day he saw him slipping guiltily out of the smelt-room as he came in. To add to Jim's annoyance, he found that not only was his shed haunted by the stranger, but Shultz also seemed to be getting into the habit of hanging round it.

Jim had heard, of course, of the mishap the day of the Governor's visit, and though he never uttered his suspicions, he was sure that Schultz was responsible, for the accident, and he kept an eye on the man since then, for he distrusted him utterly.

Schultz saw that Jim suspected him, and he returned the suspicion with hatred. It happened one day that Jim had an encounter with both Michael and Schultz.

In the morning, before the shift had started, Jim came up to the shed and caught sight of Michael slipping behind

THE FURNACE FOR GOLD

a tank. There was such a furtive air about the man that Jim followed, and saw him stealing cautiously up to a solution pipe. He drew some of the mixture into a tube, examined it, then threw it into the charcoal filter.

Jim stood in the shadow of the big door and watched his movements with growing anger, but as he saw the fellow going to his private locker with a bunch of keys and attempting to open the lock, his indignation got the better of him.

With one bound he was beside the startled man, and without giving him a chance to recover he seized him by the back of the neck and threw him outside on a bit of waste. A group of men were waiting outside for the "hooter" to give the signal for beginning work, and they greeted the flying figure with a shout of laughter, which died away as they saw that the manager was approaching.

"What's this, hey? What's this?" cried Carson, in astonishment, as he saw Hetherington standing angrily over the prostrate form of Michael.

"I found him trying to mind my business, and I've given him a lesson on learning to mind his own," said Jim in a raised voice. Carson gave him a curious glance. "What was he doing?" he asked shortly and Jim explained.

"I was not doing any harm," said Michael, as he picked himself up, and endeavored to steady his voice, "I am a bit interested in the new treatment, that is all, and I suppose my curiosity led me too far, but if I have annoyed Mr. Hetherington I do apologize."

Mr. Carson's face cleared, "It is all a mistake, you see, Hetherington. I think if you will overlook it this time it will not occur again."

Jim had nothing for it but to consent, though he did it with a bad grace, for he felt, rather than saw, that there was a veiled insolence behind Michael's apparent humility, but Carson had left him no alternative. The afternoon shift was over when the encounter with Schultz took place. Jim remained behind the men, and, sitting down in a recess, took out a note-book where he had been jotting down his calculations on the gold yield by his new treatment since the last escort had left the mine. The retorting and smelting of the mixture was not under his charge, but he was able to arrive at a fair approximation of the value of the amalgam that passed through his hands.

In this way he wished to ascertain how much of the monthly output he could hold himself responsible for. As he pored over the figures he became strangely impressed with the idea of being watched. He fancied he heard the sound of quiet breathing behind him.

He bore with the growing feeling for a minute or two, then, with one of the quick movements that he had learned on the football field, he straightened himself, twisted about, and found his arms clasping round the shrinking figure of Schultz.

The man had evidently come quietly behind him and leaning over a board of the recess had been able to read the notebook that Jim held in his hand. The remembrance of the affair of the morning did not sweeten Jim's temper. He shook the man as a cat shakes a mouse, then flung him on to the floor of the shed.

"What did you do that for?" said Schultz, rising to his feet with an evil look. "What did I do that for?" cried Jim. "Have you the impudence to ask me? I'll teach you to come creeping behind me and reading over my shoulder another time."

"Who was reading over your shoulder?" said the man sullenly, "I was only reaching up to get a billy that was hung on a nail above your head, when you swung round and nearly shook the life out of my body."

Jim looked up and saw that a "billy" as they called it, belonging to one of the men, was certainly hanging on a nail in the recess, and he felt rather foolish.

"I beg your pardon," he said with an effort, "if it really is as you say. But you know, Schultz, you've no business here, and I've had to send you away from my part of the works a good many times lately."

"No offence! Boss, no offence!" said Schultz quickly, "anyone might make a mistake. I'm not one to keep a grudge, when a gentleman begs my pardon," and he hurried away, without giving Jim time, as he remembered afterwards to ask whose "billy" it was that he had come to take away.

If Jim could have seen Schultz's face when he left the shed, his regret for the assault upon him would have vanished. The look of vindictive hatred, and impotent rage, distorted and brutalized the face.

"Everything seems out of gear to-day," thought Jim to himself, with the discomfort that a naturally good tempered man feels on being betrayed into a violent exhibition of anger. "Hang the blessed shortage of gold! It is getting on my nerves. My temper is going to rags," and he strode homewards, resolved to put the mine out of his thoughts for a night at least.

The sound of light steps behind him made him turn around.

"Oh, Mr. Hetherington," said Clara Carson, holding out her hand with a pretty impulsiveness. "I have not seen you since that terrible night. I've never thanked you for saving my life." Jim was in no humour for polite speeches, and heartily wished that he had remained a little longer in the works.

"Oh I did nothing to deserve thanks," he said bluntly, and did not add his thought. "Any danger you were in was due to your own foolishness, that might have cost other lives more valuable than your own."

"It is like you to be modest," said Clara warmly, "but I'll never forget how nobly you rescued me." "Why it was only a stroke or two," said Jim with a laugh. "Lynne did the same thing."

"Ah, yes, Pen will thank him, I know," said Clara, and her blue eyes dropped.

Jim felt intensely uncomfortable, and provoked also. "You are making a great deal too much of a very little thing," he said bluntly, but as he saw that the girl's face fell at this ungracious acceptance of her thanks, he struggled to reply more amiably. "Surely it is pleasure enough for me to think that you believe that I really did save your life."

"I wish I could repay you," said Clara, looking up for a moment, and as swiftly turning her glance up to the top of her pink parasol, with which she drew lines on the sand.

"Perhaps I'll ask you to do something for me one of these days," said Jim with a smile, that died away as the girl's eyes were lifted eagerly for a moment to meet his, and he saw the sudden flush rise to her cheek. She did not speak for a moment, and Jim looked about awkwardly for some means of getting away. The silence grew painful.

"Mr. Hetherington," Clara said hurridly, "there is one thing at least I can do for you. I think it is right that you should be told. Do you know a new man named Michael that has been taken on in the works. He is in Mr. Marlowe's shift, I believe?"

Jim looked at her in some wonder.

"I heard father tell mother," said Clara in a low tone, "that he is a detective, brought here to watch the sheds." "What!" cried Jim in dismay. "A detective?"

"Hush," said the girl anxiously. "Yes father got him up last week. No one knows about it, not even Mr. Marlowe." As Jim's senses returned, he felt annoyed and disconcerted with the uncalled for confidence.

"You mean kindly, I am sure," he said irritably, "but I'd just as soon not know since Mr. Carson clearly wishes to keep the matter secret." It was inexplicable to him that a girl should betray a family confidence, and if Clara expected to have deserved Jim's gratitude by imparting the secret she would have been bitterly disappointed, could she have read his thoughts.

But Clara would not have understood or appreciated such punctiliousness, and unconscious of his condemnation she came home in high spirits. Jim had been so kind and gentle in his manner, she thought, and as she recalled what he had said in answer to his thanks, it seemed to her that he hinted at what she had been hoping for some time.

Since the afternoon of the Governor's visit, Clara's interest in the good-looking young workman had been steadily growing, until now she confessed to herself that he was never absent from her thoughts.

She had been apprehensive at first of Pen, but since her engagement she had ceased to think of her as a rival. She believed, or persuaded herself that she believed, that Jim had saved her life that night on the lagoon, and resolved to dedicate this saved life to him. She fully appreciated her position as the manager's daughter, and considered that the thought of this alone kept Jim from declaring his feelings. His reserve she termed diffidence, and she made up her mind to overcome it.

When Jim became fully alive to the fact that she was willing to overlook his position, she felt sure that he would at once ask her to be his wife. And as the foolish girl recalled the equivocal expression he had made use of it seemed to her almost tantamount to a proposal. By the morning she had argued herself into a belief that it was meant as a proposal.

CHAPTER XXIII.

JIM MAKES AN ENEMY

Anne Hetherington stood at her own gate, and, shading her eyes with her hand from the afternoon sun, gazed after Clara Carson, who had just parted from her, and was hurrying up the path towards the works. An expression of pride, mingled with doubt, appeared on Anne's face. "I suppose she is going to call on Ellie, and tell her the good news," she said to herself. "If anyone else but the girl herself had told me I would not believe it! But she distinctly gave me to understand that she is engaged to James; well, perhaps not exactly engaged, but the next thing to it. I thought I knew anyone I know my own boy, but I'm all out of my reckoning. I fancied the poor boy was eating his heart out for the love of Pen Morgan, and now it seems he has been paying attentions to Clara Carson." Anne went slowly in, and as she looked round the familiar room, she felt more uncertain than ever. Unless in the rebound of Pen's indifference James had offered his slighted love to Clara, she could not understand how it had come about. But this conduct did not seem possible in Jim.

"No I can hardly credit it, though the manager's daughter will be a fine catch for Jim. I had my doubts about the girl, when she suddenly took to visiting me; but I never believed that James would offer himself. And to think of the work I used to have making him see her home. Why, he would do anything to get out of it! I'm sure I saw nothing that looked like love-making. I thought the love was all on one side, and that is the wrong side for the love to be on, if it is missing on the other. I cannot believe that he has given up caring for Pen; he cannot utter the girl's name in ordinary conversation, or even mention one of the Morgans, without changing colour."

The sound of her son's footsteps caught her ear, and she looked up with some curiosity as he came in. There seemed no change that she could see. He was a little paler and quieter than was his wont a few weeks ago, that was all. There were faint lines under his eyes, that seemed to have lost their old merry light, and there were curves of suffering round the mouth, that might have told a tale of heartache secretly borne. There was none of the exultation of the accepted lover about poor Jim's aspect, Anne could plainly see.

"I'll take the chance of asking him as soon as he has washed, since father is out of the way," she thought, and she went to the kitchen to see that her small, inquisitive servitor was not likely to come slipping out without notice, to listen to the conversation – a favourite trick of Tommy's. "I wonder James," she said, as he came into the dining room, and sat down at the window with some papers, "that you did not tell your mother the news first, and not let her find it out from the girl."

THE FURNACE FOR GOLD

"What news, and what girl?" said Jim with his pleasant smile, opening his eyes widely at the question.

"That you are engaged to Clara Carson," said Anne, looking at him steadily. Jim sprang up from his seat, "Engaged to Miss Carson," he cried out. "Who told you such rot mother?"

"Miss Carson told me that you were as good as engaged, and I'm sure she would not try to mislead me," said Anne, composedly. Jim stared at her, as if wondering whether she had taken leave of her senses, and Anne told him what the girl had said.

"I cannot think how she got such an impression," said Jim at length, "for nothing was further from my mind. In fact, I dislike Miss Carson, rather than otherwise, and I'm certain if we knew each other till doomsday I would not think of asking her to be my wife. Marriage is not in my mind these days, I can tell you."

"She is a fine stylish girl," suggested Anne. "I've nothing in the world against her," said Jim, "there are dozens of pretty girls in Neummurra, but that does not say I want them."

"It is no use of fretting for ever over the one girl you cannot get," said Anne in a low tone.

A dark flush rose to Jim's face, his blue eyes dilated, but he met his mother's look without flinching. "That has nothing to do with the questions." He said quietly.

"You will not find it easy to trifle with the affections of the manager's daughter. Mr. Carson could make himself very disagreeable to you if he chose," Anne went on

"He is none too agreeable as it is, but that again is outside the question. There has been no trifling with Miss Caron's affections. I can tell you, mother, in all honesty; and if I have unhappily given her a wrong impression I shall see that it is set right."

"You won't tell the girl that?" said Anne in a scandalized tone.

"I intend to tell her the truth," said Jim, "I think it would be cowardly to let her believe that I intend to marry her when I have not the slightest thought of ever doing such a thing. It would be far worse for me to let it go on, and have the poor girl telling others, and then have to unsay her words."

"If you can't get the girl you like," said Anne, hurriedly, "could you not like the girl you can get?"

"Mother!" cried Jim, in a shocked tone, and Anne was only too glad to change the subject, especially as she saw John approaching.

Though Jim had spoken so calmly to his mother about the mistake that Clara had made, yet as he went to the works next day he was much disturbed at the thought of the ordeal before him.

He tried to recall his conversation with Clara, to see if there was really anything to justify her in assuming that he wished to marry her. He remembered that she had blushed very much and seemed confused at times, but still he did not think that he had said anything sentimental at all. He had stopped her effusive thanks, and had also almost reprimanded her or betraying her father's secret. There was nothing in this, surely, that savoured of love-making.

As the day wore on Jim's mind regained balance, and he decided that he would, bluntly or delicately, as best he could, on the very first opportunity correct the wrong impression the girl had received. No sooner was the shift over and he was on his way home that his resolution was put to the test.

A few yards ahead of him was Clara Carson tripping with dainty steps along the dusty road. Jim's courage began to ooze away at the mere sight of her.

"It seems a caddish thing to do," he thought, "and perhaps mother took her up wrongly. I'll wait until I hear more about it. I'll go back to the works till Miss Carson is out of sight."

But, as though divining his intention, Clara turned round, and, observing him, stopped, till he was obliged to hasten to her. Jim noticed with dismay that she seemed confused with his greeting. She flushed and smiled until the poor young fellow was certain that his mother had been right.

"Whatever shall I say," he wondered, as he walked dismally by her side, "I'm bound to hurt her feelings any way. But I'll not be knave enough to refuse to give her a hint now that the chance is thrown directly in my way."

To one of Jim's disposition the task was cruelly distasteful, as indeed it would have been to most men, and it was little wonder that in his youthful chivalry he revolted from it. Assuredly it required no small share of courage on any young man's part to speak a rude, blunt truth of this sort to a pretty girl.

Clara herself at length gave the desired opening, for she spoke of Anne, and repeated something she had said to her yesterday.

Jim could no longer stave off the evil moment. With a face grimly set and suffused with shame he soon succeeded, in spite of his awkwardness, in making Clara understand him. He did not look at the girl, nor see the soft colour fast dying away, into ashy paleness, then deepening into a flush of anger.

In her own heart, Clara knew that she had, if not willfully, yet too willingly misconstrued Jim's words. But that the wish had been eager "father to the thought" did not lessen the fierce sting that began to burn in her heart toward Jim, as the cause of the humiliation that she was enduring. That he should dare speak so to her was the burden of her thoughts, while she strove to calm them sufficiently to allow her to answer him.

"I am afraid, Mr. Hetherington," she said at last in a haughty tone, "that I do not quite understand you. I think your mother must be labouring under a strange misapprehension; her wishes may have led her astray. I trust you will set her right. As to anything else, I did not think you were conceited enough to imagine that I required your explanation. Set your mind at rest, I have no wish to become engaged to you. I must compliment you on your courtesy in intimating that you are afraid lest I should announce the improbably fact of our engagement. Rest assured I shall not forget your kindness. Good afternoon!"

Poor Jim! His ears tingled, his face burned, his tongue clove to the roof of his mouth, as in utter silence he raised his hat and turned away. Had he seen her in her own room half an hour later, as she alternately raged and wept, he would have felt more miserable still.

She gazed for a minute at her own livid face in the mirror; then at once bathed her eyes, and did her utmost to remove all trace of the storm of passion before she went down to join her mother and father.

"He shall pay for this," she cried angrily. "If I live to be a hundred I'll have my satisfaction out of him. To think that ever I was fool enough to care for him; great hulking, awkward brute! And I told Ellie and mother that we were engaged. Well, I'll have to say I've changed my mind. As for Mrs. Hetherington, I'll never see her again, that is certain. It was a bad day's work for you, Jim Hetherington, when you tried to humiliate me." Clara's love turned at once to hatred – the cold fury of a woman scorned. At that moment she felt there was nothing she would not be willing to do to be revenged on Jim Hetherington.

CHAPTER XXIV.

DIAMOND CUT DIAMOND

Schultz suspected Michael the first day he worked with him. His former life had given him too close an acquaintance with the Criminal Investigation Department to admit of his being easily hoodwinked by a detective. There was an indefinable something in the manner of the new hand that attracted his attention, and before the week was over he was satisfied in his own mind, after painstaking shadowing, that Michael had been brought to the works in order to watch them, and he resolved to spy upon the spy.

For depth of cunning and sly ingenuity it would be a clever detective that could approach Schultz. He contrived to put himself in the way of the stranger, and it did not take him long to get into friendly relations with him.

The two men were soon, apparently, fast cronies, and were seldom seen apart; in fact, it became a difficult matter for the detective to shake off the affectionate Schultz, even when he resorted to stratagem to escape him. Schultz, with his broad, fat, sleepy face, seemed the very impersonation of foolish good nature, and Michael congratulated himself on having secured such a useful ally. He would be able to pump this simple fellow, very easily, he thought, and extract from him information almost without his knowing that he was imparting it.

He cultivated his new friendship with tireless assiduity, while Schultz lowered his sleepy eyes and poured out his foolish talk like water. Schultz posed as a simple, innocent, but good-natured fellow. A fine actor was lost in Schultz who, indeed, was an exceedingly clever man; while Michael was, after all, neither very clever nor very observant.

Now and again Schultz would hint at some mystery, of which he had received some inkling, but, in spite of his garrulity, and in despite of Michael's adroit questioning he contrived to avoid committing himself.

"He knows something," was the reflection of the detective at last. "No doubt there is a secret understanding among the men, and this simple fellow has got some hazy idea of it, but is afraid to talk about it; I suppose he is frightened in case he might get into trouble. I'll have to make him thoroughly drunk some time, and then I'll get it out of him." This was about a fortnight after the arrival of the detective.

The next day was Saturday, and Michael proposed that Schultz should show him the Falls, one of the beauty spots of Neummurra, some three miles up the creek. Schultz was evidently delighted, the more so when his friend intimated that though there would only be the two of them it was not to be a dry expedition.

The Falls were reached in good time, and then under a branching ti-tree, and to the musical accompaniment of the falling water, the detective produced his promised refreshments.

The solid portion was soon disposed of and Schultz showed no reluctance in attacking the liquid part. He leant against a rock, and drank steadily, happily, and with apparently, no more effect on his head than if he were drinking the water that flowed beside them.

In spite of his maneuvering, Michael found that he must share equally in the liquor with his companion, for Schultz, in his good-natured, yet obstinate way made a point of this, and while he complied, Michael watched him with a feeling of helpless fascination. Schultz seemed no nearer being drunk than when he started.

Schultz's face seemed to grow broader and broader, the smile more simple and foolish, but the drink, instead of loosening his tongue appeared to lock it into a maddening silence. His face did not flush, nor his small eyes waver, as he kept time with the glass to his friend.

"I'm getting drunk," said Michael, at last, solemnly. Schultz only nodded and passed the bottle to him, with an unmoved face. The detective was dimly aware that he was caught in his own snare, as the fumes mounted to his head, and he began to talk inanely, but he had passed the stage of self-control before the realization of this came to him. He knew that he was blabbing the secret, while he vainly endeavoured to check himself and recall his responsibility to his mind.

"You are a fine chap," he said thickly, in despair. "You are a fraud, that's what I mean. Why don't you get drunk answer me that you fat Dutchman?" But Schultz only smiled at him and plied him with the spirit, and the next moment Michael was calling heaven and earth to witness his love for his dear friend.

THE FURNACE FOR GOLD

"Do you know why I came to Neummurra?" he said, as he leant forward confidentially, and caught the arm of Schultz, who looked at him with quiet unconcern.

"Carson, your boss, brought me here to watch you; a set of swindling thieves that you are. I can't afford to lose time either, for if I don't manage the business in a week or two there's another man to be brought up, so Trent told me. A crack 'tec. from Sydney, so he says, though I'll eat my hat if he does any more in the time than I have done. What do you think of that?"

Schultz smiled at him and passed the bottle again with fatuous amiability.

"Why don't you speak, you stick pig! You were ready enough to talk at the works; why don't you speak now, hey?" cried the exasperated detective.

"You are doing the business yourself so well, there's no need for me to put my oar in," said Schultz, opening his lips as if with an effort.

For a moment Michael looked as if he were inclined to resent the speech, but he changed his mind, and struck Schultz affectionately on the back.

"You are a good chap, but I wouldn't do you the injustice of calling you clever; you mean well, but," tapping his own forehead impressively, "the brain is here. I'll tell you something that will make you open your eyes. You know that gold has been stolen from the mine lately. Well, I know for a certainty who has taken it, and I'm here to get absolute proof."

If Michael's sense had not been clouded by drink, he might have been startled by the change in his companion's face. The eyes were no longer sleepy but keenly watchful, a rapier-like gleam in their depths. The foolish smile vanished, as if it were rubbed off, to show that beneath it every line in the cruel face was tense and anxious. Schultz did not say a word; he knew he had but to let the fool utter his folly.

"It is Hetherington, the new boss, that's who it is. Carson all but told me he suspected him the first day I came, and my own judgment tells me the same thing. Who has the front hand in the works? Who has only just been taken out of the ruck? Who is so mighty afraid to have any one nosing round his vats? Who but Hetherington? He will come to me yet, and beg my pardon for what he did to me the other morning. But I'll not listen to him. I'll be satisfied when I see him goaled; not before."

The look of anxiety on Schultz's face had changed while the drunken man maundered on to amused bewilderment, and finally to satisfaction. Schultz had his own grudge against Jim Hetherington, and would have given a good deal to satisfy it; and the thought that the merest suspicion might touch his enemy gave him the purest satisfaction. He listened to Michael's aimless outpourings for some time longer, but seeing there was no more to be got out of him he proposed to return.

It was dark before the two men re-entered the township, or Neummurra would have seen Schultz labouring homewards with his helpless burden.

Next day Michael could recall little of the picnic but he had an indistinct idea that he had made a fool of himself.

However, after a talk with Schultz he was reassured, whatever he might have said in his cups was safe in that faithful, simple bosom, and all his fears were groundless, thought the detective to himself.

CHAPTER XXV.

A MISSING LETTER

"I say, Marlowe, do you happen to have any of these about your place," Todd, the foreman of the lower shed, held out a few small specimens of the beautiful ore that the Neummurra miners called "peacock stone". It is really black ironstone (hematite) with brilliant iridescent rainbow hues, and of stalactitic formation.

These stones, which were often met with in the early days of the mine, were rarely found now, but were eagerly looked for by visitors as curios. They contained a very large percentage of gold however.

Carson, soon after he had assumed the management of the mine, had strictly forbidden, on pain of dismissal, any man taking or giving away any of these beautiful specimens. This was one of many restrictions that had given him a hard name with the men. It was a very necessary restriction, for a good deal of stone had been taken away; some for other purposes than collecting stones.

"I have a few at home," replied Marlowe, "one or two rather fine ones. Where did you strike these? I thought we never met that ore now."

"I brought them from home, but they are such shabby specimens I don't care to give them." "Who wants them?" asked Marlowe. "You had better not let the manager hear of your giving them away, or he'll be giving you the sack," he said with a grin.

Todd laughed, then he said, avoiding Marlowe's eye, for it was patent all over the works that there was ill-feeling between the old boss and young Hetherington.

"Jim Hetherington asked me to get him any, if I could. He received a letter from a friend asking him to secure one or two good specimens, and as he had none himself worth much he spoke to me about them, and I promised to do my best to get some." Marlowe's geniality vanished. He straightened his tall figure and said stiffly. "I am sorry to disoblige you, but I prefer to keep the stones myself."

"Oh, just as you like," said the foreman, confusedly, and turned away.

"What a pity," thought Todd to himself. "It was true as they say, jealousy can turn the warmest friend into the bitterest enemy. Marlowe hates the poor lad that he was almost a father to, and all owing to Buxton showing him such partiality. I'm sorry, for they are both real good fellows. It has aged the boss terribly. He doesn't look half

THE FURNACE FOR GOLD

the man he was, and I don't like the way he is taking to the drink."

Marlowe, after walking down the shed, stood for a few minutes looking gloomily to the floor, when a voice beside him startled him out of his abstraction. "Excuse me, boss, could I speak to you a minute?"

It was Schultz, and something in his face warned Marlowe that he had some news to communicate. "This boiler don't seem right, boss. I'd be obliged if you'd take a squint at it, as I have been told off to look after it to-day," Schultz said, and his eyes added, "Come with me, but show no sign of uneasiness."

Marlowe turned to look at the pipes, and as he bent down fingering a screw here and a bolt there, Schultz said in a low, quick tone.

"That man, Michael, is a detective, brought here to watch the works and find out about the gold shortage. He suspects Hetherington, and so does Mr. Carson. Unless he finds out something definite by this week Carson is going to consult with Trent, the detective in Walsingham, and to see about getting another man, a fellow with a great reputation, from Sydney. I have spoken to the others and we have decided we have no time to lose. We want a share of the gold, so we can make tracks."

While he poured this out rapidly, Schultz appeared to the rest of the men, to be merely pointing out the shortcomings of the engine to the boss. Marlowe listened and trembled; he felt that he could not move from the spot. His head seemed turning round, he was afraid lest he should fall down. At every moment he dreaded lest Michael, who was working at some little distance away, should observe his agitation.

While he pretended to look at the engine, he revolved the matter in his mind. He was mortally afraid, yet he was doggedly determined not to part with the gold, at least not till the last extremity. He could bring himself to return it to the company; in fact, he told himself that he wished ultimately to return the gold to the smelting department, but to give it to Schultz – never.

"Innis, Achmann, and myself, will be down by the bridge by 8 o'clock to-night; can you get down by then? We can talk matters over, and arrange for the quickest way of getting hold of the gold. We want our fair share, that is all," said Schultz without looking up. But behind the quiet speech, Marlowe heard the note of threatening.

"Thanks, Boss, I think she'll do now," said Schultz hurriedly, as another workman approached. To his relief Marlowe found that he could walk away, though his limbs seemed to move jerkily, as though galvanized into movement by sheer force of will alone.

The manager entered the shed, and went to Marlowe. "I think I'll take a run down to Walsingham to-morrow, or next day," he said, looking round the shed, till he saw Michael working with a gang of men removing the dust from the hoppers, then he turned to look at the boss.

The pallor under the bronzed skin, the dark shadows under the light eyes, the haggard look of the whole face, struck him sharply.

"You are not looking at all well, Marlowe; you ought to take a long holiday. I've been noticing a great change in you lately. Why don't you ask for extended leave, and take a trip to the south. It would set you up again. You take my advice, or you'll have a break down one of these days."

"I'm all right," said Marlowe angrily, and a flush passed over his face, "I do not need any change."

"Oh, just as you like," said Carson, in an annoyed tone, "I only spoke for your good; you can please yourself, of course," and he left the shed with a displeased step. The two men seldom met without their tempers clashing.

Marlowe watched his retreating figure with a beating heart. He must have time to think, to recover himself, was his thought, as he walked slowly along the sheds, and mechanically attended to the routine of the day. He did not really fear Michael, whose suspicion of Jim was proof enough that he was not to be dreaded, but how could he prevent Carson from sending for this other, this terrible detective from the south? He wearied his brain with futile planning until it seemed to him that he could no longer think at all.

When he set out for home at the end of the shift he was as far as ever from a solution of the difficulty.

Just ahead of him, going hurriedly along the track, was Jim Hetherington, and for a moment it occurred to Dan that it would be a relief to talk the whole thing over with Jim. The utter impossibility of it drew from him a bitter smile.

In the dust a few paces from him he saw a sheet of paper. He picked it up idly, and saw it was a letter. Scarcely conscious of what he did, he read it though, and as he did, there came into his mind a sudden idea, which seemed to him to promise some little help in his extremity. This letter, so providentially thrown in his way, might it not answer his purpose of giving him a little more time, by putting off, if only for a few days, the manager's visit to Walsingham.

If Marlowe had not had the conversation with Todd that morning, he himself would have been puzzled by the letter, which ran:-

"Dear Jim.-I expect to be round your way shortly; in fact, it is on the cards that I'll be up next week at Walsingham as Crown Prosecutor in the district sittings of the Criminal Court there. Luck for me, isn't it? Things are very dull down here, and I'll be glad for a change of scene, to say nothing of the matter of fees. We poor barristers are not like you, the millionaires of golden Neummurra. And that reminds me of something I spoke of to you before I left. Could you, like the trump that you are, yet hold of a good specimen or two for me? I want some particularly. You have the run of the place, you know. I meant to have a try for some myself before I left, but being the son of the manager I had to be careful. Of course this is all on the strict q.t. I'll take care you are not mentioned in the matter.

THE FURNACE FOR GOLD

"It is no use asking a Diogenes like you any question about the girls; besides, I'll see them, in all probability, next week."

"Yours, LYNNE CARSON."

Suppose this letter were sent on to the manager, wondered Marlowe in his anxious, confused way, would it not be likely to make him abandon the idea of bringing up the detective from the south, at least for a few days, until he investigated Lynne's connection with the affair? Already he suspected Jim; it would surely be an easy matter to frighten him into believing that Lynne and he were fellow conspirators, and go give a breathing space for Dan to face the situation and arrange his plans. He resolved to show this letter to Schultz that night, and see what he thought of the proposal. He put it in his pocket and walked on. He breathed quickly as if he had been running, and his heart beat heavily against his side.

When he came home, Mary thought from his flushing face that he had been drinking again, and her heart sank. Times were hard now for the gentle wife.

CHAPTER XXVI.

TOMMY PLAYS THE SPY

Tommy Ratten was hurrying home with some fear in his heart. There was a scolding waiting for him, but he cared less for this than for the fact that he had loitered so long on the errand, that he must pass through the township and perhaps run the change of meeting in the darkness the Dummy, whom he still held in fear.

He was not so afraid while he was near the works, for the furnaces were in full blast, and the workmen were moving about, but as he left the mine and came along the creek, the way was lonely enough to frighten a braver boy than Tommy. There were no tents on this side, for the chlorination fumes, which blew over the creek, made dwelling there unpleasant.

Tommy crept fearfully along, his bare feet making no sound on the grass, when suddenly the murmurs of low voices gladdened his heart.

He stopped for a moment to listen, and rightly guessed that the speakers were on the bank at the end of the bridge, which was so brightly lighted from the works that no one could pass unobserved by them, while they themselves were in darkness.

True to his natural instinct, Tommy crept up to listen, and he heard an unfamiliar voice say. "If I had my way I'd smash young Hetherington with the greatest of pleasure, but I don't believe Carson is fool enough to be taken in with that letter."

Tommy was a coward, and he knew it himself, but stronger even than his cowardice was his love for his young master. If these men intended ill for Jim, Tommy believed he had it in him, he said to himself, to find out all about it. His native curiosity came to the aid of his courage as he made the valiant resolve. He moved forward, step by step, until he was under the bridge, then crept up till he was near enough to the men to touch their feet. One of them hung back from the rest, and kept in darker shadows.

"I'll put the letter in an envelope and address it to Carson," said Marlowe. Tommy recognised his voice. "He will, unless I am much mistaken, jump at the conclusion that his son wants Jim Hetherington to steal some gold for him, and that will give him such a scare, until he finds out the truth, that he will not be too keen on bringing a new detective up to the mine. It will give us a day or two at the least to look about us. I'll send it up the first thing in the morning by Dummy. They can't question him, and he will do anything for me."

"Rat!" said the man who had first spoken, "I don't for a moment believe such a childish thing would do any good. I'd like well enough to get a slap at Hetherington, but the idea of yours is out of the question. It beats me what you see in it!"

"I don't know about that," said another. "Anything to gain time. You say you can't give us our share to-night. What I want to know is when are we going to get it? I'm tired of shilly-shallying. I want to clear out before there is likelihood of our being nabbed. Are you sure we are safe talking here; anyone might come up and listen."

"You are a white livered coward, Innis," said Schultz. "Haven't I told you that Achmann and myself have been sitting here since before sunset, and you know yourself that no one could come along the bridge without us seeing them, or along the track either."

"But along the other way?" said Innis faintly. "Wouldn't we hear them? Besides Achmann has been on the watch all the time. Shut up now, act the man, or I'll give you a lesson on how to do it in pretty sharp time."

Little Tommy drew himself carefully into the shadows, and wished both his courage and his curiosity had failed him, sooner than that he should have come into this trap. There was something in the voice of Schultz that made his blood run cold.

"You are always wanting to rush things," said Marlowe. "You would spoil everything with your hurry. Haven't I shown you in black and white the exact amount we have taken, and when, and how, and each man's share of it?" "That's all very well on paper," said Achmann, speaking for the first time, "but I fail to see how we benefit, so far. It is all paper, it seems to me. The old way was better; if we got less, it was more certain."

"The boss knows he can't expect to get any more time," said Schultz, with quiet meaning, but insolent emphasis. "To-morrow at the latest we must have it. I do not believe the gold has gone south at all. It is all bluff; he can't think we swallow all this rigmarole he has been chucking at us. Give us the gold or its money value, or an open order to get it, and we'll cry quits. We'll give you until to-morrow to make good your promises. What do you say mates? And not a day longer."

The others agreed.

"But I can't, I can't," said Marlowe querulously. "Give me this week, and

THE FURNACE FOR GOLD

I'll see what I can do. Let me try this letter of Lynne Carson's on his father first; that will give us more time."

"You old fool," said Schultz, coarsely, with a string of foul oaths. "What different will it make to give you a week? Time to get us nabbed, while you shuffle out of it." "No, No!" said Marlowe in a panic. "Just give me to the end of the week, I'll make things straight by then."

A silence followed, Tommy held his breath to listen. "I tell you frankly," said Marlowe more firmly, "I will not be bullied, as you'll find to your cost, Schultz, if you push me too far I'll write to Buxton and tell him the whole story; he won't be hard on his old mate, I'll tell him the truth. It was made with drink and rage, and jealousy and when you, you infernal blackguard, took advantage of my state of mind to make me steal the gold."

"We've no thought of pushing you, Boss," said Schultz, in a conciliatory tone, "and if you want the week, why we are only too pleased to let you have your way." The others hastened to add their consent.

"Well, so long then, I'm off," said Marlowe, abruptly. "I'm glad to see you've got a little sense of decency left in you, after all." He walked slowly away from the group.

"What does he mean?" asked Innis after a pause, in a trembling voice. "I believe he has been fooling us all along. If I find he tries to chizzle me out of the gold I'll show him what he little expects;" but his frightened voice belied his bold words.

"The old fool! The old fool!" said Schultz, savagely, "to round on us, and put us off, when I thought I had him completely under my thumb."

"You always think you've got people under your thumb," said Innis peevishly. "It is thanks to you the whole mess has come about. Why did you go telling him in the beginning about our taking the charcoal? We were getting on so nicely, on the steady make. Couldn't you have bluffed him? You could see the man was drunk. I could have done it better myself."

"You!" Schultz gave a low laugh of utter scorn. "You do anything, you frightened cur. Why, you lay like a dog when the boss caught us, and it was only my quickness in taking advantage of the state he was in that prevented him giving us up to Randall. I saw there was just this chance, and I played on his rage of jealousy against Hetherington till I worked on him to join us. That is what I did, and now you pretend you would have done it better yourself?"

"You needn't have told him so much," whined Innis. "Oh, shut up," said Achmann, who appeared the silent member of the gang. "Put your head in a bag till you get some sense." "I want my gold, the beautiful gold he stole from me," broke in the plaintive voice of Innis, but it was peremptorily hushed by Schultz.

"No, I don't like the look of things a bit," he confessed. "But I'll watch the boss, and if I think he is trying to play us false I'll let you know. I think we can find some way of showing him the disadvantages of treachery. I know a cure for it, I fancy."

"I don't want to be mixed with any rows," said Achmann slowly. "For two pins I'd clear out now, and let the gold go. I'll be thankful to get off with a safe skin." "Well I won't. I tell you that I want the gold, and I'll get it, too, or know the reason why. So long as that idiot of a Michael is in charge there's no need to talk of clearing out."

"I think we'd better be making tracks," said Innis. "There's no need to give anyone a handle against us."

"I wouldn't be such a coward as you for all the gold of Neummurra," said Schultz scornfully. "Why, the man is shaking like a leaf. Feel him, Achmann, as if he had been dipped in the creek. What is there queer in sitting here by the bridge by the cool dam on a hot night like this, you shivering piece of jelly-fish?" Innis did not resent the description, nor answer the question, and once more a silence fell.

Poor Tommy, that at this inopportune moment of all others it should be his ill-luck to be seized with a fit of sneezing. He had retreated to a corner, and as he leant his head against a support he drew in some of the light dust of the works. He struggled bravely against the paroxysm but at last it overcame him. He gave a loud sneeze. He heard a match struck and made a dash to escape, but on the instant a strong hand closed on his arm and he was dragged out of his retreat.

He looked very small, dirty, and scared, in the brief moment of inspection as he was brought to the light.

"What's your name?" asked the man who had caught him. "Johnny Smith," he said, with ready duplicity. "Where do you live?" was the next question, and he answered quickly. "On the other side of the township, past Sandy Point."

"What does your father do? What's his name?" "He works in the mine, John Smith," replied Tommy, a faint pride in his resourcefulness struggling with his panic.

"Do you know him?" the man said to his companions and one replied. "There are dozens of Smiths. I believe the kid is lying."

"He'd better not try it on," said the first speaker. "Hold him for a minute," and giving the boy into the charge of Innis, Schultz moved a step or two away with Achmann.

"No, no, don't think of such a thing. I don't hold with murder and I won't see it done." Tommy heard the second man say, "Give the kid a fright, and he'll promise sharp enough to hold his tongue."

"Look here, I know you sneaked under the bridge to listen to us, you imp of the evil one." Schultz came back to Tommy. "You've got to give us your solemn promise not to say a word about what you've heard to-night, or I'll take and chuck you into the dam over there. Your father will think you fell into it in the dark, so I guess we are safe. Can you keep your word?"

"Yes, yes," said Tommy, eagerly, as his knees shook together with fear.

THE FURNACE FOR GOLD

"Very well then. You swear that you will not speak to a living soul of what you heard?"

Tommy was silent for a second. Had he not endured this fright for the sake of Jim, and now must he keep silent on the secret so dearly bought? Tommy had no scruples on the matter of telling a lie to anyone, but to Jim, and he thought he could make this promise with the private reservation in his favour.

"I promise," he said and repeated with a tremor the oath that Schultz dictated to him.

"To glib by half," said Schultz. "You are thinking you can tell your father, aren't you, in spite of your promise?"

"No," said Tommy faintly.

Schultz struck a match. "Now lift up your head, till I see what you are like. You will not forget me, and I shall not forget you, savee?" He closed his strong fingers over the thin arm of the boy, who cried out in agony. Tommy's pallid face looked up to the hard face of his tormentor, and his poor little heart began to beat heavily.

"Now, I shall see if you are game to tell," said Schultz, as the match spluttered out. "I think you know the kind of man you've got to deal with, and understand that you'd better throw yourself into the dam than open your lips about what you've heard to-night. I'll soon know if you blab, and wherever you try to hide yourself I'll find you out." He shook the boy savagely. "Now, run, for your born natural, and if you've got a grain of sense in that black head of yours you'll cut your tongue out before you drop a hint of anything you've heard."

The boy needed no second bidding; he shot off like a rabbit to its burrow. The three men, after a few more words, separated and went the several ways.

CHAPTER XXVII.

DAPHNE'S RETURN

"It seems like a dream being back again," and Daphne looked with smiling eyes over the little houses in the valley, the tents that dotted the hills, and the mine itself, with its great chimneys pouring out their rolling volumes of smoke into the cloudless blue of the December sky.

"I keep saying to myself, five whole weeks before I need to think of school again, for this is only Tuesday and I've pretty well the whole holidays before me. I never knew how nice it was to be at home until I sat down with the family to tea again last night."

Pen looked at her sister critically.

"Do you know, Daphne, you look somehow different; are you sure you have told me everything?"

A rosy flush overspread Daphne's face, but she replied laughingly. "Have I once stopped talking since I came last night?" "You are different though," persisted Pen. "I don't seem to know you. I wonder what has changed you."

"Oh, having to mix with strangers, I suppose, that rubs off some of the shyness, you see," said Daphne, with a queer look at her sister.

343

Pen was right. There was an added something in Daphne's face; something that deepened the lustre of her blue eyes, and gave strange sweetness to her tender smile.

"Your letters never told much. Fancy your being engaged," said Daphne. "I am longing to know what kind of a ma this wonderful Lynne Carson can be. Is he like his sister?"

"Oh, no," said Pen, "he is dark, not a bit like Clara. I haven't a photo to show you, as he is going to bring me one up next month, when he comes to Neummurra. He is supposed to be very good-looking if you really want to know; but I'm not the sort to go into raptures so you must wait till you see him."

Daphne felt a little surprised. Why, Pen, impulsive Pen, always went into raptures over everything. Her comical exaggerations used often to call down a reproof from Lew, Daphne remembered, as she noted, with a sudden sinking of her heart, that Pen spoke in a sharp, constrained tone, very different from her former frank manner.

Was her beautiful sister not happy in her engagement? Surely it had been entered into of her own free will? And what, thought Daphne, had come between Pen and Jim Hetherington.

Daphne had never felt more certain of anything than that Jim was very much in love with Pen when she left Neummurra, and she believed Pen, in spite of her willful, teasing ways, understood this, and really loved him in return. It had been with great surprise that Daphne had learned of Pen's engagement to Lynne Carson, whose name she heard mentioned in one home letter, and in the next Pen was engaged to him.

"We had better take a run down to see cousin Anne," said Pen, breaking the awful silence, "or she will fancy I'm keeping you away from her." Daphne willingly assented, and the two girls were soon at Anne's cottage.

"Daphne! You are strangers! I really do not know which is the greater," was the disconcerting greeting that met them.

Pen's colour heightened; she was clearly ill at ease; though she tried to hide it; and just as evident in spite of her efforts as Anne's lack of cordiality towards her.

Daphne came to the rescue, and with her as a go-between the two women managed to maintain some semblance of friendly conversation.

Every time Anne looked at Pen her anger rose hot within her. It was no longer the inherited jealousy of the cousins, nor the petty rivalry of the older women towards the beautiful younger one. All that had been swallowed up in her love for her son; it was now bitter indignation against the girl who had it in her power to make him suffer so cruelly.

Jim's silence had not deceived his mother. She knew him too well not to understand that in losing Pen he had lost everything. The quiet serious Jim of these days, with his forced cheerfulness and hopeless patience, had taken the place of the merry, high-spirited boy of but a few weeks past.

THE FURNACE FOR GOLD

The change was Pen's work, and Anne felt that she could never forgive her. The half timidity of the girl's manner angered her; it seemed to hint at pity, a pity that she threw back with indignant scorn to her again.

"You'll stay and have tea with us; father and James will want to see you," she said to Daphne. "Perhaps you can stay too, Penelope?" She did not look at Pen.

"Oh, no, thank you; we must both be home for tea. Another time we shall stay," said Pen, hurriedly.

"Oh, by the bye," said Anne, with the air of suddenly recollecting it, "I nearly forgot, Jim will have to hurry off to Mount Kudgee. The Roberts's are giving a big ball in honour of Miss Meta's twenty-first birthday. James is the only one invited from Neummurra, except Jack Larman, Meta Roberts's cousin."

Mount Kudgee was five miles from Neummurra. It was the homestead of a large cattle station. The Roberts were popularly supposed to be very exclusive and Meta Roberts, the only child, was a very pretty girl and an heiress.

Anne uttered her speech with an air of indifference that poorly disguised her pride. Her black eyes, resting on Pen's downcast face, seemed to say: "You see how other people value my son, though you were foolish enough to slight him. Do not fancy he is fretting for you. On the contrary he is going in for society and amusement."

Pen understood her, but the old-time saucy daring was gone. She listened in silence. With Anne in these days, Pen was embarrassed and depressed.

"How is little Tommy, is his bump of curiosity as well developed as ever?" asked Daphne, anxious to create a diversion.

Anne laughed a natural laugh. "There he is peeping in at the crack of the kitchen door," she said and with a quick step forward, she brought him out. But Tommy, too, was altered, or so Daphne thought; and she began to wonder whether the change she found everywhere might not perhaps be in herself.

"What is the matter, Tommy? You don't look as bright as usual. Been seeing Dummy lately?" she said for Tommy's fear of Dummy was now an old joke.

"Nothin' miss," said Tommy, listlessly. "No I never see Dummy lately." And his dull eyes rested helplessly on the two pretty young girls They were so bright and cheerful, while the whole world seemed darkened to his confused and terrified mind.

All day long the voice of Schultz rang in his ears and the broad, cruel face, as he had seen it in the momentary flash of the match, haunted him. Tommy understood very little of what he had overheard the previous night, but this much was clear to him, that there was evil brewing for his young master, and that he had promised not to speak of it. Not that Tommy cared whether he broke a promise or not, but to incur the displeasure of Schultz was not to be thought of. He trembled at the mere idea of breathing a word of the secret, and he felt that he would as soon throw himself readily into the dam as venture to denounce the thieves.

But to leave Jim in ignorance of the unknown danger that lurked for him, Tommy could not bear to think his silence meant this.

Between his love and his fear, it was no wonder the poor little lad was nearly distracted. When he held open the gate for the visitors Pen looked so self-reliant, Daphne so gentle and kind that Tommy almost felt inclined to drop a hint to them, but his courage failed and he allowed the opportunity to pass.

Daphne and Pen spoke little as they walked slowly homeward, with a strange, unhappy sense of constraint marring their wonted pleasure in each other's society.

"Oh, bother take the girl, what is she coming here for?" said Pen in a vexed tone, about half an hour later. "Who is it?" said Daphne, turning round. "Why it is Clara Carson. Aren't you fond of her Pen, your future sister-in-law?"

"So fond that I'm sure that fate intended her to be my sister-in-law," said Pen, as Clara came up the steps.

"I ran up to ask you whether you would mind coming up to our place to sleep with me to-night," said Clara, as she joined the sisters. "Father went away in a great hurry this morning, and mother and I are alone. We wouldn't care, but father left in his desk a good lot of money in gold and notes to pay off the men on the North Works, and Parsons has never come for it. I told mother I'd run down, and get you to sleep with me. You see, we've only the girl and ourselves in the place."

"Who didn't you send word to Parsons to come for the money?" said Pen, ungraciously. "Father said if Parsons did not come today, he would see about it himself to-morrow. He left the key with me, and I can't help feeling anxious."

"Much good I'd be," laughed Pen, "if a burglar really came. Shall I get a gun?"

"Oh we are not really frightened," said Clara, in an offended tone, "it is not the first time father has gone away and left money in my charge, but this morning a queer thing happened. Soon after father left that wretched-looking creature they call Dummy brought a letter with father's address printed on it. He wouldn't give it up at first when I tried to explain that father was not at home; but at last I got it from him, and put it in father's office. There was nothing queer in that, perhaps, but Dummy has been up to the house two or three times since then, and I think, from his signs, he wants the letter back. Well, I won't give it to him. I put it on the desk in father's office, and there it will stay till he comes back. But the sight of that Dummy hanging around the house gave me a turn."

"You will soon be as bad as the little orphan boy at Hetherington's," said Pen unsympathetically. "Honestly Clara, I am sorry, but I cannot get up to-night. Perhaps Daphne might go."

Daphne agreed somewhat dubiously and shortly after she and Clara set out for the manager's house. Daphne was surprised to meet Cousin Anne as she called, in passing, to see Ellie Marlowe, and note how much kinder she was in her manner when Pen was not present. It struck the girl, too, that there was something curious in the frigid constraint between her cousin and Clara Carson, who was obviously ill at ease in Anne's presence, and soon hurried away with Daphne on some frivolous pretext.

CHAPTER XXVIII.

MARLOWE MAKES A MISTAKE

Marlowe as he had promised Schultz, sent off the letter by Dummy in the morning, and when he got to work he waited anxiously to see whether Carson would come down to the sheds.

The morning passed away, and there was no sign of the manager.

"Was he likely to suspect who had sent it?" wondered Dan, as he tried to recall whether anything in the printed address could betray him.

The men could not help seeing that the Boss was preoccupied that morning, and the idlest of the found man a chance to 'loaf', though careful to keep a strict watch, lest they might be discovered.

A sudden change in Marlowe's face startled them, and set them to their work with an appearance of great industry, but Dan did not see either their laziness or their diligence.

A terrible thought had come to him. What had he done with the paper that contained so exact a statement of the stolen gold? He could not remember with certainty whether he had locked it away again or lost it going home, or, most cruel thought of all, whether in his confusion he had put it into the envelope with Lynne Carson's letter.

He racked his brain the vain effort of recollection and finally, with a word to Todd, he hurried off home. Mary was surprised to see him back in the forenoon, and his haggard face frightened her, but in answer to her questions he said he had forgotten something he had to bring down to the works. She heard him rummaging among his papers, then the door slammed, and she saw him walking with frantic strides towards the creek.

A sudden fear caught at her throat, for Dan had been very strange lately; but it left her as she saw him cross the bridge and hurry towards the township.

Marlowe had not found the letter, nor could he satisfy himself where he had lost it. It would be dangerous anywhere, though no names were mentioned from the beginning of the damaging statement to the end, but nowhere would it be so incriminating as if found with the letter sent to the manager.

"What is up with the Boss?" Innis managed to get a chance of whispering to Schultz. "He rushed home, then to the town, and now he is back again. He looks very queer. Do you think he is trying to play any tricks on us; have you seen any signs of the manager about?" The perspiration poured down his weak face. His hands shook.

"I'd like to see him try it on," said Schultz, grimly, "go back to your work. Michael has his eye on you, I'll keep the Boss in sight. I think he knows better than to try any tricks with me."

Schultz, while preserving his assumed expression of amiable foolishness, kept a sharp watch on Marlowe, and he was soon satisfied that something very serious had occurred to upset him. He discovered, too, that the Boss was taking pains to avoid him, and the hint of Innis as to possible treachery began to seem a more plausible thing.

"I must have put it in with the letter," groaned Marlowe, at last, as the lunch hour gave him a little leisure. "I suppose Carson is decided what he had better do; he would recognise my handwriting at once. He'll have no mercy, I know. It will be a work of pure love on his part to down me. Oh! What a fool, what a fool I was."

A dragging step made him look up. It was the Dummy, who, with evident timidity made known to him in sign language that the manager was not at home when he gave in the letter.

Marlowe had charged him to give it to no other hands. For a moment Dan felt relieved, and the poor Dummy smiled as he saw that he need not fear Marlowe's anger. He had been up to the house several times vainly trying to recover the letter, and now he saw, with joy, there had been no need for his anxiety after all.

Dan was sitting alone is his office when Dummy came to him, and, as he quickly got rid of him, he hoped that no one would have noticed his being there; for Dan's guilty conscience feared all things now.

Dummy went reluctantly; he was devotedly attached to Dan, and in his poor dim mind he felt all the more that he had received no reprimand, that he had not quite fulfilled his trust, and he wished to explain exactly why he had given up the letter to Miss Carson. He looked wistfully backward, as Dan sent him away; but the Boss did not notice his pleading face, he was sitting dejectedly, with his great head buried in his hands.

How to get hold of the letter, this was the problem that Dan set himself to solve. He rose, and even went halfway up the hill to the manager's house, when it occurred to him that it would be impossible for him to claim the letter that he had sent in such an unusual way. Suppose when he arrived he should find that Carson had returned and had read the letter, what reason could he give for seeking him? He walked slowly down the slope again, and waiting for the sound of the "hooter".

Schultz and Innis saw him as he returned and formed their own conclusion.

In the afternoon Dan heard from the "Boss of the Mine" that Carson had gone to Walsingham but hoped to be back next day. "I must get that letter back to-night. If I have to break into the house to get it," was the conclusion that Dan at last arrived at.

He went back to his office and locked himself in to be free from the exploring glances of the men. He felt that he could not endure to go through

THE FURNACE FOR GOLD

the afternoon's monotonous routine with all the curious eyes bent on him, he feared, too truly, that his disquiet and guilty terror were plainly to be read on his face.

CHAPTER XXIX.

LOVE CONQUERS FEAR

Anne did not tell the girls how much difficulty she had coaxed Jim to accept the invitation to Mount Kudgee. It was to please her, to make her believe that he was not unhappy, that Jim consented at last to go.

Tommy listened in the hot kitchen to the discussion, and debated in his own mind whether he dare risk the vengeance of Schultz by dropping a hint to his young master before he went, and as Jim came out to the back to saddle his horse, Tommy made up his mind. He trembled in an anguish of fear, but yet he held fast to his plucky resolve.

"I say, I want to tell you somethun'," Jim started at the hoarse whisper at his ear as he bent down to fasten the girth.

"Say on, sonny, say on, my lord!" said Jim, but the small boy took no notice of the pleasantry.

"You won't tell a soul what I tell you," he said in a deeper voice. "Say 'true as death, and double death; strike me dead if I let out a word'," and he drew a small grimy forefinger across his throat in a suggestive way. Jim looked at him more closely, and saw that the boy seemed ill and nervous.

"I'll keep your confidence, Tommy," he said, kindly. "Out with it my boy."

"There is a letter what you sent, no, what was sent to you, what you lost," said Tommy, and Jim nodded.

"There is somebody what wants to do you a mischief, and make out that you've been sneaking the gold, so they sent this letter to the manager by Dummy." "Who sent it?" asked the young man but the boy shook his head, and a sickly pallor overspread his face.

"I dassent let that out; no, I dassent for my life. I heard them talking it over last night by the bridge and they copped me, and was going to chuck me into the dam if I didn't promise to hold my tongue. You bet I promised lively, and if he finds I told you he'll murder me. I know he will," finished Tommy miserably.

"I think someone was playing off a joke on you, Tommy," but the energetic shake of the black head scored that supposition. "Anyhow, it was very kind of you to tell me. I won't forget how good you were. I won't ask you anymore now as I am in a hurry, but I am sure there is no need for you to be afraid, either for me or for yourself. You stay near the house, and no one will dare to meddle with you. I'll keep your secret, except that I may write about it to the one who sent me the letter I lost. You will not mind my telling him, will you?"

"No, sir," said Tommy and his face glowed as Jim thanked him and shook him warmly by the hand.

Though Jim was inclined to smile at the boy's exaggerated fear, yet as he rode on the lonely track to Mount Kudgee he began to dislike the aspect of affairs. He remembered how persistently Michael shadowed him, and he also recalled the suspicious manner of Mr. Carson towards him of late. His conscience was perfectly clear, but still it was not a pleasant thing to feel that he was being watched by suspicious eyes in his daily work. Life seemed to wear a different complexion of late to what his roseate dreams had pictured it when first Buxton told him of his appointment. As he rode sadly on he almost wished that he had stayed in Melbourne and never returned to Neummurra. But he thought of his father and mother, and their silent love and pride in him; and squaring his shoulders, he resolved to see the thing through, and bring it to a successful issue. All the dogged obstinacy he inherited from his father made him determined to keep on with the work till he had proved to Buxton that his ideas were workable.

He was soon among the brilliant company at Mount Kudgee. Mr. Roberts, a tall, handsome, elderly man, and his wife, a slender, fair, little woman, with the faintest, prettiest touch of an Irish brogue, seemed charmed to see him, and gave him in charge of Larman, with instructions to see that he had a good time.

"Hullo, old chap," cried a familiar voice, and Lynne Carson clapped him on the shoulder. "I am glad to see you. Did you get my letter?"

"Yes," said Jim in a low tone, "I'd like to have a word with you. You'll excuse me, Jack?"

"Why, certainly, Jim. Sit down and have a chat with Carson, and make yourself at home. I'll come round and look you up again directly."

Lynne with some surprise followed Jim to the end of the long verandah, where he was put in possession of little Tommy's story.

"It looks fishy; perhaps it is someone with a grudge to me that is doing it. For to tell the truth, Dad is sure to cut up rough when he hears that I've been after some of his previous specimens, especially when he gets the letter in such a way. He is such a martinet for rules, and is so strict about what he calls 'principle' of the thing that I fancy I'm in for a fine old dressing down on undermining his authority with the men, and so forth. Why, one day I was talking about stones, and Clara brought me a fine specimen that she had had given her, Dad promptly collared it and locked it up in his safe. Did you manage to get any for me," he added, with one of his whimsical smiles.

"Yes, a few very good ones. I'll have them ready for you when you come up."

"To tell the truth," said Lynne, somewhat shamefacedly, "I wanted them for Miss Meta Roberts here. She and I were fellow passengers from Brisbane just before I went to Neummurra. I told her where I was bound for and we got talking about the mine. She is just fresh from school –

THE FURNACE FOR GOLD

the most bewitching little parcel of goods; and when she said she wished to secure a good peacock stone for a collection she is making of course I promised to get one for her. However, with one thing or another it passed out of my mind. But I met her a little while ago in Brisbane; she again referred to my promise and pretended to be highly offended. I wrote to you on the spur of the moment, as I found I was likely to go up this week to Walsingham and then came the invitation to Mount Kudgee. She asked me tonight whether I mean to get them or not."

"I have them ready for you, as I said," replied Jim quietly, "but it is rather a pity you did not wait till you came to Neummurra, as I am afraid your father will be vexed. He cannot have seen the letter yet, as he left for Walsingham by the early coach this morning."

"I wonder what is taking him there," said Lynne uneasily, "you are sure he did not get the letter?"

"Quite; for your sister was speaking of it to Daphne who told it to my mother this afternoon. She said Dummy had been round several times during the morning, apparently to get the letter back. She had put it in Mr. Carson's office, I think she said."

"Look here, Jim," said Lynne eagerly, "are you very keen on dancing?"

"Not at all," said Jim in surprise, "especially on a night as hot as this."

"What do you say, then, to our riding over to Neummurra; we could easily slip away after the first few dances were over. Then we could go up to my place and get the letter before the Governor sees it. It is your letter, and I do not see why you shouldn't get it back, if you want it. Perhaps, too, you might run down to your own house and get the stones for me. I would specially like to give them to the girl before I leave. I must go straight back to Walsingham as soon as the dance is over, for the Court begins its sittings tomorrow."

"And you mean to tell me," said Jim with a smile, "that you rode up here today and after dancing all night intend riding back to Walsingham in the morning."

"Why no," said Lynne, "a fellow can only be young once," and he hummed lightly –

The best of all ways to lengthen your days,
Is to steal a few hours from the night.

"But joking apart, it was the only way I could manage to come, and as old Roberts' brother is the Attorney-General, and has put one or two things in my way, I did not like to refuse the invitation."

"I see," said Jim dryly. He knew Lynne of old, and could estimate at its proper value this setting up business as a plea for indulging in pleasure. "It seems a wild goose chase to think of us riding to Neummurra to get the letter; but honestly I'd just as soon have it in my pocket. If there is a plot formed against me, one can hardly tell what use they might be making of the letter. I can't remember much of what was in it, but my impression is that it could not do a great deal of harm."

He felt inclined to speak to the detective, who had been placed in the works, but remembering the source of the information he decided to keep silent on the point.

About an hour later, the two young men were riding from Mount Kudgee.

"I hope they are all asleep at home. I'd just as soon slip in without being noticed," said Lynne as they drew near to Neummurra, and saw that most of the houses in the township were in darkness. "Pen will fancy that if I could get as near as Mount Kudgee, I could easily call and see her; but as I must be back at Walsingham tomorrow, there was no chance of doing that, was there?"

"I suppose not," said Jim, in a toneless voice. He thought with a pang how differently he would have thought of the chance of seeing Pen were he her accepted lover, absent from her. Lynne, who had won her, evidently grudged the ride for her sake, that he was yet taking willingly for the sake of Meta Roberts, or perhaps to save himself a reprimand from his father.

A wave of jealousy passed over Jim's heart. It was hard for him to speak naturally, but with a strong effort he beat back the tide of bitterness. The manager's house looked dark and silent on the lonely hillside. The two young men secured their horses at the foot of the rise and cautiously mounted the hill from the back, as Lynne thought by so doing they might more easily escape detection.

There was a strange, breathless sensation of heat in the still air.

"I expect the doors are all open on such a night. People in the summer here never shut up all night, so I've heard," said Lynne softly, "but even if closed I can easily open the door of father's office. I know the trick of the bolt."

As they moved warily to the house both felt as guilty and nervous as if they were burglars in reality. They stepped on the verandah and tip toed to the back of the building.

"The door is locked," whispered Lynne, but in a few minutes he opened it carefully, and they went into the office. "I can light up now; they will not see the light from the bedrooms," he added, as he struck a match.

"Eureka," he whispered joyfully, as he pounced on a letter lying on the plain hardwood desk. "The very thing. Catch it, Jim' it is yours; open it and make sure."

Jim tore the envelope reluctantly, and opened it. He drew out a letter, glanced at it and tossed it to Lynne, saying.

"Yes, here it is. Read it now, and see what a compromising epistle even a clever barrister can send to a friend."

As Lynne took the note and began to read Jim saw that there was another slip of paper in the envelope.

"Something I suppose to drive the nail home," he thought as he unfolded it. But the next instant he crushed the paper in his hand. He had read enough, unless his eyes were deceiving him, to assure him that there was something terrible in this paper. At the first glance the handwriting seemed his own. There was but one other who might have written it, and if he were the writer, poor Jim scarcely dared to think what it might mean.

"Well, of all muttonheads! I could scarcely believe, unless I read it, that I could write such a letter. I'm glad Dad did not get hold of it," said Lynne, looking up from his rueful perusal of his letter; and, as Jim was silent, he continued, with a half-defiant smile at Jim's serious face, \"Do you know I've a good mind to have a hunt to see where dad planted the stone Clara gave me. I know he took it to his office, probably he has sent it down to the works, he is such a comically conscientious beggar. Perhaps it is in his desk, if I could only lay my hands on the keys. What's that?" he said, a little startled.

"It is a curlew flying past," said Jim, "sounds a bit dismal, doesn't it? I'll run over to our place and get you those specimens I have. I shall only come back again to where we left our horses, at the foot of the hill. If I'm not there when you get down, do not wait for me. I'll soon catch you up," and he turned to go. "I must have time to see this paper before I do anything else," he resolved desperately to himself.

Again the mournful cry of the curlew was borne upon the night air.

"Very well, old man! Thanks very much for the trouble you have taken," said Lynne and Jim went out.

CHAPTER XXX.

A MIDNIGHT MEETING

Mrs. Carson was graciously pleased with Daphne, whose quiet gentleness was in such marked contrast to Pen's irrepressible vivacity.

"I wish Lynne had seen this sister first," was her final thought, as Clara and Daphne bade her good-night.

It was quite an easy matter to patronize Daphne. She knew by sad experience that it was impossible either to patronize or impress Pen, whose saucy impatience made light of every attempt of Mrs. Carson to form her daughter-in-law to her own ideas of propriety.

Clara also found it pleasant to have a companion who as so submissive and trustful a listener. She had the remembrance of many disconcerting conversations with Pen, that had not added to her love for the girl of her brother's choice. Besides, Clara had her own private reasons for disliking Pen. By some unaccountable feminine course of reasoning she held her responsible for the humiliation she had endured from Jim Hetherington. Pen was her rival, also, in more things than in the affections of the young Boss.

Clara's dislike was directed against Pen for her popularity. While Pen was considered the Rose of Neummurra, Clara felt she was defrauded of her rights as reigning beauty of the township.

Daphne's unassuming and simple manner was therefore much to Clara's liking, and the two girls got on very well together.

Daphne was very tired and was asleep soon after she laid her head on the pillow and Clara, in spite of her professed nervousness, followed her example before long.

She dozed off when some sound startled her. She listened with the strained keenness of fear, and fancied she detected footsteps coming along the verandah to her mother's door. The boards creaked, the zinc roof gave out sounds, and the footsteps seemed to pass into her mother's room. She fancied she heard a smothered cry.

Clara sat up in bed, and bent every nerve to listen. A second cry came to her ears. "It must be mother," thought the now thoroughly frightened girl.

"Daphne, Daphne, wake up," she whispered into her ear. But Daphne slept heavily. She shook her, and at last awakened her.

"What is the matter?" asked Daphne, sleepily.

"Some burglars have got into mother's room and are murdering her," said Clara, hoarsely and Daphne gave a frightened cry. The two girls clung together for a minute. Daphne was the first to recover herself. "What makes you think it?" she whispered. But at the mere sound of her companion's voice, Clara began to feel a little doubtful whether she had not dreamt it all.

"I thought I heard steps in mother's room, and a cry." "Is that all," said Daphne. "Why, what a fright you gave me; very likely your mother cried out in her sleep. Let us light a candle and go to see."

"Oh no," said Clara, "we couldn't do any good if there were really burglars. If there are none, there is no need to go."

"I'm going anyway," said Daphne, rising and lighting a candle, "it is the next room, isn't it? You needn't come unless you like."

"But I'm afraid to be left," said Clara half crying, "Don't go Daphne." But Daphne only replied by putting on a white wrapper, and walking to the door. Clara followed, trembling, but as they went into her mother's room, and she saw that all was well, her courage returned. "You see she must have cried out in her sleep," said Daphne. "Come along, we'll search all upstairs and see if it is right. That will set your mind at rest. We needn't go below, or disturb the girl." The two girls went from room to room, and found all safe. The office was closed, the letter undisturbed on the desk, so they returned to their own room.

In the reaction from her fright, Clara was soon asleep. Not so Daphne. She had been in a slumber so profound that now, after being awakened, she felt that she could sleep no more that night.

She lay quite still, and listened to Clara's easy breathing.

Her thoughts returned to her perplexity ever Pen. Her instincts told her that all was not right with her pretty sister.

From Pen her thoughts wandered to her journey to the little school at Bundamango and in the darkness, a soft flush rose to the girl's cheek, as she remembered the stranger whom she had twice met in such curious circumstances. She remembered the

THE FURNACE FOR GOLD

very way he smiled, the look in his eyes, the deep tone of his pleasant voice as he spoke to her, and so from waking into sleeping dreams she drifted happily into oblivion.

Suddenly she was startled into wakefulness; the mournful cry of a curlew met her ear. Had she heard a step on the verandah, or was she still dreaming?

She lay and listened for a few minutes. Again the weird call rang out. She crept quietly out of bed and put on the wrapper again. Clara did not stir, and it seemed cruel to rouse her from her peaceful slumber. Daphne lit the candle, and went on tip-toe down the hall. All was still, but as she opened the hall door a pencil of light came from the door at the end of the verandah.

Blowing out her candle, but with the box of matches ready, Daphne moved carefully along the boards till she reached the office. The door was ajar and with an almost imperceptible movement the girl pushed it further open.

A lamp burned brightly on the table in the centre of the room, but, before the desk which contained, as Clara had told her, the precious money, Daphne saw a man kneeling down, and trying to fit a key into the lock. His dark head was bent but something familiar in the set of the shoulders made Daphne draw her breath in convulsively.

It was some hideous mistake, some trick of overwrought nerves, for surely the man attempting to open the safe could not be the hero of floor and fire at far-off Bundamango. The matches fell from her nerveless fingers and rattled on the floor.

The man raised his head, and saw the tall white figure in the doorway. The girl's feet were bare, her golden hair was floating over her shoulders, but she was utterly unconscious of this in her shocked surprise.

The blue eyes and the dark gazed into each other, as they had done in the little school house – a long troubled gaze – that was fraught with emotions of horror and grieved surprise, on Daphne's part; and utter bewilderment on Lynne's. The young man was the first to recover himself.

"Hullo!" he cried. "How did you get here?" "How did you get here, you mean?" said Daphne, sadly, finding her tongue with an effort.

"I don't think that is so strange, as to your being here; why, the last time I saw you we were hundreds of miles from this place. I belong here; this is my father's house. I'm Lynne Carson. I just ran over with Jim Hetherington from Mount Kudgee. We wanted to get something. Did you think I was a housebreaker?" he added, with a smile that Daphne remembered so well.

"Oh," she cried, with a world of relief in her voice. "I thought you were a burglar, there is a lot of money in that safe, you see, and you were trying to open it. I couldn't know you had a right here." Her innocent face showed her gladness.

"No wonder you looked so horrified," laughed Lynne, "but I'll tell you what I am looking for now. Perhaps you could help me to find it. It might be in the desk, but none of the keys of the bunch I have found will fit. It is a pretty piece of peacock stone I wanted to get. Clara gave it to me, but Dad took it away, and planted it here."

"And you came all the way from Mount Kudgee to get a bit of stone," said Daphne in a wondering tone.

"No, not for that," said Lynne, flushing, "It was for something else we came, I'll tell you about it some other time. The stone was an afterthought. But if you would not mind, I'd sooner my mother or Clara did not know of my being here to-night." Daphne looked at him doubtfully.

"You see Pen and they might wonder if I got so far that I did not stop to see them," he said awkwardly.

"Pen, my sister? Oh I see!" said Daphne. "I'll not speak of it then, if you want to keep it quiet. I'm Daphne Morgan. I'm spending the night with Clara," and suddenly, as she spoke, Daphne became aware that her hair was tumbling over her shoulders, and that her feet were bare, without another word, she turned and fled to her room.

She crept in beside the still unconscious Clara, and buried her burning face in the pillow. Her excitement soon quieted into cold apathy, and a full realization of the situation came to her, when she thought over it in the silence.

She had been dreaming a foolish dream; how foolish none but herself need know; that at least, was her comfort, as she understood too clearly how much of her thoughts since she had crossed the flooded creek, had dwelt on the handsome stranger, and how utterly without foundation were the timid hopes that she had built of some day hearing in words what those dark eyes had seemed to say, as they looked into hers, on the eventful day of the fire at Bundamango.

He was Lynne Carson. He was engaged to her sister Pen, and that was the end of the story, she told herself sternly, and she called the bare cruel facts steadily to her mind; but the dawn was growing pink in the East before poor Daphne slept the sleep of utter weariness.

As soon as Daphne fled, Lynne sat for a while, half dazed, and looked at the open door; then he put out the light and left the house. As for the stone, in the complete surrender of his mind, in the strangeness of the reappearance of the girl, whom he had often thought of since their romantic meeting, he forgot it entirely.

"To think that she could be Pen's sister," he said to himself as he loosed his horse and mounted it. Jim's horse was still fastened up to the fence, so he resolved to ride very slowly on. "Pen's sister," he continued, "and I saw her before I saw Pen. This makes the third time. That's the fatal number, so folks say," and he tried to laugh away the feeling that oppressed him. It was in vain; again and again his mind recurred to Daphne, until in the darkness he almost seemed to see her, as when, but a short time before, she had appeared to his startled eyes at the open doorway. The wide, blue eyes starting in horror-stricken intensity; the sweet pale face framed in the tumbled mass of golden hair, the trembling girlish figure rose before him in the darkness, and refused to be banished.

CHAPTER XXXI.

AN ATTACK IN THE DARKNESS

After the shift, Schultz sought Innis and drew him aside.

"Look here," he said peremptorily, "you cut to the next shed; no one will notice, and the hooter will go in a minute. Follow the Boss; don't let him out of your sight till Achmann or I relieve you. He has just come down the hill now. That makes the third time he has set out for the manager's house, though he hasn't plucked up enough courage yet to go in. I suppose he is waiting for dark. He is up to mischief. If he goes home, you keep an eyes on his house, and follow him where he goes; I'll send Achmann after you and one of you can run and tell me if he leaves before I come."

Innis looked his distaste of the duty appointed him, yet he dared not rebel openly. His fear of Schultz held him too much in check.

Marlowe lingered about the sheds, with a strange reluctance to leave the familiar scenes of his ordinary daily duties.

He was utterly wearied out; his brain seemed incapable of connected thought, and a sense of impending trouble hung over him like a cloud. He walked slowly from furnace to furnace, tested the bolts of the shaft-bearings of the chlorinating barrels, peered into the leaching vats and charcoal filters with an air of absorbed attention that was so entirely mechanical that he was, in fact, unconscious of what he did.

He left the sheds and went home in the same curious engrossed way. He did not see the thin, furtive figure of Innis slinking behind him, nor the poor Dummy watching him from the yard of the "Three Crowns" if he had; he would have paid no attention to them.

One thought only filled his brain; how was he to regain the letter before the manager returned?

Mary met him at the door, and, as she spoke, he tried to answer her, and found, to his horror, that no words would come. He staggered slightly, with sudden giddiness, which passed as he entered the cool dining room. His wife followed him apprehensively, Ellie looked up from the table and spoke to him. He was able to reply to her, for the paralyzing numbness had left his tongue, to his infinite relief.

They appeared not to notice his disturbed manner, and the evening passed as usual, until about eight o'clock he told them he must go out. They tried hard to persuade him to remain, but desisted when they saw he paid no attention to them.

He left the house, and three watchers outside followed him. As he turned towards the hill they nudged each other in the darkness. They had agreed, or, rather, Schultz had arranged, that only Innis should follow him when they reached the little rise on which the manager's house was built. The other two would hide in the clump of scrub below the house till Innis gave them the signal that the Boss was returning. The signal was to be the cry of the curlew.

They believed that Marlowe was planning to betray them to Carson, if he found him at home, and when they observed that he was making directly for the house they became certain he was playing a double game.

"He may take time to pluck up enough courage to go in," Schultz said to Innis as he left him, "but you just keep your eyes peeled, and I'll see to the rest. We are willing to wait our time, so we get even in the end."

Once again, and still more unwillingly, Innis was pushed to the front. Marlowe walked steadily, but slowly, till he came to the house, then he stopped at the foot of the steps and with an effort tried to collect his thoughts to frame an excuse for asking for the return of the letter. The verandah was high, and as he put his foot on the lowest step the giddiness that had seized him a few hours before, again overpowered him, and he sank helplessly on his knees upon the grass.

In the faint light from the window above Innis saw him in this position, and a contemptuous pity for his boss touched his heart for the moment, but the thought of the coveted gold scorched it away.

"He wants to sell us, poor beggar! But he is hardly game," he thought, half his fears leaving him, and the little man seated himself on a log near by to keep his watch in comparative comfort.

More than an hour passed, and still the huddled figure did not move. Innis grew weary and found it difficult to keep awake.

The lights above went out, and still he heard no movement from the steps. Before he was aware, he had dozed off.

A flash of light from the end of the verandah caught his eyes, and he sprang to his feet in some alarm. He ran to the steps and found that Marlowe was no longer there. With a cold fear of Schultz clutching at his heart, Innis knew that he must have slept at his post; how long he had no means of guessing.

He hurried down the side of the house, where the sound of low voices came from a lighted room. He did not see the shrinking figure of Marlowe, who had wakened from his stupor at the approach of Jim and Lynne, and following them, lay crouching among some shrubs in front of the office window.

Innis looked into the room and saw that one of the men was the manager's son, the other was out of view behind the door. He gave the preconcerted signal, and was soon joined by the two men.

"What is it?" asked Schultz. "Who is in there?" "Marlowe and young Carson," was the whispered rejoinder. "He is selling us, that's sure as death. They've got young Carson to give them the law of it." "Is he?" snarled Schultz, "we'll see about that."

"We began to think you must have gone to sleep," said Achmann his slow drawl in curious contrast to Schultz's quick, harsh accents. "In fact, matey and me was on the point of coming to find out what was up, when we heard your fine imitation of the curlew's call."

"Don't be a fool, if you can help it," said Schultz, who was almost beside himself with anger, though his strong will forced his voice into control. "Here, separate, they are coming out. No, young Carson is sitting down again. You stay here, Innis, and give the call again when he comes out. Come along back to our post Achmann, we'll make ready to give the Boss a taste of something to pay him out for to-night's work. You chaps brought your sticks as I told you? I've got mine," and Schultz gripped more firmly a heavily-mounted riding whip. "Now that we know for certain he has split on us," his voice grew husky in spite of his efforts, "I'll take some satisfaction for the gold out of his hide, the sneaking, lying, treacherous, old fool. I think you two have your share to take out of him as well," Innis swore a hasty corroboration. "But that means we must cut Neummurra. It will be too hot to hold us after to-night."

"I am as full up of the Boss as you," said Achmann shortly, "but I'll have no hand in murder, I tell you straight."

"Who spoke of murder, I didn't; I only mean to leave a beauty spot on him, our mark," said Schultz, with an ugly laugh, and the men went back to the scrub.

Jim Hetherington came quickly down the steps, and hurried along the track towards the township. He stumbled a little, for it was not easy to pick a path among the loose shingly stones of the hillside; yet even at the risk of a slip he did not slacken his pace, for he was too anxious to examine the paper he still had crushed in his hand to care for anything else.

A feeling that there was someone near him made him stop as he neared the foot of the hill.

He could see nothing. Not a sound caught his ear, not a breath of air moved in the hot stillness of the night, when suddenly a blow from behind sent him crashing downwards into the dry crisp grass, and he knew no more. He felt not the pitiless blows that rained on his unconscious body, nor heard the sudden guilty terror of his assailants, as a stumbling step behind sent them flying with the speed of fear from the cruel work they had wrought.

It was Marlowe who came stumbling after them; he staggered blindly on, hearing and seeing nothing but the lighted room, and Lynne Carson holding up a letter in his hand.

When he reached the foot of the hill the same giddiness came over him again. It passed, and he rose to his feet, and, with the homing instinct of an animal, he turned the accustomed path that led to his house. He had to stop and rest many times before he was clear of the works. He passed the "Three Crowns" which was still lighted, though it was past midnight, and as he lurched past, Dummy, who was at the gate, ran out and caught hold of his arm.

Dummy had been in his way almost as disturbed as Dan, whom he had been watching all the afternoon. He had expected to see him come into the "Three Crowns", where Dummy was at times odd stable boy. But though he hung around the verandah, and watched the bar all night, there was no sign of Marlowe.

It was not reason, for poor Dummy could not reason; some sense, such as teaches a dog to divine when his master is in trouble, enabled Dummy to feel that Marlowe was in need of his help, and kept him faithful to his watch, until he saw in the light from the bar the staggering figure pass blindly past the hotel.

Dan accepted the helping hand unconsciously, leant his gaunt frame against the misshapen shoulders of Dummy, and the two incongruous companions moved away together.

At the foot of the slope on which his house was built the giddiness overpowered Marlowe again, and he fell to the ground.

For a few minutes Dummy hung over him in utter despair, then with a strength that his spare frame gave no indication of he began to half carry, half drag the unconscious man, until he managed with incredible exertions to bring Marlowe to his own gate, where he laid him gently down. Mrs. Marlowe and Ellie were sitting anxiously together when a gentle, hesitating knock at the door awoke their nervous fears.

As the door opened they were still more startled to see Dummy there gesticulating violently, while the perspiration poured in streams off his face, and his breath came in loud pants.

"It is father," cried Ellie, snatching up the lamp; "he has brought father home." Dummy nodded as he saw the women understood him. He led the way to the gate at once. Dan was lying on his back with a strange livid look on his face.

In spite of the shock, they were filled with joy to see him, and assisted by Dummy they managed to get him into his own bed. Ellie ran off for the doctor, while poor Mary did what she could to restore her husband to consciousness.

Dummy quietly disappeared when his work was done; and when Mary, after the Doctor had gone, remembered the poor creature, she could not see him anywhere. "A paralytic stroke," Dr Mackay said at once. "It has been coming on for a long time; in fact, his brain must have been partially affected these last few months." Mary thought of those miserable months, and shuddered.

"It may pass away, and though he will never be again the strong man he has been, still he may live for many a year yet." Ellie and her mother looked at each other, and took what feeble comfort they might from the doctor's words.

Dr Mackay was a tall, florid man, a great favourite in Neummurra, in spite of his outspokenness. He was a Scotchman, as his tongue amply attested.

CHAPTER XXXII.

A WOMAN'S REVENGE

THE FURNACE FOR GOLD

When Clara awoke, she found Daphne still sleeping. The sleep was so profound that even when the other rose and dressed herself the girl did not move. "Well, she is a sound sleeper, I'll let her sleep it out. She must be tired," said Clara with some complacency, as she left the room.

As she walked along the verandah, she saw a little distance down the hill a horse, with what looked like the body of a man beside it.

"The man must have been thrown from his horse, or he is sleeping off a 'drunk'," Clara said, running down the steps; then as she got nearer she fancied she recognised the horse. "I am sure it is Jim Hetherington's," she cried. "What can have happened to him?"

She soon reached the spot, and saw that her surmise was quite correct. Jim lay in a pool of blood, while the poor horse stood patiently keeping guard over him. In the course of the night the sagacious animal had worked itself free and found its master.

Clara did not shriek, though the colour forsook her face, as she bent trembling over the battered figure. She forgot everything, except that the man she loved lay before her, and she believed that he was dead. But as she stooped over him she found that he was still breathing, and in the relief from her dread her wits returned.

"I must get help at once," she thought, and cooed loudly. "There are men in tents not so far away."

A white paper was crushed in the rigid hand. Clara bent down and touched it lightly, and the fingers closed mechanically on it.

"Pen, oh Pen," Jim muttered thickly, but Clara heard the words. Her quick jealousy flared up, and she snatched the paper from the helpless hand. She was scarcely sensible of what she did, as she began to read. But before she had read more than a few lines she saw several men coming up the hill. She looked at the unconscious man, and wondered greatly. It was past belief, but she held in her hand the evidence that would account for the mysterious shortage of gold.

"Pen, Pen," Jim muttered again. It was enough. The spring of tenderness dried up instantly in the girl's breast. Her eyes, that had been brimming with tears, burned fiercely. She remembered too well the humiliation that Jim had made her endure, and all her jealous dislike of Pen seemed to gather to a head. She thrust the paper into the lax fingers and looked up.

Half a dozen men were running towards her, among them she recognised with a gleam of spiteful pleasure Michael, the detective.

The men gathered round with shocked ejaculations, Michael alone preserving his calmness. Two of them ran back to their tent for a stretcher, and while they were gone the detective, who said he knew a little about doctoring, began an examination of Jim.

"Don't touch him," cried Pat Kelly, one of the dry-crushers, with tears streaming unchecked down his big, good-natured Irish face. "I've always heard it is better to let the doctor move wan that has been thrown. Och, the dear boy, to think that this should be the end of him. To think you played him false that was always a good master to you," he said laying a heavy hand on the neck of the poor horse.

"Shut your head, Pat," said Michael. "He is not dead at all; can't you see he is trying to move? He must have come a terrible cropper."

Clara noticed that as the detective rose the paper had disappeared, and instantly she wished, illogically, that she had taken it herself and destroyed it, as her first impulse was to do. The mere sound of Pen's name on Jim's lips had caused her, in sheer spite, to abandon him to his fate; but her natural womanliness revolted almost instantly at her own cruelty.

Clara stood looking helplessly at the doomed man, but she dare not speak to the detective. Dr Mackay was soon on the scene, and, after a few brief questions, helped by the willing men, he placed Jim on the stretcher, and the sand procession started for the township. The horse, led by Pat Kelly, followed sadly in the rear.

By the time the house was reached a large crowd had gathered and it was with difficulty that Dr Mackay managed to make them disperse.

John Hetherington came to the door, and one glance was enough to pale the fresh colour of his face. He looked dumbly at Dr Mackay, he dared not utter the awful question.

"Not dead, but badly hurt, I think he will get over it," the doctor said, answering the glance.

"It is only a bit of an accident, Anne; Jim will soon be all right again," said John, hurrying back to the room.

Anne ran past him, her ghastly face meeting the pitying eyes of the miners. "Bring him in here," she said, and her quiet voice did not falter, as she thanked them for looking so kindly after her son.

The men left, tip-toeing until they were some distance down the road. There was genuine grief on their honest, sun-browned faces. Jim was soon undressed, and Dr Mackay examined him carefully.

"I want the truth, Doctor, no smooth lies for me," said John, breaking the silence at last.

"Did you ever get smooth lies from me?" asked Dr Mackay, quietly. "He is very badly hurt, the skull is fractured, and I'm afraid there is some concussion of the brain. I'll know more by the morning. Two ribs are broken, and so is his collar bone, besides that he is very much bruised over the body. But, with good nursing, I do not see that we should not pull him through. It is the fever that we shall have to fear most. But his strong, sound, young constitution will fight well for his life. I can conscientiously tell you that I feel hopeful for the best."

The rigidity of Anne's face relaxed somewhat, and she tried to smile at her husband. "I'll fix him up now, and I'll be back in an hour again," said Dr Mackay, cheerfully.

A light tap came to the door, and, on opening it, John saw Daphne Morgan in the hall. She came into the room with

THE FURNACE FOR GOLD

the gentle, restful grace that was so peculiarly Daphne's own.

"I'm coming to help you with the nursing, Cousin Anne," she said. "I do not know much but I can obey orders, and perhaps lighten your work a little. You'll let me won't you?"

"No, I'll nurse him myself," said Anne, harshly.

"Now, Mrs. Hetherington, you'll allow me to decide for you," said Dr Mackay, quietly but firmly. "It will be a long nursing, and it will be impossible for you to do your boy justice, unless you have help. I was going to propose sending a nurse to you, but I have known Daphne since she was a child, and I can truthfully say I could not get a better nurse in Neummurra."

"Very well," said Anne, grudgingly; but Daphne's smile rewarded Dr Mackay, if he needed any reward.

It was arranged that Daphne should help with the day nursing, and sleep at her cousin's. Anne insisted on doing the night nursing alone, except when John could relieve her, and all that morning Daphne was kept busy in the sick-room.

Neummurra was thrown into a state of great excitement by the accident to the young boss and the illness of the old boss. It was seldom such a startling series of events happened, and the gossips made the most of their opportunity.

There was no talk of foul play about Jim's accident at first. It was supposed that he had been thrown from his horse; the doctor formed his own opinion, but kept it to himself. He knew those cruel bruises were never caused by a fall from a horse.

Two days went past, and there was little change in either of the patients. Jim was growing more feverish, that was all. Every symptom in the illness of both men was discussed fully in the township.

On the third day a strange rumour began to be whispered through Neummurra, though no one seemed to know where it originated. It has been discovered, so the rumour went, that Jim Hetherington was concerned in the gold stealing which, it now appeared, had been carried on for some time in the works.

Tommy heard the report with the rest, and wished that he dared to tell what he knew. Had he known that Schultz, Innis and Achmann had left Neummurra, and gone their several guilty ways into hiding, he might have plucked up enough courage to confide in some one.

The cruel rumour reached by nightfall John's ears, and he told Anne of it. "You don't believe it! Of course, you don't," she said, passionately. "James steal any gold! Our James! They must be mad, to say such a thing."

"I don't for a moment believe it. I know him better; but they say that Mr. Carson has enough evidence to goal him as soon as he gets better. It seems that fellow Michael is a detective," said John wretchedly.

"I don't care what he is," said Anne, fiercely, "they are not going to take away our boy's character lightly. We've got money enough to fight for it, if the worst comes to worst." Her husband agreed with her, though he sadly thought to what a far different purpose he had intended the money.

From that moment John's strong shoulders began to stoop, and day by day Anne noticed how thickly the once sparse grey threads began to appear among his brown hair.

Anne was glad that she had insisted on bearing the night nursing alone, for as soon as night came on, Jim, who would be quiet for most of the day, would begin to toss and mutter, "Pen! Pen! Pen!" That was the burden of his mutterings, and it wrung her heart to hear him, while her anger against the girl burned with a steady heat.

One night, the third since the accident, the pitiful muttering and the restless tossing ceased, and as Anne sat watching beside him it seemed to her that a change passed over his face.

She bent over him, and Jim lifted his fever-bright eyes to her face.

"We are in the furnace mother," he said in a strange voice; "all of us, you and father and Uncle Dan, Pen and Lynne, and all of us. You remember what it says." The brilliant glance held hers. "The fining pot is for silver and the furnace for gold, but the Lord trieth the heart. The furnace for gold, mother, the furnace for gold." He ended with a wild, strange laugh that tortured Anne's heart. Then he lapsed into indistinct muttering again.

John came to the door.

"Was that Jim speaking?" he asked. "What was he saying about gold?"

Anne left the chair, and drew John into the passage.

"He is wandering," she said, and she repeated what he had said. Then, for the first time since they had brought him to her, her stern composure gave way. "Oh, John," she whispered through her tears, "we are going to lose him. I feel it. He never spoke like that before. I know my James is dying," and she broke down utterly.

With the superstition inherent in her Celtic blood, she felt that the call had come to her boy in those mysterious words of Scripture.

"Hush, woman, hush! For the lad's sake," John urged, though a deadly coldness seized his own heart. "Don't be foolish, after bearing up so well till now. The boy is just wandering, as you said yourself. It is only the fever. What sense has he of what is saying? You go right off to bed, and I'll take the rest of the night to watch."

"But what will you do tomorrow at the store?" said Anne. "No, I'll call you about four."

"You go right away, and lie down," said John firmly. "If I'm tired tomorrow I can easily come home and take a sleep in the afternoon," and Anne suffered herself to be coaxed away.

CHAPTER XXXIII.

PEN'S EXPIATION

When first the news of Jim's accident came to Morgan's store all

THE FURNACE FOR GOLD

David's kindliness revived. He forgot, the restraint between the families.

"I'll run round and see what I can do," he said, and he hurried off to his cousin.

Lew heard the sad tidings in the bank. He wished to go home and break the news to Pen, before it was blurted out to her by some heedless neighbour. He had not attempted any interference since his luckless adventure with the Waratah. It was noon before he was free, and he hastened home, scarcely hoping to be in time. The sight of Pen's calm face reassured him.

Those who knew Lew only in his cynical, flippant moods would not have recognised him now, in the infinite tact and delicate tenderness of his manner as he told her of the accident.

Pen did not utter a word. She looked at her brother for a few moments with a face from which all the pretty colour had fled, then began in a dazed way to bring in his lunch. She did not utter a word.

"He'll soon be all right again, I expect," said Lew, doubtful as to whether he had done well or not; "the doctor is pretty hopeful, I think, more so than he is about old Dan Marlowe, who is down with a stroke of paralysis."

But Pen did not ask about Dan's illness; indeed, Lew wondered whether anything except the bare fact that Jim was hurt had penetrated her brain.

"I'll run round and get Daphne," he thought, "I don't think Pen is fit to be left alone."

"Has Daphne not come home yet?" he said, aloud.

"No," said Pen dully. "No, Daphne has not been here since last night," and Lew felt his own eyes filling at the dumb pain in the beautiful dark eyes.

"Will you come round with me to help cousin Anne?" he said.

"No! Oh, no! I couldn't. I've got work to attend to," said Pen quickly, shrinking visibly at the suggestion.

Lew left at last, with an anxious heart. As soon as he had gone Pen ran to her own room.

"He will die! He will die! I know he will die. Oh, I cannot, cannot bear it!" she cried despairingly. She was done now with all self-deception; too well she knew at last that she loved Jim, and Jim only. Her undisciplined heart was meeting its first real trial.

The selfishness of nature that unlimited admiring and petting produce that perhaps not a large share in Pen's character; but there was enough to have made it natural for her hitherto to please herself, without much thought for the feelings of others. But her heart was passing now through the furnace of pain, the furnace of human purification, and its dross was being burnt away. How long she lay struggling with the first wild grief she could not have told, but at length the storm of anguish and fierce remorse died away, and when she heard her brother's step on the verandah she rose quietly, bathed her eyes, and went to eh dining-room to meet him.

"Daphne's going to stay with Cousin Anne," Lew said, as she came into the room.

"I am glad of that. Poor Cousin Anne, she will be the better of her help,

365

and she was always fond of Daphne," Pen said steadily, and her tone set her brother's fears at rest. She was not the dazed, distracted girl he had been almost afraid to leave alone a few hours before.

"Tell me all about it," said Pen simply, and Lew obeyed. The brother and sister sat quietly talking over Jim's accident and Marlowe's sudden seizure until David returned.

When the rumour of Jim being concerned in the gold stealing came to the Morgans they discredited it at once; it was almost laughable, Lew declared, to imagine that Jim Hetherington could be accused of such a thing. Indeed, many of the Neummurra folk were at first of the same opinion as Lew, and deemed it incredible that Jim Hetherington could be suspected of any complicity with such a crime; but their views began to change as the rumours grew more circumstantial. It was astonishing to learn how many people, in spite of their confessed liking for young Hetherington, gradually found that they could not but acknowledge that they had been feeling doubtful of him since his sudden promotion.

"It is never a good thing for a young fellow to get on too quickly," Graves, the chemist remarked to his friend Finucane. "It upsets them somehow. They get uppish, and then comes the smash."

"Stuff and nonsense," said honest Dinny, stoutly, "what was there strange about a clever young chap like our Jim getting on? He is the sort that yez can't hould back. I'll go bail on his honesty wid me own life, an' I'll trash the villain who tries to blacken the poor bhoy's name, an' him on his sick bed too."

But in spite of Dinny's championship the rumours continued to circulate and find believers.

Pen, warm-hearted, outspoken Pen, did her utmost to contradict each fresh aspersion, but only a tolerant skepticism, a pitying silence followed her words. The Morgans were doing right in standing by their relations, Neummurra admitted, but it was useless trying to blind people to absolute fact; such fact being the rumours flying mysteriously through the township.

Pen had her first lessons in cynicism as she observed how more easily people seemed to find it to credit evil rather than good. Jim was lying helpless on a sick bed, and his character was torn to pieces by men who had professed friendship to him but a few months back. Yet they had no proof of his wrongdoing; they simply believed the reports, originated no one seemed to know how; and forgot all Jim's previous life from his brilliant, earnest boyhood to his steady manhood among his own townspeople. Pen felt that her heart must break, as she realized the uselessness of her attempts to defend him, to stem the current of public opinion.

One thing she resolved to do, and it gave her little private satisfaction in the midst of her trouble, for she found in it some sense of tardy justice to Jim. She would break off her engagement as soon as Lynne returned to Neummurra. She scarcely felt able now to understand how it was that Lynne and she had become engaged. A few weeks of holiday-making and laughing enjoyment of the attentions of the handsome, fascinating barrister, and she was pledged to him.

Looking back, she seemed to remember very little of what had led to it; a mid-summer madness it must have been, the outcome of flattered, girlish vanity and idle sentiment. The awakening had come before Lynne had left Neummurra, though she had to shut her eyes to it. In truth, no sooner were the fatal words spoken than she wished them recalled; for in spite of her coquetries Pen was no flirt. Though her love for admiration led her astray, at heart she was true to Jim, and she had never cared for anyone else. But Jim's silence and marked avoidance had hurt her pride long before Lynne came to Neummurra. She had allowed Lynne's attentions in the beginning in a half-conscious desire to pique her lover into making an advance; to find like many another girl has done that she places herself in the position of being obliged to accept one whom she does not love, but who considers her acceptance of his attentions constitutes a right to claim her.

"Whether Jim dies or lives," thought Pen, "I shall belong to him alone. Even if he gets better, I do not believe he would ask me now; if indeed he can at all care for me after how I treated him. Oh! What a fool, what a fool I've been. When I had his love I threw it away. He did love me once. Oh! I know he did."

CHAPTER XXXIV.

LYNNE LEARNS A LESSON

No word of the strange happenings at Neummurra reached Lynne in Walsingham. He received no letter from home, and no mention of Jim's accident or Marlowe's illness appeared in the city papers.

He wondered a good deal that Jim did not come back to Mount Kudgee, but concluded he had been detained at home, so put the matter out of his mind.

But the week that followed the dance, though outwardly quiet enough, was a momentous one to Lynne. In it he said good-bye for ever to his irresponsible boyhood, that had lasted so long. The gay, reckless Lynne's nature was left behind in that week of conflict; a manlier, steadier nature took its place.

There came to Lynne, for the first time, the meaning of a word he had often used lightly and, at heart, disbelieved in. He began to learn what love meant, and understood that he had never approached its confines in the evanescent fancies that he had termed affairs of love. He had come to believe that no woman would ever have power to hold his fickle affections since his experience had all gone to show that "out of sight" was invariably "out of mind" with the prettiest face that attracted him.

When he found, after his engagement to Pen, that the sight of the next pretty face was blotting out the memory of hers from his mind, he shrugged his shoulders and said – "Oh! It will be all right when we are married. I'll sober down, and be as devoted a Benedict as the best of them, then."

But now, night or day, he could not banish Daphne's face from his mind. He could not sleep, he could not eat, and though before this he had been so anxious to make a favourable first impression as Crown Prosecutor, now even his ambitions seemed but dust and ashes in his mouth.

There were depths in his nature that until now he was ignorant of. He found what it was to be tormented with the pangs of unavailing love.

"I have made a mistake, and I must abide by it; I've only myself to blame. I've given my promise to Pen, and I'll keep it to the utmost of my strength," he said at last; and the Lynne who came to this conclusion was scarcely akin to the selfish, pleasure-loving Lynne of but a short week before.

On Friday he received a letter from his father with the startling news of Jim's accident, and the still more startling news that he was suspected of stealing the gold. He tossed the letter angrily aside.

"Rot! Utter rot! Dad can't be in his senses. Jim steal! I'd as soon credit dad himself. I'll go up tonight and try to make him see sense. The Court won't be sitting to-morrow and I can stay till Monday morning. Poor Jim, was he thrown from his horse or set upon? Perhaps the wretches who sent on my letter to the dad had a hand in it. Well, I'll do my best to put things straight."

But when Lynne arrived home he did not find it so easy to disentangle the twisted web of circumstance. Mr. Carson was convinced for his own part, of Jim's guilt; the evidence was too strong to doubt even with his prejudice in favour of Jim's complicity at least in the theft.

He gave Lynne the paper that Michael had found in Jim's unconscious hand. "Read that, and then tell me Hetherington is innocent," he said shortly. "It is not only that paper either. Michael has a good deal more evidence than that."

Lynne read the memorandum gravely, and in spite of his firm belief in his friend, with growing uneasiness.

"I am more sorry for the young fellow's father than for himself," said Mr. Carson, "and the mother too. Poor things! Their only son and he is not out of danger yet, though I heard that he was conscious today. Daphne Morgan is down there helping with the nursing. The Morgans and Hetheringtons are some sort of distant cousins, I believe. That is a fine girl, Daphne; I don't know but I like her better than the one you picked."

Lynne flushed, but was silent; he felt his heart beating, till it seemed his father must hear it too.

"I must run over to see Pen. I feel a coward at meeting her," he thought when he was left alone; but he lingered, strangely loath to pay the visit. It was late in the afternoon before he left to go over to the Morgan's cottage.

As he came down the hill he met Pen coming up.

They stopped and looked at each other. Each was conscious of a change, and felt guiltily embarrassed at seeing each other. "When did you come home?" asked Pen, as Lynne thought reproachfully.

"Late last night," he said and could not find another word to say, his ordinary glibness had deserted him.

"I did not know you were coming up," said Pen, her colour paling a little.

"I was on my way to see your mother, but now I shall not go. I want to speak to you. Do you mind if we go down to the Creek? It is something important I have to say."

"She must have heard of the ball at Mount Kudgee," thought Lynne, "and is going to reproach me for not coming to Neummurra."

In a silence foreign to both of their natures they walked down the little track that led to the Creek. At last Pen stopped, and seating herself on a fallen log, motioned Lynne to do the same.

He obeyed wondering at the indefinable difference in Pen's manner. "I must blurt it out, it is the only way," poor Pen said to herself, as she turned abruptly to him.

"I can't expect you to forgive me, but I want you to let me break off our engagement," she said, with a face pale to the lips.

"Why?" Lynne cried and repeated in a startled tone, "to break off the engagement?"

"It was all a mistake, I should never have promised; I did not care for you, at last not as I should do, to give such a promise. It was nothing but my vanity that made me accept you. I know you can never forgive me. Will you let me break it off, and try not to think to hardly of me."

There came a slight recrudescence of the old Lynne, whose pride smarted at the blow, as he turned to meet Pen's pleading face. "There is someone else, I suppose," he said sullenly.

Pen looked at him piteously, and nodded, the tears gathering in her pretty eyes and falling unheeded on her lap.

Lynne's heart smote him. "What a hypocrite I am," he thought with inward shame, and he broke out.

"I've no right to ask such a question. It ought to be quite enough for me that you do not care for me. I hope he is worthy of you, and that he deserves so much happiness," something strangely mournful in the girl's face made him add involuntarily, "is it Jim Hetherington, Pen?"

"Yes," said Pen with a sob.

"He is a fine fellow," said Lynne, slowly, "I always liked him; he is a hundred times a better man than I." Pen's dark eyes brightened a little; "but," he hesitated, "I am sorry for you both just now, as there are hard times ahead of you."

"You do not believe the wicked scandal about him, do you?" she asked, the colour rushing back to her pale face. "The cowards! The cowards! To set such tales in circulation when the poor fellow lies, perhaps, on his death bed."

"Jim is getting better," said Lynne, "so there is no talk of deathbeds. Of course I don't believe it of old Jim; but dad does, and I must admit that he has almost evidence enough to make anyone doubtful, who does not know Jim as well as we do."

"What evidence?" asked Pen fiercely.

"The paper with the account of the stolen gold, and the curious explanation of the stealing. It is in Jim's writing, I couldn't dent it myself and it will need some explaining away."

"I'd never believe it, not if all the managers and detectives in Queensland swore it. Jim Hetherington a thief! The bare idea is preposterous," she said angrily.

"I feel the same about it," said Lynne, "and what is more, I'm going to do my level best to clear Jim's name; so that, before he is about again, the whole truth will come to light. I do not fear the truth for Jim; so Pen, you can count on me for all I can do for your sake as well as Jim's."

It was too much for impulsive Pen. She broke down altogether.

"You are far too good, and kind, and generous. You may forgive me," she said at last through her tears, "but I can never forgive myself; I ought to have been honest and told you at first that it was only my wicked vanity made me say 'yes'."

"Don't cry, for pity's sake, Pen," Lynne said in distress, "I can't bear to see you in tears. Look up, and I'll tell you something. I do not deserve your praise. I must ask your forgiveness too, though unless you had spoken I had made up my mind to keep my unhappy secret to myself. Can you forgive me, Pen, if I confess that I, too, have found out, that I care for someone else?"

The tears dried themselves on Pen's cheeks. However easy a woman may find it to refuse a lover, it is not in human nature to hear, unmoved, that he, too, prefers another.

"Someone else?" said Pen, in a bewildered tone. "Someone you saw before you saw me, or since then?"

The sudden pallor on Lynne's face started her.

"Yes," he said huskily, "someone I met before you."

"And you cared for her all the time?" Pen could not help the question.

"I believe I did; I believe I loved her as soon as I saw her, though I did not find it out till a week ago."

"Does she know?" asked Pen, but the indignant flash of Lynne's eyes answered her.

For a minute or two they looked at each other in silence; then Pen's sense of humour came to her aid. She broke into a fit of laughter and after a moment Lynne joined her in spite of himself.

"So neither of us really cared for the other," she said. "I'm glad we have found it out in time." She looked at Lynne queerly. "It is not yet a fair exchange. You have not told me who she is."

Lynne started up in uncontrollable agitation.

"I can't, Pen; I do not suppose I shall ever have the courage to tell her."

"Somebody in Neummurra?"

persisted Pen. "Is it Ellie Marlowe?"

"Good heavens, no," said Lynne, then he sat down again, "I'll trust you, Pen. It is your sister Daphne."

"Daphne! Daphne!" repeated Pen, stupidly.

Rapidly and nervously Lynne told her the story.

"So it was you who came to her rescue from the flood, and the fire. I never knew that the hero of the two adventures was one and the same man. If Daphne cares for you, you are a lucky fellow, for she is worth a dozen of me. If you win her, you will get her whole unspoiled heart; she is not a wicked flirt like me. I mean that, honestly," she said, with another sudden break into laughter, "not because you spoke so handsomely of Jim." But at the mention of the name the ready tears sprang to her eyes.

"I know I have no chance with Daphne; she can think of me only as belonging to you; or if not, too fickle to be worth a love like hers," and he told of his last meeting with Daphne.

"I did not hear of that," said Pen, "so little Tommy seems mixed up with the mystery of Jim's accident. Surely no one could have wished to hurt poor Jim willfully. I'll help you if I can with Daphne," she continued half shyly, "but she is not at all like me. I am half afraid of her, in spite of her gentleness. Well, goodbye Lynne. I must hurry home and get dinner ready."

The erstwhile lovers parted with a little embarrassment, but the utmost friendliness.

CHAPTER XXXV.

A MILLIONAIRE'S OFFER

"Did Lynne tell you before he left that Pen had broken off the engagement?" asked Clara Carson of her mother, as they sat together on the shady side of the verandah on Sunday afternoon.

Mrs. Carson nodded, "Yes, it is broken off, and I for one am not sorry." "I'm not sorry that I am not to have Pen for a sister-in-law," said Clara, spitefully, "but what beats me is why she gave up Lynne. Perhaps she is hoping to catch a millionaire. Mr. Buxton is up again, and you know what a dead set Pen made at him the night of our party. She may wish to be an old man's darling; that may be the reason she has given up Lynne,"

"Good afternoon Mrs. Carson, good afternoon Miss Clara," and the broad shoulders and florid face of Mr. Buxton appeared at the top of the steps. For once Clara lost her self-possession; she literally gasped at the sight of the newcomer.

Mrs. Carson, however, after the first shock of embarrassment, managed to greet her visitor with outward composure, and invited him to seat himself beside them. "It is very sad about young Hetherington," she said, after the usual polite queries.

"I believe he is getting on nicely now," said Buxton. "Oh, I was referring to those ugly rumours about the gold stealing," she said, sourly.

Buxton's penetrating glance met

hers. "It would take a good deal to make me believe evil of Jim Hetherington," he said, quietly; "I am not often deceived in a face, and I fancy I read that young man thoroughly."

"Very few in Neummurra are of your way of thinking," said Clara, but her eyes fell before the millionaire's keen glance, and she added hastily, "I am sure I hope he will be proved to be innocent." "When you come to my time of life, Miss Carson," Mr. Buxton said good-humouredly, but Clara flushed under his smile, "you will have learned how little there is, after all, in the clearest circumstantial evidence."

Mrs. Carson hastened to agree with him, and soon the conversation drifted from the dangerous topic. Both women felt relieved when, after half an hour's desultory chat, Mr. Buxton rose to go.

"Mother," cried Clara a few minutes later, "he must have heard me, and what is more, I do believe he is going straight from here to propose to Pen. Of course she will have him; I have not the least doubt. There is no standing her airs now, but if she is Mrs. Buxton she will be positively unbearable."

"Nonsense," said her mother, "the idea is simply preposterous."

Buxton walked thoughtfully down the hill. Clara's surmise, wild as it appeared to Mrs. Carson, was not far from the truth. If she knew it, her own words were the subject of the millionaire's cogitations.

He had been very strongly attracted towards Pen, when first he saw her merry, winsome face on the night of the Governor's ball, and her charming, natural manner had completed the conquest. But later in the night Buxton began to think that there was a tacit understanding between her and the young fellow to whom he had taken so warm a liking at the works. It was natural that they should care for each other; youth seeks youth, and Buxton determined to think no more of the beautiful girl. But again he had met her, this time in the manager's house, and Hethcrington appeared scarcely to speak to her. Half the night Pen remained beside him, and listened to him with evident pleasure. He remembered the pretty, winsome laugh that greeted his attempts to be entertaining, the flash of the white teeth, the arch glance of the dark eyes. He acknowledged to himself before the night was over that for the first time in many years he was honestly in love, and with a girl who was 30 years younger than he. Though he acknowledged the disparity in age, he left the house that night determined in his dogged way to win Pen; but business called him to the south, and when he came back, scarcely a month later, he learned that she was engaged to Lynne Carson.

Now from Clara's lips he heard that this engagement was broke, and however poor an opinion he had formed of Clara Carson's intelligence, he was yet more influenced by her speech than he knew.

A good many years had passed since Buxton discovered what an "open sesame" in society was the mere name of millionaire. He had seen in London men like himself, from the working classes, and many with far inferior educational advantages, able, simply because they were millionaires, to pick and choose from the prettiest and proudest young girls in England. He had observed, with cynical amusement, the stiffest locks in the most exclusive houses open at the touch of the millionaire's golden key. But he had never felt the slightest wish to say, "Barter your youth, your beauty, your womanly charm, your ancient name for my millions," until in the spot where fortune first smiled on him, he saw the lovely face of Penelope Morgan, one of the people, as he was himself.

He was fifty-one, but he felt and looked scarcely middle-aged. His strong athletic frame and fresh, wholesome-coloured face were still those of a man in his prime, and he felt himself so far from being an old man that before he reached the foot of the hill he had made up his mind to ask Pen to be his wife.

Pen was sitting on the verandah, behind the thick screen of creeping bougainvillea, when the click of the gate made her look up from her book.

"It is Mr. Buxton, I do believe," she said to herself. "Father will be vexed at being out when he came." Buxton showed none of the awkwardness he felt, as he came up the steps and greeted the girl.

"I am so sorry," Pen said, "father has just gone out; he went down the hill with Lew to see how Jim Hetherington is getting on." Buxton looked at the fair face, and wondered whether, after all, he had any chance. "I shall wait for him, if you will allow me," he said composedly, and Pen led the way to the shady side of the verandah.

Pen was perfectly unembarrassed. She was somewhat surprised at Buxton's visit, but she liked him, and had always found it pleasant to talk to him, so she was soon chatting to him with the bright girlish confidence that was one of her greatest charms to Buxton.

Buxton was a good speaker; he knew men and women well, and was never at a loss for an interesting subject of talk. He spoke at once of his recent visit to Sydney, which was regarded by Neummurra people as the goal of ambitious holiday hopes.

"It must be lovely," she said, looking earnestly at him, "to be able to go from place to place as you do." "Yes," he said at last, wondering whether he had found an opening for introducing his proposal. "I often go for a trip home. I am quite an old traveler now. Would you like to visit England?"

"Wouldn't I!" cried Pen. "Why it is the dream of my life! I think I'd go mad with sheer excitement if I thought I was going for a trip home." Buxton looked at the brilliant face. He resolved to tempt the girl, if he could, by painting in vivid colours the pleasures his millions could procure.

"And have heaps of money," he said; "go into society; wear pretty dresses; be presented at Court; travel all over the world – Europe, Asia, America; hear all the plays and operas;

see the best pictures!"

"Oh, stop! Stop!" cried Pen. "It will not bear talking about. Why, I should go fairly wild if I thought that such a thing was coming to me!"

"I do not see why it should not come to you," said Buxton steadily. "You've only to say the word."

"And what word shall I say?" laughed Pen.

"Say 'yes'." A slow flush rose to the strong face. "I offer you all that; will you accept? Will you say yes?"

Pen looked at him in bewilderment.

"What do you mean?" she said doubtfully.

"I mean exactly what I say. Will you be my wife? I am not young, but neither am I old, and all my life will be spent in making you happy. I can promise you all that I have said, and more, a great deal more. Say yes, Pen. You will not repent it."

Pen looked at him in distress.

"Oh, don't say another word; please don't. I never thought of such a thing; and I couldn't, I simply couldn't think of it."

"Why not?" persisted Buxton; "you do not dislike me, do you?"

"No, I like you. It is not that at all," the young face was very timid.

"Perhaps you think me too old; well, you'd be the sooner a widow."

"Oh," cried Pen, shocked and distressed, "don't say such a terrible thing. I never thought of you like that at all," she said, innocently. "I thought it was father you came to see."

A smile flickered over the stubborn lines of the man's face.

"No, I want you, and I mean to get you if I can." Pen looked at him in silence.

"Do you care for this young Carson? I heard you had broken off your engagement with him."

"No," said Pen, in spite of herself. She felt annoyed, yet was helpless before the relentless tenacity, the quiet obstinacy, that seemed to emanate from the strong personality of the man.

"Come, my girl, you can see the kind of man I am. What I set my mind on that I generally contrive to have. I may seem rough and cruel now, but I'd be kind to you, you'd find; if you do not care for anybody else, couldn't you bring yourself to take me? You could do anything you liked with me. It is many a long day since I spoke like that to a woman. You may not care for me now, but you do not dislike me, and if only you'll agree, I'm not afraid that I shall not be able to win your love, once you are my wife. Think over it, my girl, I say again, don't dismiss it lightly. For it means a great deal more than you would dream of to me."

The florid colour had paled, there was a dumb pleading in the man's eyes, but behind it all there was a grim determination that frightened Pen. Pen's colour too had ebbed away, she felt frightened and desperate, but she would not yield. She must not let herself be carried away on the current of the man's powerful will.

"But I do care," she whispered, "I can for someone dearly."

Buxton started at the whisper, and looked at her earnestly. Pen gathered

THE FURNACE FOR GOLD

her courage in both hands. With a pretty timidity yet with gently confidence, she lifted her eyes to his face.

"You cared for somebody once, for another girl long ago, didn't you?"

Buxton shrank back, but did not speak, there was confession in the look he gave.

"You loved her, that girl. I suppose she died; but you have never forgotten. You were poor then, perhaps, but suppose you were ill, or in trouble, what would you have thought of her if she allowed a rich man to coax her away from your love when you were too ill perhaps to say to her, 'be true to me'."

The tears rose to Pen's eyes. Buxton did not speak for a moment. While Pen's sweet glance was bent on his, he could not say that this lost love his dead past had indeed allowed her love to be bought from him and that it was the deceit and treachery of that time that had made him for many years a misogynist.

"If," Pen hesitated, "the one I cared for were well and happy, I might be tempted by what you offer. Indeed, indeed, I might, for I am not a noble character at all. I love luxury, I'd like to have heaps of money – but not, oh, surely not, when everyone else is against him, and he has no one to stand up for him. I do not even know if he loves me now, but I love him and I could not desert him. So please believe me when I say that I will never listen to any one else but him. I used to think that money mattered so much; but now I know, since I've been put against love. I can't explain what I mean, but you will understand, and never ask me again, for I like you very much indeed."

It was a childish appeal, and Pen's face, in its tender ingenuous gravity, was very childish, too, thought Buxton as he looked irresolutely at her. It was hard for him to relinquish his purpose, but he was more moved by the simple appeal than he cared to show. He liked the girl all the better that she had avowed the attraction that she found in his offer; and he did not despair of even yet winning her consent, and ultimately her love in the end but this appeal to his manliness upset all his calculations.

"It is Jim Hetherington," he thought, "poor Jim! I fancied they cared for each other the first time I saw them, and my penetration was not at fault; but the little witch has gone about the matter in the one way that makes it impossible for me to prosecute her with any further attentions now. She owns her weakness, yet, in spite of it, she is determined to keep true to the man she loves." Aloud he said:

"Thank you for telling so much; no, you are quite right. Stick to the man you love. I wish him every happiness; pity but more women were true to their own hearts. If you think I could do anything to help either of you, you have only to ask. I should like to do something for you. Goodbye. No, I shall not wait to see your father; it was you I came to see, not Mr. Morgan. Your decision is a bit of a blow, but I think you are right." He rose, shook hands briskly, and went down the steps. Half way down he stopped.

"In fact, I know you are right, little

girl. There is nothing in the world like true honest love. I am glad you have the sense to see it. Goodbye again. Don't worry about what I said. We'll both promise to forget it."

Pen sat for a long time without stirring. She was deeply moved. The two interviews – one with Lynne, the other with Mr. Buxton – followed so closely on each other that it was no wonder that she was strangely disturbed. Lynne had confessed that he loved Daphne. Pen became doubtful of even Jim's love; but now that Buxton desired to win her old confidence was renewed. And though she would not have confessed it, Buxton's proposal healed the wound that Lynne had dealt her vanity.

While she sat gazing dreamily towards the township she saw little Tommy Ratten passing down the street.

"I expect he is going to the chemist," she said to herself. "I'll stop and ask him about Jim," for Pen could scarcely ever summon up enough courage to call at her cousin's house. She was afraid of Anne, and fearful of her unspoken reproaches.

Tommy came at her call, and admitted that he was on his way to the chemist. Mr. Jim was just the same, he thought, but Mrs. Hetherington was crying in the kitchen when he left.

Tommy looked at Pen with bashful, admiring eyes. She was his ideal of beauty; and as she stood at the gate in her white dress, with one hand shading her soft eyes from the afternoon sun, and the other hand laid gently on Tommy's arm, she was no bad embodiment of beauty for anyone, boy or man.

Pen remembered what Lynne had told her of a letter that had been sent to the manager's house, and about which Tommy had warned Jim.

A sudden idea flashed across her mind. Suppose Tommy really knew a little about the affair, and could be brought to divulge it. Perhaps she might be able to do something to clear Jim's character, or discover at least who were his assailants, for by this time it was generally believed that Jim's terrible injuries had been deliberately inflicted.

"Tommy," she said in her sweetest tones, "come upstairs. I want to ask you something. I shan't keep you for more than a minute."

But Tommy's ever ready suspicion was aroused. His sallow face flushed a little as he muttered, "Sorry miss, but missus said I was to hurry back," and he tried to shuffle away from her gentle grasp.

"Oh, Tommy, please," said Pen, "just a minute," and against his better judgment Tommy yielded.

"You know something about a letter that was sent up to Mr. Carson's by the Dummy a little while ago – the day before Jim was hurt," Pen said, as soon as she got Tommy upstairs.

Tommy's sudden flush vanished into a sickly paleness.

"Told you so!" was his inward ejaculation; but he only set his small lips with forbidding firmness, and looked at the floor.

"Tommy, listen to me," said Pen;

THE FURNACE FOR GOLD

"look at me for a minute." The shy glance went up for a moment, and Tommy saw there were tears in the beautiful eyes, but he hardened his heart.

"You are sorry for Mr. Jim are you not?" He nodded. This did not seem to commit him to anything. "And you would like to see the wretches who hurt him punished?" A vindictive gleam shot from his eyes, and Pen felt encouraged. "I'll keep it as secret as the grave if you tell me. I'm sure you know enough to clear him. You have heard the dreadful things they say about him, that he stole gold from the works?" Tommy's indignant scorn could be plainly read. "Wouldn't you like to think that you had been able to prove it was all a lie; wouldn't you, Tommy?"

Tommy moistened his dry lips. "I dassent, miss," he whispered.

"Then you know? Oh, Tommy, won't you tell me?"

"They'd murder me, they said they would," he said fearfully.

"They need never know. Perhaps they are gone. I heard a lot of men left the works lately."

"He'd know," said Tommy, with conviction.

"Who?" asked Pen, artfully, but the boy was too sharp. "Was it he who sent the letter?" asked Pen.

"No; another of them. He wanted to get Mr. Jim into trouble. The others laughed at him for sending the letter. They said it was a fool's game."

"Tommy," cried Pen, her tears falling, "oh, Tommy, I shan't tell a soul if you don't want me to, but just tell me what you know. You can't be cruel enough to keep it to yourself, when perhaps, it may save your master's life. For I am sure it will kill him if he hears such a terrible thing!"

Tommy could hold out no longer, though he shook with apprehension as he poured out his story, yet he felt some relief in sharing the terrible secret.

"You are a splendid boy," said Pen, scarcely able to believe her ears, as she listened to the confused tale. "I'll never forget this to you, see if I shall. But surely you must be mistaken? Marlowe, the boss, joining in with the gang of thieves to rob the mine?"

"There was a paper he'd wrote out for the others," said Tommy. "I heard him read it; all about what they'd taken." Pen clasped her hands. She remembered now having heard that Jim's handwriting was almost an exact copy of Marlowe's his first master in the art. That explained a good deal.

"Didn't you hear the name of any of the others?" she said, after a few minutes reflection.

"No," said Tommy. "I never seen none of them before, except the boss. I knowed his voice, and I seen him plain when he walked over the bridge; but the other three stayed in the dark and I did not know their voices."

"Tommy," said Pen, "I won't mention your name at all, so you need not feel frightened; but I am going to try to see if I can't clear this thing up by myself, now that you have told me what you know. Anyway, the thieves will be afraid to touch you. They will have cleared out, take my word for it, as soon as Jim was hurt. You don't know anything about his accident do you?"

The boy shook his head sorrowfully.

"Never mind, it will all come right soon, so don't lose heart. Think how splendid it will be to have Jim all right, and thanking you for clearing his good name. You had better run off now. Thank you Tommy, goodbye," and before the astonished boy realized what was going to happen a pair of soft lips touched his tingling cheek.

CHAPTER XXXVI.

PEN TURNS DETECTIVE

Scarcely had Tommy Ratten disappeared than Daphne opened the garden gate. Pen ran down to meet her and they came up to the verandah together. "Was that Tommy I saw running away from here?" asked Daphne.

"Yes, I called him. He told me Cousin Anne was crying in the kitchen when she sent him to the chemist. Is Jim worse?" said Pen, anxiously.

"Not any worse, though not much better either. The fever keeps returning in the afternoons and night, and Jim is so weak now that of course there is great reason for anxiety. But I think Cousin Anne heard father and John talking about the rumours of Jim being mixed up with the gold stealing."

"Surely," cried Pen, angrily, "Anne does not believe it."

"Of course not," said Daphne, 'but the mere thought that Jim is suspected is killing her. She is terrified to let anyone see him, not so much because he is ill, as in case they should breathe a hint about the gold. As if anyone could be so cruel."

It was with difficulty that Pen restrained herself on the subject, but, after a slight pause, she said quietly. "I suppose you have heard that Lynne and I have broken off our engagement."

"Broken off your engagement," repeated Daphne blankly.

"Yes," said Pen, briskly. "I found I cared for someone else, and he found he did the same. Someone he met before he met me. A girl he saw up in the bush I believe. So we've agreed to part. We are very good friends. I like him very much; I think he is a splendid fellow. But our engagement was a mistake. He was just idle here on his holidays and that was the mischief that Satan found for him to do."

Daphne did not turn her head but gazed through the creeper to where the busy chimneys of the works poured out the rolling clouds across the setting sun, which coloured them with strange melting hues. The soft colour that flickered over the fair face might have been the reflection of the rosy sunset but Pen did not think so.

"Is it Jim?" Daphne said, softly, turning round without a shade of embarrassment. "I always thought it was Jim. I could never understand how you could have done him such a cruel wrong."

"Yes, it is Jim," said Pen. "Poor Jim, when he was well and strong, I could forget that, perhaps, he did care for me, and was suffering from my teasing. But not when he lies there, perhaps on his death-bed, and all those who envied or admired him or even pretended to care for him, are blackening his name. No I am not ashamed to say I love him, even if he does not love me, now, or if he does not get better," but Pen could go no further.

"Now, Pen, who said anything about not getting better?" said Daphne, quickly. "Of course he will get better, and I know Jim loves you, has always loved you."

"Has he ever asked for me?" asked Pen in a low tone.

"No," said Daphne, reluctantly. "He never asks for anybody. He seems to have very little interest in anything; but what could you expect when he is so weak, and not yet free from fever?"

"Don't say anything about my engagement to Anne," said Pen, a few minutes later, as Daphne rose to return. "She dislikes me more than ever. I can feel it. That is why I never care to run down to ask about Jim."

"I think it is partly your own imagination. I do not believe Cousin Anne dislikes you. She is so worn and upset over Jim's accident that she cannot be expected to think about other people, so you fancy she is unkind."

"It is not imagination," said Pen, to herself, but she allowed Daphne to go without disputing the point.

It was long before Pen fell asleep that night. She went over the materials she had gathered from Tommy, and made plan after plan for following up the information she had gained. The secret had been given into her hands. Was she clever enough and wise enough to make use of it, and prove beyond the possibility of doubt her lover's absolute guiltlessness of the charge that was laid against him?

To go to the manager, or Buxton, or anyone else, with Tommy's story and boldly accuse Marlowe and some unknown accomplices of stealing the gold, and cunningly contriving to throw suspicion on an innocent man, was, she saw clearly, but to court failure. Besides, her promise held to poor frightened Tommy.

Pen slept at last from sheer mental exhaustion, and in her dream she still struggled with the dilemma. Old Dan, like an ogre, haunted her sleep, and when she woke at daybreak she believed her only hope rested in him. She knew that he had laid paralyzed and speechless on his bed ever since the night that Jim had been hurt; but she did not know how close was the connection between his illness and Jim's accident.

"I'll call this afternoon; it is two days since I was there; perhaps they may ask me into the room to see him," she decided, and when she went to Dan's cottage her hope was fulfilled.

"Would you like to see him?" asked Mary, "the doctor thinks he is much better today; the paralysis is passing out of his limbs. He thinks he will soon be able to speak to us." Tears of thankfulness rose in her eyes.

Pen felt very cold-blooded and cruel as she followed the little woman to the sick room. Dan's strong frame had shrunken a good deal, but except for this he seemed pretty much as usual, though a strained look somewhat altered his expression. A slight smile of recognition passed over his face as he saw Pen, but it died away immediately, and was succeeded by a harassed, weary regard.

"Why, Uncle Dan," said Pen, reverting to the old childish title, and trying to speak cheerfully, "you do not look very sick after all. expect you'll soon be about again." Once more the faint smile flickered over the tired face.

Ellie and her mother exchanged pleased glances to see any sign of brightening in the invalid's face, for the doctor had said that morning what Dan needed now was to be roused to take a natural interest in life; the only thing that appeared to retard his recovery was the lack of any effort on his part to rouse himself.

Encouraged by the smiling faces of the two women, Pen chatted for a few minutes, and was rewarded by a happier and less tense look on Dan's face. "I feel sure you have done him good," said Mary. "I thought more than once that he was going to speak. Come soon again, Pen, the very sight of your bright face does him good."

Pen promised, and took her leave, but going home she felt rather conscience-stricken as she remembered her motive for visiting the invalid. "I do feel a wicked hypocrite," she said to herself, "what would they think of me if they had the faintest idea of what I suspect? Well, after all, I do not intend to do them any harm. I am very fond of the three of them. But honestly, I do believe that it is the secret of the gold that is at the bottom of old Dan's seizure, though it seems hard to credit the dear old man with such an awful thing.

There is a great deal more behind Tommy's yarn, of that I am convinced; but I feel just as certain that what he told me is true. This is the burden that is weighing on Dan's conscience, and keeping him from getting better. If only he could throw it off, he would begin to recover. But what can he do while he lies there speechless?

What sad, sad eyes; I never saw such a mournful look! I do not think I'll be brave enough to see him again. I seem torn in two between my pity for him and my love for Jim."

But Pen did go again; scarcely a day passed but she looked in for a minute or two, and with each succeeding visit she became more convinced that Dan was longing, yet dreading, to impart his secret. "I do believe he could speak," was the conclusion Pen came to at last, "but he will not, for he cannot trust himself to hide the truth once he can open his mouth."

The doctor plainly wondered that Dan made no effort to speak, and encouraged Mary and Ellie to use every means in their power to rouse him. "Unless he makes an effort now, he will slip away altogether," he said seriously. "The will has so much to do with recovery in a case of this sort."

THE FURNACE FOR GOLD

CHAPTER XXXVII.

DAN MAKES A CONFESSION

"Pen," said Lew a week later, "what do you say to a ride to the Falls in my dogcart? We could call for Ellie; I think it would do her good." Pen consented willingly, and while she was dressing a daring plan came into her mind.

"I'll get Lew to take both Ellie and her mother for a drive, and I'll propose to stay with Dan. He does not need much attention now and a drive in the open air will be good for his nurses."

On the way to Marlowe's she told Lew her plan, but he was rather dubious. However, when they came there Pen found that Mary was very anxious to see Anne Hetherington, and would be very pleased to drive as far as her place with Lew and Ellie. She would wait there till the two came back from the Falls; then they could pick her up on their way home.

Since Pen so kindly volunteered to look after Dan, Mary and Ellie were delighted to take this chance of a drive.

Dan's dark face lighted up at the sight of his pretty new nurse, while Pen wondered, as she returned the pathetic smile, whether after all her resolution was firm enough for the ordeal before her. However, she determined to screen up her courage to the point now that the opportunity was given her. She had brought with her some needlework, and after seeing to the invalid's wants she sat down by the open window for a few minutes, her brain working as busily as her slim fingers, while Dan's sad eyes dwelt on the pretty picture she made in the sunlight.

"Uncle Dan," said Pen at last, her heart in her mouth. "Can you speak if you care to try?"

There was a strange silence in the room. The frightened girl waited breathlessly for a moment, then rose and came to the bed.

The slow tears were rolling down Dan's face.

"Yes I can speak," he said in a hoarse whisper, "how did you guess?"

"I do not want to hurt you; I wouldn't do it for the world," said Pen, her own tears starting, "but I am sure it would be better for you to tell the truth about the gold stealing than keep it is and let it poison your heart."

"The truth about the gold-stealing," cried Dan in the same broken whisper, but with cruel agitation. "What, what about the gold-stealing? Who knows anything about the gold-stealing? What have I to do with the gold-stealing?"

His excitement was fearful to witness, for the numbness of the paralysis clung to him still, and though it was chained the body so that Dan could not spring from the couch, yet the will to rush away and do himself some bodily harm was expressed so plainly in his working face that Pen was terrified at the result of her work. But she did not lose her presence of mind.

"Now, Uncle Dan," she said quietly, "no one knows about it but me, and you do not think I would wish to hurt you, do you?" She laid her hand firmly on the shaking hands on the coverlet, and, after a few minutes, her calmness communicated itself to Dan, and he lay still, watching her with a pitiful intensity.

"Listen, Uncle Dan, and I'll tell you all I know, and if when I've finished you say to me 'keep my secret for me, even though an innocent man and one whom you love suffer through my silence' I shall do it for you, though my own heart breaks in doing it."

Dan controlled his agitation by an effort, and as the story went on his eyes began to lose their haunted look, and were bent in steady attention on the earnest face of the girl.

"So Jim is suspected; poor Jim," he said in a low husky tone. "Did you say Jim was hurt?"

"Very badly hurt; he is hardly out of danger yet," said Pen.

"They took him for me; I remember now. I fell down there, so queer and sick, and I heard them talking. I got up and poor old Dummy took me home, carried me part of the way, I believe, though it is all like a dream to me now to try to recall what happened that night."

Pen looked at him with shining, anxious eyes and Dan continued.

"You care for Jim don't you? I always knew you were the one girl in the world for him, though I wanted it to be Ellie, for I loved him like a son since I lost poor Johnny. I was hard on him, poor Jim! I don't believe now he meant to harm me; he meant it in good will that day the Governor came, though I wouldn't believe it then. I was hurt with Buxton, you see, my old mate. Yes I know all about the gold; I know where it is, and if only I could see my old mate Billy I'd tell him all about it. I don't believe he'd be hard on me."

The low monologue came with painful gasps and frequent pauses; but as Pen could see that it was really relieving the burdened heart she did not try to check it.

"If only, oh! If only Mr. Buxton would come up now to see Uncle Dan," she thought despairingly. She knew that the millionaire was still in Neummurra, for Lew had spoken of seeing him that morning.

She looked longingly out of the window and as if in response to her unuttered wish Buxton appeared coming up the hill.

She excused herself to Marlowe, and hurried to the verandah; but Buxton had turned to the left, along the path that led to the manager's house. She ran out and gave a faint call. He started at the sound of the girl's voice and came hurriedly towards her.

"I want to speak to you a minute," said Pen eagerly, but with some trepidation of manner. "It is about the gold stealing," she added, and hesitated to continue, as she saw the black look with which he regarded her. "I mean the gold taken from the mine," she said after a pause.

"That is what is keeping me just now in Neummurra," said Buxton, a little surprised, but willing to put the girl at her ease. "I suppose rumours of the affair are all over the township now. I have heard half a dozen versions of it already and they all agree that poor

THE FURNACE FOR GOLD

young Hetherington is the chief criminal. I find it hard to believe that I could be so mistaken in a man."

"He is innocent," said Pen quietly. "Dan Marlowe has the gold," and she briefly explained the situation.

"Dan take the gold!" he gasped. "Old Dan Marlowe turn thief! There is some hideous mistake somewhere! I'd stake my life on Dan's honesty. You must be dreaming, surely. I called this morning and he was still speechless," he cried, incredulously, remembering how recently he had seen Marlowe, and that he had not spoken then.

"He has regained his speech," said Pen, "and he now longing to see you and confess the truth. I am sure he cannot rest till he has unburdened his mind. He is in a state of such excitement that it would harm him more to be thrown back on himself than to tell the whole story to you. Mrs. Marlowe and Ellie have gone out for a drive with my brother, and I am left in charge. Please go in and see him."

Buxton regarded her steadily, unbelief still in his penetrating glance.

"He has regained his speech, you say; but do you mean to tell me he has confessed to you that he actually stole the gold?"

Pen nodded. "Yes, it seems hard to credit it, but come in and hear for yourself."

Buxton, still in a state of astonishment, followed her into the sick room. "Here is Mr. Buxton, Uncle Dan; he has come up to see you again, but you must not talk too long," said Pen and left the old mates together.

The time seemed long to her as she waited in the next room, but it was scarcely half an hour later when Buxton appeared at the door.

"He is fast asleep now, poor old chap," he said softly. "Come round to the other side of the house, I want to speak to you."

"You are quite right," he said as they made their way to the back verandah. "Incredible as it seemed, and hard as I find it yet to believe, old Dan really did take the gold."

In the millionaire's piercing eyes the usual sternness had given place to a pitying sorrow. He was visibly moved and shaken.

"Poor old Dan," he said scarcely conscious of the girl's presence. "It all began out of jealousy because he thought that I slighted him. In the old days it was share and share alike between us. Dan, it seems, was always sore that when I was let into the Neummurra mine I did not take him in with me. But I had lost sight of him for years, and it was a sheer piece of luck that I happened to run against him in Sydney, back at his old work of clerking. I honestly thought that I did well by him when I got him on at the works and helped him up the ladder there. For to tell the truth, though Dan was a good clerk he was cut out for nothing else. I don't say it to boast, but if Dan had had my chance he could not have made anything of it. I got my first start by the Neummurra mine, I'll admit, but I've had many an iron in the fire since then. But I had no idea until now that Dan felt I had not done the square thing by him." There was a droop in the broad shoulders; honest regret in the strong face.

"I think you have been very good to him; it is not every man who would do so much for an old mate," Pen ventured to say.

Buxton smiled at the earnest young face. "That is not bush creed," he said lightly, "never desert your mate, for better or worse, for richer or poorer, you know. It is as binding you see, as the marriage tie."

"I don't think many men act up to that creed, then," said Pen stoutly.

"I do not know, old Dan would, I believe," said Buxton gravely. "At any rate, he feels I have not quite played fair with him in the game. Then, again, he expected to become manager when Dundas left, but I was away in England at the time, so the directors appointed Carson. Candidly, I was glad to be away, for I guessed Dan hoped to get the position, and I knew he was not the man to suit us. A manager of a mine like this needs to have a thoroughly scientific education, and Dan has only the rule-of-thumb knowledge of the business that he has managed to acquire in the time he has been at the works."

Pen listened in silence. She could not but appreciate the compliment that Buxton paid her in thus speaking so freely to a mere girl on the matter, but she felt diffident in replying.

"However," he continued, "we must not lose time by talking now, for the others may be back and I want to take away the stolen gold with me."

"Is it here?" cried Pen.

"Yes; didn't he tell you that. It is buried in the garden. We shall dig it up and compound a felony. I take it that your ideas and mine agree on this subject. You want to clear young Hetherington's name, and yet save my poor old mate from the consequences of his crime. I am supposed to be rather an unscrupulous man, you know, but here is a case where I do feel inclined to take the law in my own hands. Do you agree with me?"

"Yes," Pen whispered, with downcast eyes, and Buxton said quickly. "Is there such a thing as a spade?" Pen found one and brought it to him.

"Just by a young mulberry tree. Dan told me. Here goes for the buried treasure," he said gaily.

In spite of her anxiety, Pen could not resist the contagion of his cheerfulness and began to smile too.

"I feel as if I were a boy again, going to act out my day-dream of discovering a buccaneer's hoard." He gave a short laugh. "What would the gossips of Neummurra not give to get a peep over the fence at us."

Pen glanced apprehensively over her shoulder but there was no one in sight, and the thick scrub hid the paddock from the township.

The spade rang sharply on metal, and in a few minutes the box was lifted out. It was locked and Buxton, carrying it into the kitchen, produced a bundle of keys, which Dan had instructed him to take from a drawer. After some little difficulty the box was unlocked.

The millionaire gave a low whistle,

THE FURNACE FOR GOLD

and beckoned Pen to look.

The girl drew her breath sharply, and bent over the glittering mass.

"It is all true then," said Buxton. "I could scarcely believe it after all. Poor Dan, and poor Jim Hetherington, too; they have both paid dearly for this gold."

Pen drew back hastily. "Take it away," she said, "I cannot bear to look at it."

"Yes, I mean to take it with me. Do you think you could get me a small portmanteau to put it in? It would be less likely to attract prying eyes than if I carried the box away with me."

Pen left the room, and soon returned with an old portmanteau. "There, at last I've got it safe. The only thing now will be to decide what we had better do, so as to attain all the ends we desire, return the gold, clear Jim Hetherington's name and shield our poor, misguided Dan."

Pen looked at him eagerly and he went on.

"It's a ticklish job, but I think we are equal to it. You see, we must not lose any time, though now I've got the gold, we are all right, even if Mrs. Marlowe returns."

"I cannot understand how Dan could take the gold at all" Pen said, after waiting a few minutes for Buxton to propose some plan.

"Oh I can," he said slowly, it was partly to revenge himself against me for a fancied slight, and partly it was jealousy of Jim Hetherington though I feel certain this illness had a great deal to do with poor Dan's state of mind. That is why I feel justified in hiding his fault. The man was not quite responsible at the time, and more than that, from what he says I am inclined to believe that it was almost a case of hypnotism."

"Of hypnotism," echoed Pen in surprise.

"It sounds foolish perhaps," admitted Buxton, "but yet I think that one of the men (Dan did not give his name) who helped in the theft was the prime mover in the affair, and, in fact, Dan seems to have been little more than a tool in the hands of the clever rascal, who first induced him to take the gold when he was half mad with jealousy and stupid with drink. The pity is, the other thieves will have to go scot free if we let Dan off. But I believe they have cleared out of Neummurra some time ago. I heard that quite a number left the mine when they heard a detective was among them; anyway, I'll get the names from Dan and find out. I'll tell him that they are not to be punished, much against the grain as that promise will be to me."

"Yes, I heard about some men leaving Neummurra," said Pen; "but what surprises me is that if that man you speak of was clever he did not manage to secure the gold."

"That's where the joke comes in," Buxton said, with his hearty laugh. "Dan kept the gold himself, and all the other thieves had for their share was the sight of a memorandum of the stolen gold. It was that very paper that brought me past this afternoon. Carson gave it to me yesterday, along with a letter from Hetherington, and asked me to express my opinion as to whether or not he had written it. I was on my way to see him when you called me in. The man Michael, the detective, cleared out after getting some money out of Carson, almost as soon as the rumour that Hetherington's injury was not due to an accident went about the township. I fancy some of the miners threatened to lynch him and he was scared into flight. I believe he was a mere fraud anyway; for a detective he was a poor specimen. As things turned out, I am glad he has gone, for it simplifies our work. Here is the paper. Have you ever seen any of young Hetherington's writing?"

The hot colour rushed up the girl's face as she took the paper from him.

"It is his writing. No, it is not after all. It looks very like it but there are differences. What a beautiful clear hand! I suppose you know that Uncle Dan used to pride himself on having formed Jim's handwriting into so close a copy of his own. You know Jim was like a son in Dan's house till he went to the University."

"No; but I confess the resemblance of the handwriting is close enough to have made me feel very doubtful about Hetherington, until of course I heard Dan's story."

"Dan told you about the paper, and how Jim obtained it."

"Yes," said Pen, "I think I understand it all now, but I scarcely see how you will be able to put things straight again. They look hopelessly crooked to me. How can you clear one without implicating the other? Mary and Ellie will never forgive me when they know it was I who made poor Dan incriminate himself."

"Nonsense!" said Buxton sharply, "why need they know about it? Why need anyone know, except, of course, I will have to explain a little to the manager? But I think I can contrive with his help, to get the gold returned and no one else need by any the wiser. Anyhow, I'll have a good try for it. If the thieves have fled and the detective is out of the way, it will not be difficult to satisfy Carson, especially when he finds that the gold tallies with the paper, and I suppose it does, for Dan is an exact creature."

"Oh, if you could only manage to do it," sighed Pen.

"Trust me for it, I'll do my best, I can promise. It shall be our secret. I'll square everybody all round," he laughed, and turned to go, but stopped at the top of the steps.

"If it comes to that, no one has suffered but Dan and Jim," he said. "I'll do my best to make up to the young man for what he has suffered, and perhaps you will, too." He glanced up quickly, but Pen did not meet his eyes. "As for Dan, now that he has unburdened his conscience of its load you will see that he will soon get better, and though I do not think he will ever be able to take up his position of boss again, even if he wished to, still I think I shall be able to find him something light and easy for him to do that will keep him employed and happy for a many a good year to come. Another thing, there is that poor fellow, Dummy.

THE FURNACE FOR GOLD

Fancy that frail-looking creature dragging a man of Dan's bulk up the hill. There were tears in Dan's eyes as he spoke. "I'd like to do a little something for him, there must be something fine about him, uncouth as he looks. What do you think of settling a small annuity on him? Enough to make him comfortable and above want for the rest of his days? I'll see about it immediately. And young Tommy, too. I'll see what I can do for him, eh, Miss Pen?"

He held out his hand and Pen took it. She lifted her swimming eyes to the strong face above her.

"I think you are splendid," she burst out. "I think you are the noblest man I ever met."

Buxton laughed heartily. "You should hear what the stockbrokers say of me. 'hard as nails, mean as chow.' Are about the mildest terms they apply to me, I believe."

"I do not care," said Pen, a smile glimmering through her tears. "I know what you really are and I'll never forget how good you were today."

For an instant the firm lips quivered, the sharp eyes softened, but the next moment, the man recovered himself.

"I'll be off with my buccaneer's treasure," he said with a smile, "and meantime I think you had better take up your character of nurse again, in case Mrs. Marlowe and Ellie return and find us plotting like a pair of conspirators, as we really are."

Pen could scarcely return the smile, and it was with a very moved face that she watched the stout, heavy figure walking steadily down the hill. "I don't wonder now," she said to herself, as she returned to the sick room, "that Dan was jealous of his old mate's affections, or that the miners all adore 'King Billy' as they call him."

CHAPTER XXXVIII.

COMPOUNDING A FELONY

The afternoon was close and sultry, the bag was heavy, and the millionaire was hot and tired when he reached his hotel.

He locked away the gold, and wiping his heated face, sat down to consider the situation.

Pen's impetuous, warm-hearted speech recurred to him, and though he smiled with a little sardonic self-amusement, for he had no allusions about himself, yet his thoughts of Pen were tender and kindly.

"I like that girl," he thought, "she is honest and sincere. I'd be pleased to do her a good turn. She received my proposal in a quiet, sensible way, none of the absurd fuss some women delight in. I admire her pluck in sticking to young Hetherington when he is down on his luck. It won't be my fault when he gets better if the company does not realize his value properly. He would do well as boss of the Lower Works in poor Dan's place, and that in itself would be sufficient to silence the rumours now flying about Neummurra. Then in course of time, probably, he will have the manager's billet offered to him.

So far so good; now let me see how I shall set about straightening the rest of the crooked state of affairs, as I promised."

He lit his pipe, and took a seat on the wide verandah overlooking the creek.

Buxton's nature was a strange one; it was no wonder he was so often misunderstood and misrepresented. He was, as he said himself, 'hard as nails'. He worked strenuously, but believed in getting his full pay in money. He could be at times unscrupulous and relentless for he had his own private code of ethics, yet to his friends he was kind and devoted, with a ready impulse to help where help was needed.

"A good friend, a bad enemy", in the common phrase, applied well to him; for if he spared no pains to help his friends he pursued with the same eagerness, and with a vindictive pleasure in injuring those who were unfortunate enough to rouse his enmity.

But his mental poise was so complete that it was seldom disturbed by passion or irritation. With his talents he might have been, might have done anything. He chose to make money, and he became a millionaire. But with all his faults, he was absolutely loyal, and in his own way straight-dealing. He honestly considered his way of managing affairs in this crisis to be not only the most expedient but to be amply justified by the situation.

The sun had set as he rose from his reflections.

"I'll go up to Carson," he decided, "and disabuse his mind of the idea that Hetherington stole the gold. I suppose I had better take him into my confidence to a certain extent if I find I can rely on him. Now the detective is gone there should not be much difficulty in fixing up the matter. Once the gold is put back in the furnace no one is a penny the worse, except poor old Dan and Jim Hetherington. I do not see that any good purpose would be served by letting the truth come out; but the question is, can I persuade Carson to agree with me? He is a bit of a stickler for what he calls principle, but I'll go up and try my persuasive powers on him."

The manager was not at home when he reached his house, but Buxton agreed to wait for his return. Mrs. Carson and Clara were delightedly surprised to find him in a complaisant mood, so much more agreeable than usual.

Mrs. Carson's faded face brightened as she observed the interest he seemed to take in Clara's conversation; and visions of a millionaire son-in-law flashed before here eyes.

Clara had been very dull and quiet of late, her pretty colour had fled, she seemed curiously depressed, and though Mrs. Carson was an ambitious woman, she was an affectionate mother. She had been afraid that Clara was more than a little interested in the unfortunate young man Hetherington, and she attributed her pale looks to concern on his behalf. She had not dared to speak openly on the subject for Clara was a difficult girl to deal with, but she had quietly endeavoured to provide

THE FURNACE FOR GOLD

distractions that might rouse the girl from her painful depression.

Several times she got her husband to bring up to dinner, Neddrie, the bank manager, whom she fancied was inclined to pay attentions to Clara. But Buxton as a possible husband was still more to be encouraged, and she smiled to think that her daughter had her fair share of worldly ambition, in spite of her transient aberration.

Perhaps Clara appreciated Buxton's exceptional amiability at its due value, but all her gushing animation was gone.

Since she had placed the paper in poor Jim's unconscious hand she had never ceased to regret it. Though frivolous, selfish and insincere, Clara was not utterly callous, and in punishing the man she loved she had punished herself. She wished in vain that she had destroyed the wretched paper, even though her jealous anger was as hot as ever against her rival Pen. So to her mother's secret chagrin she responded but lifelessly to Buxton's affability, and it was with relief that she saw her father returning.

"Brought back the paper, I suppose," Carson said, after asking Buxton to accompany him to the office. "Sad thing altogether; I am sorry for Hetherington's father and mother. I heard this afternoon that he was worse again."

The sudden whitening of the girl's face struck Buxton as he rose to follow her father.

"I believe she cares for him, too," he thought, "poor girl, I am sorry for her."

The two men talked long and earnestly. Buxton needed all his tact to obtain the manager's consent to hush up the matter, but at last he succeeded, though as he reflected afterwards he had never worked harder in his life.

"After this," he said grimly to himself, "I think I'll take to politics. I could never have a more trying time disposing of a 'no-confidence-vote-constituency' than I had in overcoming Carson's prepossession in favour of law and order and the due punishment of a criminal as a matter of principle."

"You'll keep this matter strictly to yourself, Carson," he said, as he rose to go, "excuse me saying it, I am not a married man you know, but I should not like it to reach even your wife."

"You have my promise," said Carson stiffly, "you can rely on it."

"I'll not forget this Carson," said Buxton, heartily. "You will not have cause to regret obliging me in this thing. You see, I feel myself to blame somewhat. Besides, man, your silence will harm no one, the gold is safe, the company will not suffer, so you see that it is the best and wisest policy to hush up the whole affair."

"So you say," returned the manager, dryly, "you have my promise, we need say no more. But I want to be satisfied that the gold we receive tallies with the memorandum, that is all."

"You may rest assured on that matter," said Buxton; "if not, I'll undertake to make it good, but I have no fears on that score."

They shook hands, and Buxton left the house.

"Now just to make sure that the men

who helped to steal the gold have left Neummurra," thought Buxton, "I'll have to see Dan, and find out who they are. It will not do to have them here, one of them might think of trying blackmail. If he thought there was any chance of getting it. I'll call round at Morgan's tomorrow and let Pen know of my success. Then when I've put things square all round, I'll be off for a trip to England to give my young rival a fair field with the fair lady. A year hence I'll come back to Neummurra, and if pretty Pen is not 'Mrs. Jim' by then, I'll cut in a second time and try my luck. If she is, I expect I'll get over it. I agree with Thackeray that the malady is never fatal to a sound organ. Mine is fairly sound, and a tough old organ, too, into the bargain."

Buxton found, as he expected, that the three men had disappeared and that there was no need to fear on that score.

It may be said here that the millionaire who seldom promised what he was unable to perform, had the pleasure of seeing his promises kept to the letter, as far as covering all traces of the theft of the gold was concerned. Carson kept his word; not even to his wife did he breathe a hint of Marlowe's guilt, though he made a point of making public on all occasions his firm belief in Jim's honesty while he laughed away as preposterous any hint of gold-stealing.

In fact, the story of the gold-stealing soon died away, until few were found who believed it to be more than an absurd fabrication, an idle tale got up by some sensation-monger.

Those who were the most positive in their conviction of Jim's crime were then the most ardent in attesting their unswerving faith in his integrity.

CHAPTER XXXIX.

PEN'S PERPLEXITY

For an hour after Buxton left her Pen sat watching Marlowe. The sleeping face was very quiet and peaceful; but it was, Pen felt, the face of an old man.

It was hard to believe that but three years separated the ages of the two friends, for Buxton's strong, active figure and alert, clever, fresh-coloured face were those of a man in the meridian of his powers; while poor Dan seemed but a worn out veteran as he lay there helpless and broken down before his time.

Then her thoughts wandered to another sick bed, but Anne's face seemed to rise vindictively before her, Anne's sharp voice seemed to say:

"You have no lot nor part with us in our sorrow. You gave him up, and chose another. Abide by your choice now. We do not want even your sympathy. What is it but mockery in our grief?"

Anne had never said this in actual words but Pen read that message in her cousin's eyes whenever she had ventured to call at the cottage. Anne had never liked her, and now Pen felt that she hated her – that she almost attributed this accident in some mysterious way to her influence. Everyone else was welcome to call and

THE FURNACE FOR GOLD

make inquiries; Daphne was treated as a daughter; but as soon as Pen appeared Anne stiffened into a coldness that frightened her away.

In the old days Pen had been wont to laugh saucily at Anne's dislike, but now her daring seemed to have departed altogether, and sooner than face her cousin's ill-concealed aversion she gave up all attempts to visit the cottage, and contented herself with what she could learn from her father or brother.

Now and then, as often as she could be spared, Daphne ran up to see her, for Daphne knew how unhappy her sister was; but Anne seemed sometimes to put difficulties in the way that would prevent Daphne from visiting her home.

Pen wondered, as she watched Marlowe's sleeping face, whether Daphne guessed that it was she for whom Lynne cared. There was no soreness in Pen's mind now that her sister should have been chosen before her; all her small pettiness, her little vanities, seemed swallowed up in this great sorrow that had come to her. Her nature grew in the stern discipline of that time of suspense.

"I believe Daphne loves him" she thought, "and I know he loves her, not as he cared for me – that was an idle fancy; but this is real love, and I feel sure that some day he will tell her so, and that they will both be happy. Daphne is a far better girl than I am; her character is a far higher one. I do not wonder Lynne loved her more than he could ever care for a silly girl like me."

The Pen, whose thoughts beside old Dan's sick bed were so humble, was indeed a different girl from the willful Pen who had dragged Daphne down the hill to listen to the committee meeting at the Oddfellows' Hall. It seemed to her that she could never laugh and make merry as she had done once, with the egotism of youth she brooded sadly over her changed feelings, and wondered whether indeed she had deserved so harsh a lesson from life. In her new found humility she lost her old assured self-confidence, and as she kept her watch many doubts came crowding into her mind. Suppose Jim Hetherington no longer cared for her, suppose the long trial of his love had worn it away or that her engagement to Lynne had killed it; or suppose, worst of all that she had been deceiving herself all these years into believing that the shy student, the quiet worker, had been her true lover, when he thought of her but as a friend. No words of love had ever passed between them, since they were boy and girl together, and Pen felt miserably that, in her vanity, she might have mistaken the message that his kind eyes seemed to have for her. She had believed that Lynne loved her, and, grieved at the thought of inflicting pain on him; and behold he was glad to be released from his engagement, frankly confessing that he loved Daphne.

Suppose Jim also cared for Daphne, suppose he had come to love his gentle nurse, with her sweet dignity, her gracious tender beauty, ever before his eyes; but at this point Pen sprang to her feet. She could not pursue the train of thought any further. That way lay the madness of jealousy. She would not stain her love for her sister by allowing that terrible thought to dwell in her mind.

The sound of wheels caught her ears, and with a glad sense of relief she rose to leave the room.

Lew had brought the dogcart to the gate, and was helping Ellie out as Pen came up.

There was something in Lew's face as he carefully lifted Ellie to the ground that struck his sister. The scales fell from her eyes on that instant. She could not mistake the look her brother gave to little Ellie.

"Oh, is that it?" she said mentally. "How blind we have all been! Yet who would have thought that Lew, matter-of-fact Lew, who prides himself on his lack of sentiment, could actually be in love, like any ordinary boy! I wonder if Ellie cares at all for him?" With a woman's subtle instinct Pen had guessed that Ellie was fond of Jim Hetherington, and had often noticed in the past the slight coldness in the girl's manner towards her that she believed due to the natural jealousy of a rival.

"Lew is such a persistent, dogged fellow when he takes a thing in hand," went on Pen's private reflections, "that I shall not be surprised if he wins her in the end. In fact, I am sure she will not be able to resist Lew when he really shows her that he loves her. She would have a nice, kind husband – not to speak of a pair of charming sisters-in-law." In her pleasure over the secret she had surprised, Pen's natural vivacity began to assert itself, and she ran up happily to the group.

"Uncle Dan is sleeping nicely now, but do you know he was speaking to me," she said, as Lew waited for a minute before driving away. "Mr. Buxton called, and he spoke to him to. He seems ever so much better." Her voice had the old buoyant ring in its merry tones.

Ellie and Mrs. Marlowe ran excitedly into the house after hearing Pen's remark.

"How is Jim?" Pen asked, as Lew gathered up the reins. Lew hesitated, and fidgeted in his seat.

"Not quite so well," he jerked out, and prepared to depart, but Pen laid her hand on the reins.

"Tell me at once," she said imperatively, "has the doctor given up hope?"

"Of course not," said Lew sharply, "but he has had a return of the fever, and Anne is in a great state over it. She says he is so much weaker now, he has less chance."

"What brought on the fever?" asked Pen, in a low tone. "Did he happen to hear any word of the gold stealing or anything like that?"

"No, I think perhaps it has been brought on by the hot weather; most likely his temperature will be down in the morning. Perhaps you might take a run over there, and offer to help them. Daphne and Cousin Anne look a bit pulled down, both of them. Father and I would be all right with Gwenny to look after things."

"Anne wouldn't have me. I asked

THE FURNACE FOR GOLD

her before. She can't bear me, Lew." Pen's soft lips quivered, and she turned away lest Lew should see the tears were in her eyes.

Lew looked at her uncertainly, but dared not express the sympathy he was feeling so keenly.

"You had better come home with me, then," he said after an uncomfortable pause. "It is a good walk on such a hot afternoon."

"Yes, I'll just run in and tell them I am going home. It is a great deal too hot to walk," said Pen, in her ordinary tone. When she returned her eyes were free from any suspicion of moisture and she hoped that Lew had noticed nothing unusual in her manner.

CHAPTER XL.

HEARTS IN THE FURNACE

It was no wonder that Lew found Anne Hetherington in a state of great distress and alarm. After making steady progress towards recovery, Jim had suddenly taken a turn for the worse, and Anne believe she knew to what it was owing. When Dr Mackay came in the morning he was delighted with the aspect of his patient.

"Ah, young man," he said, in his hearty way, "I can see you are getting tired of me; you are making such haste to get out of my hands."

Jim gave a weak laugh, and looked meaningly at Anne. "Ask mother if she is getting tired of nursing me," he said.

Anne's only reply was a smile, and the doctor continued his dressing with unabated cheerfulness.

He was fond of a chat, Dr Mackay, and though he would indignantly have denied it he was one of the most inveterate, though most kindly, gossips in Neummurra.

"You will soon be up and about again, making more havoc than ever in the girls' hearts. By-the-bye that reminds me. I expect you have heard that pretty Miss Pen Morgan has given the manager's son what our American friends would call the 'mitten'."

"What is that you are saying, doctor?" asked Jim, quickly, and Dr Mackay replied.

"Oh, just a little bit of town talk, my boy, that Pen Morgan has broken off her engagement with Lynne Carson. I expect it is no news to you." He glanced at Anne, who returned a blank, expressionless stare, as she said, coldly:

"Of course we know it. Pen is my cousin; but I can't say I think much of her – a fickly, flighty girl, that is what Pen Morgan is."

The doctor felt that his well-meaning effort to be entertaining was not received with good grace but Pen was one of his favorites, and he could not listen in silence to a detraction of her.

"I think you are rather hard on her, Mrs. Hetherington. Pen is perhaps a little spoilt and willful, as is natural enough in such a young beauty as our Rose of Neummurra; but she is sweet and true and natural, for all that."

"I am glad you think so," said Anne, in her most forbidding tone; and being anything but obtuse, Dr Mackay saw that his defence of Pen had not increased Anne's affection for her, but rather the reverse.

Daphne came into the room and the doctor took his departure. It was Daphne's turn for nursing just then, and Anne went to her own room to try to get some sleep, though in her disturbed state of mind she felt doubtful of securing any. The doctor's words had upset her. John had gone to the store, cheered by the doctor's encouraging report.

Two hours passed by and Jim seemed to be sleeping, so Daphne took some sewing and sat by the open window, keeping an eye on Jim while her busy fingers flew over her work. Suddenly she heard her name:

"Daphne, Daphne, come here," said Jim in a hollow voice, and the girl hurried to him.

"Is it true that Pen has broken off her engagement with Lynne?" he asked and Daphne saw with alarm, that a feverish flush tinged his thin cheeks, and that his eyes were unnaturally bright.

"Yes, Jim," she said soothingly, "Pen found out that she did not care enough for him, so she told him so, and they agreed to part friends. Now go to sleep again, or Cousin Anne will scold me, and say I am a bad nurse." Jim put out a weak hand, and caught the fingers that were smoothing his pillow.

"Daph, mother does not like Pen," he whispered.

"Nonsense," cried Daphne, briskly, "That is just a fancy of yours, but don't worry over anything now, wait till you are strong and well. Go to sleep again Jim, or you really will get me into a scolding, you know."

Jim moved his bandaged head restlessly. "I was not asleep," he muttered, but Daphne did not hear him. The hand that held hers was burning with heat, and the girl's heart sank with fear as she noted the signs of a growing fever.

Anne woke up just after midday and as soon as she saw her son she sent Tommy off for the doctor.

Dr Mackay quickly followed the messenger, and was shocked to find so great a change in so short a time. He had grown very fond of his patient; it was impossible, indeed, for most people to be brought into contact with poor Jim without becoming attached to him.

"Why, how comes this, Mrs. Hetherington?" he said sharply. "He was quite normal this morning and I find him running a temperature now."

Anne looked at him in anxious silence. "Has anyone been in here talking to him? Can any of the absurd rumours that are going about the township have reached him?" he asked, with intense irritation in his voice.

"No one has been here except yourself," Anne could not resist saying meaningly. But the innuendo passed harmlessly over the doctor's head.

"It is strange, very strange," he said testily. "Well we must just go back to our earlier treatment, and try to reduce the fever. He is so much weaker than he was at first that we must be very careful, very careful indeed. He seems inclined to be a bit light-headed, I see,

THE FURNACE FOR GOLD

but you must not let that alarm you."

He went over to Jim again and took his hot hand in his firm, strong clasp.

"Now, Jim," he said cheerfully, "you know I think a great deal of you, so you must try to live up to my good opinion, and keep yourself quiet and cool."

Jim smiled in answer, "You are very good to me, I know, doctor, and if you could only whistle for a breeze I'd soon be cool again. I am roasting now, but you can't help the day, can you?"

"I wish I could," said the doctor, rising to go. But Jim still kept hold of his hand, and as he bent over him said in a low tone. "Thank you for what you said, doctor. Tell mother not to be too hard on her. She knows I never went against her yet."

The words conveyed no sense to Dr Mackay. He fancied the young fellow was wandering; but before taking his leave he spoke to Anne privately.

"You must humour him in anything he wants, Mrs. Hetherington, for any opposition or irritation in his present state of health might be fatal. Agree with anything he says, no matter how absurd it may seem, but do not encourage him to talk. If he could only get some quiet natural sleep it would be the saving of him, but I wish to avoid giving him drugs for the sake of his head. But if he cannot get sleep naturally I must employ morphia, though I am loathe to use it."

Anne's sallow face looked drawn and haggard, as she promised to see that the doctor's directions were implicitly followed.

"I'm just going on my rounds. I'll give you a look in as I come back. I may be detained, but don't get anxious. I believe he will pull through all right. He has got youth and a good constitution on his side, and that is half the battle."

Anne returned to the sickroom, and sat down to watch in a dazed, despondent condition. She had grown so confident about Jim's recovery that this sudden relapse shattered all her hopes.

Bye and bye Daphne came in to tell her that Mrs. Marlowe and Ellie wished to see her.

Anne went out and spoken to them for a few minutes in an anxious, distrait manner, then returned to her post.

Jim's words, spoken in the delirium of the first fever, with wearisome iteration the phrase beat upon her brain, "the furnace for gold, the furnace for gold." They were all in the furnace, poor Jim had declared, Lynne, Pen, Marlowe, Clara and herself. In the anguish of her heart Anne acknowledged that she was indeed passing through the fire of suffering. But she did not know how truly the wandering words applied to the others as well. To each of them in this last month had come a strange testing of character. They had entered, as each one does once or twice in his lifetime, into the Valley of Decision, and the furnace fires had passed over them; they could never be again quite the same. For weal or for woe the mark of the furnace fire is ineffaceable on the human heart.

CHAPTER XLI.

PURE GOLD FROM THE FURNACE

The sun set, and Anne still kept her watch. John came in, his florid face flecked with patches of white, his tall figure looking strangely bowed and shrunken, but Anne scarcely noticed his entrance. Her whole being seemed bound up in her son, and though she answered John's questions mechanically, and listened patiently to what he had to say, she was relieved when Daphne coaxed him from the room.

In the growing dusk she could scarcely see the restless, tossing head on the pillow, but she forbore to light the lamp, hoping that in the coolness and darkness of the coming night, after the hot, sultry day, Jim might drop asleep.

As she stooped over him, the old murmur of "Pen! Pen" and her anger rose hotly against the girl who she felt was responsible for this relapse.

The doctor came in, and she lit the lamp. His face was grave, and though he tried to hide it, Anne saw that he augured the worst.

"No, not quite so well as I hoped. He is wandering a little again, I see, though he is not unconscious," he said in answer to the wordless appeal of the father and mother, for John had followed him into the room. "But he may drop into a doze, and that will mean all the difference in the world. I'll look in again, in an hour or so. Keep up your courage, I believe he may take a turn before midnight. There is a strange apathy upon him in spite of the fever, that I cannot quite understand. I'd like to see him making a better fight of it, a little more of a man's natural struggle against death would mean so much at this point."

Daphne was beside them as the doctor ceased speaking. Her face looked almost as colourless as her white dress. "Now, now, Daphne, none of this! I can't have you look so hopeless. Pluck up your courage, we are going to have a hard fight, and perhaps a long fight, but, please God, we shall win through yet."

Silently the three echoed the doctor's words as they watched him get into his dogcart and drive away. Their courage seemed to depart with the last sound of the wheels on the high road.

Anne motioned the others to remain outside while she crept noiselessly into the sick room.

Jim looked up at her entrance. "Is that you, mother?" he said in a natural tone.

"Yes, James," said Anne, "do you want anything I can get for you?" She took his hot hand in hers.

The young fellow turned his feverish eyes upon her, bright with a strange unearthly brilliancy against the white bandages that covered his bruised head. The thin fingers closed on hers.

"I want Pen, mother; I want Pen," he said, almost as simply as he had proffered a request in his childhood, and he looked as trustfully into her face.

"She is free now; tell her I want her."

Anne did not reply, and he turned dully away. The next moment he was wandering again; the fleeting moment of reason had fled.

Anne did not reply, because she could not. She felt unable, even in that terrible moment, to conquer the prejudices of years.

Could she humble her pride now, and ask Pen to come to Jim in his disgrace, when she had scorned him in happier times? Could she even bring herself to acknowledge that she had failed, that in the last dire extremity she was nothing to him and Pen was all? No, it seemed more than her stubborn pride could suffer.

She sank on her knees at the bedside, and fought out the battle there; and love, perfect mother love, at last cast out jealousy; the hard-fought victory was won.

With one glance at Jim's flushed face, she brought Daphne in to take her place, and briefly explained her errand to her husband she went out into the darkness.

The door of the little dining-room was open and as Anne stood on the threshold she saw that Pen was alone.

Even in the tumult of Anne's grief and impatience the girl's beauty struck her afresh with the force of a blow. It was no mere beauty of vivid colouring, for the pretty face was almost as pale as Daphne's; but as she sat there, with the lamplight playing on her dark hair and over her sweet, sad face, with all the brightness of her old vivacity, and the bewildering play of her dimples vanished, Anne at last did tardy homage to Pen's loveliness.

She advanced into the room, and Pen sprang to her feet.

For an instant the two women looked at each other doubtfully, questioningly, then Anne threw open her arms, Pen ran into them, and as they mingled their tears together, the foolish jealousy and bitter animosity of the past was washed away forever.

"James wants you," was all that Anne said, and Pen did not put her answer into words at all, but, taking Anne's arm, she suffered herself to be led away.

Daphne met them at the door of the sick room. "He is conscious again, and is asking for you," she said to Anne.

"Come, Pen," said Anne gently, and with a somewhat terrified look in her dark eyes Pen followed her.

The bandaged head and the hollow cheeks filled her with horror, but when Jim's blue eyes met hers in joyful surprise she forgot everything else as she sank on her knees beside him.

"Jim," she cried, "oh Jim!" and she took the thin, weak hands in her warm, loving clasp.

"Oh Pen," Jim's voice broke into a sob, "I wanted you. I wanted you all the time."

He had no questions to ask, no promises to give or to receive. Pen had come to him; nothing else in the world mattered.

While his strong young will held control, Jim had borne his sufferings in silence. He had never given a hint through all those trying months how much Pen's engagement to Lynne had cost him. But now, in his utter weakness, he gave up the struggle. He was quiet conscious, but felt strangely passively content. Between Pen and him at this moment of reunion, in the shadow of death, there was no need for words; they understood each other and were satisfied.

He drew the pretty, dark head down, till it rested beside the bandaged head on the pillow, then his restless eyes closed, as if the weight of sudden happiness bore down the heavy eyelids, and the next moment, as his quiet breathing told Pen that he had fallen asleep, her heart swelled with a rapture of thanksgiving. Life, not death, was in that gracious slumber. She dared not move, though she grew cramped in her kneeling position, and at length she heard the doctor's firm, quiet step behind her.

She flushed rosily, as the merry, twinkling eyes met hers, but at Anne's whispered warning she kept her place.

"The fever is going down," said Dr Mackay, in a low tone, but with intense satisfaction, "this quiet, natural sleep will be his salvation. Don't move if you value his life, Miss Pen, till I set you free," then with his strong, firm hands, he gently unclosed Jim's weak fingers and drew Pen from the room. "There now, he is so sound asleep that he did not even notice that I had taken you away from him." Then he turned to Anne. "So you found better medicine for your son that I have in my whole pharmacopaeia. I expect you will be taking out your diploma shortly."

"You were always one for your joke, doctor," said Anne, with a smile. She could smile now, and John asked eagerly.

"So you think he is on the mend, doctor?" "I don't think it, I feel sure of it," said Dr Mackay, "and I'm deuced glad to be able to say it." The two men shook hands heartily, with frank goodwill and gratification.

"Goodbye Miss Pen. I am jealous of you for you've proved yourself a better doctor than I. I think I am jealous of Jim, there, too, lucky dog! With three ladies to nurse him. Two pretty young girls, and a devoted mamma. Look at me, a poor, old, cantankerous bachelor. I think I'll ask Miss Daphne to have me, since you have deserted me, though you know you promised to be my wife when you were a little tot, in pinafores."

Pen did not answer, but one of her old dimples sprang rebelliously into her pretty flushed face, and her eyes flashed back a shy defiance.

"All the same," Dr Mackay said to himself, "I thought it was Daphne. She seemed so fond of him. I am afraid this will be a bit of a blow to her."

But as he went down the steps, he caught a glimpse of Daphne's radiantly blissful face, and the good old man felt obliged to give up his theory.

"Well! Well!" he muttered to his horse. "They are a sweet, pretty pair of girls, the rose and the lily of Neummurra. He is a lucky man who gets either of them;" and he drove off through the warm stillness of the night to his lonely home.

THE FURNACE FOR GOLD

He passed with unseeing eyes the red glow from the furnace sheds, and the pale, spectre, mysterious-looking, smoke clouds that issued from the tall, chlorination chimneys. But as the hoarse scream of the hooter tore through the air, he noted how instantly the hill-side became dotted with the twinkling lanterns of the men who were changing shifts, and it seemed to him (for the doctor had a vein of poetry in his nature, the concomitant of his Celtic blood) that these gleaming lights were faintly and fitfully flashing up to the quiet stars above them, a message from the toilers in the earth planet – the star of love and labour.

Dr Mackay drove on, and his kind heart melted as he recalled the pretty picture he had seen in the sick room; the two young faces, so close together, the girl's vivid beauty, and the serene, worn face of the sleeper. Here he thought was the perfect love; the flower, the crown of human life – the Pandora gift of compensation to the children of men.

Jim stirred uneasily at the sound of the hooter but as his steadfast eyes opened for a moment, they fell upon Anne and Pen, sitting side by side, as with an unwonted softness in both of their faces as they watched in mutual tender happiness the sleep of their beloved.

FINIS

Printed in Great Britain
by Amazon